BREATH OF HEAVEN

Other Novels by Joshua Palmatier

The Skewed Throne*
The Cracked Throne*
The Vacant Throne*

***

Well of Sorrows
Leaves of Flame

***

Shattering the Ley*
Threading the Needle*

**Anthologies Edited by
Patricia Bray & Joshua Palmatier**

After Hours: Tales from the Ur-Bar*
The Modern Fae's Guide to Surviving Humanity*
Clockwork Universe: Steampunk vs Aliens
Temporally Out of Order
Alien Artifacts
Were-

* Published by DAW Books

BREATH OF HEAVEN

Joshua Palmatier

Interior Design (ebook) by April Steenburgh
Interior Design (print) by C. Lennox
Cover Design by C. Lennox

Cover Art by Justin Adams

ZNB Book Collectors #5

"Well of Sorrows" series #3

First Printing, May 2016 (Zombies Need Brains LLC)

Print ISBN-10: 1940709067
Print ISBN-13: 978-1940709062

Ebook ISBN-10: 1940709075
Ebook ISBN-13: 978-1940709079

Printed in the U.S.A.

1

"See this gets to the Tamaell." Lord Aeren Rhysall handed the sealed missive to a jittery young page. The boy's eyes were wide as he watched the Rhysall House Phalanx and servants' frantic activity. Aeren snapped his fingers in front of the youth's face to catch his attention. "The Tamaell, no one else. Not the White Phalanx, not a clerk, not even the Tamaea. Do you understand?"

The boy nodded and Aeren pressed a coin into his palm. His mouth dropped open when he saw the denomination, then he snatched the coin into a tight fist and ran, his red courier outfit flaring in a pool of torchlight farther down the corridor before he vanished completely.

"Will your warning be delivered?" Hiroun asked at Aeren's side.

"Pray to Aielan that it is." Aeren glanced around at the four other Rhyssal Phalanx that flanked him. "Are the preparations going smoothly?"

"As smoothly as can be expected. The essential documents have already been packed and the wagons are waiting below, along with your own mount and escort."

"Very well."

Tension thrummed in Aeren's skin. The urge to leave since he'd read Moiran's report on what the Order of the Flame had been preaching in the temples within his own lands—in Artillien!—had only escalated with his rage in the last few hours. The Chosen had gone too far, but his fellow lords could not see how close Lotaern's hands were to their throats. Aeren did not intend to stand around while the Chosen throttled him. He was done attempting to warn the Evant. It was past time he turned his attention to the security of his own lands, to his wife and son.

He shifted toward one of the windows and glared out into the night without really seeing it. A servant raced past, a trunk clutched to his chest. Two more moved swiftly in the opposite direction, one giving out orders to the other in short clipped sentences. A Phalanx member approached, the tread of his boots on the stone floor unmistakable, and

Aeren heard the hushed murmur of a report being given to Hiroun.

The tension in the corridor shifted and he turned. "What is it?"

Hiroun stepped forward immediately. "I believe we should depart now, my lord. The Phalanx reports suspicious activity on the streets of Caercaern."

"What kind of activity?"

"Groups of Phalanx from the other Houses are moving about."

"Which House? Where are they headed?"

"Uncertain."

Eraeth, his Protector, wouldn't have waited for Aeren's approval. The Rhyssal House Phalanx would already be moving. But Eraeth wasn't here.

"Tell everyone to abandon what isn't already packed. We're leaving. Now."

Hiroun snapped out orders as Aeren headed down the corridor toward the yard below. His personal guard fell in around him, Hiroun trotting to catch up. As word spread, Aeren saw the first hints of panic in the eyes of his servants. At a cross corridor, one servant tripped and fell, the wooden box he held splintering as it hit the floor, sheaves of paper fanning out before him. One of the Phalanx leaped forward and hauled the man to his feet as he began to collect the spilled papers, shoving him before them with a barked, "Leave it!" Two more guards darted forward and opened a door, one vanishing down the short corridor and stairs beyond. By the time Aeren arrived, he'd shouted all clear and they began their descent. Aeren found his hand resting on the pommel of the House sword strapped at his side. His father and brother had worn this sword, had died with it on the battlefield, on the dwarren plains. His brother had passed it to him even as he bled to death in Aeren's arms.

Then they were in the yard, four wagons already loaded, men shouting orders in all directions, servants spilling from doorways and tossing crates and trunks and furniture to those handling the wagons. Aeren led his group toward the Phalanx gathered near the gate, horses waiting. The two groups merged and Aeren, Hiroun, and the rest pulled themselves up into their saddles. Aeren spun his mount about.

"Gather around," he shouted, but didn't wait for the forty or so Phalanx and scouts or the nearly sixty servants to respond. "It is no longer in Rhyssal House's best interests to remain in Caercaern. We're returning to our own House lands. Head for the main gate and be as circumspect as possible."

Murmurs broke out as Aeren motioned for the gate to be opened.

Hiroun and three other Phalanx rode out into the street, their horses' hooves clattering on the cobbles. The general unease increased as the servants picked up on the heightened wariness of the Phalanx, but there was nothing Aeren could do to allay their fears, not when he shared them. He nudged his horse forward, the rest of his House falling in behind. They wound down the street to the main thoroughfare and turned toward the gates leading down to the tier below them. Hiroun sent scouts out ahead, every member of the Phalanx scanning the darkened buildings to either side, the rooftops, the black alleys, lit only by the lantern light of the wagons and the torches a few of the Phalanx carried. They moved slowly, wagons creaking, wheels clacking, making far more noise than Aeren would have liked. The moon glowed a mottled white overhead, thin clouds crossing its face. The night smelled of winter, crisp and cold, with an acrid hint of smoke. The leaves of the Winter Tree flashed silver to one side, towering over the city. Few of the windows they passed by were lit, but all of them shuttered. Somewhere close a dog began barking, joined a heartbeat later by two others.

They'd made it three quarters of the way to the second tier's gate when one of the scouts burst from the shadows ahead at a near run. The Phalanx parted for him. He came to a halt before Aeren. "The gates are closed. They're manned by members of the Ionaen House."

The gates shouldn't be closed and they certainly shouldn't be manned by Peloroun's Phalanx. Only the White Phalanx protected Caercaern, except in times of war.

"Check the auxiliary gates."

Four runners tore off down the street. Aeren's eyes swept over the vague shapes of the servants and wagons in the middle of the street, then the Phalanx, noting that his guardsmen had tightened up their formation.

"Shouldn't we continue moving?" Hiroun asked. "We aren't well concealed here."

"Where would we go? We don't know what parts of Caercaern are safe. We'll wait here until the scouts return with a report."

"What about the wagons?"

"Be prepared to abandon them completely."

Hiroun's eyebrows rose. "With your papers? And what of the servants?"

"If necessary, we'll burn the wagons and have the servants disperse and find their own way out of Caercaern and back to Artillien."

Hiroun passed the orders on to the Phalanx. Aeren heard gasps from the servants, a muffled cry in the darkness, a few sobs. He tried not to let it affect him, turned his attention to the city. The tiers of the Tamaell's residence soared over them, but he could only see their outlines in the moonlight. The Winter Tree was closer. For a moment, his gaze lingered on the direction of the Sanctuary and his thoughts turned bitter.

"What do you think is happening?" Hiroun asked, voice pitched low enough only Aeren and perhaps the closest Phalanx members could hear.

Eyes still on the Sanctuary, Aeren said, "I think the Chosen has finally decided to act directly. I think he intends to seize Caercaern, and with it the Alvritshai."

"What of the Tamaell?"

Aeren chuckled, the sound harsh and unpleasant even in his own ears. "I don't think I, nor the Tamaell, are intended to survive the night." He thought of the letter from Moiran, of his dashed off missive to the Tamaell. "We may all have been too late."

"My lord?"

He shook his head, then both of them snapped to attention as another runner appeared and gasped, "Ionaen...at the...secondary gates." He swallowed and coughed. "And there are Ionaen Phalanx in the streets. They're closing in on the Rhyssal House manse."

Aeren spun on Hiroun. "Torch the wagons. Douse the torches and lanterns after. Send the servants away. We aren't waiting for the report on the other gates. Peloroun will already have them sealed off."

Guardsmen began issuing orders, the servants behind beginning to scatter, not without a few wails of distress and spat curses. Lanterns were put out and the oil dumped over the wagons. Flames spread quickly. Once the wagons were lit, the torches were guttered and Hiroun asked, "Where to?"

Aeren knew of only one other way out of the second tier—the tunnels beneath the Sanctuary—but Lotaern would never allow them access, and there was no way to steal past the Flame and acolytes who guarded it.

He shifted toward the towers of the third tier.

"To the Tamaell. We'll make our stand there." With Peloroun and perhaps other Phalanx in the streets, he couldn't count on the courier making it to the Tamaell in time. "Let's move."

The thirty-odd Phalanx remaining swung around into a new formation, and then they were moving, sprinting past the abandoned wagons, a few lingering servants dodging out of their way. Their horses' hooves thundered on the cobbles, slowing only when Hiroun raised a sharp fist as they neared a corner. Two guardsmen cantered ahead, signaled all clear, and they proceeded forward with more caution, winding their way up from the second tier's wall toward the lowest level of the palace, their path lit only by the silvery moon.

At one cross street, the point guardsmen hustled back with frantic motions and the group retreated into a side street a moment before thirty Licaetan guards clattered around the corner. They milled in the intersection a moment, horses snorting, then charged to the right at a sharp command. Two streets later, Aeren glanced down an alley and saw Peloroun mounts streaking past one street away, but they were moving too fast and none of them looked in their direction. Aeren nudged his horse forward to warn Hiroun, but one of his own Phalanx cried out and whispered, "Look!"

Through the break between two buildings, Aeren could see a pulsing orange-red light in the windows of another manse. It took him a moment to realize it was the glow of a fire, and then figures appeared, silhouetted against the wash of light. As the blaze grew, two of the men were cut down, one shoved out the window, his shadow plummeting out of sight into the darkness. Smoke billowed from beneath the eaves and seeped between the tiles of the roof, and a moment later a section caved inwards and flames surged into the night, all eerily silent.

"The Baene estate." Lord Terroec.

For the first time, true fear settled in Aeren's chest.

The fire verified this wasn't a simple powerplay in the Evant. Lotaern, Peloroun, and Orraen were out for blood. It was a coup, and Aeren suddenly realized that, aside from Tamaell Thaedoren, he had no idea where the rest of the lords' allegiances lay. Obviously, Lotaern and the others didn't trust Terroec to fall in line. But who else? Would Daesor give them sanctuary? Would Saetor or Houdyll?

He didn't think any of them would. Only Thaedoren had a hope of sheltering them, of wielding enough power as Tamaell to halt Lotaern at his doorstep.

"Keep moving," he commanded, dragging his mount around hard and then digging in his heels. The steed snorted and leaped forward, although Aeren kept him in check as the rest of the escort closed in on either side. Hiroun urged his mount farther forward, two others joining him. They banked around a corner onto a different street, picked up speed on the straightaway, then turned again. Aeren's ears strained for any sound of pursuit, but he heard nothing over the tread of the horses around him, the huffing breath of the animals and grunts of the guards. He knew it was only a matter of time before they ran into Lotaern's forces. He and his co-conspirators had planned this too well if they already had men at the gates, had already attacked Terroec's House. By now, they would have found Rhyssal's manse empty; they'd be searching the streets. The burning wagons may cause a distraction, but he hoped their focus would be on the gates.

Out of the corner of one eye, he caught the orange-yellow flickers of fire. The tower of Baene's manse still burned, now seething with flame down half its length. The bells warning of fire in the city should have rung by now. Aeren silently cursed and kicked his horse into greater speed.

Then ahead, Hiroun rounded a corner and cried out, the two guardsmen with him jerking their mounts to the side. Before those around Aeren could catch up to them, they wheeled their horses and continued straight ahead, Hiroun shouting something unintelligible. But when Aeren spurred his horse past the turn, he didn't need an explanation: ten men on horseback were turning their mounts toward them, their shouts echoing off the buildings on either side. The shadows in the street were too thick to see their House colors.

Aeren nearly ordered his Phalanx about to engage, but before he could, another larger group burst from a second street to their right and struck the men at the back of Aeren's escort, steel clashing as bodies slammed together. A horse screamed as it went down. Aeren's Phalanx didn't slow. A third group of pursuers broke into the street ahead and Hiroun pulled up short and cut into a side street. The Phalanx were forced to ride three abreast, but then they reached the far street and the formation regrouped. Aeren heard barked commands from behind but no horns calling the rest of the forces to them. They wanted silence. There was still a chance to stop whatever the traitors had left to do.

But they were blocks away from the palace. And their last evasion had driven them farther from its lower doors.

"Hiroun, bank left!" he roared, and saw Hiroun cut left, then immediately cut right again at the first opportunity without direction. He'd caught Aeren's intent. The pursuers were on the main thoroughfares, the most direct approaches. Aeren wanted to come to the gates obliquely.

Breath harsh in his lungs, he followed Hiroun as the guard slid into the side streets, their pace slowing as the roadways narrowed. The quick turns had left the pursuers behind, although he could still hear them calling out orders. The activity had woken up dogs on all sides, their howls and barking breaking through the silence of deep night. Lights were beginning to appear in windows in the streets they'd left behind; they were making enough noise to rouse Caercaern's residents. He considered waking those in the neighborhood around them, but he was afraid Peloroun's forces would find them before enough of the common people understood what was happening. No, their only chance was reaching the Tamaell.

With that thought, they spilled out onto the central square before the palace's lower doors. The tiers of the palace soared above them, its angles sharpened by moonlight and shadows. Aeren's force streaked across the wide plaza toward the open gate, Aeren drawing breath to shout an order to close the gates, to seal the palace. But then he realized there were too many guardsmen on watch—

And they weren't White Phalanx.

"Betrayal!" he roared, even as those at the gate spun toward them. "Traitors at the gate! Rhyssal, to the Tamaell! Protect Thaedoren!"

He kneed his horse hard, drew his sword as his guard bellowed in response, their own blades slicking from sheaths. Aeren shed all pretense of stealth. He only hoped Thaedoren was still alive.

Those at the gates—Licaetan and Ionaen Phalanx—scrambled to meet their charge. But these men weren't mounted. They'd barely formed a line when Aeren and his escort crashed through them, Aeren slicing down and up, one of Peloroun's men screaming and stumbling back a step before Aeren's horse ran him over. Aeren's focus had already shifted inward, into the inner corridor. His mount heaved forward, enemies brushed to either side. Blood splattered the walls of the corridor, White Phalanx already lying dead and crumpled. Through the clash of steel and the shouts of his men, magnified by the corridor around him, he heard distant fighting. He urged his mount deeper into the wide corridor and out into the open hall beyond, the clatter of hooves on marble echoing in the domed ceiling. More bodies littered the floor, White Phalanx mixed with Peloroun's and Orraen's men now. Two Licaetan guards leaped forward but Aeren and Hiroun cut them down. More of the Rhyssal Phalanx poured into the chamber, one of them shouting, "Ionaen forces are filling the courtyard outside. They've already retaken the doors."

Aeren swore, then scanned the three doorways leading out of the chamber with one glance. He motioned to those on the left and right. "Check them."

Four Rhyssal guards dismounted and broke toward each entrance. At least half his force was holding the corridor behind them. He pushed the sounds of the struggle from his mind and focused on what he could discern from deeper in the palace, his horse fidgeting in apprehension beneath him.

"They're on the level above," Hiroun said, looking upwards as if he could see the action through the arched ribbing of the ceiling and the painted murals between.

"But have they reached the Tamaell, yet?"

Hiroun didn't answer.

The two groups of Rhyssal returned. "Clear to the left. Everything's empty."

"Only a few White Phalanx on the right. All dead."

Aeren had expected nothing less. He knew they couldn't hold the corridor to the courtyard, not with the enemy already inside the palace. They were trapped.

He caught Hiroun's gaze. His personal guard gave him a nearly imperceptible nod of acknowledgment.

Aeren slid down from his horse, the rest of his escort doing the same.

"Form up!" Hiroun snapped, as a few guards hauled the horses off to the side.

Aeren strode toward the entryway directly across the room, the sounds of the fighting above louder. His escort assembled behind him, all thirty except for those few still holding the corridor behind.

Pulling the pendant with Aielan's Flame molded into one side from beneath his shirt, Aeren held it up to the light inside the chamber, muttered a small prayer, then kissed it and let it fall to his chest for all to see before turning. Some of the men before him straightened. All of them had swords and knives drawn.

"Peloroun and Orraen have shown their true colors. They are traitors to the Evant, traitors to Aielan and the Light. Head toward the Tamaell's personal chambers. Give the Licaetan and Ionaen forces no mercy."

He turned to the corridor and stairs beyond.

"No mercy at all," he muttered under his breath.

And he charged forward, thinking of Thaedoren, of his son, Fedaureon, and Moiran.

* * *

Thaedoren woke to the faint sounds of swordplay. At first he thought it the remnants of a dream, the clang of metal and weaponry illusory and distant. But then someone began pounding on the door to his personal chambers and the shouts escalated. Someone else cursed. He recognized Naraen's voice, had time to wonder why the White Phalanx guard couldn't get inside the room—

And then the bed beneath him shifted.

He reacted on instinct, hand flashing upward to grip the wrist of the arm and knife descending toward his chest. He wrenched the arm back and twisted, heard a woman's shriek as he rolled into the figure beside him and crushed her body beneath his weight. She writhed, her other hand raking across his face, drawing blood. He hissed at the pain but focused on the knife as he slammed the woman's wrist into the wood of the bed's corner post. Fingers loosened as the woman cried out, her other hand still clawing his face, shoulder, arm, anything she could reach, so he cracked her wrist into the post again and heard the knife hit the floor and skitter away.

He leaned back and snatched her other arm, bringing them both together up over her head against the carved wooden headboard. She continued to struggle, spitting curses, their bodies now tangled in the sheets and bedcovers. Both of them were panting, and as Thaedoren caught his breath he realized the woman was fully clothed. He couldn't see much more, a shaft of moonlight angled away from them the only illumination. Where were the candles Reanne usually kept lit during the night? Where was Reanne?

His jaw clamped shut and he transferred the woman's wrists to one grip, then grabbed at her throat. She stilled with a gasp he could feel through his fingers. Tightening his grip, he slid off the edge of the bed, then hauled her toward the moonlight. She choked and began kicking but he never allowed her to find her feet. He shoved her up against the wall.

Reanne's almond-colored eyes glared back at him, black against the pale skin of her face. Before Thaedoren could react, she spit at him. Anger flared and his grip tightened; he could feel the pulse of her heart's blood in her neck. Her chin tilted upwards as she strained away from his hold.

"Was this always the plan? Even before we met? Was I nothing to you but a pawn?"

Her eyes flashed, but she couldn't speak. He was squeezing too hard.

Behind them, the shouts from the White Phalanx changed, the guardsmen no longer pounding on the door. Instead, something heavy struck it hard. They were trying to break it down. Reanne must have locked it from the inside. Thaedoren shot a glance toward the bedroom entrance, then brought Reanne's locked wrists down behind her back and pushed her across the room into the outer chamber. Still their private quarters, this area was set up for informal meetings and a place for the Tamaell and the Tamaea to relax. Thaedoren realized one of the settees had been pulled across the outer door. As he made his way toward it, a sharp command rang out and the door shuddered in its frame. Thaedoren placed a foot against the settee and shoved it out of the way. He drew breath to shout to Naraen when someone roared, "Again!" and the heavy wood of the door splintered inwards and the stone head of a statue burst through into the inner room. It withdrew and three White Phalanx crashed through, stumbling as others poured in after them, Naraen among them. His personal guard caught sight of him immediately, but was brought up short when he realized Thaedoren held Reanne in a chokehold and that she was fully clothed while he was not.

"Tamaell?"

"Take her." Thaedoren thrust her to the floor, where she lay, coughing and choking for air. "Hold her. She tried to kill me. And report." Although he thought he knew what was happening. As soon as the White Phalanx seized her, he stormed back into his own rooms and began to dress, reaching for practical clothing and what little light armor was kept in his bedchamber. His heavy armor was kept elsewhere and there wasn't time to find and don it.

"Peloroun's and Orraen's men have seized the front doors and taken the first floor and most of the second. We're currently holding them off in the hallway beyond the main audience chamber below."

"My brother Daedelan?"

"The White Fox was woken immediately. He's commanding the forces below. All of the White Phalanx here in the palace have been roused."

"Summon the general barracks."

"Daedelan already sent—"

The harsh clang of the palace's bells rang out, jolting through Thaedoren, his arm jerking where he fumbled with a clasp. He cursed under his breath, finished by strapping on the Resue House sword, then stalked out of the bedchamber into the outer room. He ignored Reanne's scathing glare as he passed and shoved through the balcony doors, the frigid night air slapping him in the face. He bee-lined through the garden toward the wall with the greatest view of the city. The warning clang of the bell shuddered in his teeth.

His lips pressed together grimly as he leaned over the wall. "Fire in the second tier." His eyes narrowed in concentration. He could smell the smoke from here. "It looks like Lord Terroec's manse...and Lord Aeren's. Another smaller fire near the second tier gates, but I can't tell what it is. It appears to be in the streets."

"No alarms except the one bell," Naraen said. "There should be dozens of bells clanging by now."

"They've taken the tier walls and gates. Likely they've already hit the barracks in the first and second tier." He squinted toward the walls but couldn't see anything in the darkness, especially with the fires in between. He tried to listen, but the bell drowned out any sounds that he might have heard from below. "We have to assume no help will come from that direction."

He pushed back and returned to the outer room, stopping before Reanne. The urge to strike her hate-filled face twisted through the memory of touching her cheek and kissing her at their bonding before Aielan's White Flame in the Santuary.

"I know Peloroun and Orraen are involved. Who else? Houdyll? Daesor? I can't imagine Saetor would sanction such treachery."

Reanne's eyes narrowed. "You cannot escape. We have already taken the city. Your allies—"

Thaedoren's hand moved of its own volition, his fingers clamping around Reanne's jaw to silence her. He leaned in close as her nostrils flared, her breath ragged. He stared down into her eyes, his own teeth clenched tight. "Did you ever love me? Or was it all simply . . ."

He couldn't finish, but he let go of her jaw and stepped back, gave her a chance to speak.

"Houses fall." Her shoulders were hunched, her mouth a thin line. He couldn't read her eyes, too bright and fluid, but her body was rigid with anger, hatred, and humiliation.

Something in him died at that moment. He felt it deep in his gut, a flinch of resignation, of realization. Recognition of a line crossed, one that could not be redrawn.

He turned his back on his wife and rested his hand on the pommel of his sword. "Take me to Daedelan."

"And the Tamaea?"

"She is no longer the Tamaea." The stance of the Phalanx within earshot altered, more guarded, more deadly. "Bring her with us."

Naraen led him through the halls, White Phalanx flanking him on both sides and behind. Phalanx stood to one side to let them pass, all of them armed, swords bared. They descended to the second level. After two turns, the corridor grew dense, Phalanx retreating from the fight that Thaedoren could now hear clearly. Metal clanged against metal and men roared orders and screamed in pain. Naraen shouted, "The Tamaell, coming through!" and the press of bodies parted to make way, Naraen shoving forward first, Thaedoren a step behind. He waved for those holding Reanne to keep back, and then he jostled his way forward. The sounds of battle increased, nearly deafening in the close quarters. Naraen continued shouting, but there were too many bodies pressed too close together for anyone to move far.

Ahead, the corridor ended in one of the larger audience chambers and Thaedoren caught sight of his brother, Daedelan's pale blue uniform easy to pick out among the white and red of the Phalanx. His face was splattered with blood, drawn tight with a grimace, but he heaved forward, sword cutting down in a tight arc and slashing across two of Peloroun's men. Someone barked orders from the far side of the room and Thaedoren's gaze locked onto Peloroun himself.

Peloroun saw him and shock registered in his eyes, there and then gone in the space of a breath. Any last hope that Reanne had acted alone died.

"Peloroun, you Light-forsaken traitor! You've finally revealed your true colors!" Thaedoren drew his sword and shoved forward, dragging White Phalanx out of his way. Naraen protested—Thaedoren felt his personal guard's fingers on his shoulder trying to pull him back—but he slipped out of his guardsman's grip. Within two steps he emerged into the chaos of the audience chamber and punched his sword forward into a gap between his men, slicing into an Ionaen guard's neck. The man screamed and jerked back, hand flying toward the wound. Thaedoren lurched forward into the opening. He tasted blood on his lips as he hacked forward, striving for Peloroun, the elder lord hanging back behind his line of men.

"Give up, Thaedoren." Peloroun's calm voice cut through the screams easily. "We have the city. Your allies are dead. There's no place for you to run. The House of Resue has fallen!"

"Not until I breathe my last breath."

Thaedoren jabbed his blade into the armpit of an Ionaen guard. He staggered forward as the sword caught in the join of the armor and the man sagged back, but a hand clamped down on his shoulder and hauled him away as three more Ionaen guardsmen rushed into the opening. He spun on the man who'd grabbed him, realized it was Daedelan.

"Let go."

"Don't be a fool. It's what he wants. It's what *they* want."

Thaedoren jerked free of his brother's arm. "They've taken the second tier at least. Lord Terroec's manse is burning, along with Lord Aeren's. We can't expect help from outside the palace."

"Really? Listen."

Thaedoren took in Daedelan's rigid, unreadable face, and then listened. The cacophony in the room raged around him, harsh and visceral, but he forced it back, strained to hear what lay beneath.

His head snapped toward the entrance at the far side of the chamber.

A heartbeat later, guardsmen in blue and red surged through the door, tearing into Peloroun's Phalanx from behind, led by Lord Aeren. Thaedoren grinned in relief. To one side, Peloroun cursed and called out new orders.

"House Resue, push forward," Daedelan bellowed, then shoved Thaedoren toward Peloroun's faltering line, even as Naraen tried to pull the Tamaell back toward the safety of the corridor behind. His personal guard shouted for the rest of the White Phalanx to protect their lord.

Thaedoren joined his brother at the edge of the battle, the room exploding into a flurry of swords and the clash of blade against armor. The floor grew slick with blood and bodies, footing treacherous. But the White Phalanx pushed forward, taking back ground they'd lost only moments before. Thaedoren pressed toward Aeren's men, crushing Peloroun between the two, the traitorous lord backing into a corner, the table that had adorned the center of the room now tilted on its side as a barricade. Lord Aeren was focused on Peloroun, his normally placid face livid with rage. He hacked his way through the men, Rhyssal House guardsmen keeping Peloroun's men to either side at bay.

The White Phalanx had almost reached the Rhyssal House forces when suddenly the men to Aeren's right fell with a cry of warning. Aeren turned, saw Thaedoren—

And then a blade punched into the back of Aeren's right shoulder.

Aeren spun, sword flashing outwards and cutting into his attacker's chest. As the man fell, Aeren's face pinched with pain and Thaedoren saw his sword arm falter. He switched the sword to his left, but Thaedoren knew he wasn't as skilled with that arm. Tucking his right arm to his chest, Aeren hunched forward, blood already staining the back of his shirt, the hilt of the blade jutting out from his shoulder.

Aeren turned to Thaedoren. "They're behind us! They've taken the gates! They've—" He broke into a fit of coughing. When he straightened, blood flecked his lips and his face had paled. "They've—" he tried again, but then he began to topple.

"Lord Aeren!" Thaedoren hissed between clenched teeth and motioned to his contingent of White Phalanx. "To Lord Aeren. Now!" Those next to him surged forward. He caught Daedelan's confused look from the corner of his eye, but his brother halted for only a moment before concentrating again on Peloroun. Thaedoren could no longer see Aeren, the lord underfoot. His men cut down the last of Peloroun's forces between their position and Aeren's men, and then suddenly one of the Rhyssal guardsmen appeared, Aeren clutched to his chest.

Thaedoren seized the man's shoulder and hauled him and Aeren behind his own White Phalanx. Aeren hung in his guardsman's arms as if he were already dead. "Take him to the corridor beyond," Thaedoren ordered.

"Tamaell, there are more of Orraen's and Peloroun's men behind us. We were caught at the gates and then trapped in the palace. These are the only men Rhyssal has left here in the palace."

"Very well," Thaedoren said, then squeezed the guardsman's arm in reassurance. "Now go."

As soon as the man retreated with Aeren, he turned to survey the room. They'd pushed Peloroun's forces to one side, but they were holding behind the table. They'd cut them down in time...but they didn't have time. Not if what Aeren and his guard had said was true.

Thaedoren straightened, wiped a smear of blood from near his eye, then said, "Fall back! Retreat! Rhyssal House to me!"

Those White Phalanx at the back of the room began to withdraw, not without a few confused looks. Daedelan and those around him continued hacking at Peloroun's line. Ionaen lay on all sides, dead or dying, a few draped over the edge of the table. White Phalanx lay with them, the once pristine marble floor of the chamber now a sheet of dark, viscous red.

Thaedoren stepped forward. "Daedelan, withdraw!"

His brother shot him a dark look, but then his gaze darted toward the entrance, where one of the White Phalanx shouted a warning before he was cut down and Lord Orraen's men spilled into the room.

Daedelan began to retreat, hauling a few of the White Phalanx guards with him. Peloroun seized the advantage and ordered his own men forward. Thaedoren stepped back to the second door. "Get ready to seal the doors." Thaedoren watched Daedelan as he held the Ionaen and Licaeta House guards at bay. More of Orraen's men filled the room behind them, mixed with Peloroun's—thirty, then forty. He saw none of the other lords' guardsmen at all, nor any of Lotaern's Flame.

Daedelan reached the doorway. With three other White Phalanx—all built more solidly than most Alvritshai, broader of shoulder like Daedelan himself—his brother suddenly surged forward, not trying to kill or maim, but to throw those attackers in the front row off balance. They staggered back into those behind, and Daedelan and the other three spun and dodged into the corridor beyond. Thaedoren shouted an order, but his White Phalanx were already moving. The heavy wooden doors swung closed as Peloroun's men inside the room recovered and lurched toward them. But they were too late. Their bodies struck wood as four horizontal support beams were slid into place. Men retreated, Thaedoren with them, as others rushed forward, shoving heavy trunks before them. As soon as they began stacking them before the doorway, Thaedoren turned to find Daedelan.

"It won't hold them," his brother said. His breath came in harsh rasps and he was fingering a slash along his jawline. He winced, then shot a questioning glance toward where the Phalanx held Reanne.

"She tried to kill me."

Daedelan's eyebrows rose.

Behind them, a loud thud echoed down the corridor.

"They're already trying to break through," one of the Phalanx reported.

"We can't keep them out. The upper reaches of the palace weren't designed for it."

"I don't intend to stay," Thaedoren said. He'd already begun searching the corridor. He spotted the huddle of Rhyssal House Phalanx far down on one side. "Ready the Phalanx, and gather anything of value you think we should take with us."

Daedelan straightened. "The garden?"

Thaedoren nodded, then made his way toward the Rhyssal men. Lord Aeren lay on his stomach on the floor, his personal guard pressing a wad of cloth to the wound on his upper back. Someone had removed the blade and cast it to one side. Thaedoren knelt, but even without a careful search he could see that blood soaked the cloth the guard held. Not even the dark blue and red colors of Aeren's shirt could hide how much he'd already bled.

Thaedoren motioned for the guard to remove the cloth, then winced.

"Hiroun, roll me over," Aeren whispered.

Hiroun, the guard holding the blood-soaked bandage, did as his lord asked. Aeren reached up and gripped Thaedoren's arm, pulling him closer. He stared into Thaedoren's eyes, and Thaedoren felt himself snared more solidly than by the hand on his arm.

"Tell your mother that I love her. And take care of Fedaureon, even if he is only your half-brother."

Aeren's grip tightened until Thaedoren nodded. "Of course." His voice was ragged. "Of course, Lor—" He choked back the title and said instead, "Of course, Aeren."

The lord of House Rhyssal smiled and his grip relaxed. His gaze wandered to those around him, landing on Hiroun last. He chuckled, the sound thick with the blood in his lungs.

"Oh, Hiroun. Eraeth—" he choked, the sound fluid, then finished, "—Eraeth is going to kill me."

Then Aeren, the lord of House Rhyssal, the man Thaedoren had thought of as his father even though he had never said so, died.

2

"They're gone," Peloroun said.

Lotaern frowned at the bodies that littered the floor of the outer audience chamber, picking his way carefully through the blood. Their escort came behind, a mix of Phalanx and Flame. Orraen's and Peloroun's men were already cleaning up, the taint of smoke penetrating even here, although the pyre had been built in the palace courtyard. Peloroun had wanted to bury the White Phalanx guardsmen, but Lotaern had insisted they be sent to Aielan's Light. They had simply been following orders, protecting their lord. No need to punish them for that.

"Where did they go?"

"No one knows. They sealed the door to the third tier. By the time we broke through we found nothing but the dead. My Phalanx searched the entire second and third floors and found nothing."

They'd reached the doorway Thaedoren had ordered sealed and Lotaern grimaced. The bodies were piled high here. The white and red of Resue were stacked to the left, along with perhaps a dozen of Rhyssal's blue and red. A spark of irritation flickered in his chest. He had expected Lord Aeren to die in his manse, like Terroec. How had Aeren known to run? Had he been forewarned? Had someone at the Sanctuary—or perhaps one of Lord Peloroun's or Orraen's men—managed to send out a message? He would have to be more wary of who was informed of their future plans. Regardless, he had to respect Lord Aeren. He'd managed to elude all of Peloroun's and Orraen's men in the streets and had made it to Thaedoren's side.

"You are certain Lord Aeren was wounded?"

"Yes."

"And he's not among the dead?"

"No. I checked myself. They also have Reanne."

Lotaern didn't respond. He'd felt sick since he'd met with Peloroun and Orraen, announced the Autumn Tree had failed, then ordered the coup. Plans he'd spent decades orchestrating were finally in motion. And yet already they'd gone awry. Reanne had obviously not killed Thaedoren. Had she been found out? Had she had a change of heart? Was she still waiting for an opportunity? He assumed she was still alive, since they hadn't found her body.

He suddenly realized Peloroun had set Orraen to overseeing the pyre to distract him from his sister's absence. He approved. His sister had controlled him, had kept him in line. Dealing with the dead would keep Orraen occupied for a while.

"Show me the rest."

Peloroun led him down the corridor and into the halls beyond. According to Peloroun's report, none of the fighting had occurred here, but there were splashes of dried blood all around, including a pool of it in the center of the right corridor. Blood trails wound up the steps to the third tier and spread out along most of the halls there. In the Tamaell's personal quarters, trunks and armoires had been riffled through, clothes strewn about the floor. The bed had been stripped of sheets. One of the Tamaea's glass candelabras had been knocked to the floor, the shards glittering in the early morning sunlight slanting through the balcony windows.

Lotaern perused the room, ran his hand down a tapestry hung on one wall, then crunched across the shattered glass and out into the garden. There was blood even here, staining the grasses, the stones of the walk. The roar of the water cascading down the mountains behind lulled the churning in his gut and he breathed in the late autumn air, the scent tainted by greasy smoke from the pyre far below. A black column billowed into the sky, half obscuring the silvered leaves of the top of the Winter Tree.

The Chosen turned to stare at the water siphoned off from the cascades to create a stream through the garden, then moved back to where Peloroun stood at the garden's entrance.

"They left the palace somehow. There must be a tunnel or hidden room. Find it. We don't want them returning unexpectedly. And prepare for the Evant. A new Tamaell needs to be chosen, and new Houses risen. We have work to do."

* * *

Eraeth jerked awake, hand reaching automatically for his cattan. For a moment, he thought he was back in Artillien, but then the oppressive heat of the desert slammed into him. He sucked in a harsh breath, tasted the dust of stone, the aridness burning his lungs. Grip tightening on the handle of his blade, he turned, took in the cramped room, the sandstone walls, the firepit in the far corner, and Siobhaen staring at him over the flames in concern.

"What is it?"

He shook his head. His heart thundered in his chest and a horrible sense of wrongness twisted in his gut. But he forced his hand to unclench and relax.

He sought out Colin's form, resting on a shelf of stone to one side. "Is he—?"

"He was fine the last time I checked. But that was a few hours ago. No real change in his condition." Siobhaen reached forward and pulled a spit out of the flames, the carcass of some kind of rodent charred on its end. She inspected it, rotated the spit, and then tucked it back into the coals. "You didn't sleep well."

Eraeth wiped the sleep-grit from his eyes with one hand, then stood and moved over to Colin's side. A quick scan told him Siobhaen was right: no significant change. But he hadn't expected any. It had only been two days since they fought Walter and the sukrael at the reawakened Well. They'd managed to haul Colin's body out of the chamber to this place, a mostly intact building in the ruins of the surrounding city. Then they'd been forced to hunker down and hide, the activity in the broken towers at the center of the city attracting the attention of the odd snake-like Haessari living in the cliffs to the north. They'd swarmed the area, their search parties spreading out from the confluence of the dried-up riverbeds. Siobhaen and Eraeth had managed to keep themselves concealed, but patrols still passed through the area at random. Eraeth had seen them carting a litter bearing Walter's body from the ruins. He assumed they'd taken the Wraith to the north.

Reaching forward, he pulled the blood-drenched cloth covering Colin's wound away from his chest. It came away reluctantly, its edges dried even though the center of the cloth was still wet. Eraeth grimaced at the gaping wound within, filled with blood. What skin wasn't blood-smeared was mottled with the black oil taint of the sarenavriell. Colin's chest barely moved, his breath almost nonexistent, but when he did exhale, tiny bubbles appeared in the blood. Eraeth knew the wound in his back was worse, could see the trickle of red that streaked down the side of the sandstone ledge; they'd done the best they could to stanch its flow.

He heard Siobhaen approach, settled the flap of cloth back over the wound as she halted beside him and presented a slice of roasted meat.

"How long do you think he'll take to recover?" she asked as he slid it from her knife.

"I don't know. This damage is severe. I've never seen him this... mutilated before. At the Escarpment, he came to the battlefield and halted the fighting a day after having the knife embedded in his chest."

"He drank the sarenavriell's waters then. You haven't given him any of what we brought with us from the Well."

Eraeth's skin prickled at the accusation in her voice. "Because every sip taints him more and at the moment we're safe enough where we are."

"Then why'd we take it?"

Eraeth turned to snap at her, but found her staring toward the satchel where they kept the waterskin that held the Lifeblood, her body tense, one hand clutching her upper arm across her chest protectively. She didn't like having the Lifeblood so near. According to the Scripts of Aielan, the sarenavriell's waters corrupt the body and soul of those who drink it, a corruption blatantly obvious in the blotches on Colin's skin.

"You fear its corruption."

She nodded without looking toward him. "It's the cause of all of our recent problems. The sukrael, the Wraiths . . . they are the embodiment of all that is evil in Aielan's eyes. They are the reason that the Order of Aielan needs the Flame." She faced him. "There was a reason that the sarenavriell were dormant."

"And yet you want me to use the Lifeblood to heal Shaeveran."

Her hand dropping from her arm. "Because we need him."

"You handled yourself well. You called Aielan's Light and killed all of the sukrael that remained."

"I called it, but I didn't control it. It burned through me, nearly left me an empty husk." Fear edged her voice. "And there was something more, something I didn't notice at the time but now that I've thought about it...."

"What?"

She looked at him. "When I killed the sukrael, I could feel them. They were like," her hands groped the air, "like blights on the world. Voids of emptiness. I poured Aielan's Light into those voids, trying to fill them, and the sukrael burned. But thinking back I realize now that I didn't feel the Wraith in the same way." She drew in a steadying breath, glanced away. "It makes me wonder how effective Aielan's Light will be in destroying them. Lotaern—"

She cut the words off as if she'd suddenly remembered to whom she was speaking. Anger uncurled in Eraeth's chest, threaded with his suspicions about Siobhaen and all of the Flame. But before he could say anything Siobhaen made a cutting gesture with one hand.

"No. No more." She faced him directly. "Lotaern thinks he can use Aielan's Light to capture and kill the Wraiths. He's been training the Order of the Flame for this purpose for years now, beneath the mountain. If Shaeveran hadn't brought us the Winter Tree for protection, the Chosen would have been using the Flame and the Fire against the sukrael in their attacks on our lands. But we were only beginning to experiment with the power, using the Scripts as a guide, when Shaeveran appeared with the seed and thrust it into the grounds outside the Evant's Hall."

Eraeth almost told her that he'd thrust it into the stone of the marketplace, not the grounds where the Winter Tree grew now, but then realized Siobhaen hadn't been born at the time. As far as she knew, that ground had always housed the Tree, nothing more.

Instead, he asked, "He's perfected the process?"

"He thinks so. The Flame hasn't been able to test it."

"Why didn't you test it at the well in the White Wastes?"

Soibhaen's shoulders sagged. "Because it isn't like calling the Light like I did there or here. It requires preparation, groundwork laid out, and then multiple Flame members to hold the Wraith until the ritual can be completed."

"It requires a trap."

"That's why Lotaern wanted Shaeveran's knife. It was so much quicker and required so little work."

"Except Lotaern doesn't know that it doesn't work."

"You never gave me a chance to warn him."

They glared at each other, the moment broken when they heard the hissing shouts of the Haessari outside the building. Eraeth lurched upright, but Siobhaen was already climbing the pile of debris in one corner that gave them access to a secondary room, the only way in or out of their bolthole. He watched her vanish, then followed.

As soon as he reached the top of the debris, he caught Siobhaen's hand signal from the room on the far side and stilled. She was peering out through a crack in the southern wall. From his vantage, he could see a sliver of sunlight and the street beyond, and a larger section of the street and surrounding buildings through an open window to the east.

He caught movement through the crack and saw Siobhaen press back against the wall. The Haessari was too close for him to make out any details, only a shadow passing by the crack, followed by two others. They appeared on the street to the east a heartbeat later, pausing against the far buildings. Their snake-scaled skin glistened in the sunlight, one of the guards tilting his reptilian face to the light, eyes closed, as if soaking in its heat. They were dressed in boiled leather armor and carried s-shaped swords, although they were sheathed. The two not sunning themselves scanned the buildings, tongues flickering out of their snub-nosed mouths, the narrow slits of their nostrils flaring. Eraeth glanced toward the ceiling, where the smoke from their fire trailed across the stone into the secondary room before slipping into a crack that led to the upper stories. The Haessari shouldn't be able to scent it from the street.

He wasn't so certain about the roasted meat.

He gestured toward Siobhaen, who nodded in understanding and eased herself into a better position. Her hand fell to her cattan; Eraeth's did the same. He eyed the three Haessari as one of them hissed sharply, all three of them falling into heated conversation. One of them flared the hood of skin kept rolled up along their necks and the others fell silent. He pointed toward the west and the three trotted off.

Eraeth signaled to Siobhaen, who peered out through the crack in the wall again, then motioned all clear. She scrambled toward Eraeth, who backed out of her way.

"That's the closest they've come since the sarenavriell was awakened," Siobhaen said, crouching down over their supplies. "We're going to have to move."

"He isn't well enough to move."

"We'll have to use the water from the sarenavriell."

When Eraeth didn't answer, she turned from her search in her satchel, the waterskin in one hand, something in her face hardening. "He doesn't have time to heal without it. All they need is one whiff of smoke or his blood the next time they pass."

"We'll need a litter, or a sling—something to carry him in. The sarenavriell isn't like the Blood of Aielan, it won't heal him instantly. It will only give him strength so he can heal faster."

She pressed the waterskin into his hand. "I'll find what I can to carry him."

He heard her crawl up and out the hole, but didn't turn. The waterskin weighed heavy in his hand, but after a long moment he stepped to Colin's side and sat on his haunches. He touched Colin's skin, which felt hot even though he looked pale. Beads of sweat dotted his brow and his hair was damp.

He removed the stopper from the waterskin, careful to balance it so that none of the water inside escaped. The scent of loam, dead leaves, and snow tickled his nostrils. Tilting Colin's head back so that his mouth opened, he poured in a trickle of the Lifeblood as he whispered, "Forgive us." It was difficult to control the flow since the waterskin wasn't even half full, but he managed. Setting the skin aside, he reached for Colin's throat to force him to swallow but Colin spluttered and gulped convulsively. His eyes flew open and Eraeth reached forward to hold his body down, but he saw no awareness in Colin's eyes.

After a few harsh breaths, Colin slumped back to the stone. His body stilled. Some of the Lifeblood had spilled from his mouth, but Eraeth thought he'd swallowed most of it.

Relaxing, Eraeth sat back and replaced the stopper on the skin. He stood and stared down at Colin's body, at the fresh blood seeping down the side of the stone slab and the eyes that remained open. His chest ached, curling around the sense of wrongness that had woken him.

He leaned forward and closed Colin's eyes, careful not to touch the sheen of Lifeblood.

* * *

They departed two nights later.

Eraeth and Siobhaen bound Colin's wounds as tightly as possible with their remaining cloth. Eraeth wasn't certain the Lifeblood was working, but he did think the blood flow had lessened. He'd given Colin a swallow of the tainted water each morning and evening, and this last time Colin had swallowed without convulsing, as if he realized what the water was now and knew it would help.

Together, they lifted him from the slab and nestled him between the two staves of Siobhaen's makeshift litter. Between the two staves she'd lashed a hide made from one of their satchels and gut cured from some of their kills. Eraeth wasn't certain the gut had had time enough to become as strong as it needed to be, and the deconstructed satchel was barely large enough to hold a man, but the Haessari's patrols appeared to be focusing on the region of the city where they'd holed up and they were out of time. Three of the search teams had scoured an area mere blocks away that day.

They separated the rest of the supplies between them. Then Eraeth reached down and picked up the two ends of the staves. Siobhaen adjusted her knives and cattan before gathering up the other two ends. It was rigged so that the staves at one end, near Colin's feet, could be lashed together and dragged across the ground, but that would create too much noise here in the city. They'd both have to carry him until they were beyond the Haessari patrols.

"Ready?"

Siobhaen nodded.

It took them nearly an hour to wrestle the litter with Colin in it up through the hole and out into the secondary room. By then, Eraeth was ready to strangle Siobhaen, and by the irritated anger in her face, she felt the same about him. But neither of them spoke of it, both snapping out orders and suggestions like whips. Once in the outer room, Eraeth stretched his arms and shoulders and checked on Colin while Siobhaen scouted their route out of the city.

They'd decided to head south from their location, farther away from the Haessari enclave in the surrounding cliffs and opposite from their most recent patrols and search parties. Neither one of them knew what lay to the south, but they couldn't head west: that was the direction the Wraith army had gone to attack the dwarren on the plains. Eraeth guessed the Haessari were at least partially supplying that army, so there'd be scouts and caravans, more than likely watched over by those strange birdlike creatures he'd begun calling taeredacs. East was also not an option—it took them farther away from aid and further into unexplored lands. South was their best option. They knew there were humans to the south somewhere. Even if they didn't run into a human patrol or settlement, once they were far enough south they could cut west and hope to run into the dwarren rather than the Wraith army.

But first they had to escape the ruined city.

Eraeth tensed as someone approached, drawing a knife. The darkness outside was lit only by a half moon and the stars, the night clear. He moved to the edge of the eastern window, saw a shadow dart from one pool of darkness to another, but recognized Siobhaen by her movements.

She ducked into the room, low to the ground, and he coughed to catch her attention. She spun toward him, knives raised, then lowered them a couple of heartbeats later.

"It's clear as far as the ring of cracked stone that surrounds the city. Let's move."

Eraeth grabbed the litter again, Siobhaen leading them out into the night. He kept his eyes on the shadowed buildings and road to either side, trusting Siobhaen to warn him of anything overhead or behind as she skirted random debris. His shoulders began burning within the first hour, the ache starting high and spreading down into his upper back and along the backs of his arms. His fingers began to pulse with pain, threatening to cramp. After two hours, he was forced to signal Siobhaen for a halt. She nodded grudgingly, then vanished into the shadows.

He snapped his hands, trying to shake out the pain in his fingers, and sank down onto the gaping edge of a hole in one of the buildings. His breath came harsh and ragged, but it settled quickly. He wiped sweat from his brow. To the north, he could see the pinprick firelight coming from the Haessari city in the cliff faces that surrounded the ruins.

Siobhaen reappeared. She halted when she saw him, but he waved her away. She knelt at Colin's side instead, checking his wound.

"He's doing about as expected."

Siobhaen stood. "And you?"

He massaged his shoulder. "It's harder than it looks."

"I can take over for a while. Drag him, while you scout."

"No, it will make too much noise. We'll start dragging him once we reach the debris ring, beyond the main Haessari patrols."

They both reached for the litter's handles again.

Two hours later they reached the pile of debris that surrounded the city. Inside the ring, the buildings were disintegrating but they were mostly intact, the destruction caused by age and the elements. But the ring marked a dividing point. Cracked and shattered stone had heaved up in a mound, the blocks obviously from what had once been buildings. Some had quarried edges, others the faded outlines of carvings. As they heaved Colin's litter up and over the ridge, Eraeth saw what must have once been the hand from a statue, three fingers broken off.

On the far side, Eraeth assumed there had once been streets and parks and a thriving city. Instead, the ground had been churned up, whatever had been here before broken and jumbled.

They lashed one end of the litter together, creating a travois. Siobhaen took hold of the remaining handles and motioned him ahead with her chin. Flexing his hands, he began to scout, trotting forward into the night-shrouded wasteland. As he moved, searching for the easiest path while scanning the skies and the rolling ground for signs of the taeredacs and the Haessari, he wondered what could cause such strange damage. Whatever it was, it was ancient. The air and stone was laden with age, dry and dusty, older even than the Alvritshai ruins they'd wandered through in the White Wastes, by the feel.

Light had begun to touch the horizon by the time they passed through the shattered section of the city and back into a narrow band of ruins beneath the massive cliffs. They'd traded off pulling the travois twice more, but as soon as Eraeth saw the thin edge of dawn he had Siobhaen begin scouting for a place to hunker down for the day. He'd expected her to find a room in one of the buildings, but he followed her to the mouth of one of the jagged chasms that riddled the cliff face. They ducked into its cool shadow as the sun peeked above the horizon, tainting the eastern skies a vivid orange-pink, a vibrant green-blue above.

As he set down the travois and stretched out his back and shoulders, he said to Siobhaen, "We won't be able to do this for long. We need to get out of the ruins and as far away as we can, then find another place to hole up until he comes around."

* * *

"Where are they?"

Quotl frowned in annoyance at Tarramic's insistent tone without opening his eyes. "They may not be here at all. Now shut up. You're ruining my concentration."

Tarramic mumbled something Quotl couldn't hear. Gaezel stamped their feet and snorted behind him, the clan's raiding party restless. They'd emerged from the dwarren tunnels south and west of the Break fifteen minutes before and the Riders were ready for action. Since the battle at the Break, the clans had discovered the Wraith army had seized control of the cliffs, but had halted there. Reports said they were recovering from the losses caused by the dwarren and Quotl's collapse of the wall of rock north of the slide. It had killed hundreds of them, including nearly forty Riders. Quotl's chest ached at the thought, but he knew the dwarren had been desperate. If he hadn't used Ilacqua's power—the Land itself—to halt the Wraith army it would have swarmed over the Break and caught the dwarren in the open. The collapse had given the dwarren time to seal the main entrances to the tunnels and regroup.

But now the clan chiefs were ready to strike back. The Cochen knew they couldn't attack as one, on a single front; the plains were too open for that, the Wraith army too large. Instead, they intended to carve away at the army's edges, using stealth attacks on their scouts, on the supply wagons, on any group that diverged from the main army small enough for the dwarren to take. The tunnels were their greatest advantage now. Tarramic's group was only one of several spread across the Land to the north and south, searching for signs of the Wraith army.

Drawing in a deep breath of the fresh night air, Quotl centered himself. Since the battle, he had felt Ilacqua's presence inside him, throbbing beneath his skin, in his blood, warm and comforting. During the meetings in the keeva, that presence surged forward, suffusing him, as it had at the Break. And with it came an uncanny prescience of the earth around him, the stone and grass, the air and the animals that thrived there. He could feel the life flowing back and forth through them.

Those senses sharpened as he concentrated. The damp grass from the recent rain bit into his nostrils, the earth beneath saturated and thick. He tasted the bitterness of autumn in the breeze that prickled the hairs on his arm. The musk of the gaezel and the fear sweat of the Riders surrounded him, and he could hear their blood pumping in anticipation of the hunt. He pushed beyond, spreading himself out through the earth beneath his feet, Ilacqua's presence rising inside him. Unconsciously, he began humming one of the shaman chants, Tarramic and those closest quieting. His brows furrowed as he reached outwards, focusing to the east, but when he finally sensed *wrongness*, it wasn't to the east, it was west.

His mouth turned with distaste and he fought the urge to spit. Twisting in his seat, he opened his eyes and pointed behind the group with his scepter. The beads tied to its end with strips of hide rattled. "The blight on the Land is there, headed this way. There are twenty in the group."

"Orannian? Urannen? Kell?"

Quotl's eyes narrowed as he focused, then shook his head. "Hard to tell. No Wraiths. And no gruen or terren. They're medium sized."

Tarramic spun his mount toward the Riders and began issuing commands. The party consisted of forty Riders and gaezel, which Tarramic split into two groups. One of them broke away from the main force, the hoofbeats of the gaezel fading into the night. There wasn't enough moonlight for Quotl to catch their shadows on the plains after a few breaths, and they rode slow enough that the wet grass smothered the sound of their passage once they were beyond spear range. As soon as they were gone, Tarramic brought his mount up next to Quotl's.

"We'll meet them head on. Are they scouts?"

"Twenty of them?" Quotl shrugged. His fingers itched for his pipe and some of the yetope leaves; it always helped him think better. "I wonder how far west they were."

Tarramci didn't answer, but Quotl knew they were both thinking of the Summer Tree and how far its influence had degraded. The Cochen had already ordered that every clan begin harvesting whatever food stock they could and storing it in the tunnels. They would leave nothing above ground for the Wraith army to use.

Quotl stirred in his seat, removed a knife from its sheath at his belt. "They're close now."

Tarramic gestured to the right and left, then drew his own axe. The clan chief kicked his gaezel forward. Within moments they were charging across the plains, the wind chill in Quotl's face, pulling at his beard. The only sound was the thud of hooves on grass, the usual dwarren ululations before battle silenced by the clan chief's order. They wanted as much surprise as they could get.

A heartbeat later, the figures of the Wraith's creatures appeared on the plains before them, all twenty running to the east. Quotl raised his scepter in one hand and bellowed, "For Thousand Springs! For Ilacqua!"

The Riders behind fanned out, their sharp cries rising into the night as Quotl bore down on one of the shadowy figures. The runners faltered a moment at the sudden outcry, but then Quotl swung his scepter, felt its metal head strike the creature across the face, the impact jarring. His gaezel trampled the body as it fell, but Quotl was already focused on the next figure. He heard a hiss as he approached, knew it to be one of the snake people, and brought his scepter down hard. But the creature dodged, the motion fluid and quick. His scepter glanced off its shoulder, even as the Orannian's hand snaked forward and ripped him from his saddle.

Quotl heard one of the gaezel's high-pitched and eerie death screams a moment before he hit the ground, his breath knocked out of him, his scepter lost. Hooves beat the ground, one stabbing into his thigh, and he tried to roll out of the way, but struck something more solid. Grasping for a hold, his hands closed on the Orannian's legs, the material of its breeches coarse. Without thought, he brought the knife still clutched in his other hand around and jabbed it into the snake's thigh.

It screamed, the sound a gut-wrenching howl and hiss, and tried to jerk away. Quotl hung on as it stumbled backwards. He pulled his knife free and struck again, the snake stumbling and falling. Quotl clambered up his legs and stabbed the knife into its gut as it thrashed. Taloned hands reached for him, snagged in his beard, but he could feel its blood slicking the hand that still clutched the knife. Its motions slowed, but with a last burst of effort its hood flared and its head shot forward, fangs bared as it snapped at his face.

Quotl cried out and lurched back, out of range. Something liquid struck his cheek and began to burn. He rolled away from the body and scrubbed at his cheek with the sleeve of his tunic until the burning stopped, then sat gasping. Around him, the Riders fought the rest of the Wraith group in the darkness. He watched, one hand going to his chest where his heart pounded painfully.

He was getting too old for this.

The Riders took out the rest of the Orannian. Tarramic dispatched the last two with his axe. Most of the Riders had lost their gaezel during the fight, including Tarramic. He spun where he stood, axe raised, but saw the rest of the Riders already making certain the Orannian were dead. Lowering his weapon, he sought out Quotl, trotting to the head shaman's side and squatting down.

"Are you hurt?"

"I'm fine. A burn from that one's poison, but it will fade."

Tarramic remained silent for a long moment. "You shouldn't be participating in these raids. I should never have allowed you to come."

Quotl bristled. "Why not? The head shaman always follows the clan chief into battle."

"You are the head shaman of Thousand Springs, yes. But you are more. You proved that on the battlefield at the Break. And you proved it yet again today. None of the other shamans could have told us exactly where the creatures were, or exactly how many of them there were."

"Did we get them all?"

"Yes. Some tried to escape but the secondary group caught them. They're to the southwest."

Quotl shifted and saw the force Tarramic had sent to flank the group as it rejoined them, their figures black and anonymous in the dark.

Tarramic gripped his shoulder and leaned far enough forward Quotl could see the glint of the moon in his eyes. "You cannot ignore what has happened. Ilacqua has touched you. You are meant for more than being the Thousand Springs head shaman."

"The dwarren already have an Archon."

Tarramic's grip tightened. "Kimannen was powerful, once. But he has weakened. This is a Turning. The Four Winds are blowing. We cannot afford to have a weak Archon."

Quotl clenched his jaw. He had shoved his confrontation with the Archon aside as the clans regrouped. Too much had needed to be done in the aftermath of the Break—tunnels sealed, messages sent to each clan, plans made. He had immersed himself in the chaos and avoided the Archon whenever possible.

But that did not alter the fact that the power had shifted at the Break.

"Kimannen will not relinquish his hold on the shamans easily."

"No. But you know the Thousand Springs shamans will support you. And so will many of the others. They witnessed your power at the Break. It will be hard for Kimannen to counter that, not without insulting the shamans' intelligence."

"It is too soon."

Tarramic let his hand drop and stood. "Do not wait too long, or the memories of what happened at the Break will fade. But enough of such talk. Come look at the bodies and tell us what Ilacqua reveals to you. I do not think this was a scouting party."

Quotl took Tarramic's extended hand and rose with a groan, muscles already aching.

He leaned down over the snake creature he'd killed while Tarramic called for lanterns. In the darkness, the blood that saturated the creature's stomach and the grass beneath was black. Its smooth, scaly skin appeared glossy. Its head had fallen to one side, mouth open, fangs bared, hood still flared. The skin beneath the hood was pale, but patterns emerged in the scales on the creature's forehead, starting near the blunt snout and widening upwards around the eyes. Once the lantern was lit, Quotl could see that the mottling was tri-colored, two shades of brown with some red scales continuing up over the head at regular intervals. It carried the typical s-shaped sword, a few daggers tucked into its belt. A satchel was slung over the creature's head.

Using his knife, Quotl cut it free and sorted through the contents. He held up a vial of milky liquid, then grunted when he found the darts and the blowpipe inside. He guessed the vial was poison, probably the creature's own venom. He found nothing else of interest, just food, a waterskin, scraping stone and oil for the blade.

"They were in a hurry and we surprised them. None of their weapons were drawn and they were moving fast. They weren't expecting to run into us."

"Why were they coming from the west?"

Quotl shook his head. "Have the Riders check the bodies. Search their satchels. Look for anything out of place." As Tarramic gave the order, Quotl moved to the next body himself, began rummaging through clothing, searching for pockets, checking bags.

A moment later, a Rider cried out, motioning toward the head shaman and the clan chief.

Both Tarramic and Quotl hurried over, the clan chief passing a metal cylinder from the Rider to his head shaman before kneeling to search the body more thoroughly. Quotl held the cylinder up to the lantern light, the flame flickering over patterns and indentations along its silvered length. He focused on the ends, made of bronze, heavier than the rest. After careful examination, he pushed in two buttons on opposite sides of the rounded mouth and one bronze end popped off.

Tarramic looked up. A few of the Riders edged closer in order to see better.

When Quotl tilted the cylinder, a sheaf of papers fell out. Tarramic stood and Quotl began sorting through them.

"What are they?" the clan chief asked.

"Messages, I would assume. I can't read them. They're written in a language I don't recognize." He glanced down at the creature's face. "It must be Orannian."

Tarramic said nothing. Quotl scanned the dead lying on all sides. Only a few of the dwarren had been injured, none of them killed. Unease uncurled in his stomach and he felt the need for his pipe and weed more than ever. There was only one explanation that made any sense.

"They weren't scouts. This one was a courier, the others its protection. They were reporting back to the Wraith army near the Break."

Tarramic faced west, and Quotl watched the realization dawn on his face. "There is another Wraith army, and it's already deep into dwarren lands. What is its purpose?"

"I don't know."

"We must inform the Cochen."

And the shamans of Thousand Springs must meet, Quotl thought as he rolled the papers and restored them to the cylinder. They must call upon Ilacqua and the gods of the Four Rivers for guidance. Perhaps they would reveal something of what the messages contained, even if Quotl couldn't read them.

3

Deep within the Hauttaeren Mountains behind Caercaern, Tamaell Thaedoren listened to the soothing words of a chant as three members of the White Phalanx stepped forward, knelt as if in supplication to Aielan, head bowed, and held three burning brands to the tinder of the pyres. Lord Aeren's body lay on the center pyre, flanked by two other guardsmen who had died of their wounds after they'd fled into the passage hidden behind the cascade of water at the back edge of the Tamaell's private gardens. As soon as Thaedoren, Daedalen, and the last of the mixed White and Rhyssal Phalanx had passed through, the massive stone door had been pushed back into place and sealed. They'd tended to their wounded first, before moving deeper into the tunnels. The caverns had been carved from the rock, rough-hewn and serviceable, nothing more. They connected to the halls and corridors that were the province of Lotaern and the Sanctuary in a few locations, but had been kept secret from the Order of Aielan since their creation. A few caches of supplies lined the main tunnel, placed there at the tunnel's creation and mostly useless, but they had already been raided by the Phalanx members. They'd survived off of that and what little food they'd found in the upper floors of the palace. The pyres for the dead were built from old torches and odd pieces of dried wood soaked in lantern oil, and they were far enough from the palace that the smoke seeping through the cracks in the ceiling used for ventilation wouldn't be noticed from the outside.

As tinder caught, the three White Phalanx stepped back. Smoke filled the narrow chamber, harsh and acrid with burning oil and flesh, but Thaedoren forced himself to remain even though his eyes teared. Others retreated back down the corridor, coughing. Those few still chanting ground down into silence. Hiroun, Lord Aeren's personal guard, stood beside Thaedoren, his hand clenching and unclenching on the handle of his cattan. Daedalen stood, back rigid, on his other side.

As soon as Aeren's pyre shifted, consumed wood snapping beneath the body's weight, Daedalen turned and placed one hand on Thaedoren's shoulder. "It's time to move."

Thaedoren nodded. He wished he could have given Aeren to Aielan's Light more properly, in the white fires in one of the temples, but they couldn't carry the body where they were going. Nor could they keep it preserved. He didn't know when they'd be back among the normal populace, let alone free enough to perform a ritual in a temple unhindered.

Motioning to the guardsmen to either side, he headed deeper into the tunnels, leaving Hiroun and the other Rhyssal guards to mourn their fallen lord.

"Are the rest of the Phalanx ready?" Thaedoren asked.

"We've gathered whatever we could from the supplies stored here. We can get water from the pools and streams built into the tunnel. But the food we found in the upper floors of the palace won't last long. We have nearly forty Phalanx, eight of those from Rhyssal House, along with myself, you, and Reanne. At strict rations, we can make it another two days. We need to find additional supplies by then."

"We'll have to risk using the exits into the city then. Send some of the Phalanx out into the streets to collect food and to scout out what Lotaern and the others are doing. The rest of us will continue on to the exits farther west along the mountains."

"And where will we head once we're out?"

Thaedoren had no idea how many of the White Phalanx survived within the city. Had any of them had a chance to retreat? Or were they caught in their barracks and slaughtered before they could fight or escape? He had seen no signs of resistance from the height of the gardens, but that meant little. Regardless, he could see no way to rally whatever support he held within the city for a stand against Peloroun and the others. He couldn't even count on the support of his own people, the House of Resue. Not with the way Lotaern had used his position as Chosen, along with the acolytes and Flame, to taint the general populace's opinion this past year. All Lotaern need say is that the Wraiths and the sukrael were coming and the fear inspired by those creatures in the years before Shaeveran brought the Winter Tree would ignite again and bring the people to his side.

"The only House I can guarantee is not a part of the coup is Rhyssal. We'll head to Artillien. Perhaps our mother will know something of what is happening with the other Houses and where their loyalties lie."

And perhaps with the Rhyssal House Phalanx behind him, he'll have a chance to regroup, find his allies, and with them, reclaim his throne and the heart of the Alvritshai people.

* * *

"Time! Back off!"

Corim broke off his parry of Wade's swing at the swordmaster's curt command, but Wade didn't pull his strike. The wooden training blade thunked into Corim's upper arm with a slap and the older boy sneered as he stepped back. Corim glowered as he rubbed at his arm. Wade's eyes widened and he motioned Corim forward, urging him to attack. Corim's training blade rose to waist height.

Wade had been pushing him all morning, tripping him in the barracks when they stumbled awake for roll call and mumbling a fake apology, spilling his water down Corim's shoulder at breakfast, then flicking small stones at him during the laps around the practice yard and wall. As soon as they fell into line for the sword drill, he'd made certain he stood across from Corim, even though he was two years older and at least a hand taller.

As soon as the swordmaster barked, "Begin!" Wade had taken every opportunity to push the boundaries of the lesson and hurt Corim. Nothing serious—a sharp rap to his knuckles, a stinging slap of the flat of the blade against his side. His upper arm was the only one that would bruise, although he could already feel the ache in his side and his knuckles throbbed.

The most frustrating part was Corim didn't know why Wade had singled him out. There were nearly fifty boys in the group, ranging in age from ten to fourteen, Wade one of the oldest. They were taken from the refugees and the city both, all of them conscripted and set to training within a day of the Horde's arrival on the plains before Temeritt and the burning of the Autumn Tree. Corim knew of thirty such groups, spread throughout the city, but he suspected there were more. Temeritt was huge, so large and with so many people that the first few days had been overwhelming. He would have fled if the city gates hadn't all been closed against the Horde.

And if there'd been any other place he could flee to.

The grief sliced cleanly through his anger and the tip of his wooden blade dropped, point hitting the dirt. It caught him at odd moments, when he least expected it, and he fought the tightening in his chest, the burn at the corners of his eyes. The attack on Gray's Kill that had killed his parents and destroyed his life had happened months ago; he should be over it. He *needed* to be over it, needed to be strong, like Jayson and Gregson.

Gripping the handle of the wooden sword, he shoved the grief aside and faced off against Wade again as the swordmaster called for another bout. The muscle in his upper arm twinged, but he fell into a guarded stance. All across the practice yard, the others did the same, facing off against each other in pairs. Wade smirked before slipping into the stance easily. He'd had more practice before being made part of the group, had protested when he'd seen the others on that first day, demanded to be moved to an older unit, although Braxton, the swordmaster, had ignored him.

"Set!" Braxton shouted at the far end of the yard, back to them all, then turned. "Begin!"

Corim thrust forward, as they'd been shown, Wade shunting the blade aside with a sharp crack of wood against wood. But then he spun the wooden length around and tagged Corim on the back of the hand, the blunt tip gouging into flesh. Corim yelped as his hand went numb, tingling pain lancing up to his elbow. His mock sword dropped into the dust, but he reached down with his other hand and snatched it up. His breath hissed out between clenched teeth as he repositioned.

The older boy only laughed. The hackles on the back of Corim's neck and shoulders rose, and something inside him snapped.

He launched forward, sword swinging awkwardly in his left hand. Shock registered in Wade's eyes a moment before Corim's blade connected with his temple. As he fell back with a scream, Corim leaped onto him, straddling his torso as he punched with his right hand and flailed with the wooden sword in his left. Every strike with his right caused sizzling pain, but he didn't stop, even when he heard distant shouts and felt an arm wrap around his torso and drag him away. He kicked and writhed in the grip, two other men helping Wade up into a sitting position. Blood trailed down from a cut on Wade's temple and dirt from the yard speckled the right side of his face, but otherwise he looked unharmed.

"Stop it!" a voice growled in his ear. The arm that held him shook him roughly. "I said stop it! It's over. Let it go."

Corim went limp, sword dropping from his grasp. The arm holding him slowly relaxed and lowered him to his feet. Corim's anger was gone, replaced by a humming numbness that bled into a shame he could feel burning his cheeks. Jayson wouldn't have lost it, like a child.

"What happened here?" Braxton demanded, halting between the two.

"He attacked me," Wade spat. "He wasn't following the drill. Stupid farmer."

"I'm not a farmer, I'm a miller."

Wade snorted and one of the men, a guardsman, smacked him on the back of the head hard enough he stumbled forward.

"Farmer, miller, merchant's apprentice, it doesn't matter," Braxton said. "You're all soldiers now. And you will fight, or haven't you seen the army waiting outside our walls? Save the fight for them."

The swordmaster spun on the men and boys who'd clustered behind him. "Form up! You all've earned another hour's worth of practice to make up for this lost time. Now move!" He grabbed the shoulder of one of the youngest and pushed him back into position before turning on both Corim and Wade. "Both of you will do another ten laps around the yard and the barrack's wall once we're finished. No infighting, you hear? I don't care who you are—" he shot a finger at Wade "—or where you came from—" now pointing at Corim "—you'll work together or you'll die beneath the Horde."

He stalked away, and the guard at Corim's back finally released his hold, although he turned him around and caught his gaze. Corim hadn't seen him before, but then most of the Temeritt Legion looked the same to him, in their black and orange tabards. Like most, this one sported a black beard trimmed close, nicked in a few places by scars. The helm shadowed dark brown eyes.

"You all right?"

Corim flushed again under his scrutiny. "Yes, sir."

"Don't let him get to you. He isn't worth it."

Corim watched the guardsman walk away, then turned and faced Wade. The blood had already dried at Wade's temple. He brushed at the dirt on his face as he shifted forward opposite Corim, mock sword held tight and ready.

"So the miller wants to be a soldier," Wade muttered. "I'll show you how to be a soldier."

Corim scooped up his own sword, Wade's eyes flicking left and right. Two of Temeritt's Legion stood to one side, eyes on them both. Braxton also remained close, although his attention was divided between them and the others in their group who had already begun sparring, the sounds of mock battle rattling across the yard.

"Ready?" Wade asked.

Sweat broke out in the palms of Corim's hands, but he nodded.

Wade attacked, bringing his sword around hard. Corim parried, the crack of wood on wood making him wince. His hand tingled with the shock, the ache in the back of his hand reawakening. Wade's blows fell harsh and heavy, but the older boy kept to the drill. He simply didn't pull any of his strikes, using all of his strength to pound Corim back and grind down his defenses. Any slip on Corim's part and the wooden blade slipped through and hit hard, Corim hissing to keep from crying out. The Legion watched impassively, one of them growing bored after a while and glancing away. Braxton grunted in approval before wandering to the far side of the yard again.

They drilled for another two hours, Braxton's shouts filling the length of the quad, until Corim's arms felt like rubber and his entire body like one large bruise. Jayson had worked him hard at the mill, but nothing like this, nothing that strained every muscle in his body. As soon as Braxton called for a halt, half of the boys collapsed to the ground, Corim among them. He was drenched in sweat, but didn't care, staring up at the blue of the sky above, breathing heavily.

Wade leaned over him. He was sweaty, but he wasn't winded. He prodded Corim with the tip of his sword and said, "Don't get too comfortable, miller boy. We still have to run the yard and the wall."

Corim groaned.

As he clambered to his feet, the rest of the Legion who'd kept watch on them all morning were systematically rousing the rest of those who'd collapsed, herding them all toward the meal hall and the barracks beyond. Braxton stood in the center of the yard. "Ten laps. Put your practice swords away before you start."

* * *

"Vics is still favoring his left leg," Terson muttered. "He shouldn't be in training. He should be in the infirmary."

Lieutenant Commander Gregson stirred. They stood on one of Temeritt's many defensive walls, constructed over the years as the town grew into the massive city that now consumed the entire hill from the palace at its apex to a good portion of the surrounding plains. Only the lake beneath the hill's sharpest bluff broke through the serpentine streets and crush of buildings.

Gregson turned his attention back to the recruits training in the rough square beneath them. "If this were a normal training session, then he would be. But with the Horde outside our walls, every able-bodied man who can train, will train."

Terson's body grew rigid with disapproval. Gregson's newly promoted lieutenant practically slept with the Legion's codebook under his pillow. Anything that deviated from it set him on edge.

Motioning to the rest of the men, Gregson added, "The miller, Jayson, has improved."

"Yes. More so than the rest of the refugees we've picked up."

Gregson didn't like the condescension in Terson's voice, but he'd known of the soldier's prejudices since he'd been assigned to Cobble Kill and placed under Gregson's command. Terson had been raised in the city, son of a Legionnaire in a long line of Legionnaires. He'd hated Cobble Kill and he'd never hidden that hate well. Gregson secretly wondered if his assignment there had been some sort of punishment meted out by those higher in command here in Temeritt, although he would never have the opportunity to find out.

Gregson had been promoted along with a slew of other survivors after the retreat to Temeritt, the entire Legion force reorganized even as the Autumn Tree burned outside their walls and the Horde entrenched themselves on the plains around it. His new command consisted of veteran Legionnaires called back into service, a slew of soldiers who had barely finished training before the Horde's attack on the province, and nearly twice that in refugees and raw recruits from the city and those who had managed to make its walls before the gates had been sealed. Gregson had set the veterans and soldiers to training the recruits immediately.

Movement caught his eye on the far side of the square. A page in Lord Kobel's livery halted at the edge of the activity, scanning the recruits before jogging around to Marshall, the soldier Gregson had put in charge of the morning's spear exercise. Marshall didn't halt his rhythmic barks of "Thrust!" Nor did he take his eyes off the recruits, all of them lunging and shoving their spears forward into imaginary enemies before pulling them back and resetting after each command. At each lunge, a grunting "Huh!" filled the square. All of the men wore armor—what could be cobbled together after the trained Legionnaires had taken their share—and all of them were sweating profusely in the early afternoon heat. After a moment, Marshall glanced toward Gregson's position and motioned the page toward the wall.

The young boy looked up, hand shaded against the sun, then took off toward the stairs to the right.

"Message."

Terson perked up in interest.

Minutes later, the page appeared and trotted toward them. As he turned, Gregson's eye caught on the remains of the Autumn Tree in the distance. The blackened branches spiked into the sky, the bole rising higher than their position halfway up Temeritt's hill. He recalled seeing the tree the first time he came to Temeritt as a boy, ready to become part of the Legion. Its leaves—most larger than he had been then himself—

rustling in the breeze as his escort of recruitment officers herded their group toward the city. He'd asked then why the tree hadn't been placed inside the city walls, but the officers had scoffed at him, as if the question were asinine. Only later had he learned that when Colin Harten had planted the tree, Temeritt had been nothing more than a tower with a few surrounding cottages. There hadn't been a wall, or a city.

Recalling the image of those leaves burning, the entire tree a tower of flame, Gregson wrenched his gaze away to meet the page.

"Message from GreatLord Kobel for Lieutenant Commander Gregson, sir." The boy nodded stiffly, fist over his heart, then presented a folded missive sealed with wax.

Gregson took it without comment and broke the seal. He could sense Terson's anticipation as he read it, knew his second fought the urge to read it over his shoulder. When he was done, he folded the note. "Tell GreatLord Kobel and Lord Akers that my men will be ready."

The page darted away.

"What is it?" Terson asked, his anxiousness getting the better of him.

"GreatLord Kobel commands our unit to be ready for action at Kertillion Square at the seventh hour."

"What for?"

Gregson shifted toward the edge of the wall facing the charred Autumn Tree and the black mass of the Horde's camp that stained the plains beneath it. "It would appear the lords of Temeritt have tired of waiting for the Horde to come to us."

* * *

"All units have assembled, GreatLord."

Kobel didn't turn at the report, his eye sweeping the extent of Kertillion Square. Five hundred cavalry and nearly a thousand foot soldiers in full armor and the Temeritt colors of the Legion filled the open area, along with another thousand of the conscripted forces from the refugees and population. Most of the latter looked terrified, outfitted in bits and pieces of armor and whatever weapons could be found within the city. He had blacksmiths working day and night to produce more swords and armor, but in the meantime they made do with what they had. The city was crowded, and they had food enough for at most four or five months if they rationed, but he wasn't certain how much longer they could hold out after that.

He turned to Lord Akers. "And are your own men ready, Lord

Akers?"

"They are. I received word ten minutes ago."

"Very well. Pass the orders to each unit and mount up."

Akers issued orders as he moved down the line, runners darting out among the soldiers to report to unit leaders. Those not already mounted among the cavalry pulled themselves into their saddles while unit leaders shouted orders to fall in. Some of those on foot headed out, clearing the street toward the near gates. Many Temeritt citizens—their faces lined with stress and fear, but who continued on with their lives as if the Horde weren't outside the walls—scrambled out of the way.

Kobel moved toward his own mount. Once seated, Kobel nodded toward the horn bearer to his right. As the notes sounded, kept low since everyone who needed to hear was in the square, Kobel kneed his horse forward. His escort fell in around him—two standard bearers and a small personal guard of five Legion.

They wound through the streets. Faces appeared in windows in the second and third stories to either side, and merchants and customers stepped to the doorways of the shops beneath. A few people moved out onto their balconies. Most were children and the elderly, the men who were able still working in the blacksmithies or training with the Legion, the women fletching arrows, tending wounded, or helping with the organization of arms and armor, weapons and food. No one cheered, although Kobel saw some of the dread drain away in their eyes as the small force of Legion marched past. Reality had sunk in when the Legion forces had staggered into the city after their defeat at the Northward Ridge and the Horde closed in. The killing blow, the one that had sunk despair throughout the entire city, had been the burning of the Autumn Tree.

Kobel's hands clenched on the reins and his horse snorted in confusion, head tossing before he managed to unlock his fingers. He had tasted the fear of the citizens that day and in the days that followed. The fire lasted three days, longer than Kobel would have expected, but then it wasn't a natural tree. It had smoldered for another two. And during the entire time, the Horde had roiled on the plains before the city. A token force had tried to take the main gates when the Autumn Tree had first caught fire, but it hadn't been a serious threat. Kobel assumed it was some of the Horde's creatures unleashing aggression on the nearest target. Most of those attacking had been the more animalistic of the Horde's force—the trolls and giants. They'd managed to kill a few from the heights before they'd retreated. The Alvritshai and the snake-like creatures that made up most of the rest of the force had stayed well out of range, setting up camp beneath the Autumn Tree. Initially, there had been enough to encircle half of the city, spread out in a thick arc, their campfires dotting the plains at night. A week after the tree had burned, two-thirds of the army had packed up and headed to the west.

None of their scouts had managed to elude the Horde and warn the Provinces to the west or the south, or Yhnar in the east. He didn't think any of the messages sent by pigeon had reached them either.

He glanced to the sky, picking out the leathery birds that circled overhead, out of range of even the longbows. There were at least four of them drifting above them whenever the sky was clear, sometimes as many as eight. The only time they couldn't be seen was when it clouded over.

He'd seen the creatures take out at least a dozen of the messenger pigeons himself.

Shouts brought his attention back to the street and the wide plaza before the gates that opened up before them. He caught Akers' eye, then Kobel and his escort broke away from the main force toward the stairs. Dismounting, he handed the reins off to a waiting page, patted the animal's neck, then led the way up to the parapet above.

As soon as he broke out into the chill evening air, he moved to the edge of the wall, placing his hand against the gritty stone. He glared at the Horde beyond, at the creatures drifting overhead, then toward the east.

Clouds billowed on the horizon, spreading westward. Lightning flared in their depths, illuminating the layers within, although it was still too distant to hear anything more than a low grumble of thunder. But it was coming in fast.

They'd been waiting days for such a storm.

He mentally recited a prayer to Diermani, then turned to head back down to his forces. "Tell Lord Akers he may begin. We'll attack as soon as he's ready."

* * *

Jayson clutched his spear with both hands. On either side, his fellow Legionnaires fidgeted, clothes rustling and armor clanking as they brushed up against each other. They were pressed too closely together for the spears to be effective, but Jayson knew they'd be able to spread out once they reached the far side of the gate.

Overhead, the first trailing edges of the storm he'd seen earlier scudded across the sky. The sun had begun to fade twenty minutes ago.

"We aren't ready yet," someone whispered behind them.

"Shut up." Vics' grizzled features scanned the officers as orders were passed around the ranks. "We're as ready as they think we are, nothing short of that. If they say we can handle this, we can. They aren't stupid. GreatLord Kobel knows what he's doing."

Jayson fervently hoped so.

Sudden movement caught his eye. With a creak of straining wood, the massive southwestern gates began to grind open, the portcullis still down. The road and the plains stretched beyond, the arched stone walls narrowing the view to a space twenty riders could slip through at once. Jayson's eyes shot toward the height of the wall, where he could see a few of GreatLord Kobel's men, those set to watch and report from the heights.

Then Gregson rode down the unit's length. "We're to hold the gates and protect the retreat, nothing more!" Lightning flared and thunder rumbled through the stone beneath their feet as Gregson repeated the orders, passing back and forth, voice raised to fight the storm. "Hold the gates and protect the retreat! GreatLord Kobel, Lord Akers, and the cavalry will ride out to meet the Horde, not us." He said more, but thunder drowned it out, followed a moment later by a spattering of rain.

A few of the men groaned, but the overall sense from everyone was relief.

Vics nodded succinctly. "I told you."

Jayson didn't have a chance to respond, the rough clanking of chains filling the plaza as the portcullis began to rise. A roar from the Legion echoed back toward their unit as the front ranks charged through the opening and out onto the plains. The cavalry followed, and before Jayson was ready, Terson and Gregson motioned them forward.

They moved as a unit, their minimal training holding together better than Jayson would have expected. The men on all sides roared incoherently, the sound bouncing back on them as they ran beneath the gate, the thickness of the wall surrounding them. Jayson kept the line as they broke through on the far side. Terson called out orders, but Jayson only half heard them. Their unit broke to the right, only a few missing the mark or stumbling, and then they were spreading out as they'd been taught. Another unit in better armor and carrying shields had already formed up in a line from a point on the road back to the wall and Gregson's men fell in behind them, settling into crouches with their spears pointed toward the sky, each spaced between two of those in armor. The shield bearers each had swords, but Gregson's unit only carried knives. The shield bearers weren't any more experienced than Jayson's unit, he realized, but they had the armor because they were the spear carriers' protection.

Kneeling, Jayson scanned down the line, picked out Ricks and a few others from Cobble Kill. He couldn't see Curtis. Behind them, a similar line of shield bearers and another unit of spears had formed the second half of their formation. Any attack would strike the point and be split down the two sides.

But they'd have to get through the cavalry first.

Clouds roiling, rain coming down in fits and spats, Jayson shifted his attention toward the horse and riders led by GreatLord Kobel and Lord Akers. Beyond them, the Horde had begun to react. Their camp was too distant for Jayson to make out much, especially with the storm sheathing the plains in half-light, but he saw movement, heard scattered shouts and the blat of a horn.

GreatLord Kobel didn't wait. With a sudden tensing of haunches, the cavalry leaped forward, horses streaming across the plains. At the same time, the clouds unleashed their downpour, rain sheeting across the battlefield and obscuring the charge. Jayson shuddered as the chill water sluiced down his neck and beneath his armor, soaking him in a matter of moments. He wiped it away from his face and spluttered, men cursing and shifting on all sides as they did the same. The crushed stalks of grass sank into the earth as the dirt soaked up the rain and became mud.

"Hold steady!" Ricks stalked back and forth behind them. "Hold the line!"

A sudden scream pierced the roar of water and the growls of thunder and Jayson started. His hands worked at the wood of the spear as images of the fighting in Cobble Kill and the mad dash for safety at the Northward Ridge echoed in the back of his head. He thought of Corim, training in his own unit, and Ara—of all of those who'd started out with him in Cobble Kill and made it to Temeritt—and something in his chest hardened. He straightened where he knelt, and the edges of panic that fluttered through his chest calmed.

They stayed that way, tense and expectant, for what felt like eternity, rain pounding down from the skies, snatches of battle reaching them at odd lulls between the thunder. Lightning revealed nothing but gray streaks of rain and the purplish, bruised clouds above. A few of the men cringed at each blue-white streak.

Then a riderless horse bolted out of the rain and everyone started, a few crying out in shock. Spears and shields rattled and clanged as the wall tightened, Gregson shouting, "Ready!" unnecessarily. The horse slowed and whinnied as it hit the blockade, turning to canter down its length. As it passed Jayson's location, he recognized the Legion's colors and noted the slash across its flank, blood marring the animal's skin. With a curse, Ricks ordered a few of the men aside and, with the help of two others, caught and pulled the spooked animal back behind the barricade, sending it toward the gate with a slap.

A moment later, a half-heard horn call made everyone tense. Wind cut it short, but Jayson would have sworn it was a call to retreat.

"Tighten up!" Gregson growled. "Keep close and don't waver."

Jayson drew strength from the solidity of his commander's voice. He readied himself.

He heard the riders before he saw them, the call for retreat blaring out of the hissing rush of rain again, followed by the low rumble of hooves gouging into the plains. Frantic orders blazed through the officer's ranks and far to Jayson's left the wall drew back, leaving an opening wide enough for a score of horses abreast. Before those who'd withdrawn had managed to regroup, GreatLord Kobel, Lord Akers, and two-thirds of the cavalry burst from the curtains of rain and angled toward the opening. The GreatLord shouted orders as he kicked his steed into a faster gait, but he was facing away from Jayson and they were swallowed up by the storm. Seconds later, the last of the Legion riders sprinted through the opening and the shields and spears began to close the gap.

Jayson spun toward the plains, breath catching in his throat as nervous energy coursed through his arms. His body felt hot and flushed, even through the chill rain, and his hands trembled. He held the spear shaft tight to keep it from showing. Behind, the sound of the cavalry faded as they funneled through the gate and into the city beyond, but nothing appeared out of the sheeting rain—no black-and-gold clad Alvritshai riders, the eagle's talon splayed across their chest, no stone-skinned trolls or leathery cat-like creatures with luminous eyes.

When horns sounded from the walls above and Gregson cantered past ordering everyone to fall back, Jayson exhaled through clenched teeth, not quite believing that the Horde wasn't boiling out of the darkness as they'd done at Gray's Kill. He kept his eyes on the rain as he backed toward the gates, the pointed formation collapsing inwards. The men in his unit muttered and cursed, those in the shield guard shooting withering looks at the few who voiced their disgust that they were retreating without a fight.

Moments later, Jayson backed beneath the shelter of the gate and wall and heaved a sigh of relief.

* * *

GreatLord Kobel ignored the rain that plastered his hair to his head and streamed from his nose and chin. He stood staring out at the murky gray that hid the Horde. He'd barely been able to see the forces on foot that were still retreating by the time he'd made it back to the wall's height after the battle. His arms were trembling from wielding his sword, his head ringing with the tumult and chaos of the battle—men screaming, metal clashing, horn blaring—all filtered through the rumble and roar of the thunder and rain. Yet he knew that the Horde had only thrown a token force at them.

He leaned out through the crenellations to watch the last of the Temeritt forces reenter the city, heard the gates clanking closed, then waited with breath held for the Horde to appear. But they didn't come.

Why not attack when they were provoked? Why hadn't they attacked before this?

Lord Akers appeared, moving swiftly to Kobel's side. "I estimate we killed at least half of the Alvritshai mounts in the paddock before the Horde managed to organize any significant resistance."

"Losses?"

"Twenty-two men, another few dozen wounded. A score of the horses." Akers hesitated, then added, "Was the feint successful?"

Kobel squinted into the storm. The entire exercise had been a diversion, the clouds and rain a cover for the release of four scouts from the northeastern gates with messages for the GreatLords in Yhnar, Borangst, and the provinces to the west. It was hoped the storm would last long enough for the messengers to make it outside of the Horde's range. The last few attempts hadn't succeeded, the creatures above locating them long before any messages could be delivered. The scouts' bodies had been hung from the lower branches of the remains of the Autumn Tree, caged and still alive, left to starve. The Horde made certain they were visible through spyglasses.

"We won't know unless our scouts appear beneath the Autumn Tree," Kobel said. "But even if they are found and the warning and call for help dies with them, we still have one last recourse left to us." He turned to meet Akers grim expression. "Patris Raleveti is prepared to call upon Diermani's Hand."

4

"—a distinct tannic and is that a hint of cherry?"

Matthais Pavia, councilor to King Justinian, smiled at Lords Ancona and Pesavo over the top of his wine glass before taking another sip. He savored the flavor as he watched the two lords closely. Neither one of them wielded much power within the Province, but he'd found over the years that he never knew when he'd need a crucial extra voice, especially in recent years. Justinian was young—a mere eleven years of age—and the regency that had ruled through him since the death of his father had settled into complacency. But Justinian was a month away from coming of age and he had shown distressing signs of independence. Matthais had no intention of allowing Justinian his own reign, not with the promises he'd extracted from the lords of the Provinces and the Wraiths. He needed the boy pliable and dependent on the advice of his councilors.

Especially Matthais.

"GreatLord Alden has made significant strides in his wineries of late," Lord Ancona said in appreciation. "Wouldn't you agree, Pesavo?"

"Certainly. Although I still believe his vintage of three years ago was the best. Smoother and with a tart oak flavor. I've never been fond of the sweeter wines."

Matthais was no longer listening. Movement on the far side of the arboretum where he'd arranged to meet the two lords had caught his attention and he frowned in annoyance. He'd hoped to spend the entire afternoon with them, uninterrupted. He lowered his glass and followed the page with his eyes as the youth made his way toward them.

"Matthais?" Lord Pesavo prodded.

He shifted his attention back to the lordlings and sighed. "I apologize. I was distracted by our approaching visitor."

Both of the lords twisted in their seats, Ancona's eyes narrowing in interest and speculation. Of the two of them, Matthais had decided that Ancona was the shrewdest, the one that would require the most attention and care. Pesavo appeared merely to enjoy his status and exhibited little to no intelligence or ambition of his own. Ancona, however, had aspirations; not only for himself, but for those he ruled over.

"I wonder who the message is for?" Ancona muttered.

Matthais nearly snorted in contempt, but caught himself. He doubted any messengers for Ancona or Pesavo could penetrate this deeply into the palace. He'd wanted the meeting to be circumspect; barely anyone, servants included, knew where the three were.

He set his wine glass down and stood as the page caught sight of them. The youth looked flushed and slightly panicked as he bowed toward Matthais and straightened.

"Message from the king, councilor."

"What is it?" Matthais asked. When the youth's eyes shot toward Ancona and Pesavo, he waved his hand impatiently. "Out with it!"

"He requests your presence in the throne room. A dwarren envoy has arrived, from the Cochen himself."

Matthais' heart seized in his chest and for a moment he couldn't breathe. He swallowed once, tried to regain his composure, knew by the intent expression on Ancona's face that he had paled. "When did the envoy arrive?"

"Nearly two hours ago."

"And you are delivering your message only now!"

"N-no one knew where you w-were," the page stammered.

Matthais slapped him, the sound of his meaty hand striking the youth's flesh a startling crack beneath the leafy canopy and the faint twitter of the small birds of the glass-enclosed room. The page stumbled to one side at the force of the blow, and both Lord Ancona and Pesavo flinched, Ancona's mouth turning in distaste. Matthais barely restrained himself from striking the messenger again.

"We've been in the arboretum for hours," he said through clenched teeth, then caught Ancona's gaze. The contempt he saw here made him straighten, even as panic began eating at the edges of his rage. Two hours. Justinian and his other advisors would never have left the envoy waiting that long; they must already be speaking to the dwarren.

He had to get to the throne room to contain the damage.

Forcing a smile, he said to Ancona, "If you'll excuse me, I must tend to this...development. I'm certain King Justinian would like my advice concerning whatever brings the dwarren to our city."

"Of course," Ancona muttered. "It must be of extreme importance. I don't believe we've received an envoy in years."

"As you say. Lord Ancona, Lord Pesavo."

He spun and stalked from the arboretum. He made it to the far end of the corridor before he broke into a run. Within five minutes, every breath brought a grimace of pain and his face was sheened with sweat. Servants gaped as he charged past, but he didn't dare slow. Images of the Wraith Walter flashed before him, the coldness that burned in the man's eyes, the terror the darkness that writhed beneath his skin invoked. He had appeared in Matthais' chambers uninvited a year ago, nearly fifteen years after their first meeting, when the Wraith had approached him with the promise of the power of the Lifeblood. All Matthais needed to provide in return is what he'd intended to achieve on his own in the first place: control of the Provinces. He couldn't pass up the opportunity for whatever the Wraiths could provide to achieve that goal.

And the Wraiths had delivered, asking for little in return in the process. Aside from the occasional aid—such as arranging for the female Wraith's travel to Andover months before—the only real demand Walter had made was that Matthais intercept any requests for—and, if possible, forestall—any aid to the Alvritshai, dwarren, or southern Provinces. He'd already caught one such request from Temeritt, the pigeon that had delivered the message fluttering into the dovecote while Matthais was there checking up on a reply to another message from Rendell. The bird had been bloodied from some kind of attack. He'd managed to seize the message before the elderly caretaker could read it, then ordered the man to report any other such messages from the southern provinces to Matthais directly, unopened. He'd kept careful watch for riders from the south, but none had appeared.

Until now.

He rounded a corner and entered the main corridor of the palace, the entrance to the throne room off to the left. Legionnaires guarded the hall in intervals, and as he reached the first pair he saw them tense and give him a confused glance. He slowed abruptly, but as soon as he tried to regain control, he staggered and was forced to reach out to steady himself against the wood paneling along the hall. He couldn't seem to catch his breath, his heart pounding painfully. He wasn't built for such exertion; he hadn't run that far or for that long in over two decades.

The nearest guardsmen glanced at each other, one of them moving forward in concern. "Councilor? Are you all right?"

Matthais heaved in a breath, coughed, and waved his hand in dismissal. He knew his face was livid. Sweat dripped from the end of his nose to the marble floor. "I'm...fine. Just...need to...regain...my breath."

The Legionnaire frowned doubtfully and Matthais forced himself to straighten, meeting the guards' eyes with a glare. "Return to your station."

The man's head rose and he pounded a fist into his chest over his heart in acknowledgment before spinning and walking stiffly back to his post.

As soon as he turned, Matthais removed a handkerchief from the front pocket of his jacket and wiped his face. Smoothing his shirt, and tugging the jacket back into place, he took a tentative step toward the throne room doors. He was still winded, and his heart still thudded hard in his chest, but his legs didn't threaten to collapse beneath him as they had a moment before.

The steward guarding the door with four other Legion rushed forward when he saw Matthais. He was one of Matthais men, paid well to keep the councilor informed of what went on in the palace. One of many.

"Where have you been?" he muttered as he half herded Matthais toward the double doors. One of the Legionnaires had already moved to open it. "I sent someone to summon you nearly two hours ago!"

"I was...occupied."

The steward ignored his gruff tone. "The dwarren were brought before the king over an hour ago. After the obligatory introductions and formalities, the king dismissed everyone else from the room, including me. Only councilor Tyrik and Commander Roland remained behind, with a suitable guard, of course."

Councilor Tyrik had been appointed by Justinian's father and Tyrik and Matthais had been at odds since the day they'd laid Davin Gallatia in the catacombs beneath the Needle. Nearing sixty at the time, Matthais had assumed the ex-merchant would step down or die, but he continued on as spry as ever.

As they stepped through the doors into the high-ceilinged chamber beyond—the intricately tiled floor spreading to the dais at the far end in muted whites, blacks, and golds, depicting a sheaf of wheat—Matthais' gaze swept unerringly to Tyrik first. The councilor stood a step to one side and behind Justinian's throne, back ramrod straight, face pinched in concentration, worry, and anger. His gray gaze flicked toward Matthais and the steward, but his stance didn't change. Commander Roland stood on the king's other side, a step forward, almost as if he were protecting Justinian from a threat. The Legionnaire's focus was on the three dwarren who stood at the edge of the single step of the dais. His arms were crossed over his chest, as if he were restraining himself. Young Justinian sat in the depths of the throne. His arms were resting on the arms of the chair, hands clenched on the rounded decorations at their ends. Four other

Legionnaires were arrayed around the dais, most on the edge of drawing their blades.

"Wait outside," Matthais said to the steward. The man nodded and stepped back, closing the door behind him.

The echo of conversation had not ceased when Matthais entered, but it did as he made his way down the length of the chamber, his heels thudding on the tiles in a slow, measured gait. The low voice—one of the dwarren, since none of the three on the dais were speaking—cut off and the three dwarren turned. Matthais noted that the blades of the dwarren had been drawn and were resting on the step of the dais before them, a gesture indicating the seriousness of the message the dwarren had to impart.

He swore beneath his breath. The message had been given, the one Walter had wanted him to head off at all costs. Justinian knew of the Wraith armies on the plains.

Even as he began to plan how to downplay the report, how to twist whatever the dwarren had already revealed to his own ends, he wondered if the dwarren knew of the attack on Temeritt and the burning of the Autumn Tree...and what they had said that had put Roland and the other Legion on edge.

"My apologies, my liege," he said as he reached the dais and bowed at the waist. A slight bow, head bent, nothing more. The bare minimum required by etiquette. "I came as soon as I was informed of the dwarren's arrival."

"And yet they have been here over an hour," Tyrik said.

Matthais took the opportunity to rise, even though he had not been acknowledged by the king yet. He ignored Tyrik, keeping his attention on Justinian. The boy regarded him with an intensity that sent a frisson of unease through Matthais' gut. "I hope my services can still be of use."

"The dwarren have reported an attack on their lands. They claim the army is led by the Wraiths, and that it's made up of creatures from the Turning." Justinian's voice cracked as he spoke. "They've demanded that we follow the Accord and send the Legion to help them meet the threat."

"I asked for verification of their claim," Tyrik added. "They have no proof that such an army exists."

"We should need no proof!" one of the dwarren spat. He spoke Provincial Andovan, only slightly stilted, and the symbols on his arm bands marked him as a shaman of middling standing. The two who accompanied him were obviously Riders. "Our word should be sufficient! Our word, and the tenants of the Accord that your ancestors signed and you have agreed to uphold."

"We agreed to provide aid in the event there was a significant threat, one to both the dwarren and the Provinces, not to help you defend against dwarren superstitions and children's bedtime stories!"

All three dwarren stiffened. "The terren and kell are not 'bedtime stories.' The urannen and gruen are not 'superstitions.'" The dwarren shaman's gaze shifted from Tyrik to Roland. "I had not realized the human armies would cower at the first sign of a real threat, rather than stand forward to meet it."

Matthais suddenly understood the anger behind Roland's clenched jaw; he felt incensed at the insult himself. At the same time, he was elated. Tyrik had unwittingly already aided him by casting doubt on the dwarren's claims. He need only enhance those doubts, without drawing undue attention to himself in the process. Let Tyrik face the consequences once Justinian and Roland discovered that the dwarren claims were true.

"I'm sorry," he said, brow knit in fake confusion. "The dwarren have been attacked? By an army led by the Wraiths? But what of the Summer Tree? I thought it protected the dwarren."

"According to the dwarren," Justinian answered, "the Summer Tree has begun to fail. They say that the Shadowed One warned the Cochen of this before the dwarren clans headed east to confront the Wraith's army. That was when the dwarren envoy was sent to us, along with another to the Alvritshai."

"The Shadowed One?"

"Colin Harten."

Matthais' eyebrows rose. "Speaking of children's bedtime stories."

"You would speak so of one of your own?" the dwarren leader said hotly. "Do you not respect your own history, your own," he groped for a word, then tried, "legends?"

"Legend? Colin Harten has not stepped foot in Corsair or this throne room in decades. Not in my lifetime, nor Tyrik's."

"He halted the war between our people. He gifted you with the Autumn Tree. He is one of your own."

All three dwarren appeared honestly bewildered by Matthais' reaction. Matthais knew Colin Harten presented a problem to the Wraiths, but he still said, "If Colin Harten is still alive, it would appear that he has abandoned his people."

Silence followed his words, broken a long, tense moment later when Tyrik cleared his throat. "I would think the journey from the Land has exhausted our visitors. Might I suggest someone escort them to rooms and perhaps provide them with food and drink?"

"An excellent idea, councilor Tyrik." Matthais drew breath to order the steward summoned, but the king shifted forward on his seat and spoke instead.

"I should have thought of that. Please, rest and relax while I talk to my advisors about this situation."

"The Cochen is awaiting your response."

"We will summon you when we have that response," Matthais said.

The shaman heard the dismissal and shot a heated glare toward Matthais before gesturing to his fellow Riders. Roland muttered orders to the guards as they were escorted to the doors at the far end of the hall. No one spoke until the echoes of their footfalls had faded in the empty room.

"They dare to insult the king, the Legion, and the Provinces?" Roland began pacing to one side of the throne. "We could have crushed them decades ago at the Escarpment. We would have if King Stephan hadn't halted the battle. We were on the verge of destroying them, along with the Alvritshai!"

"Speaking of the Alvritshai," Matthais interrupted, turning to Tyrik, "the dwarren said they sent an envoy to Caercaern?"

"To Tamaell Thaedoren, yes."

"I wonder what the Alvritshai response will be."

"It doesn't matter," Justinian said forcefully. He winced when his voice rose in register on the last word. "The Alvritshai do not decide what we will do. We are the Provinces. I will make my own decisions."

Matthais had meant the comment more out of curiosity, knew that the Wraiths had a plan for the Alvritshai and wondered what it involved. But Justinian had taken the comment as an affront.

"Of course we will decide our course of action for ourselves," he said carefully. "And what do you think our course of action should be?"

Justinian straightened at the direct question, surprising Matthais. He'd thought the young king would be mollified and then panic, falling back on his regents as he had in the past. "I think we should honor the Accord and send the Legion to the dwarren's aid."

Roland's agitated pacing halted. Matthais saw the commander's instant support of Justinian's suggestion, even as Tyrik spluttered.

"How can you suggest such a thing? You would raise the army at the word of three dwarren, without any sort of intelligence verifying their claim? It's utter nonsense! Have we taught you nothing?"

Justinian's back stiffened and he frowned.

Matthais stepped forward. "I have to agree with Tyrik. I respect the dwarren, and of course we are responsible for upholding our end of the Accord, but I feel we must make certain that the dwarren are not simply drawing our army away from our lands for some ulterior purpose. They have created an army out of whole cloth, using their own myths and legends to populate it. They claim it comes from the east and is led by the Wraiths, when the Wraiths have not been seen in our lands in over a century."

"Because of the Seasonal Trees," Roland rumbled.

Matthais shot a glance toward the commander, caught a confused frown crossing his face before the Legionnaire replaced it with a bland look. A shock of worry lanced down into Matthais' core, but before he could figure out what had caused Roland's suspicion, Tyrik gave a sharp laugh.

"The Seasonal Trees, yes. But the dwarren claim the Summer Tree is failing, that the Autumn Tree is under attack as well. Yet we have heard nothing from GreatLord Kobel in Temeritt, nor heard news from Tarken Sohn in Yhnar about an army to his north."

"No, we have not," Matthais cut in quickly. "Doesn't that strike you as odd?"

He focused the question on Justinian, saw the conviction in the youth's blue eyes waver, but kept his attention mostly on Roland. The commander was still watching him closely, but this time in reaction to Matthais' point.

"If the Autumn Tree were failing, we would have heard from Kobel long before an envoy from the dwarren could have arrived. That's what the messenger pigeons are for."

"And we have received no such word. I spend an inordinate amount of time in the dovecotes, receiving messages from my trading resources in the Provinces. There has been no such warning."

Justinian's shoulders sagged and Matthais suppressed a sigh in relief. "Very well. I can see that you and Tyrik are against it, and I cannot overrule you."

He did not utter the word "yet," but Matthais could hear it in his disconsolate tone. The young king's blue eyes flashed as their gazes met and for the first time Matthais felt true fear slice through him. He had thought the regents had grown complacent earlier, had been worried about Justinian's new streaks of independence, but what he saw in the young king's gaze now told him that he had underestimated the boy significantly. That boy—who sat slumped in the throne, dirty blond hair slightly tousled beneath the gold circlet of his crown, his small-framed body diminished even more by the size of the chair—had been biding his time beneath the regents' thumbs. He knew that with Tyrik and Matthais in agreement, he couldn't order the Legion to arms, even with Roland's support. Not officially. Only Tyrik's, Matthais', and Roland's vote counted.

Roland suddenly spoke. "I agree that the lack of word from Temeritt and GreatLord Kobel is significant, but perhaps we should send a small force of the Legion to investigate the dwarren's claims? I can have a unit sent out from Temeritt and Yhnar to see what's happening to their north along the dwarren Flats."

Matthais made to protest, but Tyrik was already nodding his head. "Yes. This would allow us to send the dwarren back without a firm refusal. We could say that we are sending an envoy of our own to speak with the Cochen, to determine the dwarren's precise needs. A middle ground, with no commitment from us either way."

"That is acceptable to me," Matthais said, shifting his gaze toward Roland.

"Agreed."

Justinian's head had dropped, his gaze locked on the floor. "Summon the dwarren."

By the time the dwarren had returned, ushered into the chamber by the steward and four more of the Legion, he had straightened in the throne, his bearing regal, verging on imperious. Matthais couldn't quash a small surge of pride, even if the boy's actions didn't bode well for the future.

"We have taken your request under advisement," Tyrik said, "and would like to send an envoy back with you to discuss what the Cochen needs and what we can provide based on the tenants of the Accord."

"We need reinforcements," the shaman said immediately. His gaze shifted to Roland. "We need the Legion."

The commander stiffened at the intensity of the dwarren's words, but he said nothing. The shaman traded glances with both of his Riders before turning back to the king, addressing him directly.

"These are the king's wishes?"

Justinian's jaw clenched. "They are."

"Then we accept. It is not enough, and by the time you decide the threat is real it may be too late, but the Turning moves and the Four Winds continue to blow. We will leave in an hour, with or without your envoy."

He didn't wait for a response, all three dwarren marching from the chamber, the steward rushing to open the far doors.

"I will arrange for the envoy immediately," Matthais said, moving to follow. He wanted to make certain it contained some of his own people. Perhaps they could stall the Provinces' involvement even further.

He looked back when he reached the doors. Roland had shifted closer to the throne, had one hand resting on its back. Both he and Justinian were watching him, the young king angry.

He stilled for a moment, a shiver prickling along his arms. Something had changed, had shifted, and suddenly he felt his carefully cultivated control of the regency slipping through his fingers.

He needed to regain control. Now. Before it slipped any further.

* * *

Roland waited until Matthais had left before pushing back from the throne. His gut seethed with suspicion, but he knew he couldn't speak to Tyrik about it, nor Justinian. Not yet.

Matthais had said the Wraith armies had come from the east, when he hadn't been here for the dwarren's full report. Roland kept replaying the conversation since Matthais' arrival in his head and he didn't think Tyrik, the king, or the dwarren had mentioned the armies were attacking from that direction. He supposed Matthais could have deduced that, but he had stated it as if it were fact.

He didn't know what it meant, but his gut was telling him it was significant. He had never trusted Matthais, had always been at odds with the regent. But he assumed that Davin, Justinian's father, had planned it that way—Matthais would look out for trade, Tyrik would guard Justinian's interests, and Roland would support the Legion. That was the way it had worked for the last decade.

But what if Matthais was looking out for more than the Provincial merchants and their interests?

He turned to Justinian. "I'll send word to the GreatLords in Yhnar, Temeritt, and Borangst immediately to determine if they have heard anything of this army. At the same time, I'd like to order their Legion commanders to begin training exercises. Extensive training exercises."

Justinian stared at him hard, then glanced toward Tyrik for reassurance. The elderly regent simply sighed. "The Legion is Roland's purview. I see no reason why we cannot be prepared in case this Wraith army actually exists."

"Do it," Justinian said. A flicker of excitement lit his eyes and he grinned, his entire posture changing.

For a brief moment, Roland saw the man—the king—that the boy would become.

* * *

"We must call upon Ilacqua," Kimannen stated flatly. "You can send scouts to the Four Winds to determine what the Wraiths and their armies are doing, but it will take time for them to gather their information and return with it, even if they use the drums."

The clan chiefs who were gathered—the Cochen, Tarramic from Quotl's Thousand Springs, and Iktamman from Silver Grass—all nodded in agreement. Soma, clan chief for Claw Lake, and Oraju's head shaman had not yet returned from their most recent excursions to the plains with the Riders. This was not a formal Gathering. They were not even meeting in a keeva, merely sitting around a small fire in the warrens on the border between Painted Sands and Broken Waters. Quotl and Tarramic had traveled the last few days to meet with the Cochen and Archon with the Wraith army's intercepted courier's papers, which rested on the floor before the Cochen now.

"What of the signs?" Tarramic asked. "What do they say?"

Tarramic looked toward Quotl, but Kimannen cut in quick and sharp. "The signs tell us only what we already know: that the Wraith armies are moving, that they have entered deeper into dwarren lands than we suspected. They do not tell us their purpose. We have sealed the warrens on all fronts, and they have not attacked any of the entrances. They know that, once sealed, they are nearly impossible to break. The stone of the Ancients is thick and heavy, not easy to crack. Even the kell cannot penetrate the warrens."

Quotl's eyes narrowed as the Archon spoke. He drew deeply on his pipe, inhaling the yetope smoke, holding it, then exhaling slowly. "All they need do is find one of the breaches that nature had caused and they will have access to the warrens."

Kimannen scowled. "Those breaches are minor. Armies cannot be moved through such openings."

"You underestimate the patience and guile of the Wraiths and their following."

"And you give them too much credit!"

An awkward silence settled over the group. Attanna, head shaman of Silver Grass, had bowed his head, his thick eyebrows drawn close in a frown. The clan chiefs traded glances.

"Do you truly feel the breaches in the minor tunnels are a threat?" Tarramic asked.

Quotl shifted where he sat cross-legged on the floor, the stone beneath him suddenly hard and uncomfortable. An urgency prickled across his skin. He felt the need to move, to be doing something more than simply arguing over trivial matters.

"It is a threat, yes, but not the main threat. Kimannen is correct. The breaches are narrow, although there are enough of them that dismissing them makes me uncomfortable. And not all of them are known. But the main threat is the army that has already entered our lands. What is their purpose? Where are they headed? That is what should be our focus."

"As I said earlier," Kimannen muttered.

The Cochen straightened and tapped the orannian courier's missives. "So you agree that a call to Ilacqua needs to be made?"

"His advice must be sought, yes. Perhaps he will reveal more of the Wraith's plans than what can be determined through the Riders or the signs of the Land."

The Archon nodded and began to rise. "I will have the keeva readied and begin my preparations then."

Quotl's gut clenched, even though he'd known this moment was coming. He'd been planning for it since he and Tarramic had attacked the orannian group on the plains three nights before.

He carefully set his pipe aside, resting his hands on his knees. "I believe I should accompany you, Kimannen."

The clan chiefs stilled. Attanna gasped.

Kimannen stiffened. "You are not the Archon. A call to Ilacqua is the Archon's domain. Only the Archon may enter, only the Archon may commune with the god—"

"I call your status as Archon into question."

Kimannen recoiled as if struck. His hands tightened into fists; his entire body trembled. "You cannot demand a new Archon. The shamans have not been summoned for a conclave."

"No, but this is a Turning. Ilacqua speaks to the People through the Archon, acts through the Archon, especially in times of need. I do not believe Ilacqua acted through you at the Break, Kimannen. And in these darkening hours, I do not think we should risk Ilacqua's aid over the pride and dignity of a single shaman."

Kimannen's gaze shot toward the Cochen. "You have not spoken. You would allow this challenge, here, now?"

Oraju's face grew grim, eyes carefully blank. "I have no say. This is a matter for the shamans."

Kimannen glanced toward Tarramic and Iktamman, then turned on Attanna. Some of the tension in his shoulders relaxed. "Attanna, as head shaman of Silver Grass, you are the only one present to witness this betrayal of the conclave. You must recall this when the conclave next convenes. I would have Quotl stripped of his title as head shaman of Thousand Springs for his temerity, not just here, but at the sealing of the warrens after the Break. He oversteps his bounds."

Quotl held his breath. He recalled Kimannen's rise to Archon, so many years before. Attanna had supported Kimannen then, and since, fervently, because Kimannen's connection to Ilacqua, his strength and power, had been so obvious.

Attanna's eyes grew pinched. "You may hold much power politically, Kimannen, but I fear your spirit has drifted away from Ilacqua. Quotl is correct. It did not appear that Ilacqua worked through you at the Break, no matter how you may have shaded Quotl's actions and your own afterwards in the warren before the Riders. Everyone saw, and everyone knows in their heart what they felt on those treacherous slopes."

Attanna faced Quotl. "You should both enter the keeva and call Ilacqua, see who the god favors with his vision, his insight. I will witness the result, and report to the conclave when it is time for a proper challenge for the Archon's position."

Quotl heard the note of warning in Attanna's voice. If Ilacqua spoke to Kimannen in the keeva, he would have to remove himself as head shaman of Thousand Springs. If he did not, Attanna would make certain his actions were called before the conclave for judgment, with the clan chiefs as witnesses.

"I would request that you ready the keeva then, while Kimannen and I prepare ourselves."

"Of course." Attanna rose and gathered the orannian courier's papers from before the Cochen before moving off. Quotl heard him summon a few other shamans, his orders clipped and hard.

Quotl's gaze flicked to Kimannen and met the elderly dwarren's hatred directly. He reached for his pipe, packed a few pieces of the dried yetope leaf into the bowl, and lit it, taking a long pull on the resultant smoke.

* * *

Quotl ducked through the opening of the keeva and the heat and scent of the yetope that had already been placed on the fire struck him. He began to sweat immediately, the small room hotter than usual. This keeva was not as large as those found in the main chambers of the dwarren underground cities, but it retained the same shape: an oval room with a ledge of stone around the edge, a depression for the fire pit in the center. The walls were smoothed ages past by water erosion, stained with the soot and smoke of a thousand fires since. Attanna had filled the far side of the ledge with enough yetope to send Quotl and Kimannen to the spirit world permanently, which may be his intent. He did not look happy. Quotl wondered whether Kimannen had cornered him while they were each supposed to be preparing, and what the Archon had said if he had.

He shoved such concerns aside as he moved opposite Kimannen. He'd attempted to calm himself in the last hour, had secluded himself, spread a sheaf of dried grain on the floor, prostrated himself, and sought the power that pulsed in his chest even now, although quiet and subdued. But the grain had itched, the stalks crackling with every fidget, and the grain heads had gouged into his chest. After twenty minutes of seeking his center by controlling his breathing and focusing on the pounding of his heart, he'd sat up and pulled out his pipe. It had soothed him in moments.

All of that was lost as he met Kimannen's gaze across the fire pit through the thick smoke.

"You will regret questioning my power," Kimannen said. His voice throbbed, thick with malice, and Quotl wondered if the smoke had already begun to affect him. It felt as if Kimannen's voice reverberated throughout the room.

"You should have given up your power at the Break," he answered, and his own voice shivered through his bones.

"I will leave you," Attanna interrupted. He placed the rolled sheaf of papers with the orannian scribbles next to the supply of yetope. "I have brought the intercepted courier's messages. The keeva has been blessed and protected. Once I depart, the door will be sealed until one of you opens it from within." He stepped around the fire, Quotl shifting to give him room, but hesitated at the rounded door. "May Ilacqua's eyes fall upon you and help you both to see."

Quotl grunted at the reprimand in the head shaman's voice, saw Kimannen scowl, but Attanna hadn't waited for their reactions. The door closed, cutting off the torchlight from the outside and leaving them with only the red hot coals of the fire pit and the few flames that danced up from it. A moment later, through the thrum of power in his chest, he felt a pulse and knew that Attanna had warded the door against false spirits and interference from outside the room. He ran his hands down through his beard, a nervous gesture he abhorred, then forced himself to settle onto the ledge behind him. On the far side of the fire, Kimannen did the same, after tossing fresh yetope leaves onto the coals.

Slowly, the smoke and heat took effect. Quotl sagged back against the stone wall behind him. His breathing tightened, then relaxed as he adjusted to the stifling chamber. Blood throbbed through his skin beneath the brass armband encircling his right bicep, as if his arm had swelled and was now constricted. Sweat trickled in droplets down his back, chest, and from beneath his armpits. His shirt was already soaked, but he didn't move to pull it away. Lethargy had set in, his arms leaden. The coals pulsed with a pattern he could almost make out, and the enclosed room suddenly felt larger as the orange-yellow light grew brighter and the shadows thickened. The power that resided in his chest began to fill him, seeping out into his arms, tingling down through his torso and into his legs, suffusing him.

"Why did you not step down at the Break?" Quotl asked, surprising himself. He hadn't meant to speak. But the heat...he could feel his barriers breaking down, slipping away, even as his sense of the world expanded.

"Because I am the Archon." Kimannen's voice came from the smoke, soft and threatening, and Quotl realized that he could no longer see him. What he thought was Kimannen was merely a shadow, nothing more. "I am the voice of Ilacqua. It is my responsibility, has been my responsibility for nearly a generation, my burden to bear."

Clarity seized Quotl. "You are afraid. Afraid of what will become of you if someone else becomes Archon."

"No! I am afraid of nothing!"

But Quotl could hear the truth, could feel it in the pulse of the fire. "You are afraid that it will mean Ilacqua has abandoned you."

"Silence!" Clothes rustled and the coals suddenly flared, revealing Kimannen as he dumped more of the dried leaves onto the flames. A twinge of surprise rippled through Quotl that the Archon could move, and then he noticed the roll of papers Kimannen held in one hand.

Quotl looked into the Archon's eyes, saw the demons that haunted him there, saw other visions and shadows dancing behind against the wall and at the edges of the room—visions of terror, of beauty, of want and need. The entire room vibrated with them, like a nearly imperceptible hum.

"Let us see who Ilacqua favors now," Kimannen said. His voice rumbled from his chest like distant thunder. He tossed the rolled pages stolen from the dead courier into the flames and green-black smoke writhed upwards and concealed him. It continued to rise, expanding to block off the other half of the room, lit from beneath by the coals. Within its depths, white tendrils appeared, snaking back and forth, forming patterns on the green-black background. Quotl's heart squeezed in his chest, pain shooting down his left arm as he recognized the tendrils as the orannian script from the pages, and then the smoke billowed outwards and enveloped him.

He cried out and lurched back, head striking the stone wall behind him, and with his next breath he drew the green-black smoke and the tendrils of script inside him. It burned down into his lungs, harsh and acrid, and he coughed even as he felt himself slide down the wall to the ledge. Heat suffused him, his skin flushed hot with fever, and the power he held within exploded in a dazzling spray of white behind his eyes. He choked on air—

And then the visions began. The Land rushed beneath him, a field of wind-swept grassland, rolling hills and copses, patches of exposed rock and the deep pockets of cisterns and springs. He soared over it all in the body of a hawk, the shadow of his wings beneath him. The sun settled into the horizon to the west, dusk falling, but ahead he caught the movement of riders, five of them, on horseback, driving to the northwest. He followed them, banking in the winds, until firelight sparked on the plains farther distant: campfires, hundreds of them. He ascended and pulled ahead of the riders, circled over the Wraith army that waited below. A dark stain interrupted the silver-limned grasslands to the east, and Quotl recognized the sacred forest that had once housed the urannen. But the hawk continued to climb, its wings spreading wide, and in the vision the Land opened up before him. His sight expanded to encompass all of the plains and beyond. He saw the Wraith armies waiting beneath the walls of the human city of Temeritt, the destruction it had already wrought on the Province surrounding it, the skeletal remains of the Autumn Tree, and his heart quailed. To the north, he spied the remnants of the army the dwarren had fought at the Break, half the size it had been when the dwarren sealed the warrens behind them. As if scorched into the earth, he saw two paths breaking away from each army, one from the Break and one from Temeritt, converging on the plains and striking westward, turning north, and he realized the truth: the Wraith army was marching for Caercaern, for Alvritshai lands, for the Winter Tree.

He began to fall, the hawk diving back toward the earth. Yet as he fell, he realized there were other paths burned into the Land, other tracks, thinner than that of the armies, and other blackened marks on the world. One rested in the human city of Corsair. One trailed westward across the Arduon Ocean toward Andover. There were others, snaking across the plains, through the forests and hills, but it was the smudge of darkness that stained the breadth of grassland near the Confluence that seized Quotl's attention as he plummeted toward the ground. Hundreds of small paths, coming from hundreds of directions, all converging on one location.

Quotl glanced downwards to see the grassland rushing toward him. He flinched back—

And gasped, heaving upwards on the stone ledge in the keeva, one hand clutching his chest over his heart, the other scrabbling for purchase on the smooth stone. Smoke seared his lungs as he sucked in another breath and then he fell over the ledge onto the stone floor, the impact jarring his heart back to beating. The first thud sent lightning sheets of pain into his left arm and down into his legs. He levered himself up onto one arm, saw Kimannen staring at him through the cloud of natural smoke from across the pit. He made no move to help. Quotl turned to face the door of the keeva, began dragging himself across the floor toward it. His left arm trembled, weaker than his right, but he hauled himself forward, kicked with his legs, pulled himself to his knees using the ledge. Then he leaned forward and tumbled out through the keeva's door.

Blessedly cool air washed over him and he gulped it in as he rolled onto his back. He heard shouts, picked Attanna's voice out of the melee ordering the healing Sacred Waters brought, then felt someone dragging him from the keeva completely and sitting him upright. Cool water spilled over his mouth and down into his beard and he gulped at it as hungrily as he'd gulped for air a moment before. It washed the acrid burn from his throat, soothed the searing pain in his chest.

"What happened?" Attanna asked, taking the waterskin back before Quotl was finished.

Kimannen stepped from the keeva. "Ilacqua has spoken," he said, staring down at Quotl. None of the hatred and rage Quotl had seen inside the keeva showed; none of the fear he'd heard inside touched the shaman's voice.

Somehow the lack of emotion was more frightening than the anger.

Attanna's attention returned to Quotl. "What did he say?"

"He showed me the Wraith armies," Quotl muttered hoarsely, then snatched at the waterskin and drank so fast he spluttered and coughed.

Wiping his mouth, he croaked, "They're already inside the warrens. They're headed for the Sacred Waters and the Summer Tree."

5

Tuvaellis tucked her shawl in closer about her face and glared at the elderly couple who had entered the sanctuary of Holy Diermani's main cathedral in the heart of Trent. Light lanced down through the tall stained glass windows along both sides of the hall and through the large rosette set into the peak above the altar. Niches along the walls held statues of saints and martyrs, or small reliquaries, while between the windows and the soaring stone supports painted murals depicted scenes from the Codex, the most prominent feature being the glowing presence of Diermani's Hand reaching from the heavens, wreathed in clouds or vines, or emerging from the depths of a lake.

The murals had originally intrigued Tuvaellis, even more so after Patris Sandreo had begun speaking to her and explaining the stories behind the images, but today they were merely an additional source of irritation. She hadn't intended to speak to anyone when she'd come that day a month before, had merely meant to sit in the back of the cathedral and observe. She'd spent the last month attempting to integrate herself into the Bontari Family, the ruling Family here in Trent, but she'd discovered that getting close to the Dom was nearly impossible. Becoming a member of a guild and proving her standing and usefulness to the Family would get her in, certainly, but it wouldn't provide her access to the upper echelons, the literal family members who would be able to aid her. True family members rarely stepped outside of their own social circles within the court. Walter had warned her that her task would not be easy, but she hadn't expected the aristocracy here to be so...interbred.

She'd realized she would have to take a different approach: attempt to infiltrate the Church of Holy Diermani directly. But she'd known nothing of the church, and Walter had told her little before she'd left. So she'd come to the cathedral to see what she could find out—about the location of the Rose, about the hierarchy of the priesthood, and in particular, how she could deliver the stone Walter had entrusted her with into the Rose's heart. Time was running short. She knew Walter's plans were moving forward in New Andover. If she was going to help bring those plans to fruition, she needed to plant the stone inside the Rose by the end of winter. After that it would be too late.

So she'd come to the cathedral, had seated herself in the last pew, had stared at the murals and the vaulted stone ceilings and let the scent of ancient wood, dust, and tallow envelop her. She'd taken in the trappings of the church on the altar and throughout the large hall, the symbolism and the imagery, and had snorted in derision.

That was when Sandreo had spoken to her for the first time. She hadn't known he'd entered the sanctuary behind her, hadn't realized he'd been watching her for some time. The shock had brought her to her feet, automatically hunching to hide her height, one hand checking the shawl's placement, the other falling toward the sword concealed beneath the multi-layered robes of her disguise.

"Ah, good woman, you have nothing to fear here," he'd said with a smile.

And that was how it had started. She couldn't remember what he'd begun to say that startled her in the first place, but she remembered those words. And nearly everything he had said since.

She'd found out it was almost as difficult to get close to the hierarchy of the church as it was to the members of the Court, and that the priests kept the secrets of the church in an iron-clenched fist.

Her irritation spiked higher at the thought as the couple she'd scowled at earlier found their way down the nave, knelt and genuflected, then seated themselves a few rows away from the representation of the tilted cross Diermani had sacrificed himself upon ages past. A few others were scattered around the pews in various states of prayer or contemplation. One man was asleep, his snores faint.

She heard Sandreos approaching this time, the tread of his sandals barely audible. She sometimes thought he made purposefully more noise when approaching her, after that first incident. She didn't turn.

"Jarell," he said, his tone mildly surprised. "I didn't expect to see you here today."

Tuvaellis turned her head as Sandreo halted at the end of her pew, careful to keep her face in shadow. She had tried numerous methods to conceal the Well's oily taint beneath her skin, had even altered her age so that she was a child, from a time before she had drunk from the Well, but the taint remained even then.

"I hadn't planned on coming," she said curtly. She hadn't. But when she'd woken that morning and realized that it was nearing the end of autumn, a restlessness had seized her. Walter had given her the responsibility of delivering the stone, now secreted in a smaller, more portable wooden case, but she had met nothing but failure since reaching Andover. She needed to know the whereabouts of the Rose, its exact location in the Borangi Desert, and Sandreo hadn't revealed anything during any of their talks. She was frustrated, impatience clawing at her skin. She needed to *move*.

"I see. Is it your illness? Is the ache worsening?"

Tuvaellis bowed her head. When he had questioned why she hid her face, she had told him she was disfigured by an illness, that she would not show her face to anyone. "A little, patris. But nothing I cannot bear."

She heard a rustle of cloth, the wood of the pew behind her creaking as Sandreo settled down. Not so close as to intrude on her personal space— she'd made it clear she did not like anyone touching her—but certainly closer than he'd ever come before.

"Suffering is part of life, of course. I believe, from what you have told me, that you have suffered greatly. You should not let that color your faith in Diermani and the church."

Tuvaellis barked out a short laugh. "My faith? I have no faith."

"That is what you claimed when I first met you. Yet here you are. If you have no faith, then why did you come? Why do you continue to return?"

"Because I need something."

"What is it that you think you need?"

The location of the Rose. Her frustration boiled up inside her chest and threatened to burst forth. But she knew being so blunt would never work with Sandreos. Nothing appeared to crack his shroud of calm. She had thought it due to his age—he was ancient by human standards—but over time she'd realized that it came from something deeper.

She stood and turned on Sandreo. "How dare you? You expect me to believe in Diermani, in his benevolence, when you have shown me none of your own?"

Sandreo's eyes rose. "I have been nothing but benevolent. I have tried to bring you closer to Diermani, tried to get you to see how he can help you find peace."

"I don't want peace!" He flinched at her sudden vehemence. "I want healed. I want to walk through the plazas of Trent without wearing a shawl. I want to walk the docks with the sun warming my face, not cowering in the shadows. I want to discard these clothes and stand tall."

Sandreos said nothing when she finished, only her panting breath interrupting the solitude of their corner of the nave. Tuvaellis was shocked at the intensity of her own words. For a brief moment she wondered if there wasn't a kernel of truth to them, to give them such force, even though her "illness" was fiction, a ruse so that she could remain hidden behind the shawl. The thought sent her anger even higher and she unconsciously stood up straighter.

"Well?" she demanded. "What does your god have to say about that?"

Sandreos stood slowly. "He would pity you, that you cannot stand tall as you are and that you could not enjoy the sunlight without fearing what other people think of you."

This only enraged Tuvaellis further. This wasn't working. She'd been playing Sandreos for weeks and had learned nothing. Nothing of importance.

"Everywhere I go, the people speak of Diermani, praising him, cursing him, thanking him for his mercy, his protection. Everywhere they speak of the miracles he performed, of the healing powers he has given to the church in the form of the Rose. You know of this Rose. I know it, I can see it in the way your face closes when I mention it during our talks. And yet you do not see fit to tell me of it, of its whereabouts, even though you know it would heal me!"

Sandreos' eyes hardened and for the first time since Tuvaellis had known him, he looked angry. It accentuated the wrinkles in his face, yet made him seem more vital at the same time, more powerful. "The Rose is a gift from Diermani, yes, but its power is too great to be trifled with. The Feud was fought over that power, and that Feud nearly tore the Court and the Families apart. It would have, if it had not been decided that the power was too great for any one Family—or even a group—to wield. It was given to the church in order to protect the people. We—the patri, arruli, and caddoni—are its guardians. It is not something we speak of often, and it is not something that is given out lightly. I suggest that if you seek healing, you search within yourself first. Your anger and bitterness is what keeps you from finding peace. Relinquish that, and the healing will flow from within you."

He began to turn away. Tuvaellis lunged forward, snagged his arm, and hauled him around to face her. "Tell me the location of the Rose."

He recoiled from her and it took her a moment to realize why. She'd forgotten about her shawl. It had slipped, part of her face now lit by the patterned light of the rosette. Sandreos had seen the oily black taint of the Well. She saw his shock shift to horror...and then pity.

"You are one of the Wraiths," he said. "Is that what you seek to heal?"

Tuvaellis' fingers tightened on the patris' arm and he gasped. Furious at how he had so completely misunderstood her ruse, and at her own impatience and careless mistake, she drew her sword from beneath the folds of her clothes. "No." She calmly slashed his throat. "I have no wish to heal the gifts of the sarenavriell."

He staggered backwards as she released him. Blood sprayed across the pews as he struck one and spun, clutching at the bench for support. More splattered across the painted murals between the glass windows, dripped from the face of the statue of a martyr tucked into the adjacent niche. Sandreos sank to his knees and Tuvaellis felt power build, realized that it came from the priest. She instantly raised her defenses, but Sandreos had called forth his energy too late. He sagged to the floor, already dead, and the energy ebbed. Tuvaellis shuddered. Sandreos had been more dangerous than she'd suspected, and the thought forced her to reevaluate the entire church—the priests, the hierarchy, and Diermani himself. She had not known the patri wielded *real* power. She would not make that mistake again.

Someone screamed, the sound penetrating the stillness that had enveloped her. She spun with a curse—she had forgotten the others within the nave—reaching to slow time as she did so. Drawing the shawl back over her face, she counted nearly ten witnesses. A smile tugged at her face as she thought of slaughtering them all, here, in their holiest of places, and she streaked toward them.

But as she moved, she felt a presence press down upon her, slowing her, even though she had nearly stopped time. She fought it, her fluid run toward the center aisle faltering as she reached the middle of the church. The elderly couple stood, clutching each other. Another woman, the one who'd screamed, had a hand over her mouth, her arm pointing toward where Tuvaellis had been a moment before. Two children—a boy and a girl—partially hid behind her. A group of three men had begun to turn from where they knelt at the base of the railing and the dais of the altar.

But it was the priest who had emerged from somewhere behind the altar who caught Tuvaellis' attention. He wasn't watching the corner of the nave, where Sandreos' blood would be forming a pool beneath the pews. No, he was watching *her*.

She staggered against what held her back, struggling to push forward. But it held her, as if a hand had been raised to shield those who had seen her.

She stopped trying to push forward. The pressure ceased, but she could still feel the hand—the Hand of Diermani, she realized—hovering before her. She glared at the priest, but realized that he was caught in time like the others. She didn't understand how he knew where she was, or how he had raised the Hand against her—he must have called it forth before she slowed time—but it didn't matter. She couldn't reach the others in the nave.

Snarling, she spun and fled the church, keeping time slowed as she burst out onto the wide steps leading down to the plaza beyond. She didn't let time return to normal until she'd wound her way through the sunlit streets of Trent to her room at The Painted Vine.

She began to pack, removing a satchel and tossing it onto the bed, barely aware of the sudden clanging of bells in the city, starting with one set, then spreading to the others. She pulled the smaller wooden box that contained the stone from its place within the broken trunk that had brought it across the Arduon Ocean and placed it into the satchel, along with a few of the clothes she'd picked up to help her blend into Trent. Then someone knocked at her outer door.

She stilled, then drew her blade, halted time, and stalked to the door, standing to one side, before allowing time to resume. "Yes?"

"Mistress, there has been a murder."

Tuvaellis could hear Irina's suspicion through the door, knew that she was disappointed Tuvaellis was in her rooms. The two of them had been at odds since Tuvaellis' arrival, the keeper of The Painted Vine threatening to throw Tuvaellis out at every opportunity. But she didn't dare, not with Tuvaellis' supposed connections to the Bontari Family and the repercussions of offending them. Irina couldn't afford that. She had fled the Scarrelli Family moments before her capture and resided in Trent at the Bontari Family's sufferance and beneath their protection, although Tuvaellis had not discovered what Irina supposedly knew that would warrant keeping her alive.

"A murder? Is that why the bells are ringing? They woke me up."

"Yes. Someone has killed one of the patri at the cathedral!" Her suspicions allayed, Irina's voice vibrated with the horror and shock of the crime. Tuvaellis could picture her genuflecting. "They say it was an old woman, hunched forward with a cowl pulled over her face. If anyone sees such a figure, we are to report it to the Armory immediately."

"I see." And Tuvaellis did see. Irina would have recognized her description, which was why she was so disappointed to find Tuvaellis in her rooms. No one could have run the distance from the cathedral to The Painted Vine in the time it had taken the word to be spread by the Armory and the bells. They probably assumed she was still hiding somewhere close to the cathedral.

But the description meant she would have to discard her disguise, at least until she was outside the city. And it *was* time to leave Trent. She didn't know where she would go from here, perhaps down the coast to Carrente. It would keep her close to the Borangi Desert, more so than going north to Avezzano.

"If you were thinking of heading into town," Irina said, "I'd wait. They're going to be eyeing everyone for the next few days, unless they catch her. You won't be safe."

Tuvaellis was mildly surprised. Perhaps Irina's constant scowl and brusque attitude was merely a façade. "Very well."

She waited, listening. Silence stretched for a moment, then she heard a quiet snort and the soft tread of Irina's footsteps heading away from her door. Tuvaellis sheathed her blade and returned to her satchel. She pulled out a new set of clothes and changed quickly, discarding the slightly worn shawl and layered clothes she had on. Blood had splattered on the fabric, although it was hard to notice among the pattern of colors. She left it all where it had fallen, finished packing, then drew the satchel over her shoulder and adjusted the stylized hood of her new dress.

She didn't know exactly what she would do, but she was tired of pacing here in Trent, attempting a subtle approach. She needed to move.

* * *

Moiran frowned in annoyance. "Careful taking that wagon over those ruts! The squash bruise easily and we don't want half of our winter storage rotting before we get a chance to eat it!"

The man guiding the wagon waved a hand, but continued on at the same pace, the bed behind his seat jouncing as it rattled over the ruts in the field from the last few days' worth of harvest activity. Moiran shook her head and turned back to Sylvea and the rest of the work crew. Men and women were scattered across the field of dying squash vines, picking up the green and yellow gourds and carrying them to the wagons waiting throughout the field. Most of the workers wore the flat, conical straw hats typical of the commoners, even though the sunlight was weak today. The wind carried a nasty bite of chill and the threat of frost, which was why Moiran had ordered the work crew into the fields as soon as she'd stepped into the garden at the manse and breathed it in. Winter was coming early this year it would seem, by nearly a month.

She had wondered if it was a harbinger of worse things to come, but shrugged the sudden chill in her shoulders aside. Those thoughts had returned when she'd reached the fields to discover a third of the workers had yet to arrive.

"Where are the rest of the workers? It's been two hours already. They're late."

Sylvea bowed her head as if in shame. "None of those who were missing from this morning have come."

"So where are they?"

Sylvea said nothing and avoided Moiran's gaze.

It was all the answer Moiran needed. She cursed, her hands clenching in frustration, but forced herself to calm down. "It's the Order of the Flame, isn't it? They're convincing the people to abandon the Rhyssal House. Many of those who have stopped reporting are gone, their houses and cottages closed up and empty." When Sylvea hesitated, she added, "Tell me the truth, Sylvea, if you have any love for Rhyssal at all."

Sylvea flinched. "The people are fleeing to Caercaern, my lady. The members of the Order are convincing them that Lord Aeren has betrayed them."

"I see. And how many have left already? Do you have any idea?"

"No, Lady Moiran. Most of those who have left are from the outskirts of Artillien, the younger sons and daughters of age of families with too many mouths to feed. They're going because the Order offers them more than they expect to find here. Only a few of them truly believe Lord Aeren has betrayed the Chosen. Most are conflicted." Sylvea looked miserable. "Only a few of those who've left work in the manse, my lady."

"From the manse? Servants?"

"A few servants, a cook." She swallowed and said in a barely audible voice, "A couple of the Phalanx."

This shocked Moiran to the core. Phalanx members? They were sworn to the House, to protecting Lord Aeren, Fedaureon, and herself. If they were abandoning them, then this situation was more dire than she thought.

"The Phalanx? Truly?"

"Only a few. Two, maybe four."

Moiran turned to stare out over the field without actually seeing it. Did Fedauroen know already? Had he simply not told her? It was possible, if it were only a few.

"I should have let Fedaureon take care of the Flame earlier."

Before the anger and guilt could set in, one of her Phalanx escort shouted and pointed toward a runner cutting across the field. He was headed toward the cluster of Phalanx members, but as soon as he saw Moiran and Sylvea standing off to one side, he changed direction, coming to a panting halt before her, kneeling before he'd caught his breath.

"Message...from...Fedaureon," the servant gasped.

"Sylvea, get him some water," Moiran said, then motioned the runner up. "What message?"

The young man stood, the red and blue of his House clothing dusty from the road. When Sylvea presented a cup of water from the barrel on one of the carts, he drank it all in one draught. He must have run the entire distance from the manse and she suddenly stiffened. For him to have run such a distance...

"What message?" she repeated, her voice commanding.

"Word has come from Caercaern. There has been a coup. Several lords have seized the city and taken control of the surrounding lands."

For a moment, Moiran couldn't breathe, her worst fears realized. But then, before the runner could say more, she snapped, "Caitan Wodraen, leave a few Phalanx members to finish off the harvesting in this field. Prepare the horses. We're returning to Artillien."

Wodraen nodded and began issuing orders, Phalanx members already rushing to gather the horses. As they brought her mount around, Moiran turned back to the runner. "Any word of Lord Aeren? Of my son, Thaedoren?"

"The servants said it was chaos. No one knew what had happened."

"The servants?" She grabbed her mount's reins, gathered the folds of her riding dress, then swung up into the saddle. "What servants?"

"Servants of the House. They claim Lord Aeren ordered them to flee Caercaern and to bring word of what was happening here, any way they could."

An icy chill tingled down through Moiran's arms, her fingers going numb. Without waiting for Wodraen, she spun her mount about and kicked it into motion. It grunted and surged forward, the harsh autumn air burning Moiran's cheeks red in moments as she charged across the field. She heard shouts of protest, but she didn't care. The fear that numbed her fingers had begun creeping down into her gut. She fought it. She knew nothing for certain. There was no reason to believe that her husband and son were dead.

She focused on that thought—she knew nothing for certain—as she reached the edge of the field and swung out onto the rugged road that led back to Artillien and the manse. Behind, the dull sound of horses churning dirt clods from the field changed to the clop of shod feet on the harder earth of the road and a moment later she was surrounded by Wodraen and three other Phalanx. Her caitan didn't try to slow her down, though, and she smiled grimly. He knew her too well.

They pushed hard, Moiran's face going numb as the road wound past fields already harvested, then through forest, the smell of cedar cloying. Twenty minutes later they emerged onto the road outside the town but didn't slow, people dodging out of their way as they tore past the main square, the marketplace, and Aielan's temple, toward the incline that led to the manse. The market wasn't as crowded as usual for this time of year. Smoke issued from the temple, but she saw none of the acolytes or members of the Flame outside. Terciern services must have begun.

Moiran allowed Wodraen to pull ahead of her as they approached the main gates, the doors already open. She slowed and halted as they cantered into the courtyard, the entire manse in turmoil.

"What's happening?" she asked Wodraen as she dismounted. None of the stable hands came to fetch her horse. They were all frantically saddling other mounts, Phalanx members running in every direction. Wodraen didn't answer, but grabbed one of the younger members as they passed and spoke to him briefly before letting him go.

He turned back to Moiran. "Fedaureon and Mattalaen have called the Phalanx to arms."

Eyes widening in surprise, she said, "Find Fedaureon."

"He's not in the yard."

"Inside then."

Wodraen led the way, pushing past clusters of servants and groups of Phalanx, pausing only to ask curt questions about Fedaureon's whereabouts. Moiran followed, her apprehension ratcheting higher as they cut through the main rooms, heading toward Fedaureon's personal chambers. By the time they stalked through the open door into the feverish activity within, she was so taut her voice cracked as she said, "Fedaureon, what is the meaning of this call to arms?"

All of the servants present fell silent and turned, a few ducking their heads; she hadn't meant to speak so forcefully. Those helping Fedaureon into his armor—battle armor, Moiran noted, not that used for ceremonies—never paused as they tightened straps and buckles. Daevon, Fedaureon's Protector, stood against the back wall, eyeing the servants carefully, stepping forward to make adjustments when necessary.

Her son shot her a glare. "Not now, mother. I have to take care of the Flame."

"The Flame? I thought there was a coup in Caercaern."

"There has been, and I'm betting Lotaern and his cohorts are behind it. We've tolerated the Flame long enough. It's time to act."

Moiran would have protested, would have told him he was acting precipitously, but she thought about the absent workers in the field and kept silent. Fedaureon obviously expected her to protest, for he turned when she remained silent.

She straightened as the last strap of his armor was cinched tight and met his gaze squarely. "I agree. Do what needs to be done."

He motioned toward a servant standing to one side. "Livae can fill you in on what has occurred in Caercaern. I've already sent runners to the main garrisons about the call to arms. As of this moment, House Rhyssal is at war." A servant held out his sword and he strapped it on as he made for the door.

Moiran halted him with a hand on his arm. He turned toward her, his expression hard and grim. She had never seen him this focused, this intense. She could see the man he would become—no, that he was becoming, even now, before her eyes. "Aielan guide you."

His hand rose to squeeze hers a moment before breaking away, Daevon already at the door. She heard him shouting orders as the two trotted down the hall, Phalanx falling into step behind them. Moiran didn't wait, turning to Livae immediately, the woman weary and drained through the thin sheen of fear in her eyes.

"Tell me what you know."

* * *

"Is the Phalanx ready?"

Mattalaen turned at Fedaureon's words. "Only about half of the main unit. The others are still donning armor or saddling mounts."

Fedaureon cut him off. "Gather those that are ready. We're heading to the temple now."

Mattalaen's eyes flicked toward Daevon, but he shouted to those in the courtyard to mount up as he moved toward his own horse.

Fedaureon patted his own mount's neck, the animal snorting and tossing its head, before he stepped into the stirrup and swung into the saddle.

Daevon, already seated, shifted closer. "Perhaps we should wait until the entire unit is ready."

"No. I've waited long enough."

Daevon said nothing.

As soon as Fedaureon received a nod from Mattalaen, he stood in the stirrups and roared, "Rhyssal House, to me!"

As those ready fell into line, he sat back and kicked his mount toward the gates, charging toward the town below, Daevon to his right, Mattalaen catching up on his left. Wind lashed his face, bitter and cold. He thought of Livae's haggard face as she stuttered through her report of the night of the coup. She'd hidden in the upper tier after Fedaureon's father had ordered the Rhyssal House servants to scatter, seeking shelter with a few merchants she had befriended years past. They'd brought her food and water, kept her hidden in a back room of their house as Peloroun's and Orraen's forces purged the city of the Resue, Rhyssal, and Baene Houses. Any Phalanx or servants of any of those Houses were dragged into the streets and slaughtered. Livae's voice had hitched as she recounted the tale, her eyes staring into the distance. She'd fallen silent, only continuing when Fedaureon had prodded her.

But there wasn't much to tell after that. The merchants had smuggled her out of the city in one of their carts, beneath a pile of bolts of cloth and stacked crates. As soon as she was free of the city, she'd made for Artillien. She only knew that Lords Peloroun and Orraen were behind the coup, that they'd attacked the Tamaell's palace, and that there were rumors they were seeking more than simply servants and Phalanx members from each of the three Houses. Some said that the Tamaell had escaped, and no one had seen Lord Aeren's body. This news had sent a flush of hope through Fedaureon's chest; perhaps his father was still alive, as well as the Tamaell. Terroec was certainly dead, killed in the fire that had destroyed his house in the city. Livae knew nothing of what was happening in the Evant, and nothing of what Lotaern's role had been, if he'd been a participant at all. She only knew that the Order of the Flame had been seen in the streets and had manned the walls, and that they didn't appear to be halting Peloroun's or Orraen's Phalanx from their hunt.

Fedaureon had no doubt that Lotaern was involved, even if he had made it appear the Order of Aielan was removed from the killing. But the information Livae had given was frustratingly sparse. He needed to know what had happened, needed to know if Thaedoren, his half-brother, still lived, if the other lords had been involved, and if his father—

He broke the thought off with a shake of his head. No, he needed to focus on House lands, on keeping Rhyssal intact. There had been coups in the Evant in the past. He intended to make certain Rhyssal House survived this one.

And the first order of business was to take care of the traitors already inside House lands.

They'd reached the edge of Artillien. Fedaureon and his escort pulled up sharply in front of the temple of Aielan, black smoke rising from the roofline indicating the terciern services were still taking place. The chill air smelled faintly of some kind of spice used in the fire. Fedaureon wrinkled his nose and pulled his horse to one side so he could face Mattalaen and Daevon.

"Send a few men around back. No one leaves the temple until we have the Flame in custody."

"Are you certain you want to interrupt the service?" Mattalaen's tone was bland, almost disinterested.

"I only want the Flame. We'll take them, and leave the other acolytes alone."

"What if the Flame fights back? Or the acolytes, for that matter?"

"Then we take them by force. If the acolytes rise against us, seize them as well. Otherwise, leave them and the supplicants alone."

"Very well." Mattalaen slid from his mount and gestured once. Five of the twenty broke away and rode to the back of the temple. Ten others dismounted and formed up around Fedaureon and Daevon, both handing the reins of their horses to a watcher. As the smaller group made their way toward the temple's door, the sound of hooves rose from the direction of the manse and a moment later twenty more Rhyssal House Phalanx appeared. Mattalaen ordered them to wait outside, sending another group to the back of the temple as reinforcements.

As soon as Mattalaen turned back, Fedaureon gripped the iron rings of the temple's double doors and swung them open. They thudded against the outer walls, but he was already inside the darkened foyer, reaching for the doors to the sanctuary. He jerked these open as well and stalked into the intense heat of the inner room. The member of the Flame at the front of the room, standing before the white fire in the basin, halted in midsentence as the acolytes and another member of the Flame bristled to either side. Two of the acolytes headed toward Fedaureon, but Mattalaen motioned with one hand and the Rhyssal Phalanx blocked them. A murmur rose from the people of Artillien who'd come for the service, a few crying out in alarm when the Phalanx moved forward, but Fedaureon kept his attention focused on the two members of the Flame. The one farther back shifted slightly forward, his stance threatening, but the one addressing the sizeable gathering didn't appear upset in the slightest.

His blatant disregard of the threat the Phalanx posed irritated Fedaureon far more than anything else he could have done.

"Welcome, Lord Presumptive," the member of the Flame said, his voice filling the stifling room. "Have you come to participate in the services?"

Fedaureon sensed his Protector's subtle warning movement, but ignored it. He already knew he was treading on the edge of a blade. "No, Heffaeren." He repressed a smile when the member of the Flame frowned at his own name; Fedaureon had made certain he learned all of the Flames' names early on. "I've come to enforce the edict of the lords of the Evant by removing the Order of the Flame from Rhyssal House lands."

Heffaeren recovered fast, chuckling and shaking his head. "But we are not on Rhyssal House lands. Here in the temple, we are within the Order of Aielan. That law was established eons ago. You have no power to seize me here."

"I doubt the Evant would agree with the abuse of that ancient law in this matter. We've tolerated your blatant disregard of their orders for long enough."

"I think you'll find the Evant has a different interpretation this time around."

The words hit Fedaureon like icy lake water thrown in his face. They were innocuous, but he knew with sudden certainty that Heffaeren knew what had transpired in Caercaern.

His grip tightened on his sword. Through clenched teeth, he ordered, "Take them."

The Phalanx rushed forward, drawing swords as they moved. The commoners in the temple cried out, but Fedaureon kept his attention fixed on Heffaeren, shoving forward through the acolytes with his Phalanx. Heffaeren reacted instantly, sword flaring in the white light of the basin as he drew it and roared, "See how the lords of your own lands ignore their own laws? See how they twist their words for their own ends? These are the true colors of Rhyssal House! These are the true intentions of its rulers: the subjugation of Aielan's Light!"

The clash of weapons shattered through Heffaeren's outcry and the screams of the commoners as the two members of the Flame met the Rhyssal House Phalanx with drawn blades. Heffaeren used the basin of fire to shield his back, but as the Phalanx pressed their advantage in numbers he was forced to focus on defending himself. Fedaureon heard Mattalaen shouting orders, but his own blood pounded in his ears, dulling his hearing. Something crashed behind him and the screams from the commoners escalated, but he was in range of Heffaeren now.

"What has the Order done with my father?" he demanded, but he didn't give him time to answer. Their swords met, grating against each other as rage enveloped Fedaureon and his months of intense training took over. Smug satisfaction flicked through Heffaeren's eyes and Fedaureon slashed forward again and again, barely aware that his Phalanx kept his flanks protected as chaos broke out behind him. He was entirely focused Heffaeren, on beating the Flames' sword aside as they set upon each other with a furor Fedaureon had never felt before. It suffused him, amplified by the heat of the room, by the adrenalin coursing through his body, by the scent of the spice in the air. Their blades clashed, snicked apart, struck again. Vibrations shuddered through Fedaureon's arm. He parried, countered, snatched an opening, and with sudden force hit Heffaeran's fingers with the pommel of his sword. The member of the Flame cried out, his cattan falling from his numbed grasp, clattering on the stone floor beneath the basin. Fedaureon pulled his blade back for a killing strike, met by Heffaeren's steady gaze.

It caused Fedaureon to hesitate.

Heffaeren flung his arms out wide, chest exposed. "Kill me. Kill the heart of Aielan."

There was no fear in his eyes, only a cold, hard purpose, a singular intent.

Before Fedaureon could ram the blade through the Flame's heart, someone struck Heffaeren in the back of the head from the side, the member of the Flame crumpling to the ground.

Fedaureon spun on Daevon, his Protector. "He was mine!"

"We need him." Then he nodded toward the rest of the temple.

Fedaureon lowered his sword and turned. Behind, the temple was littered with overturned benches and the scattered bodies of commoners and acolytes. Two of the Phalanx lay among them, all unconscious and bleeding from scrapes and more serious wounds. The second member of the Flame, Saederis, was slumped over a pew to the right.

Mattalaen stepped up to Fedaureon's side. "A few of the commoners and acolytes attempted to intercede. We subdued them as quickly as possible."

"Was anyone killed?"

"Two, an acolyte and one of the supplicants. Another commoner may not survive his wounds."

Fedaureon nearly cursed, but hardened himself. "Take the Order of the Flame and any of those that resisted to the manse and secure them. I'll want to talk with Heffaeren when he rouses. He has news of what happened in Caercaern."

"And the commoners? Word of what happened here will spread. It won't be looked upon kindly."

Fedaureon flinched at the reprimand, wondered what his father would have said if he'd been there, wondered what his mother would say. But he couldn't show doubt here, not in front of the Phalanx. It hadn't gone as he'd expected, but then he'd assumed the Flame would be reasonable. "We'll deal with that later. Get them to the manse, and have healers see to the wounded."

"And what will you do?"

Fedaureon knew he didn't need to answer, but he met Mattalaen's gaze and said, "I intend to report this to my mother."

He saw his Protector's nod of approval from the corner of his eye.

6

"What have you done?" Lord Saetor's voice echoed in the chamber where the Evant met, his anger directed at Peloroun. But his gaze didn't rest long on the lord who had just finished addressing the remaining members of the Evant. It leaped to Orraen, who stiffened, before dodging toward the Chosen. "What have you *all* done?"

Lotaern shifted in his seat. Vaeren stood protectively at his back, but there would be no threat here in the Evant, not with each lord in attendance having only five members as escort—three of their own personal Phalanx and two note-takers. The limited numbers had been necessary in order to get all of the surviving lords to come. Saetor, Daesor, and Houdyll had retreated behind barricaded doors while Peloroun and Orraen seized control of Caercaern over the last month. It had taken Lotaern to coax them out. But they were still wary, even with Lotaern's assurances that the coup was over. The rigid stances of their Phalanx and their grim faces were testament to that.

And Lotaern needed them—or rather, their Phalanx—if he were to continue with his plans.

"They have done what should have been done by the Evant years ago," he said. "Lords Aeren and Terroec, and Tamaell Thaedoren, betrayed Aielan and the Alvritshai with their collusion with the human known as Shaeveran. They have weakened us to the point where we are nearly beyond redemption. Peloroun and Orraen saw this, and they have given us the chance to save ourselves."

Saetor snorted. "Shaeveran 'weakened' us? By saving us in the battle at the Escarpment? By providing us with the Winter Tree, the only protection we have against the Wraiths and the sukrael?"

"Wrong!" Lotaern punctuated the word by slamming his palm flat against the table he had been provided as soon as the Evant had seen fit to regard the Order of Aielan as a proper House. He surged to his feet and stepped out onto the rounded floor at the center of the tiers of steps that encircled the chamber, Vaeren a step behind. Nearly every seat in the hall was empty, including the three thrones on the raised dais where the Tamaell would normally sit as he presided over the meeting. Only five of the desks were occupied by lords and their minimal retinues today, a sixth by Lotaern and his own escort of acolytes and members of the Flame. But Lotaern shoved the emptiness of the chamber aside and disregarded the visceral tension that roiled about the room. He focused on Saetor, Lord of House Uslaen, even as he addressed everyone present.

"Wrong," he repeated, now two paces from Saetor, the lord's Phalanx bristling behind him. "The Winter Tree is not the only protection we have against the Wraiths, against the darkness of the sukrael. That is a lie that Shaeveran made us all believe. He convinced Aeren, who convinced Thaedoren and Terroec. He convinced us all! At least, initially."

"Because it worked," Daesor countered mildly.

Lotaern shot the Lord of House Nuant a scathing look. "I never said it didn't work. But it made us dependent on him, and it made us complacent. We were content to let the Winter Tree protect us, even though we were never given a choice in accepting it. Shaeveran brought it to us and before we could decide as to whether we wished to take it, he thrust it into the ground in our central marketplace and its power was thrust upon us. It towers over us even now, looming over Caercaern, a constant reminder of our dependence on a human." Daesor frowned in thought and Lotaern returned his gaze to Saetor. He knew Uslaen's lord would be the most resistant; he was certain Daesor already agreed with him.

"Even I was relieved when the attacks by the sukrael stopped. The Order of Aielan couldn't halt them then, I admit. We were being overwhelmed. But I never trusted Shaeveran, or the Winter Tree. According to the Scripts, the Order of Aielan had protected the Alvritshai from the sukrael in the past and I was determined to find a way for Her fire to protect us now."

"And have you done it? Have you found a way to protect us?" Saetor asked.

"I've done more. I've found a way kill them."

A few note-takers gasped, but none of the lords nor their guards reacted. Lotaern kept his eyes on Saetor and, surreptitiously, Daesor. Peloroun and Orraen already knew of his plans, and the only remaining lord, Houdyll of Redlien, was weak and easily influence; he would follow whomever he felt was the strongest.

And yet it was Houdyll who broke the tableau by clearing his throat nervously. "You say you can protect us, but does it matter? We have the

Winter Tree. We don't need protection."

"And even if we did, was it necessary to stage a coup, to kill Lords Terroec, Aeren, and Tamaell Thaedoren?" Saetor added. "Why didn't you bring this news before the Evant?"

"Would you have listened? Would you have even had the chance? From what I've observed in the Evant over the past few decades, Thaedoren would never have allowed it."

"You never gave him the chance."

"Do you truly believe he would have allowed me to speak? You forget the hold that Shaeveran and Aeren had over him already."

A seething silence settled over the room, broken by Peloroun. "Tell them."

"Tell them what?"

"Tell them why we need protection from the sukrael and the Wraiths. Why we need to halt this petty bickering and choose a new Tamaell, one that can bring the Alvritshai people together in what may be their greatest time of need."

Lotaern drew in a harsh breath through his nose, released it in a huff. He scanned the hall, catching Peloroun's gaze, Orraen's, who dropped his eyes, then Vaeren's, the caitan who served as his Protector and led the Order of the Flame.

"What Lord Peloroun speaks of, the real reason he and Lord Orraen rose against House Resue, Rhyssal, and Baene and killed their lords, is because one of the Seasonal Trees—the Autumn Tree—has failed."

The room was utterly silent, shocked into incomprehension. The realization of what he had said dawned on the lords' faces first, their retinues only a moment behind.

Saetor reacted first. He closed the distance between them—two short steps—and grabbed a handful of Lotaern's shirt in his, jerking him forward. "What do you mean it has failed? How do you know this? How is this possible?"

Before Lotaern could respond, the room exploded as everyone began to demand answers at once. Phalanx closed in on their charges. Vaeren and the other Flame and Lord Saetor's Phalanx faced off, each tight behind their own charge, bodies bristling. Lotaern let the wave of fear and panic wash over him, never taking his eyes from Saetor's face as the lord glared at him. Lotaern gloated for a moment, until he realized that unlike everyone else in the room, Saetor was not afraid. No.

He was merely angry.

"How long have you known?" Lord Saetor demanded. "How long

have you planned this? Don't claim it was Peloroun and Orraen—or even his sister, Reanne. I know better. I see the snake in the grass."

"It doesn't matter." Saetor had pulled his shirt so tight it constricted his chest, but he refused to let the lord see that in his face or hear it in the tenor of his voice. He reached up and clasped Saetor's hand about the wrist. "I am the only one who can save us now."

Saetor released him and stepped back. The lord's hand fell to his cattan. His Phalanx tensed.

But then Houdyll's voice broke over the hall. "What of the Winter Tree? If the Autumn Tree has failed, what of the Winter Tree?"

Everyone turned toward the Chosen.

Lotaern held Saetor's gaze, willing him to draw his blade. It would ruin him; Houdyll and Daesor would turn on him in an instant. But Saetor's grip on the hilt relaxed.

Lotaern broke away, faced Houdyll. "With the loss of the Autumn Tree, the Winter Tree is weakened, but it holds. I verified this myself."

"How?" Saetor asked.

"I touched the Tree. I communed with it."

"No, I meant, how do you know the Autumn Tree has failed? We have had no word from the human Provinces, no message from their king. Nor have we heard from the dwarren. Unless you've intercepted those messages yourself."

If Saetor had hoped Lotaern would stumble, he would be disappointed. "The wardens of the Tree informed me. They felt its loss through the connection that lies between all of the Seasonal Trees. I know of no messages sent by the human Provinces or the dwarren clans."

"And when did the wardens inform you of this devastating news?"

Lotaern hesitated, realizing what Saetor must already know. "Two weeks before the intended closing session of the Evant."

Saetor did not need to point out that the coup was staged that night; Houdyll sucked in a sharp breath.

Peloroun stepped forcefully into the silence, drawing everyone's attention to himself. "What matters is that the Winter Tree holds and that our Chosen and the rest of his Order of the Flame can protect us from the Wraiths and the sukrael if—no, *when*—it does fail. We must prepare ourselves. And the first order of business now that the city has settled down is to vote one of the surviving members of the Evant as Tamaell and raise new Houses if we so desire."

"And who would you suggest we raise as the new Tamaell?" Lord Daesor asked dryly.

"Myself, of course."

"Of course."

"I am the most powerful lord of the Evant remaining."

"How convenient."

Peloroun bristled, so Lotaern interrupted. "Would you deny that he is the eldest left, the most experienced? If we are to face the Wraiths and the sukrael, it would be best if we had someone who has dealt with them since they first became a problem. Peloroun was alive and lord of House Ionaen at the time of the Escarpment. No one else here can claim as much."

"Agreed," Daesor muttered. "Yet I would argue, if we are to face the Wraiths and the sukrael again, that we should have a Tamaell who is experienced in *fighting* them. None of us dealt with them as much as Lord Saetor. His House was the one attacked most frequently. He knows how destructive they can be. And he was trained to be a caitan in the Phalanx. He understands the strategy of warfare better than most of us here."

"He has a point," Houdyll said, then flinched when he caught Peloroun's look.

The Ionaen House lord turned that same look on Lotaern. Neither of them had expected resistance. Peloroun was the obvious choice to replace Thaedoren. If Daesor and Saetor formed an alliance against them, if they convinced Houdyll to back them...

The Evant would be at a stalemate, one that they could not afford.

"Does Lord Saetor even wish to become Tamaell?" Peloroun asked.

The hall fell deathly silent, Saetor scanning the rest of the lords. "If it is the Evant's wish."

Lotaern nearly cursed as a wave of rustling cloth and muffled gasps swept the hall. Peloroun and Orraen made their way to Lotaern's side, their escorts following, while Saetor stepped closer to Daesor, leaning forward to speak to him in a low murmur.

"It will come down to Houdyll," Peloroun said immediately, his voice low.

All three of them watched the lord of Redlien as he retreated back to his own desk. His caitan spoke to him briefly and he nodded, but his hands twisted in the folds of his sleeves.

Peloroun's mouth curled in disdain. "A shame. His father led the House with strength and nobility."

"Even if Jydell didn't always agree with you?" Orraen asked.

"My hatred of Jydell did not taint my respect."

"The question remains," Lotaern said, before the two could begin sniping at each other in earnest, "will Houdyll vote for you or Saetor?"

Peloroun motioned one of his pages forward. Snatching a piece of paper from Lotaern's desk, he scratched out a hasty note, folded, and sealed it. The runner scrambled across the room. Saetor and Deasor watched silently, Daesor already reaching for his own paper and quill.

But Peloroun straightened. "He will vote for me. Call for the vote."

"How can you be so—"

Peloroun cut Orraen off with a look. "Call for the vote."

Lotaern stepped forward. With no Tamaell to end the discussion and call the Evant to order, he took the duty upon himself. Daesor was still frantically folding his own note, handing it to his page without even sealing it, when Lotaern cleared his throat.

"In the absence of the Tamaell, and as the Chosen of the Order of Aielan, I call for the remaining lords of the Evant to vote for the Tamaell's replacement." Daesor's page handed the note to Houdyll, who read it, lips pressing into a thin line. Lotaern ignored him. "I believe everyone's vote is obvious, except for Lord Houdyll." He waited for acknowledging nods from Saetor and Daesor on one side, and Peloroun and Orraen on the other, then turned on Houdyll. "I cast my vote for Peloroun. What say you, Lord Houdyll? Who do you choose as Tamaell of the Alvritshai people?"

* * *

"How did you know he would vote for you?" Lotaern asked.

"Because Houdyll was less than discreet in his youth, much to his father's distress."

"You mean—"

"He bedded every servant who ever entered his rooms."

He and Peloroun stood outside the gates of the Winter Tree's garden, waiting for the wardens to admit them to the grounds. They had met inside the gardens a few times in the past, but always in secret. Such secrecy was no longer necessary. As the door creaked open and a hooded warden motioned them inside, bells began to sound, starting near the Hall of the Evant and spreading outwards, announcing the selection of a new Tamaell. Somehow, the sound made what they had done more final than anything he'd experienced so far, including seeing the bodies of the fallen in the halls of the Tamaell's House and the pillars of black smoke from the pyres.

"Such actions, no matter how dishonorable to the House or his father, are hardly unheard of in Lords Presumptive. I fail to see—"

"I have, within my care, one of the unfortunate results from one of those liaisons."

Peloroun said it softly, but the undercurrent of malice set Lotaern's teeth on edge. He couldn't help the tight frown of disapproval—he was the Chosen of Aielan after all. Threatening one of Houdyll's bastard children was not something Lotaern would have condoned if he'd known ahead of time. But he had to admit that revealing Houdyll's indiscretion would not have brought enough shame to himself or his House to have swayed him at the Evant. It would have been devastating if it became public knowledge, but it would not have destroyed him. And such a tactic would have taken time to have any real effect.

They had needed a new Tamaell now.

"Your methods are questionable," Lotaern said, as they passed beneath the boughs of the Winter Tree. Its shadow was bitingly cold, even in the last few hours before dusk.

"My methods have made me the Tamaell. You would be wise to remember that, Chosen."

Lotaern's skin prickled and his eyes narrowed. Peloroun chose not to acknowledge the look, facing forward, head held high.

After a few paces, Lotaern looked back to the path leading toward the base of the Winter Tree. "Have you secured the palace?"

"My Phalanx was already in place. Servants have begun moving my household into the upper levels."

"Have they discovered how Thaedoren and Aeren made their escape?"

"Not yet."

"What of our forces outside of Caercaern?"

"*My* forces have secured our borders to the south and set up a secondary line along Baene's boundary, in case the new Lord takes it upon himself to retaliate. Orraen is doing the same along Saetor's border, even though the lord of Uslaen is trapped between him and Houdyll and is unlikely to make any serious moves against us. My main concern is Rhyssal and, after today's Evant, Nuant. I have no idea what Lord Aeren will do, and Daesor certainly exhibited more backbone than I would have expected by backing Saetor. If he, Aeren, and Thaedoren combine forces, they will be a significant threat."

"Thaedoren no longer has the White Phalanx at his beck and call."

"He doesn't? We did not find the White Fox's body in the tower. And not all of the White Phalanx was within Caercaern at the time of the coup."

"You took care of those within. That should have weakened the White

Phalanx and Daedallen's power significantly."

"We hurt them, yes, but it was not a killing blow."

There was more to it than that. Lotaern heard it in Peloroun's voice. "What have you heard?"

Peloroun halted.

"You may be the Tamaell, but you would not be here without me."

Peloroun's jaw clenched. "We have not found all of the White Phalanx within Caercaern. I do not believe they are *in* Caercaern any longer. They have been smuggled out somehow, and battalions of the White Phalanx have gone missing outside the walls, their posts abandoned. What little my men have been able to discover leads me to believe that they have retreated to the west."

"Aeren."

"I seriously doubt anyone else would have reacted this quickly. Lord Daesor has been trapped within the city. It's unlikely he had a chance to send a message back to Nuant. Even if he did, it would take time for his sons to gather his forces or prepare for the White Phalanx's arrival. Lord Aeren, on the other hand..."

"Lord Aeren has been on guard since last winter," Lotaern finished. He clasped his hands behind his back, more troubled than he was willing to let on. They walked in silence, Lotaern aware of Peloroun's growing agitation even within the calming gardens beneath the tree. They had nearly reached the massive trunk, the Winter Tree's gnarled roots already beginning to surround them.

"What of the Wraith army?" Peloroun asked, his voice low even though they hadn't seen any of the wardens since leaving the gate. "Where are they? How much time do we have?"

"Their location is unknown. The last I heard, their army was marching across dwarren lands, headed here."

"Then the time schedule has not changed. We will still meet with Khalaek-khai as planned at the edge of Ionaen lands. Is the Order of the Flame prepared to deal with him? With all of the Wraiths?"

"The Order is ready. Vaeren has seen to it hims—"

Peloroun turned toward him as he cut off. Lotaern wiped the shock from his face in the space of a breath, but he was still too late. Peloroun had seen.

"What is it?" the lord—no, the Tamaell—spat. His head jerked in the direction Lotaern had been staring, latched onto the Winter Tree itself, onto an area of mottled darkness on the bark nearly an arm's-length across. The normally rich, craggy brown had blackened, traces of white mold threaded through it. Lotaern remained rooted in place as Peloroun stepped forward and reached out to touch the spot. The rough bark sagged beneath his touch, soft and spongy, and Lotaern's stomach roiled as a fetid stench puffed outwards and surrounded them. He would have bent over with nausea, but Peloroun snatched his hand back, spun around, and advanced.

"What is that?" Lotaern shook his head, stepped back in retreat, but Peloroun's hand latched onto his throat and jerked him forward. "What's happening to the Winter Tree?"

"It's weakening," Lotaern gasped, both hands clutching at Peloroun's appallingly strong grip. He couldn't gain any purchase, Peloroun's fingers tightening the more he struggled. He halted his struggle and said bluntly, "It's dying."

"You said it would hold. You said the Wraiths and the sukrael would not be able to reach Caercaern."

"And they won't. It will hold until the Order can deal with them."

Peloroun's grip did not loosen. He drew Lotaern closer, cutting off more air, although Lotaern sucked in enough to smell the wine sauce that must have flavored his mid-afternoon meal. "We are walking a blade's edge here, Chosen. One misstep, one minor shift in balance, and one of us will get cut. I do not intend that person to be me. So, I ask again, will the Wraiths or the sukrael be able to reach Caercaern?"

"It...will...hold."

Peloroun held his gaze, searching, then abruptly released him. "Make whatever preparations you need, Chosen. My Phalanx will be ready to escort us to our meeting with Khalaek-khai as planned."

Lotaern watched Peloroun retreat into the shadows beneath the Winter Tree. He waited until the new Tamaell was merely a blur, then turned his back and forced himself to approach the spot of blight, breathing through his mouth. The stench still made him gag, but he touched the bark, recoiled at how it squelched beneath his fingers. It left a slick residue on his skin. He rubbed it off on his sleeve.

There shouldn't be damage like this. Not yet.

He followed the trunk of the Tree upwards, stared up into its boughs, and wondered how much of the blight they couldn't see. How deep did it go?

There was only one way to find out.

Reaching out, he laid his palm flat against the normal bark beside the blighted area, closed his eyes, and sank into the trancelike state he needed to commune with the Tree. It took longer than usual, the rot from the blight heavy on the air, distracting him, but slowly he felt himself sinking into the sensations of the Tree. Wind rustled in the leaves and he sensed snow falling high above, touching the outer branches, already heavy and thick. Sap flowed through him, slowed by the cold, but still pulsing with life. He hissed in pain at the rot, like a dark bruise, tender to the touch, but moved beyond it, searching for more.

And found it. Splotches of the darkness riddled the Tree on all sides, all the way to the top, on the branches, in the roots. He winced as he flowed toward each location, an ache shuddering through his own body where it slumped forward against the trunk. The Tree fought back against the degradation, pulling strength from where it had tapped into the White Fire beneath the mountain and the deeper resources of the Lifeblood, but it wasn't enough. The disease was spreading too fast, accelerated by the loss of the Autumn Tree. Lotaern could feel that Tree's absence, like an arm that had been torn free. He could sense the weakening of the Summer Tree as well, but couldn't ascertain the extent of the damage done there. He wasn't Shaeveran. His experience was with the White Fire only, his link to the Trees limited. But he could tell that the mantle of protection the Trees provided from the Wraiths and the sukrael had been severely diminished, worse than he had imagined or predicted.

He pulled himself back from the Tree, but it clung to him, as if seeking his help. He struggled to disengage, jerking back with a weary gasp and slumping to his knees before its massive trunk, then heard a creaking groan of wood, like a moan. Lotaern listened to the branches high above thrash as if in a stiff wind, then settle. He waited a moment longer, swallowed against the dryness in his throat, then clambered to his feet, using the trunk as an aid. His legs trembled and his hands shook. Something sticky lay against one side of his face and with horror he realized he'd brushed against the blight while searching through the Tree. He scrubbed at his cheek with the corner of his sleeve as he staggered down through the roots to the garden below.

By the time he'd reached the edge of the Tree's coverage and stepped out into the accumulating snow, he knew he had to speak to Vaeren and the rest of the Order of the Flame. Because Peloroun was right. They walked a blade's edge with Khalaek-khai, the Wraiths, and the sukrael.

And the Winter Tree was failing much faster than he had ever anticipated. By the time they met with Khalaek-khai, he doubted it would be enough to protect them from the sukrael at all.

* * *

The horncry snatched GreatLord Tarken Sohn out of an intense study of the reports from his freeholders, commanders, and scouts. He'd set patrols on the outskirts of his lands since the strange sightings to the north along the dwarren Flats and the edges of the Thalloran Wasteland had begun this past spring, had confirmed the rumors from GreatLord Kobel in Temeritt, but had heard nothing from that Province in over three months. That silence was disturbing, especially with the approach of winter, but his own Province of Yhnar was the most isolated out of all of the Provinces. It was not unheard of to receive little to no word from the other GreatLords or King Justinian.

The horncry repeated itself.

He rose and headed to the window overlooking the city of Yhnar, eyeing the outer stone walls. A flag had been raised at the central gate— yellow, signifying a messenger.

"It's about time."

He moved to the double doors across the large room, opened them abruptly. The two guards outside turned.

"Messenger at the gates. Have the servants prepare the secondary audience chamber. And forewarn Laurelen. We may have guests for dinner." One of the guards rapped his closed fist against his chest, armor clanging, then turned on his heel and headed off as Tarken turned to the second guard. "Pellin, you're with me."

"My lord."

Tarken headed toward the audience chamber, slowly enough the servants would have time to prepare it. His thoughts were already on the messenger, the reports that he'd been absorbed in already forgotten. Did they bring word from King Justinian about the unusual activity reported from the dwarren? Or was it something else entirely? His patrols had reported seeing movement far out in the desert and the salt flats, along with strange creatures flying in the skies overhead, but whatever it was, it had been too far away to investigate further.

Halfway down the stairs to the main level, another horncry echoed down into the center of the palace, the walls unable to dampen the urgency in its notes.

Tarken glanced toward Pellin. "A summons for the healer?"

Tarken charged down the steps, through the corridors, and out into the main hall. Guardsmen and servants jumped out of his way. He caught sight of Kent, his commander, coming from the opposite direction at the same speed. They met before the central doors to the hall.

"What have you heard? Why is there a call for a healer?" Tarken asked as they slowed.

"I've heard nothing."

They breached the main doors and stumbled to a halt on the palace's stairs. Twenty guardsmen surrounded three figures bent forward over someone on the stairs, half of them facing outwards to protect those within, the other half attempting to control the center. Tarken's hand fell to his side where his sword would rest if he'd had it strapped on, but he saw nothing threatening anywhere on the promenade or courtyard below.

Then Laurelen's voice cut through the confusion.

"Back off! Everyone, quiet, and back off! He needs room to breathe. And where's the god-cursed healer?"

Tarken headed down the stairs. One of the guardsmen shouted, "Make way, the GreatLord has arrived," and began leading Tarken and Kent through the outer edges of the group.

A moment later, Tarken caught sight of a man in armor in Temeritt's colors sprawled on the steps, Laurelen checking his pulse with one hand, the other cupped along his cheek. The man—Tarken guessed he was twenty at most—was pale. Day's old blood stained his tunic and trailed down his breeches. As Tarken knelt beside his wife, she dropped the messenger's wrist and began checking his chest, arms, and legs for wounds.

"What happened?"

Laurelen glanced up at him, mouth pursed. "From what I gather, the patrol found him in this condition. They brought him here immediately. Those at the gate asked if he needed a healer, but he insisted on seeing you first, so they signaled and sent him on up without calling for one, but he collapsed here."

"He didn't want to wait," a lieutenant Tarken assumed had led the escort to the palace said defensively. "And the blood on his clothes is old. There weren't any obvious wounds—"

"It doesn't matter," Tarken cut in. "What's wrong with him?"

"Nothing serious, so far. He's cut up and bruised. It doesn't look like the cuts are from a blade, more like...more like claws. But he's feverish, even though his skin is pale, and his pulse is fluttery." She'd worked her way down to his legs. When she pressed a spot on his left hip, the man moaned and began to thrash. Laurelen leaned back. "There might be a fracture there. The healer will know."

The man suddenly lurched upright, eyes flaring wide. He reached out and clutched at Laurelen, Tarken's wife crying out in pain at his grip. "The GreatLord! I need to see the GreatLord!"

"Right here," Tarken said. "If you'd release my wife."

The man glanced down at his hand, then let go as if burned by fire. His body began trembling, but he swallowed and forced words out through cracked lips. "Temeritt was attacked. The city is under siege. GreatLord Kobel requests aid."

Laurelen cast Tarken a startled glance while those that surrounded them—guardsmen all—tensed, suddenly more alert. Tarken felt Kent's hand fall to his shoulder as the commander leaned in closer, but Tarken spoke first.

"Who's attacked? Where did they come from? How many are there?"

As if passing on the message had drained him, the messenger slumped and the trembling increased. He began to sag backwards, but Tarken caught him, surprised at how light his body felt. He lowered him to the stone of the steps, the man gasping as he tried to report.

"They came from the northeast. Demons. Creatures...creatures I haven't seen before...featherless birds...leathery cats with eyes...eyes like lanterns...Alvritshai." He winced as he shifted his hip, his face writhing in pain, turning even whiter. Through gritted teeth, he continued, "They found me...halfway here...killed...horse..."

With a strangled moan, his eyes fluttered shut and he sagged back against the stairs, body going limp. Laurelen immediately pressed her fingers into his neck hard. "He still lives."

"Let me through!" someone snapped. Tarken recognized Marten's voice.

"Let the healer through." He caught the shocked looks on those who stood close enough to have heard the man's report and added, "Now!"

Marten stumbled into the cleared space at the center. He shook his head, mumbling imprecations under his breath, but then his attention was caught by the Temeritt guard.

"What's this? A messenger from Temeritt?"

"He was momentarily conscious, enough to make an initial report, but then he blacked out. Can you bring him around enough we can ask him additional questions?"

Marten sent him a scathing look. "I haven't even looked at him yet." He clucked his tongue when he pulled the man's eyelids back, but moved on with a shake of his head.

Tarken turned to the lieutenant. "Did he carry anything with him, lieutenant?"

"The patrol found him on the plains about two hours walk distant, no horse, no supplies, nothing. He said he carried a message, but refused to pass it along to anyone but you. He appeared exhausted, but he was coherent."

"I need to know more. Temeritt attacked? Under siege? By the Alvristhai and...and demons?" He looked to Kent, but his commander wore the same confused expression he knew lined his own face.

Marten sat back. "He's certainly been attacked by something, but hell if I know what. Not a bear. The marks are wrong. I'd say there are internal wounds. Nothing life threatening. He needs rest. We should move him to a room in the palace, carefully, try to get some water into him. He's dehydrated."

"Can you force him awake?"

Laurelen placed a hand on his arm. "The wounds aren't serious, the man's simply exhausted. You can wait, Tarken. Whatever has happened, another few hours will not matter."

Tarken damped his irritation. He wasn't certain he agreed. "Can you handle this?"

"Of course."

Tarken stood and stepped back, Pellin to one side, Kent to the other. Kent ordered all but three guards back to their posts, then shooed the gathered servants away with one hand. Tarken had no doubts that the rumors about the Temeritt guardsman and what little news he'd had was already spreading through the halls and into Yhnar's streets below. He watched as Kent spoke with the three guardsmen remaining, including the lieutenant, then dismissed them.

When Kent turned back, Tarken asked, "Demons? Alvritshai attacking Temeritt? Any clue as to what in hells is going on?"

"No idea. It can't be good if he came in as beat up as he did. I can't think of anything in the local area that would have mauled him like that."

"But?" He'd heard the hesitation in Kent's voice. He motioned both his commander and Pellin up the stairs toward the open doors of the palace.

Kent didn't answer until they'd entered the main hall, Tarken directing them toward his personal study.

"But...we've been receiving reports for months now of attacks on the villages and towns in the outlying edges of Yhnar. They've all claimed some kind of demon or creature out of folklore. I dismissed these accounts out of hand. They're commoners. They frighten at every twisting shadow and are generally superstitious. But still." Kent rolled his shoulders uncomfortably. "When I inspected the patrol routes, what we saw hovering in the distance over the wasteland and then on the ground on the Flats wasn't any animal I recognized. And when we camped one night, I would have sworn something was watching us from the grass."

Tarken smothered his initial response. He'd known Kent since they were in training in the Legion. He'd always been pragmatic, and was never one to accept rumor or suspicion as truth. But whatever he'd seen during the patrol—demon or otherwise—had disturbed him.

And that disturbed Tarken. He'd dismissed the reports as well, believing that all of the sightings were merely mistakes—hawks or fear-driven hallucinations. But now, with the arrival of the bloodied messenger, his report, and Kent's own doubts...

"Double the patrols and the guardsmen on the walls. Send out a general warning to the citizens of Yhnar. Have them report anything they see, no matter how strange or insignificant. And begin preparing the Legion for a march. If what the messenger from Temeritt said is true, GreatLord Kobel will need our help to break the siege, no matter who is at their walls. We'll wait until he can give us a full report, but it doesn't hurt to prepare. Keep me updated."

"Very well, GreatLord." Kent saluted and broke away. Tarken paused, considered heading toward the room where the messenger would be kept, but decided he would only be a nuisance. Marten and Laurelen could handle it, and he knew they'd summon him the moment the man woke.

Instead, he continued on to his study. He needed to revisit those reports.

* * *

"Anything?" Lord Akers asked abruptly. He'd been pacing behind Kobel on the narrow balcony the entire time the GreatLord had been scanning the distant Horde and the burnt husk of the Autumn Tree with his spyglass.

Kobel ignored him, his jaw clenching ever so slightly in irritation as he focused on the blackened branches at the base of the Tree. Most of the upper branches had been consumed in the conflagration as the Horde surrounded Temeritt and laid siege. But the lower branches, while stripped of their fiery autumn-colored leaves by real flame, still remained and were strong enough to hold heavy metal cages. Those cages now held the remains of men and women of Temeritt caught by the Horde. Most had simply been luckless enough to be outside the city walls when Kobel had ordered the gates closed and sealed. But a few of them were guardsmen caught in the few forays Kobel and Akers had made against the Horde from the wall.

Three of the most recent additions were the messengers they'd attempted to send during their last sortie. They'd appeared nearly a week before, and as Kobel scanned their bodies, bile burning at the back of his throat, he felt a sense of relief creep over his shoulders. Two of the messengers had finally died. While he was certainly far too distant to have heard their screams, he had watched them through the spyglass long enough his wife, Echeri, had finally scolded him and taken the instrument away. He'd had to appeal to one of Echeri's ladies to retrieve the spyglass two days later. He'd been careful to use it only when Echeri was otherwise occupied since.

When the third captured messenger twitched as a carrion crow plucked at the already mangled flesh of one arm, he dropped the cylinder and collapsed it, handing it over to Akers, who seized it instantly and began scanning the black army before them.

"What did you see?" Akers said.

"Two of the messengers have died. The third still lives. I did not see the fourth."

"Then there's hope that he got through."

"Or there was nothing left to place in the cage to antagonize and demoralize us."

"Who's demoralized? We're trapped inside Temeritt, running short on food, and no one knows that we need help. I was thinking of taking my wife and children down to the market for a treat of skewered rat and burnt pigeon."

In spite of himself, Kobel smiled. "We aren't that desperate yet."

"Not yet, but if someone doesn't arrive soon, with an army at their backs..." Akers trailed off. "It's hard to tell, but it appears that the scout missing was the one bound for Yhnar."

"So it would appear. Which means that even if he did make it through, we're still in trouble. Yhnar doesn't have the resources we need to end this siege. And they're too isolated to spread the word quickly enough to the other Provinces to help before starvation kills the majority of us here."

Akers didn't answer, shifting the spyglass so he could scan the Horde itself. Kobel had done the same, but hadn't seen any significant change in the Horde's encampment. They were settled in, entrenched, waiting.

Waiting for them to starve? Or waiting for something else?

He snapped his fingers in frustration and motioned Akers to follow him back inside the room. "The citizens of Temeritt are getting restless. Commanders have begun reporting an increase in violence in the streets and general rumblings from the populace that we aren't doing anything."

"What do they expect us to do?"

"Attack, of course. They know half of the Horde left the walls after the siege began. They know that supplies are running low and that they won't last much longer. They can feel winter sinking its claws into their skin already. I can feel it myself." Kobel rolled his shoulders as he headed toward the far door of his personal chambers, Akers following without comment. As soon as they hit the corridor outside, Kobel's usual escort of four guardsmen fell into position around them. "I can't blame them—we've been cooped up inside the walls for over two months now—but we can't let it escalate. Issue orders that anyone caught rioting or looting will be conscripted into the Commoner's Army or executed, their choice. Also, prepare the commanders for more sorties. We need to begin harrying the Horde. They've become too complacent."

"I'd noticed that as well. They didn't even respond during out last attempt, merely roused themselves enough to make certain we retreated back to our walls. No retaliation at all, not even a token show of mockery."

"I intend to take advantage of that."

Akers halted at a cross corridor, Kobel and his escort continuing on without him. "Where are you headed?"

"To see Patris Raleveti. It's time to call upon the Hand of Diermani."

* * *

Kobel found Raleveti in the main hall of the cathedral, tending to those who'd gathered for solace beneath the vaulted ceilings and the tilted cross of Diermani. Kobel's escort's boots echoed hollowly in the solemn silence of the hall, even though there were at least a hundred citizens of Temeritt scattered throughout the rows of pews, sitting quietly or kneeling with head bowed. A rustle intruded as a few of those in prayer turned at the disturbance, but Kobel ignored them, his gaze latching onto the robust figure of Raleveti to the left of the main altar, beneath the cross. As soon as he caught sight of him, he headed down the central aisle, the patris glancing up from blessing a man and woman as Kobel drew near. Raleveti was twenty years Kobel's senior, had been Kobel's tutor when he was a boy, and had the shock of gray hair and weary eyes to prove it. That weariness had deepened in the last few months, carving harsh lines in the patris' face, especially around the mouth. As Kobel came closer, he realized the portly priest had lost weight as well.

Raleveti withdrew his hands from the two supplicants' bowed heads as he murmured, "May Diermani guide you in the days to come and cast His blessing on you and yours in this time of darkness."

Both muttered a response that Kobel didn't catch, but when they rose to their feet, the man helping the woman by taking one elbow, he realized that the woman was pregnant, close to term. He stepped aside, swallowing back the sudden bitter taste in the back of his throat. The two noticed who he was and genuflected. "GreatLord," the man said.

The woman reached out to touch Kobel's arm. "You have to stop it," she whispered fiercely. "You have to stop the Horde. My baby can't be born into this. He can't live in such a world. Do something! Make them go away!"

The presumed husband snatched at his wife's arm and dragged her away, his face a mask of apology and horror and despair. But the woman's words had echoed throughout the hall, louder than they would have been had they been shouted on a street corner. Kobel stared around at those faces, some angry, others afraid, a few pleading, most glancing aside as his gaze swept over them.

Kobel turned Raleveti. "I need to speak to you."

Raleveti clasped his hands before him, the sleeves of the patris' robes nearly obscuring the gold rings on his fingers. "I've been expecting you. You've come for the Hand of Diermani, I assume?"

"Yes."

"You realize that it hasn't been activated for decades. I'm not even certain it will work. And someone must notice its activation within Corsair and the other Provinces for it to be effective."

Kobel straightened. "It needs to be done."

"Very well. Follow me."

The patris lead them around the curve of the altar's dais, pausing only once to ring a soft-toned bell before passing through a shadowed doorway that led behind the altar into the rooms reserved for the priests and the servants of Diermani. Two priests approached them, headed toward the main hall, and Kobel realized the bell had summoned them as Raleveti ordered them to light additional candles and lead those gathered in a prayer of protection.

Moments later, Raleveti halted outside a simple wooden door, one like all of the others they'd passed in the winding corridors. "Wait here. I must retrieve something from my quarters."

He pushed through the door, leaving it slightly open. Kobel heard the sounds of rustling paper, a cascade of books falling over, followed by half-muttered curses, then more rustling and the sound of drawers opening and closing. Finally, a barked, "Aha!"

Raleveti reappeared, expression serious. He shut the door behind him and continued down the hallway without a word.

Ten minutes later, he led Kobel through latticed double doors inset with intricately-carved panels with symbols and images from Diermani's Codex and into a small sanctuary that must have been reserved for the patris' personal use. Six kneeling mats lined the narrow floor, facing an altar containing the tilted cross, reliquaries, a copper basin containing water, and other small religious objects, all on a shelf inside a niche. The walls were as intricately carved as the doors, the two to the left and right containing their own smaller niches behind latticework. The tiny room smelled of incense—myrrh and cloves and something Kobel couldn't identify. The scent was heavy enough Kobel found himself drawing shallow breaths through his mouth so he wouldn't cough. Raleveti didn't appear affected.

After scanning the room, Kobel told his escort to wait outside; the space would be cramped if they all entered at once. They left the doors open.

Raleveti knelt before the altar, hand flowing smoothly through the standard genuflection as he murmured beneath his breath, his other hand clutching the chain and cross that adorned his neck. Kobel knelt behind him and to the left, listened restlessly to their breathing in the silence that followed, but started when Raleveti suddenly rose.

"The Hand of Diermani," he said, and motioned to one of the side niches.

Kobel rose. "What needs to be done?"

"I looked through our records when this all began, before the Horde arrived here at Temeritt, but they weren't exactly precise in their description. The general principle is simple." He pulled an iron key from an inner pocket, unlocked the small lattice door, reached into the niche, and withdrew what looked like a simple clear glass orb. He held it out toward Kobel. "It works like the bonding vows. Place your hand on top. I'll support it from below."

"Like the bonding vows?" Kobel did what Raleveti suggested, resting his hand on the top of the orb. He knew of the bonding ritual. His wife's vow rested against his chest beneath his shirt, the vial that contained their mixed blood suddenly warm against his skin. The vial was inset in an intricate knot of wires of copper, bronze, and gold. Echeri wore a similar pendant. "Will this require blood?"

Raleveti met his gaze. "Yes."

Sharp pain stabbed up Kobel's arm. His teeth clenched in reaction and he stifled a grunt, hissing instead, as the pain ended as quickly as it had come.

"Was that necessary?"

"The Hand of Diermani requires the blood of the current GreatLord and the residing patris."

"That wasn't what I meant."

Raleveti smiled.

Kobel dropped his glare to the orb. His hand still clutched it, clawlike from the unexpected pain, but he released it now, shaking the dull ache from his fingers. The orb was no longer clear. Blood—he assumed his own and Raleveti's—swirled inside as if caught in moving water. But unlike blood dripped into a stream, the tendrils remained intact, rather than fraying and diluting. At the heart of the orb, white light glowed, pulsing slightly.

There was no indication of how the blood had entered the orb—no aperture, no stopper—just like the bonding vows. And when Kobel glanced at his palm, he saw no marks. There was only a faint tingling in his skin, as if he'd been pricked with a thousand tiny needles.

"That was *not* like the bonding vows," Kobel muttered, clenching and unclenching his fist. "The bonding was not that painful."

"The pain was...unexpected. The description in the records didn't mention that." Raleveti turned and set the orb back in the gold circlet holder where it had rested in the niche, then closed and locked the lattice screen. The orb's glow could still be seen, casting strange shadows from the latticework onto the walls. Kobel was silently gratified to see the patris massaging the palm of his own hand. "But it appears to have worked. Now...we wait."

"No. It's too late to wait. They won't arrive in time. Now, we prepare to defend ourselves, to hold as long as possible, to attack when we can."

"Then what was the Hand of Diermani for?"

"A warning to the king and the other GreatLords." Kobel turned and headed toward the door. "Let us hope they notice and take heed."

7

Colin woke with a start.

His first instinct was to suck in a deep breath, but his entire chest felt hollowed out and empty, yet dense, as if someone had stacked layers upon layers of blankets over top of him. He managed a thin wheeze that choked off at the end with a thick gurgle that tasted of blood. He gagged on it, tongue slick as it spread the viscous fluid around his dry mouth. His lips were cracked, the skin across his face tight and gritty with dust. He opened his eyes and blinked up into the half-lit shadows of striated stone, gouged and smoothed by water.

He frowned. The taste of blood, the hollow in his chest, the cracked lips...it was all familiar. He'd woken like this once before. The time that he'd tried to kill himself. The time he'd thrust his dagger deep into his—

Memory flared, brighter than the sun, blinding him to the stone of the ceiling even though his eyes shot wide open. Sheared off towers filled his vision instead: the bowl, the building clutched in its center, the massive open pit of the Well surrounded by shards of crystal caught in the white-blue glow of the Lifeblood as it surged higher, the Well awakening, pulsing with life. Then the appearance of the Shadows.

And Walter.

Pain seared through him as he felt again the sword pierce up through his chest from behind, its tip jutting out from his torso as his own blood gushed from the wound and smeared its length. Walter's hand clutched at his shoulder, fingers digging in to hold him steady as the force of the thrust eased. Then the Wraith's breath touched the skin of his neck, shockingly hot and humid—or perhaps it was his own skin that had abruptly cooled—as Walter whispered, "You never did open yourself completely to the Lifeblood and all it offered as I did, did you?"

Colin hadn't answered, couldn't have answered, even after Walter drew the blade free and let him fall. Blood filled his mouth, his lungs; bile burned his throat. His entire body seethed with excruciating pain, but even that was fading, his arms and legs going numb. A haze of yellow infiltrated the edges of his sight, seeping inwards, obscuring Walter, the chamber that housed the newly awakened Well, the stars and the night sky above. A moment before he lost consciousness completely, he thought he saw arrows streak past, trailing white fire.

He forced the vibrant flare of memory back, focused on the striated stone above, forced himself to feel the heat in the air that surrounded him, to draw that heat into his protesting lungs, even though it woke a deep-seated ache in his chest. He tried to lift his arm, couldn't, but found he could use his fingers to crawl across his feverish skin toward the hollow in his torso. Before he reached it, he ran into bandages tied tight beneath his armpits.

He had nearly finished exploring these with his fingers—mostly dry, with a spot of slick wetness near their center—when he heard someone gasp, followed by the clatter of loose stone.

Siobhaen appeared above him, her shadow blocking out some of the light. "You're alive," she breathed, then muttered a short stumbling prayer to Aielan as she felt his forehead, pinched the skin near his eyes, pressed fingers hard into his throat beneath his jaw.

He batted at her hands feebly. "I'm all right."

"You're far from all right." But she withdrew slightly. "You should not even be alive."

"I should have died two hundred years ago with Karen." His hand suddenly flew to the bandages around his chest. "My pendant...the vow. Where is it?" Panic clawed up his throat, more sickening than the taste of blood, but Siobhaen caught his hand and squeezed it.

"It's right here. We had to take it off to bandage you."

She shifted away, out of sight. He heard rummaging as she pawed through a sack, then she returned, carrying his own bags. She pulled out a small, empty vial caught in a crescent of metal, then set it in the palm of one hand. His fingers curled over it protectively and a tightness in his chest eased. His breathing relaxed.

"What is it?" Siobhaen asked as she leaned over Colin's chest and pulled out a water skin.

Colin almost didn't answer. The vows were private, meant only for those who chose to take them, made public only during the blood ceremony before the patris and the church. But this vow had never been confirmed, never had the chance to be confirmed.

"It's a marriage vow, given from one partner to another. It's a sign of the bond taken. This one was given to me by Karen. We intended to be wed, our blood mingled in the vial to seal the marriage, but it never happened."

"Why not?" Siobhaen unsealed the skin and dribbled a little of the water onto his lips. He drank it greedily, used it to wash the blood from his tongue and throat. His stomach clenched on the third swallow, so he pulled away, spluttering. Siobhaen waited, then offered him some more.

When he'd had enough, he answered her. "We never got the chance. The dwarren attacked and drove us into the Shadows. They took her... took everyone but me and Walter." His fingers clenched on the pendant, its edges digging into his hand. He shook his head. "It doesn't matter now." His voice grated less, and the water gave him strength. He began to struggle into a sitting position.

Siobhaen cursed, set the water skin aside, and helped him. By the time she'd propped him against a stone wall, he was short of breath again, the ache in his chest radiating down into his gut and his arms. Sweat had popped out on his skin, had slicked his hair to his scalp.

He scanned the cave where Siobhaen had sheltered him, nothing more than a shelf of rock overhead. A litter leaned up against one wall, tied with rags and draped with a few blankets. Satchels were piled at its base. Stones ringed a small firepit and he caught the faint scent of smoke, greasy coals, and roasted meat. His stomach growled. The mouth of the cave opened up onto a vista of red-burnt stone and sand hazed with ripples of heat beneath a pale blue sky scudded with straggly white clouds.

He didn't see Eraeth and a sudden certainty seized him. "Where's Eraeth? He isn't—"

"Dead? I should be so blessed. The Protector is out hunting. And keeping an eye out for the Haessari and the taeredac. They've sent out patrols, although we haven't seen one in two days. But the leathery birds fly much farther afield. That's why we're undercover." She motioned to the ledge overhead as she stood, then moved to the satchels and began digging through them again, removing something folded up inside a swatch of cloth.

She crouched down at Colin's side and pulled out a length of dried meat. "Chew on this. You haven't eaten for weeks."

"Weeks?" he asked, taking the hard meat and sticking it into his mouth. He bit down, but it was too hard to chew, so he sucked on the smoky flavor, working moisture into it slowly. "What happened back at the Well? How long have I been unconscious?"

"Over two months."

Colin choked, coughing roughly. The wound in his chest spasmed violently and fresh dots of blood bloomed on the bandage. He regained control and collapsed back against the rock wall.

Long moments later, he gasped weakly, "I knew it took weeks for me to heal when I tried to kill myself in the Ostraell—I was covered in leaves when I first woke—but months?" He tucked his chin in to look at the freshly-blooded bandage around his chest. "This must be significantly worse than before."

"The Wraith drove the entire length of a sword through your chest. Aielan alone knows what could be worse."

The image of the blade's tip jutting from his chest returned with gruesome clarity. "I've often wondered. Would a limb grow back if I lost it? What about burns? I've healed from them before—when embers from fires scarred me, for example—but nothing serious. I've never been willing to test the limits."

Siobhaen said nothing, had moved to the edge of the overhang and stood staring out at the heated landscape, troubled.

Colin watched her, returning the length of salty meat to his mouth.

"We gave you the waters of the sarenavriell," she said abruptly. "We gave you the Lifeblood. We didn't know what else to do. After the attack at the Well, after we defeated the sukrael and brought down the Wraith, we gathered your body and hid in the ruins of the city. The Haessari hunted for us. They were getting close. We had to move you, but...You were still bleeding, the wound..." She swallowed hard, still not looking toward him. "We had you drink the Lifeblood so that we could move you." She turned to him then. "Eraeth said the waters of the sarenavriell would hurt you, that you would not be happy with our choice."

Colin glanced down at his body again. He'd been so preoccupied with the bandage and the blood that he hadn't taken a close look at the black oil that swirled beneath his skin. He'd become accustomed to it, had almost accepted it, but when he realized that the darkness had increased, that it covered nearly all of the exposed skin below his wrapped chest, that it snaked down his arms and the backs of his hands like living tattoos, his throat closed off. He drew in a few deep breaths, thought of Walter's words, whispered into his ears with the sword thrust through his chest, then forced a smile.

"You did what you had to do."

Based on Siobhaen's expression, he didn't think he'd eased her mind at all, but before he could add anything more, stones clattered outside the ledge.

Siobhaen reacted instantly, ducking down into a crouch and settling to one side of the wide entrance, her cattan drawn smoothly and soundlessly.

Colin tried to move, but he was too weak to do more than adjust his posture and ease the throb beginning in his lower back. He didn't even have a knife for protection.

Eraeth appeared, caught sight of Siobhaen, then shot a glance toward Colin.

A complex knot of emotions twisted across his face, quickly shuttered behind the implacable wall of a Protector. "You're awake. Finally."

"It's good to see you, too, old friend."

"What did you find?" Siobhaen asked. "Anything?"

"These." Eraeth pulled a strap up over his shoulder, two scrawny rabbit carcasses dangling from its end.

Siobhaen took them with a muttered, "Something besides snake."

Colin pulled the hunk of meat from his mouth and stared at it in distaste.

Eraeth shrugged out of another satchel and removed a few water skins. "I also refilled our water supplies at the pool we found. No sign of the Haessari, and no sign of the taeredac either."

"We haven't seen either of them for a few days now."

"Not since we heard that strange whirring sound. I think it was a summons. It came from the north and west. The scouting party headed in that direction almost immediately after. I think they were called away for something else."

Siobhaen was already gutting the two hares, while Eraeth began making a fire using wood from a pile stacked near the makeshift stretcher. Colin watched in fascination, chewing on the softened snake meat; he'd managed to tear a chunk off with his teeth. The two of them moved in tandem, without arguing, without snapping at each other, neither one giving the other any direction. Eraeth started the fire with flint and tinder, piling sticks on top as curls of white smoke began to rise from the dried grasses. Siobhaen handed over the skinned rabbits, already mounted on spits. Eraeth dug in another satchel and found some kind of spice to sprinkle over the meat as it cooked. The scent of roast and rosemary filled the hollow and Colin's stomach growled again. Siobhaen removed a small tin pot, filled it with water, and set it on a stone next to the fire, tossing some dried leaves into it a moment later. Outside, the sky darkened to the right, the clouds on the left horizon now a burnished gold deepening to orange as the sun began to set. But it was Eraeth and Siobhaen that held his attention. He'd never seen them cooperate with each other, let alone work together with such ease.

Eraeth looked up and caught him staring. "What is it?"

"Nothing." He motioned toward the land outside. "Where are we?"

"The Thalloran Wastelands," Siobhaen said, casting a glare at Eraeth. "Still."

"We didn't know where to head, but knew we needed to get as far from the Haessari as we could. Our only option was to head south. The Haessari enclave was to the north, and last we knew the Wraith's army was to the west."

Colin began struggling into a standing position.

Eraeth cursed and dashed to his side. "You should not be standing. You shouldn't even be sitting."

"I'm fine," Colin wheezed, as Eraeth supported him with one arm draped over his shoulder. Except he wasn't. His legs were weak, trembling already, and stiff. His breath felt clogged in his chest and the bright patch of blood on the bandage grew. He felt something trickling down his back as well, knew the wound back there must be worse, but he wanted to see where they were—*needed* to see. And he felt better with the movement, more alive.

He swallowed a new bubble of blood in the back of his throat as Eraeth eased him forward and halted at the edge of the overhang. Siobhaen had moved to watch over the spitted rabbits.

Colin straightened with effort and stared out at the vista. The sun was a glowering firepit on the horizon, the few clouds now a deep-seated red. The land stretched out before them, flat, riddled with stones, most no larger than Colin's torso, but a few the size of a horse here and there. They cast long shadows. To the left and right—east and west, Colin realized—a few plinths like the one where Eraeth and Siobhaen had sought shelter were silhouetted against the sun or flared bright with its last rays. The air tasted of salt and burned in his lungs. He drew it in deep, savored it.

"We're on the edge of the Flats." Colin squinted into the distance. "We'll have to travel at night, try to take shelter during the day. And we'll need as much food and water as we can carry." If he'd been alone, he would have slowed time and crossed in the space of a night, even wounded. But he couldn't take both Eraeth and Siobhaen that way, not in his condition.

"Where are we headed?" Siobhaen asked.

"Yhnar. We need to find out what's happening now that I've failed and the Well has been reawakened, and Yhnar is the closest Province."

Eraeth said nothing. Colin knew it was because of the bitterness he couldn't keep from his voice, the self-recrimination. He knew Eraeth would claim he'd done the best that he could, that they'd arrived too late, that it had been a trap and Walter had been waiting for them.

But he couldn't keep Walter's last mocking words from echoing in his head:

You never did open yourself completely to the Lifeblood and all it offered as I did, did you?

* * *

Tuvaellis tugged her cowl closer about her face. Alvritshai rarely sweat—it was uncouth—but drops slipped down her back and trailed down from her forehead nonetheless. One touched her cracked lips and she winced at the burn, tasted the salt on her tongue. She'd endured the Aielan-forsaken heat of this desert that consumed the center of the Andovan continent for a week already; the burn had become familiar. It didn't help that she couldn't remove the cowl and bare her skin to the gusts of wind that crossed the sand, as the others did, without exposing the Well's taint within her. She already knew what that would provoke—instant and violent condemnation from the Andovan church and its priests.

And the priests were a mere twenty paces away.

She ducked her head as the leader of the pilgrimage she'd run across as she fled Trent passed by, his robes flapping about his feet, his sandals slapping against his heels. The caravan of nearly forty men, women, and children—the sick and the dying and their families—were headed into the Borangi Desert in search of enlightenment...and the healing powers of the Rose. Unconsciously, she hefted the stone in its more portable case secured in the satchel over her shoulder. There were three priests in the pilgrimage—the eldest, Paulle, with a scraggly gray beard, carrying a staff taller than himself, who'd just walked past, and two acolytes beneath him who were now tending to the sick during their rest. Tuvaellis had barely spoken to Paulle since the caravan entered the desert, but she despised him for the threat he represented, especially after the unexpected power the patris had displayed in the cathedral in Trent.

She felt a tug on her sleeve and turned, one hand slipping toward the knife beneath her garments. Orren, one of the other priests, held a water skin out to her. "You should drink. The desert heat is deceiving, and we won't be resting here for long."

Her eyes narrowed in suspicion, but she took the skin, squirting a spray of water into her mouth by massaging the leather bladder. It was warm and tasted of some mineral, but it soothed the dryness of her throat.

She handed the skin back, then watched Orren as he drank himself and settled down on the rough stone beside her.

She shifted uncomfortably. Orren had attached himself to her almost as soon as the pilgrimage left Trent, finding her during the breaks, hovering near when the desert winds picked up and the group had to slog through driving sand and stinging salt. She didn't know why.

"Why do you keep yourself covered?" Orren asked. "It would be cooler if you dropped the cowl."

"You know why. I'm diseased. The leprosy has eaten away at my skin, my face. Those in this pilgrimage would not find my appearance... pleasant."

"Most of the priests who lead the pilgrimages have worked in wards, helping the sick. They would not react to your disease, no matter how gruesome you feel it appears."

"Have you worked in a ward?"

Orren turned to her, then away, staring out over the undulating sand of the desert. Unlike the Thalloran Wastes or the Flats, the Borangi Desert was like an ocean of sand, the winds carving its surface into rippling dunes and ridges that changed overnight. The pilgrimage followed a road—the hard stone scuffed red beneath her sandals where they'd halted—but most of the time that road was obscured, so that only Paulle, Orren, and the third priest, Garanti, knew where they were headed. If the route had been clear, Tuvaellis would have broken away from the group and traveled to the Rose on her own long since. She could not determine how the priests knew the route, although she had caught Paulle taking measurements from the stars at night. During the day, though, the desert was an ever-changing, yet monotonous, deep blue sky over sear wasteland, broken only by an occasional column of stone, exposed ruins, or an oasis where they replenished their water.

"I worked in a ward for five years," Orren said, "helping those crippled by the red plague."

"I haven't heard of it."

Orren glanced at her again and she cursed herself. Was it something everyone in Andover would know of? But Orren said, "It appears at first as a boil on the skin, along the neck here and here." He pointed to either side of his own neck, back beneath the hinge of his jaw. "It progresses to black lumps in the armpits, sometimes in the groin. The boils usually break and run, but the lumps simply swell. Eventually, the skin becomes striated with red lines, like the veins of a leaf, covering the chest and face, and the victims begin to cough up blood. Patients usually only last a day once the striations appear. It is a horrible, disfiguring disease, if you survive."

"If it was so virtuous a task, then why are you here now?"

At the head of the caravan, Paulle shouted that the break was over. Those in the pilgrimage began to rise, some grumbling, others anxious as they comforted their sick family members. A few began urging the pack animals that pulled the half dozen carts and litters forward.

Orren stood, tucking the water skin into the fold of his robes. He pulled his collar back and exposed a web of red latticework across his chest, like blood vessels. "Because I caught it myself. Only the Rose saved me. I hope to bring its healing powers to those in the wards with the red plague." He covered his scars, motioned to her cowl. "I've heard that the heat of the desert helps with leprosy."

The priest moved off and Tuvaellis rose from the stone, keeping herself hunched over to obscure her stature and heighten the pretense that she was a stooped elderly woman. Ahead, Orren paused to help a woman with a club foot rise.

Tuvaellis' mouth twisted in distaste. She would take out her blade and relieve all of them of their suffering if she didn't need them for her ruse. She'd considered killing them all and forcing Paulle to show her the way to the Rose, but the priests had proven more stubborn than she'd thought. If Paulle refused to take her to the Rose, she'd be forced to start over again.

No, the caravan might be moving slowly—she was still uncertain how close they were—but there was still time. She could afford to be patient.

Clutching the strap of the satchel holding the stone in one hand, her knife in the other, she plodded forward with the rest of the pilgrims.

She did not join in when Garanti began leading them in a chanted prayer to Diermani for the absolution of their souls.

* * *

Quotl drew his gaezel to a halt amid the raucous noise of a thousand dwarren doing same at the edge of a large room in the dwarren tunnels beneath the plains. The headdress of the Archon wavered and tipped as he dismounted and steadied it with one hand. He hated it, and all the other accoutrements that came with the duties as Archon, but he hadn't been able to discard them, not after the vivid dream sequence Ilacqua had seen fit to bestow upon him in the keeva.

"Archon, do you need help?"

Quotl cast Azuka a withering look, ready to snarl a response, then reconsidered. "Find the Cochen, and clan chiefs Tarramic and Iktamman. Have them meet us—"

Before he could finish, the sound of war drums boomed through the hall. Quotl listened intently until the message noting their location and urging the rest of the dwarren clans to the Sacred Waters began to repeat, then continued.

"Have them meet us beneath a fire tent. I want to attempt a vision, to see if Ilacqua will show us the Wraith's current path. Send someone to erect and bless the tent."

"What of Attana and Kimannen?"

Attana had accepted Quotl's vision in the keeva as the sign from Ilacqua that it was. He had expected resistance from Kimannen. But the former Archon had been surprisingly silent. Glowering from a distance, unquestionably angry, but agreeable.

"Send for them both." As Azuka turned to dash off, Quotl shouted after him, "And bring me my pipe!"

The shaman vanished in the milling confusion of the dwarren army pulling packs from their gaezel, setting up makeshift campfires, leading the animals to the river coursing down one side of the chamber, and resting before the next push toward the Confluence. They'd been riding hard since Quotl's vision in the keeva, the drums pounding incessantly at every halt, warning the rest of the clans of the Wraith's convergence on the Sacred Waters and the threat to the Summer Tree. Claw Lake and Shadow Moon were coming in from the west; Asazi and the Broken Waters clan were behind them; Painted Sands had been the closest to the Sacred Waters and was already inside the ceremonial chambers protecting the Summer Tree, along with the shamans and Keepers who lived there year round and the contingent of dwarren Riders who had been left behind to defend the heart of the dwarren clans while the others faced off against the Wraith army at the Break.

Quotl handed his gaezel over to a waiting shaman, then wove his way through the throng to the eastern side of the cavernous room, the Riders around him stepping aside in respect, a few offering him slices of cooked meat, a heel of bread, a cup of water. He paused to drink the water, and took the first few chunks of meat and bread, but waved all other offers aside.

The top of the fire tent reared over the mixed Red Sea, Silver Grass, and Thousand Springs clans and he angled toward it as it wavered, then steadied, the fold of cloth forming its sides growing taut as they were tied to the supports. When he broke through into the cleared area around the tent, he found Azuka and Attanna circling the tent, the head shaman of Silver Grass waving a scepter and chanting, the other following behind with a bundled sheaf of grain and feathers, brushing the stone floor of the chamber, mumbling beneath his breath to the gods of the Four Winds. Two Riders were finishing the last ties for the tent. One of them ducked inside with a bundle of sticks and one of the braziers.

"You seek the advice of Ilacqua, Archon?"

Quotl turned, although he recognized Kimannen's voice from the sarcastic tone and the bitter twist of his new title. "I do not seek advice. I seek information...on the elloktu's whereabouts and the location of their forces."

"You seek reassurance that this is the correct path."

Quotl uttered a short barking laugh that caught the attention of the surrounding Riders and both Azuka and Attanna. He waved away the two shamans' looks of concern, then stroked his beard. "I have been accused of many things in my time, but never have I been accused of a lack of confidence. No, I need the vision so that we may plan our defense."

"You have made it clear that my powers are not necessary. I will remove myself from your presence so that I do not taint your vision."

Quotl said nothing as Kimannen stormed off, his fingers still tangling with the braids and ties of his beard. In truth, he wanted Kimannen inside the tent—not for fear that Ilacqua would not bless them with a vision, but because he feared what the vision might reveal. At the keeva, the gods had shown him the armies of the elloktu marching toward Alvritshai lands, had shown another army to the south in the human Provinces. The forces within dwarren lands had been minimal in comparison, yet they were closer to the Sacred Waters and the Summer Tree than most of the dwarren Riders.

He was afraid that the vision would show them they were too late.

Whitish smoke began to rise from the hole wound into the tent's roof near the supports and a moment later the two Riders emerged. Quotl's gaze flicked to where Attanna and Azuka had nearly closed the circle. "Is everything prepared?"

The older of the two Riders nodded. "The fire is set, the brazier prepared. May Ilacqua's gaze guide you, Archon."

He and the second Rider stepped out of the circle, passing before Attanna and Azuka, who continued their chants uninterrupted. With a last flourish, Attanna and Azuka closed the circle, everyone who would participate already inside. Quotl felt the lines of power solidify. The sounds of the encampment outside the circle dampened, as if he's stuffed wool in his ears. His skin prickled as the sensations in the interior heightened. The scent of smoke sharpened, the sweat of the clan chiefs and the musk of the gaezels they'd ridden layered beneath. Quotl's own beard felt suddenly coarser beneath his pads of his fingers and he ceased stroking it, stepping forward instead.

"We're ready."

"What of Kimannen?" Oraju asked.

"He was invited and chose to see to the Riders instead."

Oraju frowned, staring out over the chamber as if searching for the shaman, then ducked down to enter the tent. The others followed.

Inside, the brazier had already been lit, incense infusing the small enclosure as smoke curled from the ornate brass filigree sides. The fire beneath crackled, sending heat out in waves. The clan chiefs and shamans were seated around the fire, directly on the floor, Oraju already packing leaf into his own pipe. Azuka stood to one side and handed Quotl his pipe, already lit. Quotl puffed on it twice, sucking the smoke deep into his lungs, then releasing it in a weighted sigh. His perceptions of the tent sharpened further as he shifted toward the remaining two positions with Azuka, settling in so close to the heat he could feel his exposed skin turning waxy. He drew on his pipe again, then handed it to Azuka. The headdress of the Archon shifted, one side digging into his temple. He grimaced and reached up to remove it, catching Oraju's look of shock as he set it behind him near the edge of the tent.

"The headdress isn't necessary for the scrying." When Tarramic raised his eyebrows as well, he added, "It's nothing but a symbol, something for the Riders to look to for reassurance! Besides, it itches and pinches my head."

Iktamman chuckled. "Kimannen would never have been caught dead without it, especially during a ritual."

"Let's get started."

Oraju glanced toward the headdress, still troubled, but stopped chewing on the end of his pipe long enough to ask, "What are we attempting to do here?"

"We're asking the gods for the location of the elloktu's armies."

"We'll need a map and seeds from the harvest," Attanna said.

Azuka pulled out a satchel tucked against his back and withdrew the rolled leather of a map and one of the small pouches every shaman carried for use as part of their daily rituals. Attanna took the map, setting it on the floor near the fire, Oraju and Tarramic shifting back to make room.

Azuka withdrew stones to hold the corners in place, then handed the pouch to Quotl. The seeds inside shifted and ground together as he gripped it, the sounds of husks scraping against husks too loud in Quotl's ears. He could feel the presence of the gods descending upon them already, the heat beginning to make his blood pound in his temples, sweat tracing paths down his face and neck.

"Begin the ritual," he said, motioning toward Attanna. After a moment's hesitation, Attanna began the low, nearly subvocal chant that called for the gods' attention, the sound threading beneath the muted sounds of the dwarren army outside the circle, slowly drowning it out. Quotl closed his eyes, breathed in the heavy air of the tent—not as dense as that inside a real keeva, but near enough—and exhaled slowly, repeating it before opening his eyes again.

The entire tent appeared hazy, as if filled with smoke, the fire a bright, leaping flame in the center. Across from him, Tarramic nodded once, as if in encouragement. Iktamman also looked serious, his gaze focused on the map spread out before him. The Cochen sucked on his pipe, mouth downturned in a look of disapproval. Attanna and Azuka both shimmered—not with light, but like heat waves above a wide, flat field of grass.

When he glanced down at the map, the colors and impressions made into the leather leapt forward.

Someone spoke, the words lost to him, meaningless. As he looked up, he realized that between Attanna's rumbling chant he could hear other voices, whispering in hushed conversation. Only a word here and there was discernible, but he caught enough to know that the voices weren't all speaking dwarren. He heard Alvritshai and human, the hissing language of the orannian, others he didn't recognize.

Tarramic spoke again, concerned, but Quotl waved a hand to silence him in irritation. He reached for the pouch of grain, ready to grab a handful of seeds and fling them over the map to see where they landed, but before he could work the ties free, the presence of Ilacqua pressed down on him. He moaned beneath the weight, sagged forward over his crossed knees. Azuka cried out, a steadying hand suddenly gripped his shoulder—

And then something buried deep within the fire popped, spraying blackened embers and burning fragments outwards. At the same time, the pressure forcing Quotl forward vanished and he jerked upright, blinking, his vision clear, sounds no longer muffled. The clan chiefs were cursing, Iktamman patting out coals that had landed in his beard. Tarramic had jumped to his feet, stomping on dull red embers scattered around the floor, Attanna exclaiming and rising to help. Oraju sat stunned, a few flakes of ash touching his flushed cheeks, pipe pulled away from his face.

The Cochen glanced down, snuffed out a bright red coal singeing the center of his beard, then stuck the pipe back in his mouth. His gaze fell on the map at his feet. "I guess we'll have to start over. You should have worn the headdress."

He reached for the map—to shake the blackened coals from it, Quotl imagined—but Quotl seized his outstretched arm at the wrist.

Oraju looked up, startled. But that quickly shifted to anger. Around them, the other clan chiefs and shamans stilled; the grip Azuka had on Quotl's shoulder tightened in warning.

"You presume too much, Archon," Oraju said. "I am still the Cochen."

"Look at the map."

All eyes dropped to the rolled leather, to the scattered black embers, to where they had fallen.

Iktamman swore.

"The elloktu," Attanna said, voice low and filled with awe.

"And their armies."

Oraju gave a shallow nod of grudging respect, then pulled from Quotl's grasp. The clan chiefs and shamans gathered around the patterns of black char that told of the dark armies' whereabouts. Black smudges dotted the human Provinces, one near Temeritt, another—larger—south of the Cut, headed northwest. A third marred dwarren lands, but was already on the verge of the southernmost Alvritshai Houses.

Quotl ignored those, focusing on the smears of black throughout the Land, caught between the Four Rivers, all of the dotted trails converging on the Sacred Waters. Even though the elloktu's armies within dwarren lands were smaller than any of the others, because of the singular clarity of sight brought by his vision—the map still vividly *deep*—he could see that the creatures of the Turning—

"They're in the tunnels," Azuka said.

"We knew that from Quotl's vision in the keeva," Attanna muttered.

"Where are they?" Oraju demanded. "Will we be in time?"

Quotl's eyebrows drew together. The cinders had clustered around the Sacred Waters, had burned into the leather. The stench of charred hide filled his nostrils as he leaned farther over the map, his breath disturbing ash that had settled to the ground into the air again.

"They're nearly there. They're coming in from two fronts." His eye caught on a third cluster, much smaller than the other two, too small to be a significant threat against dwarren Riders. He shoved that aside, thought about where they were, the distance left to cover, how fast the elloktu's forces had moved since his vision in the keeva...

"At our current pace, their forces will arrive before us. By nearly a day."

Creases appeared in Oraju's forehead. "Corranu and Painted Sands will have to hold. And we must move faster."

8

Thaedoren emerged from the cave's entrance into filtered sunlight, brushing aside the dead hanging vines and roots that obscured it from casual observation. He breathed in the fresh winter air, dredging the stale must of the mountain caverns from his lungs. His gaze flicked toward the White Phalanx who had exited the tunnels beneath the Hauttaeren Mountains before him to make certain it was clear, settling last on his brother, Daedelan, who listened to a scout's report as Thaedoren approached. Snow drifted down through the branches of the surrounding pines, the ground lightly dusted already, the chill bite of the air promising more to come.

Daedelan dismissed the scout and turned as Thaedoren halted, the guardsmen Naraen and Hiroun at his back.

"Report."

"We've entered Nuant lands, as expected. No sign of Lord Daesor or the House Phalanx, but that's not unexpected. We're far north of the main road, nowhere near any of Nuant's major towns. There's a village within a day's march southwest, but it's not large enough to provide us with many supplies. The nearest town is three day's march east, but we'd risk detection by traveling the road."

"Lord Daesor was in Caercaern at the time of the coup. We won't run into him here."

"Unless he was part of the coup, working with Peloroun and Orraen."

Thaedoren turned to Hiroun. "Did you see Nuant's maroon and gold that night, when Lord Aeren fled to the tower?"

"We did not see any Nuant guardsmen that night, my Tamaell."

Thaedoren met Daedelan's gaze. "Daesor was not part of the coup."

"We should not make assumptions. When we left Caercaern, Daesor was participating in the Evant with the remaining lords. All indications were that he was cooperating with the traitors. We should avoid Nuant's people as much as possible."

Thaedore didn't want to think that his influence on the remains of the

Evant had crumbled so far, but his brother was right. They knew almost nothing. They'd sent the White Phalanx into the city dressed as commoners to gather what supplies and intelligence they could, but they hadn't wanted to risk discovery, not with Lotaern's Order and Peloroun's and Orraen's men scouring the city for them and any remaining members of Aeren's or Terroec's Houses. Consequently, what they'd found out had been limited to gossip and rumor.

And Reanne had been uncooperative in confirming what they'd discovered.

He turned as the Tamaea was led from the cavern surrounded by six of the Phalanx, her hands bound before her. Her hair hung about her face, ragged and dirty, her clothes smudged with dirt and blood, her lips dry and cracked. Her wrists were covered in scabs where she'd struggled with her bonds. She'd screamed herself hoarse the first few days, had refused to utter a word since.

She glared at him as the rest of the Phalanx emerged from the cavern, the snow beginning to fall more steadily. Thaedoren wanted to brush his hands down the side of her face, as he had during their courtship; he wanted to strangle her, the anger so intense his fingers curled at his side.

He turned away from the conflicting emotions. "We'll camp here. Set up a patrol and have those who can hunt for fresh meat. We've been inside the mountains too long. We'll rest here for a day, then head south."

"Our goal?"

"Rhyssal House lands. We have to warn my mother."

* * *

"You could go with him," Wodraen muttered from his position to Moiran's right, a step behind her. Sylvea stood to her left, farther back. All around them—and in the courtyard before the manse—the Phalanx had gathered, but without the frantic intensity of the seizure of the Order of the Flame weeks before. This call to arms was orderly, and on a scale much larger than that raid. Over a thousand guardsmen filled the yard in rank after rank of columns, those on foot to either side, those who'd be mounted in the center, where Fedaureon, Mattalaen, and Daevon were talking in low, terse voices.

Moiran could see the strain on her son's face and her hands clutched the fabric of her dress. "I could go with him, but it would undermine him in the eyes of the Phalanx. He can't afford that. Not now."

Wodraen didn't respond.

"Did the supply wagons depart on time?" she asked.

"Yes, Lady Moiran. And preparations for the next are proceeding as planned. Would the lady of the House like to peruse the reports?"

"That won't be necessary, caitan."

Below, servants frantically pulled the last ties of saddlebags and buckles of harness tight. Horses stomped the ground fitfully, ready to depart, their breath clouds of mist on the chill air. Storm clouds rolled across the sky above, low and dark, threatening snow, although so far it had yet to manifest. The Rhyssal House banners hung slack in the quiet air. The Phalanx caitans were beginning to report their readiness to Mattalaen and Fedaureon when those Phalanx still watching the gates cried out in alarm.

Everyone in the courtyard tensed, although no one drew their blades. Mattalaen and Fedaureon turned toward the closed gates as one of the guardsmen shouted, "Messenger, on horseback. Moving fast up the main road."

Fedaureon met Mattalaen's gaze, then turned toward Moiran questioningly. Lips pressed thin, Moiran merely shrugged.

With Daevon and Mattalaen at his side, Fedaureon shifted through the gathered Phalanx and horses toward the front gate. "Open the gates. Let them in."

The guardsmen rushed to comply, the gates unlocked and opened barely a minute before the messenger and his mount appeared on the road outside.

He bore Rhyssal House colors, and Moiran unconsciously took a step forward, one hand rising toward her chest. She fought down a surge of hope. "Is he from Caercaern?"

"No. He's from one of the posts along the eastern border of Rhyssal House lands."

"I see."

She felt Wodraen's eyes on her, but she refused to look at him.

The messenger converged on Fedaureon and Mattalaen, pulling his mount up sharply before slipping from the saddle and nearly collapsing as his legs folded up beneath him. He caught himself with the saddle as Fedaureon and his caitan surged forward, supporting him on either side, two servants dashing to take the horse, the animal lathered in sweat. The messenger attempted a few limping steps, then straightened, Mattalaen and Fedaureon stepping aside. Heads bent close, they listened to the messenger's report, the man removing a letter satchel tucked inside his armor. Fedaureon took the satchel, but listened to the rest of the messenger's report before motioning servants forward to lead the man away. He broke the satchel's seal and pulled a sheaf of papers free.

"Sylvea, see to the messenger. Make certain he gets food and fetch a healer."

"Yes, my lady."

Moiran moved down the steps to the courtyard, but halted on the bottom step. Sylvea dashed around her, joining the other servants bringing the messenger up the steps and into the manse. Moiran saw no blood or other obvious wounds as he passed and relaxed slightly.

"He rode hard to get here," Wodraen said, low enough only Moiran could hear.

Fedaureon read through the pages quickly, then handed them off to Mattalaen before heading straight toward her. The caitan scanned the reports and dogged Fedaureon's heels.

"What is it?" Moiran asked.

"A report from the border. Our scouts near Caercaern report that Peloroun and Orraen have combined their armies and are headed south, gathering additional forces as they move. Lotaern and a significant number of the Order of the Flame lead them. They've left a minimal force along our border."

"What about the other Houses? Redlien and Uslaen?"

"No word except that Lords Houdyll and Saetor remain in the city and that messengers have been seen leaving for their House lands. Daesor also remains in the city, although there have been no messengers sent to Nuant lands as yet."

"Which could mean anything," Mattalaen muttered. "It says here that forces have been left along the Nuant and Baene borders, approximately the same number as on our own."

"But why is Lotaern headed south? Why take the Flame with him, as well as Peloroun and Orraen? Peloroun's lands are to the south. There is no threat from that direction. If they wish to retain control of the Evant and the Alvritshai, they should be turning their attentions west, toward us."

Fedaureon glanced toward Mattalaen in uncertainty, the elder caitan shaking his head. "There must be a more significant threat than us to the south."

"Like what?" Fedaureon asked.

Moiran's heart stuttered in her chest and her skin went cold. "The Wraiths. The sukrael."

All eyes turned toward her, Mattalaen with a skeptical frown, Wodraen in surprise.

"Father did travel to the north because of Shaeveran's warning that the Wells had been disrupted somehow. And Shaeveran himself warned me personally one night in the gardens overlooking the lake."

"Shaeveran spoke to you in private?" Moiran asked. "Alone?"

Fedaureon glanced toward her in irritation. "I sought him out, mother, he did not come to me."

Somehow, Moiran did not find the words comforting. The thought that Shaeveran had spoken to her son without her knowledge, behind her back...it sent a shudder of foreboding through her. She knew he had power over time, but she did not understand the extent of the sarenavriell's taint. If he had had foreknowledge of what would happen to Aeren, to her son—

She cut the thought off. Shaeveran had always worked in the Alvritshai's and Aeren's best interests. She could not begin to doubt that now. But if Lotaern and the others were headed toward a confrontation with the Wraiths and the sukrael, it begged the question of where Shaeveran was now. Should he not be here, helping the Alvritshai defend against them?

"What of the Winter Tree?" Mattalaen demanded. "It protects us from the Wraiths and the sukrael."

"Shaeveran and my father feared that the sarenavriell had been tampered with by the Wraiths. That's why he traveled to the north, to check on one of the Wells. They ran into one of the Wraiths and the sukrael there. If the Wraiths are experimenting with the sarenvriell, it wouldn't surprise me to learn they've found a way to circumvent or even destroy the Winter Tree. Lotaern is at the front of the army, with the Order of the Flame for support. They wouldn't be there if it were simply a matter of the dwarren attacking, or even the humans. And neither one of those two races have threatened us recently."

"Even if that is true, does it change our plans?"

Fedaureon stared off into the distance, toward the southeast, brow furrowed.

Then, abruptly: "No, the plans remain the same." He turned to Mattalaen. "We'll head toward Baene, gather as many men as we can along the way, and hope to find welcome from Lady Sovaeren and her son. We'll need Haedrian's Phalanx if we have any hope of stopping Lotaern, Peloroun, and Orraen and surviving this coup, regardless of whatever threat Lotaern sees to the south."

"Then we're ready to ride. At your word."

"The word is given."

Mattalaen turned on his heel and snapped a command. The rest of the Phalanx jolted into action, warriors mounting their horses, servants dashing to make last minute adjustments. The riders began filing out of the courtyard, through the gate, and onto the road beyond.

Moiran clasped her hands before her. Fedauroen reached forward and gripped her forearm. His mouth opened, but no words came out. In that moment, he appeared young, vulnerable, afraid—but not weak. She could see the strength in him, the strength she'd seen in Aeren, that had drawn her to him.

Fedaureon squeezed her arm once before moving toward his own mount. A moment later, without a glance back, he rode out through the gate around the side of the rest of the Phalanx, racing to catch up to Mattalaen at the head of the army.

Wodraen shifted closer to her. "Shall we see to the next train of supplies?"

Offering her an out, Moiran realized, a distraction. But she steeled herself.

"No, I want to visit the captives. Fedaureon and Mattalaen got nothing from them. I want to see if perhaps I can."

* * *

The draft of air that came from the door to the cell that held the members of the Order of the Flame reeked of old blood, shit, urine, and damp straw. Moiran's nose wrinkled in distaste, but she did not hesitate as she stepped forward, between the two Phalanx guards, and into the close, cramped interior. One of the guards had already hooked a small lantern to a ring of metal in the ceiling. The light it cast was minimal, but it was enough for Moiran to see the bruises that mottled the two acolytes' faces, see the weeping cuts and scars on their exposed flesh where they lay, wrists and ankles shackled to the floor. Their robes were ripped and soiled, the crispness of the white flame symbols now stained into a dull, listless gray, spotted with blood. In the month since their capture, the Phalanx had not treated them well, the layer upon layer of bruising obvious. Moiran had asked to question them herself numerous times, but Fedaureon had always refused. She could have come regardless—she was his mother after all, Lady of the House until it was known for certain that Aeren was dead— but she hadn't wanted to undermine his control if it wasn't necessary. She couldn't guarantee she'd gain any more information than Fedaureon and

Mattalaen.

But now Fedaureon was gone, gathering forces, gathering allies, the Alvritshai at war. She needed as much information as she could get.

"Come to gloat?"

The voice was dry and cracked, barely rising above a whisper. Moiran's eyes fell from the motionless figure on the left, who appeared asleep, to the man on the right, met his defiant gaze squarely. She recognized him as the leader of the Flame at the temple when she and Sylvea had visited. Heffaeren.

She knelt down beside him, nostrils flaring at the stench. "I came to see how you've been treated."

"Your son has been the consummate host, my lady."

"I see he has. But what can you expect. You invaded our House, our lands. Attempted to subvert our people."

"I sought to bring them back to Aeilan's Light!" He said it with such intensity he choked on the words. By the time he'd recovered, he was trembling, body slumped against the straw-covered stone floor.

"Your conviction would be honorable if I believed it. But you care nothing for their redemption. You are Lotaern's pawn, sent to undermine Lord Aeren's hold in his own lands. There's no need to pretend otherwise now."

Heffaeren's eyes narrowed. "Why? What has happened?"

Moiran didn't answer. She reached forward, gaze shifting from Heffaeren's eyes to the wicked gash near his temple caked with dried blood, but Heffaeren jerked his head away.

Hand poised over the acolyte's body, Moiran said, "It looks infected. It needs to be cleaned." She let her hand drop and half turned toward the door to the cell. "Sylvea?"

Her servant appeared at the door. Moiran had asked her to wait until she could see the prisoners herself first. "Yes, Lady Moiran?"

"Bring the healing salve, some warm water, and plenty of rags. We need to clean up our two...guests. This room as well. The straw needs to be swept up and replaced. And have someone bring some tea—mint, I think—and fresh bread."

Sylvea met her gaze, eyebrows raised, then nodded. "Very well."

She vanished, and Moiran turned back to Heffaeren a moment before standing and shifting to Saederis' side. The younger acolyte's forehead was burning with fever and he moaned when she touched him.

"He's been that way for a while," Heffaeren muttered.

"How long?"

"I don't know. It's difficult to keep track of time in here."

Moiran ignored his caustic tone, motioning Sylvea forward when she appeared in the doorway a moment later, tray in hand. Grabbing one of the rags, she soaked it in the bucket of water another servant brought, wrung it out, then began to wash Saederis. "Help me. As soon as he's relatively clean, I'll begin applying the salve."

Another third servant arrived carrying a broom and began sweeping out the straw while Moiran and Sylvea worked, others arriving with fresh straw. Within half an hour, the room had been cleaned and Saederis had been bathed and his wounds attended. His acolyte robes had been removed, replaced with a simple tunic and breeches. He'd moaned and thrashed occasionally while they worked, but never woke, settling into a deeper sleep as they finished.

No one touched Heffaeren, at Moiran's orders, but now she turned to him.

"Sylvea, please stay. The rest of you may go."

As the two servants left, Moiran knelt, picked up a cup from a second tray, and brought it to Heffaeren's cracked lips.

He jerked back. "What is it?"

"Mint tea."

He continued to glare, but drank when she brought it to his mouth again, Sylvea helping to hold his head high enough. After the first few tentative sips, he gulped down the rest and asked for more. She cut him off after the second cup, Sylvea beginning to wash him down as Moiran fed him small pieces of bread. As soon as his wounds were cleaned, Moiran began spreading the salve into his cuts. Heffaeren hissed and pulled away at the sting, but Moiran was relentless. They worked in silence, until Heffaeren broke it.

"Aren't you going to interrogate me?"

"Is there something I should interrogate you about?"

Heffaeren laughed, condescending, but with an uncontrolled edge. "The Chosen? His plans for the Order, for the Evant, for the Alvritshai?"

"I already know Lotaern's plans."

Heffaeren frowned in confusion and Moiran dabbed the sudden sheen of sweat from his brow, noting the slight dilation in the Flame's pupils as she did so.

"You know the Chosen's plans? How? Who told you?"

"No one told me. The Chosen's plans are obvious." Moiran shifted to continue treating Heffaeren's wound, but he grabbed her wrist, his grip so tight she felt bones grinding together. She merely clamped her jaw tight, kept the pain from her face as she met the acolyte's gaze.

"What do you know?"

"I know of his alliance with Peloroun and Orraen, of his intentions to seize control of the Evant. I know of his plans to kill Lord Aeren and Tamaell Thaedoren, my husband and son. I know he meant for you and the rest of the Flame to foment rebellion in our House lands so that his ascension to become Tamaell would be easier. And I know that he has failed."

Heffaeren's eye flew wide. Moiran leaned in close, smelled the acrid taint of the willowart they'd dosed him with in his sweat. His breath quickened and he tried to draw back from her, his grip on her wrist loosening. "The coup failed. The Tamaell escaped, with Lord Aeren. Fedaureon rides to meet with them even now, the Rhyssal House Phalanx at his back. I don't need to interrogate you, Heffaeren. You and the Order of the Flame are nothing."

She thrust herself back from Heffaeren's wild eyes and wrenched her arm from his grasp. She motioned to Sylvea, who began gathering the rags and medicine, the cups and tea, her motions swift and efficient. Heffaeren's eyes darted between her and Moiran, one hand raised and clutching at the air pathetically as Moiran gathered her feet beneath her and stood, staring down at him imperiously.

"Lotaern's rule is already over, before it even really began."

"No," Heffaeren whispered. "It can't be. You can't destroy the Flame. We'll be needed. If you destroy the Flame we'll be defenseless against the Wraiths!"

"We have the Winter Tree to protect us!"

Heffaeren's grasping hand fell to his chest. "No, we don't. It's dying. The Wraiths are killing it. That's why the Chosen made a deal with them!"

Sylvea gasped, even as coldness gripped Moiran's heart.

"What deal?"

"He invited them onto Alvritshai lands in exchange for control of the Evant. He promised to destroy the Alvritshai resistance."

"He did *what*?"

"He meant to betray them, lead them into a trap. But it won't work if you destroy the Flame. We're the only ones who can control the Wraiths, the only ones who can stop the sukrael!"

"Nothing can stop the Wraiths!" Moiran nearly choked on the words. Swallowing back the sour taste at the back of her throat, she stalked out of the room, Heffaeren shouting something at her back, but she didn't listen.

Her mind was roaring, thoughts flaring across her consciousness so fast she couldn't focus. Sylvea scrambled behind her, tray in hand, but it was Wodraen standing stoically outside in the hall who caught her attention, his eyes grim.

"Did you hear?"

"Lotaern is in collusion with the Wraiths."

"Lotaern has forsaken us! We have to send word to Fedaureon immediately, as well as Sovaeren and Halceon. Sovaeren, in particular, will want to know the reason her husband died." She halted suddenly. "Lotaern's heading south with the Flame."

"So we've been told."

"Don't you see? He's going to meet with the Wraiths right now. He's going to betray them. If he fails, if the Flame cannot do what they believe they can do—"

"Then the Chosen will have unleashed the Wraiths and their armies upon the Alvritshai."

Horrified silence hung in the air between them, but then Moiran spun, moving purposefully toward her rooms and the parchment and ink that waited there. They had always been her greatest weapons, during her term as Tamaea with Fedorem, and again, after being bonded to Aeren as the Lady of Rhyssal House.

"What are your orders, Lady Moiran?"

"Prepare messengers, with the swiftest mounts we have. Fedaureon and our allies must be forewarned. And pray. Pray to Aielan that for once the Chosen has not overstepped his bounds."

* * *

"Am I interrupting, Chosen?"

Peloroun's voice—formal, yet tinged with a hint of derision—dragged Lotaern out of his meditation. He knelt on a cushion before a single, thick candle burning with a cool white flame, representing Aielan. Its light— and that of the lantern hung from the center of the room—glinted on the gold thread embroidery of the cloth he'd draped over the trunk used as a makeshift altar. Brass braziers were set to either side, trails of scented smoke rising from their filigreed faces. Wind gusted and ruffled the tent, the wooden posts creaking. Through the protective walls, he could hear it soughing through the cedars and pine that surrounded the army encampment.

Peloroun stooped at the flap to his central chamber, cloth held back with one hand. Lotaern took in the lord's pale skin, the avidness in his eyes.

"You are not interrupting, Tamaell Peloroun. Enter." Lotaern rose as Peloroun stepped through. He motioned toward a low table and two large pillows. A kettle sat in the center of the table. "Tea?"

Peloroun shook his head, but Lotaern reached for the kettle anyway and poured for them both, then settled onto one of the pillows.

"I assume you've come out of concern for the Flame."

"Are they prepared? We've reached the end of the game, Chosen. If the Flame falter, if what you claim they can do is false—"

"The Flame is ready. And their preparations are based on the teachings of the Scripts. Our plan will work. Or do you doubt the words of Aielan?"

"I doubt the abilities of the Flame, not the words of Aielan. They have not been able to test these rites in any meaningful way, not against the Wraiths. They were designed to work against the sukrael."

"And they did work. Do not forget that they were used on your own lands to protect your people from the Shadows, Peloroun. You have seen it yourself."

"But I ask again, will they work against the Wraiths? At the time of the Scripts, there were no Wraiths!"

Peloroun's words woke the anxiety Lotaern had fought so long and hard to crush during his meditations that afternoon. To hide it, he sipped from his tea, but found it hard to swallow. He set the cup aside with a clatter.

"According to what I could learn from Shaeveran, the Wraiths are created by the sarenavriell, from its essence. It's a taint, like a poison, that seeps into their souls and transforms them. He believes that the sukrael were created in the same way, ages past, that the sukrael and the Faelehgre in Ostraell were once flesh and blood mortals like the Alvritshai, and that the exposure to the sarenavriell changed them into the elemental forces they are today. If that's true, if the Wraiths are truly beings at the beginning of the transformation that the sukrael suffered, then what works against the sukrael should also work against them."

Peloroun brooded for a moment. "You are risking our lives on this, Chosen. On what is, in essence, an act of faith."

"I am the Chosen. Faith is my specialty."

Peloroun was not amused.

Lotaern leaned forward. "If you doubt me so much, why did you agree to this plan years ago? We have been working toward this end for what feels like decades. Are you so weak that you would falter now?"

Peloroun stiffened, stilled.

Then his hand leaped across the table. Fingers twisted in the cloth over Lotaern's chest and hauled him forward. The table lurched between them, Peloroun's cup upsetting, spilling tea across the surface, but Lotaern focused on Peloroun's eyes, now inches from his own. The lord's lip curled as he scanned the Chosen's face.

"The weakest link in this plan is you, Lotaern—you and your abilities to control the Wraiths and destroy the sukrael. If you fail, I will personally slit your throat in the courtyard of the Sanctuary and spill your blood across its stone."

"If I fail, you and your blade will be the farthest thing from my thoughts. Now let me go. I—and the Flame—have work to do tonight."

Peloroun held him steady for a moment longer, then shoved him back. Lotaern resettled his clothes as Peloroun stood.

"Do not fail in this, Chosen."

Then the lord left, tent shaking as he stormed through the flap and into the camp beyond.

Lotaern stared after him, then let his gaze drop to the table and the spilled tea. He rose and found a cloth to sop up the mess. His earlier calm shattered, he paced the small space before his pallet, then halted before the still-burning white candle. Wetting his fingers, he extinguished it, then removed the candle, braziers, and cloth, and opened the trunk beneath.

It was packed with clothes and the accoutrements he needed as Chosen—candles and the wide bowl used for rituals before the army; the pouch of powder that caused fire to burn white. He ignored all of these, digging deeper, beneath the robes of his office. For a terrifying moment, he thought the pouch containing the fine metal mesh and the wooden dagger was missing—that somehow Shaeveran had stolen it back—but then his hands brushed leather. He pulled the leather case free, untied its flap, and removed the folds of metal mesh inside. They slipped open with a faint chattering of metal against metal, exposing the wooden knife to the remaining lamplight. It appeared to glow, its markings dark and rich with warmth.

He hadn't intended to bring it tonight, not for this meeting. Tonight depended solely on Vaeren, Boreaus, Petraen, and the rest of the Flame. But Peloroun's words had fed the seeds of doubt already planted inside him. Because the lord spoke the truth: the Flame had not been able to practice the ritual on a true Wraith, had only been able to practice the words and the summoning of the Fire. And if that failed...

"Then there will be only Aielan and the knife to protect us all."

He wrapped it back in its metal cloth, shoved it into the leather case, and tied it closed. Moving with purpose, he stashed it in the satchel already prepared, then glanced around the small tent's chamber before muttering a small prayer to Aielan for guidance and ducking out into the night.

* * *

"Is everyone ready?" Lotaern asked as he joined the small group of figures on the road south of the encampment. Thin clouds obscured the night sky overhead, the moon a soft glow behind them. Vaeren, Boreaus, Petraen, and the seven other members of the Flame were mere shadows scattered about the stone road.

"Everyone is ready, Chosen. Boreaus and Petraen will provide the anchor, the others the shield."

"Good." Lotaern's hands clenched around the strap of his satchel, sweaty with tension, even though the night was chill. The army had moved far enough south they'd passed out of the region threatened by the latest snow storm, but he could taste it in the air. He glanced in the direction of the moon. "The meeting is in two hours. That gives us an hour to reach the area and then another hour for you and the rest of the Flame to prepare."

"Then we should move now."

Vaeren turned to those gathered and with a silent gesture, four broke away and jogged further south down the road. Vaeren fell in beside Lotaern and they followed, the rest trailing behind. When they reached the prearranged meeting place—a field off the road that now lay fallow for winter—the four Flame who'd scouted ahead were waiting.

"The field is clear. They haven't arrived yet."

Vaeren turned to Boreaus and Petraen. "Begin setting up the shield. Once you're satisfied that it's stable, you can begin your own preparations." Petraen grinned, but Vaeren caught his arm. "This is not a game, Petraen. If something goes wrong with the shield..."

"The shield will hold, we've practiced it often enough."

"Not with someone trapped inside."

Petraen said nothing, but his brother spoke up. "You and the Chosen are the ones at risk."

"Let us worry about that," Lotaern said. "You and Petraen must anchor the shield and hold it, no matter what happens. If you fail, we're all dead."

They watched as the Flame scattered, some heading for the trees that lined the field, others beginning to form patterns in the soil using staffs and branches. Lotaern didn't need to watch to know what patterns they'd create. He'd worn the Script pages where they'd been found thin, scouring for any hidden meanings, anything that the acolytes and the Flame might have missed that would cause their plans to fail. He hoped that the coming Wraith wouldn't notice the freshly churned soil, and if he—or she—did, that they wouldn't recognize what the patterns meant. They shouldn't. None of them had been alive when the Scripts were written and the patterns last used. He couldn't say as much about the sukrael.

But none of the sukrael were to attend the Wraith. That had been the agreement.

"Do you need to make any preparations?" Vaeren asked.

Lotaern pulled the satchel from his shoulder and let it fall to the ground. "No. We only need to meet with the Wraith and keep him inside the sigil until the others have activated the shield."

"How will we do that?"

"By talking."

Vaeren wandered away to oversee the preparations. Lotaern considered removing the knife that Shaeveran had created, but resisted. He watched the Flame work instead, watched them as they shifted farther away, fading into the darkness. The clouds overhead began to tatter, the moon appearing more often. The wind lessened and the scent of tilled loam caught Lotaern's nose.

The members of the Flame vanished into the trees. A moment later, Lotaern felt Aielan's presence, starting to the north, where he knew Boreaus and Petraen were forming the anchor for the circle. He knelt and reached for the ground, dug his fingers into the soil as the energy of Aielan's Light grew in strength, lines forming as the other members of the Flame surrounding Lotaern's position joined the anchor, creating a net that encompassed the entire field. When the last member of the Flame joined in, he felt a pulse surge through the earth, tracing out the sigil and coursing up through his hands and feet before settling back into the earth. It faded down to a dull throb, deep underground, and Lotaern sighed. He drew a chunk of soil with him as he stood, let it crumble between his fingers and rain back to the ground, then turned to Vaeren.

"It's ready. It needs only to be released now."

Before his caitan could respond, the night grew quiet. The wind still gusted overhead, but the faint night sounds of animals stilled. Lotaern hadn't even been aware of them until they were gone. The skin at the back of his neck prickled and he shifted to one side, Vaeren moving up beside him. "The Wraith's early."

On the far side of the field, the Wraith stood at the edge of the road, cloaked in shadow. As the figure began moving toward them, Lotaern bit back a curse. He should have taken the knife from his satchel earlier. He thought he'd have time before the Wraith arrived, but now it was too late.

He glanced down at where the satchel rested near his feet.

Clutching a fold of his sleeve in one hand, he stepped forward, placing the satchel behind him, and steeled himself. He had never met one of the Wraiths. Peloroun had been the one to speak to Khalaek on the dwarren Flats during the tour of the Provinces; Lotaern had remained with the rest of the entourage. And at the Escarpment, Lotaern had not been inside the parlay tent when Walter killed Fedorem. Even those who had been had only seen the Wraith for a few seconds. There had been another Wraith at the initial meeting at the Flats, an Alvritshai named Courranen that neither one of them had known. He did not know who had been sent to meet with him here; he hoped it was Khalaek.

But as the Wraith halted four paces distant, bootfalls sinking into the unnatural quiet of the surrounding forest, Lotaern realized it wasn't. The features were Alvritshai, pale in the moonlight, slightly more angular and prominent than usual, the scar of banishment slicing down one cheek. The cut of the shirt, the boots, and the styling of the cloak and breeches were from a time before Lotaern's birth. He carried a cattan, a knife visible on the opposite hip, but no pouch or satchel. But it was the signs of the sarenavriell's black taint shifting beneath the exposed skin of his hands and face that caught and held Lotaern's attention. He nearly muttered a prayer to Aielan, but caught himself. Who knew how the Wraith would react?

"Chosen," the Wraith said. His voice was soft and silky smooth, but he twisted the title with enough derision to stiffen Lotaern's shoulders.

"Yes, I am the Chosen. As an Alvritshai, you should recall the respect that the title demands."

"I am fallen, Chosen. I respect no one, least of all you." His words carried a faint archaic accent.

Vaeren shifted his stance and the Wraith shot a glance toward him. "Ah, yes. I'd been told that the Order of Aielan had created its own Phalanx." The Wraith blurred and vanished, suddenly appearing at Vaeren's back. The caitan of the Flame whirled, but the Wraith was already moving, blurring and reappearing as Vaeren spun, his cattan snicking from its sheath as Lotaern's caitan attempted to keep track of the fallen Alvritshai. The Wraith laughed, the sound filling the silence of the field.

Before it had faded, the Wraith vanished, leaving Vaeren breathing hard, half crouched.

"Pitiful."

Both Lotaern and Vaeren spun toward the voice, the Wraith behind them, standing perfectly still, not even his cloak drifting with movement.

"I could have killed you both a hundred times over."

"Who are you?"

The Wraith's gaze fell away from Vaeren. "Maenaed, of House Bellaerus."

"I've never heard of that House."

"It is long dead. I destroyed it. After they betrayed me, banished me to the south." He tilted his head, exposing the scar down his cheek to the moonlight. "They paid for their arrogance."

Lotaern wondered what was taking Boreaus and Petraen so long. The sigil had been laid, activated. The shield should be ready, even though he knew it was more complicated than that. Still...

He waved the Wraith's words aside with one hand. "Enough. You have a message for us?"

"I have orders, yes. The Winter Tree is not yet dead. I can feel its influence even here, though it is severely weakened. It must be completely dead by the time our armies reach Caercaern. There must be nothing left, no root, no branch, no leaf."

Lotaern's eyebrows rose, but he said nothing.

"Your armies and people must retreat to the central House lands. Anyone who remains within the outer Houses will be taken by the army that follows me."

"There are forces within Alvritshai lands that are not under my control. The coup was not as successful as I had hoped."

"Those forces will be dealt with."

"And your army," Vaeren said. "Where is it now?"

The Wraith's attention shifted. His eyes narrowed. "It is close. We know of the army you came here with. If you wish it to survive, you will retreat with it back to Caercaern in haste."

Beneath his feet, Lotaern felt Aielan's Light pulse. He gestured toward Vaeren, who nodded; the caitan had felt it as well.

Tensing, the Chosen said, "I don't think so."

The Wraith's gaze snapped back to him. "What did you say?"

Feeling the Light gathering power, Lotaern took a step backwards, knelt in one smooth motion to retrieve the satchel he should no longer need, then straightened. "I said, I don't think so. I don't believe that the Wraiths intend to honor our agreement. I believe you intend to herd us into Caercaern and slaughter us there. As, perhaps, you did to the members of your own House. So, no. I don't believe we'll be retreating back to our city to await our deaths."

The Wraith hesitated, as if he couldn't quite understand what Lotaern had said.

But then he snarled and reached for his cattan.

At the same moment, Lotaern felt the energies of the shield around them lock into place.

Light flared—the harsh, white Fire of Aielan—in the trenches of the sigil the Flame had etched into the field, and then a ring of that same fire flared up around them, twenty paces distant. The Wraith screamed, in defiance and in pain, but Lotaern didn't flinch, didn't pause. Spinning, he cried, "Run!" and charged toward the nearest wall of white, the field and the forest beyond obscured by the conflagration. He didn't wait to see if Vaeren had heeded the order; the caitan knew the risk. As with all of the Flames' defenses against the sukrael, it required time to implement. Someone had been needed to keep the Wraith inside the shield long enough for it to be activated. But that meant the person would be caught inside the trap with the Wraith, at least for a moment. Lotaern hadn't been that concerned, had assumed he'd have enough time to escape the trap before the Wraith could react.

Until he'd seen the Wraith blur out of existence in order to taunt Vaeren.

Now, visions of the Wraith flickering back and forth as the caitan spun uselessly flashed across his vision as he plowed toward the edge of Aielan's Flame. The earth gave beneath his feet, treacherously soft. His breath scoured his lungs, huffing from his chest as he clutched the satchel tight. His legs burned with effort.

Then, ten steps from the white fire, the Wraith coalesced before him, his blade already swinging.

Lotaern flung himself to the ground to the right, his shoulder hitting hard, earth gouting up into his face, into his mouth. The blade whirred overhead, but he let momentum carry him into a roll, tumbling away. He halted on his back, spat out dirt, and lurched upright.

In time to see the Wraith blur, whisper back into form above him, sword descending—

Vaeren roared as he crashed into the fallen Alvritshai, the two spinning as the Wraith was carried to the ground. Lotaern scrambling into a crouch as the two rolled apart, began backpedaling toward the protective wall as both began to rise. Vaeren charged, cattan snaking forward, and stabbed the Wraith before he'd made it halfway up. The fallen Alvritshai bellowed in pain and backhanded the caitan, sending him hurtling away, opposite Lotaern. Vaeren crashed to the ground as the Wraith straightened, cattan jutting through his shoulder. The Wraith gripped the handle of Vaeren's blade and, with a smooth sucking sound, pulled it free of his flesh.

Lotaern felt Aielan's Flame at his back and paused long enough to shout, "Go, Vaeren! Now! The wall is right behind you!"

He saw Vaeren crawl toward the wall as he dodged into the white fire himself, shoulder hunched protectively against it.

He tripped on the far side, slammed into the ground again, but gathered his feet beneath him and stood. Shouts rose from all sides as the Flame who'd constructed the shield converged on him. He shoved their concern aside. "Vaeren should be coming out on the far side of the shield. Find him!"

Two of the Flame took off, circling the white fire.

Lotaern searched those that remained, picked out Boreaus and Petraen, the two standing off to the left, concentrating on the wall. As the anchors, they were the ones holding it together now, the ones controlling it. If they faltered...

He stumbled toward them. "Is it holding? Is the Wraith contained?"

Before they could answer, an unearthly shriek split the night air. Lotaern's head snapped toward the shield as the Wraith's hand appeared, reaching forth from the fire, followed a moment later by the Wraith's head and shoulders. One of the Flame swore. "It's not working. He'll kill us all."

But then the Wraith stopped. Face a rictus of pain and fury, contorted with effort, he stretched toward Lotaern. The oily blackness beneath his skin—the taint of the sukrael—appeared to be boiling, and still he strained forward. But Lotaern could see him weakening. Lotaern stepped forward. "We have you. And shortly, we'll deal with the army you brought with you."

The Wraith snarled, but retreated back behind the wall of fire that contained him.

Lotaern turned back to the Flame, to Boreaus and Petraen. "Close it."

Both nodded, and the wall of fire began to contract, closing inwards toward its center. Inside, the Wraith shouted a curse.

"He's fighting back," Petraen said, then winced. "Hard. He's trying to break the seal."

"Hold it."

Petraen never wavered. As the fire tightened around the Wraith, both brothers stepped forward. The rest hung back. The Wraith's cattan pierced the encircling wall, the motions more frantic as the radius decreased to twenty paces, then ten.

"Traitors! You have betrayed me as the Order betrayed me during my own time. The Alvritshai and the Evant are nothing but a nest of snakes, preying on their own for the sake of power. I destroyed my own House, my own flesh and blood, because of that betrayal. Do you not think I will destroy you as well? I will slaughter you all, then hunt down your families, your kin, and every last soul who ever took your House name as their own!"

As the fire shrank closer, he howled in agony and slipped into an even more archaic form of their language, one that Lotaern did not understand. He could only make out a few words scattered here and there, each one bitten off in hatred and defiance.

When the wall had closed to the point where it had become a pillar of flame, just large enough to contain the Wraith and nothing else, it halted. The Wraith's tirade cut off sharply. Lotaern saw Vaeren on the far side, one arm held awkwardly to his chest.

The pillar began to shrink, the flames abating. They lifted from the earth, exposing the Wraith within. He tried to lash out, but even though the flame had decreased to a ring hovering at neck level, his arms struck an invisible barrier a hand-span from his body. He glowered as the ring began to contract further, settling into position around his throat, a collar of white fire that glowed in the night.

The shield of Aielan's Light had become a leash.

Lotaern hesitated, then stepped close, near enough he could see the Wraith's nostrils flare as he tried to reach out to kill him.

"I think it's time to return, to show Lord Peloroun what the Order of the Flame can do. And to prepare."

"Prepare?" one of the Flame asked.

"For the Wraith's army. We have much work to do."

9

Deep inside the dwarren's tunnels, in the chamber that held the Sacred Waters and more recently the Summer Tree, a sudden barrage of war drums crashed down one of the numerous corridors and echoed into the open space that formed the main chamber, cutting through the roar of water cascading down the northern dome's walls and the channels and reservoir in the center.

Inside his chambers, clan chief Corranu of Painted Sands sat bolt upright on his pallet, one arm flailing and striking the stone wall beside him. He cursed at the pain, but it brought his groggy mind into sharp focus. Halfway through bringing the numbed elbow to his chest, he paused and listened to the pounding drumbeat.

A moment later, he leaped from his bed, grabbed the nearest piece of armor—he'd only half undressed the night before—and began pulling it on, motions hurried but not frantic. Not yet.

Riders burst through his door. "Clan chief! The drums—"

"I hear them, you oaf! Skeen, help me don the rest of my armor. Rannu, warn Peyo and have him ready the shamans, and don't forget to inform the Keepers!" This last was shouted at Rannu's back. He mumbled deprecations into his beard, then turned on the last Rider, Terrannen, his son. "Gather the Riders. Have them mount their gaezel and prepare to defend the Sacred Waters." He drew a deep breath, thankful that they had sent all of the rest of the dwarren—the women and children, those not needed to help with the defense or the care of the gaezel—to their own clan enclaves. Only Riders and shamans remained. "And have the sappers prepare to seal the tunnels."

"What of the Cochen and the other clans?"

"They're on the way. We must defend the Sacred Waters until they arrive. Now go."

Terrannen glowered, but obeyed.

"We must preserve the Sacred Waters," Corranu muttered under his breath. Skeen glanced up as he tugged on a buckle, gaze shying away at the expression on Corranu's face. "The Wraiths and the armies of the Turning cannot be allowed to touch it."

"How far away is the Cochen?"

Corranu let his fingers play through the knots and beads and feathers in his beard in reassurance of his past deeds, past victories. "At last report, a day, perhaps a little more."

The silence was eloquent. Skeen did not think they could hold the chamber for a day. He didn't think so himself. Perhaps half that, if they sealed most of the corridors.

Skeen gave the last buckle a tug, then stepped back. "You're ready."

Before Corranu could answer, the stone floor beneath them shuddered, the tremors coursing up through Corranu's legs, followed by a low rumble coming from the central chamber.

Corranu ran for the door.

He emerged into chaos. Three levels below, the dwarren of Painted Sands were scrambling to mount their gaezel. Some already sprinted toward the southern tunnels. Others charged toward the western tunnels, circling around the massive red-lit pool of water that formed the heart of the Sacred Waters chamber. Opposite his position, the Keepers of the Summer Tree had assembled, the shamans converging at the base of the massive root system. Peyo and the remaining shamans of Painted Sands were scattered through the ranks below, helping the Riders and no doubt chanting to Ilacqua and the Four Winds, to the Land and the Sacred Waters, even though he couldn't hear them over the tumult of the waters, the drums, and the chaos below. But what seized his attention was the plume of dust that spewed out of one of the southern tunnels.

Someone had collapsed part of the warren.

His gaze raked the Riders below, picked out Terrannen instantly. Turning, he stalked back into his chambers, picked up his axe, his knives, sheathing them as he circled the chamber, then exited and began the descent to the floor below. Skeen followed without a word.

Ten minutes later, merging with the chaos, weaving between gaezel and Riders, shamans and servants, Corranu reached Terrannen's position and shouted, "What happened? Who collapsed the tunnel?"

"The order didn't come from me. My guess is that a faction of the Wraith army reached one of the sappers positions and they couldn't hold it. They collapsed it instead. I think we should collapse a few more."

Corranu tugged his beard. "Which tunnels do you suggest?"

Terrannen motioned a Rider who held the leather folds of a map forward. "All of the tertiary ones, a few of the secondary. Force the

Shadow Army to approach along the primary routes."

"According to the Archon, the main forces are approaching along these routes," Corranu said, pointing to two difference places on the map. "We should seal all of these tunnels, funnel them directly toward us."

"We need to leave these tunnels here open for the Cochen and the other clans."

"Agreed. Do it."

Terrannen began shouting orders as he turned to mount, closing his fist in respect to Corranu before kneeing his gaezel toward the eastern wall. The drums relayed the orders down the corridors as Corranu turned to Skeen.

"Bring Ischt."

Skeen headed for the paddocks. Riders approached Corranu as he waited, giving reports and receiving orders, then racing back into the fray. Corranu fingered the haft of his axe in between.

Thunder rumbled through the chamber and the floor shuddered, another plume of dust surging from one of the tertiary tunnels. It was repeated twice more in the next five minutes, then again five minutes after that, one of the rumbles louder than the others, signifying a secondary tunnel had been collapsed. As he waited, Corranu watched the clan organize and assemble, the chaos shifting into order. He nodded in approval and a certain grim pride.

Skeen appeared, mounted, with Ischt in tow. Corranu patted the gaezel's neck, ran hands down his sides, then swung up onto his back, grabbing the horns to steady himself. Ischt snorted and shook his head. Corranu could see the southern and western tunnels easily now, Painted Sands Riders split between the two main corridors. Terrannen appeared to have taken over the southern ranks, so he kneed Ischt toward the west, passing south of the pulsing fiery light of the Sacred Waters. A group of ten Riders moved with him and he raised a questioning eyebrow toward Skeen.

"Terrannen ordered it."

Corranu said nothing, but he nudged Ischt into a trot, passing through the center of the Riders gathered at the western mouth.

"Report."

Those assembled outside the corridor—two of Corranu's most trusted Riders, their beards thick with victories, and a third who'd shown promise—cut off their argument and faced him.

"Last communication indicated the Shadow Army was closing in fast, a hundred lengths out," the eldest, Metter, said.

"Beyond the Riven Chamber, then. What are we facing?"

All three of the men shared a look. "Gruen, kell, and a significant number of the terren."

"None of the urannen? No elloktu?"

"Peyo said that the Summer Tree is still active, although weakened. We're still under its protection. There shouldn't be any urannen or elloktu in the Shadow Army's forces. He said the rest would have a hard time once they reach the chamber. This is where the Summer Tree is strongest."

"Then we can hold them, Metter. We can hold them until the Cochen and the Archon arrive. And then we will crush them." His voice rumbled with certainty and he saw the others begin to nod. Their backs straightened and their hands moved involuntarily to their weapons. Metter was not as reassured, but even his chin rose.

Just as Corranu began to feel his own spirits lifting, shouts rose from the Riders around them. Moments later, Corranu heard the familiar sound of gaezel hooves, racing at full speed—

And then three Riders burst from the mouth of the tunnel, swerving and pulling up sharply as they ran into the gathered forces. Corranu moved without thought, kneeing Ischt toward them. "What is it?"

One of the Riders turned, eyes young and wild, blood staining his armor and splattered across his face. Not dwarren blood. The black ichor of the tainted.

"The Shadow Army! It's less than twenty lengths distant!"

"What? Why was there no report? What's happened to the forward defense?"

"The Shadow Army outflanked us." The Rider spun his gaezel around to one side. "We were attacked from behind. We hit them hard, but only twenty of us managed to break through. We've been hounded by the gruen since. We're the only three left. The rest are trapped back there. The gruen fell back, but they're close now."

"What of the sappers? Can they collapse the tunnel?"

The Rider shook his head, face grim. "They were already dead when we passed them."

Corranu swore, so colorfully even Skeen raised his eyebrows in surprise. He spun in his seat. "Sound the call to war! Warn the Keepers and the shamans! Metter, get your Turning's-damned Riders moving before—"

He cut off and whirled as from the mouth of the main tunnel a horrendous roar overrode the frantic sounding of the drums. Corranu hewed his gaezel around hard and jerked his axe from its straps. Even had they not battled the beasts at the Break, Corranu would have recognized that roar from the legends of the Turning told at nearly every festival and feast. "Terren."

The three Riders who'd fled the forward ranks to warn them echoed him with a shouted, "Terren!" even as they broke toward the protection of the amassed dwarren army.

The first terren swept out of the shadowed opening, stooped over at first but standing upright with another roar that shuddered in Corranu's chest. The creature stood five times as tall as any dwarren. Its gray-brown leathery skin rippled, its tusks broken and mangled, with teeth the size of Corranu's head. Spittle flew from its gaping maw and as its second roar ended it dropped onto its knuckles, the ground trembling at the impact. Its beady, pinkish eyes—too small for the rest of its bulk—latched onto Corranu.

The clan chief noted the flicker of unexpected intelligence there and then he charged, axe held high, bellowing the Painted Sands' ululating battlecry. Metter and the other Riders took up the cry behind him, but he kept his eyes focused on the terren, saw its head pull back as if surprised at Corrranu's move. But then it drew back one of its massive hands and swiped at him.

Corranu gave Ischt his head and drew a knife. Knees tightening in order to hold his position, he felt Ischt's muscles tense a moment before the gaezel swerved out of the terren's reach.

At the same moment, Corranu swung.

His axe dug into the terren's tough skin on the upper arm—skin nearly hard enough to be stone—and lodged there.

He was jerked from Ischt's back as the terren reared. With a growl of pain, it staggered forward into the oncoming Riders. A second terren stepped from the tunnel, and as if the first terren's movement were a signal, kell and gruen skittered from the darkness, swarming up the side of the chamber before leaping toward the attacking forces, or scampering between the terren's feet.

Screams broke through the roar of wind in Corranu's ears as he clung to the axe's haft. He nearly lost his grip when the terren brought his arm down in a sweep that knocked three dwarren and their gaezel to one side. The axe shifted and he cursed, saw the black ichor of the creature's blood welling up near where the blade was embedded into the skin, and then, arm wrenched sharply as the terren changed its swing yet again, the axe broke free.

Corranu flew over the leading edge of the dwarren army, arms flailing. He caught a few startled glances beneath him—

And then he plowed into the back ranks, at least twenty dwarren deep from the front line. He knocked one Rider from his saddle, slammed into the side of another's gaezel, then dropped to the ground with a jarring thud and clang of armor. His entire left arm went numb. The knife bounced from suddenly limp fingers, but he held onto his axe. A gaezel close by screamed, the high-pitched sound piercing deep into his brain, and then a hoof slammed into the stone floor beside Corranu's head.

He lurched away, scrambled to his feet as quickly as possible, surrounded in a crush of gaezel bodies all trying to press forward. He caught sight of the Rider who he'd knocked from the saddle, reached down to haul him upright, but the Rider was limp. His skull had been crushed, trampled before he could recover.

Corranu grimaced, then spied the Rider's mount.

He hesitated, but a sudden shove thrust him forward into the Riderless gaezel. Corranu heaved himself up across the gaezel's back, then used the animal's horns to slew himself into proper position.

Chaos reigned across the entire chamber.

Four more terren had appeared, the massive creatures wading forward in a path of rending limbs and blood. The gruen and the kell had overrun the front ranks, clinging to bodies and slashing and biting throats as they leaped from Rider to gaezel. Their hisses sizzled across the chamber, underscoring the screams of the gaezel and the shouts and bellows of pain from the Riders. The rest of the dwarren were trying to push forward, shamans scattered throughout their ranks wielding scepters and chanting to Ilacqua and the Four Winds. But they did not wield the power that Quotl had at the Break. Their voices did not resonate with Ilacqua's will, did not vibrate in Corranu's chest or imbue the shamans with invisible strength. Yet he could feel power emanating from the Keepers. They'd circled the Summer Tree and were chanting with hands and scepters raised. Even where he stood, an invisible presence pressed against his skin, prickling the hairs on his arms and making his beard crackle. The air shimmered between the Riders and the Keepers, as if heat waves rose from the stone. Younger Keepers raced from behind that wavering distortion, seized hold of the wounded or dead, and dragged them back to safety beneath the dark green of the Tree, where they dosed them with pink-tinged healing droughts from the Sacred Waters.

Another roar and a mass cry of dismay drew Corranu's attention to the southern entrances.

Terrannen's forces, fighting at three different tunnel entrances, were suddenly thrown backwards as four terren barged from the largest opening. His son fell beneath the onslaught, gaezel shrieking as they were trampled by the terren's charge. He heard the crack of dwarren bones even though the chamber was already reverberating with the cries of a thousand deaths.

His son did not rise again.

Something inside him snapped. It shuddered down into Corranu's core, and then grew still. The cacophony of the cavern muted, the screams deadened, the sight of crushed bodies dimmed. Yet the smell grew sharper. Blood—thick and dark and vibrant. Fear—rank and wretched and hopeless. Even the acrid earth-stone of terren musk and the bitter-cold night scent of the kell and gruen filled his nostrils. He breathed it in deep, noted that his vision had narrowed down to one goal: the arched supports of the dome overhead. They appeared to glow. It was the same glow he'd seen on Quotl at the Break—Ilacqua's touch.

"We can't hold them back. We need to protect the Sacred Waters." His gaze traveled up the long arch of one of the supports, past the already cracked dome, to the apex, where the arches converged in a large oval. Parts of the ceiling had already collapsed in places. The gaps were obvious, signs of decay that the dwarren could do nothing about. The dwarren had sworn to protect the Land. They'd been commanded to protect the Waters at all costs by Ilacqua himself, taken a sacred vow that had been passed down from generation to generation for hundreds—no, thousands—of years. And yet it came down to this.

"The dome must fall." His gaze swept across the shamans scattered among the Riders, found Peyo pushing his way forward through the ranks.

Sitting as high as possible on his gaezel, Corranu shouted, "Peyo!" and waved his axe, still dripping with terren blood. "Peyo, to me!"

It took long moments to catch the head shaman's attention, even more to meet at the back the battle.

"What is it, Corranu?"

"We have to bring down the dome."

Peyo drew a deep breath as if to protest, but then his gaze traveled over the battle. The hand not holding his scepter tugged at the fringes of his beard. Feathers and beads jounced, clicking and clattering together. "You're right. It would normally need to be agreed upon at a Gathering, taken care of by the Archon and the Cochen."

"We don't have time."

Peyo pursed his lips. "We will be remembered as those who lost the

Sacred Waters, those who destroyed it."

"We will be remembered as those who kept it from the Shadow Army, from the elloktu and the urannen. If we are remembered at all."

Neither one of them voiced what they both knew wwould happen: the dwarren within the dome would die. There would be no chance to escape.

But the Shadow Army would die with them.

"We'll need two teams—"

"No, four. Two to head north and start working on the supports in both directions, and two east and west, heading south. It's the fastest way to bring it down without sending teams to every support. And we shouldn't need to crack them all. It will fall before they're done."

"Agreed."

They both turned, Peyo toward the Keepers and Corranu to the back of the Riders still attempting to keep the Shadow Army at bay. The initial push to the south had been halted, but they'd lost ground on a third of that part of the chamber, with more of the Shadow Army pouring in. The terren, kell, and gruen were making steady progress at the eastern tunnel.

Corranu grabbed five Riders for each team, dragging them away from the fighting. Peyo chose four of the shamans, one for each of the Four Rivers. When Corranu explained their task, the entire group was stunned into silence.

Then Peyo stepped forward, raised his scepter, and blessed the groups, using one of the most sacred verses, riddled with protections. When he finished, his voice cracked. "Now go. Go, and may Ilacqua watch you with hawk's eyes and protect you with its talons."

They watched the groups split off, heading north, east, and west, behind the dwarren ranks, circling the red pulse of the Sacred Waters.

"It is done."

"Yes," Corranu said, straightening. "Now we give them the time needed to finish their task."

* * *

"Archon, to your left!"

Quotl spun, hands already slick with the blood of the kell that had swarmed from the main tunnel ahead of them as they'd raced toward the Sacred Waters. They'd continued the charge without slowing, trampling the twisted black creatures in the front. But even the gaezel couldn't keep the momentum going as the gruen joined the kell in the attack and the passage became jammed with the denizens of the Shadow Army.

One of the gruen leaped from the shoulder of a dead Rider to the wall, then launched toward Quotl, claws extended. Quotl swung his scepter, cutting off the creature's sibilant hiss in mid-arch. The bone-crunch shuddered through the wood and into Quotl's fingers and he grunted in satisfaction, then twisted around in his saddle. Twenty paces away, the Cochen and his clan pushed forward through the Shadow Army, leaving broken bodies and slick blood-smears behind, but the progress was slow. They were still a thousand paces from the main entrance.

He knew from the scrying that the Shadow Army was attacking from the west as well. They needed to get into the main chamber. They'd never get a foothold here.

"Azuka!" He pulled back even as he crushed a kell's skull and kicked another gruen from a fellow Rider's mount. The shrieks and death-cries drowned out his voice in the close tunnel, so he reached forward and grabbed Azuka's shoulder, his fellow shaman nearly braining him as he turned to attack. The younger shaman looked horrified as his scepter glanced off of Quotl's shoulder instead, but Quotl merely tightened his grip and pulled Azuka closer so he could shout into his ear.

"We won't be able to break through here! We need to use some of the secondary corridors!"

They began pulling back, seizing some of the Riders who were doing nothing in the rear. Most hesitated, until they saw Quotl leading them.

They charged down the passage, passed the gruen-slashed bodies of the sappers who'd been in charge of collapsing the tunnels, and hit the first cross corridor. Quotl motioned left, then led the way forward, reaching the first branch and turning again.

He tasted dust and dirt before he realized the corridor ahead had been plunged into darkness, the oil sconces that usually lit the tunnels gone. A moment later, he ran into the outer debris and then the solid wall of collapsed rock and he cursed.

"Back. Try the Gaezel's Run and the Little River. Check all of the branches for one that's not blocked."

As the group split, he realized they'd brought more than just a hundred Riders with them. A full two hundred had followed behind, and they were led by Kimannen.

He scowled as he saw the former Archon, slowed as the Riders streamed past.

"Archon."

"We don't have time for this, Kimannen. Why did you follow? Do you hope to supplant me if I die? Searching for the opportunity to kill me yourself?"

"If only Ilacqua were so kind. But no, the gods made it clear in the keeva that you were to be the Archon."

"Then why are you here?"

"Because you were not the only one to receive a vision in the keeva, Quotl. I may not be the Archon, but the gods still have a purpose for me. And I cannot carry that out unless I make it to the Sacred Waters."

Quotl tried not to let his shock show, but knew his eyebrows had risen. He had never heard of two shamans receiving different visions while within the keeva, especially during one of such import.

His shock slid into doubt. "What is this purpose the gods have given you?"

"To save the dwarren race." It was said without Kimmanen's usual arrogance and self-importance.

Before he could come up with a response, he heard shouts from one of the corridors and a Rider appeared.

"They've found an unblocked tunnel," Kimannen said, then kicked his gaezel into motion.

Quotl followed suit.

As they rode, the Riders surrounded them, so that they burst from the secondary tunnel into the southeastern part of the main chamber as one group.

Quotl's gaze took in the mass of dwarren fending off the Shadow Army at the two main corridors, the terren plowing forward into their ranks. A dull throb of power coursed through the army from the shamans who wielded the scepters, with the much deeper and distinct surges of the Sacred Waters and the Summer Tree to the north. The Keepers had erected a wall of protection around the Summer Tree using its remnant strength, so diminished from what it had been after the Shadowed One had thrust its seed into the stone of the chamber so many years before, when Quotl was merely a child.

But it was still significant. That power seized hold of Quotl and pulled him in. In the space between breaths, the entire dome slid into sudden heightened focus, as the battlefield at the Break had done. The air shuddered with the cries of the dead, with the echoes of the dying and the movements of those still alive. Invisible eddies coursed around and through him, outlining the darkness of the Shadow Army, giving its name deeper meaning. Others lit the Summer Tree and its shield in brilliant colors, gave the reddish light of the Sacred Waters a new pulsing depth.

He caught Azuka's attention as the group ground to an uncertain halt.

"Take a few Riders and report back to the Cochen. Tell him of the open tunnel."

Azuka nodded and took off, trailed by his escort. Quotl turned back to the others, caught Kimannen watching him intently, realized that the other Riders were doing the same. He knew he'd taken on the aspects of Ilacqua's touch, what Azuka had called a glow at the Break. He heard the throb of it in his voice.

Irritated, he asked Kimannen, "Do you see your purpose yet?"

"Not yet. But your purpose is to give them hope." He pointed his chin toward the faltering Painted Sands forces. "They need to see that their Archon has arrived."

Quotl jerked at his gaezel's horns. "Then we will show them."

He pulled his gaezel around, raised his scepter, and began chanting, the ancient words flowing from his mouth without thought as he kneed his mount forward, the rest of the Riders falling in around him, raising their own ululating battlecries as they swept down around the Sacred Waters and across the bridges over the two easternmost rivers. Before they'd reached the back of the army, Quotl heard answering cries from behind. The Cochen and his forces had arrived. He watched those ahead turn, saw their despair and desperation transform into determination as they caught sight of him, of the Cochen's much larger force behind him, and then he swerved to pass along the back of the dwarren army, headed toward the western part of the chamber and the Summer Tree. The dwarren in his wake rallied, surged hard against the Shadow Army, shoved it back with sudden force. He glanced back at an ear-splitting bellow, caught two of the terren tumbling into the raging waters of the Estuar River, their stone-like bodies vanishing beneath its surface. Looking forward again, he focused on the Summer Tree, on the Keepers beneath, and picked out Peyo, angling straight for the head shaman of Painted Sands.

Behind, he felt the approach of the Cochen's forces. It rippled through the energies that surrounded him, like wind in the grass signaling the approach of a storm front, building and building as it approached, until it slid smoothly into the already gathered dwarren forces and struck the blackness that was the Shadow Army.

Quotl shuddered at the collision, felt the Shadow give.

Then he caught the look of shock and horror on Peyo's face. It wasn't the reception he'd expected. He drew back from it automatically, his gaezel picking up on the subtle movement, slowing as they approached.

"What's wrong?" he shouted over the heightened noise of the battle competing with the roar of the cascading water and rivers.

Peyo gestured frantically at the surrounding walls. "We—we thought you weren't coming. We thought—"

But a sudden crack of splintering stone reverberated throughout the chamber, snapping Quotl's attention to the northern part of the dome. The sound cut through the air and trembled up through the stone floor in a teeth- and bone-grating ripple. Quotl clutched at his gaezel's horns as it instinctively shied away from the noise; other Riders were not so lucky as their mounts bolted.

Quotl paid no attention to them, or to the suspended chaos of the battlefield. Yet he still couldn't pick out what had changed, what had happened.

Then a chunk of the smooth white stone—dirtied by time and a thousand years of smoke from the dwarren—slid free from one of the supports. A thousand times the weight of Quotl himself, it plummeted to the floor below, and as it fell Quotl noticed the cracks that riddled the rest of the support, from its base all the way to the ceiling overhead.

The chunk of stone struck, splintering into a thousand pieces and cracking the floor north of the Sacred Waters. Quotl felt the concussion on the eddies around him, felt the new flaw in the support as he'd felt the flaw in the stone of the cliffs at the Break. The tremor from the impact broke additional stone from the ceiling, debris raining down onto the northern rock wall of stone and cascading water, clattering down its face.

Quotl turned to Peyo slowly. "What have you done?"

"We sought to protect the Sacred Waters. We meant to collapse the Ancient's dome."

Quotl would have staggered if he hadn't been mounted. "We have to stop it."

"We sent four teams. Two to the north and one each to the east and west." He spun, arms gesturing Keepers forward, stumbling over his orders before practically pushing the four shamans toward the tunnels that led below ground, where the supports that held the dome could be broken.

A second splintering crack shivered through the chamber, its report making Quotl cringe, but the battle around him barely reacted. Stone was already falling from a crack-riddled support to the east.

"You should have waited!" Quotl snapped, turning back to Peyo. "You should have had faith!"

Peyo's mouth opened and closed, but no words came forth.

Then the guilt-stricken shaman's gaze suddenly shifted, away from Quotl, centered on something to the east. His brow furrowed in confusion.

Without turning, Quotl knew why. Their presence caused a ripple on the eddies of power around him, another darkness like that cast by the Shadow Army, but this one much smaller, nearly lost in the tumult. He thought suddenly of the char scattered across the map at his last seeing, at the smear of it that had caught his attention to the east, so insignificant he'd dismissed it.

He felt something else as well, something buried in the darkness: a heart that beat with a faint pulse, yet promised a power of much greater potential if it were unlocked.

He yanked his gaezel around, eyes locking on the small force of skittering gruen as they scampered across the now debris-riddled floor. Those in the center carried what looked like a satchel, held high above them. They moved fast and were utterly silent.

And they were headed directly toward the Sacred Waters.

* * *

Kimannen remained calm until the first support cracked.

He watched Quotl lead his advance group of Riders—and moments later, the Cochen's forces as well—into the fight already going on at the two main entrances.

He should have led that charge. As Archon, he would have donned the official headdress that Quotl had left behind and ridden directly into the fighting. It would have given the Riders hope, the symbolism of the Archon—and thus Ilacqua—riding into battle beside them, bolstering their courage and eradicating their fears. It would have had *meaning*.

The five Riders he'd commanded to stay with him, all from Kimannen's own Claw Lake clan, shifted nervously. Their desire to join the battle was obvious, but his voice still carried weight, even if he wasn't the Archon.

And the gods had spoken. Ilacqua had a higher purpose for Kimannen. One that transcended becoming the Archon and leading the People of the Land. One that had taken him days to accept and come to terms with, even though it would be the ultimate achievement. It would make him a legend and would be spoken of for generations to come.

Quotl would never be able to surpass it.

Then the first support cracked.

Kimannen nearly fell from his seat, managing to catch himself with one hand on the gaezel's horns while keeping hold of his scepter. One of the Riders helped him upright while the others surrounded him protectively. He slapped the Rider's supportive hands aside as soon as he regained his balance, then froze in shock as the chunk of the support broke free and fell. When it hit, causing more of the support—and part of the ceiling—to fall, he pushed his gaezel forward through the Riders protecting him.

"Fools. They're all fools."

The urge to rush forward, to seize control, suffused him, so intense a compulsion that he'd grabbed his gaezel's horns and tightened his knees before he caught himself. The gaezel tensed in anticipation, but he forced himself to relax, pried his fingers free with effort. The vision had been clear.

A darkness was coming, here, to the Sacred Waters, slipping with stealth and cunning around the dwarren army, hiding in the shadows, waiting for the moment when the dwarren were distracted by the Shadow Army and the battle. According to the vision, it would bring destruction of a magnitude that the dwarren had never seen before, that the dwarren would not survive.

And the gods had chosen Kimannen to stop it.

But the vision hadn't been clearer than that. Everything had been blurred, feverish, distorted as if seen through deep, cloudy water. He'd seen the blood-red glow of the Sacred Waters, heard the screams of the dying and the clash of battle, and felt a dull, menacing, heart-throb of power pulsing over it all. That overriding malice had come from an ink-spill of oil beneath the water, streaming toward the glow of the Sacred Waters, a pin-prick of cold blue light at its center, and when it reached the Sacred Waters, the Meeting of the Rivers, the Heart of the Land—

The vision had roared, deafened him with a rumble of thunder a thousand times louder than even the vicious, unnatural storms that once again riddled the plains. Purplish lightning had stabbed forth from the Sacred Waters, blinding him. He'd lurched up from the ledge in the keeva, gasped at the intense heat of the fire, the dense scent of the yetope leaves' smoke, and found Quotl writhing on the floor, hand clutched to his chest, body wracked with tremors...

The second support snapped, this time closer to Kimannen's position, yanking him from the thoughts of the vision that had tortured him since his time in the keeva. His escort of Riders shouted warning and herded him back from the edge of the debris field as more stone tumbled from the ceiling. Kimannen allowed it without protest, confused. He'd sensed nothing like this in the vision, heard nothing like splintering stone.

Then one of the Riders shouted, "Look!" and pointed with his drawn short sword.

Kimannen followed his sword, and the doubt and confusion fled.

A group of the cat-like gruen with glowing lantern eyes flowed across the central chamber like a spill of ink, moving directly toward the Sacred Waters. Kimannen hadn't seen where they'd come from, but they carried something on their backs, a satchel of some sort.

Kimannen stiffened in his seat, the gaezel beneath him snorting and stamping one foot.

"We have to stop them before they reach the Sacred Waters."

He didn't wait for a response. He kicked hard into the gaezel's sides, leaned forward between its horns for balance as it hunched back, muscles bunched, then leaped, cutting toward the reddish glow of the central pool of water, angling to intercept the gruen. Kimannen barely registered the ululating cry of the escorting Riders, finally allowed to release their pent-up battle lust. His entire being centered on the gruen, on the satchel. He sank into the gaezel's fleet movement, slid into its rhythm as it dodged the chunks of fallen debris. The shattering of a third support of the dome overhead registered as a dull crump in the sudden pounding of his own blood in his ears. The gruen were thirty paces from the Sacred Waters... fifteen...ten...

And Kimannen struck, grunting with effort as he leaned to one side of the gaezel, the sharp point of its horn scoring a searing slash across his cheek, raking up alongside his ear and into his hair. His scepter slammed into the pack of gruen with jarring force as his gaezel charged straight through its center. Shrieks and hisses pierced the thundering noise already filling the chamber, escalating a moment later as the Riders at Kimannen's back descended on the scattered group. Kimannen hoisted himself upright and hauled the gaezel back around in a tight arc.

Three gruen had been trampled, two dead, one trying to crawl away, its hind legs twisted and limp, dragging behind it. The Riders were occupied with the rest, slashing with their swords, their gaezel striking out with their hooves. Two Riders were fending off gruen that had leaped onto their mounts.

But four of the gruen were still hauling the satchel toward the lip of the sacred pool.

Kimannen spat a curse, nudged the gaezel into greater speed as he tucked his scepter under his armpit to free one hand. Blood coated the side of his face, poured down his neck and soaked his shirt, but he barely felt it. The gruen had reached the lip of water, had thrown the satchel down. They began shoving it over the edge, their black bodies and lantern eyes tinged blood-red by the pulsing light of the rings of fire that rotated about each other deep inside the lake. Kimannen's breath caught as the satchel began to tip, whatever weight it carried pulling it over the side—

With a cry of defiance, Kimannen grabbed for the satchel, the gruen turning to hiss at him as his gaezel bore down on them. Two of them leaped for the gaezel's neck, the animal screaming as their claws pierced fur and skin, but Kimannen's hand closed on leather, gripped tight, and hauled the unexpectedly heavy satchel away from the Sacred Waters. He barked in triumph as he rose, his laughter feral and harsh, and then blood splattered his face as the gruen tore out his gaezel's throat.

The animal staggered, still attempting to run as it had been built to do, but its legs gave out. It fell, Kimannen thrust forward over its head, its other horn slicing across his hip, and then he slammed into the stone floor and rolled. His scepter snapped between the floor and his body, sent tingling pain down his arm. His forehead cracked into stone.

He came to a rest, stunned, eyes blurry, ten paces beyond his gaezel. Pushing himself up onto hands and knees, the leather satchel closed tight in his fingers, he heard hissing and glanced up. Blinking, he tried to focus, made out dark shapes creeping toward him through the haze of his vision. He lurched to his feet, the remains of his scepter falling to the floor beside him. He hefted the unnaturally heavy satchel as dizziness nearly overwhelmed him, but steadied himself by sheer force of will. His sight cleared enough he could see the two gruen as they approached. Beyond them, his gaezel gasped once more and died, and beyond that the Claw Lake Riders were finishing off the last of the gruen pack.

Kimannen swung the satchel once, twice. "You failed."

The gruen leaped, but Kimannen slammed the satchel into them in mid-air, heard bones crack, one of the gruen squealing. They were both flung to one side, their bodies coming to rest against part of the collapsed ceiling of the dome.

Kimannen laughed, but choked on the sound, falling to one knee and a supporting hand as his strength gave out. He stayed there, hunched over, then sat and pulled the satchel into his lap. He heard the other Riders approaching—only four now, one of them dead—as he worked at the satchel's knotted clasp.

When it finally gave, the flap fell open, exposing a smooth, rounded stone the size of Kimannen's two fists placed side by side. Except it wasn't simply a stone. Its power pulsed with the slow menacing heartbeat of his vision in the keeva. Blue light suffused its center, and threads of light, tinged purple-white like the lightning of the storms on the plains, reached out from the center and played along its surface.

"What is it?" one of the Riders asked.

Kimannen reached out to touch it. "I don't know."

When his fingertips brushed its edge, the blue light within flared. It reached out—reached *in*—and seized on the power that Kimannen held inside himself, that he used as a shaman to connect himself to the Land, to Ilacqua.

Kimannen's head jerked up. "Oh, no."

Snatching the stone up in both hands, Kimannen leapt to his feet and began to run.

* * *

Quotl flinched when the third support cracked, but his eyes never wavered from Kimannen's attack on the gruen across the breadth of the chamber. He sucked in a sharp breath when the former Archon tumbled from his dying gaezel, heaved a sigh of relief when he rose and dispatched the last gruen, but he couldn't see what Kimannen had found in the satchel. He only saw the elder shaman reach forward and touch it, saw his face go slack in dismay, felt a spike of power in the eddies that flowed around him—

And then Kimannen ran, whatever he held cradled close to his chest, headed straight for the eastern wall that housed the dwarren, a riddle of doors and ledges and walks that scaled upwards toward the ceiling between the arched supports. The eastern wall looked oddly empty, with no dwarren on those walkways or in those doors, but then Quotl realized why: the rooms had been emptied of all but the Riders and the shamans, everyone not essential to the defense ordered to leave.

That was why Kimannen was headed there. Because it was empty.

His eyes widened in sudden understanding.

"Peyo!" He reached down to grab the shaman's arm and haul him forward for emphasis. "Sound the retreat!"

"But the Shadow Army—"

"Forget them! We need to retreat now or we'll all be lost!" He shook the shaman, then thrust him away in disgust and wheeled his gaezel about, kneeing it hard toward the nearest group of Riders with drums, the urgency inside him escalating as the spike of power he'd felt when Kimannen touched the stone surged higher.

"Sound the retreat."

The drummers stared in bewilderment, mouths open in confusion.

Quotl singled one of them out, a Rider half his age, with only a few significant achievements woven into his beard, and roared with all the force of Ilacqua behind him: "Sound it now!"

The youth jerked as if slapped, then began to beat out the cadence. It stuttered at first, then found its rhythm. Quotl kicked his gaezel toward the Keepers holding the shield around the Summer Tree erect, locating the shaman in charge, a dwarren his own age that he'd known since he was a youngling.

"Retreat, Sirrano." He pointed toward the southeastern tunnels. "The chamber is going to collapse."

"But the Summer Tree still lives!"

"It's dying. It's been dying for months. Take the Keepers and escape now. That's an order, as your Archon."

Sirrano hesitated, but the drummers on all sides had taken up the call for retreat, the sound growing throughout the chamber. Where the dwarren battled the Shadow Army, those at the rear had begun streaming toward the southeastern tunnels, breaking away from the fight. Those at the front began pulling back, the terren, kell, and gruen surging forward with roars and shrieks of triumph.

Sirrano gestured to the Keepers stretched out to either side. "Abandon the Tree!" He grabbed the nearest Keeper and shoved him toward the southeast. "The Archon has spoken. Abandon the Tree!"

The shield wavered and broke as all along the line the Keepers released the Summer Tree's power and began streaming toward the edges of the retreating army, merging with it as Riders defended the bridges over the four rivers. The Shadow Army already filled the southwestern section of the chamber, was pushing toward the Summer Tree and the Keepers' position. Yet Quotl noticed they slowed the closer they came, veering away from the Tree itself.

It still held power, even if it was dying.

Sirrano touched his arm. "Are you coming?"

Quotl glanced toward the east. Kimannen had vanished into the warren of chambers the dwarren had lived in, but he could still feel the strange spike of energy building. The four Riders the former Archon had had as escort had followed him, covering his flank.

"Yes. We don't have much time."

As if to emphasize his words, another one of the supports shattered, this time to the west, near the Summer Tree. Stone rained down, ripping branches from the Tree, showering the western side of the chamber in verdant leaves, their undersides flashing silver as they fell. Sirrano uttered a gasp of dismay, other Keepers around them crying out as if in pain.

Quotl began herding the Keepers and shamans toward the retreating army. All around them, chunks of the ceiling fell, shattering as they hit the floor or splashing into the rivers or the central lake of the Sacred Waters itself. The Shadow Army had pushed far enough into the chamber that Quotl and the Keepers were forced to skirt the Waters' edge. Quotl stared down into its depths at the rings of red fire there, submerged but still burning, rotating around each other, a central core of fire at its heart. It was distorted by the now roiling water, but it still caused Quotl's chest to tighten—with pain and regret.

A massive boulder struck the bridge that arched over the center of the Sacred Waters and the bridge snapped. Quotl wrenched himself away. He didn't know what Kimannen had found, what he had done, but the spike of power had nearly reached its peak. The rising energies had begun to slow, had taken on a tremor, one that buzzed in the roots of Quotl's teeth, itched in his bones.

Dwarren streamed into the southeastern tunnels. The Cochen defended the bridges over the westernmost Tiquano River, but eventually they fell to the Shadow Army, the Estuar's bridges taken almost immediately after. Riders fell, their bodies left behind as the terren rampaged forward, the kell and gruen behind. As soon as Quotl passed the Andagua, the easternmost of the sacred rivers, he pushed through the mass of dwarren toward the largest tunnel entrance, began bellowing orders to move faster, dwarren and gaezel funneling past him out of the chamber.

The Cochen lost control of the Oulleout bridges, the dwarren pressed back to the Andagua. The Shadow Army's howls rose higher as they broke free to the north, hitting the dwarren along their flank, pressing them hard against the half-collapsed tunnels in the southeast corner. The fighting became desperate, dwarren falling on all sides. Quotl swallowed down bile at the slaughter, fought against despair, against the sense that there was nothing he could do. His voice grew cracked and ragged from shouting, from the choking dust and the taste of blood on the air. Another support shattered, the sound deadened by distance—

Then the buzz in his teeth and the itch in his bones halted.

Quotl sucked in an anticipatory breath, held it.

And watched in mind-numbed shock as the entire eastern side of the chamber cracked and exploded outwards in an avalanche of stone. Debris arched out into the room, a wall of merciless rock, disintegrating even further as it traveled. Quotl watched, frozen, as it began to engulf the eastern edge of the Shadow Army, crushing them, then realized that it had started a chain reaction. The remaining supports of the dome crumbled and the ceiling began to fall, starting at the eastern wall and working towards the west in a ripple. The initial roar began to build, escalating as more and more stone cascaded down from the heights. Dust billowed outwards in clouds, reaching towards the southern walls. He saw the northern cascades shatter, the run-off from the northern mountains that gathered here flung upwards and out violently. The water in the lake beneath churned, then vanished as it was buried beneath the falling stone, the blood-red light from the fires within extinguished in a heartbeat.

Quotl staggered back, then realized that the stone avalanche hadn't stopped. The front lines of dwarren had turned, had barely begun to flee toward the southern tunnels, when they were overtaken. Thousands upon thousands of pounds of stone rolled down on them, heading toward the southern tunnels—toward Quotl—like a wave.

Quotl spun. "Run!" he shouted, his voice nearly drowned out by the crushing thunder from behind. "In Ilacqua's name, run!"

The nearest dwarren kicked their gaezel hard, those on foot turning on their heel and racing away. Quotl gave his gaezel its head, hunched forward between its horns as it dove beneath the tunnel's entrance into the corridor beyond. He clenched his jaw against the shuddering rumble that approached from behind, prayed to Ilacqua, to the Four Winds, to all of the gods of the Land as he became nothing more than another dwarren scrambling to get as far from the destruction of the Sacred Waters as possible.

He'd made it perhaps a hundred feet down the tunnel before the blast of dust caught up to him and shoved him forward, as if Ilacqua himself had placed a hand against his back and pushed. He lifted off the back of his gaezel, heard it squeal in panic and fear, felt stone brush past his cheek—

Then he struck something, hard, and darkness seized him.

10

Legion Commander Roland Dubanar stood ramrod straight outside the training grounds inside the Legionnaire's barracks inside the palace at Corsair, mouth pulled down into a tight frown. Hi eyebrows were so knit they'd merged into one across his forehead, the edges of his eyes lined with what the hundreds of young men training beneath his eye assumed was anger but was in fact worry. The Legionnaires walking up and down the two sets of practice lines, working the boys into a sweaty lather, assumed it was anger as well and pushed them harder, their curt commands filling the yard with noise punctuated by the crack of wooden swords against wooden swords, steel armor, and the occasional dull thud when one hit actual flesh. Three of the young men had already been pulled off the field with bruised or broken hands or wrists. Any sign of frivolity had died an hour ago, just after Roland appeared to watch the morning session.

Everyone on the field—trainees and trainers—would have been surprised to find that Roland had barely noticed them.

Reports had been flowing in for the last two months. The first had been ignored. Why should he pay attention to notices from the outermost outposts along the dwarren border that the dwarren had . . . well, had vanished? The Legion was not in the habit of babysitting the dwarren, and since the Accord, the dwarren had given them little cause to worry. Certainly there were confrontations, usually misunderstandings or misinterpretations of the Accord, but nothing that had actually come to significant blows, especially during Roland's term as Legion Commander. And the dwarren had always been circumspect with their own patrols. Hells, they lived underground, didn't they? Half the time, the outposts never even saw their patrols, even though when any Legion groups wandered out too far into their lands, whether by accident or not, the dwarren appeared almost immediately to chase them back home.

So why should he take notice if the outposts reported no dwarren at all?

Except then the dwarren envoy had arrived, demanding the Legion's aid. They'd sent the dwarren back to the Cochen with an escort of Legionnaires, ostensibly to work with the Cochen and determine what the dwarren needed from the Provinces. Roland had come to believe the escort had been sent simply to stall them—to meet the terms of the Accord without actually aiding the dwarren in any way. That envoy and escort had disappeared. The last anyone had seen of them, they'd ridden into the grasses of the plains, the dwarren on their gaezel, the Legionnaires close behind on their horses, topping a rise, penants flaring in the wind, and then slipping over the far side.

Then...nothing. No reports, no messengers. Nothing.

Followed by nothing from Yhnar, Temeritt, and Borangst as well. Messages had been dispatched by pigeon and by horse to all of the Provinces to verify the dwarren claims, but those three in particular. Roland knew the messengers had reached Portstown and headed east...but there had been no word after that. No word of any kind, not even a regular dispatch.

"If the dwarren weren't lying, then where did the army that attacked them go after that? Did it head south?"

But that didn't make sense.

He glanced toward Justinian in the practice field below—a foot shorter than the other twelve-year-olds, although quicker on his feet.

After meeting with the dwarren envoy, he'd stepped up the training here in Corsair and the rest of the Provinces, had sent a dispatch that indirectly told every Legion commander to begin pulling in their forces and consolidating the Legion. He'd added additional forces to the patrols along the border as well, and most recently—overstepping his bounds— sending scouts into dwarren lands. The fact that those scouts had not been summarily repulsed had set him on edge.

What they'd reported finding on dwarren lands had brought him here.

"Nothing good can come of this."

The tension throughout the entire yard suddenly registered on his consciousness and he winced internally.

"Commander Litenn!"

"Legion Commander Dubanar, sir!"

"Enough for today. Release the men. Have them report back to their barracks to clean up, then the mess hall."

"Very well, sir. Company halt! You heard the commander. Fall out, clean up, and report to the mess hall in one hour. Dismissed!"

At least twenty young men collapsed instantly amid the groans and cheers of relief, roused and led from the yard by their fellows. Roland suppressed his smile, remembering his own days in the yard. He motioned a page forward. "Inform the king that I would like to see him in the western audience chamber immediately."

The page slipped out into the quickly emptying yard, catching Justinian a moment before he entered the barracks. The young king— crowned less than a month ago—glanced in Roland's direction and nodded in acknowledgment. Roland bowed slightly in return.

Then he spun on his heel and made his way to the audience chamber to await his king.

* * *

Matthais crumpled the summons in one fist. "Tell the king that I will be there shortly."

The young page darted off. Matthais watched him vanish around a far corner, then began making his way back to his rooms. He'd just returned from his now twice daily hike up to the dovecotes to retrieve messages, but he hadn't had time to read them yet. Not that there were many. In fact, the number of messenger pigeons had decreased dramatically, many of those sent to the southeastern Provinces never returning. Matthais' contacts reported that the trade routes had been completely disrupted. Caravans sent to Borangst or Temeritt disappeared, and now few merchants were willing to risk sending anyone to the east. Rumors had begun trickling in that entire towns had been laid waste, nothing left but pillars of smoke rising on the horizon, and that a vast, dark army had been seen in the distance.

Reaching his rooms, Matthais nodded to the Legionnaires who stood guard outside, then entered and closed the door behind him. He didn't pause in the sitting room, but moved directly to his personal office to the left, shutting that door as well. He tossed the summons from the king into the flames, then drew a chair closer and pulled the latest tiny missives from one pocket.

The first two were from Rendell with nothing if import, at least to Matthais: a warning of severe storms rolling down from the northern mountains and an invitation to the GreatLord's Winter Ball. The third was the first sign of significant concern from the GreatLord in Portstown. He'd sent men to the east, toward Temeritt, but only one had returned verifying the rumors of burned out villages and towns. Matthais swore and tossed that scrap of paper into the fire. Of the remaining five messages, one was a second note from Portstown with the same concerns, two regarded trade negotiations, one reported the loss of a galley off the cape, and the last...

Sitting back, Matthais pulled a handkerchief from one pocket and wiped the sweat from his forehead. He stared into the fire without seeing the flames.

He couldn't keep word of what the Wraiths and their armies were doing to the east secret much longer. The messages from Portstown were evidence of that. GreatLord Berand would have sent messengers by horse, and now that Justinian was of age there was little Matthais could do to stop them from seeing the king directly. His only hope would be to catch the messengers as they arrived. But the last message, from Borangst...

He glanced down again at the note, the scrap of paper no larger than his finger. Blood stained one end a rust-brown, and the scrawl was wobbly, as if the person who'd transcribed it had been weakened or panicked.

Walls fallen. GreatLord dead.

Matthais tossed the slip of paper into the fire, watched it curl, blacken, and burn.

Then he rose, the remaining safe messages back in his pocket. He moved to his desk, poured himself an inch of brandy in a small glass, and downed it in two gulps. It burned all the way down, but he was already headed out the door, through his sitting room, and back into the hall. He didn't acknowledge the Legionnaires as he passed. If Borangst had fallen, Temeritt would soon follow. It was only a matter of time before the Wraiths and their armies fell on Corsair, and then Matthais would kill Justinian and seize control of the Provinces in the Wraith's name.

Then he would taste the Lifeblood and become a Wraith himself.

He swept through the door into the audience chamber and found Roland, Justinian, and Tyrik waiting for him.

He halted at the door, one hand on the handle, suddenly aware of the four Legionnaires that had been stationed outside. His gaze flicked from Roland to Tyrik, standing to either side of the king, then settled on Justinian. The king looked angry.

Matthais bowed his head sharply, not quite as low and deferential as was proper, and eased the door closed behind him.

"My king, you requested my presence?"

"Where were you?"

"I was at the dovecote. I felt it prudent to review the messages before coming here in case there was news of importance to this meeting."

"Oh." Justinian relaxed slightly, but Roland did not. Roland had watched him carefully at every meeting since the dwarren envoy had arrived and Matthais had yet to determine why.

"And was there?" Roland asked.

"Was there what?"

"News of import."

Matthais retrieved the small notes from his pocket as he moved forward. He set the papers to the king's left, beside a scattering of other parchment, noted the tray containing bread, cheese, and fruit had already been picked over, that the wine bottle was already nearly empty.

The meeting had been going on long before he had been summoned.

"Nothing serious, no. A winter storm claimed one of Corsair's ships off the cape—not unheard of this time of year—and GreatLord Went warns of harsh snows from the north. He has also invited us all to his Winter Ball."

"No news from the east?" Tyrik asked.

Matthais shot him a look. "No, nothing from the east. Why do you ask?"

"Because we have a report from the east," Justinian broke in, his anger of a moment before transformed into an edged, barely controlled excitement.

"Was it from Temeritt? Borangst?"

"Neither," Roland said. He shifted from behind Justinian's seat, leaned forward onto the table. "I've been receiving reports from the outposts along the dwarren border and the Escarpment for weeks stating that the dwarren have apparently disappeared, withdrawn back into their warrens. I discounted them at first, but the recent silence from the southeastern Provinces coupled with the dwarren envoy that arrived two months ago gave me pause. I sent scouting parties into the dwarren plains."

Matthais hid his relief by raising his eyebrows in disbelief. "You violated the Accord?"

"I did what I felt necessary."

"You did what you wanted. You risked a war with the dwarren over what? A hunch? A misgiving? Without the king's permission! You are no longer the king's regent. You can no longer act on your own." An intense surge of satisfaction coursed through him. Roland had thrown this fact in Matthais' face at least twice since Justinian's coronation.

Justinian jerked forward in his seat. "He had my permission."

Matthais turned his attention on the king at this blatant lie, words of challenge on his lips. But then he met the young king's defiant glare, the determined set of his jaw. "I apologize, my king. I did not realize. And what have these scouts who should never have been on dwarren lands found?"

Justinian was too young to flinch at Matthais' undertone. "Signs of an army. A large army. The dwarren were telling the truth. They have been attacked."

Matthais swore mentally. He'd never be able to contain the Legion now.

But he had to try.

"'Signs' of an army? Did the scouts see the army itself?"

Justinian turned an uncertain eye on Roland. "Did they?"

"No, my lord, they did not."

"Then it could have been the dwarren, perhaps gathering their forces to meet this imagined threat from the east—"

Roland cut him off with a wave of his hand. "It was not the dwarren. The scouts said the tracks were larger than those of a dwarren, most of them human-sized, a few of them larger."

"Larger?"

"Larger than a bear's prints. The regular footprints didn't appear to be human. There were strange curved markings mingled with them, almost like the tracks left by a lizard. And claw marks, from animals about the size of a cat."

Matthais let his silence emphasize his incredulity. "You wish me to believe that an army of lizards and cats and bears has attacked the dwarren?"

"If what the dwarren said is true," Justinian said, not quite able to control the childlike awe and wonder in his voice, "then this is a Turning. According to my tutors, there are creatures—hideous creatures—that the dwarren believe reappear at the time of the Turning and wreak havoc across the Land. Some of those creatures are trolls—huge, lumbering beasts with skin like stone. Others have claws, used to dig and to rend. And still others have the faces of dogs or snakes or hawks!"

Brow furrowed, Matthais muttered, "I believe I should have a word with your tutors about the fanciful subjects they see fit to teach you in the future."

Justinian looked crestfallen, but then his face hardened. "You don't believe the dwarren histories?"

"Dwarren legends, my king. Their mythology. A religion to explain away the world and its harshness, its evil. We have our own. There is no mention of such creatures in Holy Diermani's Codex."

Justinian tensed. Roland placed a placating hand on his shoulder.

But it was Tyrik who spoke. "There is no mention of the Wraiths and the Shadows in the Codex either, and yet we know from our own history that such creatures exist. If there are living shadows in the world that feed upon our souls, or men whose skin writhes with darkness beneath its surface, who's to say there cannot be trolls or diggers or hawk-faced humans?"

"You surprise me, Tyrik. I did not realize you could be so gullible." As Tyrik stiffened in affront, Matthais turned back to Roland. "So where is this army of mythical creatures headed?"

"North." Roland searched through the papers on the table and pulled out a map of the Provinces and dwarren lands. "The scout found the army's path here, cutting northward through dwarren lands from the south and east. Best guess is they're headed toward the Alvritshai. It's impossible to estimate the numbers in the army, but the width of churned land left in their wake suggests that it's at least a thousand, probably more. There were also signs of supply wagons, perhaps a day or so behind the main army."

"Ah, yes, because this army of cats must have its ration of mice."

No one laughed, and when Matthais glanced up from where Roland had pointed out the signs of the army on the map, he found the Legion commander's eyes boring into him, his mouth set in a hard, compressed line.

"You may joke and posture all you like, councilor, but the fact remains that there is an army on the move in dwarren lands. A sizable army. I'd be surprised if it contains less than five thousand men, regardless of what the scout has reported. That army, coupled with the warning the dwarren gave us months ago, the fact that we have heard nothing from the envoy we sent back to the dwarren Cochen, and the lack of any significant communications from our own southeastern Provinces, indicates to me that there are enemy forces moving against us. That we have been unaware of them to this point makes the hair at the nape of my neck stand on end. We cannot ignore these warnings any longer. We must act now, before this army—an army I believe has already attacked the dwarren and our own eastern Provinces, and is now poised to attack the Alvritshai—decides to turn its attention toward us."

Matthais heard the warning in the commander's voice, realized he'd pushed the Legionnaire and fellow advisor too far. He heard something else as well, something buried deep but tainting the words—a strong current of suspicion. The same suspicion he'd first noticed in Roland's eyes in the throne room during the dwarren envoy's visit.

He needed to change tactics. Fast.

"My deepest apologies, Councilor Dubanar, Councilor Tyrik, and my liege. I can see that you all feel the threat is significant, and I must admit that I have been worried myself, of late, mostly due to the rumors that trade routes to the east appear to have been cut off completely. These are rumors only, at the moment. I had intended to inform you, my king, as soon as I could have them verified, but given this news..." He shrugged. "Perhaps evidence of an army is verification enough. What do you suggest we do?"

"We were already discussing that before your arrival," Tyrik said, moving to Roland's side of the table. "We must warn the Alvritshai first, since it would appear the army is moving in their direction. We should also attempt to contact the dwarren and determine what has happened since their envoy was here. They may be able to provide vital information regarding the forces arrayed against us."

"After the envoy's visit, I sent orders to all of the Legion commanders in the various Provinces instructing them to begin assembling our own army under the pretext of training exercises. At this moment, every garrison and outpost is on alert and ready to move. Based on our scant information, GreatLord Went should assemble his men and move them to the eastern borders. I'd also suggest sending scouting parties north and east from his lands to see if we can determine where this army is currently located, who they are, and what their target is."

"We also need to re-establish contact with the eastern Provinces. Sending messengers and messenger pigeons has obviously failed. I think we should have GreatLord Berand send a force of Legionnaires out from Portstown to determine what's happened to Temeritt and Borangst."

"Berand should also put his forces on alert," Roland added. "I'll have him close the borders along the Escarpment. All civilians in the towns on the edges of the upper plains should be evacuated to areas below the cliffs."

"What about the coastal cities?"

"There've been no signs of trouble from Andover. Aside from placing the Legion on alert, I see no reason to panic the citizens of the coastal cities at this point."

"And supplies? Armor? Weapons?"

"I'd hesitate to begin full scale preparations until we know more about what we're facing. The Legion has sufficient resources for what we've proposed so far, but perhaps plans should be drawn up in case we find there is a significant threat."

"I can do that." Tyrek's gaze shifted to King Justinian. "If, of course, the king wishes it."

Matthais nearly choked on a bark of laughter. The entire scene had been orchestrated by Roland. The Legion had been ready for such orders for months. How Matthais' spies had been kept unaware of it was...no, they *had* been aware. He'd seen the reports of the Legion's "training exercises" himself, had dismissed them. But Roland must have been sending secret messages to the Legion commanders in the different Provinces, ordering them to prepare, and Matthais' spies had failed to intercept those.

But what of Tyrik? Was he involved? The king was obviously being manipulated by the Legion commander. Even as the boy nodded his assent to Roland and Tyrik's plans, he could see the strings Roland used to direct him—a nudge here, a suggestion there, an appeal to the boy's tendency toward heroics. This had all of those trademarks and more.

As he watched the three discussing the placements of the armies and the shifting of resources, the king huddled between the two advisors, an intense look of concentration creasing his young forehead, he realized that whether Tyrik had been involved before this or not didn't matter. He was involved now.

Which meant Matthais needed to abandon his attempts to keep them uninformed and make himself indispensable instead. He needed to be integral to the planning of this war.

"Goran," he blurted.

The conversation between the others cut off abruptly and Roland looked up in irritation. "Goran?"

"Yes, Goran." Matthais noted the contempt in his voice and tempered it, speaking as he moved to the other side of the table, insinuating himself between Roland and Justinian so that he could point to the map. Roland stepped back reluctantly. "Goran is the last major city between Portstown and the Provinces farther east that have fallen silent. I have been receiving communications from Goran on a regular basis. The first reports of missing traders and shipments came from there, and at this point they have warned everyone from any trade at all to the east. They're also the ones who sent back the sightings of razed towns and missing townsfolk. If any action is to be taken, you should stage it from there." He turned to the king, Justinian staring up at him from his seat with a look of consternation on his face. "Although I would advise against hasty action at all, my liege, especially with so little information. You wouldn't want to send the Legion to Goran only to have this army—wherever it is—ride up to Corsair from the east and seize the city from beneath you."

Justinian shot Roland a frightened glance, his back stiffening. "What should we do then?"

"That is for you to decide," Roland said. "I agree with Matthais that Goran would be a good base for the Legion if we decide to head southeast. It's a trading city, but it also has a castle and walls. Nothing as large as here in Corsair, but large enough to house a significant portion of the Legion while we are there."

"And they should have ample supplies for the army."

A look of irritation crossed Roland's face at Tyrik's interruption, but he continued without comment. "My main concern is that the signs of the army we *have* seen indicate the army is moving northward. That leaves Rendell and Corsair as potential targets. We will have to leave forces behind for their defense, which means we'll be divided and thus weaker than before."

"I thought you said the army on the plains was headed toward the Alvritshai."

"It is, as far as we can tell. But armies rarely move in straight lines. They may be planning an attack on Rendell instead. There's no way to know, not until we locate the army itself."

Justinian leaned forward over the map. Matthais heard him mumbling under his breath, his focus so honed he no longer looked twelve, but older, lines appearing around his eyes, wrinkles in his brow, all of the boyish fancy and excitement gone. This was the deadly serious youth he'd caught a glimpse of when the dwarren envoy was here, the man who'd patiently sat back and suffered beneath his three regents' reign until the day he had become king. Matthais strained to hear what he said, but only caught a few words, nothing of consequence.

Until Justinian raised one hand to his brow to rub at his temple. "What would my father do?"

Matthais seized the opportunity. "Your father would have protected his people at all costs. If the eastern Provinces have fallen, then Goran is their next target. Do you really wish to leave those people, those you've given an oath to protect, to their mercy?"

"Think carefully, my liege," Roland added. "Splitting our forces could be a fatal mistake. You cannot protect the people if the Legion is destroyed."

Justinian's lips pursed in frustration, but Matthais kept himself from further prodding, choosing instead to scan the other papers that surrounded the map on the table. Lists of supplies, manifests, and scrawled notes and reports, most bearing the Legion's seal, a few with the official wax stamp of the king, most likely taken from the archives by Tyrik. One, near to Matthais' hand, appeared to contain a list of Legion forces—their locations, strengths, and current resources.

When Justinian finally turned to face Roland, Matthais shifted and set his fingers lightly against the sheet of paper.

"Can GreatLord Went defend himself against the army we think is heading northward?" Justinian asked.

"If the army contains five thousand men, then yes, he should be able to defeat them with the Legion in Rendell. But as I said earlier, there may be more than that."

"I need to protect the people in Goran. They're my vassals. They vowed allegiance to me at my coronation. I will not abandon them." Justinian drew in a deep breath, held it, then let it out in a slow sigh. "Send half of the Legion here in Corsair to Goran. The other half will remain to defend Corsair. Warn GreatLord Went in Rendell of the threat of an army to his east."

Roland appeared about to protest, but thought better of it. "As you command, my king."

Justinian nodded, then slid from his seat. All three of his former regents bowed, Matthais taking the opportunity to slip the sheet containing the Legion's whereabouts into his hand. As the king made his way toward the doors, Tyrik reached forward and gathered all of the papers together. Roland followed in Justinian's footsteps, Matthais and Tyrik mere moments behind. In the corridor outside, Justinian headed down the northern wing toward his rooms, the Legionnaires who'd waited outside the door as his escort, while Roland moved toward the Legion barracks. Tyrik followed the Legion commander, leaving Matthais at the door.

He slipped the sheet of paper free from where he'd secreted it inside his sleeve, then began making his way back to the dovecote. He had messages to send.

* * *

Tyrik nearly stumbled in his haste to catch up to Roland. "You were right. Matthais is acting suspicious. And I saw him take one of the pages from the table at the end."

"Which page?"

"The one with the Legion positions and strengths."

Roland smiled, his attention shifting from Tyrik back toward the barracks and the orders Tyrik assumed he was headed there to issue.

"Why are you smiling?"

"Where do your loyalties lie, Tyrik? Are you loyal to Justinian? Or do you serve for your own purposes, like Matthais?"

"I serve King Justinian, of course. As his father, the man I served before him, asked me to do!"

"The safe answer. The expected answer. But I believe you." He fell silent, long enough Tyrik thought perhaps he wasn't going to continue. But then: "The list Matthais stole was false. Most of it is correct, but not all. I may have...exaggerated the placement of the Legion in certain areas, and left off some units altogether."

Tyrik's shock rooted him to the floor, his paralysis broken when Roland continued on without him. They passed through the main doors of the palace and out onto the sunlit steps and courtyard beyond. Roland angled left across the flagstones, toward the yards used for training and the main barracks. Birds wheeled overhead, spiraling around the thin spire of the Needle, their cries mingling with the shouts and clangs coming from the practice fields.

Except, as they drew nearer, Tyrik realized that the Legion weren't practicing as he'd thought. They were already suited up in their armor, horses saddled and ready to depart.

"You're already ready to depart. But the king hadn't given his orders yet! And you lied to him about the Legion's whereabouts? Why? What do you intend? Are you even going to follow Justinian's orders, or was all of that talk of planning a ruse?"

Roland rounded on him sharply. "Of course I'll follow his orders, even though I think splitting our forces a mistake. I don't know what Matthais hoped to gain by suggesting it. But neither am I going to sit here and allow Corsair and the Provinces to fall due to his interference. Half of the Legion will go to Goran, as commanded, but the rest can do more than simply sit here in Corsair and train."

He motioned one of the Legion commanders forward. "Uthur, gather ten men and prepare them to head north. I'll have the message for GreatLord Went ready in half an hour. Tell Commander Terent he will oversee the forces to be sent south."

"South, sir?"

"Yes, south, to Portstown, where they will join up with GreatLord Berand's forces. I'll have his orders ready shortly as well. After that, report to me."

Uthur bowed, fist to chest, and stalked off to pass on the orders.

"What do you hope to do?" Tyrik asked.

"I intend to find out where this army to the north is and how many men—or whatever—it contains."

* * *

An hour later, horns blared in a fanfare, echoing up from the wide courtyard before the palace. Matthais glanced up from his desk, then made his way to the windows overlooking the square. He watched as, below, banners flapping in the breeze from the inlet, the ordered ranks of half of Corsair's Legion marched out of the gates of the palace and down toward the city along the water below.

* * *

Quotl woke with a start and immediately began coughing, the air choked with dust. He blinked repeatedly, but his vision didn't clear, and when he tried to move he realized why.

The tunnel had collapsed. He couldn't see because he was trapped in darkness, pinned down by the weight of a ton of stone. He couldn't move at all, and when he tried, his body screamed with a thousand aches and pains, too many to locate individually. He could barely shift his head, stone scraping against his cheek. He tried to lift it, but hit another stone above him. His wriggled his fingers, his arms shifting slightly, but he couldn't move his legs at all. He couldn't even *feel* his legs.

He panicked. He thrashed around, even though pain shot up through his spine and spiked into his head, creating white-hot sparks in his vision. A bellow broke from his lungs, ragged and dry from breathing the dust of the collapse. A daggerlike pain dug into his right chest. His head bashed against the unseen rock above him and he choked on his own breath, the building scream dying. Something wet trickled down the side of his face and into his beard and mouth. Blood.

Panting heavily, he forced himself to calm. He was the Archon, one of the leaders of the dwarren. He had to stay focused and controlled. His body wasn't quite horizontal, his torso leaning forward, one arm pinned beneath his chest, the other off to his right, pinched at an awkward angle. His head was twisted to the right as well. When he tried to adjust his hips, he found his left hip pressing into something soft—certainly not stone—

and pain tingled down into his legs, angled beneath him. He heaved a sigh of relief at the sensation.

When his breathing had become regular and his blood no longer pounded in his ears, he licked his dry lips and croaked, "Is anyone there?"

Nothing but the steady rush of his heart, loud in the silence.

He sagged against the stone beneath him. The stones above shifted and pebbles and dirt cascaded down onto his face. He tensed and spluttered, blowing the dirt out from where it had caught in his beard. Then he stilled. If the rocks were loose enough to shift...

He thought about the battle at the Break, about finding the flaw in the cliff side and *twisting* it.

Sucking in another breath, he sank into the Land around him, into the stone and crevices. The earth was alive with tension, everything unsettled, poised to shift and slide. Stone encased him, pockets scattered through it here and there, but to his right he felt the emptiness of a hole. Part of the tunnel, he assumed, although it was closed off on both ends. But it was close.

Cautiously, he sank into the stress of the stone, felt his way along its edges. If he gave a gentle shove right...*there*.

The rock around him began to slip. Then the motion picked up speed and with a yelp of surprise he tumbled out of his pinned position into the gap he'd sensed, a minor rockfall coming with him. He let himself be carried with it, lay still until the last sounds of creaking stone and settling debris ended, then attempted to move.

A groan escaped him, even though he'd prepared himself for the pain. He forced himself to his knees, his legs tingling with what felt like the bites of a thousand fireants. His hands brushed against fur and he realized the softness that had pressed against his left hip had been the body of his gaezel, twisted and broken and tacky with blood. He patted the animal's side in the darkness. "Ilacqua guide you." The words sounded inordinately loud to him.

And then the magnitude of what had happened crushed him. The Sacred Waters, the Wraith army, Kimannen and his sacrifice. He didn't know what Kimannen had done, but he'd sensed the power of whatever the gruen had carried, knew it had caused the explosion that had brought the Sacred Waters' chamber down. How many of the dwarren had died? What of the Sacred Waters? Did they survive? Had they been protected?

In his mind's eye, he saw the roof of the chamber caving in, saw the stone raining down, consuming the lake of water, extinguishing its light and entombing it. A wave of sadness rolled through him.

"We protected the Land as best we could. Ilacqua, forgive us."

Grimacing, he stood, hands outstretched to either side, even though he could sense the surrounding stone through his connection to the Land. He edged around the gap, fingers brushing against the smooth wall of the tunnel to one side, meeting only fractured stone elsewhere. At one point, his hands found the protruding hand of another dwarren, cold in death. His lips pressed tightly together as he mentally whispered a prayer, then moved on. He found two more bodies buried in the rubble, a third actually free of the stone, lying on the floor. His questing fingers found where the dwarren's head had been crushed by what he assumed was a falling rock. He did not recognize the pattern of beads and braiding woven into the dwarren's beard.

He settled down at the base of the tunnel wall, patted his armor futilely for a moment. "No pipe, no scepter. This is a terrible way to die." He snorted laughter.

He didn't know how long he sat in the dark, staring into nothing, before the sound registered.

He tilted his head to listen. It sounded like...dripping water.

He stood, stepped toward the jumble of stone to his left, reached out tentatively—

His hands brushed stone. Damp stone.

He felt frantically to either side, up and down. Water was seeping between the rocks. When he knelt, the floor was already damp, a thin layer of water pooling to one side of the debris-strewn floor.

Quotl thought of all of the water that had fed the Sacred Waters and the four underground rivers of the plains. Its natural course had been disrupted. It would be seeking out new channels, new pathways.

He swore. Using the tunnel wall as a guide, he shifted to the far side of the gap in the collapse, began pulling stone down from above and tossing it behind him as he stretched out his senses ahead. He couldn't see what he was doing, but he could feel the tensions in the stone and he used it, pushing and pulling with both hands and mind. Pulling one rock free loosened others. Another caused an avalanche as the heap before him shuddered and collapsed, but he didn't stop, climbing up on the fallen stone. His hands began to ache and cramp, scraped raw and bloody, but he continued on doggedly.

An indeterminate time later, he tossed a stone backwards and heard it splash.

He paused, breath harsh in his ears, hands trembling.

Then he reached for another rock—

And heard the scrap of stone against stone from farther ahead. Faint, nearly lost beneath his own heartbeat, but there.

Reaching out through the Land, he sensed movement and another, much larger, gap ahead.

He cried out involuntarily, seized the nearest stone, and began beating it against the rock heap before him. "Here! Here! I'm alive!"

He didn't know if they heard him or not, but it didn't matter. He began digging in earnest, clawing his way forward, heedless of where he threw the stone.

When those from the other side broke through, a dwarren hand reaching into the narrow burrow Quotl had dug near the top of the tunnel, Quotl gripped it tight, his fingers refusing to let go. A moment later, enough stone was cleared that Quotl could see the outlines of the face of the dwarren he held onto, light pouring past him from the open tunnel beyond. The dwarren's eyes opened wide in shock. "Archon." Then he spun around, hand ripping from Quotl's grasp, and shouted, "It's the Archon! We've found the Archon!"

Ragged cheers erupted and Quotl's brow creased in irritation.

When the dwarren looked back, he said, "Yes, you've found the Archon. Now get me out of here. There's water seeping through the stones behind me."

11

"We're almost there."

Tuvaellis gave a start, unconsciously reaching to seize time and halt it, her knife half drawn before she realized it was Orren. The priest had come up alongside her and she silently cursed this desert and its heat and sand and unending sameness. Her lips were cracked and dry, even though she drank regularly, if sparingly, from the caravan's reserves, and the unmitigated sun had drained her of energy, making her lax. Orren should never have gotten so close to her unnoticed. She fought the urge to punish him. If she killed him, she'd have to kill the rest of the pilgrimage as well and she had suffered too much to destroy her chances of reaching the Rose at this point.

She glanced around at the rest, frozen in mid-trudge. Most hung their heads with weariness, if not despair. They had been traveling the desert for weeks. Five of their number had died—four of them succumbing to the illnesses that had set them on this Aielan-forsaken path, and one to the venom of one of the desert's black snakes. Those remaining had settled into a silent, steady plod. The priests attempted to keep their spirits up, but no one responded to the promptings of the chants anymore, or the forced lightness of their conversation as they wove among the group during their breaks at oases or waystops along the occasionally glimpsed road. Even Orren showed lines of strain around the eyes and mouth.

Tuvaellis resheathed the blade and looked into Orren's face, into the gray-green depths of his eyes. Even through the signs of weariness, his soul was alive and hopeful. He was sincere in his quest for the Rose, in his fervor to bring its healing powers back to the sick in need, in his belief in Diermani and the righteousness of his cause. His strength had not flagged at all, not even during the sandstorm three days before, when they'd huddled in the lee of scoured stone outcroppings.

He found her at nearly every break, spoke to her, or simply sat in silence sharing a waterskin, staring out over the beauty of the desert.

Tuvaellis snorted in contempt, but something deep inside her, locked away beneath the bitterness that had consumed her since her banishment from the Alvritshai, stirred. She turned away from Orren and stared out into the undulating sands of the wasteland around her.

Untold years ago—she had long lost count—she had been a lord's daughter. Her House had been prosperous, her father a member of the Evant. The cold that would eventually consume the Alvritshai's lands north of the mountains—her lands, her rightful heritage—had only just begun to blow southward. No one yet knew what those harsh gusts from the far icecaps would bring.

She had been happy then, raised to be a lord's daughter, taken to the courts for the festivals, the rituals of Aielan, to the dances and the balls and the courtings. Her role was set, her life decided. She would bond to one of the lord's sons, preferably a lord presumptive. She would preside over his House and his lands. And she *had* bonded, as intended, had caught the eye of a lord presumptive. Tallusaen had smiled at her at the midsummer rites, had danced with her, had trailed his fingers down the sides of her neck and kissed the nape of her hair scandalously in the dark seclusion of her father's gardens. Her laughter had drifted through the trees, nervous and tight. Even at the bonding ceremony, the white fire of Aielan burning bright behind them, Tallusaen had smiled.

But the smiles had faded almost as soon as the ceremony ended. As soon as they were in the carriage that would take them to Tallusaen's House lands, he had turned from her. She hadn't understood why he pushed her away, the unfettered joy of the bonding catching in her chest, souring into tears of confusion as they rode to their manse on opposite corners of the carriage. She'd watched the countryside drift by in a daze, blurry and indistinct.

She'd hardened then, she realized, on that long carriage ride. In the months that followed, Tallusaen remained distant, looking at her in contempt when he glanced at her at all. He gave her nothing—no affection, no physical contact, no place in his home—left her to her rooms, her garden. The bitterness had blossomed then, and grew. The first time she confronted him, he struck her, so hard she crashed to the floor, her face bruised for a week. The second time, she'd been prepared, had caught his wrist, had glared at him over their straining arms and told him if he hit her again, she would kill him.

He'd beaten her, enraged, bellowing that she was nothing but a pawn in the games of the Evant, that her father had sold her to form an alliance, that she was nothing but a commodity to be traded and used. Then he had stormed away, leaving her bloody and broken on the marble floor of the foyer. Servants had found her, had taken her to her rooms and healed her. It had taken months.

As soon as she could move again, she'd taken the knife she now carried and found him in the gardens talking to his father. He'd smiled at her in the seconds before she'd drawn the blade and stabbed him in the neck. The blood covered her entire arm, from wrist to shoulder, had splattered her pale yellow dress. His father had sat in stunned shock, making it easy for her to yank the knife from Tallusaen's neck and plunge it into his chest.

She'd walked away then, covered in blood, knife in hand. She'd returned to her father's lands. She hadn't believed Tallusaen's words, had thought her father would welcome her, protect her.

But when she arrived, he'd met her between the gates and the main entrance to the manse, surrounded by guardsmen. His expression had been hard, his eyes like flint, his arms crossed before him. The guards had seized her, roughly, and the muscles in her father's jaw had twitched, his only reaction. Once bound, all he'd said was, "What you have done?"

Then he turned his back on her and walked away.

Tallusaen had been right. Her father saw her as nothing more than a commodity.

She snarled into the stillness, the memory of that betrayal still harsh and violent. The urge to lash out, to *harm*, was nearly unbearable. But she contained herself.

They had intended to try her, to brand her a traitor and banish her. But she'd escaped, her father's guards too lax, their contempt of her so great they underestimated her, and she fled.

But not before killing her father.

Her hand clenched around the hilt of her knife. She seized the part of herself that had woken beneath the bitterness and ruthlessly buried it again. She wanted to kill it, had thought she'd succeeded, decades ago. But something within this priest—his attempts at friendship, the depths of caring in his eyes; emotions she had expected from Tallusaen, from her father—had stirred those long forgotten memories.

Turning back to Orren, she composed herself, tugged the cowl into place to shadow her face, then let time resume.

Orren gave a start and halted. She must have shifted position without realizing it.

"Almost where?" she asked.

Confusion flitted across Orren's face. "We've almost reached the Temple of the Rose. See that ridge of sand? Beyond it is a valley of stone, the remains of an ancient city we think, long buried but now exposed. The Temple of the Rose was built on the edge of the city. We should reach it by nightfall."

The rest of the pilgrimage had shifted past them as they spoke, trailing out along the top of the dune. Tuvaellis stared at the ridge beyond avidly. The burden she had carried across the Arduon Ocean and through the Borangi Desert suddenly pulled heavily upon her shoulder. For the first time in weeks, she sensed its power, throbbing low, asleep inside its case. She had checked on it nearly every night of the journey to make certain it remained unharmed.

"Is the pain of your disease so great?" Orren asked.

Tuvaellis hunched her shoulders; she'd unconsciously straightened to her full height gazing at the ridge. "Why do you ask?"

"Because of how you look so intently in the direction of the Temple. The scars of the leprosy must be hideous, for you to have endured so much to journey here."

"Of course they are. Have you not journeyed this far to heal your own scars? The markings of the red plague?"

Orren's hand rose to his chest. "I didn't come to heal myself. I came to petition the caddoni of the Temple of the Rose for the right to bear the waters of the Rose back to Trent in order to heal the plague victims there. I intend to keep my scars. They remind me of what I endured, and they give hope to those suffering from the plague now that they may survive."

"Then you are a fool. If you have the power to heal yourself, you should use it. You should not *ask* the caddoni for the healing waters, you should *take* them. Don't be a pawn of the Temple. Don't let them control you. Show them that you are in control of your own destiny."

Orren regarded her in silence after this outburst, more vehement than she had intended. But then he said, "The Rose will heal your leprosy. I pray that it will heal your scars."

He broke away, moving to catch up to the rest of the pilgrimage, leaving Tuvaellis standing alone. For a terrifying moment, she thought he knew about the taint of the sarenavriell that roiled beneath her skin, that he had seen beneath her cowl, and a new thought occurred to her: could the Rose heal the damage done by the sarenavriell? Could it reverse the taint of the Lifeblood, destroy the darkness that had seeped into her soul? Would it redeem her in Aielan's Light? The possibility flared brighter than the sun, glinted hard like diamond, and she reached for it—

Reality crashed back down, snuffed out that hope. It left an ache in her chest that she quickly smothered with bitterness, as she had smothered every emotion since her father's betrayal. Orren hadn't seen the taint of the sarenavriell. If he had, he wouldn't have walked away so carelessly. He would have condemned her. Or he would have called upon the power of Diermani to strike her down, as the priest in Trent had done. No, he'd meant something else, some other scar. But what?

She shifted the satchel containing the stone from one shoulder to the other and followed in Orren's footsteps.

Three hours later, she stood by the priest's side at the top of the ridge, the sun sinking into the far horizon, the desert and the ruins of the vast city jutting up from the sands tinged a deep, burnished orange. Twilight hung heavy to the east, stars glittering in the emerging darkness. The shadows of the ruins and the Temple before them were long.

The Temple itself was small, made of yellowed stone, ten pillars supporting a flat roof in the front, the entrance set deep inside, with no windows visible. Beyond it, sand-scoured buildings thrust upwards, their edges long smoothed by wind and erosion. Yet Tuvaellis could see rooflines, canted at odd angles where walls had given way, pillars that supported nothing, a fallen statue, even what must have been a road. The strange stone—not sandstone, nor any kind of stone Tuvaellis had seen in the Borangi—gleamed in the fading light, windows empty sockets, doors gaping mouths. A dead city, once buried but now unearthed, its bones exposed.

She wondered if this city were related in any way to the ruined city at the center of the Thalloran Wasteland, where Walter had discovered the Well.

"When can we see the Rose?" she asked, her voice husky.

"The Rose isn't in the Temple. Only the caddoni and a few of his arruli know the true location of the Rose. But you can petition for the waters you seek here. The caddoni listens to all who come."

Tuvaellis gripped the straps of her satchel tight, a scream of rage building inside her. She needed the Rose, not its waters. She needed the source of its power.

Then, abruptly, the anger ended, as if she'd severed it with her knife.

The Rose was near. She could feel it. All she had to do was find it.

* * *

"What do you intend to do with her?"

Thaedoren drew himself up out of his desolate inner thoughts and glanced toward his brother, Daedelan, also known of as the White Fox.

His brother had gotten the name during their tenure on the border patrol, the White Phalanx scouring the edges of House lands to the north as part of their training while their father, Fedorem, ruled from Caercaern. Both of them had known that the patrol was more self-inflicted exile than training. As young lords, they'd grown restless, too constrained by Caercaern, so they'd taken to patrolling the land with the White Phalanx, running exercises, honing their abilities, carousing.

Ignoring Daedelan's question, he asked, "Do you remember the hunt when we were younger, when father was still alive? We were north of the Hauttaeran Mountains, in the White Wastes, on patrol, and we'd had far too much to drink."

Daedelan settled back into the saddle. "We argued. I don't even remember what it was about now, but you challeneged me."

Thaedoren chuckled. "We agreed to split our forces. I'd travel east, chose a location, then attempt to defend it. You'd have three days to find and capture me and all of my men. It was supposed to be nothing more than a game, but somehow, somewhere along the way, it became more serious." He paused, some of the humor seeping out of his voice. "I set up in two different locations, all within clefts of the snow-packed mountains and the hills below. The first was in the ruins of an ancient church, the last remnants of a small town at the base of a waterfall. I left most of my men there, thinking it would be easy to defend. Then I took a small escort of five out into the wastelands."

Daedelan took up the story. "You found a drift of snow beneath an upthrust section of rock, dug a narrow passage into it, and hollowed out two rooms. Then you packed the opening back up with snow and sealed yourself and your men in, with only a small opening along the rock face to let in air and let out smoke."

"All I needed to do was remain hidden for three days, until you were forced to give up and concede. I thought I'd succeeded, until late on the third day I heard movement overhead. I hissed everyone to silence, to listen. We were still reaching for our weapons when the ceiling caved in. I remember snow and ice collapsing on top of me, slipping down my neck and beneath my armor. I saw a body rolling, a flare of black cloth—"

"And then I seized the front of your shirt, yanked you close, and said, 'Surrender.'"

"A little melodramatic, don't you think?"

"I was young."

"But what else could I do? Without having drawn a blade, I surrendered." He shook his head. "My men told me you hunted me for a day and half after taking them at the church. And even though the wind had scoured away our tracks, on the third day you halted, sniffed the air, then crept up onto the drift where we were hidden. But you didn't simply attack. You circled to the top of the ridge of stone we'd sheltered against and then, like the foxes we'd seen hunting snow-buried prey, you pounced and dove head first into our burrow from above."

"And I became the White Fox." He stared off into the distance a long moment, both of them silent, then turned to face him. "You stopped arguing with me so often after that."

Thaedoren grimaced. "It was the first time I saw you as someone other than my younger brother, to be tolerated and nothing more. I realized you were a better strategist—a better warrior—than I was. That's why I gave you control of the White Phalanx when I ascended to the Evant." He glanced back toward the White Phalanx and Rhyssal House guard trailing behind them. "Now look at where we are."

Daedelan lips pursed. They were riding through a rocky defile along a small creek, roots hanging down on either side, the ground covered with water-smoothed stones from when the winter snowmelt flooded the ravine. Trees loomed over the top of the walls above, their branches laden with heavy clumps of snow from the storm the night before. The creek burbled to their left.

"What do you intend to do with her?"

Thaedoren sighed and pretended he didn't understand. "What do I intend to do with who?"

"The Tamaea, Reanne. We can't continue hauling her around with us. We can't—"

"What do you expect me to do? If we were in Caercaern, in control of Alvritshai lands, I would denounce her as a traitor and banish her. She would be thrust from our lands as khai, left to fend for herself. But we aren't in Caercaern. We aren't in control of our lands. We've been forced out, practically khai ourselves. If I brand her and let her go, she would return to her Aielan-forsaken brother Orraen and Peloroun and reveal our whereabouts, tell them how we escaped and of our strength. We can't afford to let her loose, branded or otherwise. She's too dangerous."

"Then kill her."

"You mean execute her."

"She's a traitor. And as you say, she's dangerous. Or are you unwilling to kill her because of...something else?"

Thaedoren jerked his head forward, guided his horse around a canted bole of a tree trunk that had fallen down from above. Its branches brushed his shoulder, left a pattern of dampness across his shirt.

But after a moment of turmoil, his shoulders sagged. "I thought we could obtain information from her, that she would reveal Lotaern and Peloroun's plans. As soon as I realized she would reveal nothing, I should have had her killed. But I couldn't. I convinced myself that she could still be useful. As a hostage. As leverage against her brother. But those are merely rationalizations."

"They are."

"Blunt as always, brother."

Daedelan gripped his shoulder and he turned.

"I understand why you are reluctant, Thaedoren. But she is a traitor, and you are the Tamaell."

Thaedoren caught sight of Reanne, riding with eyes downturned, head bowed, her hair covering half her face.

Ahead, a whistle pierced the midmorning stillness. Both Thaedoren and Daedelan jerked their mounts to a halt. A moment later, one of the forward Phalanx wheeled his horse about and cantered back towards them. Thaedoren found himself surrounded loosely by the White Phalanx before the forward guard reached him.

"Tamaell."

"What is it?"

"Phalanx in the Nuant House colors. They're waiting for us up ahead."

"Take me there."

Daedelan motioned their escort to follow and they moved down the ravine, their horses' hooves loud on the stone scree of the bed, a few horses splashing in the creek as they tried to keep formation around Thaedoren. When they reached the leading Phalanx, Thaedoren drew up short.

A hundred paces farther downstream, ten Phalanx wearing Nuant's maroon and gold waited, one bearing the House banner. Motion drew Thaedoren's eyes upward, to the lip of the draw on either side. More Nuant Phalanx stood there, arrows trained down on them.

Thaedoren turned his attention back to those waiting ahead. One of them nudged his mount forward. "Welcome to Nuant House lands, Tamaell Thaedoren."

Thaedoren kicked his horse ahead, felt its muscles tense as it picked up his own tension. "I'm afraid you have the advantage."

The man laughed, still not close enough for Thaedoren to recognize, not with the hood pulled up, although he knew it was not Lord Daesor.

"Of course. You are on our lands uninvited after all. You and the White Phalanx. I see you have a few of Lord Aeren's guardsmen with you as well. And is that the Tamaea held hostage behind you?"

Thaedoren heard the Phalanx just behind him shift into new positions. They had no idea how they would be received, whether Nuant was allied with Peloroun and Lotaern or not. They had hoped to make it to Rhyssal House lands undetected.

"It is."

The figure ahead nodded. "Strange times, indeed."

He gestured toward the archers without glancing away from Thaedoren. All of them lowered their weapons, bowstrings loosened. But they kept the arrows nocked, ready to draw at the first sign of trouble.

"My father sends his regrets," the man said. "He is unable to escape Caercaern, but he told me to welcome you to Nuant and to help you with whatever it is you require."

Thaedoren's eyes narrowed. "Caeden?"

Caeden, Lord Presumptive of Nuant, pulled his hood back and bowed briefly in Thaedoren's direction. "Nuant House is loyal, my Tamaell, no matter what my father was forced to do in Caercaern."

* * *

"You're saying Daesor stayed in Caercaern against his will?" Thaedoren asked.

They were ensconced in the main room of an inn, the entire structure seized by the Nuant Phalanx, the rest of Caeden's men camped outside, along with most of Thaedoren's men. Thaedoren, Daedelan, an escort that included Naraen and Hiroun, Caeden, and Caeden's highest commanders sat around the inn's longest table, a fire crackling in the hearth. The innkeeper and his servers had filled their glasses with wine and set out trenchers of bread, cheese, and sliced meats, then were ushered from the main room so that Caeden, Thaedoren, and the rest could talk.

Caeden leaned back, eyeing Thaedoren carefully. He had his father's rounded face, dark hair, and penetrating gaze, although his eyes were his mother's. "He was trapped there, yes. Lords Peloroun and Orraen made certain no one could escape the night of the coup. Their men had already seized the gates by the time my father realized what was happening. Lord Terroec's rooms were already ablaze, Terroec himself dead by all accounts, and Lord Aeren had already fled."

"He didn't flee," Daedelan said. "He came to the palace. He tried to warn us, but it was already too late."

"Lord Aeren lives?"

"No. He died outside my rooms in the palace. We gave him to Aielan's Light before we fled Caercaern." Thaeodoren's brow creased in confusion. "Peloroun and Orraen sealed the city. How is your father communicating with you?"

"I could ask how you left the city, but I won't. Peloroun couldn't keep the city closed for long, and from what my father said, Peloroun is the one in control. Orraen merely follows orders. My father has been pretending to go along with the newly formed Evant. As such, he's allowed to send couriers home. All messages are read beforehand, of course, but my father has managed to get some messages through without their knowledge. We have...our own code."

"What has happened since the coup?"

"What do you know already?"

"Practically nothing. Terroec and Aeren are dead. Peloroun, Orraen, and Lotaern seized the city. They killed nearly all of the White Phalanx, at least those they could find. They've subdued the remaining lords enough to have called a meeting of the Evant. Other than that..."

"More informed than I expected, but there have been new developments in the last few weeks."

"Such as?" Daedelan asked quietly. His brother had not completely accepted Caeden's apparent benevolence.

"Lord Peloroun has been declared Tamaell by the Evant, although the remaining lords were divided. My father and Lord Saetor opposed Lotaern and Orraen. Lord Houdyll was the deciding factor. Since then, Peloroun has gathered up his forces and, with the Chosen, headed south."

"South?"

"Yes, south. He collected more of his Phalanx along the way. I have received no word on where they are headed, nor why, but Lotaern did take a significant portion of the Order of the Flame with him. Orraen remains in Caercaern. The city's gates have been opened and trade has resumed.

"At my father's urging, I have gathered together the Nuant Phalanx. We have been watching for your arrival, Tamaell, and gathering information. Fedaureon has called Rhyssal's Phalanx and has headed south and east, I believe to rally Baene's forces and confront Peloroun and Lotaern."

"I see."

Caeden let the silence hang for a moment, then shifted forward. "My father believes Lord Saetor will align with us, given the chance. But he is trapped between Orraen, Peloroun, and their allies. Lord Houdyll cannot be trusted. Myfather believes that Peloroun has some kind of hold over him, based on what happened during the Evant.

"Peloroun and Lotaern think we are weak, because we are scattered and because Lords Aeren and Terroec are dead, and my father and Saetor are confined to Caercaern. But I am not weak, and neither is Fedaureon. I know he has already acted. He seized the members of the Order of the Flame who remained in his lands and confined them. I have done the same here. I only waited to act because of my father's belief that you escaped and would come here. Now that you have arrived, Nuant is ready to follow you, ready to take back Caercaern and your throne from these usurpers."

Around the table, men from both Nuant and Thaedoren's own forces shifted in their seats and grumbled or muttered in voices too low to hear. Thaedoren stared hard into Caeden's eyes. "How would you suggest we do that?"

The young Lord Presumptive straightened in his seat. "We should join forces with Fedaureon and Terroec's son, Renaerd, and attack Peloroun and Lotaern while they're separated from Orraen and their forces in Caercaern."

Daedelan caught Thaedoren's attention. "I agree. They are more vulnerable outside of the Caercaern's walls."

Out of the corner of his eye, the Tamaell could see a few of the others nodding in agreement.

"Then prepare the Phalanx," he said. Men began to rise, but he forestalled them with a raised hand. "But there is one thing we must do before we leave."

* * *

"You don't have to do this yourself," Daedelan said.

Thaedoren's chin lifted. "Yes, I do."

At the central square of the town, the combined army parted. Naraen and Hiroun escorted Reanne forward, her hands tied before her, her head held high. They were flanked by members of the White Phalanx, the rest of the army closing in behind them as they halted before Thaedoren, Daedelan, and Caeden. She thought she knew what he intended. She'd been anticipating it since Thaedoren hauled her into the catacombs of the mountains.

Thaedoren faced Caeden. For the sake of all of those assembled, but in particular Caeden's men, they had decided that a formal announcement of support was necessary, to solidify the ranks.

"Lord Presumptive Caeden," Thaedoren intoned, voice raised so that it would reach most of those gathered, "you have welcomed the White Phalanx, and myself, to Nuant House lands. By extension, you have also welcomed those with us from Rhyssal. But these are dark times. The Evant is divided, the Houses of the Alvritshai in turmoil. I must ask, do you pledge the Nuant House, in your father's name, to me?"

Caeden faced him. "Thaedoren Maen Resue, in the name of my father, Daesor Kae Nuant, and as Lord Presumptive, I here formally recognized you as the true Tamaell of the Evant and foreswear as traitors Peloroun Troic Ionaen, Orraen Desor Licaeta, and the false Chosen, Lotaern."

Thaedoren's eyebrows rose. Caeden only needed to recognize him as Tamaell. He had not expected the young Lord Presumptive to denounce the traitors as well, especially Lotaern. By doing so, he had essentially pledged to summarily execute any of the three if they happened to be captured by Nuant House Phalanx. In these times, Peloroun and Orraen would be written off as casualties of the games of the Evant, but Lotaern...

As Chosen of the Order of Aielan, and now the Order of the Flame, his death may have more serious consequences.

But Thaedoren could not call Caeden's brash words back. Everyone in the square had already heard them, had borne witness.

To one side, Reanne gave a disparaging snort, but Thaedoren didn't acknowledge it. At the end of his oath, Caeden had lowered his head in fealty. Reaching forward, Thaedoren gripped Caeden's shoulder long enough to signal his acceptance, then released him, turning to those assembled as Caeden straightened.

"As the rightful Tamaell of the Alvritshai, I recognize the House of Nuant and Caeden as Lord Presumptive."

There was no sound from the White Phalanx or those from Nuant. Not even the townsfolk who peered at the assemblage from the second story windows of the surrounding houses, or from the edges of the square and corners of the buildings, stirred. The solemnity that had descended over the square as soon as Thaedoren, Daedelan, and Caeden appeared deepened instead, as the Tamaell's gaze finally returned to Reanne.

"And now I ask you, Lord Presumptive, as well as those assembled, to bear witness." He stepped forward, felt a twinge of satisfaction when Reanne flinched back. Her façade of contempt and derision wasn't as solid as she wanted him to believe. "Reanne Yraell Resue, you are a traitor to the Alvritshai people, conspiring with lords of the Evant to murder the Tamaell, your own husband, and to seize control of the Evant by force. You have betrayed the trust and loyalty given to you as Tamaea of the Alvritshai and of House Resue. You have betrayed me. As such, your life is forfeit."

With those words, he drew the knife at his side, a flood of memories assailing him from the last time he'd drawn this knife for this purpose. It had been dark then, on the churned and muddy battlefields of the Escarpment. Surrounded by representative lords of the Evant, and King Stephen and his escort from the Provinces, he had said similar words and passed a similar sentence against Khalaek, the lord of the House of Duvoraen. His heart had been filled with hatred then, along with grief over his father's death and what would have amounted to the near destruction of the Alvritshai people, if not for Shaeveran's intervention on their behalf.

His heart was filled with hatred and grief now as well, but also a deep pain over Reanne's betrayal. Love could not be snuffed out so quickly, so easily. And he had loved Reanne.

He reached forward and grabbed her neck, his eyes burning with tears he refused to shed. He tried to focus on the bitterness of his anger, but his voice betrayed him, coming out broken and choked.

"Our bonds are broken. The ties that bind us as husband and wife, as Tamaell and Tamaea, are severed. I mark you as traitor, so that all will know of your deed." He placed the blade of the knife against her cheek, near her eye, drew it down to the edge of her jaw in a smooth, sharp move. Reanne hissed and jerked back, but two of the White Phalanx behind her held her still, Thaedoren's own hand, around her throat, squeezing tighter. She strained upwards onto her toes. Blood dripped down from her eye, as if she were weeping. But Thaedoren didn't release her. He twisted the hand holding her neck instead, exposing her other cheek, and sliced down that side as well.

Then, before she could react, before he could have second thoughts, he punched the knife into her ribcage, seeking her heart. He wanted it to be quick. But he must have missed.

Reanne sucked in a hoarse gasp of shock around his chokehold. He felt her throat working beneath his palm. He released his hold on her neck and pulled her close, resting her chin against his shoulder. Her long black hair blew into his face, caught in his tears as he whispered, "You thought I'd save you. You thought I'd keep you alive. You underestimate me. So do Lotaern, Peloroun, and your brother Orraen."

He drew his knife free and Reanne gasped again. Then he stepped back.

She fell, her legs already too weak to hold her. She turned her head toward him, her eyes searching, wide in disbelief. Her lips were stained with blood, the front of her dress drenched. One hand flopped toward him and she arched her back.

Then she collapsed in upon herself with a sigh and didn't draw breath again.

12

Moiran threw down the missive from Lady Sovaeren in frustration. "The woman is worthless."

Sylvea sat quietly in one corner working on needlework and tending to the fire when necessary. When the servant glanced up in enquiry, Moiran waved toward the slightly crumpled paper.

"She writes to inform me that Fedaureon and the rest of the Rhyssal Phalanx arrived in Hallieas safely and that they have joined forces with Renaerd. But then instead of expanding on that, perhaps telling me of their plans, she spends the rest of the letter bemoaning her husband's death, fretting about her son, and complaining about the sudden turmoil the Phalanx are causing in the town. I thought Sovaeren would be more sensible in this situation. Instead, it appears Halceon from Nuant is the more practical."

"Perhaps Sovaeren simply has no one else to talk to in Baene. You do share similar circumstances."

"You would think she'd take my lead. I asked specific questions in my last letter and yet she has answered none of those, focusing instead on herself and her troubles."

"Not everyone is as steadfast as you, my lady."

Moiran reached for the next letter in her stack. "She could have at least enclosed a note from Fedaureon. Or Mattalaen. One of them could have spared a thought for those of us waiting here in Artillien."

"Perhaps none of them wanted to risk revealing their plans in case the messenger was intercepted by Peloroun's or Lotaern's forces."

"You've met my son, yes?"

Sylvea replied with a smile.

A moment later, they heard heavy boots in the corridor outside the room. A muted discussion unfolded outside the chamber door, the words too low for Moiran to pick out. She stood, one hand braced on the desk for support, before the conversation ended and someone knocked at the door.

"Enter."

Wodraen opened the door and stepped inside. Another Rhyssal Phalanx member could be seen in the hall behind him, a scout by his dress, recently returned to Artillien.

"What is it?" she asked, too sharply.

"We have received word of a force approaching from the north. They've entered Rhyssal House lands and are heading toward Artillien." Wodraen hesitated, then said bluntly. "They carry the Resue, Nuant, and Rhyssal House colors...but Lord Aeren is not with them."

Moiran's hand rose to clutch at her shirt. "And Thaedoren?"

"The Tamaell—your son—leads them."

Moiran leaned forward onto the desk on one arm, her head bowed. She breathed a prayer of thanks to Aielan, then gathered herself. "We must prepare for their arrival. Wodraen, ready the Phalanx. Sylvea—"

She turned to find Sylvea had already set her needlework aside. "I'll inform the rest of the servants and staff."

"Have the kitchens prepare something to eat. I'm certain Thaedoren will be hungry."

Sylvea nodded as she slipped past Wodraen at the door. Moiran caught her motioning to the scout to follow her.

Moiran moved to the window overlooking the lake, stared out at the snow that fell in large, fat flakes—snow that had been falling since the night before. The lake was frozen, a flat, white, treacherous field below the rocky crags of the bluff on which the manse sat. A gray landscape, lit only with washes of lantern light from the few windows that could be seen from this vantage.

Behind her, Wodraen issued orders, then closed the door. She heard him move across the room to stand behind her.

"I'm...cold, Wodraen."

He moved to the fire and added more wood, even though the room was already stifling. Then he left, hesitating before closing the door behind him.

* * *

Wodraen returned an hour later. Moiran sat behind the desk, the papers before her in order, composed and waiting.

She rose. "Are they close?"

"They are heading up the road to the manse now. The majority of the army has begun setting up camp in the eastern fields. Thaedoren, Lord

Presumptive Caeden, their escorts, and most of the Rhyssal House Phalanx who made it out of Caercaern are coming here."

"We will meet them in the courtyard."

The servants stepped out of the way as they made their way to the front door. Those of the Phalanx they met stiffened.

When they emerged onto the stairs leading down to the courtyard, Thaedoren had already arrived, had dismounted and handed his horse off to the scurrying stableboys. He was speaking to Caeden, the young lord presumptive taking in the manse and the waiting honor guard of Rhyssal Phalanx Wodraen had arranged to be on guard in the courtyard. Caeden's eyes fell on Moiran and he said something to Thaedoren, her son turning to face her.

Moiran managed a tight smile. "Welcome, Tamaell, to Rhyssal House." Her gaze shifted. "And welcome Lord Presumptive Caeden. It is good to see you both."

"It is good to finally arrive," Thaedoren said formally. Then the formality slipped. "I have news, mother."

"I know. I have news as well. Come inside, both of you. We have rooms and food prepared for you and your men."

"We won't be staying long."

"You will at least stay the night."

That elicited a thin smile. "Of course, mother."

Moiran led them to the same room where Shaeveran had met with Aeren and Fedaureon. Food had been laid out, and both Thaedoren and Caeden selected some from the variety of platters while Moiran poured them all wine. As she did, she noticed that the Phalanx that had escorted them to the room included Hiroun, the guardsman who had survived the trek to the northern wastes and become Aeren's personal guard upon Eraeth's departure with Shaeveran.

Eraeth.

Moiran fumbled, the decanter clinking against the glass, wine spilling onto the table. She set the decanter down hard as a wave of lightheadedness passed through her, driven by the realization that Eraeth, Aeren's Protector, would not know of Aeren's death. And there was no way to get word to him. She had no idea where Shaeveran was, let alone whether he and Eraeth still lived.

For a moment, it felt as if her entire world were swaying wildly out of control. Nearly everyone she loved was lost or dead. The Evant was torn asunder. The Alvritshai people divided. Everything that had once been stable and steady had now crumbled beneath her.

A hand found her shoulder and she returned to the room with a start, found Thaedoren watching her closely.

Moiran pulled herself together. "I just realized Eraeth doesn't know of Aeren's death. He should be told, but there's no way to let him know."

"Where did Eraeth go?" Caeden asked.

Thaedoren's hand dropped and he turned toward the lord presumptive. "Shaeveran and Lord Aeren discovered evidence that the Wraiths were interfering with the sarenavriell. He and Eraeth, along with one of Lotaern's Order of the Flame, went to warn the dwarren and to find out more about the Wraiths and their activities if they could. We have not heard from them since they left Alvritshai lands."

Thaedoren motioned to the chairs waiting for them around the fire and they all took seats, the tone of the room shifting toward that of a council. And Moiran realized that's exactly what it was: a war council.

"I've heard that Peloroun and Lotaern have left Caercaern with an army and are traveling southward," he began.

"According to our scouts," Moiran answered. "Fedaureon has taken the majority of the Rhyssal Phalanx to join Renaerd and his forces in Baene. My last report, received today, was that he'd arrived in Hallieas safely, but no news from Sovaeren on what their plans were after that. Given that the letter is a few days old, I'd be surprised if Fedaureon is still in Hallieas."

"He wouldn't wait. And Renaerd would not be able to detain him. Which means we'll have a hard time catching up to him if he's intent on attacking Peloroun and Lotaern's forces while they are outside of Caercaern."

"He will attack if given the chance." When Thaedoren raised an eyebrow in question, she sighed. "Even though we received no official word that Aeren had died, we both knew. He's taken it hard, blamed himself. And he's impulsive and somewhat rash. He hasn't learned patience."

"None of us had learned patience at that age. Daedelan and I would have done the same."

Moiran straightened. "Is Daedelan with you?"

"Yes, he was in Caercaern at the time of the coup. He's seeing to the White Phalanx and Caeden's men. He'll join us as soon as he can."

Moiran glanced toward the door, in the direction of Artillien and the fields where the army would be encamped, then forced herself to settle back down. "Tell me what happened."

She did not need to clarify.

"He died honorably, as did Lord Terroec."

"I expected nothing less. He was...an honorable man. That's why I bonded with him."

Thaedoren had never really accepted her decision, had always thought her bonding to Aeren had been a betrayal of his own father, Fedorem. But he nodded now, as if he finally understood.

"Peloroun and Orraen attacked at night. They took the gates in both walls first, so that neither Terroec nor Aeren could escape. Then they went after them both in their manses. They caught Terroec unprepared, although he fought. His manse burned, and by all accounts he died fighting. Lord Aeren—"

"Lord Aeren had already ordered us to leave."

They all turned to face Hiroun.

"Go on," Moiran said.

Hiroun's gaze flickered back and forth between Moiran and Thaedoren, but settled on her. "Lord Aeren ordered the servants to run, to try to escape if they could. Then he took the Phalanx with him to the palace, to warn Tamaell. We arrived to find that Peloroun and Orraen had already attacked. We struck them from behind, managed to push all the way to the Tamaell's outer rooms, but—but he was cut down."

"I saw him fall," Thaedoren said. "The White Phalanx pushed the traitors back far enough to drag him into the highest tier of the palace with me. He was still alive then. He held on long enough to deliver his warning, then he died. We escaped through the mountain, taking his body with us. He was given to Aielan before we gathered what supplies we could in Caercaern and headed west."

Moiran remained still for a long moment, fingers gripping the wooden arms of her chair. She had already grieved, had been grieving for months now she realized, since the servant had arrived to tell her of the coup. Hiroun and Thaedoren had merely filled in details of a tableau that she had already imagined in her head.

So she drew in a deep breath and let it out in a long sigh, the tension that cramped her hands and shoulders releasing. With the outrush of air, she let go of Aeren, of her grief, her hope that perhaps he still lived. Her second husband was dead. She would not bind herself to another again. She would not allow herself to suffer this heartbreak a third time.

She'd faced the windows and the softly falling snow without realizing it. Now, she spoke without turning back.

"You will find Fedaureon and with him you will kill Peloroun, Orraen, and Lotaern. For Lord Aeren and Lord Terroec. For all of those who died during the coup in Caercaern, and all of those who will die in the battles to come." Her tone left no room for argument. "Swear it, Thaedoren."

"I swear before Aielan's Light."

"As do I."

Both of them spun to find Daedelan and Wodraen standing in the door, snow still melting on Daedelan's black armor.

Moiran stood. She would have embraced her son, except that there were others present. Instead, she nodded formally. "Thaedoren has told me of Aeren's death."

Daedelan stepped into the room and reached for a few slices of the sauced meat, chewing as he poured himself a glass of wine. "We should attempt to catch Fedaureon before he reaches Peloroun's army...and whatever it is that Peloroun has sent his army after."

"Do you know?" Caeden asked.

Moiran shot Wodraen a glance.

"What is it, mother?"

"We believe Peloroun and Lotaern are going to meet an army being led by the Wraiths."

No one reacted for a long moment. Then Caeden stirred. "But what of the Winter Tree?"

"According to Lotaern's own Order of the Flame, the Winter Tree is failing. Before he left, Shaeveran feared the Wraiths had found a way to counter it, using the sarenavriell. It appears he was correct. The Chosen believes the Flame can stop them."

The disbelief was palpable, no one daring to speak.

Moiran leaned back into her seat. "You can speak to the two members of the Flame we captured in the temple here in Artillien if you'd like."

Thaedoren raised a hand. "It doesn't matter. Peloroun and Lotaern would not have taken their army south unless it was necessary. Someone is attacking from that direction. It could be the Wraiths, or even the dwarren or the humans. Regardless, we will depart for Hallieas tomorrow in the hopes of catching up to Fedaureon, then we will head east in search of Peloroun, Lotaern, and their forces." At nods from both Caeden and Daedelan, Thaedoren turned to Moiran. "You have supplies organized for Fedaureon and the Rhyssal Phalanx?"

"Of course. And I'll warn Sovaeren of your arrival."

Thaedoren set his wine glass aside, all of them rising and moving toward the door. Moiran slid ahead of them, catching Hiroun's arm before he could turn to follow them.

"Lord Aeren's death was not your fault, Hiroun. You could have done nothing to prevent it."

"I could have died protecting him," he said stiffly.

Moiran could say nothing to that, so she let him go.

Thaedoren and Daedelan paused beside her, watching as Hiroun walked down the corridor, not meeting his fellow Rhyssal guardsman's eyes.

"He's been this way since Aeren's death," Thaedoren said quietly. "I thought assigning him to my personal guard would help, but it hasn't."

"Only battle will help," Daedelan added. "He needs to expunge his guilt with his blade, on the field, against Peloroun and Orraen."

"I fear only his own death will help."

"Then better on the field than for him to take his own life here or elsewhere."

Moiran wanted to refute his statement, but couldn't. Fighting a wave of weariness, she asked, "What of Reanne? I expected her among your entourage."

A stricken look flashed across Thaedoren's face, so pained that Moiran reached for him before she could catch herself. "She attempted to kill me in our own bed the night of the coup. She's been executed."

She let her hand drop. "Was it a clean death?"

"Her ties to my House were severed and she was declared a traitor to the Alvritshai, but it was a clean death. I made certain of that myself."

"Good. You did what was necessary then."

Thaedoren's eyes closed and his head bowed slightly.

When they reopened, his gaze skipped to Daedelan. "We have little time if we are to leave at first light."

"I'll issue the orders to the Phalanx."

"I'm certain Caeden already has, but we should coordinate with his House."

The two began moving away, leaving Moiran behind.

She turned back to her rooms. She had missives of her own to write and send on their way before morning, not least of all to Sovaeren. And she would have to inform the temple of Aeren's death. The people of Rhyssal would need a service, a remembrance ceremony before Aielan's Light, even if Aeren's body had already been burned.

Rubbing at a throbbing ache starting near her temple, she moved to the desk and drew out a fresh sheet of parchment and her quill.

* * *

Fedaureon held up a hand for silence and brought his mount to a halt.

On all sides, the Rhyssal House forces, combined with that of Baene, came to an abrupt stop, flags flashing in the twilight back through the ranks in warning. Everyone held still, the army as silent as it could be. The soft clang of metal and creak of leather filled the road behind, but Fedaureon filtered out those sounds, focusing ahead.

Mattalaen kneed his horse to Feaureon's side, leaned in close. "What did you hear?"

"A moan, I think." Fedaureon tilted his head, straining. "Something."

Daevon sidled up on his other side. "The scouts would have reported anything untoward."

"We haven't heard from the scouts in over an hour. And we're nearing a village. We crossed into Peloroun's House lands yesterday. The scouts should have reported back by now."

"Lorannen is just ahead, at the crossroads." Mattalaen tugged at his horse's reins, surveyed the darkening forest ahead, then motioned six of the nearest men forward. Behind, Fedaureon saw Renaerd making his way to the front of the army and cursed silently to himself.

"Split into three groups," Mattalaen ordered, "and search the road ahead and on either side. Report back in twenty minutes."

The men nodded and dismounted, one group heading up the road, the other two branching off to either side. Within moments, they'd vanished into the gloom.

Renaerd's panting breath warned Fedaureon of his approach long before Daevon leaned forward with a murmured, "Lord Presumptive."

Trying not to sigh, Fedaureon turned as Renaerd reached the back of Fedaureon's escort.

"Why have we stopped?" the lord of House Baene demanded.

Since his arrival in Hallieas, his opinion of Renaerd had plummeted. He'd met the lord presumptive on many occasions in Caercaern, at bondings or ceremonies before Aielan, or events held by other Houses, but he had never had to deal with him on a regular basis. The newly risen lord was arrogant, condescending, and in many ways childish. He'd been protected by his mother, ignored by his father, and carried about him a sense of entitlement that grated on Fedaureon's bones.

Fedaureon would have abandoned him at Hallieas, but he needed Renaerd's Phalanx if he had any hope of defeating Peloroun and Lotaern.

"We're coming up on the village of Lorannen, yet we haven't heard back from our scouts yet. Something's wrong."

Renaerd looked in the direction of the village. "Are you certain? Maybe—"

Mattalaen suddenly grabbed Fedaureon's arm, cutting Renaerd off with a sharp, "My lord."

Fedaureon turned to find two of the guardsmen Mattalaen had sent out sprinting through the forest toward them.

"What is it?" Fedaureon asked, suddenly tense. His escort shifted position to protect him.

"One of the scouts, my lord. We found his body ahead, off the road."

"How did he die?" Mattalaen was already gesturing orders to the Phalanx behind him. Fedaureon heard softly barked commands, the ranks behind shifting, the newly fallen night suddenly tense. "Could you tell? Was it Peloroun?"

"I don't think so. I saw no wounds from a cattan, only claw marks. He'd been disemboweled."

"Claw marks?" Renaerd spat. "Are you saying he was killed by some wild animal?"

"No wild animal I know of," the guardsman said, then added a hasty, "my lord."

Fedaureon thought instantly of the Wraiths. But none of the stories he'd heard from his father and Shaeveran had mentioned claws. The Wraiths were Alvritshai, dwarren, and humans turned by the sukrael.

Yet the dwarren legends spoke of other creatures.

"An animal attack may have claimed one scout's life, but all of them? Where are the others?"

"They should have reported in. We'll continue forward, but I want an advance group ten minutes ahead of us to give us warning, and I want you surrounded by an escort until we know what we're dealing with. No arguments."

Another group of Phalanx broke off from the main force, heading forward without their mounts, crashing through the forest with less stealth than the previous scouts. Fedaureon found himself and Renaerd at the center of a combined group of Rhyssal and Baene Phalanx, Daevon at his side. Mattalaen led the force as they started up again, moving slower, the men more wary than before. Some had drawn their weapons, blades readied, others riding with hands on their cattans. Fedaureon's gaze darted to the shadows beneath the trees on either side. The forest appeared darker than before, deadlier. He twitched at every sound, his attention distracted only by Renaerd's incessant comments to his own Protector on one side.

Fedaureon smelled the smoke before they arrived at the village.

Most of the buildings appeared intact, giving the illusion that nothing was wrong, that the villagers were simply sleeping. But there was no warm glow of candlelight seeping from the cracks around windows or doors, and no welcoming barks from dogs. Nothing in the village moved, except for their own advance force, sweeping from building to building ahead of them.

Then Fedaureon caught sight of low embers pulsing in the husk of what had once been the village's temple. Half of the building still stood— two walls canted at odd angles, charred supports spiking up from the rubble of the other two walls and the collapsed ceiling. As soon as Mattalaen saw the ruins, he motioned additional men forward, the Phalanx spreading out on all sides. A few of the men paused and knelt, and Fedaureon suddenly realized that certain pools of shadow weren't shadows at all, but bodies.

Fedaureon nudged his mount to Mattalaen's side, the elder Phalanx caitan's face hardened into harsh lines, his seat on his horse rigid.

"What's happened?" Fedaureon demanded.

"Someone attacked the village."

"Peloroun? But why?"

"I don't think it was Peloroun. He wouldn't attack his own people, on his own lands. It must be someone else."

"Who?"

Both Fedaureon and Mattalaen turned. Fedaureon hadn't heard the lord of House Baene approach.

Before either could answer, someone cried out from deeper inside the village. The call was taken up by others, and someone close shouted for Mattalaen.

The caitan kicked his horse into motion, Fedaureon, Renaerd, and their Protectors falling in behind. They trotted through the village, Fedaureon picking out more bodies, more damaged buildings. Carts in the street were overturned, and Fedaureon saw no horses or goats or chickens—no animals of any kind.

Ahead, a group of Rhyssal Phalanx stood over a scattering of bodies. "Here, caitan, Lord Presumptive!"

Fedaureon dismounted along with the others. The group of Phalanx peeled back to let them in. Mattalaen knelt by the nearest body, grabbed it by the shoulder, and rolled it over onto its back.

Renaerd cried out and lurched back. Fedaureon's entire body prickled with a cold shudder, but after a few moments he forced himself to step forward and kneel beside Mattalaen. As he did so, he realized the caitan's hand was trembling where it rested on his knee, his other clenched into a tight fist.

"What is it?" Fedaureon asked.

"I've never seen or heard of anything like this before. Have you?"

The creature's skin was smooth but scaled, like that of a snake, but its colors were washed out by the darkness. "Light torches," Fedaureon ordered, the Phalanx passing the order along with relief. As he waited, he leaned closer, caught a whiff of some kind of spice coming from the body, almost like cinnamon, but muskier. The head was rounded, the snout protruding forward, eyes to either side, beneath bony ridges. The neck was thick, bony, heavily muscled, and there appeared to be folds of skin on either side. It wore clothing—a shirt in a thickness and style Fedaureon had never seen before, heavy breeches—made from an unidentifiable fabric, coarser than that of the Alvritshai or humans, more fibrous, although the boots were made of leather. Its hands were scaled as well, with four fingers, each ending in a sharp talon. One clutched an oddly-shaped sword.

"I guess we know what killed the scout," Mattalaen murmured.

Daevon brought one of the torches and held it above the body. The scales were dun-colored, with a few tan and red patches. In the new light, they could see the slits of its nostrils.

Removing his knife, Mattalaen pried open the creature's mouth, revealing the pinkish interior and two whitish fangs. Blood stained the left front of its shirt, where someone had slashed through the cloth and cut deep into the skin beneath with a cattan. Blood had also pooled in the creature's throat, and a clear liquid dripped from its fangs.

"I wouldn't touch that," Mattalaen warned.

"I wasn't planning on it. Is this the only one? Are there others?"

Daevon answered. "It appears this is the where the villagers managed to resist the attack. My guess is that the army—"

"The Wraith army. It has to be. It's certainly not the dwarren or the humans."

"The Wraith army, then. They attacked unexpectedly and without warning. They killed most of the villagers, but a few managed to get weapons and defend themselves." Fedaureon stood as Daevon motioned toward the rest of the bodies strewn around them. "There are four villagers dead here, all carrying cattans, and two more of the creatures. It looks as if they were covering some villagers who were trying to flee."

Fedaureon glanced up the now torch-lit roadway heading north and saw scattered bodies all along its length. With Mattalaen, Fedaureon checked them all, lingering over the strange snake men. The last carried a satchel, hidden beneath his body. Fedaureon began sorting through it, Mattalaen standing over him, perusing the village.

"Most of the villagers died by the sword. If this is the work of the Wraith army, do you know what that means?"

"We're behind them. We missed Peloroun and Lotaern. They must be fleeing north, toward Caercaern."

"Unless they're working with the Wraiths," Daevon said.

Before Fedaureon could come up with an appropriate response, Renaerd stamped to a halt five paces away. "I heard you talking about a Wraith army. The Wraiths can't travel these lands. We're protected by the Winter Tree."

Fedaureon clutched a few of the items from the snake man's satchel in his hand and stood, facing Renaerd. "The Winter Tree is failing. It has been for over a year now. Shaeveran and my father warned the Evant, but they refused to listen, and Shaeveran was warned that the Wraith armies were already moving. This creature, whatever it is, must be part of that army. And they're headed toward Caercaern."

"Why haven't I heard of this before now?"

"You should have heard of it. It was brought before the Evant. Your father should have informed you." Renaerd shifted uneasily. "You haven't been reading the missives from Caercaern, have you?"

"I never needed to read them before. My father always told me what was important after he returned."

Fedaureon stepped carefully through the bodies, halting barely a hands-breadth away, far too close by Alvritshai protocol. "Your father didn't return this time. Or hadn't you noticed? You're the lord of House Baene now, Renaerd. You'd better start acting like it."

Renaerd huffed in protest, then spun on his heel and stormed off, motioning his Protector to his side.

Fedaureon watched him in silence.

"What do you intend to do now?" Mattalaen asked. "Facing Lord Peloroun was foolhardy. Facing an unknown army of creatures under the command of the Wraiths..."

Fedaureon glanced down at the two vials of clear liquid, hollow tube, and bundle of feathered darts in his hands. "We have no choice. We follow the Wraith army."

"And if Peloroun and Lotaern are working with them?"

"Then we fight them all."

13

The deep-toned bells of the main cathedral in Corsair rang out over the city as dawn broke, rays of light streaming through the narrow defile that pierced the cliffs to the west and allowed ships access to the large inner bay. Men were already moving along the docks, loading cargo holds, or offloading shipments to the warehouses strung all along the northern shore. The lower streets teemed with carts and wagons heading toward the markets, smoke rising from baker shops and inns. Gulls wheeled overhead, their raucous caws harsh against the smoother clangs from the church. Moments later, additional bells joined the first from all across the city, and those not already awake began to stir.

Deep inside the cathedral, the priests of Diermani roused themselves, some heading toward the kitchens to prepare the daily meals given to the poor, others tending to the lightly attended early morning service, still others moving toward the great library for study and to work on transcribing and copying illuminated texts.

Patris Vorati had walked the hallowed halls of the cathedral for nearly forty years. His sandals flapped against the worn flagstones of the ancient halls that had once been part of the main public chambers until the church had been expanded, the new nave build adjacent to this building nearly three times as large and as grand. He brushed a hand against the aged wood frames of the stained glass windows as he passed, smoothed by decades of polishing and care. He'd long ceased paying attention to the scenes from the Codex depicted in the windows, although he still enjoyed the splash of colors against the stone of the hall.

He passed through the heavy oak doors at the end of the corridor and into the Learner's Hall, so named because this was where all of the artifacts of the church's long history were stored. He grunted in approval as he saw three other younger priests already dusting, a fourth working at a small desk, cataloguing what looked like a small chest with inscriptions carved into its side. He paused at the desk long enough to see that the priest was painstakingly sketching the carvings onto parchment, including the words written in the original tongue of Andover, a translation provided underneath. Patting the priest on the back, he moved deeper into the room, passing tables with stone statues of Diermani with his hand outstretched, paintings of every size, various stylized tilted crosses, armor from the Legion, tapestries, chests containing vestments and chalices, silver braziers and gold scepters, and a thousand other objects collected over the last two hundred and fifty years, since the church here in Corsair was founded, nothing more than a stone building at the center of a tiny port on the edge of unknown lands.

Vorati brushed a few of his favored artifacts as he passed, pausing to pick up a carved wooden bowl once used during the marriage rituals, running his hand down the side of a silk banner with a depiction of the ten Families of the Court from Andover. Then he reached his own desk, a massive piece, more like a table, carved with intricate scrollwork on its sides. A dusky mahogany, it contained animals rampant, detailed etchings of leaves and vines, and multiple symbols from the Codex woven throughout. He had spent twenty years at this desk, in this room, and every week he still found details in the carving that he hadn't noticed before.

He sat and opened the massive tome set before his seat, flipping toward a new page. The desktop was littered with an assortment of objects he had not yet catalogued. Removing fresh ink and a quill from a drawer to one side, he dipped the nub and began to write, recording the date, location, and his name. Then he reached for the nearest object, a small knife used to open missives when the wax seal needed to be preserved.

He'd just begun to draw the knife's shape into the tome when he felt a pulse of energy.

He paused, knife held up to the lantern one of his fellow priests had lit for him, and stared out into the room, a frown touching his lips. The priests of Diermani used His god-given powers, of course, but no one should be using them here, in this chamber. They were reserved for rituals, for marriage vows, for the services performed in the nave and the cathedral's main chambers. They were rarely used elsewhere.

Yet he felt the pulse again. And now that he was attuned to it, he realized that it continued with a steady beat, like a heartbeat.

He set the knife down, placed the quill back in the inkpot and stood, his frown deepening. "Gregori, Bacchurus, what are you doing? You know you cannot use Diermani's power here, even in order to practice."

Gregori appeared around the side of a large armoire, his face creased in consternation. "What are you talking about? I'm not using Diermani's power. And neither is Bacchurus. He's right here."

Bacchurus' red head popped up on the other side of the room. "I don't feel anything."

Vorati huffed in disgust. "Well, someone's using it. I can feel it from here. It's a low throb." He began searching the nearby area, ignoring the look that passed between the two younger priests and their shrug as they went back to work. Mumbling to himself about youth and its arrogance, he moved deeper into the artifacts, turning when the intensity of the pulse faded, moving forward when it strengthened. Dust rose up around him and he cursed the other priest's inefficiency in dusting, then tripped over a footstool and caught himself against a lattice cabinet.

Straightening, his eye caught a faint light to one side.

He sucked in a sharp breath. "Gregori, Bacchurus, come here."

"Where?"

"Here. Just follow my cursing!"

Struggling over a low settee, he pulled aside a cloth covering a large mirror. Behind it sat a small, ornate, wooden table, an orb resting in a scrolled indentation in the center. The orb glowed with a soft white light, but there was something darker trapped within.

Vorati leaned forward, the sounds of the other two priests struggling to reach him coming from behind. He reached out a hand to shade his eyes, trying to see what was inside the orb.

He stood abruptly, just as Gregori and Bacchurus came up to his side. Both of them gasped and genuflected, but Gregori was the first to recover.

"What is it? And what's floating around inside it?"

Taking a deep breath to steady himself, Vorati said, "Blood. And this is the Hand of Diermani."

Both of his fellow priests looked confused.

"Send for the caddonis and the arruli. Now!"

                              * * *

"What is it?" Justinian said.

Standing two paces behind him, next to the throne, Roland had the same question.

Caddonis Liandau hunched his shoulders, although his face remained sober. Two of the patri flanked him, the elder man on the left fidgeting as if he were restraining himself from speaking, clearly agitated. The patris on the right appeared bored.

"It is the Hand of Diermani," the caddonis intoned, his voice full and rich enough to reach the corners of the throne room. Its cadence was soothing, although Roland knew it could contain a sharp edge when needed, based on the masses he'd attended at the cathedral over the years.

"That doesn't answer the King's question," Matthais said.

Roland half turned in the other advisor's direction. Matthais mirrored Roland's position; Tyrik stood with Roland. Members of the Legion lined the walls and guarded the door, even though the caddonis and his escort were well known. Tensions had been high since half of the Legion's forces had departed to the south. Rumors had spread through the city like a disease and the citizens had grown restless. Some had even packed up and departed, although Roland wasn't certain where they intended to flee; the rumors weren't specific enough about the dangers. The plains were no haven: everyone knew of the storms and the resurgence of the deadly Drifters, not to mention the still-feared dwarren. Which left only the Arduon Ocean and the Court of Andover to the west, and the Alvritshai to the north.

"I believe what the king's advisor meant to ask was, what is the Hand of Diermani?" Roland said.

Liandau bowed toward Justinian, with a slight inclination toward Roland. "My apologies, my liege. The Hand of Diermani is..." the caddonis hesitated, twisting toward the agitated patris before continuing, "...well, it's a signal of a sort. A warning."

"A warning of what?" Tyrik asked.

"I believe Patris Vorati would be better at explaining its purpose. He is responsible for the cataloguing of Holy Diermani's artifacts and is more familiar with our history."

Liandau gestured toward the elder patris, who stepped forward with a stiff, formal bow immediately. He began to speak before he'd finished. "At the time the Families were setting up colonies here in New Andover, the church realized that the major ports were extremely isolated and vulnerable, especially on a coast that had not yet been fully explored. They decided they needed a way to warn each other of potential threats, something more reliable and faster than sending a messenger overland, or a ship up along the shore. So they created the Hands of Diermani."

He motioned to the low table and the softly glowing orb that rested at its center. Everyone's attention returned to the pulsating light as he continued, Matthais stepping forward for a closer look.

"Each of the major cathedrals in each of the Provinces has one of the Hands. When the Province is threatened, the head of the cathedral, along with the lord of the city, can activate the Hand in their respective church, which will cause all of the orbs in each of the remaining Provinces to begin pulsing like this. It is a warning that one of the Provinces is in trouble. It is a call for help."

"What's swirling in the orb's center? It looks like blood."

Roland frowned at Matthais' question, shifting forward so he could see the orb better as well.

"It is blood. In order to activate the orb, the lord of the Province must be present. This is the blood of one of the lords."

"Which one? Which Province is threatened?"

"I believe it is Temeritt."

Matthais' eyebrows rose. "You believe? You aren't certain?"

Liandau answered. "Once the orb is activated, members of the church should be able to communicate with each other by touching the orb. We have all attempted to speak to those in Temeritt, but we haven't made contact yet. I don't understand why they haven't responded. I would have left one of the patri in attendance at all times until the message had been passed on."

"Perhaps the threat is not that serious," Matthais said dismissively.

"Or perhaps it is so significant that they did not have a patris to spare," Roland countered.

"Or it may be neither. It may be as simple as those in Temeritt not knowing that the orb could be used for communication. The Hands of Diermani were created over two hundred years ago and have been used rarely since. They may not truly understand how they work. Or they may have attempted to communicate, but gave up when there was no response. Our own Hand was locked away in the artifact room, lost among stacks upon stacks of forgotten objects and lost items. I have no idea how long ago the Hand was activated before it was noticed. It could have been months."

Roland turned toward Justinian. "I believe this verifies our suspicions that something has happened within the eastern Provinces, my liege."

Justinian edged forward onto his seat. "Enough to warrant joining our army headed to Goran?"

"That is for you to decide. You are the king."

Justinian glanced toward Matthais and Tyrik out of habit, but neither one of the two advisors said anything. Then he stood. "Ready an escort. We will depart for Portstown on the next tide."

"As you command."

Justinian descended from the dais and headed to the door, Legionnaires falling into position around him. The caddonis and patri bowed low, Liandau genuflecting and muttering an invocation under his breath.

"My lord," Matthais said, voice raised to catch Justinian before he'd made it halfway down the throne room's length. "As you and Roland have pointed out many times in the past, I do not have a military mindset. I do not believe I'd be of much use to you as an advisor during this... excursion. I would like to remain behind, here in Corsair."

Justinian's eyes narrowed in suspicion, but Tyrik interceded. "I, too, do not feel I would contribute much on this journey, my liege. At my age, I may simply slow you down."

The king glanced between the two before saying, "Very well. You both will be responsible for Corsair while I am gone."

Roland waited until the king had left before confronting Matthais. "Watch yourself, Matthais."

The former regent scowled as he straightened. "I will watch over Justinian's kingdom as if it were my own." Then he sidled closer and whispered, eyes wide, "But what of your mysterious army headed north? Have you abandoned that nonsense?"

Without waiting for a response, the rotund advisor trailed after the king.

"Don't fret," Tyrik said. The elder councilor had drifted up behind Roland. "I'll keep an eye on him."

"I'm not leaving you here alone to deal with him yourself. Commander Houndell will remain behind to oversee the Legion. I'll get Justinian to proclaim all three of your as overseers while we are gone. Then you'll have the power to overrule Matthais, if necessary."

Someone cleared their throat and both advisors turned to find the caddonis and the patri standing unobtrusively to one side. Roland motioned to the pulsing orb.

"Caddonis Liandau, please keep trying to contact whoever activated the Hand of Diermani. Any information you can learn from them would be appreciated."

"Of course, Commander Roland. I will pass on anything we learn directly to Tyrik and Matthais."

Roland nearly asked him to report only to Tyrik, but couldn't figure out a way to do so without appearing to counter the king's orders. He merely nodded, then walked with Tyrik to the hall's doors.

As soon as they were in the corridor outside, he said, "Send whatever they may find directly to me. Use the Legion. Don't rely on Matthais and the messenger pigeons."

"I wouldn't dream of it."

They halted at the main entrance to the palace and Roland gripped Tyrik's shoulder. "Be careful."

"Always, commander. This is the palace after all."

* * *

On the edge of dwarren lands, GreatLord Went of Rendell leaned forward over the neck of his steed as it charged across the snow covered plains behind Legion Commander Uthur. A string of Legionnaires trailed behind them, their mounts galloping across the low rolling hills beyond the Highplains River, the official boundary between Rendell and what the dwarren called the Land. Frigid wind struck Went's face, his skin already burned red with the cold. His breath came in puffs of white that had frozen in white particles in his short-cropped beard, yet sweat plastered his underclothes to his body, slick and tacky from the exertion of the ride. He cursed the heavy clothing that he knew he couldn't discard, not with the cold that had sagged suddenly southward weeks before and seized hold of the northern Province. Every augury posed by the believers and the charlatans in Rendell predicted that this cold snap was only the beginning; there was even more bitter cold to come. The roiling bank of clouds he could see to the north, now that they were beyond the lesser mountain range of the Claw, supported those claims. It obscured even the Alvritshai's Hauttaeren Mountains, and it was moving slowly south.

Ahead, Uthur shouted and pointed to the northeast, his horse angling in that direction a moment later. Went caught sight of a group of Legion against the white landscape, one of them waving the yellow banner of the king.

Wind roaring in his ears, Went veered after the Legion commander, thinking that this excursion had better bear fruit or he would have sharp words with Uthur, no matter that the orders had come from the king. Justinian was still young. He owed Went's loyalty not to his actions, but to the Gallatia name and Went's respect of the boy's father, Davin. Justinian had yet to prove himself.

As soon as he crested the next low ridge, all of Went's doubts died. Even half obscured by wind-blown snow, he knew immediately what the wide tract of churned dirt and mud and grass meant.

An army. A large army, since the roiled earth cut a path across the plains at least five hundred feet wide.

He pulled his horse up sharply, even though Uthur had continued on toward the waiting group of Legion. He was still scanning the path of the army—the swath running north-northwest to south-southeast—when Brandon, Legion Commander of Rendell, drew to a halt beside him.

"Diermani's Balls," the Legionnaire swore, twisting the reins of his anxious mount and dragging it back under control. "The bastard's report was right."

"My thoughts exactly." Went wasn't certain who Brandon meant to be the bastard, but he assumed it was Uthur, not the king.

Uthur was waiting on foot when they arrived, one hand steadying Went's horse as he dismounted.

"How long ago did they pass through?" Went demanded.

"The last storm passed through here five days ago, according to your reports. It didn't drop much snow, but it did freeze the ground pretty hard. Best guess is that the army passed through here a few days before that." Uthur passed Went's horse off to a Legionnaire, then led Went and Brandon past the group. They crunched across the crusted layer of snow, grass flattened to the ground beneath it, then onto the rough earth where the army had marched through.

Brandon knelt immediately, digging into the ground with one hand, holding up a clump of dirt, then letting it fall as he began pacing across the stretch of land, staring intently at the footprints and marks the army's passage had left behind. Went watched him a moment, then turned to Uthur.

"What of the dwarren? What did they say about this?"

"We haven't seen the dwarren since we came here."

"We're on their lands right now, entered their domain as soon as we passed the Highplains River. You weren't stopped and questioned once you crossed?"

"No. We expected to be met by a group of their Riders, but we've seen nothing. No Riders, no patrols, no sign of them or their gaezel. The plains are empty."

For the first time, a niggling worm of fear crept into Went's stomach. "Where have they gone?" He glanced down at the tracks in the earth. "Was this made by them?"

"No," Brandon said, approaching them again. He motioned to the soil. "These tracks were not made by dwarren or gaezel. They're too large."

"Then who made them?"

Uthur seemed about to speak, but waited to hear Brandon's response.

"Some of the tracks are obvious. There's a large contingent of cavalry. They appear to be leading the force, which means most of their

tracks have been obliterated by those following behind. The other tracks,"
he shook his head, pulled on the short hairs of his gray-peppered beard at
the jaw. "They haven't been made by any animal I know."

"What do you mean?" Brandon had always been one of Went's best
trackers.

"I mean, I can't identify them. They aren't human, Alvritshai, or
dwarren. They aren't made by pack animals—not horse, mule, oxen,
gaezel. There *are* some of those types of tracks, along with wagon ruts, I
assume for the army's supplies, but the majority of the tracks and spoor...
it's not made by any creature I've ever seen."

Uthur didn't appear surprised. "What can you say about them?"

Brandon stared at the king's Legion commander a long moment before
kneeling and pointing to the depressions in the earth to one side. Both
Uthur and Went crouched down as well.

"See this tri-toed impression, with a fourth toe toward the back? This
belongs to a lizard, except that it's about ten times larger than it should be.
And based on the depth of the track and those around it, this lizard is
standing upright."

Went snorted in disbelief, but Uthur's face was serious as he said, "Go
on."

"Then there's this mark here." He pointed to a much lighter
indentation behind the lizard's print in the shape of an S. "This appears
with all of the other lizard prints. I'd guess that whatever they are, they
have tails that they use at least partially for support. This is the swish of
the tail as they move. These lizard men were marching at a fairly steady
rate."

Uthur sat back slightly, met Brandon's gaze. "What else?"

Went's chest tightened. "You can't possibly believe that there are
lizard men walking the dwarren plains?"

"The king sent me here to find out whatever I could. I intend to do
that."

"There are no such creatures as lizard men!"

"You know this for certain? Before humans landed on this shore, we
would have said there were no such creatures as Alvritshai or dwarren,
Shadows or Wraiths. The dwarren came to the king with a warning that
the Wraiths had formed an army, and according to the king, the dwarren
mention snake-like creatures in their legends of the Turning."

"You heard this from the king?"

"From Roland Dubanar, Legion commander and advisor to the king.
He gave me a full report before sending me north to find this army.

Tracks like these were found east of the Escarpment months ago.

"Now," he turned back to Brandon, "continue."

Brandon stood and led them to another part of the churned earth, Went trailing behind. He wanted to call all of this nonsense off, except he knew Roland, had sparred with the commander on occasion, had hunted with him when the former king had accepted one of Went's invitations. Roland would never have sent Uthur with that information if there wasn't some basis for it. But...lizard men!

"Here," Brandon said.

"That's a boot print."

"Yes, but it has the swish of the lizard men's tail behind it. I think some of them wear boots. Judging by the weight, probably armor as well, since these depressions are deeper than the others. And here. This is a track I've never seen before, man or beast." He motioned to a rounded mark with three blunt toes along the front edge.

"It's huge."

"Nearly two hands across. And much deeper than any of the other markings. Whatever it is, it's massive. Every now and then, the tracks are accompanied by this." He pointed to another depression. "It looks like the imprint of a fist, as if the creature lumbered across the plains and caught its weight every now and then with one fist."

"Trolls," Uthur muttered under his breath.

Went threw up his hands in disgust and stalked away, halting only when he realized that Brandon and Uthur had not followed. Instead, Brandon was pointing out further tracks in the frozen ground, the two shifting back and forth as Brandon spoke. Went was too distant to pick out the entire conversation, but he heard Brandon speaking of claw marks, cat-like creatures, and more about boot prints. He fumed as he scanned the edge of the storm building to the north, black clouds roiling, then turned east.

His disgust faltered when his thoughts returned to the dwarren and the strange emptiness he felt here on their lands. The dwarren plains had never felt empty. Whenever he'd ventured onto the Land before, his neck would prickle, as if he were being watched.

But not now.

When Uthur and Brandon drifted back toward him, Went asked, "Which direction is the army of beasts headed?"

"North."

"The dwarren would never have allowed an army of such size through their lands." He turned on Uthur. "You intend to follow it, don't you?"

"The king didn't order such, but yes. I want to know who they are and where they are headed. I need to know if they're a threat to the Provinces."

"I and the Legion of Rendell will join you."

Uthur's eyebrows rose in surprise. "What of the Winter Ball?"

Went waved a hand negligently. "The Winter Ball is my wife's affair. She can hold it without me. I prefer to hunt."

"Ready your men, then. And send for any others you wish to join us. We'll head north tomorrow, following the army's trail."

The king's commander broke toward his own men and Brandon stepped up to Went's side as they headed toward Rendell's forces. Went's commander waited until Uthur was out of earshot before asking, "What changed your mind?"

"The dwarren. Can't you feel it? They aren't here. They've abandoned their lands, and I've had enough dealings with the dwarren to know that they would defend the Land to the death. And yet now an army marches through it unmolested. I don't know who was in that army, but I don't intend to let it roam so close to my own Province without finding out why and where they are headed.

"It still leaves us with a disturbing question," he added, casting one last glanced over the plains as one of his men brought his steed forward to meet them. He patted the animal's side, then heaved himself up into the saddle, the Rendell Legion around them assembling as Brandon did the same.

"What's that?" Brandon asked as they kicked the animals into motion.

"Where in hells are the dwarren?"

* * *

"I do not think we will find any more survivors, Archon."

Quotl looked up at Azuka from the fire he had been staring at for...he didn't know how long, he realized. He raised a hand and wiped at the exhaustion around his eyes, felt the tightness of the skin there, the grittiness from lack of sleep and the constant dust that filled the tunnels as the dwarren attempted to dig through the collapse of the Sacred Waters. Many of the tunnels had been abandoned as they filled with water, the great confluence of the northern rivers attempting to find new pathways now that the main conduit they had followed for thousands of years was blocked. Of those tunnels they had been able to reach, only a few dwarren had been rescued. Most of those they found were already dead, their bodies removed from the rubble and laid to rest in a few designated side chambers where the combined shamans of the clans performed last rites and ushered their spirits into Ilacqua's arms.

But even those they found were few. Thousands would remain buried in the chamber they'd attempted to flee. Their deaths weighed heavily upon Quotl's heart, but he shouldered that burden without regret as he focused on Azuka's face in the fire-lit room he'd secured for himself. With the Cochen dead, along with all of the clan chiefs who had been with them, responsibility for the dwarren who remained had fallen to him. He had been the one to pull the dwarren left out of their despair and get them organized into search parties. He had used his station as Archon to send out war parties to clear the tunnels of any remaining factions of the Wraith army.

And now it was time for him to gather whatever remained of the dwarren race and lead them in the Cochen's stead.

Rising, he acknowledged Azuka with a weary wave. "Call off the search and have all of the clans assemble in the main chamber. I'll address them from there."

"What are you going to do?" If Azuka hadn't been at Quotl's side for the last twelve years, Quotl would have simply glared at the impertinence of the question, but here, now, he merely sighed.

"I intend to escort the dead into Ilacqua's arms. And then I intend to lead our army from this place."

"But where will we go? What will we do?"

Quotl thought of the last vision given to him by Ilacqua, in the spat out char of the fire. "The Turning continues. There are still battles to be fought."

Azuka straightened and nodded before stepping out. Quotl heard him speak to the Riders who stood guard outside, then his footsteps faded into the distance.

Reaching down to the pouch at his side, Quotl withdrew his pipe, tapped it out on the edge of the firepit, then packed it with leaf and lit it with an ember from the fire. He puffed contentedly a moment, then began roaming around the small chamber, collecting his few remaining things, packing them in pouches and saddlebags. All of the ancient accoutrements of the Archon had been lost in the tunnels, buried with all of the rest of the dwarren, gaezel, and Wraith forces. He felt no great loss himself, but a pang of regret tightened his chest at the loss of his scepter. He had carried the symbol of the head shaman of the Thousand Springs clan nearly his entire life, knew its worn edges and smoothed depressions like the back of his hand. He'd tied many of the feathers and beads and snake rattles to it himself.

Now, he picked up the replacement scepter he'd been given. No carvings had been etched into its side, although he had taken the time to tie a few symbolic elements to its end with lengths of cured gut. A few rattles from the other shamans, a hawk's feather in honor of his vision in the keeva, a braided length of his own beard. The other shamans had also provided him with ritualistic elements from their own satchels—seeds and pouches of dirt, vials of water and packets of dried spices. He gathered all of these, then settled before the fire again and enjoyed the last of his pipe.

A short while later, Azuka reappeared. "We're ready. A few of the Riders are still out on patrol or are guarding the tunnels."

"Are the shamans ready?"

"Yes, Archon."

Quotl followed him out the door. They filed down the corridor, Riders falling into guard both ahead and behind. That was also new. Before, the Archon would have been nearly autonomous, going where he pleased more or less unaccompanied. The Riders stuck with their Cochen or with their clan chiefs and clans. Now, there was only one clan, and the Riders had adopted him as their clan chief. They hadn't allowed him out of their sight since he'd been found in the rubble. There were never less than four of them within spitting distance no matter where he went, except the privacy of his own room, and even then they were waiting less than ten feet away, outside the door.

As soon as he entered the large chamber they'd retreated to after the collapse, the hall fell silent, those nearest at first, conversations ending in a ripple as he cut across the crowded floor toward the stone ledge at the front. The rush of flowing water from the channel that sliced through the chamber along the eastern wall created background noise, nearly muffling the creak of armor as those assembled shifted to follow his passage. The water had run black with sludge for five days, but had finally cleared enough it could be drunk.

His escort of Riders stayed on the floor as he climbed the stone steps to the wide ledge, Azuka following. His fellow shaman motioned a group of six other shamans onto the ledge as well, the dwarren fanning out behind Quotl as he made his way to the edge and cleared his throat.

His gaze swept those assembled, nearly three thousand battered and bruised dwarren, Riders and shamans alike. All that remained of the Cochen's army, the forces of the four clans who had come here to defend the Sacred Waters. Beneath their gazes, he thought suddenly of Kimannen and his last words to Quotl: *Your purpose is to give them hope.*

He raised both arms, scepter in one hand. The room stilled.

"We have suffered a tremendous loss," Quotl began, his voice echoing out over the room, somehow amplified by the architecture. Even Quotl could hear the undertones brought on by the power of the Land flowing through him. "Thousands of dwarren died protecting the Sacred Waters, keeping it from falling into the elloktu's hands. Thousands more would have died if the elloktu's army had succeeded. In fact, everyone in this chamber would have died along with the Cochen and Corranu, Iktamman and Tarramic. It was never the ellokus' intention to seize the Sacred Waters. No, their intention was to destroy it."

At this, a low murmur rose, dwarren shifting position nervously, the mass of Riders and shamans before him eddying like the currents on the surface of a river. Quotl didn't wait for them to settle.

Lowering his arms, he began pacing back and forth at the edge of the ledge.

"The army that we fought, that poured into the chamber from the south and west, was there to divert out attention from the true threat. That came from the tunnels to the east, a small group of gruen who were carrying something of great power. I did not see what it was, but I know what happened.

"Kimannen, your former Archon, was given a vision from the gods at the same time as I. It was Ilacqua's will that I become Archon in Kimannen's place, but not because Kimannen's power was waning. The gods had a different path for Kimannen, head shaman of Claw Lake. In his vision, he saw these gruen and the power they carried. He saw their intention to destroy the Sacred Waters, and he saw that his path was to stop them.

"I watched him, along with his escort of Riders, kill the gruen and seize the object they intended to throw into the Sacred Waters. But something happened." Quotl shook his head. "Something terrible. Whatever the gruen carried awoke. I felt it from my position beneath the Summer Tree. I felt it unleashed. Kimannen must have felt it as well, for he clutched it to him and fled into the catacombs of the eastern wall."

Quotl paused. He knew Kimannen had saved them all, and yet his contempt for the former Archon still roiled within him. He had contemplated for days how to bring the disparate clansmen who had survived together, had prayed to Ilacqua, had attempted to call the gods of the Four Winds and their wisdom to him using the visions brought on by the yetope, yet the gods had remained silent. Because he already knew how to bring the clansmen together, even though it galled him.

He raised his eyes to those gathered. "Kimannen sacrificed himself to save us. Everyone in this room owes their life to him, including me. He gave his spirit to Ilacqua so that we would survive, so that we could continue our fight against the elloktu's forces and bring about the end of this Turning. Darkness is walking the Land. It has crept into our warrens and buried the Sacred Waters and the Summer Tree beneath its weight, but it cannot be allowed to survive. Kimannen has given us this chance! And we will not allow it to slip from our grasp. We will fight the dark armies of the Turning. We will fight to protect the Land!"

A roar rose from the Riders, an ululating cacophony of shouts, battlecries, and yips. The sound enveloped Quotl and he raised his scepter, nodding toward Azuka and the six shamans behind him, who began to chant a death dirge, moving slowly in a dance that would guide the spirits of the massed dead that they could not bury into Ilacqua's arms.

Watching the roar of defiance from the Riders change into a release of pent up grief, Quotl allowed the sorrow that had settled in his own chest to ease. Even the distaste of using Kimannen's sacrifice—one that would undoubtedly become legend—dissolved.

The dwarren remained. And the dwarren had sworn to protect the Land. They had done so in Turnings past, and Quotl would be damned if he'd allow the dwarren to fail during this Turning.

He turned to Azuka. "As soon as the ritual is completed, sound the drums. Call all of the Riders. We're done here."

"Where will we go?"

"To where the elloktu and their armies are. To Caercaern and the Alvritshai. They're going to need our help."

14

Colin trudged forward, feet cracking the brittle layer of salt and dirt that crusted the ground in the Flats. He leaned heavily on his staff as he moved. The sun glared down harshly, and the wind tugged at the layers of clothing he, Eraeth, and Siobhaen wore for protection, but all of the sensations had grown muted and distant. He'd been numbed to them by the weeks spent crossing the gods-forsaken salty land. A parched, arid trek, there had been nothing to break the monotonous flat earth except an occasional plinth of rock or lonely boulder. They'd sheltered during the day as much as possible in the shade, resting so that they could move at night. They'd hoarded their water, after filling their skins before leaving the edges of the Thalloran Wastes. But even then, their water had finally dwindled, the last drops squeezed from the pouches days ago, and they hadn't always been able to find any shade. Colin's lips were cracked and bloody, his skin chafed and burned by the sun, scrubbed raw from the gritty wind, even though he was covered head to toe in cloth. Eraeth and Siobhaen had fared even worse. At least Colin knew that no matter how bad it got, he'd survive.

His foot caught on a protruding edge of bedrock and he fell forward, his body not reacting fast enough to catch himself. He slammed into the soil, salt and dirt particles rising around him in a plume before being caught by the incessant wind and carried away. A deep-seated pain flared in the center of his chest—finally scabbed over—and he gasped and coughed up blood, its taste thick at the back of his throat. Wheezing, he struggled to get his arm beneath him, then froze.

A single withered bunch of grass flailed in the wind a foot in front of him, its highest stalk bent and broken halfway up, its roots partially exposed at the base.

It was the first sign of plant life he'd seen since entering the Flats.

He heard someone cry out, then the crunch of approaching feet, and a moment later both Siobhaen and Eraeth were kneeling at his side.

"Shaeveran! Are you all right?" Eraeth demanded. Siobhaen's hands were already checking along his body.

"I think I tore something in my chest. But look." He pointed toward the dried husk of grass, even as Eraeth rolled him over and sat him up. The pain flared again and he coughed up more blood, the liquid staining the cloth that covered his mouth, but he didn't care. He realized he hadn't even let go of his staff.

"It's dead grass," Siobhaen said hoarsely. Both of their voices were dry, and even though he couldn't see their faces through the coverings, he knew that their lips were as chapped and split as his.

He worked some of the blood he'd coughed up over his lips, wincing at the pain. "When was the last time you saw a plant of any kind? We're close to the end of the Flats. We must be."

He heaved himself to his feet with a groan, leaning heavily on Eraeth. They turned to look south.

Heat smeared the horizon a short distance away, but they could still pick out a few more tufts of dried grass through the haze.

Siobhaen laughed. "Aielan's Light. We made it."

They stumbled forward. The shimmer above the salt plain receded before them, more and more grass appearing, some beginning to show hints of green. Then the ground began to rise. They staggered up the slope and halted at the view spread out before them. Yellowed grass covered the ground, gradually shifting to darker and darker greens. Larger bushes dotted the landscape, and a stand of maybe five scraggly trees. Far distant, Colin thought he saw the shimmer of actual water—a creek or river, its banks lush with greenery.

At his side, Eraeth collapsed to his knees, bent forward at the waist, his hands resting on his knees.

Colin knelt beside the Alvritshai. "Eraeth?" The Protector's breath came in ragged gasps, each intake harsher and more strained than the last, as if he couldn't get enough air. "Eraeth, what's wrong?"

"I can't—" Eraeth rasped, then broke into a fit of coughing. "Water."

When he canted to one side, Colin caught his weight. But the Alvritshai was too heavy—or Colin too weakened by their crossing—and he was knocked to the ground.

"Shaeveran," Siobhaen said.

Colin as he crawled to Eraeth's side. "Siobhaen, help me." But the warrior of the Flame remained standing, her eyes shaded from the mid-morning sun. Eraeth was still breathing, the cloth covering his mouth still moving, but when Colin ripped it aside, he gasped.

Eraeth was worse off than Colin had thought, his lips a deathly white, except where they'd cracked and bled and split again. His eyes were crusted with salt, his eyelashes caked, and his already pale skin had dried to near translucence. Patches had cracked and peeled away, one spot on his upper cheek rubbed raw and bleeding by the covering over his eyes.

"Siobhaen!"

"Shaeveran, look."

Colin glanced up, a curt retort dying on his lips as he saw a group of riders heading straight toward them.

He stood, pulling himself up using his staff. "Who is it? Can you see?"

"The banner they carry is some kind of tower against a red field."

"Yhnar, then." He moved ahead of them both. "I'm surprised they're patrolling this far north."

They waited in silence, the group separating until Colin could pick out five individuals, all on horseback, all wearing light armor in the colors of Yhnar. They vanished behind a low hill, but as they neared, they kicked up dust from the dried grasses, the wind taking it east. Neither Siobhaen nor Colin moved as the men slowed their mounts to a trot.

They halted ten paces away, the lead Legionnaire glaring down at Colin, gaze flicking toward Siobhaen and the prostrate Eraeth before returning. "Who are you and what are you doing in Yhnar Province?"

Colin tried to speak, but his voice cracked and splintered into a hacking cough. He spat blood into the grass, one hand raised to keep Siobhaen back behind him when she started forward. He wiped his mouth and tried again. "I'm Colin Harten, and these two Alvritshai are my escorts. We're here to speak with the GreatLord of Yhnar. Do you have any water?"

At mention of the Alvritshai, all of the guardsmen stiffened, but none of them drew weapons. The leader considered for a long moment, but then he fumbled at his belt, producing a water skin. He tossed it to Colin, who immediately turned to Eraeth, his hands shaking as he crouched down and unstoppered the leather pouch. Water spilled across his hand, warm, but glistening in the sunlight. Its rich scent flooded his senses and he gave out a low moan. But Eraeth needed it more and so he dribbled it into the Protector's mouth.

Eraeth choked on it, spluttering without opening his eyes, then began to drink almost reflexively. The liquid stained his skin dark, his clothing darker, what escaped from his lips colored pink with blood.

He let Eraeth drink a little, then withdrew the skin, handing it off to Siobhaen, who stood over them both protectively.

"You should drink first."

"I'll live. You first."

Siobhaen's eyebrows rose, but she didn't argue, taking a pull, swirling it around her mouth, then swallowing it with a grimace of pain. She took another few swallows, then handed it to Colin.

Eraeth hadn't opened his eyes, his breathing steadier, but still shallow.

Colin dribbled more water onto his lips. "Come on, you bastard. This isn't how it's supposed to work. You're supposed to be saving me. That's how it's always been. Aeren would never forgive me if I let you die."

Eraeth drank some more, then began coughing, his eyes fluttering open.

Colin sat back.

Eraeth's eyes found his, his forehead creasing in consternation. "Why am I on the ground?"

Colin snorted and took a long swallow of water. It tasted like the finest wine in all of New Andover...and Andover as well. Washing the blood from his throat, he worked the moisture into his mouth and tongue, then stood and handed the water skin to Soibhaen, turning back to the waiting guardsmen. He heard Siobhaen speaking softly to Eraeth behind him.

"Take us to Yhnar, Lieutenant..."

"Craig. Craig Mills."

"Lieutenant Mills. I need to speak with Tarken Sohn immediately."

"The GreatLord is not in Yhnar."

This startled Colin. "Where is he?"

The lieutenant opened his mouth to respond, then snapped it shut, as if suddenly realizing he may have already said too much. "We'll take you to Yhnar. You can ask your questions there."

He turned and ordered three of his men to dismount. Siobhaen helped Eraeth up into the saddle. The Protector slouched forward but remained seated. Siobhaen took a gelding, while Colin took the third, a muscular brown mare with a black mane. He could have slowed time and reached Yhnar within hours, but he felt too weak from his wound and the trek across the salt flats. Besides, he didn't want to leave the Alvritshai alone with these men, not after the sharp looks of suspicion once they knew who they were. Something had obviously happened in the southern Provinces to set these men on edge. Colin needed to know what as soon as possible.

Seated, he spun his horse toward Lieutenant Mills. "Lead the way, as swiftly as possible."

The Legionnaire gave orders for those unmounted to return to the patrol camp and report, then kneed his horse into motion, heading south and slightly east, his second close behind.

Siobhaen and Eraeth followed, Colin bringing up the rear.

* * *

Two days later, Colin's group and their escort—now grown to seven Legion, the other five men picked up at various camps along the way— broke from the edges of a forest, the road ahead leading down to the banks of a river, then snaking into the distance. The river split, one branch heading east, the other south. In the land between, grassland rose in wide, rolling hills toward a fat, rounded tower surrounded by a formidable wall. Smoke rose from the tower and from numerous unseen buildings inside the wall. Yhnar wasn't as sprawling as Temeritt—it certainly didn't hold as many people—but it was still a sizable city. Unlike Temeritt, there was only the one set of defensive walls outside of the one that surrounded the palace, barracks, and cathedral; it hadn't been around long enough to grow enough in size to warrant more.

"Is that Yhnar?" Eraeth asked as Lieutenant Mills led the group along the road toward the river without pause. The Protector had recovered slowly over the last two days, but he still wasn't back to his usual strength. Siobhaen had fared much better.

"Yes. The farthest eastern Province, on the edges of human lands."

"Because no one has dared to venture through the Thalloran Wastes to the lands beyond," Siobhaen said.

"There are other options besides the wastelands," Colin said. "Ships that have set out from the cliffs along Yhnar's coastline have reported land not that far off. In fact, it appears to be merely a massive inlet, or perhaps an inland sea. No one's completely certain. All they know at the moment is that there's land, the shore surrounded by massive cliffs, their heights typically shrouded in fog or clouds. They haven't discovered a safe port or beach yet, although sailors report seeing massive stone ruins on some of the cliff heights."

"Like the ruins we saw in the desert?"

"They haven't gotten close enough to tell. They've only seen them at a distance."

Siobhaen muttered under her breath, "There's more to this continent than we know, even nearly five hundred years after the Abandonment of the North."

"The humans have explored more of this land in the two hundred years since they've landed than either the dwarren or the Alvritshai in the last thousand. Yet I do not think even we have unearthed even half of the mysteries it holds."

Before either could respond, he felt a tingling through his skin and he turned, facing back along the road they had already traveled.

Far distant, well beyond the forest, black clouds boiled along the horizon, their depths flashing a dark blue-purple bruised color with occasional lightning. The storm was too distant for them to hear thunder, and was traveling away from them, southwest, but Colin didn't need to hear it to know that the storm was unnatural.

"The sarenavriell are still unbalanced," Eraeth said, his voice low.

"The activation of the new Well would have made it worse." Colin turned his back on the storm and what it meant. "I haven't felt the presence of the Autumn Tree since we left the Flats either. We need to find out what's happened while we were in the wastelands."

They crossed the eastern branch of the Serpent River, their horses' hooves clopping on the stone of the bridge, then swept up along the road to the gates of Yhnar. The walls were higher than Colin had estimated, those manning them tense and alert, but Lieutenant Mills cantered through with only a brief pause to speak to the gatekeeper. The scarred man, older than Mills by at least twenty years, eyed Eraeth and Siobhaen suspiciously, but nodded at Mills' words. His eyes never left them as they trotted past.

They rode through the streets, Mills' men closing in on either side. Colin noted they'd picked up five more Legion at the gates. Those on the streets stepped out of the way, most ignoring them, a few giving them curious stares. A procession of children followed as they wound past three and four story buildings crammed tightly together, broken only by alleys or narrow passages that led to courtyards in the back or stableyards at inns or taverns. They passed two small churches, the tilted cross of Holy Diermani reaching into the sky from the spire of one. Signs hung above shop doors, sporting brightly painted depictions of candles, loaves of bread, charging horses, or butting rams. Shingled roofs pitched sharply over gables and dormer windows, and second floors often jutted out over the street. In two places, buildings were built over the street, the horses passing underneath as if through a tunnel. They skirted a marketplace and a plaza, both small in comparison to those in Caercaern or Corsair, but bustling with hawkers and venders nonetheless.

As they drew near the massive tower that Colin knew was Yhnar's palace, he felt Eraeth nudge him from one side. The Protector nodded discreetly to a small group of Legion at the corner of a cross street as they passed. "They have Legionnaires strewn throughout the city. There were extra guards at the gates and patrolling the walls as well."

They passed through a second gate into the tower's courtyard. A stone cathedral, twice the size of any of those they'd seen in the city, rose multiple spires to the sky to the right, a massive barracks with training yard and outbuildings to the left. The rounded base of the tower lay straight ahead.

Colin craned his neck back to stare up at its heights, the banners above flapping in a gusting breeze. Twice as wide as it was tall, the squat tower was riddled with small windows. It was essentially its own self-contained wall.

His gaze fell to the steps leading up to the open double doors banded in iron, flanked on either side of five Legionnaires, all at stiff attention. Lieutenant Mills and their escort had drawn up to the steps and dismounted, stable hands scurrying forward to take their horses after Colin, Eraeth, and Siobhaen removed their pouches, cattans, bows, and staff. Mills spoke to a steward, whose gaze shot toward the three in surprise. Mills motioned them forward.

"Steward Dobbins will show you to a waiting room," Mills said, removing his riding gloves. "I'll speak to Lady Laurelen about your request."

"Thank you, lieutenant."

Mills disappeared up the stairs. Dobbins bowed slightly. "If you will follow me."

They entered the main doorway into a narrow inner room, not much larger than a corridor, another set of iron-bound doors inside that. Colin glanced up and saw murder holes above, caught Eraeth and Siobhaen doing the same. Then they passed into a large foyer with stone flags, a set of steps curving upwards to the left, banners and tapestries lining the walls on all sides between lanterns worked in brass and polished to a high sheen. Dobbins didn't give them time to admire any of it, shuttling them down wide corridors lined with artwork, a few sculptures, and finally depositing them in a small room that contained multiple chairs, tables with arrangements of dried flowers in vases, and an unlit fireplace, all surrounding a low oval table made of inlaid wood. As Colin moved to one of the chairs, he noticed the pattern in the table: a depiction of the known continent of New Andover, including rough outlines of the treacherous straits and the archipelago to the south.

"Wait here," Dobbins said. "A servant will bring you some wine."

The aged steward stepped out and closed the door behind him.

No one sat.   Siobhaen and Eraeth scanned the room, their gazes meeting a moment later.

"At least they didn't take our weapons."

The door opened abruptly, a servant taking a step in before giving a startled cry at the sight of the Alvritshai.   She recovered swiftly, a stern look settling on her face as she trooped to the central table and set down a platter containing a decanter of wine, fine glasses, cheese, bread, and sliced apples.

"Dobbins said to bring you wine," she said, her hands clasped nervously in front of her.   "I thought you might like something to eat. Would you be needing anything else?"

"That will do nicely, Gina, thank you."

The servant spun to the open door, then slid into a curtsey before dashing out behind the regal woman who stood there.   Her gaze swept over all three, intense and intelligent, but landed on Colin last, her lips pursed.

"Who are you and why do you bring Alvritshai into my lands?"

Colin stood frozen, eyes widened, his throat locked.   With his free hand, he reached toward the brown-haired, green-eyed, freckled woman in the doorway and managed a strangled, "Karen?"

The woman's harsh expression broke, eyebrows knitted in a frown.   "I am Laurelen Sohn, Lady of Yhnar and Tarken Sohn's wife."

Even as she spoke, he realized it couldn't be Karen.   He'd left Karen's body on the grassland outside the Ostraell, along with everyone else who'd been a part of that ill-fated wagon train: his parents, Karen's father, the Armory commander Arten, dozens of others.   All dead.   All killed by the life-eating Shadows of the Ostraell.   He had thought that wound had healed over the last two hundred and more years, but it hadn't. And he realized that it would never die, no matter how much time passed, no matter how long he distracted himself.

He heard his breath catch in his throat and he let his arm drop.

"Of course you are," he managed, suddenly feeling too weak to stand, even with his staff as support.   He fell back into one of the chairs.   "Of course you are.   You just look...you look so much like her."

He fumbled with the front of his shirt, his fingers finally finding and closing hard about the vow hidden beneath.   Its edges bit into his palm.

He felt a hand fall to his shoulder and his head jerked up and met Eraeth's gaze.   "You do look like her.   Or at least, what she would have looked like if she'd lived."

"Who was she?"

"If she had survived, she would have been my wife," Colin rasped.

Laurelen's gaze dropped to where his hand clutched his shirt, her head tilting back slightly in understanding. "My sympathies."

"It was a long time ago."

An awkward silence fell, but it did not last long. Laurelen shifted further into the room, two guardsmen slipping in behind her, another barely visible outside. "Who are you?" she asked again, her tone less imperious, but still demanding.

"Colin Harten," he said. He stood, letting Eraeth's hand fall from his shoulder. "Called Shavaeren by the Alvritshai. The Shadowed One by the dwarren."

"Colin Harten is a name out of legend, stolen from the histories of the Provinces. He helped end the conflict between the three races, gave us the Seasonal Trees to protect us. But that was over ninety years ago. Even with the hints surrounding his legend of mystical powers, I find it hard to believe that you are the same man."

Colin pulled back the sleeves of his shirt, revealing the oily darkness that now trailed beneath his skin all the way to his wrists, tendrils reaching toward the backs of his hands.

Laurelen's eyes widened, her breath catching...but only for a moment. "Colin Harten was not the only man tainted by the so-called Well of Sorrows. The Wraiths were as well."

"The Wraiths could not travel this close to the Autumn Tree."

"The Autumn Tree is dead. Burned to a charred husk by the army that surrounds Temeritt even now. Forces that contain Alvritshai warriors." Her gaze shot toward Eraeth and Siobhaen. "So I ask again, why do you bring Alvritshai onto my lands?"

But Colin didn't hear the question. A roaring filled his ears, as if a great wind screamed past him, like the scouring winds of the Flat. "Dead?" he heard himself whisper, as if from a distance. "The Autumn Tree is dead?"

Someone else was speaking, and he saw Siobhaen moving forward, the guards reacting by drawing swords, stepping in front of Laurelen, Siobhaen halting, hands raised. Reaching with his powers, he tried to sense the presence of the Tree. He had known the Tree was under attack over a year ago, had felt the attack while they were at the Sacred Waters through the Summer Tree, but he had not thought the Wraiths and their armies would have been able to move so quickly as to have destroyed the Autumn Tree already, even with the activation of the Source in the wasteland.

Yet he could not feel the Autumn Tree's presence, could not sense its protective shroud. And what else had Laurelen said? Alvritshai at Temeritt?

Alvritshai...

He snapped back into the room, the winds receding, replaced by Eraeth, Siobhaen, and the two guardsmen threatening each other, two additional guards now protecting Laurelen. Only the Yhnar Legion had blades bared, but he could tell Eraeth and Siobhaen were close to drawing their cattans.

"Hold! Eraeth, Siobhaen, quiet!"

The two Alvritshai backed down, the Yhnar Legion breaking off after a quiet command from Laurelen.

Colin caught the Lady of Yhnar's gaze. "The Alvritshai attacking Temeritt—"

"Besieging it," one of the guardsmen interjected.

"—besieging it, then...they wear black and gold, yes? With an eagle's talon as a House symbol?"

"So we've been told by the one messenger that managed to break free of the siege and bring us word."

"Those are the colors of House Duvoraen, led by Lord Khalaek."

"The lord banished and executed at the Escarpment, bringing about the Accord?"

"You've read the histories."

"They were part of my training, yes."

Colin shifted toward the untouched tray of wine and food and poured four glasses. "What you do not know is what happened after Khalaek's banishment and death. His House fell and a new House was risen— Uslaen, led by Saetor. Those of House Duvoraen became members of Uslaen immediately, but not all. Some of them felt the Alvritshai's Evant had betrayed Khalaek and House Duvoraen, even knowing what Khalaek had done. They felt cut off, adrift, disillusioned, and Houseless. So they left."

"They abandoned their House for another?" Laurelen hadn't moved, still shielded by the Legion. Eraeth and Siobhaen had stepped back.

Colin picked up one of the glasses of wine and sipped it. "Some of them abandoned Alvritshai lands altogether. No one in Caercaern knew where they had gone. I think they formed their own House, a version of House Duvoraen, in the Thalloran Wasteland, where they were found by the Wraiths and absorbed into the Wraith army. I've seen them. They were traveling with an army of creatures I've never seen before, heading toward dwarren lands."

"What were you doing in the wastelands?"

"I was attempting to stop the Wraiths from destroyed the Seasonal Trees. I failed."

Laurelen still appeared suspicious, but she said something to the guards and they parted, letting her through. They did not sheath their blades. "Describe the creatures you saw in this army."

"About a third of it was Alvritshai, all dressed in black and gold. Another third were snake-like people, a race that lives in the Thalloran Wastelands, in cliffs on the edge of a ruined city. The rest were a conglomeration of many kinds of creatures: bird-like flyers with leather wings, hulking creatures with skin like stone, smaller cat-like ones with luminous eyes, a few others."

Laurelen shared a glance with one of the guards. Looking closer, Colin realized he was of higher rank than the rest, a lieutenant commander.

"Like those described by the messenger," the Legionnaire said.

"Some." She turned her attention back to Colin. "There were no snake-like creatures at Temeritt. But the rest..." Her lips thinned. "If you are who you say you are, why have you come here, to Yhnar? What do you intend to do?"

"I was hoping to speak to the lord of the Province, find out what has happened since I've been in the wastelands, determine where I should go next. What news do you have? Where is Tarken Sohn?"

"The Lord of Yhnar is headed to Temeritt to aid Lord Kobel," she said succinctly. "Now, tell me how you and the Alvritshai ended up here in Yhnar. If I believe you, then I will tell you what I know of Temeritt, the Autumn Tree, and the Wraith army that has attacked us."

* * *

Gregson lurched back from the crenellation in the outer wall of Temeritt, an arrow from the Horde snapping hard into the stone and shattering on impact. Flecks of stone and wood pattered against the side of his face. He cursed and jostled back into position, leaning out over the edge to stare down at the dark throng of the Horde below, moving like waves on an ocean. Their roar of anger and hatred slammed up the wall, drowning out the screams from the Legion defending the parapet. To the left, a group of Legion upended a cauldron of hot oil onto the forces below, the creatures below shrieking as it struck, while arrows lanced from the black and gold ranks of Alvritshai at the rear of the Horde's forces. A soldier next to Gregson took one in the chest, his scream fading as he toppled from the rampart, his body vanishing below. To the right, men rallied around where the Horde had managed to get two ladders up the walls, throwing stones onto the cat-like creatures as they scrambled up the ladder's length. Someone hooked the top of the ladder with a spike and shoved, the ladder tilting back, then beginning a slow fall into the army below, the cat-like creatures hissing and shrieking as they lost their grip on the way down. The ladder cracked as it hit the backs of the creatures below, one of the trolls seizing it and tearing it apart in annoyance. It tossed the pieces toward the wall, then lumbered to the stone and began beating against it.

But the real focus of the attack was the main gates.

Gregson scanned down the wall's length, sweat dripping from his forehead and nose, and assessed the situation at the gates. Most of the Horde's forces surrounded the sealed entrance, trolls at the front, battering the iron-banded outer gate. Gregson did a rough count, then glanced farther back, where the Alvritshai leaders watched impassively from their mounts, two banners flapping in the afternoon breeze behind them. A black and gold eagle's talon marked the first, a white flame on a black background the second. The blackened husk of the Autumn Tree stood against the horizon like a scar.

To the right, the cat-like creatures scaling the second ladder reached the top. Gregson pulled back from the edge. "Reinforcements to the right! Breach on the wall!"

He heard the shout echoed down the length of the parapet, stood aside as men—mostly shopkeepers, farmers, bakers, and boys barely old enough to be growing beards—charged down the wall, their eyes wide in fear, their faces dirty but set with deadly purpose. As soon as they passed, Gregson hustled in the opposite direction for the nearest stairwell and the steps down to the streets below. He'd intended to stay atop the wall, but with the breach he'd never get past the blockage, not until they threw the ladder away from the wall and killed the creatures who'd reached the parapet.

He skirted the men huddled under cover, then jumped over a man as he slumped backwards from the crenellations, an arrow shaft jutting out of his eye. He tagged another man and pointed the body out before continuing, falling in behind two others carrying someone else from the wall. They noticed him, noticed his rank and impatience, and halted long enough for him pass. He hit the stairs as another wave of arrows whirred overhead, charged downwards past men in arrow slits firing steadily into the sea of creatures beyond, and emerged onto street level.

Even here, it was chaos, men and women running back and forth, carting the dead, seeing to the wounded. Men had been set along the base of the wall, moaning as they clutched shoulders or legs, some with blood coating half of their faces, a few unconscious. He caught sight of Ara, the tavern keeper from Cobbleskill, as she washed one of the men's wounds, her hands and clothes already bloody from the day's fighting, and gave her a quick nod when she glanced up. Her smile was weary. Children raced amongst the activity, toting water skins, food, wine, rags, and even one carrying a saw.

At the inner gates, the sound of the pounding from outside muffled but still audible, he glanced up toward the tower, to where the Temeritt flags snapped in the wind, arrows arching over the wall even here, black against the sky. He ducked into the cover of the nearest stair, began climbing upwards at a rough trot. By the time he reached the top, he was gasping and had to stop, one hand clutched to his side. Before the stitch had faded, he pushed away from the wall and made his way to the edge of men grouped near the center of the main tower.

He searched for Commander Pearson, caught sight of the stocky salt-and-pepper haired man's full beard in the throng, and shoved his way forward. Pearson saw him as he approached. "Report, Lieutenant Commander."

"As far as I can tell, all of the Horde's forces are at the wall. There are two thousand or so beneath the gates, the rest of the creatures strung out on both sides from there. The Alvritshai have their mounted units gathered behind their leaders, with lines of archers to the left and right. I see no other reinforcements behind them, near their camp, or near the Autumn Tree."

Pearson's eyebrows rose. "You're certain?"

"There's nothing else to the northwest."

Pearson shifted toward another lieutenant commander to his other side. "And you saw nothing to the south?"

"Nothing."

Pearson chewed on his lower lip, his beard jutting outwards as he did so. Then, abruptly, he motioned to Gregson and the other lieutenant commander. "Follow me."

They pushed through the runners, commanders, and Legionnaires to the front of the tower, breaking through to a small area where GreatLord Kobel stood with Lord Akers and two other Legion commanders, all four of them in deep conversation, the GreatLord frowning, staring out over the field before him.

Pearson waited until he was acknowledged by Lord Akers, then stepped forward, Gregson and his fellow Legionnaire to either side.

"GreatLord, Lord, I sent these two out as requested and they both report that they see no other signs of the Horde to the northwest or south. It would appear that the Horde has committed all of their forces to this attack."

Lord Akers turned to Kobel. "I told you. Some of their forces departed in the night, heading southwest. This is the smallest their force has been since they laid siege to Temeritt and burned the Autumn Tree."

"But where did those forces go, Lord Akers?"

"I have no idea. But a significant portion of their army departed immediately after burning the Tree, and they have not returned. We've been harassing their forces for the past two months, sending out the Legion from the gates at every opportunity. They've only recently begun attacking our walls in retaliation. I thought at first that they were simply responding to our continued feints. But now I think they're trying to keep us penned in while the rest of their force is off wreaking havoc elsewhere. We need to break this stalemate. This may be our chance!"

"And this may be a trap. What if those forces that departed in the night are waiting out of sight for us to leave the safety of our walls?" Kobel's eyes were locked on the three leaders of the Alvritshai dressed in the black and gold of their House. Those three were not the leaders who had initially broken the GreatLord's line of defense to the north and forced Kobel and the Legion behind Temeritt's walls. That leader had left while the Autumn Tree still burned, taking over half of that original army with him. Three months ago, another quarter of the army had left, angling south before they'd disappeared into the haze on the horizon.

And now another group had left. There'd been enough of the Horde at the walls to keep the Legion from breaking the siege earlier, but now...?

Now, Gregson thought the odds were even. With a hard enough push from the Legion and the men they'd been training since the siege began, they could break the stranglehold on Temeritt.

Lord Akers shifted as the silence held, began to say, "We've heard nothing from the King, nothing from the Provinces—"

"Enough," Kobel cut him off. "You've already convinced me. Even if this is a trap, it's an opportunity we can't let pass. Lord Akers, assemble your men at the southeastern gates. Send out scouts to make certain the Horde's forces aren't lying in wait for us. Take Commander Higgins with you, along with his men. Pearson, you and your men are with me."

"You, GreatLord?"

"This isn't a feint. I intend to break this siege. I'll lead the forces exiting from the northeastern gates. We'll circle around Temeritt both north and south, attack the Horde on two fronts. We'll use all of the Legion forces and any of the battalions that you feel are up to the task. Commander Leighten, you'll be in charge of the walls. You'll only have untrained farmers and boys, but you need to hold the wall. Spread the archers along its length, and as soon as we attack, hit them hard. We may have only one chance at this."

Everyone snapped to attention. A sizzling sense of urgency spread out from the group in a ripple as both Lord Akers and GreatLord Kobel broke apart, one heading south, the other north along the wall. Kobel gave orders as they moved, Pearson, Gregson, and the other lieutenant commander hoofing it to keep up. Runners scattered, dodging through those gathered on the tower even as it began to break apart.

Then they were on the stairs, emerging minutes later in the courtyard beyond the gates. The sounds of the trolls pounding on the outer gate had grown louder, although Gregson could barely hear it above the roar of his own blood in his ears. Fresh sweat already soaked the clothes beneath his armor, his hair plastered to his forehead and back of his neck.

Once they reached the middle of the courtyard, Kobel said, "Pearson, send your lieutenant commanders to ready your soldiers at the northeastern gates. You're with me." Then he mounted a waiting horse, spinning it around toward the main thoroughfare. Another horse waited for Pearson.

The commander reached for it. "You heard the orders. Pull your men from the walls and gather at the gates."

He swung up into the saddle, then both GreatLord and Commander kneed their mounts down the thoroughfare.

"Where are they going?"

Gregson turned. "To gather the Legion." Then he spun on his heel and headed back to the walls.

He needed to get his men armed and in order before either Pearson or the GreatLord arrived.

* * *

Corim's breath burned in his throat and lungs, but he couldn't slow it. He gasped, grabbed one of the stones piled in a box, then heaved it up onto his chest. The others from his unit—boys his age, none of them more than fifteen—scrambled aside as he staggered with the weight to the crenellation and then threw the stone over the side. He collapsed into the opening, watched the stone fall into the morass of black creatures below. He saw it strike, but couldn't tell if it had hurt or killed anything. The monsters below were too numerous, nothing but a sea of arms and legs, talons and teeth, flesh and claws.

Then someone gripped the back of his breeches and hauled him back.

"No time to gawk!" Braxton snapped, dropping him to the stone of the parapet. "Heave and throw, that's all you have time for. Now move!"

Corim scrambled to his knees, heard Wade mutter, "Stupid farmer," as he passed, a stone held up to his chest. The merchant's son tossed it over the side, then, hunched over, made for the wooden box of stone. Corim followed in his wake, wiping sweat from his brow.

They both grabbed stones, Corim taking the larger. "You might want to throw something other than pebbles."

They both reached the break and tossed the stones over.

"Arrows!" someone bellowed.

Both immediately ducked behind cover, the sharp retorts of arrows striking stone following a moment later. One of their unit screamed and staggered back, an arrow jutting from his arm. Braxton appeared instantly, hand covering the boy's mouth to muffle his cries. "Stop it! Stop it now!"

The boy's screams descended into racking sobs. Braxton removed his hand and inspected the wound.

"It didn't hit bone. Get down to the lower level, they'll patch you up." The swordmaster shoved the boy toward the stairs, but the boy hadn't taken two steps before another arrow shot through the crenellations and took him in the neck. He stiffened, half turned toward Corim and Wade, then crumpled to the parapet.

Braxton swore, dropping to the boy's side. A fleeting look of pain crossed the swordmaster's eyes, there then replaced with the hardness Corim had come to associate with the aged task master.

Braxton glanced up. "You and you." He motioned to two others crouched near where the boy had fallen. "Take his body down to the black tents. The rest of you, keep moving. We need more stone! Drop the box and raise the other!" He shoved a few of the unit into motion, three of them grabbing the ropes attached to the box and kicking it over the side, letting out the line fast, the box dropping to be reloaded below. Ten paces away, three others began hoisting the second box back up to the top of the wall.

"Come on." Corim snagged Wade's arm as he moved to help with the boxes, but Wade didn't move.

He turned to find the merchant's son staring at the dead boy's body, even as the two Braxton had picked out hauled him up beneath the arms and legs and headed for the stairs. Wade's gaze dropping to the smear of blood on the parapet where the boy had fallen.

"He was already wounded."

"And then he died. There's nothing you can do now." Corim pulled on Wade's arm.

Wade jerked his arm from Corim's grip. "How can you just brush it off? He died! In the space of a breath!"

"We can all die in the space of a breath! I've already seen it a hundred times! They killed everyone in my village, except me and Jayson. They killed more in the towns and villages between there and here. An arrow in the neck is nothing."

When Wade simply gaped at him, he brushed the merchant's son from his mind, darting forward and grabbing the end of the rope hauling the box up from below. Within moments, his fingers were rubbed raw and his arms and shoulders ached. Moments later, the box hit the bottom of the parapet.

"Hold it," an older boy named Harden shouted. He leaned out over the side, hooked the crate on one side and dragged it up to the ledge. Corim dropped the rope and rushed to the box to grab another stone.

When he saw Wade still cowering behind the crenellation, rage bit down deep inside his chest. He used that rage to heave the stone as far out from the wall as possible, then turned.

He wanted to snap at him, to ridicule him, the way Wade had ridiculed him during training. He wanted to laugh in his face and tell him this was real, this was what war was really like, not the games Wade had likely imagined in his head, the heroic charge onto the field, sword swinging. But all of that vindictiveness died as he thought back to that first attack in Gray's Kill, the subsequent flight to Cobble Kill, and after. He'd been terrified then, too, had shrunk in upon himself, like Wade was doing now. They'd only been stationed at the wall for two days, and this was the first day of real fighting for the group. They were only here now because nearly all of the rest of the Legion and the trained fighters had been pulled back.

Corim's anger dampened. He ignored Wade and returned to the box.

He lost count of how many stones he heaved over the wall. The motions became rote: trudge to the box, lift a stone in his scraped and bloody hands, carry it to the aperture and either throw it out if it were light enough, or roll it off the edge if it were too heavy. Sweat sheened his face, stung his eyes, but after a while he stopped trying to wipe it away. He tasted stone grit and dirt, knew his skin was coated with dust. A some point, he noticed Wade had begun moving again, the merchant's son tossing stones with a terrified desperation. He ducked his head when he saw Corim watching.

Then one of the guardsmen roared, "Ladder!"

Corim turned to look, muscles aching, body awash in exhaustion—

And heard the clatter of wood against stone. Close.

He lurched toward the crenellation, hit the raised edge and leaned out, squeezing in beside the dark-haired Harden. The ladder had slapped against the wall an arms-length below their post. Down its length, Corim could already see some of the cat-like creatures scrambling upwards.

"Diermani's Balls," Harden breathed. "What are they?"

Corim didn't answer, shoving back from the wall. "We need a stone. A big one."

To one side, Braxton shouted, "Arm yourselves. Swords and knives." The rest of their unit darted for the crates that contained swords. Not the weighted sticks they'd used for hours upon hours in practice, but actual blades. "One each, then to the walls. If anything reaches the heights, kill it!"

Harden headed for the weapons, but Corim snagged him and steered for the stones again. "We can get a sword later."

"What are we doing? We can't kill them all with a single stone!"

"But we can break the ladder." Corim knelt over the box, began discarding stones to one side. "It has to be big. It has to have weight. *That* one."

They quickly pulled the lose stones around it away, Braxton bellowing, "Steady!" behind them. Harden grabbed one end, Corim the other, and they lifted it, both groaning at its weight. The cords in Harden's neck stood out as they sidled toward the crenellation. Braxton saw what they were doing and shouted those at the opening out of their way, but they couldn't lift the stone up onto the ledge; it was too heavy.

Suddenly, another set of hands appeared and Corim glanced up to see Wade's determined face. Together, all three rolled the stone onto the lip, Harden releasing the stone with a cry of triumph. He began to roll it toward the edge, but Corim stopped him, squeezing beside the stone to check the placement.

As he leaned out, the first of the cat-like creatures reached the top of the ladder and leaped.

Corim screamed as it attached itself to his face, claws digging in to the sides of his neck and forehead before it leapt off again with a dry, whispering hiss. Corim slammed into the side of the crenellation, pain lancing down from his shoulder. Chaos erupted behind him, even as blood from the slices on his brow blinded him in one eye. The pain was silvery and intense, but he reached out and latched onto Harden before he could scramble away as two more of the creatures slipped through to the parapet. Braxton roared orders and the rest of the unit screamed, blades flashing as the three creatures attacked, but Corim pointed to the stone.

"To the left!"

Harden, Wade, and Corim shoved the stone hard to the left, rolling it forward as they did so. Three more creatures appeared in the opening, two leaping over the three boys, chips of stone stinging Corim's face as their claws dug in for purchase. The third got caught as the stone rolled forward, but they didn't falter. The stone rolled to the edge, crushing the creature beneath it, and then Corim yelled, "Now!"

With one final shoved, the stone slid over the lip.

Corim leaned forward to watch the stone fall, his hands in the black ichor oozing from the crushed remains of the creature on the ledge. Arrows pocked into the stone to either side, but he hardly noticed, his breath caught and held as the stone tumbled.

It struck the wall and bounced outwards, missing the top of the ladder and the three creatures preparing to leap the last few feet. They hissed in irritation, their lantern-like eyes blinking, turning to follow the stone's fall. One of them turned back—

Then the stone hit the ladder, the wooden supports bowing in towards the wall before snapping. The three creatures shrieked, their cries joining those from lower on the ladder as it buckled and spun away from the wall. One of them leaped, claws scraping against the stone, but tumbled down in the ladder's wake.

Wade let out a whoop and ducked back behind protection. Harden gave a choked laugh.

When Corim turned, Braxton and the others were dispatching the last of the creatures that had ascended the ladder. One of their unit, Rory— who they all called Rat because he was so short and had a sharp, pointed nose—snatched up a dead body and threw it over the wall.

Braxton wiped his sword on his arm, a few of the others mimicking the gesture, although only one or two were actually stained with the creatures' black blood. The swordmaster motioned with the blade when he was done. "Good job. Keep the swords, but back to the stone throwing. Hopefully we won't have another breach."

Eyes bright, the unit hastened to follow orders, sheathing swords and picking up the stones Corim and Harden had tossed aside in their search. Braxton caught Corim's gaze and nodded.

Before Corim could feel anything—pride, relief—horns sounded, one close, the other farther away, almost an echo.

The unit crowded up against the crenellations, including Braxton. All along the wall, men began to shout and cheer, the sound passing along the wall toward the main gate's tower in a wave. Corim jostled between Harden and Wade. He glanced to the ground first, the Horde still pushing up against the wall at the base, but near the edges, the creatures had turned their attention north.

"Look!" Harden shouted, pointing.

From around the curve of the wall, a force of a thousand Legion on horseback, two thousand behind on foot, charged forward. Corim sucked in a sharp breath as he caught sight of the lead horsemen—GreatLord Kobel and those closest to him in command. They drove forward in a wedge formation, those behind them beginning to fan out onto the grassland in a flanking maneuver.

The Horde reacted, the creatures beneath turning with a roar. The Alvritshai archers scrambled to reform their line.

They didn't have enough time.

The GreatLord and his forces hit them hard, two lengths down the wall from Corim's position. The horses plowed through the front ranks, the Legion's swords slashing downwards in smooth arcs. The roar on the wall intensified and blood flew, the cat-like creatures leaping out of the morass onto the horses, clawing their way onto the armored men above. Shrieks and screams melded, the cavalry's charge halted twenty feet deep. Corim saw two Legionnaires pulled from their saddles, saw Kobel slice one of the cats in half in mid-leap—

And then someone grabbed his shoulder and hauled him back from the edge, flinging him aside. An archer, Corim noted, as he steadied himself behind the crenellation. Another archer yanked Harden and Wade back, then both were leaning out over the edge, bows drawn and arrows loosed before Corim had caught his breath.

All along the wall, archers were spreading out, a Legion commander shouting, "Target the trolls! Target the trolls!" while Braxton ordered Corim's unit to step back and give the archers room.

Corim crawled to Harden's and Wade's side, where they sat with backs against the inside of the outer wall. Wade chuckled. "The GreatLord will take care of them. Nothing can beat the Legion on the field."

Corim said nothing. He'd seen the Legion lines collapse at the northern ridge.

"Who was with them?" Harden asked. "They weren't all Legion."

"All of the other trained fighting men, I expect," Wade answered, wiping at the blood and grit that had caked to his face. "Anyone who can wield a sword or pike with any skill. We should have been with them. We're just as good as any of them."

Corim stared at him. None of the terror he'd seen in Wade's eyes remained. He'd returned to being the sniveling, arrogant merchant's son.

He turned away in disgust.

But then what Wade had said registered.

"Anyone who can wield a sword or pike," he whispered. "Jayson."

* * *

Jayson's unit trotted forward behind the ranks of the Legion on horseback, spear clutched tightly in both hands. His armor weighed heavily on his arms, a newer addition to their armament. From his vantage, he could see nothing but the walls of Temeritt off to the left, stones and oil and arrows dropping or shooting down from the heights, while other arrows arching up from the Horde's forces on the ground. The charred spire of the Autumn Tree sat off to the right. Only the backs of the shieldbearers and the asses of the cavalry lay ahead.

Horns sounded, close, followed in instant later by an answering call from the forces to the south. He shot a glance toward Gregson, on horseback to one side, Terson beside him. Both were watching the field ahead.

Then the cavalry in front charged, clods of dirt and grass from the churned ground flying up and back, a few of the shieldbearers biting back curses as it rained down on them. Vics barked tense laughter, a few other chuckling, but Terson snapped, "Keep the line! Hold steady!" and everyone quieted. Vics shot the lieutenant commander a black look.

"As if some laughter will break the line," the grizzled elder muttered, spitting to one side. "We'll be seeing plenty of blood and death in a few moments."

As if in answer, the Legion cavalry roared down a small slope, and for the first time since they'd marched through the northeastern gates, Jayson saw the Horde they faced.

A ripple of despair cut through the line, felt more than heard in the low gasps and faltering steps of those around him. Jayson kept silent, fresh sweat prickling in his armpits and down his back.

The Horde appeared black on the field, turning toward the sound of the horns, toward the Legion's charge. The cat-like creatures Jayson had faced in Gray's Kill streaked across the grass, larger creatures that those in Temeritt had started calling goblins and orcs behind them. The trolls continued to pound against the stone walls, still unaware of the attack.

And then there were the Alvritshai.

"Company halt!" Gregson bellowed, as the Alvritshai archers began to reform their ranks. "Shieldbearers, form the wall! Spearsmen, form up! Ready shield wall and hold position."

All along the line, the men Jayson had been training with for the last eight months sank to the ground, the shieldbearers digging their shields into the ground, bracing for potential attack. Once set, they drew their short swords, Jayson and his fellow spearmen falling into position behind them, leaving enough space for the cavalry to slip through their ranks when they returned, but tight enough they could close ranks quickly. Each spearman was partnered with a shieldbearer. Jayson was paired with a man named Owen, a hand shorter but broader of shoulder. He cut Jayson a quick glance, then focused forward, watching the battle. Watching the archers.

Behind them, the rest of the reinforcements—Legion in armor and on foot, weapons at the ready—formed up into their own lines

Terson charged past, glaring at the unit's line, shouting a few corrections. Gregson did the same in the opposite direction, turning his horse as the front line of Alvritshai archers suddenly sank into crouches.

"Shields up! Shields up, you bastards!"

Jayson heard the release, watched the hundreds of shafts shoot up into the mid-afternoon sky, like a flock of birds. He followed them as they reached their peak, separating as they arched downwards.

"Cover!"

Jayson ducked and stepped forward, knee coming down hard on the trampled grass, his chest pressing up against Owen's armor as Owen jerked the shield up to cover them.

Seconds later, the rain of arrows hit. Shafts pinged off of the shields. It sounded like hail from a storm. Someone close cried out; someone screamed, a grating shriek. An arrow sank into the ground a hand's span from Jayson's foot.

The storm ended and through the relative silence Gregson said, "Reform! The cavalry is returning!"

Jayson shoved back, noted a few spearmen had fallen to the arrows along their ranks, but the shieldbearers remained. Behind, the Legion footmen had pulled farther back, out of the archers' range, while leaving room for the returning cavalry. Jayson braced himself, spear still pointed to the sky but body ready. Owen dropped his shield, arm and shoulder against its inner side, left hand gripping his short sword protectively across his body. On the field below, the cavalry were galloping across the intervening grass in a ragged line, the Horde trailing close behind them.

"Here they come," Vics muttered.

"How close?"

"Twenty feet, but the gap is widening. Get ready."

Owen tensed, Jayson gripping his spear so hard his knuckles were white. The Legion thundered up the slope, the horses' hooves flashing, their necks straining forward. Jayson waited until they were ten feet away before shouting, "Now!"

In a practiced motion, Owen shifted stance, shield swinging out and opening a space, Jayson dropping, ground shuddering beneath the cavalry's passage. The lead horse charged past Owen and Jayson, a gust of wind buffeting them both, heavy with the scent of horse sweat, tainted with blood, and then Owen shifted again, closing the line. Jayson lurched back into position, lowering his spear between Owen and the shieldbearer to the left—

And then the Horde struck. The cat-like creatures leaped onto the shields and launched up over them toward the spearmen's faces with dry shrieks and sibilant hisses. Jayson didn't have time to react, kept his spear in position for the front ranks of the Horde. The creatures that had appeared black from the wall's heights were actually a range of dark, dusky browns and tans. They hit the shields and spears in a solid wave. Owen cursed as three threw themselves at his shield. Jayson turned the angle of his spear at the last minute, felt it shudder into one of the creatures' bodies, impaling it through the shoulder. The creature screamed, an ear-rending sound that sank claws into Jayson's mind. He lifted his spear and heaved the body up and over his shoulder, jerking the weapon free as men from the Legion behind surged forward and fell on the creatures who'd broken through. Jayson only had time for a glimpse and then his attention returned to Owen, the shieldbearer thrusting the creatures back and jabbing forward with his sword, skewering one and slicing another along the arm. Jayson called to Owen, the shieldbearer crouching down behind his shield as Jayson heaved the spear through another creature's gut. He heaved the flailing creature over and behind him. Something splattered against his face and he realized with numbed shock that it was blood.

But he had no time to think, no time to react. As the Legion behind finished off his latest kill, he jabbed the spear forward again. The Horde was pressed too close to miss, but it was only a glancing blow, the sharpened tip opening up the side of a shorter creature's face. It roared at him, mouth gaping wide, needle-like teeth glistening with spit even as Jayson yanked his spear back and thrust again. Owen shifted, short sword swinging out from his shield, and skewered the creature through the throat, black blood spouting from the wound. Two more creatures surged forward, half-dressed in mock armor. Jayson shouted something incoherent and sank his spear into one creature's side, Owen taking care of the second. Blood coated the end of his sword, sheeted down the shield, but neither Owen nor Jayson halted their attack. Arrows rained down again, killing Legion and Horde indiscriminently. One sank into the boot of the shieldbearer to Owen's right. The man spat curses, but held, blood soaking through the leather.

A moment later, Gregson shouted, "Prepare to advance! Three, two, one, mark!"

Drawing a deep breath and pulling a roar from deep inside his gut, Jayson fell in beside Owen a moment before he lifted his shield. Together, they shoved forward, feet digging into the ground, the Horde pressing hard from the other side. Two steps, three, five, and then they heard Gregson call for a halt, Owen slamming the shield back to the ground, nodding to Jayson as soon as he was braced. Jayson stepped back, spear already lowering, but before he was ready one of the creatures punched a blunted sword hard against his armored upper shoulder. The pain was intense, but he shrugged the blow aside and stuck his spear into the creature's armpit, its weapon dropping to the dirt. It fell back, more of its ilk pushing forward.

Jayson and Owen fell into a rhythm, interrupted occasionally by a call to advance or retreat. Men fell on either side, Jayson and Owen taking glancing blows from makeshift weapons, nothing serious. A break occurred five men to their left, the Legion behind surging forward to shove the Horde back, the shieldbearers and spearmen closing ranks to seal the opening. And still the Horde attacked. Jayson expected one of the trolls to appear at any moment, but they didn't come and he couldn't spare a moment to see where they were. He heard horns, but didn't know what they meant. He listened for Gregson's and Terson's voices over the tumult, and fought even though his arms were exhausted, his shoulders numb. He saw the same weariness in Owen's face.

Then the order came to withdraw, the Legion who'd been held in reserve, protected behind their wall, surging forward to take their place. Jayson staggered backwards, Owen beside him, clapping a hand on his back before stumbling and falling to one knee. Jayson halted, the Legion surrounding them.

Owen waved him away. "I'm fine, just tired."

Jayson heard Gregson calling to rally. He gripped Owen under one arm and hauled him up. "Time to check in."

Swinging Owen's arm over his shoulder, they hobbled toward where Gregson and Terson were gathering what remained of their unit. As they fell into line, Jayson was shocked to realize that hours had passed, the sun already obscured by the walls of Temeritt. He scanned through those in their unit, picking out Vics and Curtis, Vanson and Ricks. They'd been reduced in number by nearly half. Sickened, he glanced behind, to the field they'd fought for over the last few hours and the dozens, perhaps hundreds, of bodies that littered it, trapped in awkward poses where they'd fallen. Carrion crows were already circling overhead, or were pecking at the remains.

His stomach heaved, and not far distant he heard others vomiting into the destroyed grassland. He straightened, jaw clenched, and forced his own gorge down, swallowing back the bile in the back of his throat.

"Quiet!" Terson barked, and some of the men near Jayson and Owen muttered imprecations under their breath. "Quiet, I said. We have new orders!"

The unit moaned in unison, a few of the men giving in to exhaustion and settling to the ground. Nearly everyone was covered in blood and gore. Most were nursing wounds, clutching shoulders or arms, a cut along a leg.

Gregson glared Terson into silence, while Ricks and Curtis circled the group, helping some of those who'd collapsed back to their feet, patting shoulders or saying a few words of encouragement.

"You held well today," Gregson said, his voice carrying over the group even though the fighting continued near the gates. "Held longer than I expected, longer than Kobel expected as well. He was impressed. If he weren't currently smashing in Alvritshai heads and stomping on the Horde, he'd tell you that himself."

Some of the men laughed. Jayson glanced toward the battle, saw the GreatLord's banners in the thick of the fighting. The sight lifted the weariness from his shoulders a little, made his chest swell with pride.

But movement caught his eye, beyond the battlefield, far in the distance.

"Kobel wants us to hold here, regroup and reorganize, in case we're needed again. Terson will see to rearming those of you who've lost or broken your weapons. The Horde is trapped between the GreatLord's forces here and Lord Akers' forces to the south. He may need help keeping them hemmed in."

"Lieutenant Commander!" someone shouted.

Gregson continued, as if he hadn't heard. "We're to reform farther to the east, near the main road, and watch for any of the Horde that manages to break free. We're to take them ourselves, or use our line to corral them in if it's a sizeable force."

"Lieutenant Commander!"

Gregson cut off with a frown. "What is it?"

"What's that?"

Nearly everyone turned toward what Jayson had seen on the horizon. A ripple of unease broke through the group, even as Gregson kicked his horse forward, Terson at his side.

"What do you see, Terson?"

"Something on the horizon, but it's too distant to make out. It's moving like—"

"An army," Gregson suddenly said. He sat straighter in his saddle, motioned toward Ricks. "Lieutenant, sound a warning. Those on the walls should be able to—"

Before he could finish, a blat of horns sounded from the tower over the gates, harsh and dissonant and desperate. The warning cut across the field, everyone in their group listening intently even as the forces attacking the Horde faltered. The horns sounded again, less panicked, more concise, and Jayson realized they were issuing orders.

Gregson shared a quick glance with Terson, then spun toward the group.

"Retreat! Back to the northeastern gates! Prepare to hold them open long enough for our forces to return behind the safety of the walls. Move, move, move!"

Jayson glanced toward the streak of black on the eastern horizon, still too distant to make out any details, then hefted Owen and began staggering toward the northeastern gates. They seemed impossibly distant as the entire unit stumbled over the churned field, dodging bodies, broken spears thrust into the ground, blood-slick mud, dismembered limbs, and severed heads. Gregson and Terson charged out ahead to meet those Legion set to guard the gates, readying for their arrival.

At his side, Owen tripped and nearly dragged both of them to the ground. Half of their unit was already in front of them.

"I can't," Owen gasped. "Leave me."

"Like hells. Get up! Get up and move!" He heaved Owen upwards, the man crying out—something must be broken inside him, Jayson realized, something serious that he couldn't see—but he clutched the man closer and began moving again. "Walk, damn you. One foot in front of the other."

Owen complied, legs moving, even though Jayson was doing most of the work. They staggered up to the gates, Ricks appearing out of nowhere. "Form up."

"Owen can't. He's hurt. Something inside his chest."

"Take him inside, leave him with the healers, then get your ass back here."

Jayson dragged Owen inside the walls, then off to one side, the streets behind the wall already covered with bodies, some moaning, others still. Owen slid from his grip and he called out to one of the healers moving among the men. The nearest glanced up, then picked his way to him.

"What's wrong?"

"Something in his chest, something internal. I have to get back to the gate."

"I think it's too late for that."

Jayson spun. At the gates, the Legion cavalry and footmen began pouring into Temeritt. More and more came through, then GreatLord Kobel and his entourage, banners flaring. The GreatLord turned as soon as he'd entered, his shout to close the gates echoing against the walls. But the gates were already drawing closed, those above taking the initiative. Gregson and the rest of Jayson's unit scrambled in after Kobel's men, even as the space between the doors narrowed. The last of Temeritt's men slipped through a moment before they slid shut with a resounding thud. A portcullis began lowering with the clanking of chains, braces being slid into place. Jayson heaved a sigh of relief.

Kobel watched the gates in silence, his horse prancing in agitation. Then, without a word, he spun his mount and ordered his entourage to follow him to the main gates.

* * *

"What in hells happened?" Kobel brought his escort to a halt at the base of the main tower of the outer wall. He dropped from his mount before it had come to a complete stop, already stalking toward the stairs and the heights. A flurry of panicked activity surrounded his escort as they dismounted, but he ignored them all, focused on Commander Leighten, who stood waiting to receive them. "We had them. We could have slaughtered them all before the gates and been free of them!"

"And you would have been trapped outside the walls when the army coming from the southwest arrived."

"What army?"

"See for yourself."

They ascended to the chaos of the parapet. Kobel moved directly to the edge of the wall to look out over the battlefield.

The grassland in either direction was churned into mud and littered with dead, both those from Temeritt and from the Horde. Carrion crows already covering the field with their black, glistening wings. But there was nothing they could do for those beneath the wall, even those that were not yet dead. And he knew there would be some, too wounded to move, or unconscious where they'd fallen. He could only hope they died quickly, before the crows found them.

Or the Horde.

The group he and Lord Akers had attacked had withdrawn back to their camp around the base of the Autumn Tree. Kobel couldn't see what they were doing, but he assumed they were preparing for the arrival of the army that even now filled the southwestern horizon.

"Spyglass." Leighten handed it over. He snapped the spyglass open and brought it to his eye.

"What is it?" Lord Akers asked, huffing as he shoved his way to Kobel's side. His face was lined with the same annoyance, anger, and frustration Kobel felt. "Why did you pull us back?"

"It's the Horde."

"We had the Horde beneath our heel! We could have finished them!"

"Not the Horde beneath our walls. The Horde that left in the first few days of the siege. The part that marched off to the west. They've returned."

Lord Akers slapped his hands onto the parapet, still catching his breath. Kobel lowered the spyglass and handed it off to him, noting the lord's flushed face and the gore that splattered his armor. Akers pushed himself back to take the spyglass. His breathing slowed as he scanned the approaching army.

"They have more trolls. And...what are those things off to the left?"

"I believe they are some type of standing lizard people."

A few of those near Kobel chuckled uncertainly, as if they thought Kobel were joking. They quieted as they realized neither the GreatLord nor Lord Akers were smiling.

Lord Akers watched in silence, the Horde marching steadily toward them. Kobel could pick out individual groups now. Messengers raced between the coming army and the one beneath the scorched Autumn Tree.

"What's your estimate as to their numbers?" Kobel asked.

"At least five times what was beneath our walls his morning. I'd guess around eight thousand." The spyglass settled on the head of the army. "What are the leaders carrying with them?"

Kobel held out his hand and Akers handed back the spyglass. The army was almost close enough he wouldn't need it. Still, he brought it up and closed his other eye, shifting it until he found the head of the army, the rest of the Horde a dark stain behind them. There were two Alvritshai and one of the lizard men on horseback, ranged behind another Alvritshai with the mottled skin of a Wraith. They were surrounded by an assortment of creatures, an escort of representatives from the Horde. But the image was unclear. He shifted the focus of the glass, stilled the beginnings of trembling in his arms. Exhaustion would hit shortly as the battle rush faded.

"Do you see it?" Akers asked.

He opened his mouth to say no, but then the spyglass settled on the pikes being carried by the creatures immediately behind the leaders.

"I see it."

"What are they?"

"They're heads on pikes. GreatLord Alden from Borangst is being paraded around at the front."

15

"What should we do, GreatLord?"

Tarken Sohn steadied the spyglass, elbows resting on the ground at the top of the knoll. Grass shielded him, Commander Kent, and the scout that had led them up to the perch from both Temeritt and the area where the force Tarken had brought with him had halted and made camp. They'd arrived at Temeritt that afternoon, exhausted from the forced march, yet for a brief moment it looked as if Tarken would be leading a charge to help Kobel in his attack on the creatures beneath his walls. But the main gates were on the opposite side of the city from their approach, and by the time Tarken had turned his men southward so they could skirt the city, scouts had reported another army approaching from the west.

He'd halted immediately and ordered the scouts to take him to a vantage point. He needed to see the city, Kobel's forces, the army laying siege, and the army coming from the west.

Now, he lowered the spyglass and handed it off to Kent. "We make camp. No fires. Pull back even further from the city, since this new army has some kind of fliers overhead. We can't stand up to the forces moving on the city. There are too many of them."

"It would appear that the reports from the outlying landholders of Yhnar weren't superstitions after all. I make out snake-like things, and something small and black racing along the outskirts of the main force. And what are those huge creatures lumbering in the back? Not to mention Alvritshai. What the hells are they doing here? Have they broken the Accord?"

Tarken said nothing, although he unconsciously made a gesture to ward off evil and caught himself muttering a prayer to Diermani to protect them.

"How many enemy forces?"

Kent responded immediately, his tone that of a military commander taking stock of the situation. "Around eight thousand combined. They're halting near the charred remains of the Autumn Tree. The camp and surrounding lands appear well worn. I'd say that what the Temeritt scout told us was the truth: Temeritt has been under siege for at least six months, probably longer. They've likely been here since the spring."

"Then why haven't we heard from them? Why hasn't someone else come to help them?"

"I'd guess that those fliers kept any word from reaching us by messenger bird. The messenger who finally did make it to Yhnar said they'd tried multiple times before that and no one had made it through."

"We didn't see any of those fliers on our initial approach."

"No, we didn't. They must have been called away for some reason."

"Why? What for?"

Kent looked toward him, then returned to scanning the army, his attention fixed and intent, searching for something.

Tarken knew when he'd found it by the sudden tension in his shoulders.

"They have GreatLord Alden's head."

Tarken nodded. "I think the forces—this Horde, as the messenger called it—besieged Temeritt and as soon as their position was fortified they split off over half of their army and headed toward Borangst. It's a smaller city than Temeritt, but it's in the mountain ranges. It would take them a while to march up to the city's height and attack. But they did. It's taken them this long to break Borangst's walls and march back here."

"Why not attack Yhnar? We're one of the Provinces."

"Likely because we're so isolated."

"And small."

"They targeted Temeritt because of its size and its central location. And because of the Autumn Tree, of course. It makes a good base camp for attacks on the rest of the southern Provinces. I'm certain they intend to attack Yhnar eventually, but they don't see us as a threat yet."

Kent lowered the glass. "So what are we going to do now? I don't see how we can help those in Temeritt with the two thousand men we've brought with us. We're outnumbered, and with those fliers overhead, we aren't going to be able to communicate with GreatLord Kobel to let him know we're here. Not without exposing ourselves to this Horde."

"For now, we stay hidden and wait. And we keep an eye on this army. We need to know what they intend for Temeritt, and see if we can't figure out what Kobel intends to do in response. We need to be ready to act, when the opportunity arises."

Kent grimaced. "I hate waiting."

Tarken Sohn gave a mirthless smile, his mind already trying to work

out how to notify Kobel they were here without alerting the Horde. "So
do I, commander. So do I."

* * *

Lotaern ducked down beneath the flap of the tent and into the outer room,
where two of the Order of the Flame stood guard. Both came to attention,
one nodding in the Chosen's direction, although neither spoke. Lotaern
moved between them and into the tent's inner room, where four more
members of the Flame stood around the Wraith who knelt at its center, the
band of white light—Aielan's Light—still encircling his neck. It throbbed
slightly with power. The four inside the tent were there to keep it
anchored and the Wraith under control, although Lotaern was taking no
chances. Besides the two in the outer room, there were another eight
scattered around the outside of the tent, ready to take control of the anchor
if something went wrong.

The Wraith could not be allowed to escape. Lotaern had plans for
him.

The prisoner was on his knees, bent forward, back hunched, head
lowered. His long black hair covered his face, hanging loosely. Tension
lined his shoulders, evidence that he was still fighting the leash Lotaern
and the Flame had placed on him, even after a week of captivity. He
would have thought the Wraith would have given up by now, but then the
Wraiths were used to long lives, according to what Shaeveran had said.
Some of them had existed for over a hundred years, trapped in Ostraell's
forests. A week would be nothing to them.

The Wraith, Maenaed, raised his head at the sound of Lotaern brushing
through the tent's partition. He leaned back as one of the Flame reached
for a wooden chair, placing it four paces from where Maenaed knelt. The
Wraith's hands were unbound, his feet as well, but Lotaern knew that with
the collar of light around his neck he could barely move. Maenaed had
tested the limits of the leash during the first few days. Each morning,
before Peloroun's army stirred and prepared for the march, Lotaern came
to this tent and sat in this chair. He hoped to learn something from
Maenaed, about the Wraiths' plans, about the army that trailed behind
them. Something that could be used to halt their attack on Caercaern.

But he was running out of time.

"Maenaed."

The Wraith's eyes narrowed with hatred; a patient hatred, Lotaern
thought. He leaned back, shoulders no longer hunched, back straight. The

blackness beneath his skin came into stark relief in the lantern light, and once again Lotaern suppressed a shudder at the sign of the sarenavriell's taint. The ragged scar from his banishment appeared particularly livid.

"Chosen." The muscles of his jaw worked as he clenched his teeth, then he visibly relaxed, nearly smiled.

"Why do you smile?"

"Because it is almost done. The Wraith army is nearly here. Once they attack, once they reach your guardians," he glanced toward the four who held him, "then I will be free. And you...you will die."

The Wraith's soft, slightly accented words sent a shiver through Lotaern's skin. But Maenaed had been offering up such cold threats for the last seven mornings and Lotaern was unwilling to let the Wraith know how much they unsettled him. Everything about this...creature...unsettled him. The air of superiority, the arrogance, the frigidness that permeated the air around him, not to mention the power he knew the once-Alvritshai wielded. The image of him blurring into and out of existence in the field where they had captured him still haunted Lotaern's sleep. He knew Shaeveran had the same powers, but Colin never flaunted them.

Lotaern had to give the tainted human a certain amount of credit for that, even if he didn't trust him. Shaeveran retained more of his humanity than Maenaed did, but Lotaern didn't know how long that would remain true. At some point, the sarenavriell would turn him, as it had Walter, Maenaed, and all of the others.

He focused on Maenaed's eyes. "Your army is moving slowly. They're two days behind us, and we are only a day's march from the walls of Caercaern. We will reach it today. And the Winter Tree is still alive."

"Moving slowly yes, but not because of the Winter Tree. Do you not hear the screams of the Alvritshai you've left behind? Does Aielan not trouble your sleep with their terror, their tears? All of those people you've abandoned in the villages and towns in the outer lands. They are all dying beneath the Wraith army's rage."

Lotaern shifted uncomfortably in his seat. "They were not abandoned. The acolytes and the members of the Flame told them to flee to Caercaern, to its walls."

Maenaed laughed, a soft, low, knowing sound. "And you expected them to listen? They are simple people, Chosen, and you ask them to leave their homes, their lands, everything they have worked for their entire lives for the uncertainty of Aielan's favor?"

"The Order of the Flame will protect them."

"But only if they leave everything behind and travel to Caercaern. I think you'll be surprised at how few of them have enough faith to do so at your word."

"At Aielan's word. They should have more faith."

"Never fear. Their faith is being tested. Even now, most of them have been given to Aielan's Light."

Lotaern's stomach turned and he closed his eyes, head slightly bowed. He had known there was risk. That's why he'd sent the Order of the Flame out into the House lands earlier, why he'd attempted to spark true belief in the common people before they reached this point. He'd known it would undermine the lords' authority, had even ordered the members in particular Houses to use their positions to do just that; he needed to maintain his power within the Evant after all. But he hadn't expected the lords to protest so vigorously.

Or rather, he hadn't expected Lord Aeren to gather so much support, so quickly.

He shook his head, raised it again, eyes open. "You seek to distract me. Tell me of the army that approaches. Who leads it? What creatures is it composed of? How many are there and what is their plan?"

Maenaed's cold enjoyment faded into boredom. "Their plan is to destroy you."

Lotaern was surprised. This was the most significant response he'd gotten from the Wraith since his capture.

"How? How do they intend to destroy us? How do they intend to break Caercaern's walls? How do they intend to get close enough with the Winter Tree still alive?"

"The Winter Tree is weakened." Maenaed's voice was bland, his eyes drifting from Lotaern's. "The Summer Tree is dead. Did you not feel it? Perhaps you were too enthralled with collaring me to notice."

Lotaern's eyes widened, even as the members of the Flame—silent and inconspicuous until now—fidgeted, trading glances. Lotaern had felt the Autumn Tree die, but the Summer Tree?

Reaching out, he tried to sense the Winter Tree's protection. He knew it was dying, but he *had* been distracted since he last touched it.

Now, he couldn't sense it at all, even straining to the limits of his power.

But the Summer Tree was protected.

"You lie. The Summer Tree is protected by the dwarren."

Maenaed's gaze returned to Lotaern. "It was."

Lotaern didn't want to believe it, but Maenaed was so certain. If the Summer Tree had died, the Winter Tree would be weakened even further.

He wasn't certain it could survive such a blow. He had expected the Summer Tree to be the last to fall. It was the most heavily guarded, being underground and protected by the dwarren, who were near fanatics when it came to preserving the Land. But if the dwarren had failed...

What did that mean for the dwarren? Did they still live?

He would have to check on the Winter Tree the moment they returned to Caercaern, verify that the Summer Tree was dead, that the Winter Tree still provided some protection. And he would have to inform Peloroun.

He rose.

"Leaving so soon? You haven't even begun to ask your usual annoying questions. I must admit, though, I will miss our little talks. They were highly entertaining."

Lotaern strode from the room, barely noticing the two guardsmen stationed in the outer room.

He found Peloroun waiting for him outside the tent.

"Good. I need to speak to you."

"Is your little morning ritual done?" Peloroun asked. "I'd hoped to get the army marching to Caercaern a little early today."

"Yes, yes, we can leave as soon as the army is ready."

Peloroun hesitated at Lotaern's dismissive tone, then ordered two of his accompanying Phalanx—guardsmen Lotaern hadn't even noticed—to break camp immediately.

"I must say I never understood what you hoped to gain from talking to him. He obviously wasn't going to provide us any meaningful information."

"You made your thoughts on that abundantly clear after the first day." Lotaern began moving toward his own tent. "But it has borne fruit."

Peloroun's lips thinned. "Has it now."

"He claims the Summer Tree is dead."

"And you believe him?"

"I don't know if I believe him. But if you recall, the scouts reported a sudden increase in the Wraith army's pace just after we captured Maenaed."

"They were moving at a slow but steady pace before that, as well as a tight group. Then, suddenly, they spread out and their pace quickened. It was as if they had been unleashed."

"That's when the Summer Tree must have died. It would have been a blow to the Winter Tree's strength."

"And you didn't sense this?"

Lotaern bristled at Peloroun's reproving tone. "I was dealing with

Maenaed at the time."

Peloroun didn't respond. "What else?"

"I can't sense the Winter Tree any longer.   And this close to Caercaern, I should."

They continued on in silence, Peloroun's brow creased in thought. Finally, he asked, "How does this affect our plans?"

"It doesn't. Not to a great extent, at least. The Winter Tree was never part of the final defense. It was merely there to hold the Wraiths and the majority of the creatures in their army at bay for as long as possible. If it has weakened, or even died, then we may have to hasten our timeline, nothing more.

"What's more important is the fact that the dwarren protected the Summer Tree. It was planted underground, at their most sacred and centralized location. If the Summer Tree has indeed fallen, then the dwarren must have been decimated, if not completely destroyed. Any hope of calling on them for aid has died with the Summer Tree."

Peloroun snorted in contempt. "I never intended to call on the dwarren for aid, nor the humans. If you recall, I never agreed with Shaeveran, Lord Aeren, or the Accord, even with the threat of the Wraiths. They killed both of my sons, when all they were doing was protecting Ionaen House lands. The dwarren can fend for themselves, and we will protect our own. Let the dwarren die."

He halted abruptly. "We'll reach Caercaern today. As soon as we enter the lower tier gates, have the Order of the Flame and the acolytes within the Order of Aielan prepare their defenses of the wall. I'll take care of the Phalanx of the combined Houses. We need to be ready for the Wraith army, especially if they'll be arriving sooner than expected."

Lotaern ground his teeth at the tone of command in Peloroun's voice, but he said, "The warriors of the Flame will be ready."

"Make certain of it."

Peloroun spun and stalked off, his remaining escort falling into place to either side. Lotaern watched his retreat.

The Flame would be ready.

But he would check on the health of the Winter Tree first.

*   *   *

"It's the same as the last," Renaerd muttered, then spun his horse around and fell back among his own House Phalanx.

Fedaureon forced himself not to say anything. Daevon shifted into

Renaerd's vacated position.

"Doesn't Renaerd feel anything?" Fedaureon kept his voice low enough only Daevon, and Mattalaen on his other side, could hear. "He acts as if they died simply to inconvenience him."

"That's probably exactly what he thinks," Mattalaen said. "But calling him out for it wouldn't improve our situation at all. The more villages and towns I see razed to the ground like this," he motioned toward the smoking ruins in the small valley stretching out before them, "the more I realize we need the Phalanx that follows his lead. Even if he is an arrogant, self-absorbed bastard."

Fedaureon had never heard Mattalaen be so blunt before. Renaerd must be grating on his caitan worse than he thought.

Daevon glared in reproach. "We need his men, yes. Which means none of us should be voicing such thoughts, especially where someone may overhear."

"Always the teacher, eh, Protector?" But Mattalaen shook his head. "But he's right, Lord Presumptive. I spoke impulsively." He waved toward the destroyed village. "What are your orders?"

"Same as for the last. Search for survivors, potential supplies, and then we'll continue on." His eyes fell on the storm gathering over the mountains, the leading edge of the clouds already beginning to streak toward them. "We still have a few hours left before dark, even with the storm approaching."

Mattalaen turned away to pass on the orders.

Fedaureon asked, "How far behind them are we now?"

"I'll need to take a closer look, but the ruins are still smoking. I'd guess at most a day."

"We're only three days from Caercaern."

Daevon didn't comment. He didn't need to. They weren't going to find any protection from the walls of Caercaern.

But he hadn't expected that anyway. Not from Lotaern, Peloroun, and Orraen, at least.

They'd spent the last week trailing in the Wraith army's wake, each day edging closer to the army, forced to witness the destruction the army was wreaking on Ionaen House lands. Villages and towns had been burned to the ground. The dead lined the streets, caught in the act of fleeing. Even more bodies were found inside the husks of the ruins, women and children who'd hidden and died in the flames or where crushed when stone buildings collapsed. They'd found nearly no survivors. In the last town, a mother and her two young girls had been trapped in the root cellar beneath their home, the charred timbers of their house fallen across the doors. Two villages before that, a man had been mauled by one of the snake creatures, but had crawled into the stream and washed beneath the bridge, where one of the Rhyssal Phalanx heard his cries and found him clinging to the bridge's supports. He'd reported that the army had come out of nowhere, attacked with no warning. He'd raced toward the village center, but the snake creatures had already overrun it. Before he could turn and flee, they'd fallen on him. He'd only escaped because the creature that had attacked him had been distracted by another man, hissing and striking the other man with its fangs. He'd crawled away in horror before the creature had disengaged, the man's body already turning black from the venom. He was thankful he'd only been attacked with the creature's claws.

"Any sign of any creatures other than what we've heard from the survivors we've found?"

"Besides the snake people, we've seen signs of the cat-like creatures the man from Ettaeren mentioned. There's also something much larger in the army—nothing we've heard of or seen is strong enough to knock over some of the stone buildings we've passed."

"Check the village below, see what you can find."

A moment later, a shout rose from the rear of their army.

Fedaureon spun, his chest tightening as he saw those at the back of the long line of Phalanx from both Baene and Rhyssal drawing weapons and spinning to face back along the road they'd been following. They fell into defensive positions, the panicked outcry from the first men rippling backwards toward Fedaureon through the ranks.

"What in hells." Fedaureon made to knee his horse down the line, but Daevon clamped a hand down hard on his arm, holding him back.

"Wait."

Farther down the road, the front ranks of an army appeared.

Fedaureon shouted, "Mattalaen!" but his voice was drowned out as all along the line the caitans and Phalanx sprang into motion. The lord of Rhyssal caught sight of Mattalaen at the front of their column, expression perplexed, and he realized the caitan couldn't see the approaching force; the road dipped down toward the village, the surrounding trees blocking his view. He shook off Daevon's restraining hand. "We have to get to the rear of our army. Mattalaen can't see what's going on."

"Lord Presumptive," Daevon said, his voice calm. "Look."

Fedaureon saw Renaerd, with an escort, emerging from the rear of the forces now arrayed in a defensive position toward the approaching army.

He cursed beneath his breath. But he'd never make it in time, not with over half of the Rhyssal and Baene Phalanx between him and Renaerd.

Renaerd halted twenty paces beyond the end of the supporting Phalanx. At the far end of the road, still barely visible, the other army halted as well. Fedaureon found himself reevaluating Renaerd. He would never have expected the pompous lord to actually lead his Phalanx into battle, but Renaerd hadn't hesitated to take charge.

"They aren't attacking," Daevon said.

"No." The stalemate held. "Can you see who they are?"

"Not from this distance. But they're mounted. And they're carrying a banner."

"What colors?"

"White and...red?"

Fedaureon sucked in a breath of hope, even as Renaerd nudged his horse forward. Someone broke from the other army to meet him.

"He didn't send a proxy," Daevon muttered, echoing Fedaureon's own thought. Then the Protector added, "Mattalaen is looking for orders."

"Tell him to hold position for now."

Fedaureon remained focused on Renaerd. The lord was in deep conversation with the envoy from the other army, but it didn't last long. The two broke apart, Renaerd riding back to his own Phalanx, the envoy heading back down the road.

A moment later, Renaerd's escort signaled that all was well, even though the army had begun moving toward them again.

"It's Resue," Daevon said. "Tamaell Thaedoren."

"Signal Mattalaen to continue on to the village. We'll go to meet the Tamaell."

Daevon ordered a runner to pass on the news as Fedaureon headed toward Renaerd, the Rhyssal and Baene Phalanx parting before him. Excitement radiated from the men, low conversations and barks of laughter erupting from them as Daevon rejoined him. Fedaureon felt the same tingling sensation in his own skin, but he kept his face neutral. He didn't want Daevon, Mattalaen, or even Renaerd to see the hope that gnawed at his heart—hope that Thaedoren wasn't alone, that his father had come with him. The only word they'd heard from Caercaern before he'd left was that Aeren had vanished along with Thaedoren. No one knew where they had gone.

He entered the small circle surrounding Renaerd, the lord's Protector coughing lightly, Renaerd turning at the noise. He caught sight of Fedaureon and motioned him forward imperiously.

"Is it Tamaell Thaedoren?"

"Yes, along with Caeden, lord presumptive of Nuant."

"I know who Caeden is. Our Houses are adjacent." Fedaureon hesitated. "No one else?"

Nonplussed, Renaerd said, "They have another three thousand Phalanx with them, a few from Rhyssal and Resue but mostly from Nuant. They've been following us for the past week, trying to catch up. I didn't learn much of anything else."

Something in Renaerd's tone caught Fedaureon's attention, but the lord of Baene refused to look him in the eye, his chin tilted upwards, head high, turned toward the approach of the Tamaell's forces. Fedaureon realized Renaerd knew exactly what he'd really wanted to know but was attempting to be tactful.

Before Fedaureon could figure out what to say, Renaerd gestured toward the road beyond and said, "Here they come."

Tamaell Thaedoren rode forward, flanked on the left by Daedelan and the right by Lord Presumptive Caeden. Each had a caitan as escort.

All conversation ceased around them as Thaedoren halted, scanning both of them before nodding formally. "I greet you, Lord Renaerd and Lord Fedaureon."

Their eyes met, and if the title the Tamaell had used had not been enough, he saw the truth in Thaedoren's eyes.

"So he's dead."

The Tamaell's mask slipped. "Yes, half-brother, your father is dead." He looked as if he wanted to say more, but ducked his head instead. When he raised his eyes again, the mask had been replaced. "We need to speak, all of us."

"We've just discovered another razed village in the valley beyond. My caitan, Mattalaen, is searching for survivors. We can talk while we wait for him to finish."

"Very well. I'll have my men erect a tent, since what I've seen of the past villages makes me suspect there's no building left standing in this one."

"No, there's not."

Thaedoren's eyes narrowed at the anger in Fedaureon's voice, but he raised a hand, the guardsman at his back spinning his horse and returning to his army. Within moments, a group of Phalanx moved off to the side of the road, scrambling to erect a tent in whatever space was available.

"Do you know if Peloroun, Orraen, and the Chosen are working with these creatures, this Wraith army?" Renaerd asked.

"We came from Nuant, by way of Rhyssal and Hallieas, following your own path. You know as much as we do," Daedelan answered. "But from what we've seen, there has been no active fighting between Peloroun's army and the Wraith army. All of the casualties have been commoners. They're either working together—"

"Or Peloroun and Lotaern are more cowardly than we thought," Caeden finished.

"What advantage would Lotaern gain by siding with the Wraiths?" Thaedoren asked. "He is the Chosen. The Wraiths and their minions are the antithesis of everything he believes in. And even if he has sided with them, the members of the Order of the Flame and all of those in the Order would not follow him that blindly, not to mention the general populace. It makes no sense for Lotaern or Peloroun to have allied with the Wraiths. Something else is going on here."

"We've been following their trail for days now," Fedaureon said. "As far as we can tell, Peloroun and Lotaern are racing for Caercaern, the Wraith army behind them. We'd hoped to catch Peloroun and Lotaern outside of Caercaern's walls, but they're too close to the city for us to catch them now, unless we rode all night."

"Hopefully we can sort out this mess," Daedelan said. "I believe the tent is ready. We should send the rest of our forces into the village for a short rest, send hunters out to forage for whatever we can find."

"Do so," the Tamaell said, already moving toward the tent. "But tell the caitans to have everyone ready to move out again in an hour. If Lord Fedaureon is right, we may have to continue on after dark."

* * *

As soon as Lotaern reached the gates of Caercaern, he turned to Peloroun, ignoring the fanfare of horns and shouts from Orraen's men on the walls above as they passed through the door into the first tier. "You know what needs to be done?" he asked over the roar, the street ahead lined with the citizens of Caercaern, although the main thoroughfare had been kept clear. He caught sight of Orraen waiting off to one side, the younger lord looking haggard and unhappy.

But he had no time for the weak lord. He needed to prepare the Order of Aielan and the Flame. And he needed to check on the Winter Tree.

"Of course," Peloroun said. Lotaern saw the strain around the lord's eyes, something he hadn't seen in the long years he'd spent in the Evant. Not even during the battles that culminated at the Escarpment. "You forget that I'm the Tamaell, Chosen. Now, prepare the Flame. The Wraith's army is half a day behind us. I'll take care of Orraen and the Phalanx." He glanced toward the younger lord. "The fool. He should have these people readying the walls, not welcoming us back."

Lotaern brushed Peloroun's disrespect aside and caught Vaeren's attention, motioning the caitan Flame closer as they split off from the main force.

"Have Boreaus and Petraen, along with eight others, take the Wraith to the gate tower. Make certain the anchor and collar remain in place. Have them begin the ritual as soon as they're ready. I'll bring the knife. I want you to assemble the Order of the Flame and begin the preparations for the attack. We need all of our defenses against the Wraiths in place within the next three hours." He glanced toward the sky as a gust of icy wind lashed down the street. Clouds scudded overhead, low and thick, growing darker and more bruised as they rushed steadily southward, heavy with the taste of snow.

"Where will you be?" Vaeren asked.

"I need to check on the Winter Tree."

"The Order will be ready when you return."

"See to it. This is our time, Vaeren. What we've been preparing for, what the Flame was meant for."

Vaeren's shoulders stiffened and his chest swelled. "We'll make Aielan proud."

Lotaern drew his mount around and charged up the street, the people of Caercaern shouting in welcome on either side as Peloroun's returning forces, along with his own Order of the Flame, poured back in through the gates. He heard Vaeren's first shouted orders, but then everything was drowned out in the wind blasting past him as he headed toward the gates to the second tier. He didn't halt, but noted how crowded the streets were. More so than usual. He thought about what Maenaed had said earlier, felt a small thrill of vindication. Obviously some of the Alvritshai *had* come to Caercaern to seek shelter, as the acolytes and members of the Flame had suggested throughout the House lands. Some had listened, and because they had come, they could be saved.

He passed through to the second tier, his horse flagging as the main road angled upwards. Caercaern loomed above him, the third tier and the Tamaell's tower soaring into the sky, the Winter Tree ahead, the storm skating over it all. As soon as they hit the flat, his mount picked up speed. Even so, he felt the power of the storm buffeting him from the side, the scent of snow so harsh his nostrils tingled. The nape of his neck prickled as the temperature dropped. Not one of the unnatural storms that came out of the east, but a deadly storm nonetheless. One that rarely came this early in winter.

He slowed as he entered the streets surrounding the marketplace where the Winter Tree had been planted, pulled his horse up short at the wall that had been built to create the gardens that protected the Tree. On all sides, as the storm blotted out more and more of the sun, lanterns and candle glow filled the city. At the gates to the gardens, one of the Wardens finished lighting the two lanterns outside, the glow suffusing the stone of the archway and the wooden doors, one half open.

"Who seeks the garden of the Winter Tree?" the Warden asked. "The gardens are closed to the public."

"But not to me."

"Chosen!" The Warden bowed deeply. "I apologize. I did not recognize you. I knew you were returning, but thought—"

"Take me to the Winter Tree," Lotaern interrupted. He could feel the Wraith army approaching. The prickling tension from the storm wasn't helping. "I need to check on its health."

The Warden brushed the cowl back from his face, even though the wind was biting. His expression sank claws of unease into Lotaern's gut. "Chosen, the Winter Tree...it's dying."

Lotaern barely caught the words, spoken so softly they were snatched by the storm. "Show me."

The Warden immediately turned and entered the garden. He paused to light a lantern, holding it up over his head as Lotaern took the lead, huffing to keep up with him.

Within moments, the grass became covered with leaves—the large silvered leaves of the Winter Tree. His feet kicked through them and they flashed silver as they were caught by the wind. A silver mottled with black patches of rot. Overhead, the leaves remaining on the Tree thrashed in the winds, even as they sheltered the two below. Branches creaked, and somewhere high overhead he heard cracks as some of them splintered and broke.

The Winter Tree had never shed its leaves before; its branches had never cracked.

The leaves beneath his feet grew thicker as they approached the bole of the Tree. He'd checked on the Tree before he and Peloroun left, had noticed blotches of rot then. But when the trunk of the Tree fell inside the lantern light, he gasped and staggered, fell to his knees.

"Aielan's Light." He clutched at the ground, the dead leaves crumbling between his fingers.

"I told you," the Warden said, his voice loud in the deadened silence near the Tree's base. The storm, the Wraith army, Peloroun and Orraen— all of it seemed distant.

Lotaern shoved himself back up from the ground, brushed the detritus from the leaves off on his robes, then shambled forward into the roots at the base of the trunk. They squished beneath his feet, a putrid smell rising to surround him, but he continued forward, struggling once or twice as he slipped in the rot. When he reached the bole, he hesitated, unwilling to touch the black splotches that covered the bark, striations of gray and white running throughout. There were few places where the original bark remained.

A roar rose from the wall of the lowest tier, muted by distance.

He had no time to be squeamish.

Reaching forward, he placed his hands against the trunk, fingers sinking into the fibrous, yet soft bark and closed his eyes, seeking the heart of the Tree. Disease enfolded him, smothered him, and he gagged on the putrid stench of it, fought the impulse to withdraw, and forced himself deeper into the roiling stagnation. A moan escaped him unbidden. All of the warmth of the Winter Tree, all of its richness—the smell of earth, of loam, the healthy pulse of the flow of sap, the silvery hint of snow from its leaves—all of it had died, had succumbed to the perversion of the disease. He sank further and further, yet still found nothing of the Tree's former life, of its power.

He turned back, his consciousness nearly subsumed by the layers of decay, and as he did so, he felt the faintest touch of what the Tree had once been. He lurched toward the feathery trace, but cried out as it receded. The Tree must have felt him searching.

As he neared what remained of its heart, the flicker of hope he'd felt at the Tree's touch guttered and died, replaced with a deep-seated sense of sadness and despair.

Striations of disease already threaded through the heart, fine as hairs, but they were there. The Winter Tree was in its death throes, and it knew it. It had tried to protect itself, withdrawing in upon itself and encasing its essence—its soul—in a knot of hardened wood, but the disease that consumed it had worked its way into the knot.

Tears streamed down Lotaern's face, chilled by the bitter winter air pouring down from the mountain heights as the storm spilled over the peaks. The sensation was far distant, the only outward sign of his pain. He reached out and enfolded the heartwood before him, let it feel his sorrow and grief.

It responded by embracing him in what little remained of the comforting pulse of its warmth. The flow of sap filled his ears, the rustle of leaves in a breeze, supplanting the harsh sounds of branches snapping, of the bole creaking. For a moment, the storm that tore at the Tree and stole its strength faded to nothing. There was only the heartwood and Lotaern.

But even as Lotaern sank into the Tree's welcome, he sensed its desperation. It knew it was dying, had known so for a long time, long before its connection to the Autumn Tree and the Summer Tree were severed.

In its embrace, he felt it tugging him toward something deeper, something it had kept protected.

He resisted at first, then followed it reluctantly, his thoughts already returning to the walls, to the approaching army, to the Wraith he held captive and the waiting Flame. There was nothing he could do to save the Winter Tree. It was nearly dead already. The Wraith's taunting had been correct.

Yet what the Tree showed him made him gasp.

* * *

The Warden watched silently as the Chosen of the Order of Aielan ascended to the bole of the Winter Tree and placed his palms flat against its bark. Around him, at the outer edges of the Tree's physical reach, he heard the damage the storm was inflicting. Winds screamed down from the heights, leaves already weakened by the blight torn from their branches. Limbs cracked and snapped, clattering to the ground. The main trunk directly overhead and the thickest branches shooting off from it groaned and creaked under the assault. Each splintering of wood, each moan, sent a shudder through his soul. He had stood in this marketplace the day Shaeveran thrust the seed of the Winter Tree into the stone, had witnessed the Tree's birth. The sight had changed him, had given him purpose. He'd forsaken his House, his family, to become an acolyte, his sole intent to serve and protect the Winter Tree.

He had been young then. His family had thought him foolish.

To see the Tree diseased, to see it trembling beneath the storm's onslaught...

The Chosen moaned, a strange counterpoint to the Tree, and he turned back, held the lantern up higher, squinting at the figure who now leaned heavily against the bark at the edges of the light. The Chosen's hands had sunk into the rot, his forehead resting against the bole. Tears streamed down his face, his eyes still closed.

For a long moment, the tableau held, the Chosen's breath calming, a sense of peace enveloping him, even though his tears continued. He sagged against the Tree, as if holding it up.

And then the Chosen gasped.

A moment later, the Chosen's eyes fluttered open. He shot a glance toward the Warden, his face drawn in grief, in pain—

And yet he spun to face the bole with a grim determination.

"What is it?" the Warden called, and even in the protection here at the sheltered center of the Tree, he could tell that the storm had intensified. The shrieking of the wind had escalated.

The Chosen didn't answer. The Warden took a step closer, sandaled foot settling on a softened root. It squelched beneath his weight, the liquid rot squirting up over his sandal and between his toes. He shuddered, drawing breath to shout the question louder.

But he choked on the breath instead.

The Chosen had shoved his hands deeper into the rot of the Tree. Jaw set, he braced himself and pushed harder, his arms sinking deeper and deeper. Liquid—a disgusting yellow brown streaked with black—trailed out of the two holes the Chosen's hands had made in the bark, but the Chosen didn't pay any attention to it, his arms sunk to their elbows now. And still he struggled forward. He pushed until his chest rested against the bole of the Tree, his head turned to one side, his cheek resting against one of the softened black blotches. But he strained forward, face twisted with effort. The Warden could see the muscles of his shoulders working.

The Chosen's jaw clenched and the Warden started forward. "Wait. Let me help."

Before he'd made it two steps, the Chosen sank another handspan farther into the bole, the bark near his head caving in beneath the pressure, and he yelped in triumph.

He staggered back, his entire front coated in rot, half of his face slicked with it, yet he was laughing. His arms came free of the Tree with a soft sucking sound, hands clasped around an object. Once free, the Chosen cradled the object close to his chest with one arm, using his free hand to slough off the worst of the rot from near his mouth and his cloths.

Then he stumbled down toward the Warden.

Somewhere overhead, a large branch cracked, the retort loud enough they both flinched and looked up. But the Chosen didn't slow, coming to a halt before the Warden, his face grim.

"What did you find?" the Warden asked.

The Chosen ignored the question. "I have a task for you."

The Warden bowed his head. "Of course, Chosen. What is it that you need?"

"I need you to leave Caercaern. Now. Before the Wraiths' army arrives, surrounds the walls, and blocks the roadway."

The Warden's eyes widened in surprise. "But I'm a Warden, sworn to protect the Winter Tree."

"The Winter Tree is dead. But this," he held up the object with one hand, "is its seed."

Something closed off the Warden's throat, his chest tightening. What the Chosen held appeared so small, even though it was a knot of wood the size of his fist, resting on top of a shaft the length of his forearm.

The Chosen thrust the seed into his free hand. He gripped the Warden's shoulder, even as the Warden struggled to swallow past the constriction in his throat. He felt the power of the seed in his hand, felt the weight of responsibility settling heavily on his shoulders, even before the Chosen spoke.

"The Wraiths and their brethren cannot be allowed to capture this. Who knows how they would distort it to their own purposes. You must flee Caercaern with it. You must take it to..." The Chosen halted, then grimaced in distaste. "You must take it to Shaeveran."

"But—"

"Find him, and give this to him. He will know what needs to be done. He gifted it to us, after all."

"But don't you need it? Can't you use it to fight the Wraiths?"

The Chosen stood back. "Perhaps. If it had had time to fully form. But it hasn't. It's useless to me now. But by the time you find Shaeveran—or by the time he finds you—it will have finished growing."

"But—" The Warden glanced down at the seed. "But I'm merely an acolyte."

"You are a follower of Aielan. You joined the Order in order to serve Her. Would you renounce Her now? She placed you here, on watch on this night, at this time, for a reason. This is your path: to carry the seed of the Winter Tree to Shaeveran. To see that it survives."

The Warden nearly said that he had joined the Order to serve the Tree, not Aielan, but the Chosen's last words stayed him. The Tree...

He looked up into the thick branches above, undisturbed by the storm here. He looked up and thought of the disease he had seen eating away its heart over the past eight months, small signs of blight at first, turning quickly to entire patches of rot. Disease that, no matter what the Wardens did, could not be slowed, could not be stopped.

If this was the only way the Tree could be saved...

His gaze dropped to the Chosen. He lowered the lantern. "Where will I find Shaeveran?"

"I do not know. But your first concern is escaping Caercaern. Follow me. You will need a horse, and supplies. Then we must get you outside the walls, before the gates are sealed and the Wraith army arrives."

* * *

Vaeren, caitan of the Order of the Flame, ducked his head and hunched his shoulders, turning away from the blast of frigid air that screamed down from the Hauttaeren above, his hair whipping around his face and stinging where it lashed against his cheeks. As soon as it abated he swung back and shouted, "Boreaus, check the placement of the Order of the Flame. If they're in position, have them begin the chant and lay down the lines of power now. Doublecheck their positions yourself. Petraen, swing by the gatehouse and make certain Orraen has men standing over the winches to the gates. Double the guard if you have to, but make certain they know to keep them open until the last moment. Peloroun needs to be able to get back inside, but they also need to be ready to close them at a moment's notice."

Both of the brothers nodded and tore away in opposite directions, neither responding verbally. Vaeren cursed the winds that were already drying out his throat, making his voice cracked and brittle. He worked some spit into his mouth and swallowed, reaching to check for his waterskin. He'd taken a swallow earlier, surprised to find that the cold air that had followed the passing of the leading edge of the storm had already begun freezing it.

He glanced upward again, the entire sky seething with bruised clouds skating southward. This was not a normal storm for this far south. It was more like the storms to the north, beyond the mountains. "The storms that drove us into the mountains and into this land in the first place," he said to himself. A shudder ran through him, not brought on by the fierce chill air prickling his skin, but by something deeper, an ancestral memory.

The cold in this storm could kill. If the temperature dipped much lower—and he didn't think they'd felt the brunt of the storm yet—it could kill even the Alvritshai.

A roar snapped his attention back to the wall and he stepped to the parapet and looked downwards, both hands braced against the stone for support. Far below, beneath the long, wide ramp that ran across the entire length of the wall to the gates to the west, he saw the combined Alvritshai Phalanx. Men from Ionaen, Licaeta, Redlien, and Uslaen—all of the eastern and southern Houses—were arrayed on the field. Forest had once come all the way up to the wall, but Orraen, Saetor, and Houdyll had spent the last month clearing it with a controlled burn. Under mostly Saetor's direction, the lands had been turned and shaped for defensive purposes. Trenches had been dug, pits filled with stakes and then covered had been placed in strategic locations, all of it planned to pull the Wraith army in to their deaths. Saetor had been the natural choice to devise the plan, since he'd once been Khalaek's caitan, commander of the House's Phalanx. He'd never had aspirations to become a lord, had had the honor thrust upon him after Khalaek's banishment, but he'd served his House well. Vaeren had been told by members of the Order of the Flame who had remained behind that Saetor had stepped into the role of commander again without qualm, had, in fact, appeared more comfortable in that role than he had at any time serving as lord of his House.

The roar came from the Phalanx, a rallying cry, echoing up to the heights in defiance of the wind. As Vaeren watched, the combined Phalanx broke, units separating and falling into their positions.

Movement at the gates caught Vaeren's attention. He frowned, picking out Lotaern and another man dressed as a Warden on a horse, both surrounded by a group of Orraen's Phalanx. Lotaern raised a hand and placed it on the Warden's head, the man bowing low to receive the blessing. Then the Warden pulled up his cowl, concealing his face before Vaeren could catch a glimpse, and spun his mount from the gates. He charged down the wide ramp, while behind another man—Orraen, Vaeren saw—emerged from the shadows of the gate and joined Lotaern. They spoke, their voices lost to the storm, of course, but moments later Orraen turned and motioned with one hand. More Phalanx appeared, archers, marching in formation from the gates and down the long ramp to take up positions over the battlefield below. Lotaern disappeared back into the gates.

The man on horseback had reached the end of the ramp. But rather than joining the host of Phalanx, he turned east, following the edge of the mountain wall, until he vanished into the far edge of forest and was gone.

Vaeren pushed back from the edge and turned.

The Wraith stood in the center of the square tower. There were two towers, one on each side of the main gates, both of their roofs the size of a small market square. Orraen and Daesor had taken control of the right, leaving Lotaern and the Order of the Flame control of the left for their own devices. Orraen had fought the decision, but Lotaern needed room for the Order to prepare their own defenses.

Even as Vaeren stepped toward the Wraith, he felt the first line of power from the rest of the Flame scattered along the walls in both directions fall into place. A small smile of satisfaction touched the corner of his mouth.

The Wraith—Maenaed, Vaeren remembered—lowered his head as he approached. There wasn't a trace of concern in Maenaed's eyes. He didn't even react as more lines of power snapped into position. But perhaps with the collar in place, he couldn't feel them. Maybe it was more of a prison than any of them thought, locking the Wraith away from any sense of the power of Aielan around them.

For a moment, Vaeren allowed himself to stretch out along the lines being laid. They reached from the walls all the way down to the battlefield below. In fact, most of them were centered on the field.

"Can you feel what we have planned for your army? Can you sense it? Or is the collar too constricting?"

Maenaed merely glowered, refusing to respond, a muscle at the corner of his jaw twitching.

"Is everything in place?"

Vaeren turned from the Wraith to look at Lotaern, the Chosen moving purposefully toward both of them. "Boreaus is overseeing the placements of the Flame. Everything appears in order. Petraen has gone to the gates to make certain the men at the gates are ready."

"I saw him there as I ascended. What of the Wraith?"

Vaeren's gaze flickered toward the eight other members of the Flame who stood at various positions around the tower. "The anchor holds."

Lotaern stilled for a moment, and Vaeren knew he was checking the anchor himself. He stiffened, even though he knew he'd do the same in Lotaern's place. The Wraith was too dangerous to risk letting escape. He'd proven that at his capture, taunting them with his power before they'd sprung the trap around him. And even then, he'd almost killed them both before the collar had subdued him.

Vaeren had argued that they kill the Wraith then, but Lotaern had wanted to use him as a symbol of the Order's power...and as a goad.

Awareness pricked Lotaern's eyes again and he said, "Good. As soon as the field is set below, have Boreaus return. The rest of the Flame already know what needs to be done."

"Do Peloroun, Orraen, and the rest?"

"If they don't, then they won't survive."

Vaeren followed the Chosen as he moved to the wall. He watched as Lotaern assessed the field.

"Where did you send the Warden?" Vaeren asked.

Lotaern's gaze flicked toward him. "What Warden?"

Vaeren's eyebrows rose. "The one you sent away at the main gates, before Orraen's archers manned the ramp."

Lotaern said nothing for a long moment, eyes narrowing slightly. But then he shrugged. "It was nothing of consequence."

Vaeren considered pressing for more—it had obviously been more than nothing—but felt a surge through the stone at his feet.

Lotaern and Maenaed felt it as well, both of them focusing out beyond the wall, the Chosen with a look of satisfaction, the Wraith with the first signs of concern Vaeren had seen since his capture.

And as if in answer, a cry of warning rose up. Signals flared all along the wall's length and on the ramp below, the archers—sheltered from the wind by Caercaern itself—were all pointing toward the distance, beyond the cleared area where the rest of the Phalanx waited.

Vaeren stepped forward, picking out movement among the trees.

A moment later, the front ranks of the Wraith army marched into view, spread across nearly the breadth of the wall, led by three figures on horseback, all dressed in black and gold. One of the Flame nearby sucked in a harsh breath as rank after rank of creatures filed forward. Vaeren tried to make out what they were in the ghostly light of the torches below and the storm above.

"What are they?" he asked. "They look like...snakes."

"Haessari," Lotaern said. "The oldest Scripts speak of them. I did not expect to see them here. But they aren't all Haessari." He motioned toward the center of the field.

Vaeren focused in on those at the heart of the army, most on horseback. A few were these...Haessari...but most of them were—

"Alvritshai." He unconsciously stepped to the wall. "But how? Who are they? It can't be the traitors. Thaedoren would never ally himself with the Wraiths. Neither would Aeren or any of the others who escaped the coup. So who—?"

But he halted, aware that Lotaern did not appear surprised, nor incensed, even as the colors the Alvritshai wore finally pierced deep, sinking down and reawakening emotions he had long thought dead and buried. He lurched upright. "No." But his eyes had already skipped from the black and gold armor of House Duvoraen to the three figures who led the army. The figure on the left was Haessari, the snake-like snout clear, the skin scaled and mottled with colors bleached into odd grays and blacks. On the right sat a dwarren, the shorter figure seated on a gaezel, and even from this distance Vaeren could see the black oil that marred his face. He hadn't realized there were dwarren Wraiths, but if there were Alvritshai and human Wraiths, why not dwarren? Yet it was still a surprise; he had thought the dwarren reverence for the Land would make them less susceptible to corruption.

But it was the central figure that caught and held his attention.

"Lord Khalaek."

He had pledged his life to Khalaek and House Duvoraen what felt like an eternity ago, in his youth, before the lord's betrayal at the Escarpment and the dissolution of the House. When Duvoraen fell, it had left Vaeren Houseless. Even though everyone who had belonged to House Duvoraen was given over to the newly risen House Uslaen, led by Lord Saetor, it had still caused in rift, a disassociation. Vaeren had trained as a member of House Duvoraen, had gone to war beneath Khalaek's rule. He hadn't been able to simply sever those ties and realign himself beneath Saetor. Instead, he'd cut his ties to Duvoraen and Uslaen both, became an acolyte within the Order...and eventually came to Lotaern's attention and helped create and found the Order of the Flame. He'd found his path.

There were many others disillusioned by Khalaek's betrayal and the fall of Duvoraen. Some had become acolytes like himself. Some had simply...left. He'd thought they'd found places among the other Houses, a few perhaps seeking self-banishment, but this...

The number of Alvritshai arrayed behind Khalaek was staggering. And unconsciously, Vaeren's heart soared to see the banners and colors of the eagle's talon flapping in the winds of the storm. If he had known Lord Khalaek lived, if he had known that House Duvoraen had survived—

A hand clamped down on his arm and he jerked in surprise, hand gripping the hilt of his cattan, partially drawing it before his eyes caught Lotaern's.

"That is not Lord Khalaek. Look, caitan of the Flame. Look at his face. Lord Khalaek died on the field at the Escarpment, died beneath the hands of the human, King Stephen. That creature is Khalaek-khai, an abomination tainted by the sarenavriell, twisted by its dark power. It is not the man you knew. Lord Khalaek has been forsaken by Aielan."

Vaeren spun back, searching out Khalaek, searching out his former lord—

And found the sarenavriell's taint beneath his pale skin, just like that of the dwarren.

Lotaern's hand on his arm steadied him, yet he still reached for the stone of the parapet for support. He knew others on the wall would be feeling the same—members of Duvoraen who had fled to the Order or to other Houses loyal to Peloroun, Orraen, and the rest—

And he suddenly realized that was Lord Khalaek's—no, Khalaek-khai's—intent. It's why he stood at the forefront of the army, why the Alvritshai who had betrayed their people to join the Wraith army were at its center. They were there to throw the Alvritshai defenders into chaos. He could sense the confusion running through the Phalanx even now, affecting those on the field below, the archers on the ramp, those lining the walls to either side, even the members of the Flame. Especially the members of the Flame, because many of those who'd felt abandoned by the fall of House Duvoraen had come to Aielan for solace.

He couldn't allow Khalaek-khai's tactic to work. Not on himself, and not on the rest of the Flame. They'd planned too carefully for this.

As he gathered his strength and straightened, he caught Lotaern's eyes and suddenly realized that Lotaern had planned more carefully than even he'd thought.

"This is why you couldn't kill the Wraith earlier," he said, his voice gaining strength even as he spoke, as all of the repercussions of Lotaern's plan began to sink in. "You knew Khalaek-khai led the army. You knew there were Alvritshai coming to attack Caercaern."

"I needed a rallying point. I needed to show everyone that the Wraith army before us has been forsaken by Aielan."

"I understand." Vaeren shook off Lotaern's hand and the Chosen let it fall. And he did understand. Any doubt he had harbored about the Chosen faded and he felt the warmth of Aielan's Light fill him. "What is it that you need me to do?"

16

Lotaern saw Aielan's Light ignite in Vaeren's eyes and nodded in satisfaction. He had known the sight of Khalaek-khai would affect the caitan profoundly. He had counseled Vaeren during his confusion and uncertainty after Lord Khalaek was banished and given over to the humans at the Escarpment and summarily executed. The fall of House Duvoraen had shocked the caitan to his bones and for a long while Lotaern had harbored the fear Vaeren would not recover. But with Aielan's guidance and Lotaern's support, Vaeren had, and he'd become one of the Flame's most powerful and respected members.

Now, it was time for him to put that to use.

"I need you to address the Phalanx, Vaeren. Denounce Khalaek-khai and those that follow him. And then let me speak."

Vaeren glanced down at the forces arrayed below the wall. Already, the ranks on the ground, beneath the ramp, were wavering, the Phalanx fidgeting in uncertainty and confusion. Lotaern could see Peloroun, Saetor, and Houdyll berating them, even though he couldn't hear their words. Saetor's Phalanx showed the most disruption, which was to be expected. Like Vaeren, his men had once been part of House Duvoraen, had once served beneath Khalaek.

"How will they hear me? The storm..."

"Have faith in Aielan, caitan."

Vaeren stiffened, then stepped up to the edge of the parapet. As he did so, Lotaern bowed his head, closed his eyes, and muttered a small prayer, more of a chant.

When he opened them again, lines of power radiated out and down from the top of the tower along Caercaern's wall, the ramp below, and the field beyond, stretching all the way to the Wraith's army.

"Fellow Alvritshai!" Vaeren shouted. He gave a start when he realized his voice had been amplified, shot Lotaern a surprised look, but returned his attention as those below began reacting. "Fellow Phalanx! Do not falter! Stand steady beneath the walls of Caercaern. This is not the lord of

House Duvoraen who stands before you. Look at him closely. The taint of the sarenavriell writhes beneath his skin! He has forsaken Aielan. He is khai and so, too, are those who have chosen to follow him. They have all forsworn Her Light in the name of the Wraiths! Lord Khalaek died on the battlefields at the Escarpment. This creature who leads their army was sent to make you doubt. It is a trick of the Wraiths, meant to make you quail and falter at the very moment you should stand tall and fight." Drawing his sword, Vaeren raised the cattan before him, pointed toward the roiling storm, and bellowed, "In the name of Aielan and Her Light, stand and fight!"

An answering roar rose up from below, defying the storm. Lotaern stepped up to Vaeren's side, soaking up the battlecry that had settled into a chant, the members of the Phalanx raising their own weapons, brandishing them toward the walls. Beyond them, Khalaek and the rest of the Wraith army hadn't reacted, even though Lotaern knew they'd heard Vaeren's words; he'd made certain of that. But the dwarren Wraith and the leader of the Haessari broke away from Khalaek, trotting their mounts to either side of the army in preparation.

Raising both of his arms to catch the Alvritshai's attention, Lotaern broke into the chant. "We have faced the Wraith's before," he said, his words echoing out from the walls, "and paid a high price in the past. But I stand before you now as Chosen of the Order of Aielan to say that those days are behind us. The acolytes of the Order and the warriors of the Flame have prepared for this day, for this confrontation. We are no longer powerless before the darkness of the Wraiths! As proof, I present to you the Wraith once called Maenaed, captured days ago by the Order of the Flame as Khalaek-khai and his forces approached."

Vaeren motioned those holding Maenaed's collar forward. The Phalanx below had fallen silent, tension lacing the air. It shivered through Lotaern's skin, tingling with the same intensity and energy as that of the storm, and Lotaern savored it with every breath. Maenaed struggled against the chains that bound him, chains Lotaern had researched, had resurrected from the words of the Scripts, had trained the Order of the Flame into mastering in preparation for this moment. The culmination of everything he had worked for was at hand.

Maenaed's struggles were useless. The Wraith was forced forward, the collar that encircled his neck blazed a harsh white with his efforts, burning with Aielan's Light, visible to everyone below.

Turning back, Lotaern reached for the folds of metal mesh tucked into his belt and pulled them free. He unfolded the mesh slowly, the curiosity of all of those watching intoxicating. The mesh fell away, revealing the smoothed wooden curves of the knife beneath. Vaeren's breath hissed out as he recognized the blade he had stolen from Shaeveran over a year before.

Lotaern gripped the hilt, a pulse of the heartwood's lifeforce coursing through him. He dropped the metal mesh to the stone parapet, faced the Phalanx waiting in enthralled silence, then let his gaze drift toward Khalaek-khai and the waiting army. He couldn't see the expression on Khalaek's face, the former Alvritshai lord too distant for such subtleties, but he imagined tension there, perhaps fear at the corners of his eyes.

He raised the knife with both hands, cradled it, careful not to touch its edge. He remembered how easily it had sliced his finger what felt like ages before, when Shaeveran had first shown it to him in the depths of the Sanctuary.

"I give you proof that the Wraiths are not indestructible."

He turned to face Maenaed, switching his grip on the hilt of the blade. He allowed the anger and rage over all that the Wraiths had inflicted on the Alvritshai, all that they had been forced to endure, including the interference and manipulations of Shaeveran, suffuse him.

"You are an abomination in Aielan's Eyes, and so I destroy you in Her name."

Then he raised the knife high overhead, one handed, and plunged it into Maenaed's chest, directly over his heart.

Maenaed screamed and arched back, the sound piercing the shriek of the wind, cutting deep into Lotaern's bones and making him clench his jaw. The Chosen was thrust back, the knife slicing down across the Wraith's chest before wrenching free. "Hold him!" He stumbled and caught himself against the stone wall. The collar blazed as the Wraith struggled against it, blood coating his torso from the chest wound down. Those Flame on the tower strained to hold the anchor, their postures crouched and taut, two with hands outstretched and clenched, as if they held physical ropes. Vaeren stood poised to attack, his cattan before him, his eyes watching Maenaed's every move. But the Wraith was still constrained. Only Lotaern's proximity had allowed him to be flung aside.

Lotaern shoved away from the wall and advanced, knife held ready. He could see the Wraith's strength waning. Blood continued to gush from the wound, the front of the tainted Alvritshai's clothes saturated. Droplets splattered from his arms, dripped from the folds of his shirt. The Wraith's scream died into a phlegmy gurgle and he hunched forward, spat blood onto the stone at his feet. He tried to rise, growling low in his throat. He managed only a tilt of his head, his eyes flashing hatred, and then he fell to his knees. Breath coming in harsh, wet heaves, he tried to speak, but Lotaern could discern nothing intelligible through the blood he continued to choke up.

Lotaern moved to sink the knife into the Wraith's back, but Maenaed collapsed forward and remained still.

Someone shouted something from beneath the tower and the Phalanx let out a roar of triumph. Lotaern let the sound wash over him, the tension in his shoulders releasing. Vaeren shifted forward, prodded Maenaed's form with one foot, and when the Wraith didn't move—didn't even appear to be breathing—he lowered his cattan and met Lotaern's gaze.

"It is done," Lotaern said.

He turned to the wall, stepped up to the edge and raised his hand out before him, the bloody knife still clenched tight in one fist. "It is done!"

The answering roar from below was deafening, shuddering in the stone beneath his feet. He basked in the adulation, so intense he closed his eyes. The manic energy of the storm complemented it. A shiver coursed through him, answered a heartbeat later by a blinding flash of lightning and a crackle of thunder. His eyes flew open and he shouted, "Now finish it. Aielan's Light is at your back and the Order of the Flame is at your side!"

Commands lashed out from below, echoing his words as Peloroun, Saetor, and Houdyll led their forces forward in a charge, only a few remaining behind as reinforcements. Orraen's orders bit through the winds, the archers on the ramp in the lee of Caercaern nocking arrows and readying. The Wraith's army was still too distant, the storm cutting down on the archer's range significantly, but that didn't matter. The intent was to draw the Wraith army closer to the wall anyway, within range of the archers and the Flame.

Lotaern lowered his arms to the frigid stone of the battlement as across the field the Wraith's armies charged, Khalaek-khai's Alvritshai in the center slightly ahead of the Haessari to either side. Khalaek-khai led them astride his horse, not deigning to dismount and use the powers of the Wraiths that Maenaed had taunted them with before his capture. He drew his cattan and hit the front line—Peloroun's men, Lotaern noted—with a battlecry that was lost on the winds, sword crashing down on Peloroun's shield. The muted sounds of the battle rolled upwards, punctuated with screams, hissing shrieks, cries of rage and defiance and horror. Lotaern had witnessed such battles before—his first taste at the Escarpment, when he'd introduced the Order of the Flame to the battlefields alongside the rest of the House Phalanx. There had been intense fights with the Wraiths and the sukrael in the years that followed. He had only seen the aftermath of those battles, the sukrael attacking without warning, the Flame unable to prepare ahead of time.

But they were prepared today. He could feel the lines of power that lay across the field, could sense the anticipation of the Flame along the walls.

"And where are you, Shaeveran? You, who swore to protect us?"

"Did he swear to protect us?"

Lotaern gave a start. He hadn't intended Vaeren to overhear him. But he hadn't noticed Vaeren approach, the caitan of the Flame standing beside him at the edge of the wall, staring down at the battle below, arms crossed over his chest. He'd sheathed his cattan.

Lotaern glanced behind to see if any of the other members of the Flame were close. But they were still standing at their positions, the collar around the Wraith's neck still blazing white.

"You can release the anchor." He gestured with one hand—the one that still clutched the knife.

The Flame glanced toward each other, the eldest bowing his head. "Where do you wish us to go then?"

"Find Boreaus or Petraen. They will know how you can support the Flame best."

The impromptu leader nodded and led the small group to the stairs leading down to the lower portions of the tower.

After they'd left, Lotaern turned to Vaeren. "Shaeveran did swear to protect us. Not in so many words, but with his actions. He brought the Wraiths down upon us. He agreed to help us in the years following the signing of the Accord at the Escarpment. But where was he when the sukrael were attacking our borders?"

"He is only one man. A human, at that. He could not have protected our borders any better than we did ourselves."

"Perhaps." Lotaern shrugged. "Who knows what powers he possesses? He was never very forthcoming about the extent of what the sarenavriell's taint gave him. I find it hard to believe that he did everything within his power to protect us."

"He gave us the Winter Tree."

"He forced it upon us!" Lotaern shouted, and only then did he realize how bitter his thoughts were regarding Shaeveran. His anger ran deep, an anger he'd been harboring for decades. "He forced it upon us," he repeated in a calmer tone. "As he forced the Accord upon us. And yet when he finally did find something that could be used to protect us," he raised the knife, "he refused to give it to us. We were forced to take it from him, so that we could use it as intended."

Vaeren shifted restlessly, but said nothing. Words were unnecessary.

"I know that the theft of the knife has weighed on your soul, caitan. But it was necessary. Do you see that now?"

Vaeren contemplated the field below, where Peloroun's forces held steady. He'd broken away from Khalaek-khai, the two forced apart by the ebb and surge of the battle, although Lotaern could tell they were straining to reach each other. The Tamaell's banners stayed with him, his escort using whatever openings were offered to push toward the Wraith. Khalaek-khai slew his former fellow Alvritshai left and right. To either side, the Haessari and Caercaern's forces washed forward and back, a tide of blood and pain. He'd lost sight of the Haessari leader and the dwarren Wraith.

Vaeren finally lowered his head, not taking his eyes from the battle. "I always understood that retrieving the knife was necessary. I simply wish there had been another way."

"With Shaeveran, there is no other way. He is arrogant. He believes only he knows what's right and fitting for our people. He is an interloper. I have striven to provide for the Alvritshai since long before the Escarpment. I began forming the Flame before the sukrael became a problem, before we even knew of the Wraiths. Perhaps, without Shaeveran's interference, we would not have run into them so soon and we would have been prepared for them."

"Do you lay none of the blame at Khalaek's feet? He is the one who dealt with the human Wraith named Walter. He is the one who conspired with him to kill Tamaell Fedorem."

Loatern nodded. "Khalaek's hands are bloody, yes. I hold him responsible for much of what has happened. But not all. Shaeverean— and because of his influence, Lord Aeren—share his guilt. I do not know the fate of Lord Aeren. I assume he is still alive, somewhere, along with Thaedoren. But it does not matter. Today, we will punish Khalaek for his role in what has become of the Alvritshai. Today, we will begin taking control of our own destinies. No more reliance on Shaeveran and his gifts. The Flame will show how powerful they truly are, prove they can protect the Alvritshai as well as anything Shaeveran can provide. No one will doubt the power of the Order of Aielan."

Vaeren said nothing, but his brows creased in a frown. Irritation flashed through Lotaern's skin. He'd thought the caitan understood and agreed with him. He'd thought his chosen leader of the Flame had faith in his own Chosen and the Order of Aielan.

When Vaeren finally spoke, Lotaern had braced himself for additional arguments, but he was surprised.

"We expected the sukrael here," Vaeren said. "Where are they?"

Caught off guard, Lotaern didn't answer immediately. "It doesn't matter. If they appear, the Flame is waiting, and Peloroun knows what to do. Otherwise, we can leave the majority of the battle to him and Saetor."

* * *

Peloroun smashed his mailed fist into an Alvritshai traitor's face. Bone crunched and blood splattered as the Alvritshai screamed, his nose flattened. The traitor reared back, dragging his horse's reins, the creature rising and kicking with its hooves. The lord of House Ionaen stabbed forward with his cattan as he ducked, felt one of the animal's hooves skim his shoulder with enough force to jolt him to one side, nearly out of his own horse's saddle, while sending a frisson of pain down into his arm. He cursed and jerked his cattan free, blood gouting from the wound, then turned to meet the next warrior dressed in the black and gold of the dead House of Duvoraen.

Out of the corner of his eye, he caught a flash of lightning, highlighting Khalaek, his sword descending, but that brief glimpse was all he got as he was attacked on two sides. He bellowed to his fellow Phalanx, felt them closing in from behind, as he parried one thrust, kicking out with one foot to shove the man back while slapping the other aside with the mail along his arm. He brought his cattan around, slicing into the nearest Alvritshai's neck, jerking it free and spinning so that he could see Khalaek again.

"Time to finish this," Peloroun muttered.

Without looking, he shouted, "Eraent, Bulorren, and any of the rest of you who can manage, stay with me!"

Then he kneed his horse forward, the animal chuffing as it sank back on his haunches slightly and launched itself forward. Two Alvritshai fell beneath its feet, the rest attempting to wound it or Peloroun before they were shunted aside. Peloroun hacked on both sides as his steed plowed forward, coming at Khalaek from one side, the tainted lord oblivious, his attention fixed on slaughtering his former countrymen before him. Blood flecked his pale features, as black as the oil that seethed beneath his skin. Hope surged in Peloroun's chest as he cut the distance by half, Khalaek turning away, exposing his back. Raising his sword, he brought it down in a high slant—

But a moment before it connected, Khalaek's upper torso blurred and spun, his sword arm shifting up, his cattan blocking the blow with a grating crash of steel on steel. Peloroun let out a cry of disbelief and outrage, but carried his blade's momentum through, smashing down against Khalaek's cattan again and again, until finally Khalaek twisted, the blades clashing and sliding off each other, destroying his methodical barrage. Peloroun lurched back, the roar of the battle rushing in to fill the bloodrush in his ears...along with a full, deep laugh.

He blinked at the burn of sweat in his eyes, his chest heaving from exertion, and realized that Khalaek was chuckling. He met the ex-lord's gaze, teeth clenched.

"Why are you here, Khalaek?" he shouted over the clash of armor and steel to either side of them. Thunder growled overhead, the storm clouds above roiling. "Did you come back of your own accord, or are you Walter's pawn?"

Khalaek's dry laugh cut off. "I am no one's pawn, least of all Walter's. I've come back to reclaim my rightful place as Tamaell of the Alvritshai people."

Peloroun spat to one side. "You will never be Tamaell of the Alvritshai. You are khai, banished, lost in the eyes of the Evant and in the eyes of Aielan. And the taint of the sarenavriell marks you as well. House Duvoraen is dead."

"Not while I still live."

"You expect to take Caercaern with these forces?"

"No, I expect to take them with those."

He pointed with his sword, and Peloroun followed with his gaze, looking out over the tumultuous battlefield, ebbing and flowing like an ocean. His brow creased in consternation as he searched and found nothing, but just as he was about to turn back to Khalaek, he sensed a ripple in the flow of battle at the outer edges, those closest to the trees to the east.

Squinting, he saw men on the flank begin to fall, picked off like sheep at the edge of a flock. Some of them twisted, swords flashing at nothing, but most simply collapsed, as if their legs had been cut out from under them.

A moment later Peloroun saw a flicker of darkness deeper than even the shadows beneath the trees and the storm. A darkness with a tinge of gold.

"The sukrael."

"The sukrael," Khalaek confirmed. "The prisoners of the sarenavriell have been unleashed."

Khalaek shifted in his saddle and Peloroun spun back, cattan rising to slap away the blade he expected to be falling toward his neck. But Khalaek merely shook his head.

"You should never have betrayed me, Peloroun. Was it Lotaern who convinced you to turn against me? I thought we had reached an agreement back at the salt flats. I thought we were kindred spirits, trapped in the Evant by the machinations of Tamaell Fedorem and the insufferable lords beneath us."

"We were never kindred spirits." Peloroun reined in his horse as it picked up on the sudden tension in the battle, its nostrils flaring. The attack of sukrael was being felt even here. He didn't have much time left. "You murdered Tamaell Fedorem. You betrayed the Alvritshai by conspiring with one of the Wraiths."

"Ah, yes, I remember. I believe you handed me over to the human king for execution. Do you know what it feels like to be gutted? To have your entrails sliced open and exposed to the night air? Perhaps I'll show you. If the sukrael don't get you first."

Peloroun laughed, satisfaction coursing through him as Khalaek frowned in confusion.

"You underestimate us yet again, Khalaek-khai." He bit off the end of the traitor's name. "We've prepared for the sukrael."

Spinning in his seat, he roared, "Sound the horns! Fall back!"

A horn's forlorn call blew before he'd finished shouting, the call picked up by others on the field, then on the heights above. He risked a glance toward the main tower, prayed that Lotaern was watching, that the Chosen was prepared, then swung his horse back around to face Khalaek.

Then he charged, cattan raised, a deep-throated growl erupting from the depths of his chest.

* * *

"What is that fool doing?" Lotaern shouted from the tower.

"He's charging toward Khalaek, although calling it a 'charge' is a little strong since they're already so close together."

"I can see that. But why? He's called the retreat!"

"I don't know." Vaeren leaned forward onto the stone. "But I'd guess he's either hoping to catch him by surprise, or else he's trying to throw him off enough they can retreat without being harassed by Khalaek and his men."

Lotaern's gaze snapped back to the battlefield below. To the east, the sukrael continued to spill out of the forest, attacking the flank, their shadows like ink seeping across the land. If they had simply attacked and moved on, leaving the bodies behind, they would have overrun that entire side already. But as soon as the bodies fell, the shadows fell on their victims, enveloping them, their darkness seething as they fed. Sickened by the sight, Lotaern tore his gaze back to Peloroun in time to see the lord and Khalaek trade blows, Peloroun driving the Wraith back with a fierceness Lotaern hadn't seen from him yet. Ionaen's Phalanx surged forward as well, driving hard into Khalaek's Alvritshai forces to either side. Behind, the rest of the defenders of Caercaern were pulling back, Saetor taking control. The Chosen watched as they funneled past the hidden pits, drawing the Wraith's army behind them. To the west, some of the Haessari had already reached the pits, rushing forward and falling into their depths, onto the spikes that had been hastily erected. Fresh screams rose into the air. Near the center, the press of their own forces grew too great and part of Saetor's Phalanx stumbled into the edge of another pit, at least five men falling to their deaths. Lotaern muttered a prayer to Aielan to take them into Her Light.

Then Vaeren's hand latched onto his upper arm.

"Look."

Lotaern's gaze shifted back to Peloroun and Khalaek. The lord of House Ionaen had driven Khalaek and his forces back at least twenty paces, but when Khalaek's horse stumbled, tossing the Wraith from the saddle, Peloroun turned and shouted something, the words lost to the wind long before they reached the tower. The Ionaen Phalanx abruptly halted their push forward and began to retreat, most simply spinning and running toward Saetor's forces, leaving Khalaek's men behind.

Peloroun tried to do the same, kneeing his horse forward—

But with a blur of darkness, Khalaek suddenly appeared between him and his men. No longer mounted, Khalaek simply stood there, Peloroun drawing his mount up sharply. A few of Peloroun's men saw their lord's escape had been blocked and tried to return to him.

But they were too late.

Lotaern imagined he could hear their curses as Peloroun decided to ride Khalaek down. He watched in silence as Peloroun steadied his horse, then kicked it hard, bringing his cattan up in a swing meant to decapitate Khalaek where he stood.

Except that Khalaek no longer stood there. A heartbeat before the blade would have fallen, Khalaek blurred—a smear of darkness—and reappeared on Peloroun's other side. The traitor's blade cut up and under, seeking the weaknesses in Peloroun's armor, exposed by his own swing. Peloroun flinched as Khalaek's blade scored flesh, but recovered and swung again.

But Khalaek shifted again, appearing behind him, striking, then blurring again. As Maenaed had done on the field to taunt them, Khalaek used the powers he'd gained from the sarenavriell to hound Peloroun, never letting the lord's cattan hit him. Peloroun's men rode hard to catch up to him, but Khalaek was too fast, flickering in and out of sight, blade sinking in deep, until Lotaern could see the blood trickling down Peloroun's armor, could see the lord's attempts to strike faltering as he grew weaker.

Then one of Peloroun's swings tipped him far enough he could no longer remain in the saddle. He tumbled to the ground, his horse's startled whinny heard even on the tower, the animal—who'd danced to Peloroun's command during the entire horrific fight—suddenly taking flight, leaving Peloroun behind. The lord rolled and drew himself up onto hands and knees—

But Khalaek appeared at his side.

Before Peloroun could raise his head, Khalaek brought his cattan down on Peloroun's exposed neck.

Lotaern flinched and gasped as Peloroun's head rolled to one side, his body falling gracelessly to the other, blood spurting from the stump. Peloroun's men pulled up short, hesitated, then twisted their mounts around and headed back to the main forces.

Lotaern half expected Khalaek to attack them as well, as he'd done with Peloroun, flickering in and out of existence. But the Wraith didn't move. Even his forces remained where they stood, while the Haessari attacked the retreating Alvritshai, falling into the pits on all sides. They'd already exposed over half of the traps.

"Aielan's Light," Lotaern muttered, raising a shaky hand to wipe his mouth. He felt suddenly weak. "That was—"

"Barbaric." Vaeren's hands were clenched hard against the stone of the tower, the knuckles white. "Peloroun didn't stand a chance!"

"Why didn't Khalaek use his powers earlier?" Lotaern wondered. "He could have slaughtered half of Peloroun's men in the space of ten minutes. And why isn't he or his men attacking with the rest of the Haessari and sukrael?"

"Perhaps because he was mounted earlier. But it doesn't matter. If he doesn't follow the retreat, we won't be able to seize him."

"Peloroun must have said something, given him some kind of hint of what we planned. That's why the Duvoraen Alvritshai aren't attacking."

"Then all of this is for naught!"

Lotaern felt the same...but then the gathering tension in his shoulders relaxed. "Not for naught. We can still protect Caercaern from the sukrael." He motioned toward the battlefield. "Look, they're being drawn into the center of the field."

Below, the Haessari continued to push forward, most of the Alvritshai behind the scattered pitfalls. They were using the narrow spaces between the pits to cut down the Haessari in droves. But the sukrael could flow over the pits and slipped past the steel cattans as if they were nothing, falling on Alvritshai who thought they were protected on one side. Some still fed on those that had fallen outside the pits, but as the last of those rose from their prey and sought out new ones, Lotaern said, "Ready the horn, and pray that the winds don't steal it from Petraen's ears."

Vaeren pulled a smaller horn than those used on the battlefield from where it hung at his side, wiping its mouth with a small square rag. He brought the horn to his lips.

"On my signal," Lotaern said. He watched the field closely, saw the last of the sukrael slip inside the line of pits, heard the first volley of arrows launch from Orraen's Phalanx along the ramp and the subsequent screams of the Haessari as they found targets, and flicked one last regretful look toward Khalaek—the traitor lord had remounted, he noted, and summoned the dwarren Wraith to his side—then muttered, "Now."

The horn sounded, a long, mournful note, higher in pitch than any of the horns on the battlefield below. Lotaern tensed when the note faded, Vaeren drawing breath to sound it again, and still nothing happened below. He leaned over the edge of the wall, glared down toward the lower tower, then along the wall's length to where he could see members of the Flame behind the rest of Orraen's men on the parapet. "Why are you waiting, Petraen?"

But as he pulled back, Vaeren halfway through his third call, a pulse of power surged up through his feet. For a brief moment, it felt as if the surge would topple him forward over the wall. As the sensation faded, he stepped back from the edge, a blast of stronger wind catching him full in the face. He waved a hand to Vaeren. "You can stop! It's started!"

The horn cry trailed off.

Below, beneath the surging sea of struggling men, strands of white fire had erupted from beneath the ground, tendrils of flame rising up from the soil between the Phalanx, Haessari, and sukrael. No one noticed at first, but as the fires—as Aielan's Light—rose higher and began to spread, the screams of death shifted into cries of terror. Alvritshai and the Wraith's creatures shrank away from the expanding flames, but the entire field was surrounded, the lines that the Flame had placed earlier, the boundaries that Saetor and Houdyll had drawn the Wraith army into, let no one escape. The only aspect of the battle that would have made it more perfect would have been if Khalaek-khai had been drawn into the circle as well.

"Now we see the power of the Order of Aielan and the Order of the Flame."

His gaze shifted from Khalaek-khai and his men, watching silently from the far side of the trampled field, back to the seething white light. The Haessari had drawn into scattered clumps, back to back, watching the flames warily, their strange S-shaped blades held ready.

It was the sukrael that caught and held Lotaern's attention. Their fluid black shapes, behaving like cloth although he knew they had no tangible substance to them, darted from wall to wall, frantic as they sought a way around the white fire. But the flames continued to expand, the pools of open space between shrinking, and as they grew more and more confined, the sukrael became more and more desperate. A few of them braved the fire, attempting to dart through it, but as soon as they touched it their entire shape burst into white fire, a conflagration that nearly blinded Lotaern, as hideous, piercing shrieks rose from below, faint, but loud enough and insidious enough to escape the tearing winds. The death throes sent the remaining sukrael into a panic. More and more of them were caught by the fires, a few elongating in an attempt to stretch over their height. But the flames were twice as tall as anyone on the field, even those on horseback. The sukrael were being consumed.

Lotaern allowed himself a small smile.

Vaeren tapped his arm.

Near the center, where most of the Haessari were trapped, the first of Aielan's Light had reached the snake people. They could no longer retreat, crowded into a tight circle. Those on the outside stabbed into the flames, but their swords had no effect. They hissed in rage, in fear, shrunk back further, but like the sukrael they could not escape. The fire touched those on the outer edge, a strange sibilant howl erupting from the creature's throats—

But as the flame continued to spread, those howls cut off in surprise. There were no bright flashes of intense fire, like sparking embers. The fire left the Haessari alone, engulfing them, but not harming them. It did the same to the Phalanx caught on the field, the Alvritshai shrinking from its light—except for a few followers of Aielan who appeared to almost embrace it, Lotaern noted with approval.

"Aielan's Light doesn't burn the Haessari," Vaeren said.

"I had hoped," Lotaern said, "but the Haessari aren't tainted by the sarenavriell like the sukrael or the Wraiths. They simply allied themselves with the wrong side. The Phalanx will have to deal with them. Both Saetor and Peloroun knew this was a possibility. But we've dealt with the most significant threat, aside from Khalaek-khai himself."

Below, the white fire engulfed the entire field, the lines of the Flame's power pulsing as the last vestige of ground within its confines was consumed. They held for a long moment, the last few shrieks of the sukrael tattering into the storm's gusts. Then, as if someone had reached out to place a cover over the fire, the flames dampened, shrinking to a few feet high, exposing the Haessari and the Phalanx alike, both groups registering shock and confusion.

That didn't last. Seeing that their enemies remained untouched, fear of the fire abated and after a few tentative steps and sudden harsh commands from Saetor, both groups converged again and began slaughtering each other anew.

Lotaern's gaze flicked back toward Khalaek-khai. He couldn't be certain, but he thought the dark lord of Duvoraen was looking to the tower. He thought he could feel his seething, resentful eyes upon him. "I wonder what Aielan's Light would have done to one of the Wraiths."

"We should have waited for Khalaek-khai to come closer. Or we should have tried a summoning of the Flame on Maen—"

Vaeren's voice cut off in a sudden, bloody gurgle and Lotaern spun, his breath locking in his chest as he saw the point of a sword jutting out of Vaeren's chest an inch to one side of his breastbone. The caitan of the Flame had bent backwards under the blow, arms flung back, legs straight and stiff, standing up on his toes. Blood fountained from his mouth as he tried to scream. The horn he'd used to call for Aielan's Light clattered to the stone parapet from his limp hand, and a moment later his head sagged back and tilted to one side, his eyes dead.

Lotaern gasped, the sound torn from his chest as his body demanded breath. He took a step backwards, unable to comprehend what had just happened. His eyes shifted from Vaeren's ashen face, stained and splattered with the dark red of heart's blood, to the figure that still held the sword that had punched through the caitan's chest. A figure dressed in a black cloak, shirt and breeches of an Alvritshai cut, although an ancient style. A figure with a long-healed scar of banishment down one cheek and a fresh, ragged hole in his chest over his heart.

"No." Lotaern's voice was strained. "No, I killed you. I killed you with Shaeveran's knife."

The Wraith Maenaed smiled, pulling his blade from Vaeren's body, the steel making an unpleasant sucking sound as it came free. He let the caitan fall carelessly, his attention focused on Lotaern.

"It doesn't work."

The words made no sense to Lotaern. Vaeren had seen Shaeveran use the knife against another Wraith, had seen that Wraith fall. It should have worked. It should have killed him.

"I don't—" he began, intending to say, "understand." But tremors coursed down his arms. His heart had accelerated. It beat so fast he thought it would explode. Pain tingled down his right arm, and coldness seeped into his legs, a coldness that had nothing to do with the frigid winds of the storm.

Maenaed savored his reaction, but then the Wraith's smile died.

The Wraith's body blurred, and in the space between one shaky breath and another, Maenaed's hand seized Lotaern's throat and slammed the Chosen into the ledge at the edge of the parapet. Lotaern couldn't breathe. He choked, pain searing up into his brain as the Wraith crushed his windpipe. He could hear the scream of the wind above, the echo of the clash of swords and the cries of death from below, but all he could feel was the white fear that suddenly suffused his body with a harsh, intense heat.

"Now," Maenaed said, "Caercaern will fall."

He lifted Lotaern off of his feet, the muscles in the Chosen's neck shrieking in agony. But the increased pain was short-lived.

With a heave, Maenaed thrust Lotaern backwards. The Chosen hit the edge of the parapet, one hand scrambling for purchase against the cold stone, but momentum carried the weight of his body in a roll and he slipped over the side.

Lotaern had always thought he'd die with dignity, head held high.

As the stone of the ramp rushed up to meet him, he was horrified to find that he screamed the entire way down.

Thankfully, Maenaed had crushed his windpipe, so no one heard him.

* * *

On the battlefield, Khalaek watched the Chosen's body drop from the height to the ramp, but he was too distant to hear the thud of Lotaern's landing. His gaze flicked up from where Lotaern's body had vanished to the top of the wall again, where Maenaed stood, a blacker shadow against the gray of Caercaern and the storm beyond.

The other Wraith held position for a moment, then blurred out of existence.

Khalaek turned to Arturo, the dwarren Wraith who had joined him at the edge of dwarren lands, the army that had fought at the Break merging with the portion of Khalaek's army that had broken away from the siege of Temeritt. They'd marched northwest across dwarren lands, between the Escarpment and the Ostraell forests, harried by the dwarren Riders, but undeterred. A large portion of Arturo's forces—the terren, gruen, and kell—had branched off to attack the dwarren at the Confluence. Khalaek had wanted to send the sukrael as well, but the Summer Tree had still been too strong due to its proximity to the ruanavriell. So he'd ordered the sukrael north to Caercaern, along with the combined Alvritshai and Haessari forces.

He hadn't expected Lotaern and Peloroun's betrayal, hadn't expected Maenaed to be captured. But he had expected resistance—from Tamaell Thaedoren and Lord Aeren, if no one else.

He wondered briefly where they were, but when Arturo finally met his gaze, he brushed such concerns aside.

"Prepare the men and pass word along to the Haessari general."

Arturo's aged brow creased in confusion. He rarely spoke, his shoulders hunched as if he constantly carried a heavy burden, his eyes perpetually squinted as if he were in pain.

Khalaek waved toward Caercaern's walls at the unasked question and gathered up the reins of his horse.

"The gates of Caercaern are about to open."

17

Maenaed leaned over the wall and watched the pompous Chosen of Aielan fall, the wind shrieking around him, his cloak slapping against his ankles. As soon as the bastard hit and didn't move, Maenaed pulled back and glanced toward where Khalaek and Arturo stood outside the radius of the Flame's killing white fire. He could feel the flames even from the height of the wall. Their power prickled along his skin, the sensation painful. He'd felt the sukrael's death throes. It had pulled him out of his near-death unconsciousness, their screams scraping down his bones like steel on stone.

Khalaek's head rose. For a moment, Maenaed knew their eyes had met, even though they were far too distant for him to make out Khalaek's features. But he knew what Khalaek wanted him to do.

He would have done it regardless of Khalaek's wishes.

Reaching out with the powers of the sarenavriell, he seized time and slowed it.

And began to move.

* * *

Inside the tower, Boreaus stood beside Petraen at one of the wide windows, staring down at the battlefield. Cattan ready, his fingers itched to descend to the rough ground below and dance among the cries of blood and death. His skin and muscles ached with the urge. He wanted to smell the Haessari's blood, wanted to feel his blade slicing into their scaled flesh. He wanted to be surrounded with Aielan's Light as he fought, dodging their strikes. As he watched, one of them reared back, flaps unfolding from the sides of its neck, and then it lunged forward, mouth gaping. Its fangs sank into its victim's neck and with a wrench of its head it flung Boreaus' fellow Alvritshai aside. The man writhed as black tendrils began threading through his skin toward his head and heart, but the Haessari had already moved on.

At his side, his brother said "I didn't know they could do that. Did you?"

"The Scripts aren't clear, but there were hints that their venom was poisonous."

"What are they? Where do they come from?"

"They're called the Haessari. The Scripts say we drove them from the Hauttaeren and that they fled south and east. We haven't seen or heard from them since."

"They should have stayed wherever they came from. Even if they aren't affected by Aielan's Light, Saetor and Houdyll are still holding their own against them."

Boreaus scanned the field. "Perhaps." He eyed the western flank, where the Haessari had nearly reached the base of the wall, Houdyll's men giving ground reluctantly, but still falling back. Houdyll's forces were the weakest. Saetor's men held the east, defending the base of the ramp lined with Orraen's archers and protecting the only approach to the gates of Caercaern. Peloroun's men appeared to be bolstering Houdyll where they could.

They watched the fighting in silence. After twenty full minutes of study, Boreaus still could not predict the outcome. Saetor, Houdyll, and the Haessari were closely matched, even with Orraen's archers on the ramp above.

Boreaus was watching Saetor slice through three of the Haessari when Petraen gave a sudden, surprised grunt.

He glanced to one side. "What is it?"

"I'm not certain. Something...something changed."

"What? Where?" His eyes grazed the field, latched on unexpected movement. "Khalaek's men are moving."

"That's not it, although why are they moving now? They've held back this long."

"Khalaek and the dwarren Wraith can't enter the field," Boreaus said with certainty. "Not with Aielan's Light still burning through the ground."

Petraen gasped. "It's the fire. Aielan's Light. Something's happening to the lines of power on the field. They're faltering. They're being ripped free."

"How?"

"I don't know."

His brother was connected to the construct. If he didn't know...

Boreaus spun and scanned the rest of the Flame gathered inside the tower room. There were six of them—two who had accompanied Petraen and held two of the lines holding the fire on the field, the other four those who'd held the anchor on Maenaed. Lotaern had sent them below, but neither Petraen nor Boreaus knew what to do with them. They were hanging back, out of the way. The two holding lines weren't reacting like Petraen, but Petraen was acting as the center for the entire construct.

Even so, one of the two suddenly flinched and glanced toward Boreaus with a troubled look. "I think something's wrong—"

Boreaus cut him off, dashing toward the western side of the tower, leaning far out so he could see down the wall's length. Wind bit into his face, brought tears to his eyes. Its cold burned down into his lungs, but he fixed his attention on the wall, Lord Daesor's men mixed with Orraen's Phalanx strung out along its length from the tower. Nearly all of them were hunched into their armor at the edge of the wall, looking down at the battle, waiting to see if the Wraith army made it to the ramp. Scattered through their white-green and maroon-gold raimant, he picked out members of the Flame, spaced out more or less evenly. His gaze jumped from the nearest down the line—

Until it came up short.

Boreaus' hands clenched against the unyielding stone of the window's ledge. He searched the rest of the wall to the west, but couldn't pick out any of the Flame. They were simply gone. The last one still visible, the fifth one out from the tower, stood back from the press of Phalanx closest to the wall's edge. The Flame holding Aielan's Light in place didn't need to see the construct, they only needed to be in alignment with all of the rest. But where had the others gone? What had happened to them?

A second later, a black figure blurred into view alongside the member of the Flame farthest out. Boreaus watched in horror as the man gave a start, his only reaction before the Wraith brought his cattan across the man's throat, tilting the body backwards as blood fountained and dropping it back behind the wall. None of the Phalanx staring out at the battlefield reacted. Boreaus doubted his fellow member of the Order had had a chance to cry out before he was dead, and even if he had, the storm would have torn the scream away.

As soon as the body began to fall, the Wraith blurred out of existence.

Boreaus held his breath, although he knew what would happen next.

The Wraith appeared beside the next member of the Flame, dispatching him as quickly as the first.

He swore and whirled. "There's a Wraith inside the walls. He's taking out the Flame holding the fire."

"What are you talking about?" the elder who'd held the anchor on the roof demanded.

Boreaus ignored the question. "We don't have much time. We'll need to set up another snare like the one we used to capture Maenaed." He halted abruptly, thinking back on the brief glimpse he'd gotten of the Wraith as it attacked on the wall, then swore again, more forcefully. "The Wraith inside the wall *is* Maenaed."

"That's impossible. We saw the Chosen kill him! We saw the body!"

"It doesn't matter. You three, space yourself out along the eastern wall. The rest of you do the same to the west. Orient yourselves away from the door if you can, and keep yourself hidden. Begin the chant as soon as you're all in place. Petraen, you and I will remain in the center of the room."

"What about the fire below?"

"Let it go. It's going to collapse soon anyway."

The two holding lines shot a questioning glance toward Petraen.

"Do as he says. I'm going to release the lines anyway."

The four who'd held the anchor hesitated, the younger ones moving first. The elder shook his head, but took a place in the far eastern corner of the room. "We're too confined. It will never work."

Boreaus stalked back to the window, but none of the rest of the Flame remained on the wall. He trotted across the room to the eastern side, passing Petraen. The other six began the low chant that set the snare. He unconsciously fell into the cadence, his body tingling in response.

On the eastern wall, the Flame were still arrayed all along its length.

A sound—a choked, expelled breath; a sickening patter of blood—came from behind him and he spun, his cattan snicking from its sheath in one fluid motion. A blur of darkness skated from the eldest Flame to the next around the circle, like a flowing wisp of smoke, but with deadly purpose, the second member of the Flame taken out before Boreaus even registered the sudden stain of red growing against the white of the eldest's surplice. Boreaus lunged forward, but the Wraith was already moving, the others in the room beginning to cry out in realization. Brow creased, he focused, tried to catch the elusive figure as it moved from man to man, blade flickering in the lantern light inside the room, blood splattering on walls in smooth arcs, cries cut short. But the Wraith moved too fast, circling the room in the space of ten heartbeats, each thud growing louder in Boreaus' ears. Yet by the time the sixth man fell, he found himself catching the faintest hints of the music the Wraith followed, the rhythm of his movements, the thought behind the dance.

Then the Wraith launched himself toward Petraen. Boreaus' cattan swung before conscious thought, striking the Wraith's blade in midair, Petraen stumbling back from the blow. His brother belatedly drew his own cattan and the two brothers faced off against Maenaed.

The Wraith had stilled, facing them, framed by the window that looked south over the battlefield.

"I'm impressed," Maenaed said. "Let's see if that was a lucky block."

He blurred, Boreaus shifting to counter as he bellowed to Petraen, "Warn the others!"

It was all he managed to say before Maenaed's blade slammed into his own cattan, metal clanging and shrieking as he thrust the Wraith away, already anticipating the tainted Alvritshai's next strike. Weapons whirred, steel clashing on steel for another two blows, and then the tip of Maenaed's sword sliced down Boreaus' arm. He swore, realizing that his counter had been a fraction of a breath too slow, that he'd have to think farther ahead. But Maenaed's blows were coming faster and faster.

Jaw clenched, ignoring the silver-thin pain of the cut on his arm, he feinted, parried another strike, caught a glimpse of Maenaed's features as he blurred into existence, then back out, used that glimpse and the direction of Maenaed's momentum to predict the next attack, and lunged back, the Wraith's cattan sweeping across his stomach, catching in his shirt. He drove his own blade forward, steel passing through the space Maenaed's hand had been in, then hissed in frustration when the Wraith shifted away. But he couldn't afford hesitation. He flowed into the next movement, his cattan slashing downward, shunting Maenaed's aside, then up and back, catching Maenaed's again. They danced across the room, following a rhythm that Boreaus knew was more instinct than plan. He felt the remnants of Aielan's Light from what had been called to the field stirring in the earth beneath him and he reached for it. If he could pull the light into himself, shape it and use it against Maenaed, as they'd shaped it to capture him, as they'd used it on the battlefield below against the sukrael...

The white flames had just begun to suffuse him when he realized his latest parry had met empty air.

Before he could recover, a blade punched into his side from behind. It slid up under his ribcage, into his vital organs. White hot pain seared away his vision, sucked his breath away. Not a cattan, he thought, the words strangely clear as he tasted thick blood at the back of his throat. A dagger.

Maenaed had changed the dance.

He staggered back and the Wraith caught him from behind, clasped him close with one arm over his shoulder as he choked and spat up blood. The Wraith's other hand still held the dagger deep in his side.

"You lasted longer than I expected," Maenaed said, his voice close to Boreaus' ear, his breath hot against Boreaus' skin. "Much longer."

The Wraith twisted the dagger and Boreaus couldn't contain the scream. He wrenched to one side, to escape the pain, but Maenaed held him in an iron grip.

Leaning in closer, the Wraith murmured, "You're an excellent warrior. The Chosen would have been proud. Wish him well when you see him in Aielan's Light."

Maenaed jerked the dagger free and released him. Boreaus fell to the stone floor, his legs numb, his entire lower body dead. His cattan clattered to the stone. He couldn't move his arm. He'd fallen on his side, felt blood trailing out of the corner of his mouth, pooling in his throat, blocking off his breath. His chest shuddered as Maenaed walked away from him toward the door, boot heels clunking loudly on the floor. Boreaus blinked. Blood pooled at the edge of his vision, seeping outwards across the stone. His own blood.

He wondered if he'd given his brother enough time to warn the others, and then his body stilled and his vision filled with a pure white light, like flame.

* * *

On the western tower, Lord Daesor saw the seething white fire on the battlefield gutter and then go out, the flames sinking back into the ground.

"What—?"

His gaze shot toward the eastern tower, where the Chosen had slain the captured Wraith, but the tower was empty.

No, not empty. He could see a body slumped to the stone. He couldn't be certain, but he thought it was Vaeren.

There was no sign of Lotaern or the Wraith.

His heart faltered for a single beat and then he lurched forward, leaned out over the wall toward the ramp and gates below. In his peripheral vision, Khalaek's entire Phalanx began to move, charging toward the raging battle between Saetor, Houdyll, and the snake people...charging toward the base of the ramp. But what held his attention was the group of archers who surrounded a crumpled body on the ramp to one side. Lord Orraen was pushing through that group now, shoving his own Phalanx aside. Daesor could see the anger on his face even at this distance, could see him shouting orders. Then the lord reached the body. He knelt, rolled the body over onto its back—it was clearly Lotaern; the Chosen's robes of office were obvious—and pressed a hand against Lotaern's neck.

No Wraith body, Vaeren dead, Lotaern dead...

The moment Orraen looked upwards toward Daesor's position, the lord of House Nuant spun. "Sound a warning."

Those Phalanx with the horns glanced toward each other in confusion. "Which warning?"

"We have a Wraith inside the gates. Warn Saetor below, and call those spread along the wall back to the tower." He turned to the rest of the Phalanx. "The rest of you, follow me. We have to protect the gates."

He jogged toward the stairs leading into the depths of the tower, his Phalanx falling into position around him, orders being shouted back and forth as they descended. Ten steps down, the horns cried out, tattered by the winds. After twenty he heard a choked off scream. He picked up speed, drew his cattan as he moved. The clank and clatter of the winch echoed up through the stairwell. He could hear the protests of the wood as the gate creaked open and he moved even faster, cursing as he flung himself around the last corner and onto the final flight of steps. The Wraith loomed over the winch, the gatehouse floor wreathed with dead bodies, including the member of the Flame named Petraen.

"Halt!" He raised his blade and pointed it at the Wraith.

The tainted Alvritshai turned to look at him as he charged down the last few steps. Then he thrust his blade deep into the gears of the winch and pulled the release.

Metal shrieked against metal as the gears of the mechanism began to turn, the gate beginning to drop. Then they caught against the blade obstructing their movement. The Wraith smiled, then stepped to one side. His body smeared into darkness, like smudged charcoal on paper, and vanished.

Daesor's Phalanx plowed to a halt behind him. He waited, expecting the Wraith to reappear again, perhaps directly in front of him, but after a few moments of tense silence, he gestured with his sword toward the winch. "See to the gates."

He strode across the room to the window, sidestepping through the bodies. Half of his men converged on the winch, the others fanning out. Four of them kept close to his side as he leaned out the window and glared down at the gates.

They were more than half raised. The Wraith hadn't had time to open them completely, but there was plenty of room for Khalaek and his forces to pass beneath and into the city.

He shoved away from the window. "Can you fix it?"

One of his caitans looked up from the mess of cogs and wheels. "The sword is locked in place. We can't budge it. At least two of the gear shafts have cracked. We can fix it, but it will take time."

Daesor glanced out the window. Khalaek's Duvoraen Phalanx had hit the forces at the end of the ramp hard. Saetor and Houdyll's men had been split, the snake people and Khalaek driving like a wedge toward the ramp. If they gained the heights...

"We don't have time. Forget repairing it. Can you do something to get the gate lowered?"

The caitan's brow creased in thought, his gaze shifting from the shattered gears to the surrounding walls. Daesor knew there were pulleys and weights hidden behind the stone, but he knew nothing about how they worked.

"If I can find the counterweights, I can cut them free." He met Daesor's gaze squarely. "But if I do that and the gates close, there will be no way to get them back open again on command. Everyone outside will be trapped there."

Daesor pressed his lips together. "Do it."

His caitan chose three other men. They vanished down a second set of stairs, presumably looking for the counterweights.

"What about the rest of us?"

Daesor turned toward his own Protector. He had few of his own House Phalanx here with him in Caercaern—one of the reasons he'd been stationed on the wall; although he knew another had been a certain amount of distrust between him and Peloroun—but those that were here were men he had faith would defend Caercaern to the last. He could hear others approaching, men who'd been scattered along the parapet and had answered his summons. He straightened as the first of them poured into the room with varied looks of determination, hatred, and confusion.

"Gather everyone in the street below," he said. "We'll have to defend the gates."

* * *

"Lord Saetor! Look to the gates!"

Saetor Uslaen yanked his cattan from a snake creature's throat, its head lolling to the side at an unnatural angle, then said harshly, "Torrael and Gaeghan, take my place," as he pulled his horse's reins, the steed retreating from the front lines. He slashed down toward two enemies who tried to follow, slicing across the snout of one of them, before his Protector and caitan surged forward and closed the gap. Only then did he glance away from the front line where his Uslaen Phalanx pushed hard against the Wraith's army. He frowned as his gaze swept over his forces. Khalaek and the Duvoraen Alvritshai had cut through the line, were now attacking the base of the ramp, already making headway up the gradual slope. Orraen's archers were scrambling to recover, a knot of them trying to shove the Duvoraen back. Arrows spat back and forth between the two, men falling on both sides. On the far side of the Wraith forces, he could see Houdyll's men attempting to rally as well. He didn't understand Khalaek's strategy. Taking the ramp would be worthless with enemy forces both above and below. He didn't have enough men to keep them all at bay on two fronts—

But then his gaze shifted up to the top of the ramp.

The gates were open. Not completely raised, but far enough to be a breach in their defenses.

"How? How in hells did they gain access to the gates? And where the hells is Daesor?"

He snapped his attention back to his own lines.

"Torrael, Gaeghan! Break away. We need to regroup."

He pulled back farther from the front lines, cursing beneath his breath the entire way. Torrael and Gaeghan joined him moments later, both of them splashed with blood, their cattans dripping with it, their faces hard. Torrael had a cut along his jaw and Gaeghan was bleeding from a head wound that was lost in his blood-matted hair. Both of their mounts were raked with claw marks, their sides shuddering and twitching as they were brought to a halt.

"We need a new plan," Saetor said. "The gates are open and our forces are split. Houdyll's barely holding his position to the west. We're not doing much better here. And Orraen's men..." He looked to the ramp. "Khalaek has forced his way halfway up the ramp already. Suggestions?"

"Can we retake the gates?" Gaeghaen asked. "Orraen is withdrawing back to the gate tower."

Torrael met Saetor's gaze. "If they gain the gates..."

"The entire city is lost," Saetor finished. He squinted into the distance. The gusts of wind that reached them even here in the lee of the wall forced him to blink repeatedly, but he thought, beneath the shadow of the tower—

"Are those Daesor's men?"

Both Torrael and Gaeghan turned to look, Gaeghan raising a hand to shield his face, but it was Torrael that answered.

"Maroon and gold, yes."

"He would never have opened the gates himself." He gathered the reins of his mount in one hand, his steed picking up on his sudden anxiety.

He needed to make a decision.

"We'll trap Khalaek and his Duvoraen between us and Daesor and Orraen at the gates. On my signal, we'll fall back from these damned snakes and force our way to the ramp. Have Yaeran command the flank. She'll have to hold against the snake people on her own, but her force has seen the least amount of action so far."

Gaeghan jerked his mount around as he began calling out orders, plowing through the sea of men pushing to get to the front lines around them.

Torrael raised one eyebrow. "Will it work?"

"It has to, or Caercaern will fall. Pray that Daesor can hold the gates. And that Houdyll realizes what we intend." He held out little hope the lord of House Redlien would react in time to be helpful; Houdyll wasn't a tactician. Saetor raked the field with one last peremptory glare, then motioned to Torrael. "Give me your horn."

His Protector handed it over without comment. Saetor held it in one hand, shivered at a sudden blast of frigid air from above. He looked up, watched the storm roil, barely visible in the darkness, even though night could not yet have fallen. He blinked as lightning flared, thunder cracking harshly.

A moment later, the first few flakes of snow began to fall.

He traded a glance with Torrael. His bones told him the storm had only just begun.

A hand signal caught his attention and he straightened in the saddle. "Gaeghan's ready."

Without preamble, he brought the mouth of the horn to his lips, the metal there burning with cold as he drew in a deep breath and blew, the horncry clear and defiant.

He let the note hold, then cut it off, a roar going up from Uslaen House as the entire army began to shift, caitans barking orders on all sides. As if in response, the snowfall escalated, hundreds of fat flakes skirling in the winds, biting into Saetor's skin as he shielded his face to see better. To his right, his forces fell back, Yaeran's group rushing forward to protect the flank while others retreated back toward Gaeghan's position. The caitan spun where he stood, sword pointing, shouting orders that Saetor couldn't hear.

Then, Gaeghan thrust his sword toward the base of the ramp and the entire left flank and center heaved toward their goal.

"Should we join them?" Torrael asked.

"Not yet. I want to see how Khalaek and his forces react."

On the ramp, those in Khalaek's forces at the rear, and those few snake people who'd followed in their wake, hesitated, then spun as Gaeghan's men plowed through the resistance and hit the end of the ramp, surging far enough up its length that those above them were trapped between Gaeghan and the gates. Saetor saw flags flashing, signals passing up to the front, where Khalaek battled against Orraen and Daesor. He couldn't pick out the traitorous lord, but he knew he was there.

"Now what, Wraith," Saetor murmured under his breath. "You may have more men than us, but do they follow you out of respect or fear?"

If Torrael heard him, he said nothing.

Below, on the churned earth of the battlefield, the snake people's line broke at the unexpected move. A few of their sharp hisses filtered through the wind. Some looked to the sky, at the falling snow, cringing as if in fear.

But their hesitation didn't last. Those Saetor had picked out earlier as the snake people's commanders flared the folds of skin at their necks and within moments the ranks were reforming.

"They're more disciplined than I would have imagined," Torrael muttered.

"Agreed." Shifting his gaze beyond them, he swore. "Houdyll's forces have pulled back." Even as he said it, he realized why. The Redlien Phalanx had been decimated. He could see Houdyll desperately trying to regroup. But he didn't have enough men left to protect himself, let alone help Saetor.

Before Saetor could determine what Houdyll intended, a thick swirl of snow blocked his view.

But the snakes were still in sight. With a fluidness that Saetor wished his own men could mimic, they altered formation.

"What are they doing?" Torrael asked.

"I think..." Saetor began—

And then he knew.

"Call Yaeran back now! Have her retreat to the base of the ramp!"

Torrael heeled around and charged toward Yaeran's position, shouting and flailing his arms to catch her attention. Saetor watched in horrified fascination as the snakes' formation surged forward, the front half slamming into Yaeran's forces while those in back turned and sprinted to the left, slipping down and around the end of those attacking and coming at Saetor's group from the flank. They moved faster than Saetor expected, faster than they'd moved when attacking on the field earlier. Within moments, they'd surrounded Saetor's entire force, their own lines thinned, but holding.

Saetor flicked the reins and headed toward Torrael, his Protector seizing control of the eastern forces since Yaeran was dealing with those attacking her own men. "Hold the line!" he shouted, plowing toward where the snakes were cutting down his own men. "Hold it or we all die!"

He reached the edge of the fray and brought his cattan down in a smooth, controlled arc that cut into one of the snake people's heads, lodging in the creature's skull. He twisted the blade, bringing his mount sideways to the juddering body, then pulled his foot from the stirrup, planted it against the creature's snout, and shoved hard. His cattan came free with a sickening scrape of metal against bone, but he was already swinging at his next target. Sheets of snow blinded him at odd moments as he fought, yet sweat began trickling down into his eyes. His body felt hot, prickling with anger, with desperation, with the certain knowledge that he would die here, that Khalaek and his army had won, that Caercaern would fall. Every decision he had made since he'd taken control of Khalaek's fallen House rolled through his head, especially those in the Evant. He should have supported Lord Aeren fully, not hesitated, not waited to see how the other lords would react. He should have challenged the Chosen earlier himself; he'd known Lotaern was only seeking to gain power. He should have trusted Tamaell Thaedoren.

Every regret, every recrimination drove him harder. He slashed and cut, meeting the enraged, hissing faces of the snake people with blunt defiance and the deadly edge of his cattan. One of them reared back, hood flaring, poised to strike, but he thrust his sword into its mouth as it opened, its own lunge punching the blade through the back of its head. Its fangs nearly made it to his hand. He jerked the blade free, some of its venom splattering along his arm, burning with an intense pain, but he ignored it, parrying one of their strange blades before severing its arm from its body with one blow. His body sank into the flow of the fight, something he'd trained for since he'd first made his vows to become part of the Duvoraen Phalanx. Exhaustion leached into his muscles, but he bulled through it. He lost track of his forces, lost track of Torrael, of the battle on the ramp and at the gates. Only the fight before him mattered; only the men dying at his side. They were all dying. They were all going to die. But Saetor intended to take as many of the Wraith's Aielan-forsaken army with him as he could.

He would have kept on fighting until one of the snake people scored a lucky blow, or one of their fangs sank into his flesh and poisoned his blood, but in the middle of drawing his blade from one of their scaly hides someone's hand clamped down onto his shoulder and hauled him back, nearly unseating him from his horse.

He spun in his saddle, cattan raised to strike, but met Torrael's gaze, his Protector's expression penetrating the fog of battle that enveloped him.

"What is it?" he shouted.

"Look."

Torrael pointed with his sword, not toward the walls of Caercaern, or the gates, as Saetor expected, but toward the forest to the south.

Saetor twisted, glaring through the sheets of snow, noting how much of it had already collected on the ground, although here at the wall it had merely churned the earth into mud. But beyond the fighting, through the darkness caused by the storm, he could see movement.

His shoulders sagged. "Reinforcements. Khalaek had reinforcements."

"No. It's Tamaell Thaedoren. They're carrying House Resue's banner."

"How is that possible?"

Torrael laughed, the sound brittle and cracked. "I don't know, but it's the Tamaell."

The Tamaell's forces emerged from the obscuring snow in a wave, hitting the snake people from behind. He saw Resue's colors, along with Rhyssal's, Nuant's, and Baene's.

"Aielan's Light." His voice choked, and tears pricked the corners of his eyes. His shoulders shook, tremors coursing down his arms— exhaustion and emotion both.

But he couldn't succumb yet, no matter how weary he felt. He didn't know how many men the Tamaell had brought with him, didn't know if it would be enough.

Straightening, he shot a look toward the gates, realized Khalaek-khai had penetrated the city while he fought, then turned to Torrael. "Gather a few Phalanx as escort. I need to speak to the Tamaell immediately."

Torrael nodded, gesturing to a few of those near them. Within moments, his Protector had formed an escort of seven men and Saetor had picked out Tamaell Thaedoren through the snow. The Tamaell appeared to be angling toward him, cutting a swath of death through the intervening snakes.   Saetor had intended to use his escort to fight his way to Thaedoren's side, but he decided to wait for Thaedoren to come to him. Thaedoren's men had yet to burn themselves out.

He took the time to look over his own forces. He'd lost over half of his Phalanx. But they still held the base of the ramp. He couldn't tell what was happening at the gates or Caercaern; the city and tower were hidden by the snow. There was no sign of Houdyll's men.

Twenty minutes later, Thaedoren broke through the snakes' line and headed toward his position.

The Tamaell halted a few paces away, his entourage flanking him to either side. Their horses' haunches were covered with mud, the mounts shuddering with exhaustion. Saetor took in the strained lines around the Tamaell's eyes, the sagging shoulders, and all of the other signs of weariness that lay over him like a shroud.

They may have come fresh to the battle, but they had ridden hard to get to Caercaern.

Saetor bowed his head in abject deference. "Tamaell Thaedoren. It is good to see you."

"Tamaell? You call me such after siding with Lotaern and Peloroun these past months?"

Saetor didn't raise his eyes. "I did what was necessary to survive. I could do nothing trapped within Caercaern. But I did not side with them in the Evant after they seized the palace. I did not vote for Peloroun and his House to ascend after the coup."

"So Daesor's son claims."

"Caeden is here?"

"The Lord Presumptive is here, yes. Along with Lord Fedaureon and Lord Renaerd."

Saetor took in their titles. "So Lord Aeren is indeed dead."

"Yes. I sent him to Aielan's Light myself." Thaedoren said it baldly, but Saetor sensed the sea of emotion beneath the words. Yet the Tamaell turned to the battle still roiling around them, half hidden by the snow. "Now explain what has happened here."

Saetor straightened at the command in the Tamaell's voice. "Lotaern and Peloroun intended to lure the Wraiths and their army here by pretending to work with them, offering them the fall of Caercaern in return for the taint of the sarenavriell. They planned to destroy them before the gates. But something went wrong. The Order of the Flame failed. They were supposed to prevent the Wraiths, sukrael, and any of the other tainted creatures of the Wraiths' army from reaching the ramp with Aielan's Light, and for a while it worked. But then the white flames died. The gates of Caercaern were opened from the inside. Khalaek-khai and the Duvoraen House stormed the ramp—"

"Wait." Thaedoren held up a gauntleted hand, protective mail glinting in the sparse light. "Khalaek-khai? The Duvoraen House?"

Saetor swallowed. "Khalaek is a Wraith."

"How? We left him for dead on the fields at the Escarpment. He'd been disemboweled!"

"I don't know how. I didn't know he was still alive until today. But Peloroun and Lotaern must have known. That's why they insisted they be the only ones to approach the Wraith army to the south."

"Why send a group south at all?"

"Ostensibly, to meet with the Wraiths—with Khalaek-khai—and hand Caercaern to them. But Lotaern had other plans. He intended to capture the Wraith sent to meet them. He claimed he could kill them. He had a knife forged by Shaeveran. He *did* capture one of them. Not Khalaek-khai, although I'm certain that's who he'd hoped to snare. And he appeared to kill the Wraith he captured on the walls above."

"He didn't. The knife forged by Shaeveran doesn't work. Members of his Order of the Flame stole it from Shaeveran in the northlands. If he had consulted with Lord Aeren, he would have known that."

Saetor wondered what else had transpired in the northlands. He hadn't known anyone had been traveling in the Alvrirshai's wintery homeland recently, least of all Shaeveran and Lord Aeren.

He would have asked for more details, but lightning flared, thunder followed, and Thaedoren's eyes rose toward the walls of Caercaern above them, a gray shadow through the falling snow. The orange glow of fire lit the roiling storm from below, pulsing with a slow, steady beat.

"We can talk more later," Thaedoren said. "For now, ready your men for retreat."

"Retreat!"

Thaedoren had already begun to turn his horse aside, but he halted, eyebrows raised. "Khalaek-khai has already breached the gate. Even with the forces I brought with me, we cannot retake Caercaern. It already burns."

Saetor's gaze shot toward the pulsating orange of the clouds.

"We'd be slaughtered in the streets if we tried to take the city, along with everyone else in Caercaern. And for what?"

"What about Daesor? Orraen? They manned the tower and the wall."

Thaedoren didn't answer, motioning to his escort, who broke away, a horn sounding. He didn't need to answer; Saetor already knew.

The atmosphere beneath the walls shifted. Saetor felt it, the energy of the fight pulling back as men began shouting, withdrawing slowly, the remaining snakes hissing in triumph as they attacked the army's back.

Torrael edged his mount forward. "Your orders?"

Saetor stiffened in a momentary burst of defiance, then sighed. "Follow the Tamaell. Pull back from the ramp. Let Khalaek-khai have Caercaern."

As soon as they lost the gates—as soon as they lost the Flame and the protection of Aielan's Light—they'd lost the city.

Torrael spun and shouted orders, his voice fading as Saetor stared up at the wall, at the bloody orange light that had grown in size. He blinked as a snowflake caught in his eyelashes.

Then Torrael gripped his upper arm. He focused on his Protector's grim face. The armies were departing, he realized. The snake were shifting their attentions to the city beyond. They charged up the ramp as Saetor's men pulled back.

"It's not the first battlefield we've walked away from in defeat," Torrael said.

"It won't be the last, either."

They joined the rest of the Uslaen Phalanx as they crossed the battlefield, flowing around the pits dug weeks earlier, past the cleared land, to the edge of the forest beyond.

There, before merging into the trees, Saetor paused and looked back. Snowfall obscured most of Caercaern from sight, but the storm was a glaring, fiery red-orange. From what he could tell, the majority of the city was ablaze, at least the lowest tier and a good portion of the second. The Tamaell's tower was wreathed in smoke and snow, a vague outline against the mountains behind. The Winter Tree was a blackened spire silhouetted against the flames.

A loud crack resounded, shivering in Saetor's bones, and through a short break in the obscuring fury of snow, he saw the Tree beginning to topple. A sheet of white hid it before it landed, wind shrieking in a sudden rage.

Without a word, Saetor followed the Tamaell and the remaining Alvritshai forces into the protection of the trees and the falling night.

18

"Houdyll's dead." Thaedoren stood at the head of the long table in what had once been Lord Aeren's study in the manse in Artillien. A fire crackled in the hearth to one side, the flames giving the entire room a soft, warm glow, the scattered desk, tables, and chairs—all littered with papers, maps, and the sundry items Aeren had collected over his years of travels across Wrath Suvane—lit in pale yellows, oranges, and shadow. Behind, outside the window, snow fell steadily, as it had more or less for the last week. Over four feet had accumulated before Thaedoren and his army had reached Rhyssal House lands. "Daesor and Orraen are dead. Saetor saw Peloroun fall on the battlefield before Caercaern, and we have others in the Phalanx who saw Lotaern's body fall from the walls. I expect most of those who fled to the safety of Caercaern are also dead. And now we must deal with this storm." He glanced around those seated at the table: Lords Saetor, Fedaureon, Renaerd, and Caeden, their Protectors and caitans, and his mother. All that was left of the Evant; nearly all that was left of the ruling Houses of the Alvritshai, aside from those who had been left behind on their own lands.

He straightened, rapping his knuckles against the desk. "I asked you all to bring news of what transpires on Alvritshai lands. What have you found?"

No one responded, a brooding sense of despondency cloaking the entire room.

Thaedoren turned to Saetor. "What do our scouts report of Khalaek-khai and Caercaern?"

The lord of Uslaen stirred. "Only three of the five teams sent out have returned. I believe the other two have been killed by Khalaek-khai's men. The others report that Khalaek-khai and his army have taken control of Caercaern. The city gates have been closed and there are Haessari manning the walls, along with Khalaek-khai's own Phalanx. Parts of the city still burn, although some of the smoke seen must come from funeral pyres."

Caeden snorted in contempt. "You believe Khalaek-khai cares if the Alvritshai he's killed—that he's betrayed—are given to Aielan's Light?"

"He is still Alvritshai."

"He's a Wraith! He's tainted by the sarenavriell. He became something other the moment he drank from its waters."

"Agreed," Thaedoren cut in. "Khalaek is a Wraith, nothing more, no matter what he's told the Phalanx who became khai to join him."

Moiran cleared her throat. "Some would argue he was less than Alvritshai well before that, but that is not the point. There are other reasons for him to burn the dead besides religious reasons. To prevent the spread of disease, for one." She gestured toward Saetor. "You have more to report?"

"Khalaek-khai spent the first few days solidifying his hold on Caercaern. After that, he began sending groups out into the surrounding land. They're gathering up food and supplies, slaughtering anyone they find. Entire villages and towns. Word is spreading, and refugees have already begun moving southward, although no one knows where to go. Some are fleeing to Liossae in Redlien, others to Iscaeta in Ionaen House lands."

"Lady Yssabo will take in refugees," Moiran added. "She may be mindless, but she's not heartless. And I believe Tovvain will as well."

"That won't solve the main problem," Mattalaen, Fedaureon's cattan said bluntly. "The Wraith army will not stay in Caercaern forever. They're foraging for food and supplies now, but they will run out, especially with winter coming. If this is a precursor of what is to come, then the winter will be harsh. Khalaek-khai's men will be looking for more food shortly. Lady Yssabo, Tovvain, Sovaeren...all of those remaining in their House lands, without the full protection of their own Phalanx, are in danger."

Caeden and Renaerd shifted uncomfortably at this, concern etched into their expressions. Thaedoren doubted they'd thought of how exposed their own Houses were until now.

Renaerd broke first, standing abruptly. "I need to return to Hallieas."

"Sit down, Renaerd."

"But my mother—"

"Your mother is fine," Moiran said, her tone harsh. Thaedoren looked at her closely for the first time since returning. He'd been too exhausted and too distracted to pay much attention to her, but now he saw how haggard she looked, how old. Her skin appeared loose, her eyes bruised, her face drawn with hard lines. "Your's as well, Caeden. I've been receiving missives from them on a daily basis, except for delays caused by the storm. Both of them are preparing to leave for Artillien as we speak, if they haven't left already. They're bringing what Phalanx was left in their lands and whatever supplies and food they can manage with this snow."

"What do you mean?" Thaedoren said, leaning forward onto the table. "They're coming here?"

"Yes. They aren't safe staying in their respective homes by themselves, and it makes no sense to split the forces we do have to protect them there. So they're coming here. And they're bringing as many of their people with them as they can."

"But we can't protect them here either," Fedaureon protested. "Artillien isn't built for defense. It's nothing more than a manse, with a stone wall barely high enough to thwart a hefty stone thrown by a child. The gates themselves would be breached within a day—within an hour!"

"They'll have more protection here than on their own lands. None of the lords' manses were designed for defense, not like Caercaern. And here they'll have the combined Phalanx surrounding them."

Fedaureon spluttered, something no one else dared to do. "Mother, the combined Phalanx won't be able to stop them, not for long. We would only slow them down."

Murmurs of agreement ground out from the rest of the lords, their Protectors, and their caitans. Thaedoren would like to believe otherwise, but was forced to agree with them. After what he had seen at Caercaern...

"Then what do you expect them to do?" Moiran asked. "Cower in their manses until Khalaek-khai decides to deal with them? We have no chance at all if we're divided."

"But Artillien?" someone countered, and then everyone broke out into arguments, gruff voices edged with tension and exhaustion blending into a low rumble that washed over Thaedoren and heightened his weariness. His shoulders sagged and he rubbed at his eyes, felt the grit there—from lack of sleep, from the hard march through feet of snow, from the stress of trying to figure out what to do. He'd hoped that they could come to some kind of decision here, at this meeting. But he could hear the fear in their voices, knew that what had happened at Caercaern—what had been happening to the Alvritshai for the last year—had sunk its fangs into their souls and wouldn't let go. And like the Haessari poison, those fangs were laced with venom.

"Enough!" he barked. "Enough fighting! Enough words! Enough self-pity and self-loathing and recriminations!"

The arguments cut off abruptly, his outburst slicing through them as cleanly as a blade. He waved both hands, gesturing all of them back to their seats.

"We are all tired. We are all stressed out from worry, from the march, from grief over everything that we've lost. But we are not finished yet. We need to plan, or Khalaek-khai and his Phalanx and Haessari will destroy us all."

He turned to Fedauroen. "Your mother is right, we cannot leave Lady Halceon or Lady Sovaeren alone. We cannot leave anyone within Khalaek-khai's reach. He will seize whatever advantage he can, use it against us if possible. We need to send word to those in Ionaen, Redlien, Uslaen, and Licaeta to abandon their lands."

"And have them come here?" Saetor asked. "I agree that leaving them vulnerable to the Wraiths is foolhardy, but having them come here is impossible. Even if word does reach my people in Uslaen or those in Licaeta, it would take them months to reach us. The storm itself will add weeks to the trek, even if the snows stopped tonight."

"The storm is going to cause more problems than that," Moiran said. "It doesn't have the feel of a normal winter storm, not here south of the Hauttaeren. It feels more like the storms that drove us out of our homeland centuries ago."

"What are you saying?"

Moiran glanced around all of those gathered, some of them shifting uncomfortably beneath her gaze. "I'm saying that this storm came too early and is too strong. It is a harbinger of a harsh winter, yes, but it's more than that. I think the ice and snow and cold that drove us first into the catacombs of the Hauttaeren, and finally out into these southern lands, is finally moving farther south."

"Do you think it's something the Wraiths have done? Are they controlling it?"

"Of course not. But that doesn't mean they won't take advantage of it. If I'm right, then the snows won't stop tomorrow, or the day after. They'll continue for days, perhaps weeks on end, as they did to the north long before any of us were born. And like those who were too stubborn to bow down beneath the ice and retreat, we will die."

Thaedoren suddenly understood what his mother intended to propose. He didn't like it, but he asked regardless. "What do you suggest, mother?"

Moiran straightened, her posture rigid, but regal. "We cannot stay here, in Artillien. As has already been stated, it was not designed to defend against an army of Khalaek-khai's size. None of the cities outside of Caercaern were. Even without Khalaek-khai's forces looming over us

in Caercaern, the storm will drive us south eventually. We will run out of
food, and if the snows continue as they did in the north, according to the
Scripts, there will be no spring, and precious little summer or fall. No
time to sow, no time to harvest. We need to retreat—from the snows,
from Khalaek-khai's army. We need to head south."

A few of the caitans snorted in dismissal, low murmurs breaking out as
they turned to speak to those standing closest, but Thaedoren didn't let it
degenerate into arguments. He raised a hand and slowly the room fell
silent.

"Suppose you are correct—" When a few began to protest, so he
added, "And I do not admit yet that I agree, but suppose you are correct.
Where do we retreat to? The humans control the coast, and the dwarren
the plains. And do not forget that we are not simply seeking new lands.
We will have an army at our backs. We will be seeking sanctuary. Why
would the humans or the dwarren agree to protect us?"

"Because of the Accord."

A few of the men barked out laughter, Fedaureon flinching. Moiran
didn't react. Saetor leaned back, eyes fixed on the table, but he shook his
head slightly. Caeden and Renaerd were silent, although he could tell they
were siding with their men. None of the Alvritshai lords had taken the
Accord seriously since it was signed at the Escarpment. It was a useful
tool to keep the dwarren and humans at bay, to keep them in line, nothing
more. None of them believed the humans or dwarren would follow
through on its clauses of mutual aide in the event that they were attacked.

"We would be refugees," Saetor said, his voice loud enough to quell
the rest of the discussion. "The Accord says nothing of refugees. They
would not be obligated to take us in. They would not be obligated to help
us in any way. The Accord only allows for us to ask for their aide in the
event of an attack."

"Then ask them! Take our armies, take our people, to their door and
ask them for aide against Khalaek-khai and his forces."

"And if they say no?"

"Then we are no worse off than we are right now."

Thaedoren turned away to watch the snow fall outside the windows.

It did not look like it would be letting up any time soon.

The room remained silent except for the rustle of clothes, the clank of
a buckle against wood, someone tapping their fingers against the table in
an odd pattern, and the creak of a chair as someone leaned back with a
sigh.

He let his gaze drop to the table, leaned forward again, hands planted flat against its surface. Then he met Fedaureon's eyes. "We will wait until Lady Halceon arrives with those from Nuant House."

"Tamaell—" one of Saetor's caitans began in warning, but Thaedoren cut him off.

"What? Do you deny that this storm isn't normal? Every man and woman in the room can feel it. All you need do is step outside and its strength, its determination, presses down on you like a shroud. Moiran is right. This is a precursor of what drove us from the north in the first place, and if we wait too long, the snow will trap us here and we will die beneath the cold. We need to head south, now, before the roads become impassable and before our food runs low. The sooner we move, the less likely Khalaek-khai and his forces will be able to find us and stop us. Because they will be coming for us, as soon as they regain their strength and solidify their hold on Caercaern. He knows where we will run, if he hasn't already had scouts confirm it. Artillien isn't safe."

"The snow will confound him and his army as much as it will us."

"That is true. And perhaps we can use it to our advantage. The fact remains that we do not have enough men to counter Khalaek-khai's forces even without the snow. We lost our greatest defense when Caercaern's gates fell."

"They didn't fall," someone grumbled. "They were opened from the inside."

Thaedoren chose to ignore the comment, speaking to Moiran instead. "While we wait for Lady Halceon's arrival, send word to Lady Sovaeren to remain in Hallieas, but to continue preparing her Phalanx and House for travel. We will join her there, then continue southward. Send word to the eastern Houses as well, even Licaeta. Tell them of our plans. We will wait for them as long as possible in Hallieas, but if we've already departed when they arrive, they should attempt to find us on the road."

"Where will we be headed?" Caeden asked.

"South, to the White Winds Pass toward the human Province of Rendell. If the storm has closed the pass, we'll head around the eastern edge of the Reach, skirting the plains."

"Why Rendell? Why not go to the dwarren first?"

"Because Khalaek-khai's forces came from the dwarren plains."

Thaedoren let the ramifications of that sink in before turning to Saetor.

"The Phalanx will be needed to help control the populace. Work with Moiran and the rest of the ladies of the Ilvaeren to coordinate the wagons. Caeden, Fedaureon, and Renaerd can help with the Phalanx itself. Begin sending groups south as soon as they are ready, don't wait for the arrival of Nuant. And I want scouts watching Caercaern and reporting back on a constant basis. We need to know if Khalaek-khai's forces move, especially if they leave Caercaern."

"There will be those who wish to stay," Moiran said. "What should we do with them?"

"Leave them. It's their choice."

"What of those who wish to join the Phalanx? We've already had requests."

"Begin training them. Have the caitans see to it. Use whatever weapons you can find or forge before we leave."

Thaedoren paused, but no one filled the silence. The atmosphere in the room had shifted. There was still a heavy sense of dread and hopelessness—he couldn't banish the defeat at Caercaern that easily—but now there was also a sense of purpose and direction smothering it. A purpose tinged with excitement from the three younger lords. Even Saetor's back had straightened, his jaw set with determination. Thaedoren could see the orders he intended to issue in his eyes. The caitans and Protectors all held the same stiff stance, eager to begin, poised to move.

"See to it then."

They rose with a creak of wood and the scrape of chairs against the floor. Conversations broke out immediately, Saetor moving toward the three younger lords, the rest conferring with their caitans and Protectors as they filed out.

Thaedoren didn't move, watching in silence as they departed, aware that Moiran had stood and moved to the window, arms crossed over her chest.

He waited until everyone had left, servants entering to deal with the remaining wine and glasses. He shifted to his mother's side, staring out at the snow, the fat flakes falling steadily, although not so thick that he couldn't see the glow of lights from other rooms in the manse in the wings to either side.

"You need rest," he said softly.

"I haven't slept well since Fedaureon left for Hallieas."

"It's more than lack of sleep, mother."

He hands clenched tighter on her upper arms, but then she bowed her head.

"Yes, it's more than that. When you returned—both you and Fedaureon alive—I was thrilled, but then you told me of the fall of Caercaern...and of Khalaek-khai. I thought he was dead. He should be dead. You saw him gutted by the human king at the Escarpment, you and

Aeren both. How could he have possibly survived?"

"We left him bleeding into the dirt of the battlefield. He'd already lost too much blood to survive."

"But he *was* still alive. Someone should have made certain he was dead."

"In retrospect, I agree."

Moiran harrumphed...and then chuckled, the laughter soft and still bitter, but with a touch of actual mirth to it. It sounded more like the mother he remembered, not the hardened, angry woman he'd seen at the conference table earlier tonight.

"What will we do, Thaedoren? The Alvritshai are broken."

"But not destroyed. We'll regroup. We'll seek the aide of the human Provinces and the dwarren. And we'll find a way to defeat the Wraiths, once and for all."

"There is one factor we did not take into account in our councils earlier."

"And what is that?"

"The Order of the Flame."

"Lotaern died at Caercaern. I suspect few of his Flame survived Khalaek-khai's attack on the city."

"But Lotaern sent his warrior acolytes out into House lands, remember? We have two of them here, kept as prisoners. I'm certain there are many more who did not return to Caercaern, since Lotaern never ordered them back, in defiance of the Evant. His most powerful acolytes were in Caercaern, but I doubt that those here and spread throughout the rest of the Houses are untrained. If we have any hope of defeating Khalaek-khai and his fellow Wraiths, we're going to need them."

* * *

Quotl rode out of the dwarren tunnels into a blast of frigid air and the pin-prick pain of particles of ice. Not quite snow, the precipitation immediately began collecting in his beard and he huffed in annoyance, turning toward Azuka, who rode to his right.

"It's worse than the forward scouts reported."

Azuka said nothing. There was nothing to say.

As the rest of the dwarren emerged from the tunnels behind him, ducking beneath the onslaught of the gusting wind and the abrasive ice it carried, Quotl urged his gaezel toward the nearest ridge. His animal plowed gamely forward through the layer of snow that covered the plains.

A thick layer of clouds rolled by overhead, blacker and more threatening to the north and west. It was obvious the snow would start up again soon; this break was only a small reprieve.

He contemplated the northern darkness, running a hand through his beard as he did so. Accumulated ice crackled as it broke and pattered down into his seat. His exposed skin beneath his newly donned helm already felt red and tight with the cold.

He turned to the south. Sunlight broke through the clouds in patches, the shafts of light spearing down onto the snowy plains for long moments before the roiling movement closed up the holes. The interplay of light and shadow was beautiful, but Quotl found it hard to appreciate fully.

Especially when he saw Ikterru approaching, the eldest Rider who'd survived the battle at the Sacred Waters and who'd taken over as the leader of the dwarren warriors. If there had been any semblance of clan divisions left, he would have been a clan chief, and for all intents and purposes he was, except in name.

But he didn't agree with Quotl's decision to lead them to Caercaern to help the Alvritshai. He had followed Quotl's orders up to this point, voicing his opinions only in the company of Quotl and Azuka, but Quotl could see the anger on the Rider's face as he urged his gaezel through the knee-deep snow.

"Archon!" he called, his voice loud, even if it was broken by the wind. "Archon, we need to speak."

"I hear you, Ikterru. No need to shout."

Ikterru's breath plumed in the air as he passed Quotl's constant escort of four. Quotl returned to looking to the north. Lightning flared in the darkest part of the storm, but it wasn't the strange purplish lightning of the unnatural storms that came from the east. This was natural.

Ikterru drew up on his left. The Rider shot a glance around to make certain no one was near enough to hear. "You can't possibly expect the Riders to travel in this. It's already knee deep on the gaezels. And by the look of that storm, there's more on the way."

"The elloktu's army is to the north."

"How do you know? Are they creating this storm? Is it to keep us away?"

Quotl's brow furrowed and for a moment he allowed himself to sink in to the power of the Land surrounding them. It flowed with a slower pulse with the onset of winter, but it was still strong, still powerful. Yet he sensed nothing out of place with the storm. He sighed. Ikterru had perked up with the possibility the storm was unnatural.

"No, the storm is natural. But the elloktu's army is there nonetheless. Ilacqua and the Four Winds revealed it during my last scrying."

"It doesn't feel natural. We've seen snow on the plains before, but never this early."

"I agree, but I have received no warnings from the gods." He drew in a deep breath, scented the air. He could smell the coming snow, the cold crackling in his nostrils. A deep abiding cold, coming from far north, beyond the range of mountains the Alvritshai called the Hauttaeren. "And the storm smells of strength, of permanence. We cannot wait for it to pass. It will be here for days...days in which the elloktu's army will be attacking the Alvritshai."

"What of our own? Why should we concern ourselves with the Alvritshai? We should join clan chief Asazi and the rest of the surviving Riders in the east, protect our women and children and what few dwarren remain."

"If we were not caught up in the middle of the Turning, I would agree with you, Ikterru. But this *is* a Turning. The world shifts. The Land will shudder, seas will rise, the skies will burn. Already, the storms gather. It will not matter where we run, where we flee. The elloktu and their followers will find us. If we do nothing, they and the forces they unleash will destroy us." Ikterru had stiffened in affront at the thought that what he suggested could be considered a cowardly flight. His mouth worked as if he'd bitten into a piece of bitter tarrow root. Quotl let that taste settle before continuing. "But you are right to question me. There is a reason we split the responsibility of the Archon and the Cochen, why even they call for meetings in the keevas between their advisors. There is danger in allowing one voice to dictate every decision."

"You have barely listened to anything I have said."

Quotl chuckled. "That's not true. You suggested I send those dwarren who were not Riders, along with most of the shamans, back to Broken Waters. You suggested that all remaining dwarren from all of the clans gather there, beneath clan chief Asazi's protection. I listened. The drums sound out those orders even now." Although he knew those drums would end soon, as soon as they headed overland to the north. A niggling thread of doubt worried through him, burying itself in his chest. He didn't know how badly the elloktu and their creatures had infiltrated the warrens. The pounding of the drums may be echoing down empty and abandoned corridors. Or, like the chambers around the Sacred Waters, halls filled with dead.

Ikterru considered for a moment, then straightened in his saddle, his gaezel pawing at the snow-covered earth before them. "Travel through the snow will be difficult. It is already deep."

"It will likely get deeper."

"Ai, likely. That means it will be slow going. And we are not used to the cold."

Quotl nodded ruefully. His own bones already ached from the exposure. But he heard the warning buried in Ikterru's tone. Some of the Riders would succumb. The dwarren were used to retreating beneath the earth those few times ice storms had driven this far south. But retreat was not an option. Quotl knew this in his soul.

"The Riders will persevere," he said.

Ikterru spun his gaezel around, kneeing it toward where the Riders were still emerging from the tunnel onto the plains. Quotl watched him go, thinking of all of the dwarren Riders with him, and all of the dwarren gathering to the south and east in Broken Waters.

"Where is my pipe?"

He began patting his pockets when someone cleared their throat. He spun, startled, to see Azuka holding his pipe out toward him. He bit back a sharp reprimand when he saw that the pipe had already been packed with yetope and that the shaman held the ember box in his other hand.

He plucked the pipe from Azuka's hand and stuck it in his mouth. "I suppose you're proud of yourself for anticipating your doddering Archon's needs," he said as he leaned forward, Azuka pressing one of the coals from the box to the bowl of the pipe, shielding both from the frigid gusts of wind. Quotl sucked on the end of the pipe until he felt tendrils of the soothing smoke entering his lungs. He drew it in deep, leaned back and closed his eyes as it warmed him from the inside out, dispelling some of the cold. He moaned slightly as he exhaled and drew in deep again.

Azuka dropped the coal back into the box and snapped it shut without comment.

The low throb of the drums from the tunnel behind them ended. The last of the dwarren Riders emerged from the tunnel's mouth. Quotl watched as they fell in around Ikterru, the Riders' new leader giving out orders without looking in Quotl's direction.

Five minutes later, the dwarren Riders headed out into the storm, leaving a wide trail of churned snow behind them.

* * *

Colin stood at the top of the wide tower in Yhnar, a dry, hot wind tugging at his hair and shirt, blowing from the north. It smelled of salt from the Flats, and the scent made his lips burn with the memory of the trek through that barren land. He ran his tongue over them, imagined them cracked and bloody. His hands rested on top of his staff, his feet planted shoulder-width apart. The crenellations of the fat tower cut off his view of the surrounding city of Yhnar, but he could see the river to the north, gleaming in the sunlight, and the rolling hills and grassland beyond, yellow where it wasn't broken by the browns of plowed fields. He could see the orange dots of pumpkins in one of the nearest fields, another with what he guessed were squash. Small figures hauled wagons through the patches, while others were threshing grain closer to the river. But his attention wasn't focused on the people of Yhnar or their work. His thoughts were farther north, beyond even the Flats.

"You've been standing here for nearly two hours."

Colin lowered his gaze, but did not turn toward Laurelen. "I've been... thinking."

"Is that all?" He heard her move forward, tensed as she came up beside him. He could see her out of the corner of his eye, her hair catching in the breeze, her chin lifted defiantly. Just as Karen would have looked, if she had survived the encounter with the Shadows.

And somehow been raised up into a royal house. Colin had a hard time visualizing Karen in the dusky, deep red dress Laurelen wore, gold embroidery at the neck and along the sleeves, the cloth so fine it appeared to shimmer in the sunlight. He knew if he touched it, it would be as soft as baby's hair.

"You've been rather reclusive since you arrived here, Colin Harten. If I had to guess, I would say you've been avoiding me. Is it because I remind you of Karen, of your lost love?"

"Yes and no. When I look at you, I see her. And not just physically. You have some of her mannerisms—a hand gesture, a lift of your chin, a twist of your lips when you smile. Seeing that, being forced to remind myself that you aren't her, that she's gone...it's painful."

"I've seen you watching me, clutching the vow beneath your shirt. Always from a distance. Which is what I pointed out to Commander Renolds when he came to me with...concerns."

"I'm sorry. I didn't realize I was being so..."

"Obvious?"

Colin couldn't help smiling. He realized his hands had clenched on the top of his staff and he forced his fingers to relax. "I suppose I should speak to Commander Renolds myself, make certain he realizes there is no threat."

"Not necessary. I've already assured him of that." She looked toward him for the first time. "You pose no threat, correct?"

"Not to you, no. And not to your people."

"Good. Now, care to explain what you've been looking at for the last two hours?"

He shifted. "Nothing...and everything."

"That's the least helpful statement I think I've heard from anyone my entire life."

"That's exactly what Karen would have said. Although she likely would have slapped me first."

"Don't think I didn't consider it."

He turned and met her gaze. Her smile didn't quite fill her eyes; still wary of him.

He glanced behind and found two Legionnaires standing to either side of the open cavity of the stairwell leading down into the tower. Both were watching them carefully, their expressions hard.

He turned back to his search of the hills and the wasteland he couldn't see beyond them.

"Tell me what's bothering you," Laurelen said. "I need to know, especially if it may affect the people of my Province."

"The Winter Tree has fallen."

Laurelen stiffened. "How? Who destroyed it?"

"I don't know. But I sensed its death. Like the Autumn Tree and the Summer Tree, it was already failing, but even so, I expected it to last much longer. Yet the power being wielded by the Wraith using the Well in the Thalloran Wastelands...that power is tremendous. I should never have allowed it to be woken. I should have stopped it."

He jumped when Laurelen touched his arm.

"From what I've gathered speaking to Siobhaen and Eraeth, you fought to stop it."

"Not hard enough." In his head, he could hear Walter's voice, tainted with mocking laughter: *You never did open yourself completely to the Lifeblood and all it offered as I did, did you?*

"Is that what you're doing up here? Berating yourself for something that has already happened? Picking at the scabs of a wound that should already have healed? What you should be doing is asking yourself how you can help all of us deal with the situation the way it is now."

Colin felt as if he'd been slapped, even though Laurelen hadn't moved. He nearly stepped back, but her hand on his arm kept him from moving.

Her words bit deep and he felt a flush of shame, but something in her tone forced him to focus on her more closely. "What's happened? Why did you come up here? You weren't looking for me, were you?"

Laurelen let her hand fall from his arm. "No, it wasn't. I come here to think, or to get away from the court. To relax."

"So what's happened? Have you heard from your husband?"

"He says he's arrived at Temeritt, but the city is surrounded by an army of creatures he would never have thought existed, except that he can see them. GreatLord Kobel has sent out forces to harry them, but there are too many for Kobel to repel, even with my husband's help. Tarken has kept his forces hidden, but he's afraid there's little he can do, and it's only a matter of time before he's discovered. There are flying creatures keeping patrol overhead, so he's been forced to keep his Legion a significant distance from the city itself."

"Eraeth calls them taeredacs—the flying creatures."

"Whatever they're called, he says they remain too high for his archers to take down. They've only managed to kill one, when it came low to feed on a dead deer. But the most disturbing news is the Wraith army— and there's no doubt that's who they are—has apparently already destroyed Borangst. They've hung the GreatLord's body from the remains of the Autumn Tree, along with several of Alden's Legion commanders and—" she paused to swallow "—and his wife and children."

"What about the king? Why hasn't he sent the Legion to help them?"

"I don't know. Yhnar is so remote. We rarely know what's happening in the western Provinces, even Temeritt."

"You've received no envoys from the west? No messages by courier?"

"Not even messenger pigeons. Which is strange in and of itself. We usually receive something from merchants or the other GreatLords a few times a month."

"The Wraith army must be intercepting them. There must be some other way to find out what's happening in the west."

Before he could say anything more, Laurelen straightened. "Perhaps there is."

Without explanation, she spun and ran for the stairs. The two guards were startled at the sudden movement, but after a confused glance at Colin—who shrugged—followed her down into the tower. Colin trailed after them.

The tower smelled of stone and smoke from the candles, torches, and lanterns that were used to light the interior. Laurelen and her guards wove down through stairwell after stairwell, along corridors and through long narrow rooms, the scents shifting. He knew the servants placed sachets in most of the rooms to hide the mustiness, so one hall smelled of lavender, while the next of roses.

They'd just exited a large hall redolent with pungent cedar when he realized where they were headed: the GreatLord's personal chapel.

One of the guards stepped ahead of Laurelen and opened the door to the small inner sanctum, closing the door behind Colin. Laurelen hadn't appeared to notice his presence, her attention fixed on the far side of the room. It was small, perhaps twenty paces wide, with mock columns rounding out from the walls to either side, arching to points on the ceiling at least twice Colin's height above. A short walkway separated two sets of four pews to either side, leading to a single step up to an empty dais. The wall opposite the door was filled with niches of the same shape, one large central one containing a carved skewed cross draped in a pure white cloth embroidered with Diermani's Hand, a gold bowl filled with water beneath. The cross was surrounded by tall candles, their light soft and diffuse. Relics filled most of the rest of the niches—a thick tome that Colin presumed was a copy of the Codex, a filigreed brazier, an ivory scepter, multiple chalices...

And one niche that held a single glowing glass orb.

Laurelen headed straight for the orb. "Send for one of the patri."

"Which one?"

"Any of them. The arrulis if you can find him, but any of them will do."

"What's wrong?" Colin asked, moving down the aisle himself. The farther he moved into the room, the deeper the scent of rosemary grew, along with something else. He unconsciously pulled in a deeper breath, tested it...

Blood. The scent beneath the rosemary was blood.

"The Hand of Diermani." Laurelen halted before the glowing orb. "It's never glowed before."

Colin reached out with his senses as he drew near. "There is power here. What is it for?"

"The original intent was communication. There is one in every main city in each Province—here, Temeritt, Borangst, Portstown, Corsair, and Rendell. They were created by the caddoni of the Holy Church of Diermani at great expense, to be controlled and used by the patri and GreatLords in each of the cities in the event of emergencies. And, according to the histories, for a while they were. But as roads were built between the Provinces, as more and more trade developed between us, the GreatLords found themselves using the Hands of Diermani less and less. In some cases, the GreatLords refused to use them for political reasons, since they were under the control of the church. After a while, they fell into disuse. I only know of them because we are a newer Province." She grimaced. "And because I was forced to read the histories of the church by my mother. She was...extremely faithful."

Colin thought of his own mother, who had kept Diermani's cross alongside her own vow. She had been faithful as well, more so than his father.

First Karen, now his parents...even this small sanctuary that smelled of rosemary reminded him of the cathedral he'd entered once in Portstown, before the fateful confrontation with Walter. The old memories churned in his chest, producing a dull ache.

"How does it work?"

"The journals and notes I read only said that patri and the GreatLords could use them. They didn't reveal why."

"Perhaps because the patri possessed the power."

"But what about the GreatLords?"

Colin shook his head, leaning forward. "What is swirling around inside the orb? It almost looks like—"

"Blood." Both Colin and Laurelen straightened and turned toward the door, where the guard stood with another man dressed in the dark gray vestments of one of the arruli. His hands were clasped in front of him in disapproval.

His gaze shifted to Laurelen. "You brought him here?"

"He is a guest, Arrulis Cuneo. And he does have his own...history."

"Yes, he does." He moved deeper into the room, the second guard entering behind him. "Some of that history causes concern."

"But he is still our guest."

Cuneo fixed his attention on the orb without comment.

"You say it is blood," Colin said. "Whose?"

"That would depend on who has activated the Hands."

"How do we find out?" Laurelen asked.

Cuneo glanced up. "We touch it."

And he reached out and set his hand on the orb.

19

Colin expected a reaction from Cuneo when he touched the Hand of Diermani—a gasp, a flash of light from the orb, perhaps a surge of power rippling away from the arrulis like a gust. Instead, the arrulis simply frowned in annoyance.

"What is it?" Laurelen demanded. "What's happening?"

"Nothing is happening. I can hear someone talking though. No... arguing. But it's from a distance, as if they were behind a closed door."

"What does that mean?" Colin asked.

"It means," Cuneo said impatiently, "that they're in the room with the Hand of Diermani, but no one is currently touching it. Now shut up and let me listen."

Laurelen pressed her lips into a thin line and shot Colin an apologetic look. Colin didn't respond. He'd lived long enough, and encountered enough people, including men of the church, not to let the arrulis' words or attitude affect him. He wanted to seize the Hand of Diermani himself. He thought it would respond to him, even if the lore surrounding it said that only those within the church or the GreatLords could use it. He could sense its power, as he could sense the Lifeblood in the Wells, or the white fire that the Alvritshai called Aielan's Light. This didn't feel quite the same as either of those, though. Nor like the healing powers of the Confluence. It was new, with a flavor that was vaguely familiar. As if he'd tasted its power once before.

"They're arguing over whose turn it is to watch over the Hand. If they'd simply touch it, we could speak to them!"

"We need to catch their attention somehow."

"I know that. But I don't know how to reach them from here. I could shout, but unless they're physically touching the orb, they won't hear me no matter how loud I bellow."

Colin looked to Laurelen. "May I try?"

The lady of Yhnar hesitated, suspicion wrinkling her forehead briefly, but nodded assent.

Cuneo stepped aside. "I think this is a mistake. You trust him too freely."

"He has done nothing to warrant my distrust, as yet."

"History proves that death follows in his wake."

Laurelen's eyebrows rose. "Does it? My interpretation is that he has always attempted to help."

Colin settled his palm over the Hand, felt its power surge up his arm and into his chest, warm, like sunlight, prickling beneath his skin as if he'd stepped suddenly from the cool shade of a portico. A memory of the ocean flashed through him, the scent of salt strong, the startlingly blue waters of a harbor in the background. Yellowed stucco buildings with red tiled roofs stacked on top of each other rose up along cliffs to either side. A breeze blew into his face, fresh with the hints of a storm.

He staggered slightly as the image faded.

"What happened?" Laurelen asked.

"Nothing. Just...just a sudden, sharp memory of when I was a child. A vivid image of the harbor of Trent, in Andover, from a few days before my father grabbed me and my mother and we boarded a ship for New Andover."

"What caused it?"

"I don't know." He suddenly heard voices. As Cuneo had said, they were muffled, as if Colin's ears were stuffed with rags. Only a few words stood out, loud enough to understand. The more he focused on the thread of the conversation, the more his connection to the room in Yhnar blurred as well. He heard Cuneo speaking, but the words meant nothing. Laurelen said something in response, but then their voices grew more tenuous. It almost felt as if he had shifted from the Hand in Yhnar to wherever this second orb was resting, as if he were inside the orb itself. The light within swirled around him, its essence tainted by the signature of blood. He didn't know who that blood belonged to, but he tasted its metal, slick and acidic against his tongue.

The argument in this other room began to fade, as if those arguing were moving away.

Reaching out, he seized the power of the orb flowing around him, gathered it, and threw it outward. He acted on instinct, afraid that whoever was in the room would leave and not return. They needed information. Short of having him Travel to the west to scout, which would drain him and still take time, this was their quickest option.

If those they could hear through the Hand were even in the west.

Outside the Hand, the voices had fallen silent. He couldn't hear anything.

Gathering the power around him again, he flung it outward a second time, then a third, and held his breath.

All he could hear was his heartbeat.

Then, an incomprehensible exclamation.

He repeated the gathering and flung it out two more times.

A presence approached. A shadow fell across the orb, as if a lantern had been shuttered.

And then a palm fell down on the Hand of Diermani in the unknown city. Colin was wrenched back to the room in Yhnar, flung back into his own body so hard he cried out. Both Laurelen and Cuneo jerked back, startled, and one of the guards at the door stepped forward. But Colin's attention fixed onto the man in priest's robes who now stood before him. The youth—he couldn't have been more than twenty years old—stared at him in shock. Both of them were reaching for the Hand of Diermani, but where they touched the orb their hands overlapped, making Colin's skin crawl. He couldn't feel the youth's hand, but it appeared to be inside his own.

Not only could he see the young man, he could see the room he stood in and a second priest, red-headed. The chamber looked formal, as if it belonged in a palace, not a church. The Hand of Diermani rested in the center of an ornate wooden table, nestled in an intricate iron cradle. The walls of the room were adorned with banners and tapestries, the table surrounded by multiple chairs, a few decorative urns, another table with a platter of mostly eaten food, and a nearly empty decanter of wine.

The room looking vaguely familiar. Colin's gaze locked onto the young priest. "You're in Corsair, in an audience chamber of the palace. Who are you?"

The young man swallowed. "Gregori. My name's Gregori."

"Who are you talking to?" the other priest demanded. "Is someone else touching the Hand?"

"Can't you see them?"

The other priest stepped forward. "Them? I don't see anything."

"I can see and hear both you and your friend," Colin said. "I assume you can see me and those behind me."

Gregori nodded. "Who are you?"

"My name is Colin Harten, and this is Laurelen, the Lady of Yhnar, and Arrulis Cuneo. This room is the private sanctuary of the GreatLord. Why did you activate the Hand of Diermani? What's happening in Corsair?"

Gregori shook his head before Colin could finish. "We didn't activate it. It was Lord Kobel in Temeritt. We were trying to reach him to find out—"

But the other priest hissed a warning and lurched forward, slapping Gregori's hand away from the orb. Gregori, the second priest, and the audience chamber vanished on the echoes of Gregori's startled outcry.

Colin's shoulders slumped.

"What happened?"

Colin turned toward Cuneo, surprised the arrulis had spoken first. He didn't remove his hand from the orb. "I made contact with two young patri in Corsair. It was obvious they were set to watch over the Hand of Diermani, in case someone chose to communicate with them. They claim the Hand was activated by GreatLord Kobel. They were expecting someone from Temeritt to respond."

"Where are they now? Why did they break contact?" Laurelen asked.

"I think one of the priests is simply being wary. He slapped the first priest's hand away from the orb. I suspect they're going to find someone with more authority who can deal with us. As I said, they were young."

"So we wait?"

"I don't think it will take long. They were in the palace in Corsair. And they've been hoping for contact."

"But for how long? When was the Hand activated?"

Power washed up through Colin's hand and the audience chamber blurred into existence again, but this time with an elderly man in much finer robes of state than the two patri. The two younger priests stood behind him on the left, a third priest—older than the others, but younger than the nobleman—stood to his right.

The nobleman glared at Colin, his frown tight with appraisal, then shifted his gaze toward Laurelen, Cuneo, and the guards behind. He relaxed when he recognized Laurelen, bowing his head slightly. "It is good to see you, Lady Laurelen."

"She won't be able to hear you," Gregori said, then flinched when his fellow patri slapped his arm. "I mean, she isn't touching the Hand. Only someone touching the glass can see or hear the others in the chamber. Your grace. I mean, Councilor."

"Shut up already," his friend hissed.

The councilor had turned slightly to listen, but now faced Colin. "Is this true?"

"As far as I can tell, yes. I haven't used the Hand of Diermani before. Who are you?"

The man's eyebrows rose. "I believe, under the circumstances, that you should verify your own claim first, Colin Harten."

Colin pulled back his sleeve, revealing the blackness roiling beneath his skin.

"So you are touched by the Lifeblood, as the legends say. But how do I know you aren't one of the Wraiths, posing as Colin Harten?"

Colin drew breath to respond, but suddenly realized that his usual proof no longer applied.

He exhaled. "Normally I would claim that I was within the protection of the Seasonal Trees, but they are all dead." The councilor's eyes widened in shock. "Without them...I'm not certain how I can convince you I am Colin Harten."

"I see." The man's eyes flickered toward Laurelen again. "I suppose, given your current company, I am forced to take you at your word. I am Tyrik, councilor to King Justinian. We thought GreatLord Kobel had activated the Hand of Diermani, not Tarken Sohn."

"It may have been Kobel. Tarken Sohn received a messenger from Temeritt warning him the city is under siege by the Wraith army. GreatLord Sohn has taken his Legion to Temeritt to see if he can be of help, but the reports we have received are not encouraging. The Wraiths have apparently already destroyed Borangst. That city's GreatLord and his family are hanging from the charred remains of the Autumn Tree."

"I see. You say the Autumn Tree is dead?"

"The Summer Tree and Winter Tree as well."

"We had not heard. The dwarren came to us, but we did not listen."

"What do you mean they came to you? What has happened to the dwarren? What's happening in the remaining Provinces?"

Tyrik hesitated, then straightened, as if he'd come to a decision. "The dwarren sent an envoy, warning us that the Wraith army had attacked them to the east. They asked for our aide, under the auspices of the Accord. We...hesitated. Councilor Matthais wanted verification, so we sent an escort back with the dwarren envoy. But they never returned."

"Because the Wraith army *had* attacked them! You signed the Accord. You should have sent aide immediately. That was at the heart of the agreement. That was practically its sole intent!"

"King Justinian wanted verification! We needed to know it wasn't some kind of trick!" But after his initial outburst, Tyrik hung his head. "But you are correct. We should have done more. Commander Roland did prepare the Legion all along the coastal Provinces. In fact, after more significant signs of an unknown army's presence on the plains, and then the warning from Kobel through the Hand of Diermani, he and King Justinian have taken the bulk of the Legion south, to Goran."

"What about the Alvritshai?"

"We have had no communication from the Evant at all."

Colin clenched his jaw in frustration. At least he now knew that the Legion was headed toward Temeritt. "Send word to the king. Warn him of what he and the Legion are marching into. Tell him of Borangst's fall, and the deaths of the Seasonal Trees. He will be facing the full wrath of the Wraiths and their armies. And tell him that GreatLord Sohn is waiting outside of Temeritt. He doesn't have enough men to break the siege himself."

"What of Yhnar? Is it under attack?"

"Not yet. But if Temeritt falls..."

"I understand."

"You should also prepare yourself for the arrival of refugees or aide. The dwarren are a proud race, as well as the Alvritshai, but if the Summer Tree and Winter Tree have fallen, either one may arrive in Corsair or the Provinces seeking sanctuary. Or the help they didn't receive before."

Tyrik's shoulders slumped at the reprimand. "If they do appear, Corsair will welcome them."

"Good." Before Tyrik could say anything more, Colin broke the contact, pulling his hand away from the orb. The audience chamber in Corsair, along with all of its inhabitants, vanished.

"What did you learn?" Laurelen asked.

"They know less than we do. But King Justinian and the Legion are headed toward Temeritt as we speak. They thought the warning came from GreatLord Kobel. I assume it did as well, although I suppose it could have been the GreatLord in Borangst. We'll have to leave someone here to monitor the Hand in case those in Corsair have news they wish to share."

"I'll have the patri attend the orb in shifts," Cuneo said.

"They'll have to be touching the orb. I doubt any of those in Corsair will figure out how to catch anyone's attention here as I did with them."

"But what can we do here in Yhnar?" Laurelen asked. "There must be something more that can be done, some way that we can help."

He thought a moment, then met Laurelen's gaze. "I don't see what else Yhnar can do but continue the harvest. Gather as much food and supplies as you can inside the walls. Fortify the battlements. Prepare yourself for refugees from Temeritt. If King Justinian and his Legion do not arrive in time, then Temeritt will fall, and the Wraith army will turn its attention to Yhnar next."

Laurelen drew in a sharp breath as if to protest, but she stifled the words, her face hardening, chin lifting. "Very well. Yhnar will be ready."

She headed toward the door with purpose, motioning her guardsmen around her, one of them sprinting out ahead of the group at her command to find Commander Renolds. Colin watched her go, seeing again the echoes of Karen in her stride.

"And what of you, Colin Harten? What will you do?"

Colin started at the voice. He had forgotten Cuneo was there.

"I intend to stop the Wraiths."

* * *

Tyrik lifted his palm from the Hand of Diermani, his skin tingling with warmth and the same residual pain from when he'd touched it initially and Vorati had done whatever the patris had done so that he could use it. He frowned at the swirling blood inside the orb, shuddered at the thought that his own was now mixed in with whoever had activated the Hand in the first place. Vorati claimed that the blood would fade over time and the orbs would eventually be clear.

Unless they continued using them, of course.

He heard a rustle of cloth as one of the priests behind him. "What did they say?" Vorati asked.

"The situation is worse than we thought. The dwarren were correct. There is an army, and it's already attacked Borangst. It's currently laying siege to—"

He caught himself abruptly, realizing who he was speaking to, what he was revealing. He mentally cursed himself. What he'd learned had rattled him, enough that he was speaking to the patri of the church as if they were lords or councilors. None of them were even arruli, let alone caddoni.

"It doesn't concern you. Continue monitoring the Hand. Report to me immediately if those in Yhnar have new information to pass on. Or if any of the other Provinces report in."

All three of the patri straightened. Vorati bowed slightly. "Of course, councilor."

Nodding at the restoration of formality, Tyrik made for the audience chamber's door, stepping into the hall before hesitating. He needed to inform Matthais, but Colin's reproachful voice still prickled the nape of his neck. Because the legendary figure was correct—the Accord had been designed with exactly this situation in mind, and when the time had come for it to be implemented, the Provinces had failed.

Tyrik spun and strode toward the Legion's barracks with renewed purpose. He would inform Legion Commander Houndell of the situation first, have him send messengers out immediately to the other Provinces—Rendell and Portstown—and then prepare his own missives to be delivered by bird. It was time for the Provinces to uphold their part of the Accord. The Legion should send scouting parties out into the dwarren plains and Alvritshai lands as well, try to determine how badly their allied races had fared and whether they needed Corsair's help. He and Houndell would have to bypass Matthais. He already knew what Matthais would counsel anyway—cautiousness and insularity. He'd grown tired of being cautious, and tired of Matthais' mercurial decisions. Besides, he had no idea where the rotund councilor was at the moment. It could take hours to find him, and hours more of arguing before they reached an agreement. King Justinian needed information immediately. He would need all of the support Tyrik and Houndell could gather, if what Colin Harten had said about the Wraith's armies were true.

He halted abruptly in the center of the corridor. "Andover."

The Provinces had treaties with the Court, of course. Most of those were non-aggression pacts and laws regarding trading rights, salvage, shipping lanes, and import and export taxes. None of those treaties were like the Accord between the Provinces, the Alvritshai, and the dwarren. But certain trading houses were too closely tied to the Provinces to ignore an attack on New Andover's territories. The Provinces may have severed their political ties generations back, but the bonds of trade remained intact. Andover couldn't afford to sit back and watch the Provinces fall.

He needed to send a missive to Andover as well, on the earliest ship. If nothing else, the king may be forced to trade with Andover for supplies—weapons, food, and medicine.

Tyrik pushed through two sets of doors and out into the winter sunlight. He squinted upwards, one hand shading his eyes, and noted the mass of storm clouds to the north, the front slowly moving southwards toward Corsair. As he moved down the steps and across the yard toward the barracks, a gust of chill wind slapped him in the face. It smelled of snow.

"This early?" he mumbled to himself, then set the troubling thought aside.

He had business to attend to.

* * *

Colin halted in the entranceway to the rooms Laurelen had provided for himself, Siobhaen, and Eraeth.   The three doors to their individual bedrooms were centered in the three other walls of the common area. Both Eraeth and Siobhaen were seated around the low table in the center of the room, a game of Kingdoms laid out before them.   Half-empty glasses of wine rested to one side, along with a platter containing a mostly eaten loaf of bread and a carved-up wedge of white cheese.

Siobhaen was in the process of shifting one of the black pieces on the field of inlaid wood.

"That's not a legal move," Eraeth said. He'd mostly recovered from their excursion across the Flats. His voice cracked when he spoke, as if his throat were still parched, and his words sounded like stones grating together.   "The gaezel's move is two hexes straight, one angle left or right."

Siobhaen hissed in frustration. "How can the humans play this game? What kind of movement is that? It makes no sense!"

"It's supposed to represent the arc of attack that the dwarren favor in combat. You've seen it on the battlefield."

"No, I haven't. I was born after the Accord, remember?"

Eraeth frowned, and for a heart-wrenching moment, Colin saw the weight of his age in his eyes, a weariness that lined his face and dulled the sheen of his hair.

Then Eraeth's gaze rose from the game board and caught sight of Colin. He straightened, Siobhaen turning at his movement. Both of them rose.

"We're leaving," Siobhaen said.

"No. I'm leaving. You two are staying here with Laurelen."

"I don't think so." Siobhaen was already moving toward her room. "We've been waiting here for what feels like an eternity. If you're going, we're going with you."

"You can't. There isn't time."

Siobhaen flung open the door to her room and stalking inside. Colin and Eraeth stared at each other from across the room.

"What's happened?"

"It doesn't matter," Siobhaen said from the other room. They could hear her pulling open drawers, slamming them shut, moving swiftly. "We aren't staying here any longer. I can't sit here, trapped in these rooms, another day!"

"The Winter Tree has fallen."

Siobhaen appeared in the door to her rooms. "What?"

"The Winter Tree has fallen."

"What does that mean for Caercaern? For the Order and the Evant?"

"I don't know. I don't know what's happened in Caercaern, to Lotaern and the Order, to Tamaell Thaedoren...or Lord Aeren."

Eraeth looked past Colin's shoulder toward the northwest. Siobhaen took a single step toward the Protector, one hand reaching toward him before she caught herself and let it drop back to her side. Her other hand held a bundled shirt.

"But I do know what it means for me. All of the protections I put in place to keep the Wraiths and the sukrael—anything tainted by the sarenavriell—at bay have now collapsed. All of Wrath Suvane is exposed. I can't allow that to continue."

"So what do you intend to do? You can't take them on yourself. Look what happened in the White Wastes, at the city in the Thalloran Wastelands."

"I don't intend to face them myself. But I can do something to blunt their powers."

Colin moved through the outer chamber into his own room, began packing up what little he'd removed from his satchel during their stay. He heard Siobhaen follow him, ignored her as she watched him from the edge of the room. Eraeth stood behind her. He checked the bottom of the satchel, made certain it still contained its most valuable item, wrapped in muslin that had once been as white as Aielan's Light, but was now stained and yellowed with age. Beneath its folds, he could make out the rough surface of a length of wood about the size of his forearm, with a gnarled knot at one end the size of his fist. The seed of the Spring Tree, unplanted, unused, carried around for over a hundred years in case the three races expanded even further and it was needed. But now it would be needed to protect the Source from the Wraith's abuse. If he planted the Tree near the Source, it would keep the Wraiths from using its full power, giving him the chance to repair the damage that had already been done.

He began laying his few belongings on top of it, burying it deep—clothes, a few knives, a battered steel pot, flint. He'd need some food, but he could get that from the kitchens before he left.

He reached for his staff, turned to find Siobhaen, arms crossed, blocking the doorway. "How can you blunt their powers?"

It would take nothing to slow time, slip past her and Eraeth both, and escape.

He sighed. "The only reason they are so strong, the only reason the Seasonal Trees have died, is because of the Source they found in the Thalloran Wastelands. We tried to stop its activation and we failed. I failed. Because I was weak."

"We failed because we arrived too late—"

"No!" Colin cut Eraeth's words off with a swipe of his staff. "It wasn't because we arrived too late. We failed because I wasn't strong enough to do what was necessary. I didn't have the conviction. I failed you all. Walter spoke to me after punching his sword through my chest. He whispered into my ear as I hung from his blade. He said I hadn't embraced the full powers of the Well as he had, hadn't given myself over to it, and he was right! I failed to halt its activation because at the last moment I pulled back from its power. I could have stopped it, but I didn't. Because I was afraid. And it was because the Source was awakened that the Wraiths managed to kill the Seasonal Trees!"

Both Eraeth and Siobhaen remained silent, caught off guard by the tirade.

Eraeth spoke first. "And if you had embraced the power of the sarenavriell...what then?"

"I could have stopped its awakening."

"But at what cost? What would it have done to you?"

Colin sucked in a breath, felt it catch in his throat. He knew what it would have done to him. The taint that he had fought since he'd first drunk from the Well would have consumed him; the black oil that swirled beneath his skin would have taken him. His last shreds of humanity would have been stripped away and he would have become like Walter, one of the Wraiths.

He exhaled, seeing in both Eraeth's and Siobhaen's eyes that they knew this. "It doesn't matter. Not any longer."

"It matters to us. It matters to Lord Aeren, to Lady Moiran. None of them would ask you to sacrifice yourself in order to protect them from the Wraiths."

"They don't have to."

Eraeth's chin lifted. "I still fail to see why we can't accompany you."

"The Wraith army is already moving. They have destroyed the human province of Borangst and have laid siege to Temeritt. I suspect they have attacked the dwarren as well. There are signs of the attack from Corsair, and I see no other way for them to have killed the Summer Tree, not with its location at the dwarren's most hallowed and protected grounds. I fear what the Winter Tree's death means regarding the Alvritshai. If I am to stop the Wraith army from using the power of the Source to destroy the Provinces and whatever remains of dwarren and Alvritshai lands, I need to move fast, across the Flats and back to the Thalloran Wastelands. King Justinian is already halfway to Temeritt. He will arrive within the next few weeks. I don't have the power to take both of you back to the Source in that amount of time."

"Then take one of us," Siobhaen said.

Colin smiled. "I don't know if I could manage even one. But regardless, I will not risk it. You both need to remain here, to help Lady Laurelen with the preparations here in Yhnar and to aid GreatLord Sohn with the siege at Temeritt. He's there now, although I don't believe GreatLord Kobel knows it. Kobel doesn't even know that Justinian is on his way."

"And what do you expect us to do? There are only two of us."

"Both of you have fought the Wraiths and the sukrael before." Colin looked at Siobhaen meaningfully. "And you can call on Aielan's Light."

"What do you hope to accomplish at the Source? It's already been awakened. Do you think you can put it back to sleep?"

Colin used his free hand to shift the satchel slung over his shoulder, felt the muslin-wrapped shaft of wood at its bottom. "I may be able to put it back to sleep eventually, but it took me years to find a balance for the other sarenavriell. We don't have that much time now. Not if the rest of the Wraith army is already marching toward Temeritt. And I believe it is. I can't reverse what Walter and the Wraiths have done now. But I can prevent them from using its power."

Siobhaen drew breath to ask how, but Eraeth placed a hand on her shoulder and she subsided.

"How much time do we have?"

"I can't say for certain, but those in Temeritt only have a few weeks at most."

Eraeth's face grew grim in consideration. Then, using the hand that still rested on Siobhaen's shoulder, he pulled her out of Colin's way.

"Go. Do what you can."

Colin walked past them into the outer room. He paused at the door, nearly turned to say something more, but didn't know what.

So he left without turning back.

* * *

"You were sworn to protect him," Siobhaen muttered as soon as Colin's figure vanished around the corner. She wondered if he had already seized time, if he were already outside the human's keep, outside Yhnar's walls.

"I know."

Siobhaen closed her eyes and, beneath her breath, muttered a small prayer of protection to Aielan in Shaeveran's behalf. Then she shrugged out from beneath Eraeth's hand and moved back to her room with purpose, shoving the shirt she still held in one hand into her satchel before moving to retrieve her other clothes.

"What are you doing?" Eraeth asked from just inside her room.

"Packing. You heard Shaeveran. The Wraith armies are in Temeritt. I don't intend to sit here waiting for them to come to me."

Eraeth said nothing. When she glanced up, he was gone.

By the time she'd finished, he'd returned, his own satchel slung across his shoulder, his cattan strapped to his side.

Neither one of them spoke as they left the rooms in Yhnar behind.

* * *

In the Temple of the Rose, deep in the Borangi desert, Tuvaellis opened her eyes on the darkness of her room—shared with four others from her own pilgrimage and a slew of travelers who had arrived before their group or had stumbled in off the sands since. She listened to the sounds of deep breathing, the rustle of blankets as someone shifted in their sleep, a few muffled snorts and snores, her eyes adjusting to the low flickering light cast by the lanterns in the corridor beyond. The rows of cots that lined both walls of the room slowly emerged from the darkness, the rumpled forms of bodies on top of them. The open entrance to the room beckoned, a thrill of urgency coursing through Tuvaellis' bones, but she remained still, stretching her senses out beyond the room instead. There were many priests of Diermani in the temple, most of the patri rank like Orren and the others who'd led their pilgrimage. But there were caddoni and arruli as well, and after what she had seen and experienced in Trent in the cathedral, she would not underestimate their unknown powers again. She was too close to her goal to risk it.

Satisfied that none of the priests were near, and that those in the room were safely asleep, she folded back her thin blanket and stood beside her cot, standing immobile when one of the others nearby stirred, hand rising to rub fitfully at their face before rolling to one side without opening their eyes. Touching the handle of her knife, Tuvaellis waited until the woman's breathing had deepened, then reached for the satchel that contained the stone Walter had given her. Pulling the strap over her shoulder, she seized time and halted it, slipping from the chamber and out into the corridor beyond, moving swiftly, but pausing at corners and intersections to catch her bearings and to search for the caddoni and arruli.

She'd been searching the Temple for days, knew nearly every corridor, every hall and room, every doorway. Most of the outer rooms were barracks like the one she'd just left, filled with cots for those that traveled here to be healed, or for other spiritual reasons. The men were housed on the eastern side, segregated into those who were sick and those who were simply family members or companions to those who were ill. The women were divided similarly, but had rooms to the west.

Tuvaellis passed the secondary women's quarters—the one holding the family members—and emerged into the central corridor that ran from the main entrance and its set of massive stone double doors all the way to the main spiritual chamber. Here, she slowed and let time resume. She didn't trust the caddoni and arruli not to sense her. After all, the priest in the cathedral in Trent had seen her. So she gathered her shawl and cowl about her, hid her face, and hunched forward before stepping out into the corridor. Moving like the aged and illness-wracked woman she purported to be, she made her way to the great hall, lined with pews like the cathedral in Trent. But she did not sit. Instead, she continued down the main aisle, the room opening up around her, the stone walls carved into stone figures and scenes from Diermani's Codex. Unlike the wooden cathedrals she'd seen in Trent and Andover, this structure was new, the dust of the stone still clinging to the air. Yet even without the provenance of age, the temple felt more solid, more permanent than the cathedrals. There were no windows filled with colored glass, no heavy tapestries along the walls, no wooden latticework lining the altar at the front, but the stonework was awe-inspiring nonetheless. The statues to either side of the room, framed by carved arches that reached to points in the ceiling high above, were more alive and present than the etched woodwork on the cathedrals. And the altar that was the focus of it all—

Tuvaellis paused as she reached the end of the pews and looked up at the stone tilted cross of Diermani that rose from the central platform, its white stone standing out in the light cast by the dozens of candles that lit the altar. The cross was more of a sculpture, its edges beveled, its form somehow imbued with a pulsing life of its own. Its façade was flat, unembellished, unlike nearly every other surface in the chamber. But the most striking effect of the altar was not the cross, but the hands that appeared to emerge from the back wall to either side. As large as

Tuvaellis, they'd been sculpted from huge blocks of marble, shaped palms cupped, as if reaching forward from the living rock not in supplication but in support of those who'd gathered before the cross. The Hands of Diermani, Tuvaellis knew, one of the Codex's most potent images, here made manifest. And she felt their power. The urge to step forward into the comfort and relief those hands offered tugged at her. But she resisted. She'd been through the chamber in her search for the heart of the Rose too often to succumb at this point.

She had turned away when someone said, "Restless night?"

She reached to seize time instinctively, but forced herself to halt and turn. "Nearly all of my nights are restless, Orren."

The annoying priest who'd continuously pestered her on the long trek to the temple stepped out from the shadows of a corridor leading off to the right of the altar and into the glow of the candlelight. He glanced up at the cross, bracketed by the hands, then turned his attention on her.

"So you come to the audience chamber for comfort?"

"Sometimes."

"I find it helps. When I'm uncertain, or when I have doubts."

"What do you doubt? I traveled with you for weeks. I never saw your faith in Diermani waver."

"I had doubts when the first boil appeared, when the red marks of the plague began. I railed against Diermani and the unfairness of it all, even as I succumbed to the fever. I was there to help the victims, not become a victim myself! I lost my faith then." He laughed quietly to himself. "I blamed my loss of faith on the fever when it broke, at least at first. But that wasn't the truth. I'd been filled with anger long before the fever hit, before the first sign of the plague appeared, honestly. But you didn't come on this pilgrimage to learn of my doubts. Haven't the priests taken you to the Rose, yet? Haven't they cured you?"

Tuvaellis turned away. "They don't simply hand the waters of the Rose out on arrival. They guard it, to protect it, they say. But that's not the real reason."

"What do you think is their real purpose then?"

"To control it! Whoever controls the Rose has the power. That's what the Feud was truly about all those years ago, wasn't it? The Families wanted the Rose for themselves, nearly tore the Court apart trying to gain control of it. But it was the church that seized control in the end."

"The church took control to make certain the Rose was used wisely, for the good of all. So that it couldn't be influenced by the Families and their politics."

Tuvaellis broke into a deep-throated chuckle. "So young. So naïve. The church seizing control had everything to do with politics. The true victors of the Feud weren't the bondsmen or the Families, it was the church." At Orren's angry, troubled expression, she sighed in exasperation. "Whatever the truth is, the church has control now. And they make their supplicants wait for the cure. Of those that traveled with us across the desert, only two have been given its waters. The rest of us are forced to attend their sermons, to hear of Diermani's holiness, of his great deeds, of his kindness and gentleness and purity, all while we wait for the sacred attention of his patri so that they may bless us with the healing powers of the Rose." She spat to one side. "I did not come to be lectured by men who withhold cures in order to retain their power."

Orren stared at her, his expression unreadable. Then his gaze dropped to the stone floor, before shifting up toward the cross and the outstretched hands. "Come with me."

He passed in front of her as he moved toward the corridor to the left of the altar. Taken aback, she hesitated, then followed, aware of where he was leading her as they progressed through the halls and chambers of the less public areas of the temple. This was where the priests resided, those who led the pilgrims to the temple, and those who lived here on a regular basis. Tuvaellis had already visited every room here, knew the corridor Orren took led to the source of the Rose's waters used for healing here in the temple. Not the true source of the Rose itself, but one of the tributaries.

As they neared the entrance to the sacred chamber, Orren told her to wait, then proceeded ahead. She heard murmured conversation as he spoke to the guards stationed at the chamber's entrance. She had been forced to halt time to slip past them in her explorations.

Orren reappeared, motioning her forward. Keeping her head lowered, he escorted her past the two guardsmen, then through the entrance to the top of the stairs beyond.

Steps encircled the room in tiers, descending toward the pool of pink-tinged water below. Orren stepped down ahead of her. The chamber was only half-lit with oil sconces to either side, much of the room in shadow, so she followed carefully. At the bottom, she crossed a narrow section of warm sand, her feet sinking into the shifting grains, then stepped onto the stone ledge surrounding the pool to Orren's side.

"The waters of the Rose," he said.

The stone steps had been hewn by human hands, but the pool was natural, the red-tinged water bubbling up from some underground stream, surrounded by rough sandstone. Tuvaellis could see the channel the water had carved out of the desert rock through the ripples of the current on its surface, its walls vanishing in darkness.

The power of the tributary prickled across her skin. But Walter had been clear. For the greatest effect, she needed the source of the Rose, needed its heart. Planting the stone in this tributary would not do enough damage to keep Andover and the Court from helping the Provinces defeat the Wraith armies. Andover needed to be focused on their own troubles at home. Their resources needed to be tied up saving themselves, not being shipped across the Arduon.

With a start, Tuvaellis realized Orren was watching her intently. She'd inadvertently moved closer to the pool, had been staring down into the waters longer than necessary. A prickle of unease crawled across her skin as she stepped back and faced the priest.

"Why did you bring me here?" Suspicion gnawed at her gut. She shot a glance toward the tiered stairs, the open doorway.

"So that you could drink the waters of the Rose and be healed."

"No. You're only a patris. You do not have the power to grant the waters of the Rose to pilgrims. That's a decision only the arruli and caddoni can make."

Her knife snicked free of its sheath.

Orren took a single step forward, one hand raised, palm forward. "The waters can heal many things, even diseases for which we have never found a cure. I know you do not have leprosy, Oranelle. And I know that is not your true name." His gaze flicked toward her satchel and he licked his lips. "Whatever you have come for, set it aside. With the power of the Rose, and faith in Holy Diermani and his Codex, you can be healed."

Tuvaellis snarled. "Can he heal this?" With one hand, she reached up and pulled back her cowl, standing straight in the process, so that she towered over him, her mottled skin revealed, her knife bared.

Orren flinched, took a step backwards, but she saw in his eyes that he was not surprised.

"You knew." The entire trek across the Borangi suddenly took on new meaning, new depths. All of the conversations between her and Orren, all of the times he'd sought her out to speak to her of Diermani, of salvation, of healing...he'd known the entire time that she was one of the Fallen, tainted by the sarenavriell, *shaeveran*.

Her hand tightened on the knife as the shock shifted into anger. "You knew."

Orren's hand dropped to his side. "I knew you were Alvritshai, yes, and one of the Wraiths. Did you think we could travel for weeks together and your height, your skin, would not be noticed?"

"How long? How long have you known?"

"Less than a week after you joined the pilgrimage."

Tuvaellis' eyes widened. All this time she'd thought she'd been safe. She could have killed them all, tried to find the elusive road they'd followed herself. She wouldn't have had to endure Orren's lectures, his mindless talk of redemption, of the church and how it could save her.

"If you knew I was tainted, why didn't you attempt to kill me as they did in Trent?"

"Because there weren't enough of us to guarantee success," someone said from the height of the tiered stairs. Tuvaellis spun to see Paulle, the leader of the pilgrimage, emerge from the doorway. Others filed into the room behind him, including the two guards from the corridor outside; ten additional guards and a dozen priests. "And because he thought he could save you," Paulle added as they filed in, the words laced with contempt.

"I had to try. The Codex demanded it."

"I believe it's now obvious you failed."

"She wavered. I can sense her uncertainty. All she needs is hope that what has been done to her can be undone."

"She's had her chance."

All of the guards had swords drawn, but the priests were what drew Tuvaellis' attention. All of them were arruli or caddoni, and she could feel the power radiating from them. Power like what she'd felt in the altar room and the cathedral back in Trent, suffused with warmth, a strange heavy lethargy, somehow seductive and compelling.

Tuvaellis drew herself up, all of the uncertainty of the past weeks fleeing, all of the doubts—doubts brought on by Orren and his words—fading. "I made my choice hundreds of years before any of you were born. I am Fallen. I am *shaeveran*."

Spinning, she brought her blade up and across Orren's chest, felt it slice into clothing and then flesh. At the same moment, she halted time, but met resistance. The power wielded by the priests blocked her, even as she realized that their attempts to halt her were not complete. Time had slowed. She saw Orren's startled expression as he lurched backwards, saw the blood arc out across the rose-tinged waters of the pool as he stumbled on its ledge and began to fall. Its metallic scent assaulted her nose and regret twisted deep inside her chest at his look of betrayal, but she quashed it and spun to face the priests.

None of them had moved, except for Paulle. His hand rose, motioning to the guards, all of his actions slowed as Tuvaellis continued struggling to halt time. The guards weren't waiting. Several had already begun descending the stairs, leaping between the motionless priests.

Tuvaellis surged forward, her motions sluggish, as if she were moving through mud, but she was still moving faster than the guards. Charging up the steps, the weight of the stone Walter had given her thudding into her back, she met the first guard head on. He swung his sword, but misjudged how fast she could move. She ducked under his swing, her blade sinking into his side, up beneath his armor, in and out, her other hand shoving him to one side as she engaged the next man, who'd compensated better for her speed. His sword slashed across her upper arm, but she didn't slow, punching her knife into his stomach while reaching to yank him off balance and thrust him behind her. She heard his startled outcry—long and drawn out by the slowed time—heard his body hit the stairs as he fell, but had already turned to the next two guards, converging on her from opposite sides. Reaching deep, she wrenched at time, crying out as something tore in her chest, but bounded three steps closer to Paulle as the two guards slammed into each other, their blades shrieking against armor.

The other six guards were off target, heading down the stairs toward a position she had already left behind. Tuvaellis locked gazes with Paulle, the realization that the power he wielded, the power drawn together by the priests around him, wasn't going to be enough only now beginning to dawn in his eyes.

"You should have tried to kill me in the desert," she said, uncertain whether Paulle would be able to understand her with time slowed. "At least then you would have had the advantage of surprise."

She stalked up the last few steps, Paulle just beginning to reel backwards as her blade found his throat. Blood splattered her face as she moved past him. The other priests cried out in dismay, but she could already feel their hold on her loosening as Paulle died. She gathered time around her as their hold weakened, moving into the corridor beyond, where four more guards were running toward the chamber. Their motions were nearly frozen, slowing even more as she gathered strength. She slipped past them without bothering to attack, confident she would appear as nothing more than a blur of darkness.

By the time she reached the main halls of the temple, the resistance from the priests had died. Her sense of freedom and conviction soared as she stalked through the corridors, past rooms and private chambers, a small chapel, the kitchens, and then through a servant's door out into the desert night. Heat radiated up from the stone and sand into her feet, but the night air against her face was chill. She turned from the temple toward the shattered walls and crumbling buildings of the ancient city that lay exposed beneath the night sky. Brittle stars—thousands upon thousands of them—pricked the darkness overhead, the thickest band, called the White Road, stretching out toward the west. The sliver of the moon rode above the horizon to the east, casting faint light.

Tuvaellis headed into the heart of the lost city, her eyes adjusting to the deeper night as she moved farther away from the temple. She crawled over tumbled stone, the remains of crushed walls and fallen pillars, barely taking note of the carvings and designs that riddled most of it. She followed the growing power of the Rose, its essence guiding her like a lantern in the darkness. She had thought the church would have built their temple around the source of the Rose in order to protect it, but she had been wrong. Then she had assumed that they would at least have a path or tunnel to the Rose's location somewhere in the temple. If they did, she had failed to find it. And now, with the discovery that they knew she was *shaeveran*, there was no more time to search and no more need for subtlety.

She would find the Rose tonight and finish what she had come for.

Climbing over the massive chest of a fallen statue—a man holding a sword upheld to the heavens in both hands—she found herself on the edge of a street, sand drifted across its length, piled high against the walls of the buildings to either side. She paused to stare at the empty windows and gaping holes in the mostly intact structures, impressed in spite of herself at their solidity, at their strength. They rivaled the architecture of the Alvritshai in the abandoned wastes of her homeland. Most were taller, or larger, although they lacked the elegance of the Alvritshai buildings. Their lines were rigid, the facades plain, without character.

She headed down the street, feet sinking into the sand, drawn forward by the lure of the Rose. The cracked shells of the buildings loomed to either side. Streets intersected her own, most smaller and narrower, smothered by the night. With time frozen, there was no wind, but she could smell the age that permeated the stone, dry and dusty. The entire earth reverberated with an unidentifiable nascent energy, humming in her skin. She shuddered, shrugging the sensation aside, and focused on the Rose, letting it pull her in.

Then the buildings ended, the road she followed emptying out into a wide circular space, more structures rising around the area's edges. But the space at its center was clearly delineated. Whatever it had once been—a park, a lake, a marketplace—it was now a field of undulating sand, broken only by towers of giant crystals, their faceted surfaces reaching toward the sky. Tthe weak moonlight caught in their faces, making them glow with inner, colored light.

Tuvaellis' breath caught. She had seen nothing like this before, not in the wastelands of Alvritshai's history, not in the birth of the human Provinces, not even in the ruins of the Thalloran desert. She wondered what it would have looked like in daylight, could imagine the prisms suffused with the fire of the sun, blinding in its intensity.

She stepped forward toward the crystals, noted broken shards glittering in the sand as she moved closer. Then she stood among them, some reaching as high as the buildings that surrounded the bowl, many of them broken or cracked. They trembled with a strange dissonant energy, at odds with the energy she'd felt from the stone of the city. It itched at the base of her neck, vibrated in her teeth and bones. She avoided the prisms as much as possible, only touching them when she was forced to climb over a few that had fallen across her path. Their slick surfaces shuddered beneath her touch, the vibration in her bones increasing.

But then the crystals ended, a large rounded building at their center.

"The Rose."

She moved toward the building, circled it until she found the gaping doorway, half buried by sand. She slipped and slid down the drift into the darkness inside, then began moving toward the building's center, using one hand along the wall to guide herself through the pitch black corridors. Her unease grew as the faint starlight and moonlight from the entrance faded and the darkness closed in, but then she realized she could see faint light from up ahead. A pulsing reddish glow, darker than firelight, almost like blood.

The corridor she walked curved inwards and then emptied out into a central circular chamber, its walls reaching to three times her height, broken by pillars into panels of carved stone. The ceiling mosaic spiraled inwards to a central point, its colors darkened by the light thrown up from the round pool that filled the middle of the chamber.

Tuvaellis released time and stepped toward the pool, barely registering the architecture around her. Her gaze was fixed on the placid surface of the pool and the undulating rings of fire that rotated deep below. Three interlocked circles, twisting around a central ball of fire that burned with the deep pulsing red of coals, even though they were submerged in water.

She halted. There was no ledge, no raised lip of stone. The floor simply ended, the water coming up to the stone's edge.

Without looking away from the Rose, Tuvaellis pulled her satchel from her shoulder and set in on the stone at her feet. She untied it, pulled the box inside free. She unlatched the case, opened the lid.

Only then did her gaze drop from the Rose to the stone nestled in protective folds of cloth. And only then because the stone had changed. Instead of the dull surface flecked with gold and a pulsing blue light deep inside that sent a few tendrils of energy snaking outwards to its sides, the stone now glowed with a harsh blue light and dozens of tendrils danced from that bright core.

She recalled Walter's words as he'd handed the box to her, so many months before. "Don't touch it or it will destroy you. Even at the end."

And she could sense its power. It was feeding off of the energy released by the Rose, an energy that pulsed all around her, through her, sinking into her bones. It seeped into the stone beneath her and spread outwards through the earth, through the water, and into the land beyond. An ancient energy. A healing energy.

Picking up the box, she stood, her hands trembling, her heart thudding hard in her chest. Her breath had quickened. She had traveled across the Arduon, had suffered the heat of the Borangi desert, for this moment. She had accepted this task without reservation, had vowed to Walter that it would be done.

And yet, arms outstretched, she paused.

Unbidden, her throat closed up and tears pricked the corners of her eyes as she relived the crossing of the Borangi desert in her mind. All of her conversations with Orren, all of the memories they'd evoked, memories she'd thought were long dead: her life before she'd been betrayed by her husband Tallusaen, before she'd killed her father. The life she'd lived since her banishment from the Alvritshai and the poisoning of her soul by the sukrael and the taint of the sarenavriell. Walter had given her purpose, had given her life meaning. He'd given her a chance at a final revenge.

Orren had believed she could be healed, could be saved. He'd believed she still had a choice.

But in the lurid red pulse of the Rose, she could see the black swirl of the sarenavriell beneath the skin of her outstretched arms. More darkness than light. She had been tainted and lost long before.

Tears streaming down her face, Tuvaellis released her pent up breath in a deep, heavy sigh and tipped the case.

The stone dropped into the pool with barely a sound, a ripple spreading across the smooth surface even as the harsh blue light of the stone sank toward the bottom. It curved toward the heart of the Rose as it fell, as if drawn to the light. Tuvaellis took one step back from the pool's edge as she felt the energy of the stone spike. Then it began to drink in the power of the Rose greedily, the energy building with every breath, escalating higher and higher. It sucked it into its heart, its bluish light expanding, filling the pool until it outshone even the blood-red fire of the Rose, the swirling rings of fire engulfed by blue flame. Tuvaellis sobbed, half in awe, half in terror, as the energy that suffused her, the energy that had somehow cascaded and expanded to something much larger than anything she'd ever felt before suddenly pulsed even higher—

And then contracted down to a central point at the heart of the pool, at what she knew was the heart of the stone.

Walter had told her to run. He'd told her to drop the stone into the source of the Rose, then halt time and run.

But she didn't. She didn't want to. She didn't think, even if she had, that it would have mattered. She could never have escaped this much energy, this much power. It was unfathomable.

She didn't move as the stone and all of its gathered energy exploded.

20

Matthais emerged from the stairwell of the main tower of Corsair's palace into the brisk wind blowing from the north, the air smelling of ice and pine, a distinct difference from the usual scent of brine and dead fish wafting up from the bay. He paused to catch his breath—the last stretch of stone steps was rather steep—and scanned the northern horizon, where the storm that had loomed for days appeared to have stalled out, its dark shadow lingering just within sight. He imagined its black swirling clouds covered the entire breadth of the Alvritshai nation, the northern parts of dwarren lands, and even the Province of Rendell.

Corsair's skies remained clear.

He squinted up into the pale winter blueness above, then turned toward the dovecote on the far side of the flat expanse of roof. To the west, over the stone ridgeline of the cliffs and beyond the thin spire called the Needle, he could see whitecaps on the ocean's waves, stretching all the way to the horizon. Below, to his left, the city of Corsair tumbled down the low hills, smoke rising from the chimneys. Ships filled the bay, bells clanging faintly, whistles trilling. Closer in, shouts echoed up from the courtyard along with the clang of weapons from the practice yard, a sound that had become constant since Roland's departure with King Justinian for the south and his orders to remain ready. Matthais frowned, his annoyance at Roland, Tyrik, and Justinian unabated. But he had stalled their discovery of the Wrath armies as long as he could, so he shrugged, fingering the multiple tiny messages rolled into cylinders he carried in his pocket. Since Roland's departure, he had had the run of the entire palace. Even Tyrik hadn't been as much of a nuisance as usual. In fact, he hadn't seen Tyrik in the last few days except from a distance, the councilor and once-regent passing through the halls with an intent, focused expression.

Matthais had used his fellow councilor's distraction to his own advantage. He'd increased his control and influence with the lords and merchants of Corsair and the surrounding Provinces, not to mention met with one of the premier trading companies of the Court of Andover. He'd negotiated a rather lucrative contract, one that would help solidify his hold on the Provinces once he seized control from Justinian with the Wraiths' help.

He was so caught up in thoughts of his plans for Corsair and the rest of the GreatLords—whoever remained standing after the Wraith armies passed through anyway—that he had nearly reached the door of the dovecote before he heard voices.

He halted abruptly, hand stilled as it reached for the dovecote's latch. Beneath the coos and rustling feathers from the pigeons and other messenger birds housed here, the caretaker muttered, "Are you certain?"

"Yes. Send this one immediately. It needs to reach Goran and the king before they depart for Temeritt. If they haven't left already."

Matthais snatched his hand back, his heart thudding hard once in his chest as he recognized Tyrik's voice.

"As you command, it shall be done."

"Good. And you're certain no messages have arrived from the king? Nothing from Portstown or Rendell?"

"Nothing, councilor."

Floorboards creaked and one of the birds fluttered as if startled. Matthais tensed. "Recall what I said earlier. We know of your collusion with Matthais. If you are keeping something from me, from the king . . ."

Matthais' hand clenched into a fist over his chest. They knew! But how? He'd been careful. He'd covered his tracks at every stage, made certain Tyrik was busy or distracted—

Except Tyrik had said "we." Which meant it went deeper than simply Tyrik. Roland must be involved as well. Which meant he'd been discovered months ago.

What did they know? What *could* they know? If they'd managed to compromise his communications link through the caretaker, they could know nearly everything. Most of his messages had been couched in vague terms—a necessary evil when you only had space for a few words—but they could surmise much from those messages over time. It all depended on how far back the caretaker had been delivering messages to them.

"—never in collusion against the king," the caretaker whimpered, and Matthais snapped his attention back to the dovecote and the roof. "You must believe me. The councilor brought the messages and I sent them out."

"You passed all of the messages received into Matthais' hands, even those meant for the king. That in itself is treason. So I ask again, no messages have arrived from the king or the other GreatLords?"

"No, no messages from the king. I swear on the king's name."

"Very well. I trust you will continue to bring me all messages you receive or send out for Matthais."

"Of course, councilor."

Footsteps sounded, approaching the dovecote's door. Matthais reacted without thought, stepping quietly back and around the side of the small cottage-sized building. He'd just rounded the corner when the dovecote's door creaked open and he heard both men step out onto the roof. Risking a look, he watched Tyrik move toward the stairwell, the short, thin, grizzled form of the caretaker halting a few steps from the doorway. The older man clutched a pigeon between his hands. As soon as Tyrik began descending the steps, the caretaker brought the pigeon up close to his mouth and whispered something to it, too softly for Matthais to hear, and then tossed the bird into the sky. It fluttered away, wings flapping violently as it spun around twice as if orienting itself, then took off to the south. Sunlight winked on the tiny metal capsule strapped to its leg.

The caretaker eyed the bird silently, then nodded in approval to himself before heading back inside the dovecote.

Matthais hesitated, listening to the caretaker as he rumbled around inside the small building, the birds that were his wards occasionally muttering throaty protests as they were disturbed. The caretaker muttered under his breath, the mildly angry words punctuated by deep, regretful sighs.

A few minutes later, Matthais moved back around to the dovecote's door, opening it hard enough its flimsy wooden frame cracked against the side of the building.

Inside the dovecote, the caretaker gave a startled cry, a few of the pigeons attempting to take panicked flight in their cages.

Matthais stepped into the dusty shadows inside, split by shafts of light filled with drifting motes and downy feathers. The sharp ammonia smell of bird shit assaulted his nose, concentrated within the confines of the building. Cages lined the walls, the birds behind the wire and wood frames cocking their heads to look at him as he halted just inside the entrance. The few who had been startled settled back down, while the caretaker squinted at him from where he'd shrunk against the back wall.

"I have some messages that I need to send immediately."

"Of course, councilor. Where to?"

"Two to Portstown, one to Rendell, and another to Borangst."

"Of course, sir." The older man—shorter than Matthais by at least a hand—bustled forward and began retrieving birds from various cages.

"Do you have the capsules?"

Matthais reached into his pocket and produced the messages, the capsules clinking together as he set them on a small table near the door, their ends color coded to the specific locations. He watched silently as the man worked.

After a long moment, the caretaker realized he hadn't left yet. "Was there something else, my lord? There's no need for you to stay. I can handle it from here."

"Oh, I don't mind. There's nothing else that needs my attention at the moment. Besides," he said, letting his gaze drift from the fidgeting man— he didn't even know his name, he suddenly realized—to the birds in the nearest cage, "I think I'll stay to watch you release the pigeons. I rarely allow myself such small pleasures."

The caretaker licked his lips, his gaze flicking toward the messages waiting on the tray. Matthais could almost visibly see him trying to figure out how to satisfy Matthais, while at the same time keep his word to Tyrik. Sweat beaded on the man's forehead, but he drifted slowly to the messages, picked them up, retreated back to his pigeons, and began attaching them to the pigeons' legs.

Matthais poked a finger through the wires of the cage before him, the pigeon inside eyeing it warily. "I've always loved the way pigeons move. And their soft cooing. So soothing." He withdrew his finger. "Are the messages ready to send?"

The caretaker swallowed before answering. "Yes, councilor." He held up a small, portable cage with the five pigeon's already inside.

"Then let's release them."

The man merely nodded, the sweat dripping down his face now. He held the smaller cage before him like a shield and tentatively moved past Matthais and out the door. Matthais fell into close step behind him, stepping to one side when the man stopped in the middle of the roof and set the cage down. He knelt and, with a quick twist, threw the top of the small cage back. Four of the birds took immediate flight, circling twice before heading off in slightly different directions. The caretaker had to shoo the fifth one from the cage with a wave of his hand, but it followed the others after a moment.

As soon as they were mere specks against the blue sky, Matthais turned to the caretaker.

"Now, tell me how long you've been passing my messages along to Tyrik."

"Wha—what do you mean?" the man stammered.

Matthais stepped forward, the caretaker shooting a panicked glanced toward the dovecote, as if he'd be protected somehow if he managed to reach it. But Matthais was positioned between the man and the small hut, forcing the caretaker to back away, towards the far side of the rooftop... and the stairs, Matthais suddenly realized. But if the man tried to flee, he'd simply have the Legion arrest him and his family.

"You know exactly what I mean," he said, still advancing. "You're passing along my messages to Tyrik, perhaps even to Commander Roland. Personal messages. Private messages."

"But it was by order of the king!"

"I've been sending messages for the king for years from this rooftop! Because Tyrik and Roland couldn't be bothered. I thought we had an unspoken understanding, if not a formal agreement. Obviously, I was wrong."

The caretaker had backed up nearly to the stairs. Matthais reached out and grabbed hold of the man's serviceable but worn shirt, the caretaker emitting a startled gasp. He struggled as Matthais jerked him close. "How long you've been handing my messages to Tyrik?"

The man's hands grappled with Matthais', but he couldn't break the councilor's hold. Whimpering, he opened his mouth to speak—

And then his terror-stricken eyes shifted off of Matthais face and over his shoulder, slipping from abject fear to slack-jawed wonder.

Matthais shook the man to recapture his attention, but failed.

A flicker of light caught at the corner of his eye and he turned to look out beyond the cliffs, to the ocean beyond.

For a moment, he couldn't comprehend what he was seeing. Light flickered across the western horizon in flashes, as if lightning were playing out beyond the skyline, too distant to hear. But the sky was clear in that direction, only a few shreds of clouds visible. And the light wasn't the pale blue of heat lightning, but a harsh, erratic white that hurt Matthais' eyes. He'd never witnessed anything like it in his life. The few clouds were suffused from beneath by the pulses, which continued flickering like the flames of a fire—an intense, white-hot fire—before they began to die down. His fingers slackened in their grip on the caretaker's shirt, and the man's struggles eased as they watched the display in silence.

Matthais found himself thinking of the Alvritshai Wraith he had helped secure passage across the Arduon so many months before. "What have you done to Andover?" he murmured to himself, as the flashes of light ended, leaving nothing behind but a low burning light above the dark blue line of the ocean's edge, like a cold, white sunset. And then even that died.

The caretaker saw his opportunity and acted.

Twisting free of Matthais' clenched hand, he lurched toward the stairwell.

Matthais spun, one hand reaching out to seize the man again. But then, instead of grabbing for the man's shirt, he placed his hand flat against the caretaker's turned back—

And shoved.

The caretaker tripped on his own foot, staggered one step, two...

And plummeted forward into the mouth of the stairwell. Matthais heard a barked cry of denial, then the thuds of a body hitting and tumbling down stone. Then the sounds halted and silence fell, broken only by the bells and bustle of Corsair and the ships in the harbor.

Matthais moved carefully to the height of the stairs and stared down at the crumpled form at their base. Even from here he could see that the caretaker's neck had been snapped, his arms and legs askew.

He glanced back toward the western horizon. He didn't know what the strange white lights portended, but it didn't matter. Not here in Corsair anyway. What mattered was Tyrik and his interference. He'd ignored the elderly councilor long enough. Too long, obviously. He would have to be dealt with.

He descended the stairs, sidestepping the caretaker's body.

He'd let one of the guard or another servant discover the man. He had preparations to make, and a certain meddling councilor to kill.

* * *

"Tamaell Thaedoren!"

Moiran turned at the ragged shout, her horse plodding forward through the drifted snow trampled mostly flat by those who forged a way ahead of her in the long column of men, women, and children slowly making their way southward out of Alvritshai lands. The group had grown, nearly tripled, since they'd left Artillien behind, picking up families, soldiers, and supplies in each town they passed. Moiran had long ago lost count of exactly how many the contingent contained, especially after they'd reached Hallieas in Baene, where the insufferable Lady Sovaeren had joined them. Since then, others from House Ionaen and Redlien had been added, with rumors that refugees from Uslaen and Nuant weren't far behind. And with the refugees came tales of horror from the Wraith army's attacks. Those from Ionaen and Redlien had been hit the worst, the dark army forging a path of destruction through their lands as they made their way to Caercaern. But the army hadn't waited long to begin attacking the surrounding towns once they'd seized Caercaern. According to the reports, every House had been attacked, and the Wraith army was only spreading outward from their central location, driving farther east, west, and south from the capital city. Thousands had been killed, and thousands more were dying even now as the snows continued to fall in sporadic bursts. The storm had only augmented the misery. Even though the first initial blast of cold had settled into something less violent, the cloud cover hadn't broken and snow showers or spats of ice were common. Some within the column were succumbing to the weather, the acolytes of the Order of Aielan pausing every evening to gather the bodies and give them to Aielan's Flames.

Moiran had attended the first few nights, but as the days continued and the number of bodies grew, she found she didn't have the emotional strength.

What made her even more heartsick were the people in the towns and villages they passed who refused to join them, choosing instead to wait out the storm, ignoring the warnings given by the acolytes that the storm wouldn't end any time soon and that the Wraith army would eventually make its way far enough south to attack them. Most of those who stayed were simply stubborn, unwilling to give up the life they knew, to accept change. But some of them...

Some of them had simply given up hope completely. Moiran could see the despair in their eyes, and could think of nothing to say or do. Standing beside her eldest son as he spoke to those they could find in the town square or on a snow-cloaked frozen field, she looked into their lost faces and felt their desperation creeping into her soul.

"Tamaell Thaedoren!"

Moiran's gaze fixed on the rider as he drew abreast of her position, then continued on toward the front ranks. The White Phalanx—what remained of it—and a portion of the Phalanxes from all of the remaining Houses led the column with Tamaell and the gathered lords. The ladies of the Houses followed, the rest of the Phalanx stretched out along the entire length of the column for protection.

She watched the rider as he made his way toward the Tamaell's banner, noted that Thaedoren motioned the man forward but didn't stop the slow progression southward.

A few days before, they'd reached the edge of Alvritshai lands, had passed through the last of the forests and into the rolling northern plains of dwarren lands. The bases of the mountain range the humans called the Teeth could be seen to the southwest, their peaks hidden in the clouds. They would have to begin bearing eastward soon.

Ahead, someone shouted orders and a moment later Daedelan and a large group of Phalanx plowed out ahead of the column. Moiran straightened in her saddle, glanced around at the rest of the riders near her—a few of the ladies of the Ilvaeren and their servants, all oblivious of the activity at the head of the column—and then caught the attention of Wodraen. She pointed with her chin toward Thaedoren, got a nod in acknowledgment, and the two began edging forward at a slightly faster pace.

Before they managed to reach Thaedoren, the White Phalanx closed protectively around the lead group, including Lords Saetor and Caeden. Brow furrowed in annoyance, Moiran angled toward Fedaureon instead, riding alongside Renaerd.

Her youngest son spotted her a moment before she pulled up alongside him, even though his attention was focused on the activity ahead.

"Mother," he said.

"What's going on?"

"We aren't certain. The scouts have spotted a large group of humans headed in our direction."

"An army?"

"It's not large enough to be an army. Maybe a hundred men in all. Thaedoren has sent Daedelan to meet them."

Moiran relaxed slightly. For a moment, she'd though the humans had somehow joined with the Wraith army, that they were simply walking into the teeth of another enemy. She doubted they would be able to survive such a turn of events, not physically or mentally. Everyone had suffered too much already. Another blow would break them all.

They'd lost sight of Daedelan, another snow squall blowing fat flakes across the plains. Orders were passed down the line, the Phalanx from behind coming forward to join those at the front. The rest of the Ilvaeren and their servants were sent back, although no one approached Moiran. She kept close to Fedaureon, ignoring the veiled warning looks from Wodraen until he finally gave up.

And then the skirl of snow fell away and Moiran gasped as she caught sight of Daedelan, his escort of Phalanx, and the group of men they'd gone to meet on a rise not far ahead.

"That's GreatLord Went's banner," Renaerd said.

"But what is he doing this far north…and on dwarren lands?"

No one answered. Ahead, Thaedoren eyed the group and at a signal from Daedelan ordered the column to continue onward. Then, with Lords Saetor and Caeden in tow, along with another group of Phalanx, he broke away toward them.

Fedaureon hesitated. "Should we join them?"

"You're a lord of the Evant," Moiran said.

When he still paused, Renaerd kicked his heels into his horse's flanks. "I intend to."

They galloped forward, the horses' feet kicking up clods of snow, slowing only when the drifts grew deeper off the column's main path. Wodraen, Daevon, and Renaerd's Protector followed behind.

"—see here is the remainder of our forces, those that have been able to join us since Caercaern's fall," Thaedoren was saying to GreatLord Went as they approached. "The rest are refugees from the Houses of the Alvritshai. Caercaern and our lands are lost. As Tamaell of the Alvritshai, voice of the remaining lords of the Evant, I humbly request the succor and sanctuary of the Provinces for my people." Then Thaedoren bowed his head in submission.

A hush fell. No one dared to speak. Saetor and Caeden lowered their heads as well, followed by Daedelan, Fedaureon, and Renaerd. The rest of the Alvritshai, with a rustle of cloth and armor, were quick to mimic their lords, Moiran one of the last.

With head bowed and eyes closed, she listened to the huffing of the horses and the clatter of movement from the human delegation. She heard sudden whispered conversation, between Went and his captains, between his men.

It cut off abruptly, and Moiran risked a glance upwards, barely raising her head.

Went gathered the reins of his horse in one hand, eyes shifting nervously over the contingent of Alvritshai, then half coughed, half grunted and said, "Yes, well."

Tamaell Thaedoren raised his head.

"On behalf of the Provinces, and in accordance with the Accord, we welcome you to seek sanctuary in Rendell." He glanced back over the column of men and women still making its way southward and his lips pressed tightly together. "I'm not certain how many we can accommodate, but—"

"Any refuge and supplies you can spare would be appreciated."

"We will do all that we can." Went turned to one of his captains. "Brandon, send word to Rendell. Tell my wife to expect guests and have her prepare accommodations."

"Yes, sir." The Legion Commander began giving orders.

An older man to Went's other side, another Legion Commander, but of superior rank and from a different Province, grabbed Went's arm to catch his attention. "Rendell will not be able to support all of the Alvritshai." He turned toward Thaedoren. "I am Uthur, Legion Commander of the northern Provinces. On behalf of King Justinian and his Legion, you will be welcome in all of the Provinces. Send those who are able to continue farther south. GreatLord Went and I will provide escort and written word to Corsair."

"In that case, if you agree, GreatLord Went, I will leave those who are wounded or are sick here in Rendell and send the others farther south."

"Of course."

"Lord Saetor, head back to the column and inform the Phalanx. Have them spread the word."

Saetor bowed his head once, then wheeled his mount and galloped back through the churned snow toward the column.

As soon as he'd departed, Thaedoren faced Went and Uthur. "We need to talk."

"I agree. I have questions regarding this army who has seized Caercaern, such as who leads it, and what kind of creatures it is composed of. We were tracking it, until this storm obliterated any sign of its passage."

"All of your questions will be answered. And I have questions of my own."

"We will need privacy, and I am traveling with only the bare essentials."

"I will have the Phalanx erect a tent—"

A faint horncry drifted out of the south, cutting Thaedoren off. Everyone shifted toward the sound, hands falling toward weapons as the horncry sounded again.

"What is it?" Thaedoren asked.

"One of my scouts. Brandon."

Without any additional orders, Went's Legion commander began spouting orders, the ranks of human Legionnaries on horseback springing into action. Within moments, they'd formed up defensive ranks between the oncoming scout tearing across the snowy slopes at a reckless pace and the Alvritshai and their GreatLord.

Thaedoren looked toward the Alvritshai column, Moiran turning to see that the Phalanx were already forming a protective wall between whatever the scout heralded and their own Alvritshai...and that the column had not stopped its march south. She did notice that it had begun angling toward Rendell.

Then cries of warning rose from the Legionnaires and she spun back to see the scout charging into the nearest ranks, men lurching out of the horse's path as the scout jerked it to a halt and slid from the saddle. He patted the animal's sweat-slicked sides as he tossed its reins aside and made his way straight toward GreatLord Went, dropping to one knee in the snow.

"Rise and report."

The scout's eyes darted toward the Alvritshai waiting to one side, but he didn't hesitate. "GreatLord, there is a dwarren army coming up fast from the south, and another army heading southward to the east."

"A dwarren army?" Uthur broke in, at the same time Brandon spat, "What army to the east?"

Went raised a closed fist and they both fell silent, although murmurs rustled through the Legion's ranks behind them. "What army moves to the east?"

"Unknown. It was too distant to make out, but it was clear against the snow. Hatch sent me back to report. He went ahead to get a closer look. We were returning to report the dwarren army when we saw them."

Went swore, eyes falling on Thaedoren. "Do you have any idea who it is?"

"It isn't Alvritshai. As I said before, this is all that's left of our Phalanx. Those of the other Houses died at Caercaern. It must be part of the Wraith army. We knew they were sending raids out from Caercaern when we began this march. They must have sent part of their force back south."

"That must be why we haven't had many refugees from Uslaen and Licaeta," Caeden added. "They were cut off by this force."

"Or killed."

"If they've already seized Caercaern, and aren't meeting any resistance from the Alvritshai, then where are they headed?" Went asked. "I'd think they'd be entrenching themselves behind its walls for the winter, not heading back out on march. Especially with this weather."

The Alvritshai all bristled at the implied insult at the lack of resistance, even Thaedoren, but the Tamaell simply said, "I have no idea. We have had no word of what's been happening to the south."

"Neither have we. Not recently. The last we knew, the dwarren had vanished and Commander Roland had ordered the Legion to begin extensive training exercises and prepare for orders. He sent us to check out reports of signs of an army moving northward through dwarren lands."

He contemplated in silence, then asked his scout, "How far away is the unknown army?

"Nearly a day. They're too far east to have seen us.

"And the dwarren army?"

"Half a day's ride through this snow. I don't think they're aware of us, the Alvritshai, or the other army."

To Thaedoren: "Do you think they're hostile? Could they have an alliance with the Wraiths?"

"Their entire religion is based on preservation of the Land. The Wraiths are nothing but destructive."

Went nodded agreement. "Brandon, form an escort and go to meet the dwarren. Tell them we wish to speak. All of us. It's time to find out exactly what's happening on our lands, and how we intend to fight back."

"Yes, sir."

"Uthur, I think it's about time we called Rendell's full Legion forth, don't you?"

"Agreed."

He turned to the waiting scout. "No rest for the wicked, as they say."

The scout moaned, but stood and brushed himself off. "Orders?"

"Catch up to the messenger we've already sent to Rendell. Add the call to arms to his report."

"Very well."

The scout spun on his heel and snagged the reins of a fresh horse, swinging up into the saddle and charging off to the southwest.

Thaedoren edged forward, motioning Caeden with him. "I think it's time we pulled the Phalanx away from protecting our refugees. They should be safe with a minimal guard between here and Rendell, especially if the main Wraith forces are to the east. With your permission, GreatLord, of course."

"With so many armies on the field, I welcome the reinforcement."

"Caeden, inform Saetor and have the Phalanx join us."

The lord of House Nuant nodded and spun toward the column.

Moiran's eyes shifted from his receding figure to the clouds and she gasped. "What is that?"

At almost the same moment, cries rose from the surrounding humans, many of them cursing, a few drawing weapons as their mounts jerked back, startled.

Above them, the low hanging clouds, perpetually gray and dark, even during daylight, were flashing with light, the pulses sheeting from west to east. Moiran thought at first it was lightning, but it couldn't be. The light was an intense white, highlighting the rumpled contours of the clouds, and lightning didn't flow in sheets like a wave across the ocean. It wasn't even the harsh flashes of light inside one of the unnatural storms from the east, because this wasn't accompanied by thunder. That simple absence of sound drew prickles from Moiran's skin.

In the distance, the men and women in the column of refugees cowered beneath the display. A few horses broke free of their restraints and charged out into the snowfields in a panic.

And then the flashes of light subsided, the pulses growing weaker, before dying out altogether.

Moiran turned toward Thaedoren. "What—? What was that?"

"I do not know." He shot a glance toward Went, the GreatLord still squinting up toward the now darkened clouds.

"Perhaps the dwarren will know."

* * *

"Councilor Tyrik! Councilor Tyrik!"

"I don't know what the flashing lights portend," Tyrik snapped as he drew to a halt in the corridor. One of the Legion commanders strode down the hall toward him, the tension brought on by the strange lights in the sky in late morning clear around his eyes. The Legion had been forced to double their guard on the palace and send soldiers into the city to help quell riots from the spooked citizens of Corsair.

The Legionnaire came to a rigid halt before Tyrik, bowing his head slightly. "This isn't about the lights, councilor."

"Oh." It took Tyrik a moment to divert his irritation. "Then what is it?"

"One of the servants found the dovecote warden dead."

"The caretaker? I spoke with him just this morning." A sudden sharp suspicion gouged into his side. "What happened?"

"It appears he fell down the stairs leading up to the roof. His neck snapped."

"Show me."

The Legionnaire led him back along the corridor and deeper into the palace. All along the way, Tyrik noticed the nervous tension in the servants and guards. Eyes flicking toward every sound, every movement. Startled gasps when one servant dropped a bucket onto the floor with a loud clang. The lights had set everyone on edge.

They rounded a corner, two guardsmen at the far end, their bodies blocking the opening to the stairwell to the roof. Tyrik could see someone on their knees, leaning over a body.

The two guards stepping aside to let him through. He drew in a ragged breath when he saw the odd angle of the caretaker's neck, the skewed arms and legs making it appear even more distorted. The man's face was deathly pale, a thin trickle of long-dried blood snaking out of his mouth. His eyes were open, but then the healer who knelt at the man's side reached up and closed them, sitting back with a small shake of his head, his long grayed beard rustling against his chest.

"He never had a chance."

"What do you mean?" Tyrik asked.

The healer squinted up at him. "I mean as soon as he lost his footing, he was doomed. Those stairs are too steep to recover from a fall."

"So he died from the fall? Nothing else?"

"From all appearances. You were expecting something else?"

"No, not really." And yet his suspicion still didn't die. He glanced around the stairwell, looking for anything out of place.

The healer watched intently, standing and following when Tyrik began climbing the stairs. The Legionnaire who'd summoned Tyrik trailed behind. Both stood to one side as Tyrik scanned the area around the top of the stairs, but he found nothing.

He stared across the flat expanse to the dovecote with a frown.

"I don't know what you're looking for," the healer hazarded, "but my guess would be that the caretaker died this morning, at about the same time as those lights lit up the sky. He probably saw them, was distracted, and didn't realize how close he was to the stairs. He missed that first one and..." He made a tumbling motion with his hand, then stroked his beard. "As simple as that."

"I don't see anything to indicate otherwise. If you're satisfied, remove the body and notify his family."

The healer nodded and left. The Legionnaire stepped closer to Tyrik.

"Do you have reason to believe something else happened here?" he asked.

"Not really. I'm simply...unsettled."

"We all are."

Then, from the west, a low growl rumbled, growing in strength until Tyrik could feel it shuddering through the stone beneath his feet and in his teeth. He clamped them down hard, his hands closing into fists at his side.

The sound rolled like thunder, faded the same way.

Behind, he heard the two guardsmen rattling up the stairs. They burst from the stairwell, the healer a step behind, their swords drawn.

"Are we under attack?" one of them gasped.

"Not that I'm aware of."

"It must have been thunder," the healer said. His voice was hardened, with a plaintive edge, as if he were trying to convince himself more than the others. "It had to have been."

Tyrik didn't point out that there were few clouds in the sky at all.

He turned to the guardsmen instead. "Send word to your commander. Have him send more of the Legion into the city to reassure the populace again, if he has any more to spare. I'm certain this will have unsettled everyone even more so than they were before."

Because, he thought to himself as the Legionnaires and the healer reluctantly departed, it means that whatever happened to the west—to Andover—isn't over yet.

* * *

The sound rolled over them with a slow and building growl, shuddering in Moiran's bones. Startled cries rose from the combined army of Phalanx and Legion surrounding her, Thaedoren, the lords of the Evant, and GreatLord Went. Orders were instantly sent out, the Legion forming up into defensive lines with impressive speed. The Phalanx reacted just as well, Moiran noted, everyone facing west as the rumbling escalated, then peaked and began to fade. The horses shifted restlessly beneath them, Moiran controlling hers with a few quick tugs at the reins and a reassuring pat on the neck.

Wodraen moved up next to her. "Thunder?"

"Given the strange lights from before...perhaps."

"But it's been hours since we saw those lights."

Uneasy, Moiran glanced toward Thaedoren, deep in conversation with GreatLord Went. "How much farther until we reach the dwarren?"

"We should be coming up on them any moment now."

"Let's hope they have an explanation."

Thaedoren broke away from Went, both of them falling back into position and continuing south, although Moiran noted that the defenses to the west had been doubled. Since they'd left the column of refugees that afternoon, they'd traveled hard and fast toward the dwarren's position, scouts keeping an eye on the Wraith army far to the east. For once, she was glad of the looming cloud cover and the sporadic squalls of snow. It kept them hidden. And the scouts had reported that the Wraith army was heading steadily southward, not even sending out their own scouts.

As if they had a destination already in mind, one that they had to reach swiftly.

Ahead, the leading edge of their own army crested a knoll and shouted. The rest of them surged forward, Moiran and Wodraen with them, until she could see what lay in the snow-covered land beyond: the dwarren army, at least twice the size of the Alvritshai Phalanx, spread across a wide section of snow with their gaezel. She could see dwarren digging into the snow to expose the grassland beneath for their mounts, large sections already laid bare. And in the center of the activity—

"They've erected a meeting tent," Wodraen murmured.

"Then it's to be an official meeting. We need to be near Thaedoren. I want to be part of this."

Wodraen urged his horse closer toward the Tamaell, clearing a path for Moiran. She saw Saetor, Caeden, Fedaureon, and Renaerd doing the same, as a delegation of dwarren headed toward them from below.

"Set up a makeshift camp," GreatLord Went was ordering as they drew near. "Pass out food and water, but no fires. Dig down to the grass and feed the horses as best you can."

The armies broke, men working quickly to keep warm, leaving only the lords and their escorts at the top of the knoll. They all turned as the dwarren approached.

One of the dwarren—a shaman, Moiran saw—stepped forward and chanted something in his own language, low enough she couldn't make it out, his scepter tracing sigils in the air as he repeated the actions in all four directions. Then another shaman stepped forward.

"My name is Azuka. The Archon wishes to speak with you. He asks that you see him in the meeting tent immediately."

Both GreatLord Went and Thaedoren stepped forward, but it was Thaedoren who spoke. "We accept. I wish to bring a few of the lords of the Evant with me."

Azuka scanned those behind Thaedoren and Went with a penetrating glare. "All will be welcome beneath Ilacqua's eyes."

He spun and stalked toward the tent.

Thaedoren turned in his saddle immediately. "Saetor, Caeden, Daedelan, with me." Moiran nudged her horse forward, the motion caught by her son's eyes. "You wish to come as well?"

"Yes, my Tamaell."

"Very well. The rest of you, stay here and see to the camp."

Fedaureon made a raw noise of protest and Renaerd swore beneath his breath, but both quieted at Thaedoren's stare.

A moment later, Thaedoren and Went led the small group down the slope toward the dwarren tent, Moiran and Wodraen trailing behind.

As they neared the dwarren, Wodraen asked, "What do you expect the dwarren to say?"

"Nothing good. Look at them." She pointed with her chin at the dwarren as they passed. "They're exhausted. And you can see the despair in their eyes. Hidden deep, but it's there."

"They've been in battle. They're wounded, in body and spirit."

"Like all of us."

Wodraen said nothing. They'd reached the tent, the dwarren shaman chanting a blessing as they dismounted before stepping aside to allow all of the lords, Daedelan, and Moiran through the outer flaps and into the small canvas corridor that spiraled toward the tent's center. All of their guards remained outside. Grass rustled beneath Moiran's feet and as she moved deeper a sharp, sweet, cloying scent struck her nostrils, along with increasing heat. By the time she stepped into the central chamber behind Caeden, she was sweating, the heat intense after the bitter cold of the air outside. The smoke from the braziers staged around the inner room hung thick and heavy in the air, forcing her to breathe through her mouth.

A low table sat in the center of the room, four dwarren seated at its far side, watching them intently. Two dwarren Riders stood guard at a second entrance opposite the one they'd used.

Thaedoren hesitated, Went and Daedelan stepping back and allowing him to take the lead. The Alvritshai had dealt more with the dwarren than the Provinces, Thaedoren in particular.

The Tamaell nodded toward the dwarren. "You wished to speak to us."

The eldest dwarren, a shaman by the markings of his armor, removed a pipe from his mouth. "The Turning is upon us. We have much to discuss."

"Yes, we do, Archon."

Thaedoren stepped forward and sat before the table, Daedelan and Went taking places to either side, Saetor taking the last position on the left. There wasn't enough room for Caeden or Moiran at the table, so Moiran remained standing near the door, Caeden following her lead.

As soon as the four men were settled, the three dwarren Riders drew their weapons and placed them lengthwise on the table before them. The

Archon set his scepter beside them, the beads and rattles clicking together with a soft sound.

Thaedoren and the Alvritshai followed suit, their much longer cattans singing from their sheaths. Went copied them, with a brief look of confusion.

As soon as all of their weapons were bared, the Archon said, "We have news from the Land. The elloktu have struck at its heart, at the Sacred Waters. We defended it to the last, but were forced to collapse the cavern to stop their dark army from seizing it or destroying it. The Sacred Waters still flow, but they are inaccessible to us now. It will require generations to free it again. But the Summer Tree is dead."

Silence settled as the Archon finished, but it wasn't a shocked silence; it was a weary silence, thick and heavy and smothering.

Thaedoren leaned back. "The news from the north is no better. The Wraiths have attacked and seized Caercaern. The Winter Tree has fallen. The Evant has been torn apart, the Houses split. The Alvritshai have mostly been scattered. And this storm...it is cold and bitter and it lingers, like the storms that drove us from the north. I do not think it intends to pass. We have sought and been granted refuge in Rendell with GreatLord Went. Those who have survived the attack are headed there now, all except the Phalanx you see with us. We expected more to join us, but there is a Wraith army marching southward to the east. They may have kept additional forces from reaching us."

The dwarren stirred at this news. The Rider seated to the Archon's left shot glances toward the other Riders in the room, then leaned to one side to whisper something to the Archon, who nodded in agreement. One of the Riders guarding the entrance stepped forward, listened to the Archon a moment, then departed, the Archon turning back to Thaedoren.

"We were unaware of the elloktu's forces. I have sent a group of Riders to watch them."

"We have scouts following them as well. They do not appear to be searching for us. Rather, they are marching hard and fast directly south, through dwarren lands."

"There is nothing of importance left in dwarren lands for them to attack. Like you, we are scattered. Our people have retreated to the lands of the eastern clans, into our tunnels. They are protected by the Riders of Broken Waters."

"Then where are they headed?" GreatLord Went asked.

No one answered, but the Archon drew on his pipe deeply, held the smoke inside a long moment, then exhaled in a heavy sigh. "We will ask

Ilacqua. Ikterru, summon Azuka. Have him bring me my pouch, a map, and a small stone bowl with coals from a fire."

Ikterru, the Rider who'd whispered to the Archon earlier, glanced toward the remaining Rider on guard, who ducked out through the entrance.

"What do you intend to do?" Went asked.

"Quotl—the Archon—will seek Ilacqua's guidance," Ikterru stated flatly.

Thaedoren broke the resulting awkward silence. "This morning, strange lights lit up the sky to the west, and then a short while ago there was a rumbling from the same direction. Do you know what caused these...events?"

"If you had asked me a year ago, I would have told you they were a sign from the gods that they were unhappy. But now...I can tell you that the Land has been disturbed. Something has happened in the far off land of Andover, something that has sent a shudder through the Land that can be felt even here. I can feel its pain. It is of the elloktu's doing. They seek to unsettle the Land as they once unsettled the Wells."

Before anyone could respond, Moiran heard movement in the corridor behind her. A human spilled from the entrance, brought up short by Caeden and Moiran. The young man gasped, his breath already short, face red, then choked on the dense smoke and heat. "A messenger...for... GreatLord Went."

Went stood. "I'll deal with this."

He pulled the young man through the entrance and out into the corridor, where the smoke wasn't as thick. Moiran could hear them speaking, Went's tone demanding, the messenger's rushed. She strained to hear more, but caught nothing.

And then she was distracted by the return of the Rider and Azuka, the shaman who had brought them here. The dwarren passed a handful of items to Quotl, who mumbled to himself as he handed the rolled leather map to Ikterru and began digging into the pouch, pulling out various stones, packets, a stray feather, and a small vial. As Ikterru unfurled the map, Azuka placed a stone bowl with glowing coals at its center, then stepped back.

Quotl snatched up two packets and brushed everything else aside impatiently. Tearing open the first, he scattered a fine powder over the coals, a hiss rising, along with thick streamers of white smoke. An acrid taint filled the tent, not unpleasant, but harsh enough to make Moiran's nose itch. Quotl tore into the second packet and added it to the bowl, the coals sizzling, then he sat back, a low rumbling chant filling his chest as he drew deeply on his pipe once, twice, and a third time, exhaling slowly. Eyes closed, he continued his rhythmic chant, Azuka mumbling a counterpoint from behind. Quotl's head sagged forward, and as it did, Moiran felt pressure against her chest. A strange lethargy suffused her, her arms and legs tingling.

And then, for a single moment, her consciousness lifted free of her body. She found herself hovering above the assemblage, staring down at Thaedoren, his body tense, at Saetor leaning back with slight and uncomfortable disdain, and Caeden frowning in mixed curiosity and contempt.

Quotl's head rose suddenly, his eyes snapping open, staring at the coals, at the map. A rush of wind suffused Moiran's senses, and she fell back into her body.

At the same moment, the coals within the stone bowl popped, blackened embers scattering across the table, smothering Moiran's light gasp. The rest of the Alvritshai gave a start, Saetor reaching instinctively for his weapon; the dwarren merely leaned forward, even the Rider at the door taking a step forward to see the map.

"What is this?" Thaedoren asked.

Before Quotl could answer, Went stepped back into the tent. "What happened? What was that noise?"

"Ilacqua has answered our call."

"How?"

Quotl motioned to the map. "He has told us the whereabouts of the elloktu's armies."

Everyone leaned forward, both Caeden and Moiran stepping up behind Thaedoren. The map was littered with the scattered embers, the largest near the human city of Temeritt. Two others lay on dwarren lands, one halfway between a mark Moiran took to be the Confluence and Temeritt, the other obviously the location of the army they'd seen marching southward to the east. A third still resided over Caercaern. A few more coals were scattered here and there—in the Thalloran Wastelands, the southern Provinces, even one in Corsair—but they were all much smaller in scale, nearly specks of ash on the map.

"The map has shifted since I last did a scrying."

"How do we know what the map tells us is truth?" Saetor asked.

Moiran was surprised when Went answered, before any of the dwarren could react with affront.

"Because it verifies the reports I've just received by messenger from

Corsair. King Justinian has sent numerous messages since my departure from Rendell. It appears that they've attacked the southern Provinces, specifically Temeritt—"

"The Autumn Tree," Moiran interrupted.

"Yes, because of the Autumn Tree. But the attack was more widespread. They've apparently already crushed Borangst, have more or less decimated our lands west of Goran. King Justinian is headed toward Temeritt now with nearly all of our combined Legion, except for Rendell. He's gathered those willing to fight along the way. He intends to free Temeritt from the Wraith siege."

Thaedoren motioned toward the map. "All of the Wraith armies, except for the one in Caercaern, are headed toward Temeritt as well."

"They've already broken the dwarren and Alvritshai," Went said bluntly, everyone else in the room bristling, "and now they intend to break the Provinces as well."

"The dwarren are not broken," Ikterru growled.

"Neither are the Alvritshai," Thaedoren added.

Went glanced from one to the other, measuring, then grinned. "I'm glad to hear it. But we must all admit that the Wraiths have outmaneuvered us all. We have been caught off guard. We have been reacting. They have been ahead of us through all of this. The Provinces knew nothing of these attacks—"

"King Justinian was warned!" Ikterru snapped. "We sent an envoy to Corsair, and one to Caercaern as well."

"We received no envoy."

"I am aware of no envoy to Corsair either. What did they say upon their return?"

Ikterru glowered. "Neither envoy returned."

"Then they must have been discovered by the Wraiths and eliminated. The Alvritshai would not have ignored your warning."

Quotl leaned forward. "What has passed, has passed. The question is, what do we intend to do now?"

All of them considered this in silence, until Moiran could not stand it anymore.

"You must stop them, of course."

"How? We are already behind most of their forces. They will reach Temeritt long before us. My own Legion from Rendell is on their way as we speak, but by the time we arrive in Temeritt the siege will be over!"

"He speaks the truth," Daedelan said. He'd remained silent the entire time they'd been inside the tent, so when his deep voice filled the tent, everyone listened. "And we will be further slowed by the snow."

"We can't simply sit here and do nothing."

"We don't need to," Quotl countered. "There's another way to reach Temeritt, possibly before this secondary army at least."

"How?"

"We bypass the snow completely. We travel underground."

The group sat or stood in stunned silence. Then Daedelan leaned forward, studying the map again intently. "This army is halfway to Temeritt already, but they will have to go around the edge of the Escarpment to the east to reach it. Do your tunnels extend all the way to the Escarpment to the south? Or do we need to go around the ridge as well?"

At a nudge from Quotl's pipe, Ikterru said, "There *are* tunnels to the south. We can follow the Estuar River. Those tunnels will empty out to the northwest of Temeritt."

"Then there's a chance." Daedelan glanced up to Thaedoren. "If we move swiftly and if the snows continue aboveground, then we can reach Temeritt before either of these two armies. It will be close, but it's possible."

"What of my men?" Went asked. "The Legion from Rendell coming to join us?"

Thaedoren leaned back. "We'll leave someone behind to show them the way. They can attempt to catch up to us. But we will not wait for them. If you are willing, Archon."

"Ikterru will issue the orders now."

The Rider glanced toward Quotl, then stood and departed with a low, half-hearted grumble.

"Then it is settled," Thaedoren said. "We march for Temeritt."

* * *

Tyrik sat at his desk, the thin knife he used to slit open missives in one hand. A stack of papers sat before him as he reached for the next unopened letter, from GreatLord Berand of Portstown. The knife slid cleanly through the parchment and he unfolded the missive and laid it out before him, scanning the first paragraph. A request for approval of a new tax levy against the import of glass from Andover.

"Even with the rumbling of war, commerce and politicking continues," he mumbled with a shake of his head.

He had reached for the next letter, noting the merchant's sigil as he did so, when someone knocked at the door.

He paused—he wasn't expecting anyone—then called, "Enter."

As soon as he saw Matthais step through the door, a bottle of wine in one hand, two glasses in the other, Tyrik thought of the dovecote caretaker's body at the bottom of the stairs.

He lowered his hands below the edge of the desk and leaned back, shifting so that Matthais couldn't see he still held the letter opener.

"Councilor Matthais. To what do I owe this honor? We haven't spoken in days."

"That is precisely why I am here, fellow councilor. In these uneasy times, I thought it prudent that we catch up. We've both been busy."

Tyrik watched as Matthais walked to a sideboard, setting the glasses down on a tray. He pulled a short knife from a pocket and began working at the wax sealing the wine's cork. Flakes of it fell to the floor, and a moment later the rotund councilor pried the cork free with a small, "Ah." He held the cork up. "Would you like a sniff? It's Andovan, a fine vintage from the Siracusa Family vineyards. I expect it will be difficult to come by in the future."

"What do you mean?"

Shrugging, Matthais set the cork on the tray and poured two glasses of the Siracan. "I'm certain you saw—or at least heard of—the light show earlier today.   General thought is that something has happened in Andover."

"Do you know this for certain?"

Matthais picked up the tray and brought it across the room to the desk. Light from the large bay window leading to the balcony glinted on the glassware and the gold buttons and gilt of the councilor's vest and jacket. "Whatever do you mean?"

Tyrik tensed as he set the tray down and handed the wine across the desk. When Tyrik didn't reach for it, he set it down before him, then turned and drifted away, toward the window and its view of the inner bay, leaving his own glass behind.

Tyrik ignored the wine.

"I mean, do you know what's happened in Andover?"

"Of course not."

"But you have your suspicions. You know something."

"I am suspicious of everything...and everyone. And I know many things. For example, I know that you and Roland have been feeding me false information about the whereabouts of the Legion. I've spent the last few hours determining that the majority of our forces are in the southern

Provinces, not along our eastern borders protecting us from the dwarren. Does the king know of this? Or is this being done behind his back?"

"The king knows. He approved of Roland's deception. It was done by his order."

"I see." Matthais drifted toward the door, and for a moment Tyrik thought that the traitorous councilor would simply leave.

Then he heard the snick of the key in the lock and his hand closed tighter over the handle of the letter opener. Matthais weighed twice as much as him, was a good twenty years younger. He had no illusions that Matthais could best him in a fair fight.

But Matthais had never fought fair in his life.

"So tell me, is the wine poisoned?"

"Of course it is." Matthais turned back toward Tyrik. "Now tell me, my good councilor, how long have you been spying on me? How long have you been reading the messages I send by pigeon? And have you been halting the messages I send out by other means?"

"Is that why you killed the dovecote's warden?"

"That was an unfortunate accident."

"A damned convenient accident." The fear that had caused sweat to break out on Tyrik's forehead suddenly shifted into anger. "You've betrayed the king, betrayed your sworn oath to protect him, first as regent and now as advisor. What for, Matthais? What was worth breaking your loyalties?"

"The usual. Power and immortality."

Tyrik's eyes widened. "You really have allied yourself with the Wraiths. Roland suspected as much. What did they offer you? What did you ask for?"

"Corsair, of course. The Provinces." Matthais had reached the desk, stood to one side. "And to drink from the fabled Lifeblood."

"You would become one of them. You would become a Wraith."

"Would I? You forget the legend of Colin Harten. He drank from the Well of Sorrows, yet he did not become a Wraith."

"What makes you think you would survive as he did? What makes you think the Wraiths would even allow you to drink the Lifeblood? They don't respect the Provinces. They seek to destroy them, to destroy everything that we have built here. They will never allow you to rule, because by the time they are done there will be no Provinces left. They certainly will not let you drink from the waters that give them their power!"

"They wouldn't dare. Not after what I've done for them."

Tyrik laughed. "You are delusional," he began, but he was interrupted by the sudden clanging of warning bells from the city below, muted by the closed window.

Both of the councilors looked at each other, bodies rigid with tension. Tyrik's fingers clenched tighter around his knife, but Matthais looked just as confused as he did.

Then, from the corridor outside, they heard the tread of running feet and the rattle of armor. Someone slammed into the locked door, barked a startled curse, then pounded on the door. "Councilor Tyrik! Councilor Tyrik! Something is happening in the bay!"

"What is it?" Tyrik demanded, already rising from his seat. Matthais made for the balcony, throwing back the glass doors and stepping out onto the stone ledge beyond. Tyrik strode toward the door, but realized Matthais held the key. He veered toward the balcony, clutching the knife close to his body.

"The bay." Tthe guard outside rattled the door again. "The water is receding!"

"What do you mean the water is receding?"

But by then he could see over Matthais' shoulder and he gasped.

Out beyond the slope leading down to the bay, over the peaks and chimneys of the rambling city of Corsair, through the smoke haze, the water from the bay had pulled back from the docks, drawing away from the shore in a bizarre reversal of the tides. Ships tied to the docks were left standing in mud, those with shallower hulls ripping free, or tearing the docks themselves down with them. And still the ocean receded, drawing back farther and farther, stranding ships lengths from the wharf. Birds wheeled skyward, circling with raucous cries, and fish flapped on the exposed bay's bottom, mere flashes of silver at this distance. The warning bells of the city rose higher and louder, spreading from church to church in a ripple from the bay upwards toward the palace.

"What's happening?" Matthais turned to Tyrik, his eyes edged with panic. "What's happening?"

Tyrik opened his mouth to respond, but nothing came out. He had no explanation. He had never seen anything like this, had read nothing of its like in all of his studies. He groped for an answer, his mind flailing for comprehension.

Matthais didn't wait, his eyes glinting with madness. "You did this," he spat, and he struck, his arm impacting with Tyrik's chest, flinging him back against the doorway. Glass shattered as Tyrik cried out and fell, shards cutting into his side as he landed hard and rolled. Gasping, he drew

himself to his knees, a shadow falling across him a moment before
Matthais' booted foot kicked into his stomach. Something in Tyrik's chest
snapped and a piercing pain stabbed into his side as he struck the stone
frame of the balcony door and collapsed to the floor. He groaned and tried
to rise to his knees, expecting Matthais to kick him again.

Instead, he heard a low roar, growing in intensity. Not like the roar
they'd heard earlier from the west. This was lower, and escalating at a
slower rate. Tyrik craned his neck upwards, saw Matthais' attention
diverted back toward the harbor. In two quick steps, the traitorous advisor
moved to the balcony's edge. "This can't be happening. He promised me.
He promised me Corsair!"

Tyrik shoved himself upwards, used the door frame for support, his
clothes splattered with blood from numerous cuts from the glass. All of
them were minor compared to the sharp, grating pain inside his chest. But
he ignored it all, focused on Matthais, on the councilor's exposed back,
even as in the background he saw the water that had receded all the way
back to the cleft in the cliffs that was the harbor's only seaside approach
begin to gush forward again. It came hard and swift, rushing forward with
a speed that was stultifying, so fast that it began to spout from the stone
rift, spewing outwards like a fountain, rising higher and higher. It roared
forth, devouring the exposed bay in a torrent, crashing over the derelict
ships and boats left behind, until it reached the docks. But it didn't stop
there. Tyrik heard screams as the water surged over the wharf, over the
warehouses and taverns and up into the streets of the city behind. And
still it fountained from the cleft, the roar growing into a rushing growl.
Tyrik saw figures running, but the water was too fast. It ripped the ships
from their moorings, tossed them up into the buildings beyond, charged
down the street and gouted from windows and doorways. Entire buildings
collapsed, the debris swept inland.

Before him, Matthais barked, "No, no, no! Stop this! He promised.
He promised!"

Then he spun, his rounded face purple with rage.

Tyrik plunged the letter opener into his chest.

Matthais gasped and flung out an arm, catching Tyrik with a
staggering blow before stumbled back himself, falling against the
balcony's balustrade, one hand rising to the blade, the other grasping
ineffectually at the stone for support. Tyrik caught himself against the
doorframe, then shoved forward, reaching to yank the knife from
Matthais' chest. The councilor cried out as he ripped it free, blood
soaking his merchant's jacket, obviously hurt but not mortally wounded.

The shock that suffused Matthias' pale face transformed into rage.

Before he could gather his strength again, Tyrik sank the knife into his neck.

Matthais' tirade cut short. He looked toward Tyrik, the aged councilor standing over him as the muted screams of the dying drifted up from the harbor. He heaved in a ragged breath. "He promised me Corsair."

Then he collapsed to one side.

Tyrik sagged against the stone balustrade, looked out grimly toward the raging ocean as it continued to pour from the cleft and surge through the city. It had spread across the entire bay, had engulfed both shores and half of the streets and buildings up the slopes of the shoreline. But the roaring force appeared to be subsiding.

He didn't know what had caused the ocean to recede and return so forcefully, whether it was an act of the Wraiths or an act of Diermani, but whatever the cause, Corsair had been damaged badly.

Already sick with the death and destruction he knew he would witness, he reached down to Matthais and retrieved the key to his chamber doors, then strode across the room purposefully. He needed to rally the Legion. And the caddonis, arruli, and patri.

Drawing a deep breath, he winced at another sharp pain in his chest. "And I need to see a healer."

21

Wind scoured Colin's face as he let go of time at the northern edge of the salt flats that had nearly killed Eraeth. The wind was hot, blowing out of the Thalloran Wastelands from the northwest, and he felt his skin turn slightly waxy. His nostrils burned with the tang of the salt.

Far to the north, at the very edge of his vision, he could see a thin stretch of darkened clouds. He'd watched them for the past day or so, but they hadn't shifted farther south. The stormfront had stalled. His eyes drifted toward the west, toward dwarren lands and the Alvritshai beyond. His heart ached to find out what had become of both races. The Wraith army—Walter's army—had been marching to the west, its numbers far greater than Colin had expected. He hadn't known about the disillusioned Alvritshai who had flocked to the Wraith's banner, believing their honor lost when they'd abandoned their homeland. He hadn't counted on the Snake People from the wastelands, either. The dwarren had warned him of them and the other creatures of the Turning, but he had discounted them. He'd thought that most had died out since the last Turning.

Instead, they'd been living in the twisted and treacherous desert, in the city at its heart.

Raising one hand to his chest to grip Karen's vow beneath his shirt, he wrenched his gaze away from familiar lands—from the friends he knew must be fighting Walter and his armies even now—and back toward the wastes. He could help the races now, he knew, could turn the tide of a few battles, perhaps even save thousands.

But it wouldn't matter. He couldn't stop the entire Wraith army himself, couldn't stop Walter's carefully planned campaign against the races of Wrath Suvane. And he saw it had been carefully planned now. He wondered how long Walter had waited before setting it in motion. Had the Seasonal Trees interfered? Had they forced him to postpone his destruction until he could find a way to circumvent them? And what of the battles he'd waged with the Wraiths in controlling the Wells in the years before? Had they slowed Walter down?

He didn't think he'd ever know the answers, even though he could travel back in time. And it didn't matter. Walter's plans were in motion, and from what he'd learned in Yhnar, the three races weren't faring well at all. The Accord he had established so many years before had done nothing to help.

And the real problem wasn't the Wraiths and their armies. The real problem was the Source—the Well in the Thalloran Wastelands that Walter had managed to tap into. If Colin and the three races were to have any hope of defeating the Wraiths, that Source and its power had to be eliminated.

Or blocked.

One hand reached unconsciously for his satchel, but he caught it before he could touch the worn leather. Checking for the Spring Tree's seed within had become a nervous habit. Snatching his hand away, he reached out to seize time again, but something flickered at the corner of his eye.

He hesitated, then turned west as wave after wave of sheeting white light washed across the wide expanse of the empty sky. It flickered and flashed, like the dancing lights in the far northern icy wastes, except those lights were full of color, vibrant and ethereal and free. This light was completely white and harsh, beautiful in its own way, but it carried an underlying sense of purpose. It didn't dance. It announced.

Colin had no idea what it announced, but he knew whatever it ordained, the lights meant destruction. They meant Walter's plans had advanced. They almost certainly meant death.

Trembling, Colin gazed up into the skies until the white lights faded and died. Then he spun, snapped out with his power and seized time, stepping out into the Thalloran Wastelands.

The stakes had just risen. He didn't know how, or why, but he knew the Alvritshai, the dwarren, and the human races had little time left.

* * *

"I don't know what the lights were," Roland growled to the array of Legion commanders who sat mounted before him in the morning's light. He could see their unease in their eyes, in the nervous twitching of their reins and their restless mounts. "Nor the thunder that followed. But you have your orders."

A few of the men traded glances, others straightening in their saddles at the undertone of reprimand in Roland's voice.

Terent nudged his mount forward a step. "Then we still intend to reach Temeritt in two days?"

"Nothing changes, by order of the king."

Terent motioned to the rest of the commanders behind him to fall out.

He turned back as soon as the others were out of earshot. "The men are already nervous, what with all of the destruction we've seen since leaving Goran. Those lights, that Diermani-blasted rumbling from the west, and that storm constantly hovering on the horizon to the north...it's all setting everyone on edge. I've had to break up a dozen fights between the men, reprimanded more than a few. Any word from the king as to what's causing these strange occurrences would go a long way toward settling their fears."

"If I knew, Terent, I would tell you. I'd tell all of the men."

"Makes me wonder what the dwarren knew when their envoy came to visit. They have legends about these things."

Roland's eyebrows rose, although he should have known that the dwarren envoy's visit would not have gone unnoticed. They hadn't tried to keep it secret at the time. He was surprised that someone had remembered after this long a time—remembered and connected it to their current problems. "I wonder as well. But the dwarren aren't here. We are. And from what we've seen since Goran, there's an army attacking Province lands. Tell the men to focus on that army, not the dwarren, and certainly not the Diermani-damned lights or storm!"

"Yes, sir."

"Dismissed."

Terent slammed his left fist into his right shoulder in salute, then kneed his mount into motion toward his unit. Roland heard him calling out orders before he even reached his men, knew the Legionnaire was venting his own frustrations on them. After a quick scan of the Legion army arrayed behind him, he wove through the ranks back toward the front of the line and King Justinian's tent. As he did, he eyed the distant town ahead of them. He could already see that nearly every building was a burnt-out husk, knew that they would find the dead scattered in the roads and fields, left for the carrion birds. It had been that way in every village and town they'd passed since leaving Goran. Each nightfall, when they stopped their march to camp, an entire unit was set to burying the dead they could find.

As he neared the tent, he caught sight of a rider approaching from the south bearing the Legion's scouting flag. Pulling up to the guards at the king's tent, he dismounted and handed off his reins. "Find out who that runner is and bring him to me immediately."

"Yes, sir."

He ducked into the tent, removing his gloves as he proceeded through the outer chamber and into the king's inner room.

Justinian sat at a small folding desk, papers spread before him, surrounded by three servants clearing away a tray containing the remains of the king's breakfast. The arrulis Civaldi stood to one side.

"There is nothing within the Diermani Codex that would explain the lights or the thunder that followed," Civaldi was saying, his aged voice quavering.

"No miracles? No signs from Holy Diermani that are even remotely the same?"

"No, nothing. There are many references to Diermani's holy fire, but that has always originated from the ground. There is mention of heavenly lights from sailors and sojourns to the far north, lights that can occasionally be seen in Taranto and Avezzano and the island chains belonging to those Families, but those were described as 'curtains of colored light of every hue and distraction.' I would not have described the lights we saw yesterday in those terms."

"No, nor would I." Justinian glanced up at Roland, his displeasure clear. "So Diermani's Holy Church can offer no explanation."

"As I've been saying for the past hour."

"Then it must have another source."

"Unless it is a warning from Diermani himself."

"Some of those within the army have already embraced that thought," Roland said, slapping his gloves down on the small desk.

"Have they?" Justinian asked. At Roland's nod, he grimaced. It made him look older than his twelve years. But then, he'd been forced to age much quicker than usual. The devastation they'd seen since Goran had taken its toll on him. Justinian's eyes were darkened with exhaustion, his skin pale and drawn. Roland had noticed, but said nothing. He knew Civaldi was concerned as well. The arruli had spoken to him in private a few days back, when they passed through a particularly gruesome scene of a field filled with villagers' bodies impaled on spikes, including women and children.

Justinian turned an eye on Civaldi. "Go. Dispell this rumor."

"Even if perhaps it is correct?"

Justinian didn't answer.

Civaldi bowed his head. "I'll send the patri out among the soldiers immediately."

One of the servants set a cup of steaming tea on the desk, the others bustling about the room putting whatever had been taken out the night before back into its appropriate trunk. Half of the room had already been packed. The servant who brought the tea gathered up the papers Justinian had been looking at and secured them in a satchel before stepping to one side.

Justinian looked up. "We're preparing to march?"

"Yes."

"Any word from Borangst?"

"No. A rider approached as I entered the tent, though."

"How about Portstown or Corsair? Rendell? Any messages from the north?"

"Nothing since last night."

"What do you suggest then?"

Roland leaned forward onto the desk. "Nothing has changed. We march to Temeritt. Today, we'll send out forward scouts, since we're close enough they should be able to report on what we're marching into. Once we know what we're facing—in better detail than we've heard from the few survivors we've found—then we can plan our own attack."

A guardsman ducked into the tent, cutting off Justinian's reply. Both he and Roland looked at the man, who put fist to shoulder and bowed. "My king, a runner has arrived from the south."

"Send him in."

The guard motioned through the flap of the tent and a runner entered, covered in dust and grit from the road, his clothes sweaty and torn.

He dropped to one knee in Justinian's direction. "My king."

"Rise. And drink." Justinian handed the tea he hadn't touched across to the young runner—young compared to Roland anyway. He was likely ten years Justinian's senior. He took the cup with trembling hands, held it delicately, clearly uncertain how to handle himself in front of the king with a fragile cup when he was used to skins on the road. He brought it to his lips, then gulped it down in three quick swallows, setting it back on the desk hastily.

"You were sent south, to Borangst," Roland said.

"Yes, sir, along with five others."

"And? What did you find?"

"Borangst has been destroyed, the city and the palace there burned and now mostly rubble."

Justinian lurched to his feet. "What? What of Lord Alden? What of his Legion?" His voice cracked on the last question.

"No sign. There were thousands dead on the road leading up through the mountains' pass to the city, mostly Legion. The city...the city was a slaughterhouse. I found no survivors."

Justinian dropped back into his chair.

"How long ago did this happen?" Roland asked.

"Hard to tell, but it wasn't recent. They'd been dead for at least a week."

"Any sign of the attackers?"

"There were some of their dead mixed in with the others."

Justinian leaned forward. "Who did this?"

"Most were...creatures of various sorts. Black and sinewy, small and large. I would call them...trolls and diggers and...and cats, sir. Black, disgusting, hairless cats. Like those we've found on our march. And there were also Alvritshai."

"Alvritshai!" Justinian leapt to his feet again. He spun toward Roland. "Have the Alvritshai betrayed us?"

"It's possible," he began, then threw in a loud, "but!" with a raised hand when Justinian clenched one fist in rage.

"But what?"

"But it makes no sense. Why would the Alvritshai attack to the south? To the east, if we are to believe the dwarren envoy? They would have to travel large distances, in secret. I do not believe they could stage an attack on the dwarren's eastern flank without the dwarren noticing their army marching through dwarren lands to get there. They couldn't travel north over or behind the mountains. And how could they have gotten to our southern Provinces without us seeing them?"

"Ships. The Arduon Ocean is vast. We can't patrol it all."

"Where did those ships come from? They have ships, yes, but nothing that could transport enough of their Phalanx to the southern lands to attack our Provinces. We would have heard of such a fleet."

Justinian backed down reluctantly. "Then who? If they are Alvritshai, where did they come from?"

"Does it matter? They are part of the Wraith army. That's all that matters." Roland turned back to the runner. "How many were there in this army? Could you tell?"

"Thousands. Their trail was obvious. They marched to Borangst from the northeast, approached along the Highland Road, and left along the same path."

"Northeast," Justinian muttered.

"They came from Temeritt, and returned there. What else?"

"They had no siege weapons."

Both Roland and Justinian paused in confusion.

"How did they break Borangst's walls, then?"

"The walls had split and fallen. Some had collapsed inwards, others out. The buildings and walls inside were the same. Those made of stone, anyway. Everything else had been burned."

So many unanswered questions. So many unknowns. How were they to fight an army they knew nothing about?

"File a report, right now. Everything you can remember, no matter how inconsequential. If any of your fellow runners return, have them do the same, and get the reports to us as soon as possible."

As soon as the runner left, Justinian sank back into his chair. "I was counting on Borangst's Legion."

"We have Corsair's and Portstown's. They will be enough."

"How do you know?"

Roland met Justinian's gaze, heard the twelve-year-old's uncertainty in his voice, saw it in his eyes. The king put up a bold front for nearly everyone—GreatLord Berand of Portstown, who led his own Legion, Arrulis Civaldi, his own guardsmen and servants—but he was still only twelve underneath that façade.

With utter certainty, which he did not feel deep in his chest, he said, "Because the Wraith army isn't expecting us. And because Temeritt's and possibly Yhnar's forces will join us once we arrive."

He watched as Justinian took in his solid stance, the steadiness of his gaze, and gathered his resolve. When his gaze dropped from Roland's, he stood, back straight, chin lifted. A king's bearing.

He motioned toward the collapsible desk and the rest of the furnishings in the tent and spoke to the servants still hard at work. "Pack everything quickly. We march in half an hour."

* * *

Patris Raleveti finished his sermon in Temeritt, the congregation rising and shuffling toward the outer doors. As he closed the massive Codex from which he'd read about the trials and tests Diermani's people went through beneath his Hand in the past, including starvation and war, his stomach growled.

He pressed a hand to the hollow sensation and grimaced.

"You should eat something."

Raleveti turned to find a member of the congregation he didn't know at the railing that separated the pews from the altar where he stood. "How can I eat when I know that those within the city are starving? I'd rather my rations went to those in greater need."

The man's gaze didn't falter. He had dirty blond hair, his face drawn with the same hunger Raleveti saw in most of his congregation, even here, within the confines of the palace walls. He wondered if the man was part of the Legion. Most of his followers lately were.

"Who will give us hope and lead us into Diermani's Hands if you allow yourself to starve to death? You're needed more than most. The people take strength from you."

Before Raleveti could respond, the man turned and left.

His stomach rumbled again and he stared at the worked leather and gilt letters of the Codex, brushing his hands across the embossed tilted cross and cupped hands beneath it. The tome was ancient, its pages redolent with the musk of age and use, the leather stained from the hands of an uncountable number of patri, arruli, and caddoni.

Diermani's teachings had helped him cope with the siege. Was it so surprising that they had helped his congregation as well? He supposed not. That's what he had been preaching, after all. He turned away from the podium beneath the altar and descended into the pews. Exiting through a side door, he made his way toward the cathedral's kitchens, picking up a small loaf of bread from the baskets being readied for the army. Nodding to the cooks, he retreated with a minor guilty feeling into the back corridors of the cathedral. He'd intended to go to his room, but the guilt drove him toward the smaller altar in the cathedral's recesses, the one reserved for the patri's personal reflection and other intimate rites.

As soon as he entered, he felt it. He halted in the doorway, scanning the small interior, the latticed niches and nooks along the walls, the small altar at the front with its shelf of reliquaries. The perpetual scent of myrrh and cloves and other spices tickled his nostrils. Nothing appeared out of place.

Then he caught a pulse of light from one of the niches and his eyes widened.

He crossed the room toward the niche in three steps, one of the prayer mats slipping under his feet. With trembling hands, he pulled the chain and key that he'd kept hung around his neck since he and Kobel had first used the Hand of Diermani so many months before, fumbling as he inserted the key into the lock and twisted. The light pulsed again as he drew the lattice-worked door to the niche back to reveal the Hand inside, a swirl of his and the GreatLord's blood still within.

Reaching forward, he touched the orb.

"Hello? Is anyone there?"

A moment later he gasped as someone answered.

* * *

Kobel strode through the halls of Temeritt's palace, flanked on either side by seven of his Legion commanders and Lord Akers, all with grim expressions. Servants darted out of their path, leaving a clear line to the massive front entrance. Legionnaires on guard there scrambled to swing the heavy doors open, but Kobel noted with approval that they were prepared to hold the doors if necessary. Heavy wooden bars stood to either side, ready to be slammed into the braces to barricade the doors shut. He didn't think they'd need such measures today—he hoped they wouldn't need those measures at all—but it was good to know the Legion was ready.

Akers must have had the same thought, for he said, "Defenses appear to be ready."

"I don't expect to need them today. I hope we don't need them for weeks to come."

Akers grunted, one hand going to his ill-fitting armor. He'd lost a significant amount of weight over the last few months and the armor that had been too tight during the campaign at the Northern Ridge nearly a year ago now rattled loosely on his frame. "Perhaps it won't come to that at all."

Kobel let the statement rest. He and Akers both knew that those barricades would be necessary eventually. Temeritt could not stand against the Wraith army waiting outside. Not without help.

And it appeared that help would not arrive in time. Temeritt had waited as long as it could.

Horses were waiting at the bottom of the steps, pages handing the reins over. His Legion commanders and Lord Akers all mounted, Kobel himself swinging up into the saddle with ease. He'd lost weight himself, even though he knew he'd eaten better than most of those within the city.

"Are the individual units ready?"

"All units have reported in from all gates within the city. We're ready."

"Good." He turned to the rest of his commanders, to issue the orders he dreaded. But the time had come. They'd been preparing for this for over a week, driven by the dwindling food supplies and the desperation building within the city. He hoped his wife Echeri was seeing to the rest of the preparations within the palace. Like the barricades to the palace doors, he hoped those wouldn't be necessary either.

He drew breath to speak, but someone from behind shouted his name. "Raleveti," he said, not hiding his irritation as the patris raced through the closing double doors and down the steps toward him. "What is it? We're about to head to the gates."

Raleveti reached the bottom of the steps. "Excuse my temerity, GreatLord. It's...the Hand...The Hand of Diermani."

Kobel's eyebrows rose in surprise. "What about it?"

"I've heard from Corsair. King Justinian is on his way with the Legion from Corsair and Portstown. GreatLord Tarken Sohn is also close by with the Legion from Yhnar. They've been watching us from a distance, unable to do anything or to contact us because of the Wraith army and their..." he waved vaguely toward the sky, "...their birds."

"The King is on his way?" Akers repeated, his horse stepping toward the patris. "GreatLord, if this is true, we should postpone our attack, wait until he arrives. Perhaps we can coordinate our efforts, even with those damned birds watching us. We could use lanterns as signals, or mirrors."

Behind him, the Legion commanders broke into excited argument, hands gesturing as they considered new options for attack. Kobel listened quietly, catching perhaps half of what they said. He let his gaze wander over the group.

But then it drifted toward the walls of the palace and something beyond those walls caught his eye: thin columns of smoke rising from multiple parts of the city.

"Patris Raleveti," he said, curt enough that the commanders around him fell silent. "You spoke to those in Corsair. Did they say how long it would take King Justinian to reach us? Days? Weeks?"

"They do not know where the king is at the moment. They only know that he's left Goran and headed our way. He left five days ago."

Kobel settled his gaze on Akers. "He could be days away still. It would depend on how many men he has with him, how fast he has decided to move, whether he's getting support from the villagers and townsfolk along the way."

"He could also arrive today."

Kobel looked again to the plumes of smoke rising from the city. "Do you know, I watched the first column of smoke from the first funeral pyre from the palace's tower. I knew what it represented. I'd issued the orders to begin burning the bodies of those who'd died of sickness or starvation after all. I watched the smoke each evening for the first few days, watched the fire's glow in the markets and squares from the palace walls, until Echeri came to get me and forced me to come to bed."

He turned back to Akers, the rest of the men shifting uncomfortably around them. "But over the last few days, somewhere, somewhen, I ceased to see them anymore. They became part of the background. I knew people were dying, but I ignored it, focused on our plans, on survival. But look." He waved a hand toward the columns dissipating into the skies over the wall. "Look at them. Look at how *many* of them there are. In those first few days, there were only two or three, but I see over a dozen today.

"We cannot afford to wait for the king. Too many will die. Too many have died already." He turned back to the gates. "We'll attack in one hour, as planned. Find your units and ready your men."

Kicking his horse into motion, he trotted toward the gates, the rest of his cadre and their escorts falling in behind, Lord Akers to one side, but back a pace. They passed through the wall's wide, arched entryway and into the city. Four of the commanders immediately split off, heading for the eastern and southeastern gates. Kobel didn't slow, wind burning his face red with cold as they wound down through the streets, passing thousands of people as they walked to the market or completed errands. Hundreds more were huddled in doorways and alleys and niches. He caught fleeting glimpses of faces behind windows or leaning over balconies. Nearly all of them were women and children and old men. Most of the able-bodied were now amassing at the gates, or were preparing food or wards for the wounded.

Or were seeing to the collection and incineration of the dead.

One of the wagons filled with bodies stood by the side of the road as they reached the second innermost wall, the men watching over it dressed in hooded black. Two men were carrying a limp body out of a shop's open door. After passing through the gates of the second wall, they entered a section where fire unleashed during one of the many food riots over the past week had demolished an entire neighborhood. Kobel could taste the desperation on the air, along with the ash. Even here, among the cinders and coals, people were digging through the rubble for anything of worth, their clothes stained a greasy black from the soot.

Within minutes they passed into an intact neighborhood again. Two more of his commanders broke off with their escorts, leaving him with Lord Akers and Commander Leighten, along with ten other Legionnaires.

When they passed beneath the third wall, Lord Akers edged his horse close enough to say, "Don't forget Tarken Sohn and his men are out there. Who knows what they'll do once we attack." Then he angled away with his own men. Leighten urged his mount into Akers' position, but said nothing.

They neared the outermost wall's gates, slowing as the streets and buildings fell away into a massive market square now packed with Legionnaires and common soldiers instead of peddlers and hawkers. He picked his way through the chaos, heading toward the Temeritt banners—oak against a field of burnt orange—at the base of the gates. Halfway across the square, a roar rose from those gathered. He straightened at the energy and tension throbbing in the plaza, soaked it in as men and women in makeshift armor parted before him. The common soldiers gave way to the more formal Legion, the roar subsiding into a sizzling buzz of excitement. The soldiers had been sitting behind the walls of Temeritt steeping in their fears and anxieties for far too long.

"Report, Commander Pearson," Kobel ordered, as he reached the center of the Legion.

"I would have preferred the army remain quiet, sir, but it appears the enemy is ignoring us. They're still camped beneath the Autumn Tree. No reports of any groups splitting off from the main force. No scouting parties were sent out. And there has been no untoward activity within the camp itself. They're just sitting there, sir. Waiting."

"Very well. I think we've let them wait long enough. You know the plan. Have the men fall in."

"Very well, sir." Pearson turned. "Archers to the walls! Shield wall, spearmen, cavalry—form up ranks! This is not a drill! This is not practice! Move your asses now, now, now!"

* * *

GreatLord Tarken Sohn looked up from oiling his sword at the faint sound of horns. One of the guardsmen beside him hissed a warning and two others who were sharpening their blades with a steady, rhythmic hiss of whetstone against metal halted their counts.

The group held still, listening intently. All across the camp, soldiers halted whatever they were doing as word spread.

A moment later, the horn cry came again.

Tarken leapt to his feet.

"That was a call to arms," someone mumbled.

Tarken sheathed his sword. "Spread the word through our forces.

Everyone is to armor up and stand ready. Be as quiet as possible. No horns, no shouted commands."

"It's about bloody time."

Tarken didn't bother to reprimand whoever had spoken, since he felt the same. Striding away from the group even as they scattered, he searched for his Legion commander. He found him headed toward the ridge that provided them a view of Temeritt.

"Do you think Kobel is finally making his move?" Kent asked.

"Hard to tell. Let's find out."

They climbed the steep slope of the ridge, the grass already trampled into the mud underneath. It had rained the previous day. When they neared the top, they crouched, crawling forward on their hands and knees, then lowering themselves to their stomachs as they came upon the outer perimeter guardsman's position. The man—Enik, Tarken thought—glanced back at them once, then returned to his scrutiny of the city.

"Report."

Enik handed his spyglass over. "It appears that GreatLord Kobel is embarking on an offensive."

"Really? What have you seen?" He raised the spyglass to his eye and focused his attention outward.

"The Temeritt army has exited the easternmost gates and is now making its way around the city to the south. That occurred before the first horn cry. They were joined by additional men at the southeastern gates. The call to arms went up when that group reached the southern gates and signaled the opening of the main gates."

Tarken had found the army, the image blurred with distance. But he could still see the main force as it spilled out from the gates, could pick out Kobel's position by the multitude of banners at the head of the force. "At least two thousand Legion with Kobel." He swept the glass through the ranks coming around the city's wall from the south. "Not many Legion in the southern flank. They appear to be mostly commoners. About a thousand of them."

"I'd assume he has a similar force coming from the northern gates as well," Kent said.

"I'd wager he has about five thousand altogether on the field." He scanned the walls. "Archers on the walls."

"What about the Wraith army? What are they doing?"

Tarken swung the scope toward the Autumn Tree. "They're scrambling to organize. The Alvritshai with the talon banners are ready."

"That was fast."

"They seem to be controlling the rest of the creatures. Their scouts have been released. They're circling out from the Autumn Tree now."

"I can see them."

Tarken remained silent for a long moment, then let the spyglass drop, handing it across Enik to Kent, who immediately raised it to his eye. "I think Kobel's run out of time, or patience, or both. He's mounting his main offensive, right now. And the Wraith army is responding in kind. What do you think?"

He waited as Kent assessed the field below. More horn calls echoed up from the wide plain below, the stretch of land marred only by the rise of the hill on which Temeritt stood, the four sets of walls easy to see, and the glinting blue of the sliver of lake visible beneath the hill on its northern edge. Dozens of thick columns of smoke rose from the city. Scattered remnant clouds from yesterday's storm drifted overhead, dotting the battlefield with shadows.

Kent lowered the spyglass. "He's outnumbered, but I agree. He's attacking all out. Things inside the walls must be more desperate than we thought."

Tarken was already moving. "Ready the men. There's no way we can hide our approach. But we can help divide the Wraith force's attention."

"Even with the additional men Laurelen sent from Yhnar, we won't come close to evening up the armies down there."

"I know, but we'll do what we can to help them. Mount up! We ride to Temeritt!"

* * *

Jayson roared until his chest hurt as his entire unit charged out onto the field, his spear angled across his body, gripped tight in both hands, Owen's shorter form pounding the earth a few paces ahead of him. Their entire group was bellowing, releasing the pent up rage and desperation that had driven them since the last failed attempt to break free from the siege. The weeks in between had been deadly, disease striking entire quarters within the city, food running short, riots breaking out as fear overcame common sense.

Images sparked across his sight, blocking the surge of bodies from the amassed army as it charged onto the field, horns crying out orders he could barely hear: Ara as he'd left her in the haphazard infirmary, tears streaking her face, her hands dropping to her sides as he reluctantly pulled away, pushing Corim ahead of him; his one-time apprentice ducking his head, then hugging him fiercely before trotting off to his own unit on the walls; his own glance over the spear bearer's unit as he arrived, half of the men there new after the devastating losses of the last attempt to defeat the Horde. He'd trained with them for months, but he still didn't know half of their names. He hadn't seen the point.

Ahead and to either side, the shield bearers suddenly dropped to one knee and planted their shields into the earth. Jayson cut his roar short and fell into place behind Owen, men mimicking his move to either side, short, curt commands issuing back and forth all along the line. Jayson slammed the butt of his spear into the ground and slid it into position without thought, his training kicking in. He nodded to Owen, who thrust out his chin and said, "Look."

Jayson looked.

Ahead of them, GreatLord Kobel and the cavalry charged toward the Horde, straight toward the dead bole of the Autumn Tree. Clods of dirt flew beneath their horses' heels, the wet ground soft. Beyond them, Jayson could see nothing except the eagle talon banners of the Alvritshai and the massive bodies of the trolls.

The banners were charging straight toward the Legion. The trolls were lumbering behind.

He glanced back toward the wall, surprised to find it only two thousand paces away. It had felt like they'd run forward forever. His gaze shot up to the heights, where he could see shadowed figures running back and forth, too distant to pick out faces.

To either side, the line of spear bearers and shields stretched in a smooth arc. But unlike their last few ventures onto the field, this time they didn't reach all the way back to the walls. Space had been left on either side, so that the forces before them now could retreat behind the shield wall if necessary to regroup.

The clash of metal against metal spun him back to the battle.

"And it begins," Owen muttered.

All along the line, the tension mounted. Spears tapped against shields, armor rattled. Jayson fidgeted as screams drifted back from the battle being fought along a line he couldn't see. He wanted to join the attack and run for the safety of the walls at the same time. Everyone had been bitching about doing nothing behind the thick granite as their friends and relatives starved to death or sickened before their eyes, yet here on the plains Jayson felt exposed.

"Here come the flank attacks," the man next to him said.

Jayson craned his neck to look left, saw the southern forces hit the

Horde's ragged side, their attack unexpected. The Horde had focused their attention on Kobel's group. Battle cries and roars of hatred and pain melded with the sounds of the battle ahead, coming from the north as well. But the flanks of the Horde were composed mostly of the strange dark creatures Jayson had once thought only stories. Shrieks of rage and terror came from the diggers, the more sibilant screams from the cat-like creatures, and bellows from the trolls. Jayson closed his eyes as vivid images from the attack on Gray's Kill and Cobble Kill flared across his consciousness, followed by the horrifying and exhausting flight to Temeritt.

Behind, Gregson's horse thudded past. "Hold the line! Ready your spears!"

Jayson wondered why, then realized that the sounds of battle had grown closer.

He opened his eyes. The GreatLord and the cavalry had been pushed back. Horns blared and the cavalry within sight suddenly wheeled and charged directly toward them. A triumphant cacophony rose from the Horde behind, even as the cavalry suddenly angled south, to curve along the shield wall.

Revealing the Alvritshai and ravening Horde behind.

"Here we go." Owen shifted his position. His short sword was drawn and ready behind the shield, his body braced.

Gregson returned at a gallop. "Steady! Keep your positions. Remember your training!"

The advancing Alvritshai on horseback suddenly slowed their charge and allowed the creatures of the Horde behind to overtake them.

Both Owen and the man beside him cursed—

And then the lithe cat-like creatures leaped for the spear bearers with dry hisses, the less agile diggers not far behind.

Jayson adjusted the position of his spear, impaling one of the cat-like creatures, then ducked. Claws scored along his scalp, but he ignored the fiery pain. Ignored the creature as well as he heard Gregson bellowing for the footmen far behind them to advance. A digger was clambering up over Owen's shield. The bearer skewered it with his sword, a quick thrust, then ducked behind his protection.

"The main force is almost here," Jayson warned.

Owen glanced behind them. "The footmen are dealing with those who got over the shields."

"Good. Ready now. In three, two..."

He didn't have to finish. Owen braced himself as the creatures of the

Horde slammed into the wall. Jayson heard someone scream to his right, heard cries of a breach, heard Gregson's horse charging in that direction, but the shouted commands were lost in the sudden roar of the creatures directly before him. Black-gray with sinewy, corded muscles and vicious claws and teeth, they tore at the shield wall, climbing up its side with malicious glee. Jayson struck out with the spear, the cat creature's body hanging limp halfway down its length, giving it an odd weight. The tip punched through one of the larger creature's shoulders and it fell back, two more taking its place. Owen stabbed over the top of his shield blindly, slicing cleanly through the claws of one, biting deep into another's arm. Black blood sluiced along the top of the shield, but Owen stabbed again, Jayson driving the wounded back. The man to his right jostled him, having retreated too far from his shield bearer, and Jayson risked a lunge to the side to give him room to recover. He lurched back into place, but a digger had climbed Owen's shield and launched himself toward Jayson's face in those few precious seconds. Instead of ducking, he head-butted the creature before it could extend its claws. The creature dropped to the ground and Jayson stomped hard, felt bones crack beneath his booted heel. He ground the creature into the mud as it squealed, fended off two more attackers. But there were too many of them, too close together. His spear was becoming entangled. He jerked it back to free it, pulled for another lunge—

And someone grabbed his shoulder and shouted, "Fall back for the footmen!"

He stepped back without thought, bringing his spear upright as swordsmen rushed forward to take his place. He must have missed the orders, for all along the line the spearmen were being replaced. Taking another step back, he nearly slipped and fell in the muddy grass. The dead cat creature slid down the shaft and struck his hand, coating it with black blood. He shifted and let it slid to the ground, lifting his spear free. Cradling the spear with one arm, he reached up with the other and wiped at his sweaty face. His hand came away streaked with red blood. He stared at it a moment, then prodded his scalp, felt the scrapes there, the trail of blood that tracked down around his ear and along his neck. Now that he was aware of it, he could feel its tackiness inside his hardened leather armor where it had soaked into his undershirt.

He couldn't do anything about it, so resisted the urge to shrug, even though it itched. Instead, he shifted his attention to the battle, keeping one eye forward as the swordsmen hacked at the Horde trying to reach over Owen's shield. Owen himself had given up trying to use his sword and was hunched low, straining to keep the shield upright as the creatures pressed in on the far side.

Down the line, one of the large trolls bellowed, an arm sweeping down and plowing through three men, flinging one of them aside. He flailed as he flew. It had breached the shield wall—all of the trolls had—and they were surrounded by the rear forces, including the cavalry. Those with spears who were near them had focused their attention on taking the beasts down. Someone flung a spear that sank deep into the nearest creature's right eye and it reared back with a hideous, rumbling scream and stumbled back. It pulled the spear out with one meaty hand and tossed it aside, but the swordsmen at its feet had taken advantage of the distraction. One sliced into the beast's hamstring, then was slapped aside. The creature roared again, but its leg crumbled beneath its own weight as it shifted and it fell, vanishing in the surge of Temeritt men.

A sudden horn cry caught Jayson's attention and he tensed, shifting the spear into a ready position. Terson charged by, the Legionnaire's face splattered with black blood. "Prepare to fall back. Spearmen ready! Wait for the mark!"

Jayson edged forward, spear half lowered. He caught Owen's eye, then the swordsmen blocked his view. A horn sounded a long note and Jayson took a deep breath. Three short notes followed.

On the last note, the swordsmen lashed out with their blades, driving the Horde back. Owen and the shield bearers surged to their feet, thrusting outward with the shields as the footmen fell back, all of them retreating in a rush. Jayson braced himself as the swordsmen brushed past on either side. Owen fell back the four paces necessary to get himself into position, then slammed the bottom of his shield back into the ground and crouched. Every shield man to either side mimicked the movement, one that they'd trained hard on for weeks. As soon as the shield men ducked and braced, the spear wielders slammed their spears into position to meet the oncoming charge of the recovered Horde.

Jayson jabbed the spear forward, its tip taking out the right side of a creature's throat. His arms screamed at the motion, so much different than on the training grounds, so much heavier, but he knew the battle had just started.

With grim determination, he tightened his grip and stabbed forward again.

The shield wall fell back four more times over the next hour.

* * *

Kobel slashed into the troll's hide, felt his blade cut deep and hit bone, the roar of wind and battle in his ears as he continued moving without pause. His mount surged forward beneath him as he cut left and right into the few creatures of the Horde who had managed to get past the shield wall. He nudged his mount into a curve, banking left for another pass at the troll, the rest of his escort following suit around him. As he did so, he took stock of the field.

They'd halved the distance between the initial line of defense and the wall. The gates remained open, men and women rushing out to drag wounded back inside. The archers on the heights were leaning over the battlements, waiting for the orders to fire. The shield wall had withdrawn far enough that the enemy lines were almost in range.

Circling back, he noted two of the trolls had fallen. Kicking hard, he urged his horse forward, the animal responding immediately. His escort rallied behind him. He leaned forward as he approached the same troll he'd hit before. Common soldiers surrounded it, the creature exacting massive damage. It reached down and snatched one man from those at its feet and crushed him with one hand, tossing the dangling pulped body aside. With its other arm, it took a swipe at those remaining, flinging them all to one side.

Kobel seized the opening, pulling the reins and cutting in sharply. His blade scored along the creature's stomach and blood splattered onto Kobel's face, burning slightly as it mingled with his own sweat. As he ducked the beast's return swing, he heard it roar, his horse staggering as something hit its haunches. He cursed, glanced over his shoulder, and caught the troll as it stumbled forward and fell to the ground, crushing one of his mounted escort. The horse screamed in pain, thrashing violently, but then the commoners surged over the troll's body, stabbing it repeatedly.

With grim satisfaction, Kobel turned back to the main battle. Horns sounded on all sides, one signaling another retreat for the shield wall. It had worked surprisingly well. He hadn't expected it to hold this long.

But then another horn cut through the clash and roar of the battle. Coming from the south.

His attention snapped in that direction as he pulled his mount up short. It snorted and tossed its head, impatient. His remaining escort drew up around him.

"Who is that?" Leighten growled, working to control his own horse.

The rest of the Legion milled about, surrounding them both protectively.

Far to the south, a force of men on horseback was charging toward the Horde. Kobel squinted, trying to catch sight of the banner at its forefront.

"Tower on a field of red," he said. "It's Tarken Sohn. He's going to hit them from behind."

"The archers."

Kobel's initial elation faded. He could feel the tide of the battle pressing against his chest, a hard, implacable pressure. Like an ocean current, it had taken on a life of its own.

As if mimicking the ebb and flow of a tide, the horn cry for the shield wall sounded, one long tone, followed by three shorter notes. By now, the Horde had learned the signal. Kobel felt the surge as the black creatures intensified their attack. His gaze darted down the lines as the shield bearers shoved hard against them, then shouted as they fell back. The line crumbled in three spots, shields falling as they attempted to retreat, but those that remained closed the gaps before the Horde could take advantage of the holes. The entire enemy line was within range of the archers on the walls now, but Tarken Sohn's men would be at risk of getting hit.

He couldn't afford not to signal the archers' attack.

He straightened in his saddle, but then his eyes caught on odd movement in the ranks of the Horde. He pointed with his sword. "The dark Alvritshai. They've seen the men from Yhnar."

"Your orders?"

"Order the archers north of the gates to attack. Summon the Legion's cavalry. We'll cut south and attack the Alvritshai from two sides."

Leighten repeated the orders at a shout, the men surrounding Kobel beginning to form up. He didn't wait, kicking his anxious mount into motion, heading toward the southern edge of the shield wall, toward the now narrow gap between the shields and Temeritt's wall. As he rode, mounted Legion broke off their attacks and joined them, their group doubling, then tripling in size. The walls of Temeritt, scarred and blackened from the previous attacks over the past months, loomed up on his left. The archers and soldiers on the walls cheered, the roar filtering down as the cavalry charged through the narrow gap and out around the edges of the attacking forces. They plowed through the Horde's thin line there, the creature's kept at bay by the threat of the archers, killing indiscriminately as they went, then arced out onto the dead grassland beyond, circling back to the west on the Horde's flank. Some of the Horde broke off their attack to come at them, but Kobel ignored them, fending off the few stragglers who angled toward him viciously, keeping his eyes on his target: the Alvritshai who had engaged Tarken Sohn's men. His horse's feet thundered in his ears, the muted screams and clash of swords filtering through from ahead. The main battle fell behind.

As he approached, he scanned the Alvritshai, searching for the leaders. He found them in the midst of Tarken Sohn's banners, the two engaged in vicious fighting, swords flickering in the sunlight as it sank toward the west. But they weren't the Wraiths. He'd seen two of the black-tainted traitors from the walls through his spyglass—one an Alvritshai with a wicked scar across his neck, the other one a dwarren with bones twisted into the beads and leather ties of his beard. He'd seen neither of them during the attack, wondered where they were.

He and his Legion hit the side of the dark Alvritshai forces hard, his own mount knocking one of the pale-skinned men from the saddle even as his blade clashed with another on the left. He bellowed as he cut the Alvritshai down, ignoring the screams of the one now being trampled underfoot. His mount strained forward into the press, the clang of metal on metal resounding in his head. He parried and blocked without conscious thought, slicing through arms, necks, any exposed flesh or break in the Alvritshai's guard. One of their cattans scraped across his upper arm, screeching against the armor. He drove his blade into the Alvritshai's face guard, yanked it back as the man fell, then turned to strike at the body he sensed next to him.

"Ho!" Tarken Sohn shouted, his own blade raised to block.

Kobel brought his swing up short, shooting a glance to either side. The two Legion forces had converged, the Alvritshai shunted off to one side.

"Good of you to join us," Kobel shouted over the noise.

"We've been watching for awhile," Tarken answered. "But now isn't a good time to talk. In fact, I'd suggest we retreat with all haste. Look."

The GreatLord of Yhnar nodded toward the Autumn Tree. Another band of the Horde, kept in reserve, was heading toward them. Beyond them, Kobel caught sight of the two Wraiths, both watching from horseback. The Alvritshai Wraith's expression was implacable, but the dwarren looked angry.

Why hadn't they attacked with their own forces? What were they waiting for?

"Make for the southern edge of our line. If the shield wall hasn't broken, we should be able to reach the gates there."

Tarken turned to bellow orders to his men. With Kobel on his heels, the two combined cavalry broke away from the remaining Alvritshai and galloped for the southern edge of the Temeritt forces.

As they neared the line, the shield wall fell back again, nearly closing the remaining gap. The Horde had gotten bolder, attacking the shield wall's flank after realizing the archers on the southern walls weren't firing.

"We're going to have to fight our way back in!" he yelled over one shoulder, then urged his horse on faster.

He watched the Horde surge forward and close the space between shields and wall like a wave—

And then he hit them hard, plowing deep into their midst, sword cutting to both sides as fast as he could swing it. Claws raked along the armor on his legs, a few sinking between the breaks and into flesh beneath. His horse screamed, its side opened up on its left haunch. It kicked out, hooves slamming into the black and gray sinewy bodies around it. He drove the animal forward hard as he lashed out. An arrow lanced nearly straight downward from the wall above, taking out the creature to his front right. His blade took the head off of the one on the left.

Then he broke through to the far side. He instantly began shouting orders to the men who'd rushed forward to protect the southern flank in an attempt to keep it open. Lord Akers led the counterattack, his white horse splattered with gore, yet still easy to see in the crushing sea of bodies. From above, he heard a command to draw and glanced up just in time to catch an entire wave of arrows release.

He ducked unconsciously, but the arrows thudded home in the middle of the Horde. A torrent of fresh screams rose above the general clamor, and for an instant, the pressure of the attack eased. Half of the combined Yhnar and Temeritt cavalry spilled into the gap made in the enemy forces, then past the end of the shield wall to safety, including Tarken Sohn. More of the Temeritt soldiers on foot rushed to take their place, pushing the Horde back.

Kobel spun toward Lord Akers. "Prepare to pull the shield wall back again! We need to close the gap completely!"

Akers conveyed the orders even as his blade found new marks. Kobel's hand clenched on the handle of his sword as he counted Legion slipping through to safety.

When nearly all of them had made it past the edge of the shield wall, he signaled the retreat.

The horn cry sounded. At the same time, he heard the order to draw from above.

His heartbeat slowed as he felt the tides shifting yet again.

The archers released, the creatures of the Horde falling like grain beneath a scythe. All but three of the Legion snaked past the end of the shield wall, and then the third note sounded and the shield bearers heaved their shields forward and pulled back, closing the gap between themselves and the stone walls of Temeritt.

Satisfied that the Temeritt forces were as protected now as they could be, he waved toward the wall above, giving the archers leave to fire at will.

He didn't watch the thousands of arrows as they flew from the wall, but he heard the thrum of their release.

He motioned to Tarken Sohn and Lord Akers.

"Have we sealed the break on the northern section of the shield wall?"

"It was sealed before the first arrows flew there," Akers replied.

"Good. Continue pulling back the shield wall to the gates, and keep up the fire from the walls. This battle isn't ended, but it's up to the archers now. Get as many of the ground forces back inside the gates as soon as possible."

Kobel met Tarken Sohn's eyes. "We need to speak."

His fellow GreatLord nodded in acknowledgment. "We've been watching from a safe distance for weeks now. How bad is it?"

"If the siege isn't broken within the next few days, Temeritt will fall."

22

Colin released time at the edge of the ruined city in the center of the Thalloran Wastelands. He'd approached the city from the south, the direction Eraeth and Siobhaen had taken to escape with his unconscious body. From this vantage, on the fractured and serrated rocks and cliffs that surrounded the city like a maze, he could see the distant shattered towers, cloaked with a thin layer of cloudy mist, and the sprawl of destruction from the edge of the cliffs to the central ring of debris. Between here and there, the ground had been churned, as if chewed up and spat out, but beyond the ridge of debris he could see entire buildings still standing, their empty windows and doorways and arches gaping black in the fading sunlight. Some had crumbled over time, roofs caved in, walls collapsed into the streets, but a few were eerily intact. Those that did remain were made of stone. Entire sections of the city were empty except for the haunting hint of foundations, where Colin assumed the buildings had been constructed of mostly wood.

His gaze shifted from the city to the northern cliffs, where in the shadows cast by the setting sun he could see the faint prickling of lights. The Snake People's city, built into cliffs like those that rose at Colin's back. His eyes narrowed. According to Eraeth and Siobhaen, the Snake People had hunted them in the days after his confrontation with Walter. He assumed they'd done so at Walter's order. He had no delusions that Siobhaen or Eraeth had killed him.

"So where are you, Walter?" he asked, a hot breeze blowing up sand and grit from the city below to the ledge where he stood. "Are you here, still recovering or protecting the Source? Or are you out there, in Wrath Suvane, leading the armies that are destroying our world?"

He didn't think it was the latter. Walter had never led directly in the past. He'd always sent someone else to do the work for him. He used people, as he'd used Brunt, Gregor, and Rick to beat Colin senseless in Portstown when he was twelve. He'd join in after Colin had been subdued, but it was always one of the others sent in first. He'd done the

same with Khalaek, using the lord of the Evant to find the locations of the
Wells and to sow the seeds of war between the three races. And he'd used
the Wraiths and the Shadows to wreak havoc afterwards, at least until the
Seasonal Trees had been created.

Now, those Wraiths were leading the armies. He'd sensed them in the
army heading off to face the dwarren at the Break, knew that they could
sense him in return if they were paying attention. If Walter were here, he
was powerful enough to feel Colin manipulating time, would sense his
approach if he traveled as he had since leaving Yhnar. But there would
likely be patrols set up. He'd passed three as he'd snaked his way through
the maze of crevasses in the broken land to reach this ledge. There would
be more in the city below.

Curling one hand around his staff, he dug into his satchel and removed
a small, sheathed knife, securing it to his belt. His hands brushed the
bundled linen of the Spring Tree inside the pouch as he did so, the fabric
soothing.

Knife secured, the strap that held it in place loosened, he began to
descend from the ledge into the ruined city, now half cloaked in shadow.
A soft bluish-white glow pulsed in the layer of clouds around the sheared
off towers. He could feel the strength of the Source even here, imagined
he could feel it feeding the Wraiths and Walter's armies.

He had come to confront Walter, but he needed to cut off the Wraiths'
strength first.

* * *

"Fall back!" Gregson roared, then watched as the entire line of shields
dropped back three paces and reset. The men closest to the walls retreated
further as the entire line shrank and closed in on the main gates, fewer and
fewer shield men needed for the front line. He shot a glance toward
Terson's end, the field now too tight for either of them to be riding back
and forth. As soon as he verified that Terson's side had held, he motioned
to an entire section of men held in reserve, ready to push to the front if a
breach appeared. "Back inside the walls." When they hesitated, he
snarled, "Go!"

They pulled back into the gaping mouth of the gates. Gregson glared
up above the gap toward the heights, arrows spitting outward from the
unseen archers into the Horde in spats, more and more difficult to see as
the sun set and darkness crept across the sky. Torches began appearing all
along the wall, their fiery light minimal here at the gates.

Farther down the wall, a cauldron of burning pitch flared bright in the darkness as it was tipped over the edge onto the Horde beneath, a sheet of flame from parapet to the ground. The wall appeared to burn where the pitch stuck to it. Gregson turned away, cursing himself as he blinked his eyes rapidly. He didn't need to be blinded by their own fires.

"Ready to retreat," he called out again, the lines so close there was no need for the horns. He eased his mount backwards to make room, slipping into the shadow of the gate's arch, then signaled to Terson. "Fall back!"

His unit roared and withdrew. One of his shield men stumbled and fell, his paired spear bearer shrieking, "Ryon!" but the Horde fell on him instantly. Gregson caught a glimpse of one of his arms being torn from his shoulder, Ryon screaming more in terror than pain, and then he was lost from sight as the Horde surged after the shields. Ryon's spear bearer hesitated, taking a step forward to help out his partner, but Gregson saw Jayson catching his arm and hauling him back. The miller's face was splattered with blood—Gregson couldn't tell if it was his own or not—but he was heartened to see a familiar face among the ranks. So many of the men were new after their last attempt to free Temeritt.

He scanned the line. Thirty shields held the Horde at bay, over fifty men with swords and spears behind them stabbing and thrusting into the mass of blackened and sinewy bodies beyond. He ordered the group that had been pressed into the area beneath the arch with him to retreat, freeing up the space. The thick stone walls rose up on either side. Above, a thick slit in the stone hid the iron portcullis; a few black openings marked the murder holes. The thick wooden gates were still open wide behind them, dark and glistening after having been soaked in water.

This would be the trickiest part. If they didn't time their retreat correctly, the Horde might overtake the gates with the doors open, and then the city truly would be lost.

He hoped the archers above and those in the tower were paying attention.

He sidled his mount sideways, drawing closer to Terson. "As long as our line is holding, let's give everyone above a moment more to prepare."

"Very well."

Looking over his shoulder, Gregson assessed the courtyard behind. One entire side had been lined with bodies, women and children working their way through the wounded. Some had already been covered in stained sheets. Four wagons were already loaded, the bodies stacked high, stripped of any clothing and armor that could be salvaged. To the other side, the men who'd retreated from the field were regrouping, a few of them dropping to the ground on hands and knees or sitting, exhausted. A new, fresh unit, led by another of Gregson's lieutenants—Marshall—was waiting to press forward once Gregson's last men pulled away from the gates, although if everything went according to plan, they wouldn't be necessary.

Turning back, he said, "Everything appears ready on the ground."

"But it all depends on those above, doesn't it?"

It wasn't really a question, and Gregson didn't answer. Instead, he shouted, "Final retreat, ready!" He motioned to Terson, who spun his mount and trotted back beneath the thick wall, beneath the portcullis' slit and the murder holes and into the courtyard beyond, to signal Marshall and those holding the doors. All along the remains of his line, Gregson's men had tensed, a few of those holding the shields searching for him. Outside, the sun had set, darkness claiming the skies, the Horde lit by their own torches and by moonlight, a mass of creatures that seemed somehow larger and more fearsome and stronger by night than by day. Gregson let the sound of the battle crash over him, then raised his sword and pointed it toward the rolling, shadowed forms beyond his line. "Fall back!"

The line shoved forward against the Horde, then dropped back three paces, squeezing into the walls of the gate arch. But before they could settle into new positions, he shouted, "Again!" With an answering battlecry that was more noise than words, his unit roared and pulled back again, the Horde surging after them. "Again!" Gregson roared. "And again!" They were beneath the murder holes now, and Gregson felt a droplet of hot oil strike his cheek through the slit in his helm. It burned, but he ignored it. "Again!" He was at the hinged gates now, the creatures of the Horde crammed into the archway's opening, his last few men pushing hard against them to hold them back.

Then: "Break away! Retreat in full!"

He held his ground, watching as the spear bearers, shield men, and swordsmen shoved hard against the Horde one last time and then turned and sprinted toward the courtyard. They broke around Gregson as he cantered his horse backwards, fanning to either side as they breached the archway and the gates. Someone in the courtyard roared orders, the sound muted. The last of his men scrambled from the archway, the leading edge of the Horde on their heels. The creatures screamed in triumph, spilling outwards like ink from a bottle, but the gates were already swinging closed. Marshall ordered the waiting unit forward, the men rushing to Gregson's side as he reined his mount about and slashed down into the front ranks of the Horde. Inside the archway, a heavy rattle of metal signaled the release of the portcullis. Gregson couldn't see it, the interior of the tunnel too dark, but he heard it grating against stone, heard the screams and thud as it slammed into place, cutting off the rest of the Horde outside. But he had no time to check to see if the tunnel was secure. At least forty creatures had made it past the portcullis, half of them still trapped inside the tunnel. The heavy wooden gates were swinging ponderously closed. Gregson and Marshall hacked at those who'd made it into the courtyard, Gregson's blade severing a hissing head from its shoulders, cutting through a clawed hand as it tore into his mount's side. His horse reared and kicked with a scream, shod feet connecting with solidly muscled nightmarish bodies. Gregson fought for balance, holding on tightly to the reins, and kept his seat as his horse landed hard. Stabbing downward grimly, the stench of oil slammed into his nostrils, overwhelming the already heady scents of fire and smoke and death that hung about the city walls. The hot oil had been poured through the murder holes onto whoever was trapped inside the tunnel.

A moment later, it was followed by a torch.

Gregson caught the fall of the torch out of the corner of his eye, a yellow-orange flicker of life inside the black archway riddled with the silhouettes of the creatures of the Horde.

And then the entire tunnel was engulfed in flames. They roared from the opening, sweeping outwards in a wash of heat and death that caused Gregson and his men to rear backwards. The hideous screams of those dying in the inferno beneath the stone walls followed, cut off a moment later as the heavy, iron-banded gates were swung shut, flames gouting from the crack between them until they were closed. Twenty men rushed to barricade the doors, the iron bars grinding into their brackets. The screams from within intensified, even though they were smothered by the doorway.

Gregson sliced cleanly through one of the cat-like creatures with the luminescent eyes as it leapt for him, ichor spraying against his armor, then spun his mount. On all sides, Marshall and his men were finishing off those creatures that had managed to reach the courtyard. As soon as he saw that the area was secure, the gates closed, he expelled a pent up breath, tension sloughing from his shoulders, replaced by pure exhaustion. He slumped in his saddle, then waved toward the men waiting at the edge of the stone wall.

A signal passed up through the tower and a moment later a second portcullis ratcheted into place on this side of the heavy doors. Inside, he knew the murder holes had already been sealed, although they could be reopened if the Horde managed to break through the outer portcullis. He knew they would, in time, but it would take them much longer to breach the iron-banded doors and the second portcullis.

Sheathing his sword, he dismounted, the men roaring in triumph and relief, even though the battle continued on the walls. Gregson pulled his helm off with one hand, Terson and Marshall coming up to him from two different sides, their men clapping them on the backs wearily. Gregson's arms felt as heavy as stone, every movement an effort, but he knew they were not done.

"Orders?" Terson asked.

"Tell the men from the field to rest here, in the courtyard. Sleep if they can. We'll be needed before long. This battle has hardly begun."

Terson slapped his fist over his heart and moved off, Gregson shaking his head at his retreating back.

"He's a military man, through and through," Marshall said.

"Take your unit to the northwestern gates."

Marshall's eyebrows rose. "The northwestern gates?"

"Find Lord Akers. He'll have orders for you there."

Marshall straightened, closed fist going to his heart. He didn't have the same fervor as Terson, but the salute was filled with more respect and integrity. "As ordered."

He motioned Curtis and Ricks forward to pass on the order. Both began organizing the unit into ranks, marching them out of the courtyard north along the streets. Those of his unit who had been on the battlefield outside the walls had found a spare square of space in the courtyard, some simply dropping where they stood, and were cleaning weapons, repairing armor, taking food or water being handed out by children, or had already slumped into sleep.

Satisfied that his men were being seen to, Gregson turned toward the tower. Time to report and find out where his unit would be needed next.

* * *

"GreatLord Kobel, the main gates are closed and sealed. All secondary gates have reported in as secure as well."

"Thank you, that is all."

The runner from the walls bowed briefly and departed. The sounds of the battle resounded through the small room Kobel and GreatLord Tarken Sohn had retreated to in the main tower of the outer wall, screams and the thud of the Wraith army against the inner gates reduced to a muted roar.

Tarken removed his helm and slammed it down on the table, Kobel rounding to the far side, removing his own helm and gauntlet. Neither of them sat.

"How long have you been watching the siege?"

"Too long," Tarken said bluntly. "Nearly two months. How long have they held you inside these walls?"

"Nearly six months."

Tarken's eyes widened. "You must be running low on supplies—food and water."

Kobel leaned forward onto the table, weight on both arms. "Provisions are growing short, yes. We have plenty of water. The cisterns beneath the city are still full. But food...there is no more meat to be found. Those in the city have begun eating rats, pigeons, even horse when they can get their hands on one of them. The palace's stores are nearly depleted. There have been riots in the streets, and disease is rampant. I had thought to hold out until King Justinian arrived with reinforcements from Corsair, but I could not wait any longer. In a few days' time, there will be nothing left to eat in Temeritt at all, even if I withhold everything we now have for the Legion and the commoners fighting on the walls."

"Whatever my forces have with me is yours, of course, but it will buy your Legion at most another day, probably not even that."

"And now your men are trapped here with us."

"Do you think this army would have stopped here at Temeritt? If we were not trapped here now, we would have been trapped in Yhnar later. You have heard, then, that the king is on his way?"

Kobel sighed. "Yes, but only recently. Arruli Raveleti spoke to Corsair through the Hand of Diermani earlier today. He and his forces may not arrive in time. Is that how you learned of the siege?"

"No. I received reports of strange creatures traveling near or on Yhnar's lands. They were dismissed as superstitions at first. But then the reports became too numerous. I had begun investigating them more closely when your messenger arrived."

"So one of our messengers made it through."

"Barely. He arrived wounded and close to unconscious. But he delivered his message."

A tremor ran through the stone beneath their feet, shaking grit from the rafters overhead. The roar of the fighting swelled, and both GreatLords looked in the direction of the gates, listening intently. But there was no bone-numbing crack of splintering wood. After a moment, the upsurge receded, but an urgency tugged at Kobel's feet, twitched in his hands. He glanced toward Tarken, saw the same itching need to be at the front lines in his fellow GreatLord's eyes.

"Did you notice the Wraiths?" he asked.

"They did not lead the attack. They stayed back, beneath the Autumn Tree."

"They're waiting for something. They've been waiting for months now, holding us here, like pigs being caged for the slaughter. I thought at first they were waiting for the army that took out Borangst to return, but when they did, they simply combined their forces and settled in."

"More than likely, it means they have another army on its way here."

"Another reason we needed to attack now. Temeritt stands no chance against a larger force than this, even if we did have enough supplies to last another year."

Tarken reached for his helm. "Then we'd better see what we can do from these walls. It doesn't sound like the Wraith army—"

"The Horde. We call it the Horde."

"It doesn't sound like *the Horde* plans on falling back any time soon. It's going to be a long night."

Kobel grinned. "Temeritt isn't lost yet."

"What do you mean?"

"Temeritt has a few surprises left for the Horde. The attack this afternoon was only our first strike."

Slipping his helm onto his head and patting it into place, Tarken said, "Tell me."

* * *

Lord Akers led his group of five hundred into the depths of the hill the city of Temeritt was built upon. The torch he carried cast flickering light onto the stone walls of the corridor before him. Dozens of other torches followed behind, glinting off the occasional rivulets of water from seepage that stained the stone or a pool where it had collected at the base of the wall. Most of the stones were still marked by the chisels from the quarry, having never seen the light of day or the harsh grind of erosion since they'd been placed. Moss and lichen scarred them in those places where the water had leached through, but there were entire sections where the unit's feet kicked up dust from the layers coating the floor, even though many others had recently passed through the tunnels before them.

They'd passed the last branching corridor ten minutes ago, after entering the passages through the floor of the storage room in the northwestern gate tower. The tunnels led into the depths of the hill, connecting with others that led down from the cellars in the palace. But the branch he now traveled led toward the natural caverns of the hill itself...and the lake beyond.

Ahead, the torchlight changed and Akers halted and raised a hand, fist closed. Hisses and muffled retorts followed as the men stopped, all under orders to keep quiet.

Akers edged forward, his torchlight revealing the end of the manmade corridor. It opened up into a wide cavern, stalactites and stalagmites casting strange shadows. Granite smoothed by water and time stretched off to the right, pocked here and there with holes, or layered in odd-shaped ridges rising toward the back of the room. Shards of crystal and quartz glittered as Akers stepped out into the space, motioning those behind him forward. He skirted the edge of the pool to the left, working his way around the southeastern shore of the lake. From the plains outside, it appeared as if the lake ended where the steepest cliff face of the hill tumbled down to the water, but early explorers had discovered that the water extended into this cavern. The original settlers of the city had taken advantage of the natural inlet, building stone docks here. But those docks had been long abandoned.

Until the siege began.

From the darkness ahead, the stone pillars of the docks rose into view. One or two of them had crumbled and fallen to one side, or been swallowed up by the lake water, but for the most part the stone moorings were intact. Turning to his right, Akers raised his torch higher and caught the curved outlines of boats. They'd been brought in through the tunnels a few months after the siege began, after it became clear it would not be broken by outside help. The original intent had been as a potential escape route, but now...

He spun about, his unit commanders already grouped behind him. "You know what to do."

As his commanders called out orders in low voices, the men in their units scrambling toward the boats, Akers made his way to the edge of the stone docks. His torchlight reflected off of the lake in ripples, calmer here than outside. But he could still hear the water lapping at the cavern's hidden shore. He wondered if the Horde could see their torches, even though he knew they couldn't douse them. Not yet.

Low cursing signaled the arrival of the first boat, twenty men carrying it forward onto the dock, then tilting it and slipping it into the water. Two more followed, one of them dropping in with a splash. Akers frowned, but said nothing, letting the hisses of the guardsmen be his reprimand. Ten boats were settled into the water, tied off, and were filling with armored men, twenty-five to each. Ten others were being hauled forward as the first few were unmoored and shoved away, selected soldiers already dipping oars into the water and guiding the boats out toward the opposite side of the cavern.

"Lord Akers."

Akers turned to find Commander Bronsin waiting.

"My lord, the last boat is ready."

"Very well."

He followed Bronsin to the boat and clambered in. The boat rocked awkwardly beneath him and he sat down forcibly, unused to its motion or to his own body after months of food rationing. He glanced around at the men in silent challenge, but no one said anything, everyone's eyes on the oarsmen or the mouth of the cavern.

They pushed away, gliding across the water in near silence. The only sounds were the clunk of armor as the men in the boat shifted position, their low breathing, and the occasional quiet plash of the oars. Akers watched the shadows of the other boats spread out before them, saw the first of them as they reached the cavern's lip. The torchbearers doused their flames in the lake with a hiss before slipping out and under the edge of stone. Akers could see the figures of those in the boats hunching down, silhouetted against the pale moonlight from outside.

The soldier in the prow muttered a warning and the last of the torches were doused. Akers leaned forward as his boat slid out onto the lake. His armor scraped against the stone lip overhead and he grimaced, straining lower—

And then they were in the open, the sounds of the battle at Temeritt's walls echoing harshly across the lake.

A shiver of mingled awe and fear swept through Akers as his boat glided out in the wake of the others, mere patches of darkness on the moonlight-flecked water. He felt that awe and fear touch all of the men, the restless shuffling ceasing for a moment as everyone sat back and stared at the battlements. The Horde was lit with flickering torches, a fire speckled field spread before the stone walls. It surged in dark eddies, forward and back, a black ocean with its own strange tides. The battlements stood out in stark relief as sheets of fire rained down from the heights, cauldrons of oil and pitch being lit and poured over the parapets onto the creatures below. The entire length of the wall swarmed with indistinguishable figures, marked by a thin thread of torches and lanterns trailing to the south. Behind it, the city of Temeritt rose into the night, the only parts visible the windows lit within by candles, the torch-lined inner walls, and the snaking main thoroughfares picked out by the lanterns along their sides rising toward the palace above.

It would have been beautiful if not for the muted screams of agony and the cacophony of the battle.

Akers turned his attention toward the lake's shoreline. He couldn't see it in the darkness, except as a vague line where the glints of moonlight ended. Of more importance was the fact that the Horde remained to the south, their focus on the main gates, although a large portion had broken off and were attacking the smaller gate to the north. Where Temeritt's walls intersected with the cliffs above the lake and all along the lake shore, the plains were dark. None of the Horde was close to their position.

Akers relaxed slightly. His biggest fear had been finding the Horde waiting for them at the edge of the lake. They'd shown no interest in the waters, or attempting to hit Temeritt from the cliffs, but he never planned anything without considering all possibilities. Their group could have been destroyed trying to land their boats.

He leaned forward and tapped the guardsman before him, motioning to the right. The man nodded and passed the message toward the front of the boat. Their approach shifted farther west. As they drew closer, he could hear the splashes as the others pulled their boats onto the shoreline and into the tall, concealing grass.

His own boat crunched into the stony bottom, lurching to a halt. Guardsmen rolled over the lip of the boat into the water, wading the short distance to dry land. He followed suit, water seeping into his boots, rising up to his knees. He dragged himself into the grasses and dead cattails, caught sight of Commander Bronsin and angled in his direction. All around him, the men were hunkering down, a few making certain the boats were hidden. Someone hissed for silence at a muttered oath and whispered conversation.

Akers gripped his commander's shoulder, crouched down, and leaned in close. "Report."

"All boats accounted for. Scouts have been sent out to make certain the Horde hasn't seen us, but I'd wager they haven't."

"I never bet with a fighting man. Don't forget their flying scouts. We have no idea how many of the damned Horde can see in the dark."

"Those cat-like things definitely, with those spooky eyes."

"More than that, I'm certain." Akers' brow furrowed, then he pointed into the darkness. "Look."

Ahead, one of their scouts appeared as a darker shadow against the rolling flatness of the plains. The figure neared the clustered group, then turned abruptly toward Akers' position.

Settling to the ground, one hand on the grass for balance, the scout said, "All clear. None of the Horde is within a hundred yards of our position."

"And to the west?"

"Nothing to the west either. They're focused on the walls."

"Good. Bronsin, spread the word. No change in the orders. We'll follow the lake's edge to the west for a hundred yards, then cut southwest. Stay clear of the Horde attacking Temeritt. They aren't our target. We'll hit their camp from the northwest. If anything goes wrong, I'll signal the retreat. Anyone still on the plains by dawn will be left behind."

"Understood."

Still crouched low, Bronsin began working his way around the groups of guardsmen. Within ten minutes, the entire unit was ready and at a signal from Akers that only those nearest to his position actually saw, they rose and began jogging along the edge of the water, bent over at the waist to keep their profiles low.

The group broke onto the plain, the scout sprinting out ahead of Akers' position. The lord lost sight of him almost immediately, so kept his attention on the walls, the battle to his left, and the ground before him. The plains dipped and rolled, portions of the battle hidden behind the swells in the land, then reemerging as the entire group worked their way southward. Akers could hear nothing but his own harsh breath and the thud of his feet against the ground; his own noise drowned out most of the muted roars and screams from the fighting.

They reached the wide main road and Akers slowed. But there was no word from the scout, so after a brief pause to make certain everyone had caught up, he crossed the rutted and trampled path and began angling toward the east again. He kept the same pace at first, but then began to slow, until the group was creeping along, everyone hunched down closer to the ground. They were nearing the Horde's main camp, the fires close enough now they could see the rough outlines of tents and the base of the charred remains of the Autumn Tree. Akers frowned in irritation. Where in hells was the scout? And where was the Horde's outer patrol? They should have run into it by now.

When the hand reached out of the darkness and grabbed him hard by the upper arm, Akers nearly yelped, barely containing it with a sharply indrawn breath. A shadow he'd thought was part of the landscape coalesced into the scout, the younger guardsman dragging Akers toward him without a sound, motioning toward the slight rise before them, then toward the ground.

Akers signaled a halt, then allowed the scout to draw him forward, to a different patch of shadow. The lord smelled the thick metallic scent of fresh blood before the dark shapes drew close enough to form into three bodies.

"The Horde's patrol," the scout whispered.

There wasn't enough light to see how the patrol had died, but he didn't need to know. "How long before the next patrol wanders by?"

"Probably no more than fifteen minutes."

"Then we'd better move fast."

He gestured toward Commander Bronsin, then drew his sword and pointed toward the fires of the Horde's camp.

He gave the Legionnaire a short moment to spread the word, and then he began to run, choosing one of the fires as his target. Out of the corners of his eyes, he caught the rest of the unit sprinting toward the camp as well, mere shadows against the moonlit plains. There were no battle cries, no emotional roars for Temeritt or the Provinces. This attack was meant to be swift and silent and to catch the Horde's reserve forces totally by surprise.

The closer he drew to his chosen target, the less concerned he grew about being silent. His charge picked up speed. Blood flowed into his arms and hands, tingling, crept up into his face. Images of the battle at the north ridge—the crushing defeat of their defenses there, the scattered and terrifying retreat to the south attempting to reach the safety of Temeritt's walls—raced across his mind and stoked the fire in his gut. Scenes of the long siege, of the city sinking into squalor and depravity as the food sources dwindled and the hope of rescue from the other Provinces died, hardened like a knot in his chest. He had fought on the fields before Temeritt's walls at GreatLord Kobel's side, had repelled the Horde's feeble attacks from their heights, but none of that compared to the satisfaction he would take now from striking at them at their heart. They had sat too long in triumph beneath the husk of the Autumn Tree. He intended to hurt them, here and now, even if it meant he never made it back to the boats and Temeritt's walls again.

Sooner than he thought possible, he charged from grassy plains into the midst of thousands of tents. To either side, he heard the clash of weapons as the rest of the group began to meet members of the Horde, but he ran into none of the fell creatures. He didn't slow though. He was close enough now to see shapes moving around the fire he'd chosen.

Those figures solidified. He grinned in satisfaction as he saw a few of them rise and stare out into the darkness, the commotion from the others beginning to catch their attention. He was twenty paces away before he realized they were Alvritshai, ten before the first of the pale-skinned traitors heard his approach.

Then he was in their midst.

His blade cut through the first's neck before he even reached for his sword; the look of surprise on his face made Akers bark with laughter. He spun and stabbed the next as the Alvritshai stumbled backwards in shock, then jerked his sword free. But his moment of surprise had vanished. As he turned, the three remaining Alvritshai drew their cattans, their faces settling into anger and hate.

Akers grinned. "Let's see which of you bastards can fight."

* * *

"There," Kobel said, and pointed.

At the top of the main gate's tower, Tarken Sohn shifted his attention from the screaming Horde below toward the blackness of the plains beyond the Horde's main force. "What do you see?"

"Fire, near the Autumn Tree." Kobel suddenly realized Tarken didn't have his innate sense of where the Autumn Tree should be in the darkness, even with the fires of the Horde's camp to guide him. "Farther south. There."

In the darkness, at the northwestern edge of the camp, the fires that marked the edges of the Horde's tents were spreading, no longer simple campfires. Tents were beginning to burn, and something exploded, the conflagration suddenly escalating. The hollow sound of the explosion was lost in the cacophony of the battle.

"I ordered Lord Akers to create as much chaos and kill as many of the Horde as he could," Kobel said.

"And the purpose of the attack? He has only five hundred men. They will not be able to do much damage."

"To hurt them. To show them that perhaps they do not have us as bottled up as they think. And to give the men defending these walls some hope." The words came out with more fervor than Kobel had intended. He realized he'd clenched his hands into fists and forced his fingers to relax.

He noticed Tarken Sohn watching him and turned away, toward one of his runners. "Tell Commander Pearson that Lord Akers has begun his assault. He should prepare his men."

The young runner nodded and sped off, vanishing into the mix of men on the tower. Kobel stepped forward, closer to the edge of the wall. He couldn't move all the way to the edge; it was too crowded with Legion archers.

Tarken moved to his side. "The Horde doesn't seem to be attempting to breach the wall, except at the gates. There are no ladders, no siege engines."

"They attempted to take the walls at first, but when we repeatedly repelled their attacks, they gave up. If they're content to simply wait for us to die, then I'm going to make them pay for it. As much as I can."

Tarken said nothing.

Then, barely audible above the battle, Kobel heard a horn call. Not one of the Legion's signals. This was a deeper sound. Darker somehow.

On the field below, the Horde began to react as the horn repeated itself. Those at the back began breaking away, heading toward the Autumn Tree, its charred base and lower limbs outlined in harsh firelight now.

"I think Lord Akers has finally made himself felt." Kobel motioned to another runner. "Ready the men at the gates. Tell Pearson Lord Akers was successful."

Tarken watched the runner depart, then tapped his helm down tighter over his head, checking his armor and loosening the straps on his sword.

"What do you intend?"

Tarken glanced up. "My men are fresh and have been waiting in those hills for far too long, gnashing at the bit. Time to let them work out some more of that stifled aggression, don't you think? I'm going to join Commander Pearson on the field."

Kobel clasped the pommel of his sword. "I agree wholeheartedly."

* * *

"They're retreating!"

Ara glanced up from her frantic attempt to staunch the blood from a Legionnaire's shoulder. Her clothes were already soaked with sweat and blood shed by the dozens of men she'd looked at since the fighting started. The boy who'd shouted as he sped past was already disappearing in the mad rush of activity in the courtyard behind the main gates. Men were gathering again, a chaotic crush of men in armor, horses, and stewards attempting to make certain everyone was armed and ready. She saw Temeritt's oak against burnt orange sigil, as expected, but mixed in with it was Yhnar's tower against a field of red.

The man beneath her hands suddenly convulsed. "Elaine!" she shouted. "Bring me more rags!" When there was no response, she cursed and glanced around. Elaine was nowhere to be seen.

She pressed harder into the Legionnaire's shoulder, one hand on top of the other, fingers intertwined. Both hands were already slicked with blood—dark, heart's blood—the rag beneath saturated. The soldier looked up at her, face a rictus of pain, his green eyes squeezed nearly shut. She could barely see them beneath his matted shock of hair. One of his hands lurched up and locked onto her arm, squeezing so tight she gasped. A low moan escaped him, escalating into a ragged shout—

And then the grip on her arm slackened. His hand fell away and his body collapsed back to the stained stone of the courtyard.

Ara continued to press down against the wound, although she could already feel the slackness in his body. She hissed with effort, until she was certain he was no longer breathing, then let the stiffness in her arms go and sank back onto her heels. Using the back of her arm, she wiped at the sweat and gore across her forehead, knowing she was merely smearing it around. She stared down at the man's gore-splattered face.

Then she shoved his features from her mind and numbly stood. She stepped to one side, to the next body, noted that the man had already died, and shifted to the next. He was unconscious, but his wounds weren't serious enough to warrant immediate attention.

The next man was holding his stomach and his breathing came in harsh, pent-up gasps through clenched teeth.

She sat immediately and gripped his hands, trying to pull them away. When he resisted, she looked him in the eyes—dark brown eyes, set in a thin face framed by a salt-and-peppered beard and gray-streaked hair— and said, "I have to take a look."

As she pulled his trembling hands away, seeing the deep slash beneath, he asked haltingly, "Is it...true? ...Are they...retreating?"

Her mind already considering how best to deal with the wound, Ara took a moment to glance toward the gates. "It looks like it. They're getting ready to open the gates. GreatLord Kobel and GreatLord Tarken Sohn are going to take to the field."

The man grinned, a ghastly expression. "Thank Holy Diermani."

Ara shook her head, then shouted, "Elaine! Where in hells have you got to?"

The young girl appeared at the door to what had originally been the medical building, until the wounded became too numerous to house there. She darted between the row upon row of bodies, heading toward Ara, flinging herself to the ground beside her.

"Here," she said, throwing an armful of rags to the ground. "What else do you need?"

"A needle and some gut. This man will live if we can get him sewn up and stop the bleeding."

Elaine scrambled to her feet and darted away.

A harsh horn sounded.

"What's happening?" her patient asked.

"They're opening the gates."

* * *

"Wait!"

Wade grabbed Corim's arm and hauled him back from the edge of the crenellation, nearly making him lose his grip on the stone he held overhead.

"What in hells are you doing?" Corim spat, fumbling with the heavy rock as Wade pulled him down behind the protection of the wall. The arrogant merchant's son was craning his neck around the lip of stone, but spun back with a glare.

"The Horde is retreating, stupid. No use throwing it down onto empty ground."

Corim let the rock drop into his lap, then looked through the crenellation himself, already aware that the frantic activity all along the wall had abated. Everyone was moving to the edge of the parapet, looking over. He couldn't see anything from his vantage, so he set his rock aside and stood, leaning out.

There was nothing below their position between the main gates and the northern gates, and the creatures he could see in the torchlight and fires were pulling back, heading out onto the plains.

"The Autumn Tree is on fire again," Wade said.

"It's not on fire," Rory said from Corim's other side, his voice tinged with excitement. "Their camp's on fire!"

"Keep alert!" Corim turned to see Braxton stalking down the length of the wall, trying to bring everyone back in line. "We don't know what the Horde is up to, so stay alert! This could be some kind of trick."

"I don't think so," Wade said, his own voice catching some of the excitement from Rory, although he didn't speak loud enough for Braxton to hear.

Corim said nothing. He'd learned in the attack on Gray's Kill and then Cobble Kill and the flight southward to trust nothing. This was merely a reprieve, nothing more. The Horde would be back.

"Look!" Rory shouted, leaning so far out over the wall Corim reached out to grab onto his hardened leather armor to keep him from falling. "The gates are opening!"

At that, Corim did look, craning past the smaller Rory.

The main gates swung inwards, the outer portcullis rising slowly. A moment later, GreatLords Kobel and Tarken Sohn spilled out onto the body-strewn plains on horseback, a thousand cavalry behind them, only recognizable in the darkness by the occasional torch-lit glimpse of a banner. They charged toward the retreating Horde, part of it turning back to meet them, all of the actions played out by the movement of the torches on the field. The majority of the Horde continued to retreat toward the Autumn Tree.

Behind the GreatLords' forces, another group of soldiers appeared, spreading out among the bodies.

"What are they doing?" Rory asked.

"Searching for wounded and killing any of the Horde still alive," Corim said.

"Picking up anything that can be used again as well, like weapons, arrows, whatever," Harden added from behind them.

"But what's happening at the Horde's camp?" Wade asked. "If the two GreatLords are below, who's attacking their camp?"

"Best not to speculate, boys. Better to take the break in stride, rest up, and prepare for whatever comes next."

They turned to see their swordmaster staring out over the plains.

He glanced down at them. "We aren't privy to the GreatLord's plans, and you'll drive yourself mad trying to figure them out on your own."

He turned and moved onwards, slapping one man on the back, speaking to a few others.

Corim looked back out to the darkness of the plains. He had no idea what time it was or how long they'd been fighting. He only knew it was dark, that his bones and body were trembling. He stank of fear sweat, the clothes beneath his armor itchy against his raw skin. His stomach felt hollow and empty, but it had felt that way for days now.

On the plains, the torches of the GreatLords and their forces suddenly turned back. They'd harassed the Horde close to half the distance between the walls and the Autumn Tree.   As they came within sight of the torchlight along the walls and began pouring back into the gates, those who'd ventured out on foot filtering in behind them, a roar rose along the wall, men chanting, pounding on the stone battlements with their hands, with anything within reach, a few bellowing battle cries for Temeritt, for the Provinces, for GreatLord Kobel. Against his better judgment, Corim felt a sense of pride swell in his chest, accepting Wade's and Rory's enthusiastic back slaps and shoving with a thin smile. Harden remained reserved, the older, taller boy's eyes weary and wary.

Braxton reappeared. "It appears to be over for now. We're to rest up with what few hours are left of the night and report back to the wall in the morning. Get moving!"

He repeated the orders as he stalked past them, taking Wade by the shoulder and shoving him in the direction of the stairs. Their entire unit was stumbling in the same direction. Only a contingent of Legion remained to guard the walls.

"Come on." Harden nudged Corim into Wade's wake. "We may as well rest while we can. The Horde will be waiting for us in the morning."

They trudged together toward the stairs.

Four hours later, Braxton shook Corim awake, moving on to the next cot before Corim had raised an arm to wipe at his sleep-crusted eyes.

"Rise and shine, boys!" the swordmaster shouted, his voice grim. "No time for rest today. While you were all sleeping like the dead, the rest of the Horde's army finally arrived from the north."

23

Colin ducked into the darkest shadows of the lee of the tower, hunkering down to reduce his profile even further. Night still held dominion in the ruined city, but he could see the gray edges of dawn leeching into the horizon to the east, and the low pulse of the light from the Source limned the towers immediately to the north. He'd spent the entire night working his way through the debris-strewn streets, through decrepit buildings and crumbling archways, to the inner isle and the scattered, sheared-off towers. The worst part had been crossing the bridge over the sunken, dried-up riverbeds; he'd been exposed then and could do nothing about it.

And the Haessari were everywhere.

When they'd come here the first time—he and Eraeth and Siobhaen—the Snake People had had patrols around the city, but they'd seen none of them on the streets or lurking in the buildings. Now, they had patrols on all of the major thoroughfares, had camps at intersections and open spaces that had once obviously been parks or markets. He'd approached one such camp earlier, discovered that it had been in use for months, probably since Colin and the others had first come here. Walter must have kept the Snake People away the first time, except for a token force, to better lure them into the trap he'd set at the Well. Eraeth had told him that the Haessari had searched for them after they'd fought Walter and the sukrael at the Source. Were they searching for them still?

No, he thought, as on the street he'd just vacated a patrol of ten of the Snake People marched past, six of them split into two groups that were scouring both sides of the thoroughfare, poking their weapons into the shadows, shining the lights of their torches into empty doorways and windows. The other four remained clustered in the center of the road, their eyes trained on the higher ground.

Colin flattened himself against the stone wall at his back and fought the urge to halt time and slip past them. They weren't searching; they were protecting the Well. If they were searching, they'd be moving from building to building, leaving no nook or crevice in darkness, especially this close to the Well. He could practically taste the cold, silvery waters, could smell the thick richness of leaves and loam. The Source's power pulsed up through the soles of his feet, through the stone at his back, suffusing him. His skin prickled, as if thousands of ants crawled across his flesh, and his bones shivered.

The patrol drew closer. The three nearest to Colin's position rounded the corner and Colin drew in a breath and held it. One of the Haessari halted, nothing more than a shadow silhouetted by the torchlight of the group behind him. A reflection from the torches ran down the snake's blade like orange blood. Colin caught the flicker of the creature's tongue as it tasted the air.

The creature hissed softly and shifted, head lifting.

Gripping tightly to his staff with one hand, Colin began reaching out to seize time—

But one of the creatures in the middle of the street hissed harshly and the one threatening Colin's position spun and responded. It glanced back, torchlight now reflecting off of its scaled hide, then shifted away, the entire group moving off toward the south.

Colin waited until they were out of range, then slipped up and over the dregs of rubble he'd hid behind. He paused, made certain the group hadn't turned back and spotted him, then edged around the corner into the cross street. The horizon was brighter now, light spreading outwards across the land like spilled ink. He could pick out the tops of the shattered towers, could see the striations and etchings in the stone, the nearest like thousands upon thousands of stalks of woven grass, the one beyond rough like bark.

Before him the street ran parallel to an open area with a low wall surrounding it. Shadows pooled everywhere, but he darted across the street to the low wall, slipped over it, grit grinding into stone beneath his chest, and crouched down on its opposite side. Peaking up over its edge, he saw torchlight coming from two different directions.

He needed to reach the towers before they arrived.

Spinning, he raced toward the nearest—the grass tower—moving as silently and swiftly as he could. He was in the inner circle of buildings now. He knew the oval depression and the broken crystal hall that held the Source lay at the center of the towers; its blue-white light mimicked the sunrise, but from the north.

He reached the base of the grass tower, stumbling in the scattered rocks on the wide stairs that led up to its gaping entrance. The stones clattered down the steps and he winced, making a sudden detour into the tower's doorway and the darkness there. He slammed his back against the wall just inside, gasping, then twisted to peer out the opening, across the dead gardens, and into the street.

The Haessari patrols were rushing toward each other. Their dry, hissing language filled the small gardens as they converged. Orders were shouted and they began to spread out, but none of them were headed toward his position. Not yet. They were focused on the area closest to the low wall.

A sudden hiss filled the silence of the grass tower's entrance, followed by a familiar flapping of skin.

The opening of one of the Snake People's cowls.

Colin spun, raising his staff defensively a moment before the creature struck. He caught a blur of movement in the darkness, felt something heavy strike his staff, and then he was driven back into the wall. The attacker crashed into him, pressing him back, its mouth caught on the staff. Venom splattered against Colin's face, burned, but he thrust with all of his strength, drawing his sword as the weight shifted away. He slashed downward, felt it connect, but only lightly, heard a resultant hiss of pain.

He needed to kill this one quickly, before it could warn the others.

But as he shifted his position, stepping forward to clear space for his sword, ready to toss his staff aside, he realized there was more than one of them here.

The entire inner room—what must once have been a foyer—was shifting. Figures were rising from rest, their motions torpid, but even in the faint light of dawn that filtered through the entrance he could see their anger. In the glint of an eye, the flaring of a hood, the flicker of forked tongues as they tasted the air, savored his fear. There were too many to count, nothing but a sense of slithering movement in the shadows. The hiss from the first was joined by others.

He'd stumbled into one of their nests.

A frisson of instinctual terror cascaded down through his body, tingling from his head down to his toes. His fingers tightened on the handle of his sword and the length of his staff; the muscles in his stomach clenched. Sweat broke out across his entire body, prickling with heat in his armpits and down his back.

The waking Haessari hissed again in excitement, began moving faster.

He'd never be able to silence them all, never be able to dodge all of their strikes. Not without slowing or halting time.

A cold calm settled over him, sluicing through the fear-sweat. He'd hoped to make it to the Well without warning Walter, but he'd never really expected it. This simply meant he'd have less time to do what needed to be done.

He took a step toward the doorway, his body relaxed, sword lowered. The Haessari closest to him lurched forward, still groggy from their slumber. In the growing light, their mottled skin glistened as if wet. They wore nothing but a breech clout. One of them, the nearest—with a slick cut along its upper leg seeping blood—hissed harshly, mouth opening wide.

Colin straightened. "Sorry to have disturbed you."

It lunged. With only a tweak of time, Colin swung his blade and loped off its head, blood spurting from the wound in a gush. Before its head thudded to the ground at the mouth of the doorway, Colin seized time and spun, plummeting out the door and down the steps. The Haessari he'd dodged were spread out in the dead garden area beneath the tower and the low wall. He darted to the side, began circling the tower's base, heading toward the pulsating power of the Source.

He'd taken five steps when he felt a fluctuation in the fabric of the world around him, nothing more than a tug, as if someone had tweaked the sleeve of his shirt.

Walter.

Sword still drawn, staff in his other hand, Colin charged headlong down the steps of the tower's far side, the orange-yellow glow of dawn to the east and the throbbing blue-white light of the Source dead ahead.

Walter knew he was here now, and he was coming for him.

* * *

Corim trudged up the stone steps to the parapet behind the rest of his unit, his mind foggy from the mostly sleepless night. Ahead of him, Wade scrambled forward, nearly knocking over those in front of him, shoving a few of them out of the way. Rory raced on his heels, along with a few other boys, but Harden hung back. The taller boy looked haggard, the skin beneath his eyes bruised.

"Couldn't sleep much either, huh?" he said, when he saw Corim looking at him.

"No." Corim had fallen into his cot exhausted, expecting to drop off before he'd even had time to think about it. But that hadn't happened. He'd closed his eyes, but his mind raced, skating through image after image of the battle, vibrating with its intensity. He'd tossed and turned for a full hour before giving up and rolling onto his back, hands behind his head, and simply stared up into the darkness above. He'd listened to the snores and restless, rustling movements of his unit, and the near constant clatter and clang in the streets and the walls beyond.

After the roar of the battle, it had sounded surprisingly quiet.

He'd drifted in and out of a half daze the entire night, until Braxton had shaken him completely awake not twenty minutes ago.

He followed Wade, Rory, and the rest onto the battlements, his stomach rumbling in protest, his hands throbbing, his arms aching and limp at his sides. Wade and Rory rushed to their positions on the wall, claiming a crenellation and leaning out over the stone to get a look at the field. Dawn's light streaked the sky to the east, most of this side of Temeritt's hill still deep in shadow, including the wall, but the plains below—

Coming up behind Wade, Corim halted abruptly. Harden gasped to one side. All along the wall, the soldiers of the Legion and the men, women, and children who'd sought refuge in Temeritt and now fought for their survival were steadily falling silent as the darkness on the plains before the walls was revealed.

Beneath the charred remains of the Autumn Tree, the Horde's camp had nearly tripled in size. Fresh pennants were flying, too distant for Corim to make out, but he knew they weren't all the same as the ones they'd been watching for the past few months. And not all of the vague figures he could see moving through the new tents were familiar either. He thought there were more Alvritshai, but a significant portion of the new army were shorter, their gait somehow odd. Not quite lurching forward, but close. And their heads—

"Are those snouts?" Rory asked, trying to push forward to see better. "It looks like they have snouts."

"Something like that," Harden said. "They certainly don't look human, or Alvritshai. Too tall to be dwarren."

"But they're walking on two legs."

"So do the trolls, and most of the other twisted creatures of the Horde. Doesn't mean much."

"Doesn't matter," Wade said brusquely. "We'll kill them all, whatever they are. Just like we've done to the others."

Corim locked gazes with Harden, saw his own despair mirrored in the other boy's eyes.

"How are we going to do that?" Rory asked. "Look at how many of them there are!"

Wade smacked him hard on the back of the head. "Don't talk like that.

We'll kill them all." Then, in a far weaker voice: "We have to."

"I heard they came from the northeast," Harden ventured after a long awkward silence. "Do you think they destroyed Yhnar before coming here? Or maybe they attacked the dwarren and that's why they haven't come to help us like they were supposed to."

Wade snorted in contempt. "The dwarren never intended to help us. They're probably part of the Horde, like the Alvritshai."

"No," Corim said sharply. "I saw them at Gray's Kill, the night we were attacked. At first we thought they were the ones who attacked, but Gregson said that it looked like the dwarren had been fighting the creatures. They weren't part of the Horde."

"Then where are they? If they were to honor the Accord, they should be here, helping us."

"Maybe they've been attacked themselves."

Wade rolled his eyes and turned back to the crenellation and the field beyond.

Harden shifted closer, exuding an uneasiness that now permeated everyone along the entire wall. "What are we going to do?"

"That isn't up to us."

* * *

"What are we going to do?" Akers grumbled.

GreatLord Kobel didn't answer. He, along with Akers, Tarken Sohn, and a few of his Legion commanders, were clustered at the top of the main gates, sealed once again against the Horde. Akers had returned a mere hour before, along with only a fifth of the men who'd accompanied him in the raid on the Horde's camp. The rest of the men had died creating the havoc that distracted the Horde from Temeritt's walls or in the flight back to the boats. Kobel knew that some of the men had likely been cut off from reaching the boats by the arrival of these new reinforcements, whoever—or whatever—they were. According to Akers' report, he'd waited until the last possible moment before ordering those that had reached the lake's edge to retreat in the boats back to the hidden cavern and its stone docks. Kobel and Tarken had watched the Horde's new forces march across the plains from the northeast, skirting the lake to the north. Both of them were exhausted, but not half as much as Akers. The once robust lord wove erratically where he stood, near collapse, although he refused to leave the tower to rest, even at Kobel's direct order.

"What do you make out?" Kobel asked. Tarken had taken the spyglass from him a few moments earlier.

"A good-sized force of Alvritshai. More than were here earlier. At least three times as many, maybe more. I'd say there are over five thousand Alvritshai on the field now."

"Which Houses?"

Tarken hesitated, shifting the spyglass over the encampment. "I only see the banners of one House, the same black and gold eagle's talon we've seen before. But some of the newcomers' armor doesn't bear the same colors."

"That doesn't make any sense," Akers said, echoing Kobel's thoughts. "If there are Phalanx from other Houses on the field, why aren't they flying their own colors?"

"What about the rest of the army?"

"They're...some kind of lizard creatures," Tarken Sohn answered hesitantly. "Or maybe snake. They're walking on two legs, appear to have arms and hands—they're carrying swords—but their heads... They have some kind of scaled skin and blunt noses."

Kobel's hand rose to rub at his eyes. He'd hoped he'd been seeing things, that the light had distorted the creatures, or that lack of sleep had clouded his vision. "I estimated close to ten thousand of the snake creatures. That, along with the Alvritshai and the rest of the Horde on the field—maybe twenty thousand in all." There were perhaps forty thousand people in Temeritt altogether. A maximum of ten thousand of whom were fit to fight, even if they were half starved.

Any chance of fighting their way free of the Horde had vanished.

"This force must have been what the group holding us here inside the walls was waiting for. They didn't need to break us. They only needed to keep us penned up, like animals waiting for slaughter."

"And now the butcher's arrived."

Kobel glanced toward Tarken Sohn at the comment, but Tarken had trained the spyglass west, toward the rolling hills.

A hard lance of hope speared Kobel's chest and he jerked his head to the west, took an involuntary step forward. But he could see nothing on the horizon. No tell-tale smoke, no plume of dust stirred up by marching feet.

"No sign of the king," Tarken said simply.

Somehow, the unexpected death of that knot of hope hurt worse than all of the wounds he'd received during the fighting the previous day and night. He leaned against the stone parapet, felt its solidity in the rough surface and grit beneath his palms.

Drawing strength from the walls that had kept them safe for so long, he pushed back and turned to face Akers, Tarken Sohn, and the Legion commanders who'd stood stolidly behind them in silence during the entire conversation. His eyes settled on Commander Leighten.

Leighten straightened almost imperceptibly. "GreatLord?"

"Commander Leighten. Go to the palace and inform Lady Echeri that the time has come to flee the city. She should begin the evacuation as planned, starting now. You are to remain with her as escort. Do not leave her side for any reason."

Leighten bowed slightly at the waist, his fist over his heart. "As you command, GreatLord."

He stalked toward the stairs leading down to the courtyard and the streets of Temeritt, motioning others from his unit to join him as he went. Kobel had already turned to the rest of the waiting commanders.

"Take your stations along the wall. The Horde may have received reinforcements, but they have not yet breached our walls. We will hold until King Justinian arrives. No more sorties. No more sneak attacks by night. Hold the walls, at all costs. Dismissed."

The commanders saluted, fists to chests, then departed.

Akers shifted forward, facing outwards as he leaned wearily against the wall. "Do you think Echeri and the others have a chance?"

"Depends on whether the Horde's scouts discover them and the hidden exit or not."

"We didn't have much luck passing single messengers through their scouts earlier. This will be an entire city of refugees."

As if on cue, church bells began to ring in the city, starting near the gates, but spreading quickly. Kobel felt the people of the city pause as the portent of the bells sank in, then resume with perhaps a little more urgency, their tasks abandoned, their steps taking them quickly toward home and hearth and family, and then from there to the palace.

Those who were still well enough and able to move about.

Akers' hand suddenly gripped Kobel's arm tight. "The Horde is moving."

"Sound the warning."

Tarken signaled and a moment later a horn sounded, repeated like an echo down both sides of the wall. Then the GreatLord of Yhnar joined him at his left, Akers on his right. A stiff breeze caught the Temeritt banners all along the parapet, snapping them fitfully. Kobel once again placed his hands on the rough stone of the wall.

They were trapped. And he could see no way out of it.

On the plains before Temeritt, the Horde formed up, the Alvritshai with the black and gold banners in the center, the snake creatures split into two on either side. The black creatures that Temeritt had fought for months flanked this group. They spread out across the grassland, far beyond where the field was already trampled and bloodied. Carrion crows were thick, scavenging on the bodies that Temeritt hadn't had the time to deal with the day before. The stench of rot and death gusted up from the field. Smoke from the fires of the Horde's camp trailed off to the southeast. The blackened branches of the Autumn Tree speared up into the cloudless sky. The new day had broken, the sun risen, all of the shadows of night dead.

Except for within the Horde.

Kobel squinted as a horn sounded from within the Horde's ranks. He snatched the spyglass from Tarken Sohn, the GreatLord frowning in surprise. But he didn't protest.

Kobel placed the glass to his eye and focused on the forefront of the army, near its center.

"What is it?" Akers asked.

"There's a group directly in front of the Alvritshai. I thought it was a shadow from a cloud, or a slight depression in the ground that the sun hadn't yet reached. But the sun's too high already, and there aren't any clouds."

"I see it," Tarken said.

"So do I. I ask again, what is it?"

Kobel lowered the spyglass. "They're Shadows, like those told of in the hearthfire tales, those reported by many of the people who were attacked and driven southward to Temeritt when this all started. The Shadows of legend that drain the life of those they touch, that can't be harmed by sword or spear or arrow, that—"

"That can pass through stone walls as if through air," Tarken Sohn finished.

Akers stiffened. "What can we do?"

Kobel didn't answer. He didn't know what to say.

"There's a group in front of the Shadows," Tarken Sohn said. "On horseback."

Kobel reluctantly put the spyglass to his eye again, his arms tingling with a faint numbness. He had no idea what to expect, what new horror this morning could bring.

But he was surprised into a perplexed frown.

"The Wraiths," he said. "Four of them, three Alvritshai and one dwarren."

"What are they doing?"

"Riding out in front of the Shadows and the rest of the army. Alone."

"Do you think they want to parley?" Akers asked hesitantly. "Ask for our surrender?"

"After what they did to GreatLord Alden and his family?"

Another horn cry, its echo forlorn with distance.

The Horde army's advance halted, still far outside of the ring of death surrounding the walls, but close enough Kobel could pick out individual figures in the separate units.

"Definitely snakes, not lizards," Akers mumbled.

The Wraiths continued moving forward.

"Should someone go meet them?" Tarken Sohn asked.

"No. They've shown no mercy up to this point. I see no reason they would do so now. Whoever went would be slaughtered."

On the field, the Wraiths suddenly broke away from each other, one of the Alvritshai—the leader, by his bearing—heading towards the main gates, the others spreading out to either side. One Alvritshai and the dwarren headed south, the other Alvritshai—the one who had led the Horde before Temeritt up to this point, with the hideous scar at his throat—north, toward the lake.

The new leader abruptly halted, far outside the range of Temeritt's arrows, and dismounted. His black and gold armor shimmered in the sunlight as he stepped forward, picking his way through the scattering of bodies that littered the ground. The carrion crows screeched in protest at the disturbance, a few taking sudden flight, wheeling around him. Most hopped or flapped out of his way.

Twenty paces from his horse, the Wraith stopped.

On the walls to either side, Legionnaires and guardsmen sidled forward, the parapet's edge crowded as everyone tried to see what the Wraiths were doing. The lead Wraith spread his arms wide, palms up. His head tilted back, his eyes closed, as if he were praying to Holy Diermani. To either side, the other Wraiths did the same.

"What in hells are they doing?" Tarken Sohn muttered.

A prickling of unease worked its way down Kobel's spine. He swung the spyglass back to the Wraith leader, the Alvritshai's head beginning to lower. Through the lens, he could see the Wraith's oil-mottled skin, his black hair, the scars along both sides of his face. Kobel recalled the scars meant something in particular—that the Alvritshai who bore them was a criminal of some kind, or had been dishonored in some way—but he couldn't remember precisely. The prickling across his skin deepened, dancing fingers across his shoulders. Around him, the men and lords of the Legion shifted and fidgeted, unsettled.

Through the glass, the Wraith's head leveled and bowed forward slightly. His eyes popped open, staring at Temeritt's walls, at its gates.

Then the Wraith's arms swung forward and down and he clapped his hands together.

The sound that followed was a hundred times louder than it should have been. It boomed across the battlefield, rolling across the walls and into the city behind like thunder, echoing in the streets and buildings. Some of the men on the wall started, one or two crying out. Kobel felt the hollow boom in his chest, thrumming in his lungs. It was followed within the space of a breath by three others, each of the Wraiths bringing their hands together to create overlapping growls of thunder.

Kobel exhaled and drew another breath to ask, "Was that it?" when he noticed movement. Not in the ranks of the Horde, or even the Shadows that writhed back and forth before them. But on the ground.

No, not *on* the ground. The ground itself.

Starting before the lead Wraith, the ground shuddered and jumped, a ripple forming, then spreading outwards like a wave on water. It grew as it advanced, becoming a ridge as it sped toward Temeritt's walls. The bodies of the dead, their weapons, anything that lay on the ground was tossed upwards, crashing back to the earth behind it. The carrion birds lifted in shrieking protest as it passed, like a black, feathery, glistening curtain rising into the air. And still the wave of earth plowed forward, rising higher and higher and picking up speed. Three other waves raced away from the other three Wraiths.

"Holy Diermani protect us," Lord Akers gasped, his voice thin.

"How can we defend against this?" Tarken asked.

"We can't," Kobel responded, then faced his men. "Secure everything on the walls that you can and hold onto something! Hold on tight!"

"What is there to hold onto?" someone shouted, but Kobel could barely hear him. The sound of the approaching wave was growing, at first nothing but a minor rumble, but now escalating into a roar, like the sound of a stone avalanche. The stone wall beneath him had begun to tremble, the shudder transferring up through his feet into his bones. Everyone on the tower had scrambled at his command, some reaching to grab and secure weapons, oil, pitch, whatever they had on hand; still others searched for something to grab onto. A few had panicked and were running for the stairs. He turned back to the plains in time to see the wave nearly at the wall. GreatLord Sohn snagged his arm and hauled him toward the crenellation, practically throwing him up against the stone. Kobel reached out and dug his fingers into any available crevice or crease, then shouted again, "Hold on! It's going to—"

And then it hit the wall.

The stone beneath Kobel heaved upwards, tossing everyone. The wall of earth sprayed up the stone battlements and rained back down to the ground like an ocean's wave hitting the rocky cliffs of a shoreline. Cries of terror and screams of panic surrounded him. The Legion was scattered, soldiers laying everywhere, moaning or groaning, a few picking themselves up. Kobel hauled himself up to his knees, his armor scraping against rock. A large dent on the left front dug into his chest. To his right, Lord Akers was pulling himself into a standing position with a wince, favoring his left arm. Tarken Sohn was already standing, looking down into the courtyard behind the gates.

Kobel moved up to his side. Below, the courtyard was a shambles. The wave had obviously shunted under the wall, blunted but not halted. Cracks and upheavals riddled the flagstones. One of the nearest buildings had collapsed along two sides and another was leaning heavily into the street. People were dragging themselves up from where they'd been thrown. Three men were trying to calm the horses; most of the animals had already panicked and were fleeing toward the central part of the city.

At least five Legionnaire bodies were sprawled on the stone directly below the wall.

"They were thrown from the wall when it hit," Tarken said.

Before Kobel could respond, another of the loud claps of thunder resounded across the city.

Lord Akers shouted, "Here comes another one!"

Kobel sprinted toward the battlement, caught sight of the second wave of earth heading toward them. Claps of thunder sounded from the right and left as well. He leaned heavily against the stone and dropped his head, trying to think. To his left, the stone of the parapet had cracked. He reached out and traced the fine line with one finger.

As he did so, a runner raced to his side, gasping, his eyes wide with fright. "GreatLord Kobel, sir!"

"Report."

"The inner portcullis is twisted, the iron bent, and one of the wooden gates has splintered. We don't think the cullis can be raised or the gates opened."

"Grab onto something."

"What?" the youth asked, bewildered.

"Grab onto something!"

Kobel reached forward and hauled the boy down to the stone a moment before it heaved upwards under the second wave. The cries of terror from the wall were louder this time, and there were more screams as people were thrown from the heights to the streets below. This time Kobel heard the wall crack, a sharp retort that sent shivers into his teeth. Far to the right, a gap opened up as part of the wall sagged inward toward the city before catching and holding. The Legion on that section pulled themselves up the small slant, one man who was hanging from the edge slipping and falling from sight.

Kobel leaped to his feet. "Sound the retreat!" he bellowed, but his voice was lost in the overlap of two more thunderous claps. He didn't even turn to look at the battlefield below, instead stalking forward and yanking one of his commanders to his feet. "Sound the retreat! Fall back to the secondary wall! Move fast, before this one crumbles away beneath us!"

Kobel shoved the commander toward his men, moved swiftly around the tower, hauling others to their feet and pointing them toward the stairs. "Descend to the courtyard. Now! Get everyone who's able to head toward the secondary walls."

The third wave hit and Kobel was flung forward, landing hard. He scrambled for purchase. Weapons and men in armor clattered around him and fresh screams arose from the courtyard below. A barrel of pitch juddered and tipped over the edge of the parapet. A jug of oil crashed to the stone near Kobel's outstretched hand and shattered, splattering him and slicking the walkway. Its pungent reek hit Kobel's nostrils like a hammer, but as it drained toward the edge where the pitch had vanished he realized that the tower was leaning.

He crawled up the slope to where Tarken was crouched down, feet braced before him, back tucked against the crenellation. Lord Akers clung to the stone with one hand, on his knees, his other hand flat against the walkway for support.

"The walls are going to come down around us if we don't move!" Kobel shouted over another growl of thunder.

Far to the left, he heard a hideous crack, as of a mountain splitting, and glanced down the parapet in that direction. An entire section of the wall had riven free and was tumbling down into the city behind, men falling or leaping from it as it descended. It slammed into a building, pulverizing it, a screen of dust rising to obscure the view.

He turned back to both lords, pulling himself close enough they could help him regain his feet. "It's already started. The outer wall is lost."

"Without even a fight," Akers said bitterly. "Bastards."

"What makes you think the secondary walls are going to last any longer?" Tarken asked.

Kobel barked a vicious laugh. "They'll have to work their way through the entire first ward first."

* * *

"Maintain your positions!" Braxton bellowed. "Stay where you are!"

Corim hadn't moved, was still huddled with Harden, Rory, and Wade against the parapet as another of the massive waves of earth hit them from behind. Rory was thrown forward, screaming, but Harden caught his leg as the entire section of wall canted toward the city. Harden strained to hold on. All along the length of the wall, soldiers were braced, clutching the crenellations for support, or crawling toward the stairs leading down to the street below. At least three were clinging to the edge of the walk, a few trying to haul them back to safety. Braxton had been thrown to his stomach twenty paces away. The sword master looked up from where he'd fallen, hands beneath his chest, his expression enraged. He shoved himself up to his knees, glared at those who were fleeing, and pointed with one trembling hand. "Come back here, you cowards! We haven't been given orders to retreat!"

Corim let go of his perch and lurched toward Rory, snagging his other leg. They dragged him back to their own position.

"This can't be happening," Wade muttered. The merchant son's entire body was shaking. "This can't be happening! What are they doing to us? How are they doing this?"

"We can't stay here," Harden said, ignoring Wade's rambling.

"But Braxton said—"

"Fuck Braxton!" Harden spat. "If we stay here, we're going to go down with the wall!"

Rory gaped, then turned a questioning look on Corim.

"Harden's right. We can't stay here. We have to get off the wall." Corim glanced toward the sword master. "Hang on. And watch Wade. I think he's lost it."

Corim didn't wait for Harden or Rory to agree. He scrambled down the slope of the walkway toward Braxton, the sword master still on his knees in the same spot, glaring after the deserters. The wall shuddered and tilted still farther to the left as he drew near, practically throwing him into Braxton's side.

The sword master jerked in shock, then caught him by the shoulders. His eyes were feral, not quite sane, somehow appearing lost in the wrinkles of his face. His graying hair hung in wispy tendrils from beneath his slightly skewed helm.

A roll of thunder ground over them as Braxton shook him. "Stay at your post! How many times do I have to tell you—"

"We can't!" Corim roared into his face, and was gratified to see Braxton rear back from him as if slapped. "We can't stay at our posts! The wall is collapsing! Look around you. If we stay here we'll be killed. We have to get off the wall now!" He swallowed, then added, "Sir."

Braxton blinked and glanced around, the frenetic rage settling back into something resembling his old self. "You're right." He pushed Corim in the direction of the open mouth of the stairwell. "Go! Now! Before the next wave hits!"

Corim twisted and motioned Harden and the others toward him, then began angling down the parapet's walkway in a half crouch. From behind, he heard Braxton ordering everyone off the wall, but he focused on keeping his feet. Stones meant to be thrown off the wall littered the way, along with abandoned weapons, helms, arrows, and other supplies. Most of the men who'd been assigned to this section of the wall had already fled, but as Braxton continued issuing orders, those that remained sprinted toward the safety of the stairs and the streets below.

Halfway to the opening, Corim looked back to see Harden and Rory urging Wade before them, the merchant's son nearly frozen in terror. They were barely moving, Harden forced to pry Walter's hands from the crenellations to get him to move at all. Rory had lost patience, spouting imprecations under his breath as he tried to drag him along from the front.

Then another one of the waves struck and the wall lurched.

Behind the other three, a section of wall swiveled inwards, a horrendous crack shattering the chaos as the stone split. Harden, Rory, and Wade were thrown to the parapet, Wade's scream shrill. Braxton and three other men closer to the crack went tumbling toward the canted edge. Two slid over without a sound. The third landed hard on his stomach and managed to halt his fall.

Braxton grabbed frantically and caught himself as his legs and lower torso dropped out into space.

At the same time, Corim heard stone grinding together, the sound coming up through his feet and hands where he crouched. He spun back around toward the stairs, no more than twenty paces away, and watched as that entire section pulled free and collapsed inwards, imploding into a spew of debris as it sagged down into the street and buildings below. The plume of dust billowed back into Corim's face and he coughed, raising one hand futilely to cover his eyes, but the breeze was already carrying the cloud away.

From his position, where there had once been wall, he could see directly out onto the body-strewn battlefield where the Wraiths and the Horde waited. A roar of triumph rolled across the distance, and the Horde began to charge forward, even though the Wraiths were still pummeling the walls with their power. All along the wall's length, the stone had cracked and split, gaps opened up at random, some sections twisted and skewed like the one Corim and his friends stood on, others fallen inwards or collapsed into rubble like the stairwell before him.

"Shit," Corim muttered. The word felt odd in his mouth—he'd never sworn before—but appropriate.

He thought suddenly of Jayson and Ara.

He glanced toward the gap that used to contain stairs, then darted toward Harden and Rory, both with jaws dropped. Wade was cowering against the battlement's edge.

"We can't get out that way anymore." Corim snagged both Rory's and Harden's attention with a punch to the shoulder. "Go back. We'll have to get to the other stairs. Rory, get Wade moving. Harden, I'll need your help with Braxton."

Relieved no one protested or balked, he and Harden half skidded to where Braxton still hung over the edge of the battlements, kicking loose weapons and supplies out of their way as they descended. The other soldier had twisted around and, still flat on his stomach, was holding onto the sword master's arm, both of their faces red with strain as Braxton tried to lift himself up over the side. Harden and Corim reached them in moments, Harden grabbing onto Braxton's other arm. But there wasn't anything he could use for leverage.

"We can't lift him," Harden gasped. "He's too heavy with the armor."

"And there's nothing we can brace against," the other soldier muttered.

"Have to...swing my...legs up. Corim...catch them."

"Hold him tight. Don't drop him."

Veins stood out in Braxton's forehead and both Harden and the soldier tightened their grip. Braxton began swinging his legs back and forth, breath puffing with effort. The soldier began to skid toward the edge to one side, but he cocked a knee and halted himself. Then, with an excrutiating growl, Braxton heaved his legs upward.

His feet hooked up over the edge, but he instantly began to fall back. One leg slipped free, but Corim snatched the other before it could drop away and hauled himself backwards on his ass up the slope of the walkway, heels digging into the stone. Harden barked, "Pull!" and both he and the other soldier drew back, Harden doing most of the work. Braxton's upper body scraped over the edge, the sound of his armor against the stone making Corim's teeth ache, but he slid back onto the parapet.

Corim dropped Braxton's leg. "We need to get off the wall. The Horde's coming."

"Then go," Braxton gasped, waving with one hand. "Don't wait for me! Get to the secondary walls, or find another unit and join with them."

Corim hesitated, but Harden and the soldier were already moving, angling toward the crack in the wall where Rory was waiting anxiously with Wade. "Move it!" Rory shouted. "The Horde's almost here!"

Corim tugged on Braxton's arm. "Come on. We didn't haul you back so you could just lay here and get killed by the Horde."

Braxton glared at him, but rolled onto his side, then hands and knees. Only when he began struggling up the slanted walkway did Corim head toward the others. The old sword master was wincing in pain, but he was moving.

When Wade paused at the edge of the crack—at least five feet across—Rory shoved him from behind. He half leaped, half fell to the other section of wall, which had tilted, but not as much as the one they were on. Rory vaulted over next, with Harden and the soldier hard on his heels. All four of them began sprinting down the empty walk toward the far set of stairs, Wade with only a little urging from Rory.

Corim leapt without slowing, landing hard and catching himself against the stone crenellation. He turned and glanced toward Braxton, then out over the parapet to the plains beyond.

Another wave of earth had almost reached them, and immediately behind it streamed the northernmost portions of the Horde—the black and twisted creatures that had held them within these walls for nearly six months.

"Run!" he screamed to Braxton. "Run, Diermani damn you!"

The sword master surged forward, his low crouch awkward. Corim waved him on as if he could somehow pull him along as the stone beneath his feet began to shudder. The roar of the wind, the screams of the approaching Horde, and the growl of the disturbed earth filled Corim's ears. He caught the wave out of the corner of his eye a moment before Braxton jumped—

And then it hit. The section of wall beneath him trembled, but the one Braxton had just left groaned and tilted inwards, the far side falling faster. Braxton hit the stone of the stable section and staggered forward, the collapsing section thudding into the ground below with a bone-shuddering crunch. But Corim was already running toward the stairs, Braxton at his side. They could hear the Horde as they hit the top of the stairs and plunged into the darkened corridor beyond. The sounds of the others echoed up from below. They passed a landing, torches highlighting the cracks in the walls, a chunk of stone from the ceiling, the sprawl of a dead Legionnaire. They spilled abruptly out onto the street, the dust from the collapsed sections of wall to their right, people—not just soldiers, but the citizens of Temeritt who'd been helping them with food, water, and supplies as they manned the wall—fleeing toward the interior of the city.

The soldier who'd helped them save Braxton took off after the others and disappeared into the crowds. Braxton glared after his retreating form, then spat to one side in disgust.

"We have to get to the second wall." Braxton was bent forward slightly at the waist. One hand rested on Corim's shoulder. "But not by the main gates. They're going to be overrun. We'll have to follow the streets east and north, try to reach one of the lesser gates before the Horde overtakes us." He began limping in that direction, Harden, Wade, and Rory on his heels.

Corim thought of Jayson and Ara again. Last he knew they'd been stationed at the main gates. His heart said to find them, to rush into the growing sound of death and chaos in that direction; his gut told him to follow Braxton's orders. He felt torn.

Then Rory called, "Come on, Corim, what are you waiting for?"

Corim jumped. At the same time, the Horde began pouring through the gaping hole in the wall to the south, the creatures shrieking in triumph as they fell on the soldiers and citizens attempting to flee.

He turned and sprinted after Rory as Braxton and the rest disappeared into the shadows of a narrow alley between two buildings. One of them had half collapsed from the destructive power of the Wraiths' waves, its roof sagging down in its center. The wooden slats of its face had splintered in a ragged tear down its front. But the alley between was clear.

Even as he slipped into its relative safety, he hoped Jayson and Ara had fled the main gates when they had a chance. He hoped he'd find them at the second wall.

And then he focused on staying alive long enough to reach the wall himself.

* * *

"Ara! Ara! What in hells are you doing?"

Ara glared at the interloper as he tore across the interior of the warehouse that had been converted into a medical ward. Rows upon rows of pallets lined the room, many still with patients in them, nearly all of them unconscious. Those who were able had dragged themselves to their feet after the second rolling wave had passed through and staggered out of the building into the streets. She was working hard on resetting the arm of one of those that remained.

Her glare faded when she saw it was Jayson.

"I'm trying to save this man's life." She cinched the bandage with a jerk. The soldier screamed, but she had to get it tight if she had any hope of saving the arm.

Dancing through the bodies, Jayson reached her side, one hand falling to her shoulder and pulling her back. "Leave him. The walls are collapsing. The Horde is already on its way."

"I can't just leave him! Any of them. All of the rest have already fled."

Jayson sank into a crouch while the man she worked on moaned. He was panting heavily. He'd bit the inside of his mouth and blood stained his lips. He stared up at Ara and Jayson with distant eyes, not really seeing them.

"I have to reset the bone," Ara said, her words strangely calm. In the background, she could hear a sudden escalation of screams, which she ignored. "It's going to hurt. There's nothing I can do about that."

Jayson grabbed her arm and shook her. "The Horde's breached the walls. Can't you hear that? We have to leave! Now!"

"I have to set his bone."

"He's already dead! If you stay here, you're going to die too!"

She was about to spit out angry, hateful words about abandoning his fellow soldiers when another hand clamped down onto the one she still held against the wounded man's shoulder.

She glanced down, caught the man's eyes—a green-flecked brown— and realized they were clear, no longer hazed with pain. His fingers dug into her own, his grip stronger than she would have expected considering how much blood he'd lost.

"Go," he whispered. "Before it's too late."

That was all the encouragement Jayson needed. He surged to his feet, dragging her up with him. Her hand slid from the soldier's shoulder, although he clutched her with his own hand as long as he could. His good arm fell back to his side as Jayson dragged her away. Tears burned her eyes, blurred her vision, which was probably good because then she couldn't see the others they were leaving behind to their deaths. She'd fought to save them all since the battle began, had staunched their wounds, reset bones, held their hands as others worked on tying bandages or sewed up flesh. She'd looked into their eyes as they died, or comforted them as the pain became too great and they passed out.

Before they reached the main door, it burst open and another soldier charged through. Jayson drew to a halt, swore under his breath. Ara caught a glimpse of the courtyard beyond, saw it overrun with strange shadowy black creatures, snake-like creatures pouring over the rubble of a collapsed section of the wall behind them. The main gates still stood, but the Horde was already slaughtering the people who remained behind. An entire section of Legion fell beneath the Shadows, the creatures darting forward and enfolding them as they tried to run. The snake creatures were catching those the Shadows left behind. Ara would have remained watching, paralyzed in horror, except the soldier slammed the door closed.

"Owen, what happened?" Jayson dropped Ara's arm as he leaped to help the man shove a nearby table against the door.

"Those damned shadows and snake things. They broke through our unit like a scythe through grass."

"What about Gregson? Terson and the others?"

"I was cut off. I heard Gregson order everyone back to the second wall, then saw them charge up the main street. GreatLord Kobel was on the other side of the courtyard and his men did the same thing. It's a free for all down here, and the Horde's pouring in through the cracks."

Jayson turned to Ara. "Is there another door out of here? There has to be."

Ara gathered herself, the realization of what was happening sinking in. "There's a side door toward the back. It opens onto an alley."

"Show me."

Ara darted toward the back of the room, weaving between the pallets, trying not to look down. Jayson and Owen were right behind her, practically stepping on her heels. Owen had his sword out, but Jayson carried nothing. She saw him stop to retrieve a sword and dagger from one of the wounded as they neared the back wall.

"Here it is," she said.

Jayson thrust the dagger into her hands and she took it grimly. Jayson eased the door open and snatched a look outside, then motioned Owen and Ara out.

They stepped into a half-lit alley, filth staining the stone of the ground and lower portions of the buildings to either side. Trash rounded out the corners and the rank smell of decay, shit, and piss assaulted Ara's senses as she turned toward the opening onto the street. In the sunlight there, people were screaming and sprinting eastwards, moving so fast she barely caught a glimpse of them before they were gone. She'd started toward them when Jayson snagged her by the shoulder and tilted his head in the other direction. "This way."

As soon as he said it, the snake creatures appeared, one of them cutting a woman down from behind. She stumbled and fell with a shriek. A man staggered backwards into sight, arms raised protectively before him, and then a wicked S-shaped blade descended and gutted him. He screamed and fell sideways into the alley, trying to hold his stomach and intestines in place. The snake creature stepped into the alley and stabbed his blade into the man's back, then glanced up and noticed them.

It hissed, a hideous sound. Ara screamed, and the creature loped forward, its tail flicking back and forth behind it.

Owen stepped in front of her. Jayson grabbed her arm again and hauled her in the opposite direction. Owen retreated with them, facing the snake creature as it charged. Their blades clashed, loud in the confines of the alley, but Jayson didn't slow. Sunlight flashed on metal, and then Owen lunged forward, his sword punching through the snake's chest. It tried to hiss, produced a gurgling sound instead, its split tongue flicking the air. Owen jerked his sword free and turned, running before its body had fallen to the ground.

"Go!"

And they ran, slipping in the garbage and run-off of the alley. Ahead, it turned and they lost sight of the street behind. The sounds of the fighting were muffled. The alley opened onto a secondary street.

They slowed as they reached the edge, but there was no sign of the Horde beyond. Men, women, and a few children were racing up the street toward the inner walls, but they weren't being chased yet. But Ara could hear the sounds of the attack clearly here, and they were getting closer.

"We don't have much time," Owen said. "I doubt the Horde will wait to search through the buildings. They'll drive straight toward the second wall, figuring they can take care of everyone who's hiding later."

"Then we'd better not waste any time," Ara said, and stepped out into the street.

They started at a cautious jog, blades raised, all three of them trying to look in every direction at once. But within a block, they were running, with what seemed like the entire first ward's population crowding the street along with them.

* * *

Lady Echeri herded a slew of families—mothers with clutches of children, others with the elderly—through the doors of the palace with a calm but forceful, "Follow the line of guardsmen to the catacombs. Don't stray or we may never find you." Her words were overlaid with the still clanging bells of the city's churches and the Legionnaires directing the column of humanity with shouts of "This way! Don't rush! Leave everything behind except what you can carry in your hands or pockets!" Already, both sides of the courtyard were heaped with carts laden with furniture, barrels, and assorted other objects that the soon-to-be refugees had thought couldn't be left behind. Guards were seizing such useless items and tossing them aside, sometimes yanking them from the clutches of their owners before shoving the hapless, often distraught, people toward the palace doors. Echeri had ordered the guards to stop attempting to explain why they couldn't be taken down into the catacombs. There wasn't time anymore. Temeritt had run out of time.

"If they don't agree," she muttered to herself, "they can take their chances with the Horde."

Another hollow boom echoed up from the plains and she turned, using one hand to pull the black strands of her hair away from her face. People were streaming from the second ward through the palace gates, its courtyard, and up the steps into the palace. Hundreds upon hundreds of people—most of them with looks of terror and panic, a few of them sobbing, all of them bedraggled and haggard and thin. Echeri's heart reached out to them, but she could offer no real comfort. Her already diminutive figure had thinned as well over the last few months as the rationing began in earnest. Her clothes may have been of finer quality, but she had survived on bread and water for the last three days, not to mention her share of pigeon and rat.

But the boom had come from the outer walls. She dragged her gaze from the disheartening column toward the city; she couldn't see the walls from this position.

Cursing, she hiked up the hem of her dress and moved swiftly toward the door to the side of the gates.

"Lady Echeri," a gruff voice barked.

She halted and asked impatiently, "What is it, Commander Higgins?"

The Legion commander stalked toward her, a frown of disapproval plastered on his face. "You should not be roaming off unescorted."

Echeri began moving toward the doorway again. Commander Leighten had set Higgins to guard her before vanishing inside the palace to oversee the evacuation. "No need to fret, commander. I'm heading up to the walls for a better view. The Legion certainly doesn't need me to help usher the populace into the catacombs."

"Perhaps not, but you should not be left alone."

Echeri didn't answer. Irritation pricked her skin when Higgins continued to follow her, all while bellowing, "Slow and steady, now! No need to rush." Then, under his breath, "At least, not at the moment."

Echeri's irritation faltered, her thoughts turning to Kobel. She ducked into the darkness of the inner wall and hurried up the stairwell, emerging onto the palace wall's battlements. A few of the Legion glanced her way, bowing slightly, but returned their attention to the city below as soon as they saw Higgins.

Echeri couldn't stifle a gasp.

Beyond the sloping rooftops of the city, the wall was nothing more than a ragged line of stone slabs. Columns of smoke were beginning to rise from the edges of the city through the breaches. The Horde pressed against the shattered defenses, a black stain on the plains, too numerous to enter even through the gaps. And she knew they had entered the city, even without the telltale signs of smoke. She could hear the clash of weapons and the screams, muted by distance but still audible.

"How long do you think we have?"

"GreatLord Kobel will attempt to gain the second wall and hold them there."

Echeri raised one eyebrow. "And how long will it take them to breach that? The outer walls fell in less than an hour, without the aid of siege engines."

"I'd call whatever those Diermani-forsaken Wraiths did a fairly powerful siege engine, but I take your meaning." He chewed on his lower lip, then scanned the people crowding the courtyard below. "We need to move these people through faster."

"We can't and you know it. The escape tunnel that leads through the catacombs wasn't built for the use of the entire city. It was meant for the

GreatLord, his family, and his escort."

"Then I suggest we use it for that purpose."

It took Echeri a moment to realize what he meant, but when she did, she stiffened in affront. "I will not abandon Temeritt or Kobel, not while its walls still stand." She turned away from him and stalked along the wall toward the south and east. She heard the clomp of Higgins' tread behind her, but ignored it until he grabbed her shoulder and swung her around.

"You are the Lady of Temeritt," he said, keeping his voice low. "Commander Leighten gave your protection into my hands, personally. If it becomes necessary, I will drag you into the tunnels myself."

"Pray that it doesn't become necessary."

Before Higgins could respond a shout went up from the people crammed into the streets below the walls. Not a cry of terror, but of hope. They were pointing out over the city toward the plains, their faces alight, their despair at least temporarily banished. Many of them were shouting, "Look! To the west, to the west!" A young woman close beneath their position clasped her hands together and cried, "Is that the king?"

Echeri spun, one arm rising to shade her eyes, Higgins releasing his hold to step protectively in front of her. Through the columns of smoke— and fire, she could see fire now, flames dancing above a slew of buildings south of the gates—an army had appeared. She couldn't make out much, the line of men and horses distorted by the heat and smoke.

"More reinforcements for the Horde?" she asked.

"Not judging by the Horde's reaction."

She dropped her gaze to the broken walls to see the black stain of the Horde near the walls beginning to change shape, reforming, spreading out as they turned to face the men on the ridge. The line was growing, more and more ranks appearing to either side.

"Look," Higgins said, and pointed.

To the north, a second group had appeared.

Echeri's heart quickened. "Diermani's Hands," she whispered. "*Is* it the king?"

* * *

"The walls are already broken," Roland muttered, hands holding tight to the reins of his horse as it pawed the ground in anticipation. He faced the king. To either side, orders were being shouted left and right, the Legion of three Provinces rushing to form up their ranks, vying for a position on the front lines. "But not the secondary walls. I think we arrived in time."

Justinian sat proud and regal on a horse that was perhaps a little too large for his small, young frame. "If we hadn't been delayed by running into GreatLord Went's forces and the Alvritshai and dwarren..." He let the thought wander, but both of them turned toward where Went and his allies were forming up on the second ridge to the north, their banners flapping in the stiffening wind from the west.

"We're going to need them," Roland said. "If what Tamaell Thaedoren and the dwarren Archon said is true, then the Wraith army is even larger than our initial count."

"My king, beware the skies!"

Both Justinian and Roland spun back to the battle playing out below them in time to see at least a dozen black shapes winging toward them.

"Those aren't carrion crows," Roland muttered. "Archers, to the front! Move, move, move!"

He heard the order repeated down the line, his hands tightening on the reins as the creatures wheeled closer, growing in size.

"What are they?"

Roland shrugged and glanced back over his shoulder. "Where are those damned archers?"

Two units sprinted forward, hastily stringing bows and nocking arrows, their commander bellowing orders. Roland heard the creak of the bows as they were drawn, turned his attention back to the field, where the creatures were now close enough he could make out their leathery wings and long wicked beaks. A second bony structure jutted from the back of their heads. Two of them shrieked, the sound like metal being scraped down stone, and then they dove. The others behind them—thirteen altogether—answered and suddenly streaked out to the left and right, moving faster than any bird Roland had ever seen.

Behind, the archer commander roared, "Fire!"

Arrows shot into the sky, the area over Roland's head momentarily dark. The two headed toward their position screamed again, attempting to dodge, but at least three of the arrows found their marks. Both creatures lurched in mid-air, one folding up and plummeting to the ground with a shriek that raked down Roland's spine like claws. His shoulders bunched as the creature hit the ground with a crunch not twenty paces away and didn't move. The second flyer twisted and turned as it fell, then recovered and winged away toward the burnt husk of the Autumn Tree.

The rest of the creatures fared worse. Roland caught their jagged shapes as they crumpled to the ground out of the corners of his eyes, but didn't look.

His attention was back on the main army attacking Temeritt. "They've seen us."

At the same moment, a horn cry blasted across the plain from the direction of Went's forces.

"The Alvritshai, dwarren, and Rendell Legion are ready," Justinian said unnecessarily. An edge of excitement had crept into the young king's voice. His horse edged forward and he drew his sword. "Ready the horn."

Roland drew his own blade. He wondered if Justinian were ready for this—for the harshness of battle, for the cruelty and brutality.

He glanced behind them, met the gazes of the Legionnaires he had hand-picked himself to be Justinian's guard during the battle, and received a nod from each. They had all vowed to die protecting the king, not just the vow all Legionnaires take upon reaching the end of their training, but a personal vow made to Roland, sealed with spit and blood.

But there was no more time for anything else.

The horn bearer drew breath and raised the silver coronet to his lips.

* * *

On the northern ridge, Tamaell Thaedoren's eyes narrowed at the battlefield below as Went signaled their readiness from the center of their forces. On the human's other flank, he could just make out Quotl and the dwarren, the Archon sitting astride his gaezel with a small cluster of other shamans and Riders a good thirty paces in front of the others. He appeared to be chanting and blessing the field, his hands raised to the sky, a few others shaking their scepters back and forth on either side.

To his right, Caeden shook his head in disbelief. "Do they do anything without first asking the gods?"

Thaedoren turned a baleful look on the young lord of Nuant. "Have you not said a prayer to Aielan this morning?"

To his other side, Daedelan muttered, "The city is on fire. We need to attack now, to distract the Wraith army and give Temeritt a chance to recover."

"I don't believe King Justinian will wait." They'd just watched them cut down the flyers. "Besides, it was you who suggested we hit them on two fronts."

"And it's still a good plan. Better now that the walls have fallen, since a good part of their forces are already inside. It will take them time to withdraw and reorganize. But there are still more of them than there are of us, and we have no way of knowing what the Wraiths can do after seeing how they destroyed the walls."

They'd emerged from the dwarren tunnels two days before, marched hard and fast through the lands south of the trailing edge of the Escarpment—rough terrain, with the ground broken by numerous chasms and gorges, running streams, and heavy forest—only to run into King Justinian's forces the day before. The two armies had nearly come to blows, both forces tense and on edge, before Justinian's Commander Roland had recognized Went's colors. They'd quickly parlayed and compared information, strategized and planned.

But the Wraith's destruction of Temeritt's walls that morning had been a shock. They'd intended to attack while the Wraith army was attempting to take the walls. Both Went and Justinian had sent runners as soon as the walls began to crumble under whatever power the Wraiths were controlling, but neither Thaedoren nor Quotl had been able to respond with more than simple determination.

"Are the warriors of the Flame ready?" Thaedoren asked. "They are our only protection against whatever the Wraiths may throw at us."

"What few of them survived Caercaern and joined us, yes."

"They are to stay back until we see what the Wraiths do."

Daedelan issued the orders. Thaedoren noted that the dwarren shamans had ended their ritual and were scrambling toward new positions, although Quotl and the Riders—including their leader Ikterru—remained out in front.

"This is historic," Thaedoren muttered.

"How do you mean?"

"All three races together on the battlefield."

"We've all met on the battlefield before."

"Yes," Thaedoren allowed, "but this time we are all allies."

He straightened in his saddle, his mount picking up on the change in stance and shifting beneath him, snorting in anticipation. To either side, he felt the rest of the gathered Alvritshai tense, led by their respective lords—both new and old—and a small contingent of acolytes from the Order of Aielan. They could all feel the tremble in the air. It prickled their skin, raised the fine hairs on the napes of their necks and backs of their arms. It clawed its way into their guts and gnawed on their bones.

And then the horn from Justinian's army blew.

24

Colin plummeted down the steps of the bowl surrounding the shattered building that housed the Source, the air here suffused with the blue glow of the Lifeblood within. The streets at the center of the ruined city were crawling with the Snake People—he'd been forced to seize time again and again as he scrambled from the tower and the snake pit he'd stumbled into—but here, within the depression, there were no Haessari. None of them had entered, even though they were swarming through the empty husks of the broken towers above. Dawn had shifted into midmorning, but the pressure to reach the Well and sever Walter's and the Wraiths' control of it pushed him forward. Because he knew time must be running short. He could feel it in his bones.

Even so, when he reached the bottom of the steps and entered the blackness of the entrance at their base, he slowed, adjusting the satchel on his back and bringing his staff and sword forward. As he slid through the darkness of the inner rooms, he listened intently and strained for any tug on the fabric of the world that would tell him Walter was near. But he heard nothing, not even the hiss and clatter of the riled Haessari on the street above. The air tasted stale and used, and he felt nothing around him but the solidity of stone and the heavy mantle of age. He felt certain no one had trespassed within the Source's walls except Walter since he, Eraeth, and Siobhaen had fought here nearly a year before, not even the Haessari. But the throb of the Source may be masking anything he could pick up. It beat against him now that he was this close, a steady pressure that pounded in his head, in his blood. He shuddered at its raw power, his mouth suddenly parched, his body screaming for the slick, coolness of the Lifeblood. It promised to quench a thirst that he knew was unending, to calm his stuttering nerves. But the promise was a lie. He'd broken himself free of the Lifeblood's chains ages ago.

But even that was a lie. He didn't have to look at his hands to see the oily taint that riddled his body. That insidious darkness that roiled beneath his skin itched this close to the Source. And he knew that to defeat

Walter, he would have to give in to the Well's taint, would have to embrace it fully. It was the only way to make himself Walter's equal.

He rounded a corner, one hand brushing along the wall to the right for guidance, and the bluish glow of the Well peeked around the curve of the hall ahead. He stepped forward carefully, moving as silently as possible. The blue light grew, pulsing with a slow, steady beat. The outlines of a wide door appeared and Colin crept to its edge, back to the wall behind him. He braced himself for a quick look into the rounded room he knew lay beyond.

"You can come out, Colin, I know you're there." Then, in a mocking tone, "Or should I call you Shaeveran?"

Colin exhaled with a sharp curse. He bowed his head briefly, thought of Eraeth and Siobhaen, of Aeren and Thaedoren far to the north, Laurelen to the south, and Quotl and the dwarren likely still fighting the Wraith armies to the west.

Then he turned the corner.

Walter stood in the center of the room near the Source, his figure silhouetted by the harsh glare of the Well's light. The broken crystal shards that littered the entire room refracted that light into a blinding dance of prisms. Colin squinted, raising his sword arm to block its intensity until his eyes adjusted. The few details of the room he could make out blurred, but slowly more and more of the room came into focus. He lowered his arm after brushing away tears, scanned the tiered room, the doors and alcoves around its edges, the open sky above, but kept his attention fixed on Walter for any sudden moves. His old tormentor remained where he stood, waiting, still cloaked by the light of the Source.

"There's no one else here. They're all outside in the city. Or off killing your friends."

He didn't trust Walter, but he stepped out into the room, moving slowly toward the Source, angling slightly to the right as he maneuvered himself around the shards of crystal. "I would have thought you'd have an escort of Haessari here."

"The Snakes? They won't set foot inside the bowl for religious reasons. They feel the city is sacred, that it holds the power of the gods. Initially they refused to even enter the streets outside. I had to kill their leader and threaten to kill their elders before they agreed to search for you and your Alvritshai friends earlier, after our last little encounter. They're only here now because I convinced them they were protecting their gods from the outsiders. But they still refused to enter the bowl, no matter how many of them I killed—man, woman, or child." Colin still couldn't see

Walter's face, but he could hear the sneer as he added, "They're a stubborn race. More so even than the dwarren. But at least the dwarren won't be a factor anymore."

Colin halted, feet grinding shattered crystal into the stone floor. "What do you mean?"

"Don't you know? The dwarren have fallen. The Summer Tree is dead and their precious Sacred Waters have been destroyed. The heart of their religion has been buried beneath thousands upon thousands of feet of solid rock. My army attacked them in their warrens and collapsed the chamber where they cowered in fear. The dwarren are dwindling. Dying.

"And they won't be receiving any help from the Alvritshai either."

A cold shudder coursed down Colin's shoulders, prickling in his lower back. "What have you done?"

Walter shifted away from the Source enough that Colin could see the black oil roiling beneath the skin of his face. He'd thrown the hood of his cloak back, his hair a wild tassle. He looked as he had the last time Colin had seen him, when he'd fought him in this place—he could have been wearing the same clothes as far as Colin knew—

Except that he wasn't the same. There were scars from that battle. Visible scars. A ragged hole stood out in his throat, just below his left jawbone, the flesh there an ugly mess, the wound where the arrow gifted to Colin by the Ostraell and shot by Eraeth had hit Walter obvious. But that wound was nothing compared to the empty socket where the fourth arrow had pierced Walter's eye. It hadn't healed. Not like Colin's wound to the chest, which could only be detected by a faint line of pink-white skin near the center of his breastbone now, and he expected even that would fade over time.

Walter's wounds remained, even though he must have drunk from the Well. Even though he had had the same amount of time to heal as Colin. He knew without looking that the locations where the Ostraell's arrows had struck Walter's chest and shoulder would be like the wound in his neck: an angry whorl of hard, knotted flesh.

"Caercaern has fallen," Walter said.

"Impossible."

"Not with the help of the precious Chosen of the Order of Aielan and the lord of House Ionaen. The city of Alvritshai fell within a day, the doors crumbling beneath my Wraiths and their army. Lotaern and Peloroun proved exceedingly helpful allies."

"They would never have allied themselves with you. Not after what happened at the Escarpment. It goes against all of Aielan's teachings!"

"Oh, they fought us at the end. Lotaern thought he could use Aielan's Light and his Order of the Flame against my army of Shadows and Snakes. But he didn't turn on me until after he'd deposed Tamaell Thaedoren and killed nearly every lord of the Evant remaining in Caercaern."

Colin felt the world tilt around him. "Aeren."

With a blurred flicker, Walter was suddenly within striking distance, sword drawn. Colin hadn't even felt him reaching to seize time. "I'm afraid your pet lordling is dead."

Then Walter's blade flashed out, a blow intended to take off Colin's head.

Colin staggered back, seizing time, slowing it, even as his staff rose to parry Walter's swing. The sword cracked off of the wood, flinging Colin to one side. He gasped—both from the viciousness of Walter's blow and the shock of hearing of Aeren's death. But he knew he couldn't trust him and anger spewed upward from his gut. He rolled as he hit the massive crystal shard to his left, tumbling across its surface. The hand holding his own blade slammed into one of the facets and the sword skittered free of his numbed fingers, halting in mid-air as it returned to normal time. He swore at its loss, but pulled the staff closer as he fell from the shard's edge to the floor beneath, cutting himself on the small crystals that littered the floor. The faint taint of blood touched the air, but he was already moving, using his anger to goad him on, to dull the thin pain of the minor cuts and the emotional ache that riddled his chest. Because even though he told himself Walter lied, he didn't believe it. The dwarren, Caercaern, Aeren...it was all too possible, too plausible.

And he had no time to be distracted by grief or sorrow.

He charged around the edge of the Well, the bluish light glowing to his left, the surface of the water frozen. His satchel jounced against his side, the strap pulling across his chest and over his shoulder. He heard Walter behind him, could feel his breath on the nape of his neck, and so he halted abruptly and spun, lashing out with his staff—another gift from the Ostraell.

It connected with a heavy thud, the shock vibrating up the shaft of wood into Colin's hands. Walter grunted as the force threw him to one side, his black cloak flapping like one of the Shadows. He launched himself forward again, Colin dashing away from the Well, up the tiers of the room, dodging and weaving. As he ran, he pulled the satchel in front of him, dug one hand into its depths, the contents jumping and leaping with every step. His fingers brushed the linen-wrapped Spring Tree within and he cursed as it slipped out of his grasp. He knew he couldn't kill Walter, just as Walter couldn't kill him. Walter wasn't here to deal with him; he was here to stop Colin from disturbing his control over the Source, over the Lifeblood.

Which meant Colin didn't need to fight him. He only needed to drive the Spring Tree's seed into the ground as he'd done with the Winter Tree in Caercaern and its power would free the Source and take care of Walter in the process.

* * *

The combined Legion from Portstown and Corsair slammed into the southern flank of the Wraith army, Roland bellowing incoherently as they charged across the battlefield toward Temeritt's walls. His roar of rage and hatred died as his sword flashed in the late morning sunlight, cutting into the thick neck of one of the snake-like creatures. It hissed as blood gouted from the wound, splashing Roland's mount as it reared and kicked out with its hooves, crushing the creature's head and shoving it back into the horde behind it. As his horse thumped back to the ground, he cursed in frustration, trying to keep it under control. Its nostrils were flaring in panic, and he suddenly realized it was because of the creatures themselves. The mounts were trained for battle, but they weren't used to creatures of this sort.

Even as he fought for control, one of the snakes to his right reared back, the skin around its neck flaring out with a snap, its mouth opening wide, revealing two fangs. It lunged forward, sinking its teeth into one of the horses. The animal shrieked, the sound driving into Roland's ears like a dagger. The Legionnaire drove his sword into the Snake's head and it fell back, dead, but Roland could see the striations of poison already blackening the horse's skin. A moment later it staggered and the Legionnaire—one of those selected to guard Justinian—was forced to pull back from the front.

Roland bellowed orders, stabbing down and out as he fought his own horse, urging it forward against its will. It continued to toss its head in protest, but shoved hard into the mass of creatures. He sank his blade into the strange scaled skin to both the left and right and deflected the S-shaped words they carried, slashing indiscriminately. His horse reared again, hooves crushing one of the creatures' head as it reared back to strike. He brought his mount back under control, kicking out with his own boot as he drove his sword through a neck, then caught Justinian out of the corner of his eye.

In the few heartbeats his mount had given him, he assessed the young king. Justinian held his ground, even though his intense, focused expression was lined with an edge of terror. His blade fended off strike after strike, and he appeared to have seized control of his own horse better than Roland had. The heat of pride flushed through Roland's chest—

And then he turned back to the creatures before him with a rallying roar.

In the distance, he could see more of the snakes pouring through the cracks in Temeritt's walls, abandoning the city streets to rejoin their forces on the field. But he didn't see any of the other creatures—the dark, twisted ones that had remained on the Wraith army's flanks during the attack. They remained inside. He hoped their attack would give GreatLord Kobel time to reorganize his own forces inside the walls.

As soon as the thought flickered through his mind, something else surged out of the inner city streets. Creatures out of hearthfire tales that nevertheless sent a spike of terror into Roland's gut.

Shadows. As if pieces of darkest night had detached themselves and infiltrated the day. They were streaming toward the dwarren and Alvritshai forces to the north.

Behind them came three of the four Wraiths.

* * *

"Tamaell Thaedoren! Do you see them?"

Thaedoren's cattan sliced through one of the Haessari arms at the shoulder and he kicked the flailing creature back into its companions with a grunt, then glanced toward Saetor. The lord was pointing toward the city's walls.

He turned, eyes narrowed, then cursed.

He pulled his mount back from the line. "Sound the warning. Get the damned Order of Aielan up here and warn the dwarren!"

He didn't wait for the horn bearer's response, but scanned their line, picking out Saetor, Renaerd, and Fedauroen to either side, all three of them desperately holding off the Haessari. He signaled the archers, noted that the human forces with them and to the south were already sending out wave after wave of arrows. The first volley thrummed on the air and screamed hisses erupted from farther back in the Haessari lines. In the midst of this, the blare of the horn sounded, three short blasts, followed by a fourth that held for three heartbeats.

Quotl—distant but still visible—jerked to attention at the warning. The dwarren Archon, wielding his scepter like a sword, a knife in his other hand, pulled back from the front lines even as the shamans who'd been holding back rushed forward.

Thaedoren would have watched longer, but a runner came gasping up to his side. "Tamaell! The acolytes of the Order say they aren't ready. They won't be able to stop the sukrael when they arrive."

Thaedoren drew breath to curse again—

And then Renaerd's line broke and the Haessari poured into the breach.

"Saetor! Fedaureon!" He wheeled his mount about, nearly knocking the runner to the ground, then raised his sword toward his own Phalanx. "Daedelan, to me!"

Through the crush of chaotic fighting, he saw his brother grin, then bellow a call to the Phalanx—the White Phalanx—and with a surge of horse and men, they pushed hard into the left side of the Haessari breach. Thaedoren kicked his mount forward and joined them. From the far side, Fedaureon roared his own orders, the words lost in the cacophony of the battle. As they shoved into the Haessari forces, Renaerd's men attempted to rally, their ranks already a hundred paces from the initial line. It had broken in half a dozen different places, groups of the Baene House Phalanx surrounded, including Renaerd and his escort. The men fought desperately, Daedelan spitting curses and hacking left and right with his blade, trying to reach the young lord's position. Thaedoren did the same, his own escort to either side. He parried one of the strange Haessari blades, stabbed his own into the creature's open mouth, the point jutting out of the back of his skull. The creature sagged to the ground, yanking Thaedoren's sword and arm with it, but when he tried to draw back, the sword stuck. A second Haessari seized the opening and lunged forward, Thaedoren lurching back out of its way. He felt the blade swish by his face, glance off of the armor on this shoulders, that entire arm tingling and going numb, and then the creature brought its blade back around for another strike.

Before it could recover, a cattan sprouted from its chest, the point angled downwards, then withdrew. The Haessari staggered, then its knees folded beneath it and it slumped forward.

Thaedoren glanced up into Hiroun's face, the Rhyssal House guard who'd once watched over Aeren giving his Tamaell a distant, flat look before turning back to the fight.

The lack of emotion in the man's eyes sent a shiver into Thaedoren's soul.

But then he shrugged the man's dead stare aside, pulled his boot from its stirrup, placed it in the center of the Haessari's snout, and yanked his sword free.

When he returned his attention to the broken line, he saw the last of the men surrounding Lord Renaerd fall beneath the Haessari blades. He raised his cattan, knees tightening involuntarily as he tried to press forward, but before he'd taken a second breath, one of the Haessari lashed forward, fangs sinking into Renaerd's leg.

The lord screamed, a hideous choked sound, his cattan flashing down and skewering the snake that had bitten him. His face was contorted in pain, his free hand releasing the reins of the horse and slapping down on the two jagged holes in the leather armor that were already seeping blood. His gaze darted around all of the Haessari before him, desperation clear in the lines at the corners of his eyes. His face—already slick with sweat—reddened as the poison seized his body and stole toward his heart. But the arrogant lord of House Baene gave a ragged cry and began cleaving left and right, kneeing his horse out toward the center of the Haessari army, where arrows continued to fall from the sky.

He made it nearly a hundred paces, the Haessari falling away from him on either side, before the poison took him. His back arched in agony, arms splayed to the sides. His cattan dropped from his grasp and then his horse reared and threw him from the saddle. It screamed as the Haessari closed in, Renaerd's body already lost from sight.

Thaedoren swore, lashing out, taking two of the Haessari before being forced to retreat. The breach was growing, the Haessari forcing Thaedoren and Saetor's Phalanx back, farther away from Fedaureon's men. Rhyssal's Phalanx would be separated from the rest within ten minutes, easy to slaughter, just as Renaerd had been. Thaedoren thought desperately, but their forces were spread too thin. There were no reinforcements; this was all that the three races of the Accord had left to bring to bear.

At that moment, one of the thunderous claps that had preceded the destruction of Temeritt's walls resounded over the plains.

And the sukrael struck.

* * *

Colin's hand closed over the linen-wrapped object, felt the rough contours of the wooden shaft within, like bark—

And Walter's sword slashed into his back from behind.

He cried out, the pain searing, but twisted. He let the linen go and punched backwards with his staff, sending a surge of power through the shaft as it connected, heard Walter cry out as he was flung backwards, striking the floor and skidding through the debris. The force of the punch made Colin gasp. So much more powerful than he'd expected, than it had been the last time he fought here. He trembled, hunched over, gasping for breath. Then he used his staff to stand up and began walking toward where Walter had fallen. His back burned in a slice from his upper left shoulder to the middle of his right side and he could feel his shirt sticking to his skin from the blood.

But there was blood on the shards of crystal littering the floor as well. They'd lacerated Walter's back as he scraped across them. He'd lost his sword as well. It hung, tip angled toward the ground. Colin paused beside it, then continued on, raising his staff with both hands. Walter writhed where he lay, limbs moving lethargically, breath coming in harsh heaves.

"You forget that awakening the Source helps me as much as it helps you," Colin said.

Then, the torn muscles in his back screaming, he tensed and brought the end of the staff down toward Walter's midsection.

Walter rolled, a pulse of power crackling outwards and striking Colin's chest at the same moment his staff jarred into the stone floor. He was hurled backwards by Walter's blast, the floor cracking and shattering beneath his own blow. His hold on time released and he hit the floor of the Source's chamber to the clang of their two swords clattering where they'd dropped them and the patter of broken stone. His breath gushed from his lungs and for a moment he couldn't breathe. Then he sucked in air, something deep inside his chest tearing with a sharp pain. He rolled to one side and coughed up a trickle of blood, the taste ferric in his mouth. He swirled around his tongue and then spat, wiping the back of one hand across his lips.

Walter's laughter echoed through the chamber. "Lord Aeren died screaming, according to Lotaern. He died screaming in the Tamaell's tower before Lotaern and Peloroun seized control of the city and the Evant. They slaughtered the White Phalanx, killed everyone from Rhyssal House and Baene. Lord Terroec burned to death when they torched his manse."

Colin rose to his feet. "You're only trying to rattle me. It won't work." He pulled the satchel around again, searched for Walter even as his hand groped for the linen-wrapped shaft.

He felt the pulse before it hit, tensed and grabbed time, crouching low and darting forward with a curse. The crackling power grazed him and exploded, hurtling him to the side. He skated across the top of a crystal shard, rolled off its far side, and then he was running. He caught a flicker of darkness out of the corner of his eye, brought up his staff in time to deflect Walter's blade. He twisted, but the sword sliced across his upper arm, leaving another clean cut that instantly welled with blood. But there was no time to check the wound. Walter was attacking full force, driving him back as he narrowly managed to block each swing. They were both tweaking time, each one slowing or halting it in little bursts, trying to gain that extra moment to pierce the other's defenses. But they were both too practiced. And unlike the last time, Colin wasn't distracted by the awakening Well.

This time, he could focus. On Walter's moves, on his disfigured face, on the hatred that permeated it, that gave it its brittle edges and flat planes. A deep hatred, one that he recognized from Portstown, when both of them had been younger, untainted by the Lifeblood. That hatred had only grown over the years, condensed and intensified. It had twisted Walter as much as the waters of the Well. It controlled him, fed him, drove him.

And Colin saw that it would never end, not until it consumed him utterly and he became...

Until he became one of the sukrael, one of the Shadows.

The realization—that it wasn't the Lifeblood that tainted him, that the Lifeblood merely allowed the transformation to happen—rocked Colin to his core. He sucked in a ragged breath—

And that was the opening Walter had been waiting for.

The bastard Proprietor's son grunted and slashed downwards. Colin caught the blade with his staff, shunted it to one side, but realized too late that Walter had never intended the sword to connect. He brought his elbow up past Colin's guard and slammed it into Colin's face.

* * *

"Eraeth, why have you—"

Siobhaen didn't need to finish as she climbed the last part of the ridge and the battle before Temeritt lay splayed out before her. The Haessari filled the plains, battling the humans farther west and the dwarren and Alvritshai on the far side of Temeritt's lake. The clash of weapons and the screams of the dying were muted here, but Siobhaen's breath still caught in her throat. To the south, barely within sight around the breadth of the hill Temeritt was built upon, she could see the crumbled outer walls of the city, smoke rising from the lower ward.

At her side, Eraeth's entire body tensed. "Aeren."

Siobhaen reached out and snagged his arm, drawing him up short. "You'll never find him in that chaos."

Even as she spoke, a thunderclap resounded over the field. Both of them startled, Siobhaen's fingers digging into muscle unconsciously. Eraeth said nothing. She relaxed her grip as she searched the battle, picking out a sudden ridge of earth spreading out from a lone figure, growing in strength as it moved. "Look." She pointed with her chin. "A Wraith?"

"There are two others." Two more thunderclaps followed, the swells of earth beginning to push toward the dwarren lines. "And there are sukrael."

Siobhaen noticed the strange flowing darkness seething across the plains at almost the same time, heading toward the Alvritshai. Her hands tingled with the remembered force of Aielan's Light seething through her in the ruined city in the wastes. "We have to help them. But how?"

"We're too distant. We need to get closer." He nodded toward a contingent of Alvritshai far behind the lines. "There. The reserve forces."

He began trotting toward the secondary forces and Siobhaen let him go, trailing after. They trotted across the plains, the grasses pattering against their legs, unable to move any faster. They'd been traveling for days, had run the last hour, once they realized they could see smoke from the city, but had hoped to arrive before the battle, not in the middle.

Now, as they cut behind dwarren lines and neared the Alvritshai contingent, Siobhaen realized it wasn't a reserve force after all.

It was a makeshift hospital.

They charged into the fray, Alvritshai lying on the grass on all sides, moaning or screaming, limbs missing, blood pouring from open wounds, a few of them obviously already dead. Most had staggered there themselves, although a few were being carried or dragged back from the lines by their fellow Phalanx. Siobhaen saw guardsmen from assorted Houses as well as members of the Flame. She searched frantically for familiar faces, but the sheer number of injuries and the intensity of the pain in her fellow Alvritshai's faces overwhelmed her. She reeled as she followed Eraeth deeper into the blood-matted grasses. He'd paused only once, to take stock, then headed purposefully for a group tending the wounded to one side.

A moment later, she knew why.

He halted ten paces away from where a woman hunched over a Phalanx member in Nuant House colors, her hands sheathed in blood up to her elbows, her fingers flying as she tied off a bandage around the man's neck. The Phalanx member grunted as she jerked it tight, but she snatched at his flailing hand and pressed it against the bandage.

"Hold this here. Keep pressure on it or you'll bleed out."

Then she stood, not even looking up, gaze already on the next man in line, an arrow jutting from his thigh. A dozen other women were doing the same all around her, trailed by two dozen younger Alvritshai carrying bandages, waterskins, and knives. All of them wore expressions of determination.

"Lady Moiran," Eraeth said.

"Set whoever it is with the rest." Moiran had already knelt, fingers probing the Alvrtishai's thigh around the arrow. The man bit back a scream at her manipulations, one hand grasping at the grass as he tried not to writhe, but Moiran ignored him. "Kaellin, I'll need a knife! And two lengths of cloth to tie this off once the arrow's out."

One of the younger Alvritshai stepped forward, knife in hand, but Eraeth said again, in a tighter voice, "Lady Moiran."

Moiran glanced up in irritation...then stilled.

A complex roil of emotions crossed the lady of Rhyssal House's face—recognition, shock, elation, followed by a grief so raw and profound that Siobhaen was forced to duck her head. Alvritshai never exposed their emotions so baldly. But more than that, she knew in that fleeting glimpse of grief that Aeren was dead.

As she stared at the ground, Siobhaen realized something else as well: Lady Moiran had aged since the last time she'd seen her, there in Artillien, before she'd left with Eraeth and Shaeveran to seek out the dwarren and the Source. Her eyes appeared sunken, shadowed and bruised, her hair dull in the sunlight. Whatever had happened, it had taken a severe toll, more than Aeren's death could account for.

"Eraeth," Moiran said. Siobhaen risked a glance, to find that the lady of Rhyssal had collected herself and stood. She stepped forward, halted before Lord Aeren's Protector. Siobhaen took an involuntary step toward Eraeth's side. She wanted to comfort him, but she couldn't intrude, not here, not now.

"He died attempting to warn Thaedoren of Peloroun and Lotaern's treachery."

Eraeth sucked in a ragged breath, let it out slowly. Siobhaen could see the effort to keep himself under control in the tension across the back of his shoulders, in the white-knuckled fist at his side.

"I should never have left him," he said.

Moiran reached out and gripped his shoulder. "It would not have mattered."

Siobhaen could tell that the words meant little. Moiran did as well, her hand falling away. "Fedaureon still lives. He fights on the field even now. If you wish to honor Aeren and his death, fight to protect his son."

Then she turned away, paused for a moment as if she would say more, then knelt back down beside the wounded Nuant guardsman and demanded, "Knife."

Kaellin, wide-eyed, passed a knife into Moiran's hand. The Alvritshai guard couldn't suppress his scream as Moiran began to cut the arrow free.

Eraeth shifted to face the battle, one hand falling to the pommel of his cattan.

Siobhaen moved to his side, already removing her satchel and securing her own cattan and knife. "Ready?" she asked.

By the time they'd picked their way throught he scattered wounded, they were running.

Straight into the heart of the Alvritshai forces.

* * *

"Archon!" Azuka shouted over the ululations of the dwarren and the clash of weapons only thirty feet away.

Quotl glanced toward his fellow shaman, but only briefly. He was too focused on the power of Ilacqua coursing through him, his body vibrating with the Land around him, with its energies. "What is it?"

Azuka pushed through the frantic shamans that surrounded him, each of them chanting, scepters in motion, faces raised toward the heavens. A few of them knelt in the earth. "The urannen have hit the Alvritshai forces."

"That's their problem. I'm busy dealing with that."

He nodded toward the slow ridge of earth rolling toward them. He'd seen the elloktu destroy the walls of Temeritt with them. The one rolling toward them would completely disrupt the dwarren lines. If he couldn't stop it—

His concentration was interrupted with two more claps of thunder as the two other elloktu sent their own pulse of power through the earth. He felt the initial burst jolt through him, the earth shuddering in response, almost in pain. Gritting his teeth, he pulled his focus away from Azuka, away from the desperate chanting of the shamans around him and the fight boiling a short distance away, and sank himself into the earth, letting the power of the Land suffuse him as he had at the Break. And like at the Break, he felt the earth respond, felt himself sinking into the bedrock beneath the soil. That stone remained solid, but the earth above and the top layer of stone beneath that shuddered and cracked as the elloktu's waves sped toward the dwarren forces. The first wave would hit them in a matter of moments, its momentum growing. He searched for a way to halt it, to counter its power, but this stone wasn't like at the Break. There, he'd used the flaws in the landscape to bring the stone of the cliffs crumbling down. Here, the land itself was being twisted, tortured into unnatural motion. There were no flaws to exploit—the stone was too solid.

Too solid.

Eyes widening, Quotl reached out toward the bedrock before the first wave. But instead of shattering it as he had at the Break, he focused on fusing all of the cracks and imperfections that ran through it together. He pulled the stone in tight, keeping his attention on the stone nearest the surface, making it more solid.

And then he braced himself.

The wave of earth rumbled as it approached, growing into a low growl. He opened his eyes, surprised to see the battle still raging before him. He'd withdrawn so completely into himself that he'd shunted the noise into the background. But the dwarren had begun to panic at the wall of earth heaving towards their line. A few had already broken away. Even the snake-like orannian were fleeing, breaking to either side.

The wall plowed into the retreating orannian, flinging them skyward as it shuddered closer. The growl became a roar, vibrating in Quotl's teeth. He tensed as the screams and hisses escalated, more of the dwarren breaking away. Azuka was shouting at the dwarren, turning to scream at Quotl that they had to run, to get out of the wave's path—

And then the wave hit the bedrock Quotl had strengthened.

Stone cracked and split. A backlash of shock rocked Quotl backwards, Azuka lurching forward to catch him, but the wall of grinding earth collapsed suddenly, all of its momentum absorbed by the rock beneath the earth. Stone and dirt slumped back down onto the plains, residual power pushing the wave forward another few feet. But its force had been significantly weakened.

The retreating dwarren and orannian turned in surprise, and then Quotl heard Ikterru bellow new orders, the dwarren rallying, the entire plains erupting in ululations and clan battlecries. The dwarren surged back toward the orannian in a wave of their own, the plains once more filled with the clash of weapons and the screams of the wounded and dying.

Quotl lurched forward out of Azuka's grasp, nearly stumbled to his knees as weakness washed over him, but caught himself, already reaching out to the Land again. There were two more waves approaching, and he could feel power building as one of the elloktu gathered their strength for another strike.

"Archon," Azuka said, reaching for him, his voice leaden with concern.

"Keep up the chanting. Call to the gods. I'm going to need all of the help I can get."

* * *

"Where is the damned Order of Aielan?" Thaedoren roared.

He spun from where the sukrael were decimating the Alvritshai front lines, their black forms flowing from warrior to warrior, the Phalanx's attacks doing nothing to stop them. Twenty of the Phalanx were already down, cloaked in the fluid black forms, screams rising from all quarters as the black, glistening shapes finished feasting on one man, then leaped toward another. They passed through raised swords, through armor, falling like cloth torn from the night. Tendrils lashed out, catching those that tried to flee, passing through their arms, their legs, the struck Alvritshai crumbling to the ground with cries for help or shrieks of terror.

"Where is the damned Order of Aielan!" Thaedoren cursed, caught sight of some of the Order's members spread out behind the Phalanx lines, but couldn't tell if they were doing anything or not.

A flicker of light caught his attention, far out beyond their lines, so distant he thought it must be a trick of the sun. But sweat ran into his eyes and he blinked, the flicker gone.

"Tamaell!"

With one last glance and headshake toward the Order of Aielan, he spun back to the battle at Daedelan's call. The Haessari were still attacking, taking advantage of where the Alvritshai lines were shattered by the sukrael. In their panic to get away from the black creatures, all sense of order had been abandoned, and the Haessari were flowing into the breaks, slaughtering the Alvritshai as they attempted to retreat.

"Thaedoren!" Daedelan shouted. "We can't hold against the sukrael. We have no defense against them. We have to pull back!"

"Where? Where do we fall back to? We have nowhere to retreat! Nothing can protect us against them."

"The Order—"

"The Order doesn't have enough time!"

"Tamaell! Daedelan! Watch out!"

Thaedoren and Daedelan spun at the warning, both of them bringing their swords up into a guard position, but it was too late. The Phalanx line before them stumbled back into their position, men screaming as three of the sukrael launched themselves into their midst. Horses panicked, rearing and kicking, shrieking or bolting. Alvritshai were thrown. Thaedoren seized his horse's reins and held on tight, the animal backing up awkwardly. He saw his brother's mount get shoved to one side, caught a glint of sunlight off of a useless blade—

Then someone shoved hard into him from the right. His mount reared back and before he could react he was falling, clutching the horse's side desperately, the beast stamping and stumbling to one side before being jostled in the opposite direction. Its sweaty, blood-matted neck slid from Thaedoren's grasp and he landed hard on the churned plains, pain jarring up his spine. His leg wrenched free of the stirrup and he cried out as he rolled away, but he kept hold of his sword. Feet and hooves slammed into the earth on either side and he pulled himself in tight. Someone kicked him in the side, a hoof grazed his temple and he jerked away, tasting mud and blood and bitter sweat. He rolled himself onto his back, stared up into the blinding blue sky, catching glimpses of Phalanx in his peripheral vision, kicked up earth pattering onto his chest, his face. His own breath came in tense, ragged heaves, overloud in his own ears. The pulse of his blood was a rush of wind.

One of the sukrael loomed into his line of sight, folds of darkness glistening with a shimmer of gold.

His heart stuttered in his chest. His eyes widened and his breath froze. He snapped his cattan toward the blackness on instinct as it reached for him, even though he knew the blade would pass right through it. He sensed the cold radiating from the creature's folds as it fell, wondered what he would feel as it passed through his flesh. A tingling sensation? Searing pain? Or would it numb him, so he felt nothing? He couldn't remember if Shaeveran had ever said.

But before its longest tendril touched his hand, a pure white light flashed into existence, blazing with intent, with a pure hatred Thaedoren could feel. It pierced the center of the sukrael's black form. The light— one of the Faelehgre—froze in midair, intensifying for a brief, blinding moment. The tendrils of the sukrael reaching for Thaedoren halted.

He gasped, his extended hand trembling.

For a long moment, the battle sounded dim and distant, far removed from his place on the trampled grass of the plains, the sukrael's form hovering above him, the Faeleghre's light burning white-hot at its center.

Then the world crashed back in and he scrambled backwards, elbows digging into the churned earth, his feet kicking out as adrenalin shot through his body. When he was twenty paces from the looming form of the sukrael and the Faelehgre that had stopped it, he ran up against the bodies of one of the Phalanx and his mount, both dead, legs and arms entangled. He couldn't see a mark on them, knew that the sukrael had killed them both. The Phalanx man's head was tilted far back, his mouth open, his eyes wide. His look was accusing.

It brought Thaedoren abruptly back to himself. He lurched to his feet, pulled the mantle of the Tamaell around himself like a shroud. On the field, the sukrael were still attacking, the Haessari a wary step behind, but at least a dozen Faelehgre were streaking across the grasses, heading straight for the amorphous black shapes that leaped from man to horse to man indiscriminately. Six of the black shadows were already frozen in mid-leap, white lights blazing at their centers, like the one who had attacked him. As he watched, two more of the Faelehgre struck, halting their chosen sukrael in their tracks. Neither creature—sukrael or Faelehgre—moved afterwards. Thaedoren felt his throat closing up as he realized the white lights from the Ostraell were sacrificing themselves to stop the tainted shadows. He didn't know how they had learned of the battle, but they had come, just as the human Legion and the remains of the dwarren Riders had come. To battle the Wraiths and their armies of dark creatures. But there were more of the sukrael than there were of the Faelehgre. There wouldn't be enough sacrifices made to stop them, not completely.

His gaze lifted from the field—where three more of the Faelehgre had died to protect the Alvritshai—to see the rolling waves of earth the Wraiths had called forth collapsing as they reached the edges of the dwarren armies. The dwarren were rallying, the Riders regrouping and attacking the Haessari who had hounded their flanks. But already the Wraiths were shifting their attack; he could feel it in a change in the tension in the air, could see them altering positions on the field. Something prickled his skin, made the fine hairs on his arms and neck stand on end. He smelled the harsh, burnt metallic scent of ozone. Farther away, to the south, the human Legion was in a vicious battle with the rest of the Haessari forces, and in Temeritt—

Thaedoren sucked in a harsh breath.

Temeritt burned.

* * *

"Keep them moving!" Echeri snapped at the guardsmen outside the gates from her vantage on the palace walls. "Don't let them gawk at the battle or the fires. There isn't time, especially if the winds change and the fire heads this way." She spun around, moved the short distance to the other side of the wall and the guardsmen inside the courtyard. "Get them inside the palace and down into the tunnels as quickly as possible! Move it! We don't know how the battle on the plains is going and we're taking no chances."

The Legion, already tense, renewed their efforts, hauling people through the gates and shoving them toward the palace doors, their motions frantic. The people—women with children, the elderly, a smattering of young men who should have been down below manning the walls—had halted their progress as soon as the king and his army arrived. Hope had flared through their midst, visible in the sudden uplifting of haggard faces, in the hands clasped together at chest or waist, in the clutching of pendants and religious symbols and the hushed whisper of prayers, not to mention the gasps and bursts of laughter and a few madcap dancers.

The elation had continued until without warning the thin columns of fire billowing up from the first ward and the crumbled outer walls had melded and intensified. Flames had leaped into the skies, and even Echeri could see their greedy reach as they spread fast from the southern edge of the main gates across the first ward to the southeast—the same direction the wind was blowing.

The looks of hope had crumpled into horror. Tears of joy had shifted back into the sobs of despair. Fervent prayers of thanks became muttered pleas for protection.

"Fools," she said under her breath. "Even if the entire Horde collapsed to the ground dead right this moment, the fire could still kill us all."

"They can't see the fire," Commander Higgins said. "They only want to see the Horde finished. It has held us here, captive, for too long."

Echeri stalked back to the other side to stare out toward the fire, smoke billowing in huge plumes from the roiling inferno. It was distant, but they could still hear a low crackling, punctuated by the rumble of a collapsing building.

She stood, her arms crossed over her chest, hands gripping tight just below her shoulders. When she felt Higgins settling into place a step behind her, to one side, her shoulders slumped.

"I don't think it will be enough. The king, the Legion, the Alvritshai, the dwarren—it won't be enough. Temeritt is burning. Yhnar will be next. Corsair, Portstown, the rest of the Provinces. The Wraiths have won. And Kobel—"

Her voice caught and she struggled to continue, tears coursing down her face, but couldn't.

A comforting hand settled on her shoulder and she stiffened involuntarily, hardening even as she felt the skin of her face burning with shame. She had never shown weakness so publicly; had never allowed herself to cry, not even in front of Kobel.

But before she could react—scrub away the tears, shrug out of Higgins' grasp, berate him for his temerity—the air around them tightened, crackled, became abruptly charged.

And in the same breath, the plains erupted in a firestorm of lightning.

* * *

Colin's nose crunched and he staggered back, blood and snot instantly coating his upper lip. Pain lanced straight back into his brain, like a knife between the eyes, and he screamed. Walter pulled his arm back for a two-handed swing of his sword, the blade cutting swiftly left to right, but Colin's foot caught on a crystal shard and he tripped, falling backwards. Walter's sword slashed through the open air above his chest, nicking his staff and shearing a chunk from the wood.

Colin landed hard, shards gouging into his back. His breath exploded from his chest, spraying blood and phlegm in a fine spray from his mouth, and a twinge rose from deep inside, where Walter had thrust his sword through him the last time they'd fought here at the Source. He groaned, but Walter moved fast, tweaking time so that he suddenly blurred into position above him, knees coming down to either side of Colin's chest, his weight slamming into Colin's gut. It cut off Colin's indrawn breath and he gagged, but Walter's hand closed in hard and tight around his throat, tilting his head back, the tip of his sword settling in at the base of his jaw. Colin still clutched the staff with both hands, its length angled between them, but he had little leverage in this position.

"Don't move," Walter said, all of the snideness and mockery gone.

Colin struggled to suck in air, managing a weak, painful gasp through the constriction in his throat and chest. "You can't...kill me."

"We don't know that for certain, do we? After all, we can be hurt."

The hand around Colin's throat tightened. "Look at what your Alvritshai friends did to me with their arrows. What were they? How were they treated?"

"They should have...killed you."

"They didn't. But it's taking me longer to heal than it should. Do you know how much of the Lifeblood I've drunk to heal this much? More than I've taken since we drank from the Well in the Ostraell so many years ago, when we were just boys. And the damn wounds still itch. An incessant itch that cannot be scratched, because it's deep inside." The point of the sword dug into Colin's neck. "But it raises an interesting question, doesn't it? What would it take to kill one of us? Do I need to behead you? Burn you? Or would you recover from even that?"

A flush of fear washed through Colin, making him break out in a fresh sheen of sweat. He didn't know what would happen. He'd healed from burns before, but he didn't think Walter was talking about charring off a piece of skin. Walter meant immolation, perhaps to the point of cremation. Would he recover from being reduced to ashes? And what if those ashes were spread out over a great distance?

And dismembering...what would happen then? Would an arm regrow, or would he need to have the original arm for it to reattach? He'd asked the question ages ago, during his time in the Ostraell, before he realized the Lifeblood was changing him. He'd come close to cutting off one of his own fingers to find out. But he couldn't do it. Even during the darkest depths of his depression at the loss of everything he'd known—Karen, his parents, his home—he hadn't been able to take the chance that it wouldn't regenerate somehow.

But a finger was nothing compared to cutting off his head.

The thoughts flashed through his mind in an instant, but Walter must have been able to read them on his face, for he smiled.

"I think we can be killed," he said. "I think cutting you into pieces and spreading them around Wrath Suvane—leaving a piece of you in Caercaern, another at the Confluence, another in Portstown perhaps, maybe even traveling across the Arduon and leaving a piece of you in Trent—I think that might kill you. It would at least keep you occupied for a long time, recovering. But I can't leave you in Caercaern, or the Confluence, or Trent. Because they've all been destroyed."

"You lie."

Walter's grip tightened again, but then relaxed. "You doubt me, even though you know my Wraiths were marching toward the dwarren, Alvritshai, and human lands with armies at their heels. Fine. Let me show you."

With a strength that shocked Colin, Walter pulled back his blade, stood, and hauled Colin across the floor, dragging his lower body over the crystals toward the Source. The shards cut into his back, his arms and legs. He tried to get his feet beneath him, but Walter moved too fast. He drew power to his chest, ready to send it surging down the staff into Walter's body, but before he could release it they reached the edge of the Well, the bluish glow nearly blinding. Walter dropped him at its lip, blood from Colin's shattered nose splattering into the water, curling and twisting as it dispersed. Colin sucked in a harsh breath, sending a sheet of white pain into his skull as he tried to pull some of it in through his nose. He choked on blood and snot instead, spat it off to one side.

Walter ignored him, reaching down with his free hand to the surface of the water. Fingers splayed, he said, "Watch."

A surge of power rippled from Walter's hand into the Well and the blue light intensified, then darkened. Tendrils of oil seeped from Walter's skin into the Well's surface, spreading like spilled ink. Walter shuddered, but the oil continued to writhe and boil, spreading until it formed a pool, like an ugly bruise.

Images began to appear on the oil, shadowy and indistinct at first, but solidifying.

Colin gasped as he recognized the dwarren's Sacred Waters, the confluence where the rivers and streams of the northern mountains met at the pool at the center of the dwarren tunnels. He watched as the Riders fought the insurgence of the Wraith army, the creatures pouring forth from the tunnels on all sides. He recognized some of the dwarren as they fought—the Cochen, Quotl, a few of the other clan chiefs—cringed as a few of them fell beneath the black army's blades. He could see the desperation in the dwarren faces, the resolution as the supports of the main chamber began to shatter. The reddish light from the Confluence pulsed in the background of the battle, until Kimannen halted some kind of attack on it. He saw the Archon flee toward the dwarren residences—

And then the entire chamber began to crumble, the ceiling caving in with a monumental surge of stone and rubble. It crushed the Summer Tree beneath it, branches snapping, slammed into the dwarren and Wraith armies alike, entombing them. The reddish light of the healing waters was snuffed out like a candle flame.

Before Colin could recover, the image flickered and changed to a view of the walls of Caercaern, the Alvritshai armies arrayed before it. Despair washed over him as Lotaern attempted to kill the captured Wraith with the knife Colin had forged, the black-cloaked figure rising and slaughtering Lotaern and the rest of the Order of the Flame on the walls before opening the gates. But when the Wraith army arrived and he saw who led it—

"That's not possible," he said, as Khalaek fought and killed Peloroun on the field. "I saw him die. Stephan killed him on the battlefields at the Escarpment."

"He wasn't dead yet when I arrived. The Lifeblood saved him."

Colin watched in horror as Khalaek and his army stormed the gates and razed the city beyond. Tears pricked his eyes as parts of the city began to burn, the Winter Tree a blackened and rotten silhouette in the background. But he also noticed that Thaedoren and a large group of Alvritshai Phalanx had survived and fled to the west amid the snowstorm.

He thought the images would end there, but the walls of Caercaern faded, replaced by an Alvritshai Wraith he didn't recognize, a woman. She stood at the edge of another Well, this one pulsing with reddish light, like that of the Confluence. Her hand was outstretched, a wooden box with a stone crackling with light held in her palm. She appeared to be hesitating, her features turned down in a heavy, thoughtful frown. There were tears in her eyes.

Then she tilted the box, the stone falling into the water. A moment later, a blinding flash forced Colin to squint and turn away, the light more intense than anything he'd seen from the Wells over his lifetime. Walter's face was lit from below, his eyes riveted on the visions he'd pulled from the Well. His skin was washed to a deathless pale white, the swirling oil beneath a pitch black. His hair was bleached to a dusky gray. But it was the mirthless joy that lined his face that held Colin's attention, the sick exhilaration that lit his eyes, that remained even as the blinding light faded.

Colin as he turned back to the images on the water. This had to end here. This rivalry between him and Walter, this battle begun on the streets of Portstown when it consisted of nothing more than a church, a merchantile, and the dreams of a few hundred refugees from the soon-to-be war-torn Andover.

On the oily surface tainting the Well, Andover shuddered and crumbled. Cities all across the continent shook beneath massive earthquakes, the ground splitting and heaving under the cataclysmic force unleashed by the Alvritshai Wraith and the stone she'd dropped into the Rose. Colin recognized Trent as the images shifted from one city to the next. Half of the port town slid into the ocean as the stone cliffs gave way. People ran into the streets from collapsing buildings, were swallowed up as the earth gave way beneath them in mile-wide fissures. Lakes and rivers became seas of churning mud. The images were silent, but Colin could imagine the cracking and grinding of stone that must have roared from every direction. The ocean churned to froth, waves crashing into cliffsides, consuming entire villages. Islands in the Archipelago sank. Mountains fell.

The images were coming too fast for Colin to process, Walter reveling in the destruction, consumed by it. Swallowing back the thick coating of blood and phlegm in his throat, Colin surreptitiously searched for his satchel out of the corner of his eye. He had hoped to seal the Source away from Walter's manipulations, had planned to control it as he had controlled the Wells before this. But that would have been only a temporary fix. Walter would have worked to circumvent him, as he had with the Seasonal Trees, laying his plans in secret. He needed to deal with Walter directly.

And if he couldn't kill Walter, not with certainty, then he needed to deal with him another way. A more direct way.

He found his satchel lying twenty paces away, its contents half spilled out onto the crystal-littered stone floor. He could see the end of the linen-wrapped bundle sticking out from beneath the bag's flap.

Walter grunted, and Colin's gaze snapped back to the images, the maddening flicker of Andover's destruction slowing, then switching to New Andover, to Corsair and Portstown and Rendell. The ocean receded, then surged forward, rushing into the streets and overwhelming the citizens. Portstown's walls along the dock were overrun, the ocean spilling into the city beyond. Rendell's port was completely swallowed by the rising water, although the main castle and city were high enough to escape the tsunami's wrath. But when the water finally withdrew, nothing remained of the port at all except a few pilings from the docks and one stone church, its doors and windows gaping holes. Portstown suffered almost as much, the water trapped behind the walls that were meant as a barrier to the tides and occasional storms. Most of the city lay in ruins, the streets choked with flotsam and debris. Corsair fared better, only the lower portions of the city on both sides of the harbor decimated.

"That is what has become of Wrath Suvane," Walter said, the words laced with satisfaction and resentment. "Andover, the Provinces, the dwarren, the Alvritshai—they have all crumbled. Soon, there will be only the Wraiths and the Shadows and our armies. Even now, Khalaek and the others are attacking Temeritt."

The image shifted from the watery destruction of Corsair to Temeritt.

Colin winced at the sight of the charred remains of the Autumn Tree. The battle played out on the plains before the city, plumes of smoke rising from the outer ward. He fought back grief as on the battlefield he saw Khalaek and the Wraiths attack the dwarren with waves of earth, as the Shadows broke the Alvritshai front lines. He caught glimpses of Quotl, of Thaedoren and Fedaureon, even Moiran pulling and tending wounded from the field behind Alvritshai lines. Then the Faelehgre streaked across the plains from the direction of the Ostraell, their fierce lights piercing the Shadows and halting them where they stood. With each sacrifice he wondered if Osserin were there, knew that the Faelehgre—that his friend—would be.

For a moment, it appeared the allied forces were turning the tide against the Wraiths and their armies, even though Temeritt burned.

But then the clear blue skies opened up and jagged lightning snaked down from the heavens, riddling the armies with scintillant columns of white heat. Entire units fell, men and horses charred beyond recognition. Some danced and juddered upon contact, bodies arched and contorted; others were thrown clear by the force of the strikes. The sheets of lightning struck indiscriminately among the Alvritshai, the dwarren, and the human armies. No army was left untouched.

"Your alliance doesn't stand a chance. My Wraiths have been trained in the use of the Lifeblood, in its powers, its uses. Lotaern had barely begun to scratch the surface of Aielan's Light with his Order. We were more motivated, more driven. We took greater risks."

Colin drew in a ragged breath, the scent of ozone and burnt skin filling his nostrils, even though he knew what was taking place was happening in Temeritt. He smelled the blood, the char, the sweat and fear. Its taste— that of battle, of desperation, of determination—coated his tongue. With that same breath, he drew even more power into himself.

Then he twisted, bringing his staff up into Walter's chest, his entire body screaming with a thousand aches and pains from the previous fight.

In the same motion, he saw Walter's smile twitch, realized Walter had been waiting for such a move, that he'd never been distracted by his display at all, that his sword was already shifting to block Colin's strike.

But Walter hadn't anticipated the strength of Colin's blow.

The sword and staff connected, and Colin sent his gathered power down into Walter's body.

The backlash flung them both away from the Source in opposite directions, Walter screaming as the power coursed through him, Colin crying out in shock. He landed hard, but rolled and lurched to his feet, already charging toward Walter's position, gathering more power. Walter's sword clanged to the stone as he lost his grip. Before he could retrieve it, Colin kicked it across the floor, then jabbed his staff down into the center of Walter's chest, releasing another surge of energy into the Wraith's body. Walter screamed again, twitching as the energy poured into him. Colin began raining blow after blow down on him, hitting his chest, arms, side, back, anything that was exposed as the bastard son of Portstown, the boy who had tortured him as a child, rolled and curled into a protective ball. A strange sense of repetition slid over Colin, and he realized he'd done this once before, nearly a year ago, in this same chamber. Except then, he'd been overcome with all of the repressed emotions he'd harbored since Walter had first bullied him in Portstown. All of the frustration, all of the anger, all of the fear that he'd only released once, when he'd attacked Walter and his cronies with the sling, had surged forth then, had been expelled and purged from his soul.

This time, only a trace of those emotions remained. He felt removed, withdrawn, calm. His strikes were precise, the power he used controlled. And he'd opened himself up to the Source more than he had before as well. It's what had surprised Walter with his first blow; he'd expected Colin to be restrained.

"But you taught me to wield all the power at hand," he said as he continued to rain down blows, Walter's screams dying down into choked sobs. He was rolling back and forth now, attempting to escape, to crawl away, but Colin slammed his staff into his extended hand, into his feet, a leg, a thigh, his groin. "'You never did open yourself up to the Lifeblood and all it offered.' Isn't that what you said? Well, now I have." He punctuated the words by punching his staff into Walter's side and holding it there, letting the energy of the Well surge through him unabated.

Walter screamed again, back arching in pain.

"And this time," Colin added, halting the flow and pulling back his staff, "I don't have the awakening of the Source to distract me."

Walter slumped onto his back, limbs limp, breath coming in ragged heaves. His skin and clothes were charred, the faint scent of burnt flesh and rank sweat rising from his form. Colin thought of the allied armies caught beneath the Wraith's lightning storm and his jaw clenched.

He turned and moved to his satchel, bent to retrieve the linen-wrapped bundle. It slid free with ease. Behind him, Walter groaned, but he didn't move as Colin approached again. He was too weak.

Colin stared down at the crumpled figure, at the scar on his neck, at the empty pit of his eye.

He tucked the staff into the crook of his arm, one end resting on the ground, and unwrapped the linen, careful to keep from touching the wooden shaft within.

"You can't kill me," Walter croaked, a broken smile touching his lips. "We can't die. Trust me, I've tried."

Colin knelt, his staff resting against his shoulder. "I tried as well, a long time ago. But I don't intend to kill you."

Walter chuckled. "Then I—and my fellow Wraiths—have already won."

Colin grabbed the wooden shaft in the linen with one hand, felt the power of the Spring Tree waiting within surge forth, begin to build. He'd felt this same power three times before, once at the meeting of the Evant, when he'd presented the lords of the Alvritshai with the Winter Tree, once at the Confluence when he gifted the dwarren shamans with the Summer Tree, and a third time outside the walls of Temeritt when he'd planted the Autumn Tree.

He'd intended to plant it here, use it to block Walter and the Wraiths from the Source.

But now he had a different purpose in mind.

"It won't kill you," he said, revealing the length of the seed to Walter. The bulbous top was already splitting, the outer layer of bark-like skin cracking open. The spiked shaft beneath trembled in Colin's grip. "But it will hold you prisoner until I can determine what to do with you."

Walter's brow furrowed in confusion for a single breath. Then his eyes flared wide and he jerked upwards.

Colin drove the shaft of the Spring Tree down into his chest, the spike piercing through cloth and skin, flesh and bone, and into the stone of the Source's chamber beneath. Blood gouted from the wound, Walter sinking back, head tilted, throat exposed. More blood trickled from between his lips as his hands curled around the top of the seed jutting above his breastbone. He choked, tried to pull the shaft free, but it had already rooted, the bulbous top splintering as the tree broke free and began to grow. His head lolled to one side. "What have you done? Oh gods, it burns! *It burns!*"

Roots shot from the side of the shaft, threading over Walter's body before piercing into the cracked floor, his screams rising as more and more of the tree touched his flesh. Colin stepped back as the roots thickened, the stone beneath his feet shuddering as it splintered and snapped, the roots far stronger as they surged deeper and deeper into the earth. The bole of the tree shot upwards from the center of Walter's chest, reaching for the dome's shattered ceiling and the sunlight overhead. The wood hissed and crackled as it grew, limbs jutting out from its sides, then splitting again and again into thinner and thinner branches. Buds appeared, then burst with tiny rustlings as leaves unfurled in the space of a heartbeat; long ovoid leaves the fine, crisp green of spring, touched faintly at their edges with yellow. The sharp musk of pollen filled the air, a haze settling downwards as more and more of the leaves uncurled. The soft, dry husks of the spent buds dropped to the ground, littering the floor in a carpet the color of light gold.

Colin stepped back even farther, his shoulders and head coated with the fine pollen and a few of the husks. His gaze dropped back to Walter, who continued to writhe and scream beneath the spreading root system. He had been almost completely encased, the tree surging around him, holding him tight, unwilling to touch him, as if he were tainted. The roots closest to him were withered, the exposed bark grayed and pocked. A black slash, as if the tree had been struck by lightning, twisted up through the thickening trunk to twice Colin's height. But the heartwood remained whole. Colin could feel the tree's strength pulsing with his own heartbeat, could feel it reaching for him, touching him, tasting. And he could sense its understanding as well. It knew what purpose it served, what Colin expected of it, both regarding the Source and the Wraith pinned beneath its bole.

Then its roots reached the edge of the Source and dove over the lip into the waters beneath, sucking at the Well's power greedily. The resultant growth spurt trembled through the ground and the top of the tree shot even higher, breaching the once crystalline ceiling above. But Colin kept his gaze on Walter. The former bully of Portstown gasped as a root tendril shot up over his head. He strained backwards, trying to keep out of its way, his neck at an odd angle. Tears coursed down from his eyes. Where the new root touched his cheek, his skin reddened, blistered, and cracked. His hands grasped at empty air, his arms already locked into place.

As he craned his neck, his eyes latched onto Colin. His face twisted into black hatred, into wretched rage. "You'll suffer for this," he said, his voice thick and hoarse. Raw. As if even his throat were blistering beneath the Spring Tree's power. "My fellow Wraiths will destroy this tree as they did the others. They will come for me. They will free me and then we will rip your precious world to pieces."

He would have said more, but another root shot forward and draped itself across his mouth, nose, and eye. Colin heard the sizzle of Walter's

skin, even as the Wraith's shriek split the chamber. But he forced himself
to watch as more and more roots twisted over and around Walter's body,
until there was no longer any part of the Wraith's body visible, until the
shriek was smothered and the accelerated growth of the Spring Tree began
to slow.

He turned away, a wave of exhaustion washing through his body from
head to toe. Head bowed, eyes closed, he stood for a moment, the last of
the birth groans and creaks of the tree echoing around him. The Spring
Tree's mantle settled over him, throbbing with vibrancy and life, but he
could feel the malignancy that remained at its heart, encased and
entombed. He let the tree's power wash over him, strengthen him, and
slowly the trembling that suffused him abated.

Even so, when he lifted his head and took his first step, he stumbled,
catching himself against one of the blocks of crystal. His body was weak,
bruised and beaten by the fight with Walter, his emotions torn and ragged
by what the Wraith had said, had shown him on the waters of the Well.
He didn't want to believe the images, didn't want to consider what they
meant—the Sacred Waters buried, Caercaern destroyed, Andover
shattered, Temeritt under attack. He wanted to think Walter had lied,
twisted the truth, fabricated it all in order to goad Colin, to hurt him.

But he knew, with a sickening certainty deep in his gut, that Walter
hadn't lied. He'd reveled in the images too much.

Colin couldn't go back and halt the destruction of the Confluence, or
Caercaern, or even Andover. But he could do something about Temeritt.

And what Walter had said about the Wraiths had been true as well:
they would attempt to free him from the Spring Tree. It would take time,
but it could be done. Colin needed to deal with the remaining Wraiths as
well, with all of the creatures of what the dwarren called the Turning. But
like Walter, he couldn't kill the Wraiths. He needed to do something
different, something like what he'd done with Walter.

Pushing away from the shard of crystal, he staggered toward the
Source, pausing to regain his balance once, to let the weakness fade,
before continuing. He dropped to his knees at the lip of the Well, reached
down into the waters and drew up a cupped handful, drank deeply. Its
coldness flooded his mouth, seeped down his throat, the taste of ice and
loam filling his senses and washing away the lethargy that permeated his
muscles. He drank again, and again, letting the strength of the Well
course through him.

Then he sat on the edge of the Well, its blue glow washing his face
with light, the Spring Tree's leaves a soft sussurus behind him. He

thought of what Walter had said to him the last time they'd stood in this chamber, what the Wraith had whispered in his ear as he'd held the sword that had pierced through Colin's chest.

"'You never did open yourself completely to the Lifeblood and all it offered as I did, did you?'" Colin whispered to himself now. "No, Walter. I didn't. I was too afraid of what it would do to me, of how it would change me. But I'm not afraid anymore."

He closed his eyes and tilted his head back slightly, his hands resting on his thighs where he knelt. The Lifeblood filled him, throbbing in his skin, in his veins, but he reached out and drew it in deeper, gorged himself on the Source's power. Yet he knew the Lifeblood alone would not be enough for what he intended. He needed more, needed something that would contain the Wraiths, that would hurt them, as the heartwood of the Ostraell had hurt them. He needed something like the Seasonal Trees, but instead of a barrier that would keep the Wraiths out, he needed something that would restrain them, that would imprison them, as Walter was now imprisoned by the Spring Tree.

There was only one force he knew of that could harm the Wraiths and the sukrael. He'd used it to forge the knife that had spelled Lotaern's doom. He'd used it to create the Seasonal Trees. The Order of the Flame had used it to protect the Alvritshai from the sukrael, and Siobhaen had used it to kill the Shadows here in the Source's chamber. He knew there was a source for it hidden beneath the ruined city. Siobhaen had found it, had nearly been burned out by its strength when she'd called upon it.

Submerged as deeply as he'd ever been in the Lifeblood's water, Colin reached for Aielan's Light. He reached for the white fire.

It answered, roaring up from the depths beneath the city and bursting up through the earth and stone of the chamber. It reached into the heavens, blazing with a blinding light, a column of pure white flame.

And then...it began to spread.

25

The energies of the Land shifted beneath Quotl's feet, the elloktu pulling away from the earth, retreating. Quotl staggered forward, releasing his hold on the rock that he had used as a barrier to stop the elloktu's waves. Azuka, who'd hovered at his side as Ikterru and the dwarren Riders rallied and struck the orannian forces, caught him and held him upright. The urge to dig out his pipe and burn some yetope was nearly overwhelming, but Quotl shoved it aside. His breath was already ragged with effort, and he didn't think the elloktu were finished.

"Pull us back from the fighting," he wheezed, shocking himself with his own weakness. Even with the power of the Land coursing through him, he felt faint.

Azuka acted instantly, drawing him backwards as he shouted for the nearest shamans and Riders to protect them. As they wove through the bloody remains of the battle, stepping over the bodies of fallen dwarren and orannian both, the Riders shunted the fighting to either side, the shamans chanting, their voices cracking with tension, their eyes wide. Quotl drew strength from the familiar words.

But he could sense the power on the battlefield shifting yet again. His skin prickled, the air around him snapping and sizzling with energy.

He glanced to the skies, searching for a storm, but the heavens were a clear blue.

He grumbled, his fingers running through his beard. A hundred paces from the battle lines, he halted and gently pulled free from Azuka. The rest of the shamans immediately gathered around, most continuing to chant their blessings or pleas to the gods.

"Have we defeated them?" Azuka asked. "The elloktu...did you stop them?"

Quotl drew himself upright. "They've merely changed tactics. We've stopped their attack by land, so they're reaching for the skies."

Nearly all of the shamans—and even a few of the Riders who guarded them—looked up.

And as if in answer, the skies split, lightning sheeting down from nothing and striking into the heart of the dwarren ranks, dancing in a blinding, erratic path across the plains. The crack of thunder shuddered through Quotl's skin. All of the dwarren lurched backwards, hands raised to shield their eyes, a few of them crying out or cursing. On the field, dwarren screamed as those close to the blast were flung backwards, bodies charred or seared black if they'd been touched. Those unlucky enough to be in the direct path of the white-hot, jagged streaks were killed instantly, bodies roasted where they stood. Quotl flinched, but did not drag his eyes from the impact, his retinas burning with an afterimage of the trapped dwarren silhouettes that fell to the ground as the lightning flared out. Gaezel screamed and panicked, their shrieks grating to the ears. Once again, the dwarren forces broke, attempting to flee the storm as more and more bolts streaked downwards from the heavens.

Quotl knew a little about how to manipulate the Land; he knew nothing about the skies.

"Archon, look!" Azuka grabbed Quotl's arm and pulled his attention to the rest of the field. "The elloktu are attacking everyone."

Across the plains, among the Alvritshai, the human forces, even within Temeritt, lightning slashed down in sheets, riddling the armies and the city with sizzling death. The growl of thunder grew as the onslaught continued, the bolts lashing at random. The battlefield was crumbling as the ordered lines broke, Alvritshai and their horses, dwarren and their gaezel succumbing to blind fear. Pockets of resistance remained, but the entire battle had degenerated into a morass of desperation.

A bolt cracked from the skies, impacting twenty paces distant, its force juddering up through Quotl's feet even as the dwarren closest to it were flung backwards. The air sizzled, Quotl's skin crawling as the energy blasted outwards. His teeth rattled at the instantaneous thunder, like the sound of a thousand tree trunks exploding under intense heat. One of the unfortunate dwarren who'd been thrust aside hit Quotl and he crashed to the ground beneath the body's weight before he could take a breath. The impact broke his paralysis, even as the scent of ozone and burned flesh slammed into his nostrils. He surged upwards, rolling the dead Rider's body to one side, and roared at the sky, his beard singed, the exposed skin of his face and hands red and waxy with burns. Two steps to one side, Azuka lay unmoving. Quotl's roar died, his ears ringing, his hearing deadened by the blast. He fell to one knee at Azuka's side, reached out to feel for a pulse, felt nothing. His fingers dug deeper into the charred flesh,

Azuka's skin crackling, falling away in blackened flakes. But no heartbeat throbbed beneath his fingers.

Numbness enveloped him. He hunched over the shaman's form, hand on Azuka's chest, and muttered a prayer to Ilacqua, the stench of singed hair thick in his nostrils. Tears soaked into his beard.

Leaning back, he scanned the field, gaze skimming over all of the fallen, across those who remained standing, continuing to fight the orannian—

And latched onto the figure standing alone between the ragged defenses and the broken walls of Temeritt.

Quotl lurched to his feet and stumbled forward, the numbness inside him solidifying into rage. Through the dampened haze brought on by the near miss, he felt the rush of power from the Land surging up through his feet. He called on it, drew it in and focused it.

Then released it with a ragged bellow of pain.

Far distant, the earth beneath the elloktu suddenly exploded upwards, flinging the Tainted One into the air. Across a third of the plains, the lightning storm abruptly ended. The geyser of earth reached its peak and fell, the figure of the Tainted One buried beneath it. Quotl knew it would not stop him for long, but he turned his attention toward the remaining two, still staggering through the battle, dwarren and orannian fighting around him now, swords and axes slashing, blood spraying, men roaring, screaming, dying, all of it muted. Quotl could only hear his own heaving breath, the winds of the Land pouring through him as he latched onto another of the elloktu's positions and let that wind surge forth.

Another section of the earth exploded upwards, Quotl already searching for the third elloktu, the dwarren, catching sight of him on the far side of the field, closer to the remains of the Autumn Tree. But he hadn't let go of the power used to halt the second elloktu, so when he pushed that power outwards again to attack the third it slashed across the plains like a blade.

The ground cracked, the sound deafening even through Quotl's already deadened ears. The earth beneath his feet leaped upwards and back as a huge rift shot across the grasslands from the second elloktu's position toward the Autumn Tree. He hit the ground hard, but pushed himself up in time to see the third elloktu spin around, then vanish as the plains opened up beneath him, the ground collapsing as the earthquake continued to rattle Quotl's teeth together. On all sides, the forces of the Turning—Alvritshai, human, dwarren, orannian—lurched and fought to remain standing. Animals bolted, both with and without riders. To the east, buildings within Temeritt's walls crumbled into dust and debris.

Then the quake faded, the tremors settling. Quotl hesitated, waiting for it to resume, then crawled to his knees. His legs felt unstable and weak beneath him, but he stood. For a few precious moments, the fighting on both sides had stopped, men regaining their feet warily, most gaping in shock at the huge chasm that now separated the armies on the plains from Temeritt's walls. It was fifty paces wide and perhaps three hundred long, but earth continued to topple from its edges into the gaping wound.

In the subdued silence, Quotl realized the lightning had ended.

Something prickled at the edges of his beard. Reaching up, he felt dampness, pulled his fingers away to find them coated with blood. He was bleeding from the ears.

Across the field, the stunned armies stirred. The snake-like orannian tongues flicked and tasted the air, which reeked of smoke and blood and acrid lightning. Dwarren calmed gaezel and the Alvritshai and humans reined in their horses, those that still had them; most had already panicked and fled. Among the Alvritshai, the white light of the Faelehgre blazed and the remaining black shadows of the urannen gorged themselves on their prey. The fires in Temeritt continued to burn, the black plume of smoke now angled farther south.

The wary tension had just begun to tilt toward action again when a section of the earth spewed upwards. Everyone flinched, but it was the first elloktu Quotl had buried, freeing himself. He climbed from the pit that had claimed him, face twisted in anger, his clothes covered in mud. Farther away, at the start of the split in the earth, his fellow stood as well. There was no sign of the third.

Quotl, his body strangely empty, as if he were a husk of grain left over after the threshing, reached for the power of the Land again, reached for Ilacqua's embrace.

But before anyone could react, the northeastern horizon began to glow with a fiery white light.

* * *

Siobhaen sensed it before it came into view.

She and Eraeth fought back to back on the plains before Temeritt, as they had done in the ruined city in the Thalloran Wasteland. They had battled their way to the front lines, searching for Fedaureon, for any of the Rhyssal House Phalanx, but had ended up simply attacking the Wraith's creatures where they stood. They'd held off the Haessari, Alvritshai from mixed Houses surrounding them. They'd survived the sukrael and the lightning storm and earthquake. But she'd nearly crumbled in defeat when the white light, like dawn, appeared in the northeast.

Until she felt its power, until she *tasted* it.

She gasped.

"What?" Eraeth asked, his voice leaden, exhausted. Siobhaen understood. She felt the same, her arms trembling with weariness, her body smeared with blood and dirt, her breath coming in pants. Her muscles were wrung out from fighting, her soul depleted.

But her heart swelled at the first flickering touches of what approached.

"What is it?" Eraeth demanded, stepping forward, his sword tilting upwards as if readying to fight it.

Siobhaen laughed, the sound deep and dark, on the edge of hysteria. She swallowed, shook her head in disbelief. "It's...it's Aielan's Light."

Eraeth's head snapped toward her in confusion. But he said nothing.

On the northeastern skyline, the white light spread, stretching across the breadth of the horizon. And it grew, intensifying, solidifying. What had first appeared to be a second dawn sharpened into a harsher light. Not the mellow golds of the sun, the blush of a spring dawn, but something harder. It grew, rising into the skies, engulfing them as it approached. Siobhaen laughed again as the first flickering taste slid into her, filled her to her depths with its savor. She'd felt this touch before, had let it fill her in the depths of the Hauttaeren Mountains as part of her ascension into the Order of the Flame. But this...this was so much more powerful, so much richer and more intense than the white fire that had nearly burned her out in the ruined city when facing Walter and his sukrael.

By the time the wall of White Fire became visible, Siobhaen had slipped down to her knees, tears streaming down her face, her sword digging into the soil before her, forgotten. Others had knelt as well; a few were prostrate. All of them were from the Order of Aielan, their faces rapt, their cheeks sheened with tears.

But as the White Fire drew closer, as the truth of what approached—a massive wall of white flame stretching from the earth to the skies, from one edge of the horizon to the other—became undeniable, more and more of the Alvritshai fell to their knees and joined the Order of Aielan. Not all. Some of them stood riveted in place, their faces masks of terror. Others sobbed, or stared, eyes vacant.

Many turned and ran, although Siobhaen had no idea where they expected to hide. The White Fire burned through everything in its path, consumed the heavens, and approached far too swiftly for anyone to outrun.

And it was eerily silent.

At her side, Eraeth stood, rigid, cattan still raised protectively before him. But with his other hand, he reached out toward Siobhaen, grabbed her shoulder as if for support. "What—?" he began, the word broken and raw, but he choked on his own voice, couldn't recover.

The White Fire was close now, blotting out the northeast completely, blazing across the plains from the direction of the Thalloran Wasteland. Siobhaen reached up and grasped Eraeth's hand and squeezed. The Protector glanced down at her and she saw the terror in his eyes.

"Don't worry," she said, the White Fire now burning across the lake, enveloping Temeritt, racing toward them so swiftly Siobhaen knew it would hit them in another breath. "It won't burn. And it's coming from the Thalloran Wastes."

She saw the words register a moment before the Fire surged upwards from the ground and filled her.

She gasped, as she'd done when she'd stepped into the white flames beneath the Hauttaeren so many years before as part of her rites as an acolyte of the Order. The fire took her, burned down into her core without any pain, stripping her bare and exposing her to herself. There were no illusions within its fire. It seared away all of her defenses, all of the walls she'd erected to protect herself. Everything from childhood to the moment the fires touched her were laid bare. She wept at the decisions she'd made that had formed her life, cringed and writhed beneath them. Her heart sang in triumph as she ascended through the ranks of the acolytes, as she stepped fearfully into Aielan's embrace that first time, as she accepted the vows of the Order of Aielan. She trembled in rage as she relived the moments with Lotaern, the trek to the Northern Wastes. She twisted and tortured herself over the decision to remain with Shaeveran, Lord Aeren, and Eraeth at the sarenavriell beneath the glacier. The agony of betraying her vows to the Order—even though she now felt she'd made the right decision—scarred her. Every moment, every emotion, all of the truths that she had lived and accepted or tried to deny lay revealed. There were no excuses, no rationalizations, no hiding behind words and reasons. She was defenseless, laid bare beneath the inexorable white flames.

And within those flames, she felt a presence. More than one. Someone gazed down upon her bared soul, tasted it, touched it, and passed judgment. Siobhaen felt its gaze tear through her, penetrating, all-seeing, all-encompassing—

Then it glanced away.

"Aielan," Siobhaen breathed, suddenly aware that the White Fire had passed beyond her. Its touch was fading, withdrawing. The wall of fire that had swept down upon her burned behind, already well beyond the battlefield, still stretching from earth to sky, as far north and south as she could see, but shrinking now, sweeping across the rest of the world.

She twisted where she knelt, reached out toward the retreating flames with a wrenching cry. She didn't want Aielan's touch to fade, even though the barriers she's built herself—the denials of truth and the rewritten history of her life—were already slipping back into place.

But the White Fire was gone.

She lowered herself to the ground, pressed her forehead into the mud and grass. Her chest ached. Her heart raced. Her breath came in ragged heaves. But slowly, slowly she regained control.

Someone shifted near her, crouched down at her side, and she suddenly remembered Eraeth, the armies, the battle. She lurched upright, but Eraeth's hand halted her, resting on her back, beneath her neck. His face was set in its usual expression, hard and unforgiving, with a slight frown. But at its edges, it was haunted by what he'd experienced in Aielan's flames. It had changed him.

It would change all of them, she suddenly realized.

"The Wraith army," she whispered, the words tense and urgent.

Eraeth shook his head, his frown deepening in confusion. "They're gone," he said. "All of them are gone."

* * *

Khalaek clawed his way up out of the earth where he'd been buried, clods of earth falling down around him. Rage throbbed through his entire body, his skin bloated with it. He'd lost his grip on the threads of lightning that had wracked the human, Alvritshai, and dwarren forces arrayed against them, but after this last indignity he intended to sear every last one of them from the land. He was shocked there was anyone within their midst who could summon such power. Walter had assured his fellow Wraiths that none of their enemies could access so much of the Wells' resources, or Aielan's Light. Only Shaeveran could wield the Lifeblood as they could, and Walter had been confident that his fellow human wouldn't have the backbone to do what was necessary to stop them.

Besides, he didn't sense Shaeveran on the battlefield. If the insufferable, meddling human were here, he hadn't halted or slowed time.

Khalaek would have felt it.

Which meant someone here held power. One of the Order of Aielan? Khalaek's lips twisted into a scowl. It couldn't be Lotaern. The Chosen was dead. And none of the rest of the Order had practiced wielding the Lifeblood like the Wraiths had over the past hundred years. Look at the insignificant threat they'd posed beneath the walls of Caercaern. None of them were at the level of Khalaek's fellow Wraiths.

So who?

He dragged himself to the lip of the crater he'd been buried within, then hauled himself upright, dirt cascading from his shoulders, his clothes. He wiped it from his face, felt it smear across his skin, and spat the taste of loam off to one side. It was caked in his hair, caught in the folds of his shirt. Grit had found its way down into the sides of his boots. Every breath smelled of wet mud.

Across the battlefield, the majority of the fighting had ceased, Alvritshai, dwarren, humans, and Haessari picking themselves up from the ground, stunned. Behind him, Maenaed pulled himself from the edge of the jagged fissure that had opened up across the breadth of the plains. He didn't see Arturo at all. He had no idea how Courranen fared inside Temeritt, if he'd even been affected by the earthquake.

Then his gaze fell on the dwarren standing at the edge of the dwarren forces, a smattering of fellow shamans and Riders standing protectively around him. The elderly dwarren faced Khalaek squarely, the fingers of one hand running through the knots and beads and braids of his beard. He was dressed like the other shamans, but even without the guard Khalaek knew he was the one who'd caused the quake. He could sense the power radiating from the small figure—wild and untamed, but potent. He must have been the one to halt their previous attacks as well, here on the plains and before, at the Break, when Arturo had led the Wraith army against the dwarren in their march east.

"How well do you handle your power when you're under direct attack, shaman?"

He stepped forward, reaching for the flow of the Lifeblood that surrounded them—

And stumbled, his momentum brought up as his reach encountered a wall. He tried to pull at the Lifeblood and found it sluggish, his access to it hindered. As if someone had slid a thick but malleable barrier between him and the channels he had been using moments before. He scrabbled at the barrier as he spun to face Maenaed, but his fellow Wraith was staring off into the distance.

To the northeast.

Khalaek turned, still clawing at the barrier, pulling as much of the Lifeblood into himself as possible, thinking that the barrier felt familiar. As he caught sight of the white fire approaching from the northeast, recognition hit like a hammer.

The Seasonal Trees. The barrier felt like that of the Autumn Tree and the Winter Tree and the Summer Tree.

"But they're all dead." The fire on the horizon grew, raced towards them, filling the horizon. As it drew closer, as he began to feel a niggling itch running across his skin, his eyes narrowed with hatred. "Shaeveran."

Then the prickle escalated, the itch spreading like wildfire through his entire body, edging from irritation into an ache into a searing pain. It felt as if his entire body had been lit on fire, and the white flames were still approaching. He clamped his jaw down defiantly, teeth aching as the pain sank deeper and deeper into his skin, but the seething ache reached his bones and he broke. He arched back, fists clenched, head tilted, and roared his hatred at the heavens. The bellow tore from his throat, echoed by Maenaed a short distance away, as the White Fire seethed across the plains and engulfed them both. The fire that charred Khalaek to the bone sank even deeper and he tried to scream louder, the roar of defiance breaking and twisting into a shriek of horror. He wanted to writhe beneath the pain, to turn and run, but the white flames held him, flayed him, exposed his core and what he saw there—the black heart at his center, tainted by the sukrael, twisted by the black oil that flowed beneath his skin—shattered his control.

He sank to his knees, or thought he did. He could no longer tell. The White Fire held him in its grip and all he could do was wait for it to pass, to sweep over him and leave the husk of his body behind on the bloody plain before Temeritt. He waited for that moment, yearned for it. The wall of White Fire had been moving so fast he could only be trapped in its center for the space of a few breaths, a few heartbeats. It couldn't possibly be much wider than that.

Except that the White Fire didn't die. It continued to burn. His flesh didn't crisp and sear away. His blood didn't boil. His muscles weren't consumed. His bones didn't split and splinter and turn to ash. All of those sensations suffused him, but they didn't end. They continued, somehow sinking deeper and deeper, permeating him.

Until he finally realized that they weren't going to end.

He was trapped in the White Fire, and he was going to burn and burn in Aielan's Light until the end of time.

And then he truly began to scream.

* * *

Terror engulfed Echeri when she saw the flames, but there was no place to run. The people in the courtyard and streets beneath the walls of the palace screamed as the wall of fire bore down upon them, attempted to flee, but they were packed in too tightly. She caught, out of the corner of her eye, people being knocked to the ground, being trampled—

And then Commander Higgins thrust his body in front of hers, shoving her behind him, back against the crenellations. Stone gouged into her back and she hissed at the pain, a bitter retort rising to her lips. After all, what could Higgins possibly think he would accomplish? How could he possibly protect her?

But the White Fire struck and she was consumed by it, the words choked off in a sudden indrawn breath.

The flames burned away her preconceptions. She saw herself as she truly was; she saw her own soul.

And then the White Fire blazed beyond her, leaving her gasping, her body trembling as she leaned onto the stone parapet for support. Stone and grit bit into the palms of her bare hands, but she relished the sensation, where a moment before she had been about to curse Higgins for them. The stone was solid beneath her hands. It was substantial and permanent. It was *real*.

Heaving in a great lungful of air, Echeri pushed herself back to see the White Fire sweeping away toward the southwest, receding. In its wake, Temeritt still burned, the fires roaring even higher, the winds blowing the embers and smoke south. The lower ward from the main gates southward were lost. Numerous buildings had collapsed during the quake, weakened by the flames—the regular flames—and then destroyed by the tremors, or simply too old and unstable to withstand the shaking. The gash that had caused the quake lay like a scar on the plains below. The burnt bole of the Autumn Tree still stood. The king and his forces were arrayed to the east, scattered from the battle, but beginning to merge. The Alvritshai and dwarren forces were doing the same to the northwest, beyond the edges of the lake. And the Wraith army—

Echeri sucked in another hard breath. One hand rose to her breastbone and she managed a weak, "Commander Higgins?"

Behind her, she heard a scraping sound, as if someone wearing armor were dragging themselves to their feet. The loudness of the sound brought home to Echeri how eerily silent the palace walls and courtyard were. The people below were just now beginning to pull themselves out of their stupors, the effects of the White Fire beginning to fade. Some had fallen to their knees. Others lay prostrate. A few had fainted. Many were sobbing uncontrollably; a few faces were vacant. One woman was screaming and beating her head against the wall beside the gates, her eyes maddened, the stone already bloody.

But Echeri could only spare them a fleeting glance. Her attention was fixed on the battlefield below. "Commander Higgins!"

"Here, my lady."

Higgins stumbled to the wall beside her and she reached out, hand flailing until it hit something solid. She grasped at his arm, held it in a death grip. "Look at the battlefield. Tell me what you see?"

"My lady?"

"Look at it! Tell me what you see!"

A look of concern swept over his face. But he looked.

"I see the king's army and our allies."

"Where's the Horde? Where did it go?"

"It's not on the field. It's...gone."

He turned to look at her in consternation.

"Do you think it was that..." he licked his lips uncertainly "...that fire?"

Echeri turned back to the battlefield. There was no sign of the snake people, no sign of the twisted creatures that had kept them imprisoned within Temeritt's walls for nearly six months, and most importantly, no sign of the Wraiths. They'd vanished, as if they'd never existed.

Or as if they'd been burned from the earth by the White Fire, by the...

"By the Hand of Diermani."

Higgins leaned forward onto the parapet with both hands, contemplating the field below.

Then, from farther down the wall, one of the other guardsmen shouted, "The Horde! It's gone!"

In the courtyard, the murmurs of wonder and terror fixed on the new voice.

"What did you say?" someone shouted from below, a voice Echeri recognized. She stepped away from the outer wall to look down into the courtyard, saw Patris Raleveti moving to the edge of the raised steps of the palace doors. He looked shaken, as if he'd seen the face of Diermani Himself. "What did you say?"

A different Legionnaire stepped forward. "The Wraith army is gone. I don't see any of their forces on the plains below or in the streets of the first ward."

The silenced murmurs of the crowd became a babble of excited voices. The patris' expression remained skeptical. He began searching the parapet, and Echeri knew who he was looking for.

She moved to the edge of the wall, regaining her poise as she did so. "You heard correctly, Patris Raleveti. The Horde is gone. I believe...I believe it was the White Fire."

The chatter in the courtyard escalated, but before it grew too overwhelming, Raleveti shook his head and said in a loud, carrying voice, "No, it was the will of Diermani. He sent the White Fire to save us all, to save the faithful. You all felt the fire's judgment! You felt its touch! He has sent his Flame to earth and seared the forsaken from its plane. We have been redeemed!"

The sentiment spread like wildfire, igniting the crowd, the tension and frenzied panic from the moments before the fire smothered behind a wave of disbelief that transformed before Echeri's eyes into relief and then a blaze of elation. It began with conversation, broken by an uncertain laugh that was followed by more laughter, all with a thin edge of madness to it. Soon, the entire courtyard was on the verge of celebration.

But not everyone was smiling.

Below, the woman was still beating herself senseless against the stone wall, the skin of her forehead split open, gushing blood, her hair matted to her head. Her hands were bloody as well. And there were others in the crowd—still dazed or unconscious, or clutching their arms to their chests, rocking back and forth, a string of drool dangling from slack lips.

"Do you believe it, my lady?" Higgins asked.

"Do I believe it was a miracle? Yes. Did the fire come from Diermani? I don't know. But it doesn't matter. There are still matters to attend to." She motioned toward the bloody mess of the woman below, the others catatonic or with signs of madness. "Send the Legionnaires down to stop that woman and gather up the rest who have been affected by the White Fire."

Higgins frowned as he began to notice them throughout the crowd. "Where should we take them, my lady?"

"Take them into the palace. We'll see to them as best we can for now. Summon the healers. And send a messenger to those who've already reached the tunnels. Tell them the Horde is gone and they can return."

* * *

Kobel swore as he fended off the Horde at Tarken Sohn's side.

They'd retreated through the streets, herding as many of the citizens before them as they could.   The streets were in chaos, the citizens shrieking and fleeing in all directions, most heading toward the main gates of the second wall.   Fires were breaking out all over as lanterns and candles and fires were left unattended or overturned in the panic.   Black smoke billowed into the sky, choking some of the side streets and alleys, creating a claustrophobic feel as the Legion from the broken main gates ran for their lives.   The Shadows had fallen on them almost instantly, cutting off the main street, and Kobel had been forced into the northern district.   Collapsed houses had funneled them farther north, slowed only by the panicked people emerging from the wooden and stone buildings on all sides.   He'd seen the snake people entering the courtyard in the moments before they left and swore again as he shouted commands to his men, all of them pushing hard and attempting to bring some order to the madness.   He couldn't see the main wall or the secondary wall from their position, the buildings and the hillside blocking his view.   He didn't even know if the secondary wall still held.

Within ten blocks, it didn't matter, as the impish, twisted creatures of the Horde suddenly leaped and bounded from every cross-street, doorway, and window on their block.   The citizens panicked even more, Tarken bellowing for the mixed Province Legion that remained to fall into lines, hacking and slashing as they slowly worked their way backwards up the street, stumbling over discarded buckets, clothes, even a few pieces of scattered furniture and overturned wagons.   Kobel jabbed his blade through one of the larger blackened bodies, lurching back from the snapping teeth as the creature died, then severed another creature's spindly arm from its side. It shrieked, high and piercing, but fell back. One of the men near him screamed as one of the creatures latched onto his face, but Kobel had no time to spare to save him.   He roared another command and they fell back again.   With a sharp glance over his shoulder, he realized the street behind them was mostly free of those they were protecting, so he ordered them to fall back past the next intersection into the next block. The men reacted instantly, turning and running, Kobel's blood pounding in his ears.   A flicker of movement down a side street and he realized if they didn't hurry they'd be outflanked as he saw more of the creatures closing from the south.   Tarken shouted more orders and the entire Legion turned and attacked, now blocking access to the next street.

"We have to move faster," Kobel said as both of the GreatLords cut into the monsters at their heels. "They're already on the streets to the south of us. They're going to surround us."

"And there's fire to the north. Our only open path is to the east."

"Then east it is, but we'll have to cut south again eventually or we'll be trapped against the second wall with no gate for access."

"We'll have to run for it."

Kobel agreed by slicing one of the lantern-eyed cats in half, then turning. "Fall back, as fast as you can. Follow my lead. Now!"

And they spun on their heels and ran. Exhaustion pulled at Kobel's muscles, ached in his chest, dragged at his feet and arms, but he pushed harder. Tarken huffed and puffed on his left, one of his commanders on the right, the rest of the Legion clomping along in their armor behind them. Someone tripped and screamed as the Horde caught him, but Kobel shoved the horrible sounds from his mind, focused on the streets ahead. They passed two alleys, a cross street, pushed hard across an open plaza at a diagonal, heading southeast to gain another block closer to the gates. At a circular intersection of at least six streets, he angled southeast again, but the Horde burst from one of the streets to their right before they were halfway across, forcing them back east. Kobel caught a glimpse of the secondary wall between two of the buildings, another of the palace farther up the hill, which was steeper in this section of the city. Bells were clanging somewhere to the east and he prayed to Diermani that Echeri was inside the tunnels already, leading as many of the people to safety as she could.

But then, halfway down another block, the street curving even farther north, he heard the thunderous claps that had preceded the fall of the outer walls.

He paused, the Legion falling into position around him, gasping. But the Horde had fallen slightly behind.

"That didn't come from the city," Tarken said.

Kobel realized he was right. He listened intently. "The battlefield? But why?"

Tarken shrugged. "Unless they're laying waste to the outer ward, clearing a path to the secondary wall."

"We don't have time to speculate," the commander said, adding a hasty, "my lords."

Kobel motioned them onward with his sword, but within a hundred feet they heard screeching and running feet from around the corner of the street ahead. Tarken called for a halt and they waited.

They didn't wait long. A force of mixed citizens and Legionnaires and general soldiers—obviously remnants from the outer wall—poured around the corner, shouts bringing them up short as they saw Kobel and his Legion. There were maybe a hundred more men and women in their group, which brought their total to just over two hundred.

One of the men dressed in a Legionnaire's uniform stepped forward. Gray riddled his stubble-beard and his face was lined with age and scars. "Swordmaster Braxton, GreatLord, from the northern ranks. The Horde is on my men's heels."

Braxton's "men" were mostly boys, and people they'd picked up on their way to the secondary walls.

"They're right behind us as well."

Braxton winced. Kobel noticed a cut along his side, bleeding profusely, another across his thigh. And blood dripped from the fingers of his free hand. "Then we'll have to defend ourselves here."

Tarken was already ordering the men into position. Kobel scanned both sides of the street, the Horde already appearing in both directions. A bitter taste filled his mouth and he spat it aside. He refused to accept defeat. Not like this.

His glance fell on the eastern houses, on their doors and windows.

"The houses. Someone check the houses behind us. Look for a way through to the southern street."

Braxton didn't hesitate. "Corim, Wade, Rory, Harden, check the buildings!"

Four boys broke away and vanished into the doors of three of the houses at their backs.

Kobel didn't have time to watch for their return for the Horde fell on them, coming from both directions. They were trapped in the corner of the curve. The sound of clashing metal and pain and death filled the hollow, echoing strangely off of the buildings as the clanging of the bells continued. Distantly, Kobel realized that the thunderous claps had ended, replaced by a cataclysmic sizzling sound and the flash of lightning, even though the sky above was clear. He didn't have time to be distracted. Men were falling left and right, their group being whittled down even as they took out creature after creature. There seemed to be no end to them, streaming from the southern street, dropping out of windows. They'd originally blocked the entire street with their forces, but the Horde had forced them into a group against one side. He shot a quick glance backwards, wondering what had happened to the boys checking the houses, saw one of them emerge from a building and shake his head.

He swore and swung, the black ichor that was the creature's blood flying up and splattering his face. It burned, but he couldn't wipe it away. A drop fell into the corner of his eye and stung, tears beginning to stream down his cheek, his eye blurring. His ears echoed with the screams coming from all sides. They'd been driven back against the houses now, their two hundred cut down by half.

And then someone bellowed in panic, "GreatLord!"

Kobel spun, realized at the last instant that the call had been meant for Tarken Sohn. Even as his gaze latched onto the GreatLord of Yhnar, even as he saw Tarken's left protective flank fall beneath the teeth of a dozen of the cat-like creatures—the animals shrieking in triumph as they leapt onto Tarken's back—claws sank into Kobel's flesh in the chink in his armor above his thigh, piercing through the mail beneath. As Tarken roared, one of the cat creatures tearing into the back of his neck beneath his helm, Kobel wrenched his gaze down to the monstrous creature before him, its snout opening wide and snapping forward toward Kobel's throat. He reared back, head turned to the side, felt the creature's teeth graze the skin beneath his ear, felt spittle slick his cheek, the creature's breath hot against his neck. At the same time, the creature jerked down with the claws caught in his armor, trying to gain more height.

Straps and buckles broke, the armor over his thigh ripping free, the talons shredding down Kobel's leg. He bellowed at the pain, his vision going white-hot as he stumbled and fell backwards, dragging the creature with him. It snapped at his head again, ripped the bottom of his ear off, that pain nothing compared to the seething hotbed of his thigh. His back slammed into the ground, his breath gushing from his lungs, the creature's weight crunching down on top of him. The claws buried in his thigh flexed as it scrambled for purchase, but Kobel clenched his teeth together and brought his sword around, stabbing blindly into the wriggling, leathery body on top of him. The creature howled, but he stabbed again and again, its other claws scrabbling across the armor on his chest and raking down his side. Blood splattered across his front as he finally hit something vital. The creature gave one last weak howl and then collapsed forward, its snout thudding over his shoulder.

Kobel gasped and blinked away the cloudiness in his eyes brought on by pain, tears, sweat, and splattered blood. He jerked his blade free of the creature's body and heaved it to one side, muscles standing out in his neck as he moved his leg. Pushing into a seated position, he stared down at the ruin of his left thigh, a wave of nausea sweeping through him.

The guard had been ripped free, hung by one remaining leather strap from his knee. The muscle beneath was shredded meat. Blood gushed from the four ragged claw lines. If he didn't get it tied off and treated, he'd bleed out.

The fighting still raged on either side, his own Legion crammed in so close they were practically trampling him. They must have closed in when they saw him fall. Shoving backwards, he dragged himself from beneath their feet onto the steps of one of the houses. One of Braxton's boys emerged from the darkness, scanning the battle, before his gaze fell on Kobel. He slid down the stairs to Kobel's side.

"GreatLord! There's no passage through—"

"Forget that," Kobel spat, waving one hand weakly. He was already beginning to feel lightheaded. "Get a belt or strap, anything. You need to tie off my leg."

The boy searched frantically, dodged away and returned a second later with a leather belt. "Like this?"

"Yes, yes." Kobel's head wanted to roll forward and he didn't think he'd have the strength to raise it again, so he tilted it back instead. "Cinch it tight at the top of my thigh. As tight as you can make it."

He nearly screamed when the boy lifted his leg to get the belt underneath. He did when the boy drew it tight, not releasing the pressure even when Kobel involuntarily slapped at him.

The pain in his leg immediately dampened. He pushed himself back up onto the stairs, noted the bloodflow had lessened dramatically, and then grasped the boy's shoulder. "What's your name?"

"Corim, sir. I mean GreatLord. Sir."

"Where is Tarken Sohn?"

"I think he's dead, sir."

Kobel's gut clenched. "What about the rest of the Phalanx? Can we retreat through the houses?"

"There are only about fifty of us left, sir. And the houses are a bust. There's no way through to the street beyond."

Kobel stilled, despair bullying through his defenses. He knew it showed on his face, because Corim's eyes widened and he pulled slightly back in denial, but Kobel didn't let go of his shoulder. He knew if he let go, he'd succumb to the despair himself.

He was considering the advantages of retreating into the houses regardless, trying to defend them—a last desperate gambit, an impossibility—

Then a White Fire suddenly poured up over the hill above them, spilling over the unseen palace and walls and down into the streets. He had time to stare up into its flames, time to suck in a shocked breath, and then it washed over him. No, washed *into* him, burning deep. He tensed, ready to release a last agonizing howl of pain, wondering how the Wraiths had summoned such a devastating wall of fire, when it passed beyond him.

He lurched forward, off balance, the sudden onset and departure of the Fire disconcerting, but caught himself. He saw others around him doing the same. Some dropped their swords, their faces shocked, terrified, or filled with awe. Others fell to their knees. A few whimpered or whispered a prayer. His grip on Corim tightened as he spun to follow the path of the Fire as it blazed down through Temeritt, leaving the buildings untouched, but lost sight of its base almost immediately. Yet from its height, he could tell it had reached the plains and was still moving, that it stretched far wider than Temeritt both to the southeast and northwest.

Corim shifted beneath his grip and Kobel brought his blade up, realizing at the same instant that his hold had been so tight it would leave bruises. "I apologize." He released the boy's shoulder. The youth rolled it uncomfortably. "I didn't realize—"

But Corim wasn't paying attention. "The Horde is gone." His voice cracked, the only sign he was rattled by the White Fire.

Kobel scanned what he could see of the remaining forces from his seat. The street was littered with bodies, both from the Horde and soldiers. The remaining Legion stood among them. But the Horde they had been fighting had vanished.

"Did the Fire kill them all?" Corim asked.

"I don't think so. There aren't enough bodies on the street for that." Kobel lowered his sword.

"Did it...incinerate them?"

Kobel shrugged. He didn't understand it. Where had the Fire come from? What had it done? What about the rest of the Horde?

What about Echeri?

He searched the men still standing in shock all around him. "Commander Pearson."

Pearson started. "GreatLord! Artines, Benjamin, the GreatLord has been hurt!"

Two Legionnaires rushed forward, Corim stepping aside as they began checking Kobel's wound. Kobel swore as one of them tugged at the belt keeping him alive. As they continued to prod, already barking orders to bring needle, gut, and whatever the rest of the Legion could find as bandages, Kobel said to Pearson, "Get the Legion together. We'll head toward the main gates. Carry me if you have to, or find a cart. Keep your guard up though, until we know what's going on. The Horde may still be around somewhere."

"What about GreatLord Tarken Sohn?"

Both men looked to where Tarken had fallen. The GreatLord's head had nearly been ripped from his shoulders, his armor splashed by so much blood it was completely red. He'd lost his helm. He appeared to be staring at Kobel, eyes wide in death, one side of his face oddly unmarked, although the other half had claw marks down its length.

"Bring his body with us."

Pearson clapped his hands together and began rousing the soldiers around them, pulling some up out of their stupors with a slap or shake. Artines and Benjamin sewed Kobel's mangled flesh up as best they could and wrapped his thigh tight, then removed the belt. Kobel writhed as his leg tingled back to life, the pain worse than the needle. Blood stained the bandages almost immediately, but the two Legionnaires were satisfied it would hold until a real healer could deal with it. Someone found a wagon among the detritus in the streets. Within short order, Tarken Sohn's body was loaded up, Kobel ensconced in the wagon's seat, and the entire group headed toward the gates of the secondary wall.

Halfway there, they'd nearly quadrupled their numbers with shaken citizenry emerging from the rubble and other scattered groups of soldiers.

By the time they came to the open gates, Kobel had nearly two thousand survivors—men, women, and children, all bruised, bloody, or soot-smeared—trailing behind him.

* * *

After the passage of the White Fire—which came out of nowhere and burned the attacking creatures of the Horde they were fleeing to a crisp, not even leaving behind ash—Jayson held Ara in one arm, trailing behind Owen as they made their way up through the streets of Temeritt toward the secondary gates. Partway there, they joined a stream of other refugees, a shudder coursing through Jayson's spine at the resemblance of the group to the flight from Cobble Kill. Except now, for some inexplicable reason, the Horde was gone, no longer hounding them, the siege miraculously broken.

As they trailed behind the group—growing in size with every street they passed—he realized Ara was sobbing and he pulled her close, hushing her and murmuring inanities. He wasn't even aware of what he was saying. He wanted to believe it was over, but couldn't accept it. It had gone on for too long. It had altered his life completely, taking him from the mill in Gray's Kill to the walls of Temeritt, battling among its streets. He expected the Horde to reappear at every corner. This was merely a reprieve. The Horde had simply...retreated. They were gathering their forces for a new assault. They had to be.

Except he knew that wasn't true. He and Owen had been fighting two of the creatures when the White Fire came. He'd thrust his own sword through one of the creatures' chests a moment for the flames took him.

And when the flames had passed, after that timeless moment that had driven him to the edge of madness, the creature on his blade was gone. Not the ones they'd killed just moments before. Their bodies remained untouched, littering the alley before them. But all of those who'd been alive—and he had to assume the one he'd skewered hadn't had a chance to die yet—were simply gone.

Ara shuddered and pulled away from him, looking up into his face. Tears wet her cheeks, but she appeared to have gathered her strength again. The stubborn, willful woman he'd first met in Cobble Kill had returned.

"Corim," was all she said.

"He was on the walls," Jayson said unnecessarily; Ara already knew that. "We'll find him." He had to have survived. Jayson wasn't certain he could handle it if Corim were dead.

A moment later, they passed through the secondary gates and into the inner city.

* * *

Thaedoren stood silently as the wall of white fire—could it be Aielan's Light?—faded into the horizon. He gripped the hilt of his cattan in a death grip, even though he'd already verified that the Wraith's army on the field had vanished. Daedelan had already begun organizing the scattered Alvritshai forces. Men were checking those fallen on the field, tagging the wounded, dealing with those who were not yet dead but would not survive their wounds, and taking stock of what remained of their forces. The reserve forces, including his mother Moiran, were already spreading out across the field, tending those wounded. The plains were riddled with calls and commands, sobs and prayers, moans and a few dragging screams. A few of the Alvritshai stood as Thaedoren did, transfixed by the fire as it grew further and further distant.

"Tamaell?"

Thaedoren turned at Navaen's voice. "What is it?"

The White Phalanx guardsman nodded toward the southwest. "It appears that the Provincial King is preparing to head this way."

Thaedoren lowered his cattan and forced his clenched fingers to relax. "Prepare a small group. We'll meet him halfway."

"Most of our horses were spooked and ran. Or are dead."

"Do what you can. We'll walk there if we have to."

Navaen nodded and began pulling Phalanx to his side to form an escort.

Thaedoren noticed his mother headed in his direction, her hair wild, her clothes stained with blood, although she still bore herself with the regal air of the Tamaea, picking her way through the litter of bodies. So many dead. All of the colors of the Houses mixed together with the bodies of the Wraith army. Interspersed among them all, the hovering, stilled shadows of the sukrael, burning white lights at each of their hearts, so intense they were hard to look at. A few surviving Faelehgre flitted about the battlefield, hovering over bodies, flashing and pulsing. It took him a moment, but he suddenly realized they were searching through the dead as well, looking for survivors.

"Navaen," he said, as his mother reached them. He motioned toward the flickering lights that had saved him from the cold death of the sukrael during the battle. "Send word to Daedelan that the Faelehgre are helping in the search for the living. They're trying to catch our attention."

Navaen's eyes widened in surprise, but he sent a runner immediately.

"Good. You noticed," Moiran said, coming to a halt a few paces away.

They assessed each other. His mother looked worn and haggard, strained. She raised a hand and tried to pull some of her loose hair back into place.

He felt the same, his body trembling slightly. The intensity of the fighting, the constant battle that had lasted all morning and into the afternoon—all of that built up adrenalin had died. He wanted to pull his mother into an embrace, wanted to collapse where he stood, wanted to simply curl in upon himself and scream or weep and allow the emotions of the last few days—no, the last several months—to drain away and leave him empty.

But he was the Tamaell.

He straightened, and saw the look of understanding in his mother's eyes.

"I think you can put that away," she said.

He glanced down, then hefted the cattan, its blade slicked with the blood. "I suppose so." But instead of sheathing it, he handed it off to one of the numerous Phalanx who'd fallen into place around him and asked him to clean it.

Then he turned back to his mother. "We're preparing to meet with the Provinces' King. I'd like you to join us."

"Very well. Thaedoren...the white fire..."

"Aielan's Light, you mean?" But he left a thread of doubt in his voice.

Moiran pursed her lips. "I suppose that's how the Order of Aielan will interpret it. And perhaps that is true. But...did you sense anything else when its flames washed over you? Did you sense...another presence?"

Thaedoren thought back to that moment when the flames touched him, to when they consumed him, before passing on and leaving him behind. He sifted through those sensations—

And realized he *had* sensed someone else in the flames. Beneath the all-encompassing judgmental presence that he associated with Aielan, there had been something even more familiar, as if someone were standing behind and to one side.

"Shaeveran."

Moiran closed her eyes and bowed her head before nodding. "I thought so as well. It would appear we owe him another debt."

"Owe who a debt?"

Both turned at Lord Saetor's voice. Behind him stood Fedaureon and Caeden, both lords worn and ragged, with numerous bloody gashes and nicks across their faces, arms, and legs, although nothing that required immediate attention.

The young lord of House Rhyssal bowed toward Thaedoren, then moved to embrace their mother, against all Alvritshai tradition. Thaedoren couldn't help but smile, although he knew the expression was weary—both because he was tired and because he could not do what the much younger Fedaureon could.

"We owe Shaeveran a debt," he said, in answer to Saetor's question. "Both Lady Moiran and I believe that the white fire was sent or guided by Colin Harten."

"He wields such power?" Caeden asked in surprise.

"Apparently, he does."

"Why did he not do this sooner?" Saetor asked. "Think of the lives he could have saved here. Or at Caercaern!"

"I would presume," Moiran interrupted, "that he used this power as soon as he possibly could. He has always been forthright with the

Alvritshai—"

"With Lord Aeren, you mean."

"With Lord Aeren in particular, yes, but with Thaedoren and most of the Evant as well. He never mentioned the white fire to any of us before he left. He may not have known about it, or whether it would work. When he left Rhyssal, when we saw him last, he was headed toward the east searching for a disturbance among the sarenavriell, something more powerful than anything he'd seen before. Perhaps this is what he discovered."

Saetor's protest died, but Thaedoren could see that his anger had not, so he added, "We aren't even certain Shaeveran had anything to do with it. It's mere supposition at this point. We should reserve judgment until we know the truth. But I, for one, am glad the white fire—or Aielan's Light—came when it did."

At the emphasis on the possibility that it was a work of Aielan, Saetor's anger faltered.

"Tamaell," Navaen said to one side. "The dwarren have sent a party as well. If we wish to meet with them, we should leave now."

"Lord Saetor, begin organizing pyres with the Order of Aielan. We'll need to send all of those we can find into Aielan's Light as soon as possible. Daedelan will be able to provide you with Phalanx. Lords Fedaureon and Caeden will help. I'll speak with the king and the dwarren."

"And then?" Saetor asked.

"And then we will convene a meeting of the Evant, as we have always done."

Saetor bowed his head in approval, then gestured to both Fedaureon and Caeden.

Thaedoren watched them retreat, already conferring with each other.

"As far as we know, only five of the Houses have lords at the moment," Moiran said. "That's not much of an Evant."

"Four. Lord Renaerd was killed during the battle."

"What will you do with House Baene then? And what of the other Houses—Ionaen, Licaeta, Redlien, and Nuant? They betrayed you, and the Alvritshai. And what of the Order of Aielan?"

"Their lords betrayed me, not their people. But we will deal with them in time. House Baene...I believe Renaerd had another, younger brother?"

"Haemae, yes."

"If he still lives when we return, he will ascend. As for the Order of Aielan...they will have to elect a new Chosen."

"This would be an opportunity to rescind the Order's standing as the equivalent of a House within the Evant."

He met his mother's gaze. "Do you think that is wise at this time, after we have all passed through the Fires of Aielan? Our people will want answers, and like Saetor, I do not think they will want to believe that they were saved by a human tainted by the sarenavriell, no matter how much that may be true. They will turn to the Order for answers instead. It cannot be coincidence that the fires that swept over us and cleansed the earth of the sukrael and the Wraiths, and those that followed them, were white, just like Aielan's Light."

Moiran hesitated, then sighed. "No, you are right. This is not the time."

Thaedoren turned his attention to the battlefield as Navaen—waiting patiently to one side with saddled horses—stepped forward. He mounted, noting the dwarren were skirting the fissure that split the plains on their gaezel, an elder shaman and a much younger Rider at the forefront, an escort of twenty mixed Riders and shamans behind them. The human king and his entourage were already in place at a central point, near where the earth had exploded and buried Khalaek. He doubted the king knew the turbulent emotions that any association with the Wraith would engender in Thaedoren, so the Tamaell attempted to shove those aside. Between the Alvritshai forces and the king's, GreatLord Went had sent out his own group, containing a mere four Legion as escort, bringing the entire human contingent to near thirty.

He glanced back at the Alvritshai behind him, noted Moiran was ready, and counted fifteen Phalanx. Navaen had chosen two or three from each of the surviving Houses on the field, including Baene. He nodded toward his guardsman in approval, then nudged his horse into motion. The animal was still skittish, so he had to keep tight hold on the reins as they picked their way down through the fallen, crows and other carrion birds already beginning to settle in and feast. But within a hundred paces, the majority of the dead fell behind as they passed beyond what had been the front line.

Thaedoren picked up the pace, scanning the city beyond. A wide plume of smoke still roiled from the lower ward, mostly to the south now, the black scar of the raging fire's path now visible. Only husks of stone buildings remained, everything else reduced to char, the cracked outer walls blackened with soot. But the secondary walls remained, and the inner city appeared untouched. But it was too distant to pick out details. He couldn't tell if there were any survivors in the outer ward at all. He doubted anyone had survived the blaze, but there were parts of Temeritt still standing in the outer ward to the north of the gates.

As they neared where the human king, dwarren, and GreatLord Went had converged, a horn cry rose from the Provincial army, sounding hollow and forlorn on the plains. At its signal, Thaedoren suddenly realized how quiet the plains were, as if the world were still stunned by the events that had played out here. A wind blew out of the northeast, pushing southwest—the only thing that had saved Temeritt from the inferno. It flapped in the banners that Navaen had somehow resurrected from the field, the white and red of House Resue stained with blood and dirt, a tear running up its left side. The eagle motif was barely discernible. All of the tabards worn by the Legion were in worse shape.

But as they drew to a halt, the three groups—human, dwarren, and Alvritshai—twenty paces apart, he realized that the dwarren and the humans were in the same shape. King Justinian sat astride his horse, one arm bandaged and in a sling, a vicious cut running down one side of his young face. Thaedoren knew he was twelve—barely a boy by Alvritshai standards—yet he held himself with the stature of someone much older. A Legion commander, also bandaged from various wounds, sat a pace behind in support, others ranged around them, including GreatLord Went, whose forces had merged with the king's.

He shifted his attention to the dwarren, noted with surprise that the elderly shaman had pushed his gaezel out in front of the Rider Thaedoren assumed was the Cochen, as if he, their Archon, were the dwarren leader. Something had shifted within the dwarren ranks since he'd last met with them years before. They'd even foregone the usual display and blessings before the meeting, although a few of the shamans were murmuring beneath their breaths and waving their scepters. He caught one scattering grain upon the earth.

King Justinian broke the silence first. "Did one of you call down the White Fire?"

Thaedoren traded a glance with the dwarren Archon. "It did not come from the Alvritshai."

The Archon raised a hand and combed his fingers through the braids and beads of his beard. "Nor the dwarren. We only used the Land to defend ourselves from the elloktu."

All three groups shifted and fidgeted in unease at this news.

Thaedoren contemplated mentioning Shaeveran, but the Cochen of the dwarren said something to the Archon too low for Thaedoren to hear.

"My Rider believes I should mention that we sensed...a presence within the fire, someone we are familiar with. A human we call the Shadowed One, although he is known by many other names, including Colin Harten. He has long been a friend of the dwarren. He came to see us before the Wraith army attacked our lands. He warned us of their approach, before heading off into the wastelands to the east, the direction the fire came from. We believe he sent the fire, with Ilacqua's blessing, and that of the Four Rivers."

"We know of Colin Harten," Thaedoren added. "We call him Shaeveran. I sensed him within the flames as well."

King Justinian's gaze wavered back and forth between them both. "This is the same Colin Harten who gave us the Seasonal Trees, nearly a hundred years ago? To protect us from...from these Wraiths and the other creatures?"

"Yes."

Justinian focused on him. "Then what happened? Why did they fail? How did it come to this?"

Thaedoren shook his head, but Moiran nudged her horse a few paces forward and answered for him. "Shaeveran discovered that the Wraiths were tampering with the sarenavriell, what you call Wells. He said they'd discovered a powerful Well outside the reach of the Seasonal Trees. He didn't know what their intent was, but he intended to find out. I think they used this new power to destroy the Trees. And I think Shaeveran used it to stop them."

"But we won't know the truth until Shaeveran returns," Thaedoren added.

"If he returns," Justinian's commander muttered, loud enough for all of them to hear.

"Commander Roland?" Justinian asked, a hint of reprimand beneath the question.

"It would appear that Colin Harten is more forthcoming with the dwarren and the Alvritshai than he is with his own race," Roland said.

Thaedoren let an awkward silence fall, knew that his mother was straining to contain herself.

Thankfully, a sudden horn cry sounded from the direction of Temeritt—a long blast followed by two short and two long—an answer to the previous call from the field Thaedoren assumed. All of the humans first tensed, then relaxed as the horns faded.

"GreatLord Kobel reports that Temeritt is safe. We have much to discuss. I suggest we move our armies closer to the city and reconvene in the palace. I'm certain GreatLord Kobel will provide rooms for all of us and any additional escort you'd like to take with you. We can wait to discuss the Accord and what has happened until we've all had a chance to rest and relax—"

"And wash," someone grumbled softly.

"And wash, yes," Justinian repeated. He smiled, but there was strain around his eyes. For the first time, Thaedoren caught a glimpse of the young, uncertain boy beneath the stolid exterior—a boy as worn and tired as the rest of them, barely holding himself upright, much less retaining his hold on formality.

Thaedoren stepped in. "I agree. We should see to our own people now. I know our Order of Aielan will be busy sending the fallen into Her Light most of the night. Should we meet again tomorrow, at midday?"

"That is acceptable," the Archon said. "The dwarren also have many rituals to perform, just as we have much news to report of dwarren lands. We have suffered severely from the elloktu army's attacks."

"The Alvritshai, as well. Until tomorrow then."

Thaedoren nodded to both of them, the dwarren already pulling their gaezel around. As he turned, Justinian's face blanched and he began to fall from his saddle. But his commander caught and steadied him, moving in close so his actions weren't so obvious. The young king recovered before he was surrounded and his entourage headed back toward its camp.

"He's so young," Moiran said.

"But he handled himself well. And it would appear that he has a Protector in Commander Roland."

"I agree."

"Did you notice the change in the dwarren leadership? Their Archon appeared to have higher standing than their Cochen."

"An interesting development. I look forward to hearing what has happened this past year in other parts of Wrath Suvane. The world has certainly Turned, as the dwarren would say. Nothing is as it was before."

"No *one* is as they were before either."

Moiran glanced at him sharply. Then she looked away. "No, I suppose not. Who do you wish to take with you into the city?"

"I'll leave Caeden, Fedaureon, and Daedelan in charge of the army. You and Saetor will accompany me, along with your escorts."

Ahead, a thin column of gray smoke began to rise into the sky from the center of the Alvritshai lines, a sign that the first funeral pyre had been lit. Soon the smoke would turn black as the bodies began to burn, their mortal remains released into Aielan's arms.

"So much death."

Moiran said nothing, but she lowered her head. The escort remained quiet, only the creak of leather, the clank of armor, the clop of shod feet on turned soil, and the huff or snort of one of the horses sullying the silence.

He thought again of the White Fire that had washed over them. He had thought, when he saw the flames approaching, that Aielan had come to claim them all, that the world would end in a white, blazing inferno, as the ancient Scripts said it had once before. But instead of destroying them, Aielan's Light had saved them. Inside of its fire, he had felt Aielan's presence, had felt Her touch.

And now, as weariness came to claim him, as the horror and grief of all that he and the rest of the Alvritshai had suffered settled upon him, he reached for that touch and gathered it in, taking comfort from it. As he knew many would over the coming days.

"The world has changed." He looked out toward the vastness of the plains, beyond the pyres, the still-burning city, beyond the charred remains of the Autumn Tree. "It has been reborn in the Fires of Aielan. We have been given another chance, another life. We need to make certain this new age is better than the old. We need to forge a new alliance with the dwarren and the humans. The Accord failed when we needed it most, because we did not believe in it, because we did not trust it. Without Shaeveran's intervention, the battle against the Wraiths and their armies would have been lost, here, on the plains before Temeritt, because of that distrust."

He said it softly, but with conviction, and no one contradicted him.

As they reached the edge of the Alvritshai forces, he straightened in his saddle. "It must never come to this again."

26

Colin released time at the top of a knoll within sight of Temeritt to the northeast. He stumbled, exhaustion weighing heavily on his shoulders. The summoning of the White Fire had drained him, had left him conscious but helpless on the stone floor of the Source's chamber, staring up at the sky and the stars through the shattered remains of the crystal ceiling. On the second day, he'd managed to crawl to the side of the chamber to get out of the merciless sunlight, harsh even with the leaves of the Spring Tree shading it out on one side. But then he'd collapsed and hadn't stirred for yet another day. He'd been concerned the Haessari would find him— when he'd chosen who the White Fire would take, he'd left those who were in the Thalloran Wastes alone, trapping only those Haessari attacking Temeritt in the flames—but then he remembered what Walter had said. He was certain the White Fire had only heightened their belief that the gods resided in this chamber. They couldn't have missed that the flames had originated there.

And they didn't come. They weren't waiting outside when he left either. They weren't even within the ruined city as far as he could tell. They'd retreated back to their cliffside dwellings at the northern edge of the desert. He saw their fires winking in the darkness from the heights to the south as he departed. More fires than he'd seen before. He assumed they were performing rituals, praying to the gods for mercy, for enlightenment, for hope. He assumed many people would be turning to religion for solace after the passage of the White Fire.

They would need it. After what Walter had shown him in the waters of the Source, all of the races would be struggling for many years to come. Recovery would be hard, and terrible, and it would come at a great sacrifice.

Especially once the races realized what he had to ask of them in the aftermath of the fire.

On the knoll overlooking Temeritt, he turned to face the horizon to the east, where two brilliant white lights bloomed, like miniature sunrises, one a handspan farther north than the other. Much farther south, a third white dawn glowed. During the day they were barely discernible, but at night...

At night, all three shifted and glowed silver, as bright as the moon.

He returned his gaze to Temeritt. The palace gleamed at the top of the hill, the lake glistening as the wind coming from the west kicked up a few ripples on its surface. Thin gray smoke rose from the city in trails from cooking fires and hearths, much heavier, darker, thicker plumes rising from the plains farther west, where the main battle had been fought.

"Five days later and they're still burning the dead."

Reaching out, he seized time again, slowed it, and headed down the hillside toward the city. He needed to find the leaders of the three races. He needed to explain to them what had happened.

And what was required of them now.

* * *

"What about Andover?" Thaedoren asked. "Have we heard anything from them?"

Lord Kobel stood with effort after King Justinian acknowledged him with a nod. His leg was still bandaged heavily, but he refused to be left out of the proceedings. A healer sat directly behind him.

All three of the races were represented in the large hall, the Alvritshai seated along one side, dwarren across from them, and the Provinces between, opposite the massive double doors of the chamber. Each of the three leaders and one or two other representatives sat at a table at the forefront of each delegation, the rest of those assembled seated behind them at additional tables. Thaedoren's mother sat to his right, Lord Saetor to his left. Members of the White Phalanx stood behind them.

"I spoke with Councilor Tyrik in Corsair through the Hand of Diermani last evening. He said the last ships to arrive from Andover came into port over a week ago. All of them claimed to have seen a fiery light and a great rumbling from the direction of Andover at the same time as we saw the lights flashing in the skies here. Those closest to Andover said that the seas churned and boiled, that smaller ships near them were capsized and lost. One of them attempted to return to port, but they couldn't get close enough to even see land. The ocean was too rough. But they said the skies were filled with fiery, roiling clouds of ash and lightning, and the waters were choked with mud and debris and hundreds of bodies. The captains of the ships all believe that, for the moment, there's little of Andover left. None of them were willing to return. It's an arduous journey at the best of times. They've asked for sanctuary in Corsair, although they all have shipping companies to house and care for them in the Provinces. Those that survived the ocean surge, that is." Kobel paused, then added, unnecessarily, "I don't think Andover will be able to aid in our own recovery any time soon, Tamaell Thaedoren."

He sat awkwardly as murmurs broke out around the room. Thaedoren stood before they could grow into full-fledged discussions.

"It would appear, then, that we'll have to rely on ourselves in order to rebuild."

"But the devastation!" GreatLord Berand from the Provinces said, rising to his feet. "The Provinces have been decimated! What the Wraith army didn't destroy outright has been flooded by the ocean. The coastal cities are reeling. Most of the inland villages between the coast and Temeritt have been razed to the ground, including Borangst. Only Yhnar was spared the brunt of the attack, and—apologies to the late GreatLord Tarken Sohn—but Yhnar is a fledging Province at best. It controls less than half the people of Portstown, let alone my entire Province. How can Yhnar help recover from such a disaster? They won't be able to shelter the masses of survivors, even with Temeritt's help. And what about food? Can they feed those who flee to its walls? The obstacles to overcome are too great!"

There was no stopping the arguments that broke out at that point. Thaedoren remained standing, but GreatLord Berand settled back into his seat, arguing with those around him. The chaotic conversations raged on all sides, as those gathered allowed the strain of the last few months some release. They had spent three days organizing the pyres for the dead and leading groups into lower Temeritt to put out the sporadic fires after the main blaze had burnt itself out. King Justinian had declared a day of rest and celebration after that, even though the food supplies from the two arriving armies were dangerously low and there was still much work to be done. The streets of the upper wards had been tumultuous, crammed with all of the races mixed together. The celebration had spilled over into the next day, and Thaedoren was certain it was still going on in certain parts of Temeritt, but the lords and leaders had finally met and begun talking in earnest the day before. Yesterday had been spent entirely on recounting what had happened in all three lands over the course of the last few years. The missed opportunities, the mistakes, the disheartening losses, and a few triumphs—all told in bits and pieces over the course of hours. All three races had suffered dramatically.

But Thaedoren had found hope in the recounting. When the dwarren's

Sacred Waters were destroyed, their Archon, Quotl, hadn't taken the dwarren who had survived and fled in order to preserve themselves. He had marched northwards, toward Alvritshai lands, to continue the fight there. Justinian and Roland may have dismissed the dwarren's first envoy, but they had still taken the warning seriously enough to maneuver their Legion into position to march on Temeritt, and GreatLord Went had taken in the Alvritshai refugees after the fall of Caercaern.

And then there was the battle before Temeritt, where all three races had come together to defend the human Province against the Wraith's main force.

It was clear the Wraiths had planned the attacks and divided their forces to keep the three races separated and unaware of what was happening elsewhere. None of them had had any substantial warning, except possibly the dwarren, who had kept vigilant even with the Summer Tree protecting them.

Now, the dwarren Archon stood...and waited, drawing on a thin pipe and blowing smoke out through his nose. Thaedoren caught a hint of the sickly sweet scent of the yetope from where he stood.

It took twenty minutes before those in the chamber began to notice the Archon. When the room had quieted down into soft mumbles, the scuff of feet against the flagstone floor, and the creaking of wooden chairs, he said simply, "The obstacles are not too great for the dwarren."

The room exploded again, this time at the implication that the Alvritshai and humans were weaker than the dwarren. Thaedoren traded looks with Saetor and Moiran.

His mother leaned closer. "He shifted the tone of the hall from despair to determination. I can see why he became more than simply their Archon over the course of the war. I believe there is reason to hope after all."

Thaedoren caught Quotl's eye, then shifted to watch King Justinian. The human king sat in silence, eyebrows creased—in anger or confusion, Thaedoren couldn't tell—but Commander Roland's hand was resting on his shoulder. The Legionnaire leaned forward and muttered something into the king's ear and Justinian glanced up, looking directly at Thaedoren. The Tamaell nodded in acknowledgement.

When the outrage began to die down, Thaedoren shifted out from behind the table, centering everyone's attention on himself.

"I don't believe the Archon intended to slight us all. But I can attest for the Alvritshai that the obstacles are not too great for us to overcome either. From what I've seen, the human Provinces will prevail as well. We simply need to return to our homes—to Caercaern, to the dwarren tunnels, to Corsair—and regroup. If we work together, we can rebuild. The Alvritshai are willing to provide stone from the Hauttaeren Mountains. The northern forests are also plentiful."

He turned to Quotl. "From what we were told, the dwarren's food storage survived the Wraith attacks." He spun toward Justinian. "Since their arrival on the coast, the humans have proven resourceful and adaptive in terms of construction and innovation. And your people are numerous, especially now. Even with the destruction inland and along the coast, I'd wager that there are still more human survivors than dwarren or Alvritshai. You have the manpower.

"If we work together, share resources, if we aid each other, we can rebuild Wrath Suvane the way it was, without the help of Andover!"

As he spoke, those assembled began to stir. The dwarren behind Quotl had heads bowed together, deep in conversation. The GreatLords present were also animated, although Berand's dour expression hadn't faded. But the real leaders were not participating, were waiting and watching, letting the building excitement over the proposal grow. Quotl nodded in Thaedoren's direction and took a long draw on his pipe. Justinian appeared about to speak, but Thaedoren saw Roland squeeze his shoulder, halting him. The young king lowered his head slightly and fiddled with the sling that held his injured arm close to his chest.

Then someone else spoke, cutting through the mounting enthusiasm.

"No, you cannot."

Thaedoren spun, the voice coming from behind him, near the doors. The rest of the room gasped, a few of the soldiers, Riders, and Phalanx leaping to their feet, reaching for their weapons. Those stationed at the doors reacted instantly, their blades whisking from their sheaths as they turned toward the figure who stood behind them, obviously startled, as someone cried out, "He appeared out of thin air! I saw him!"

To Thaedoren's right, Moiran leaped to her feet. "Shaeveran!"

Without pause, Thaedoren raised one hand, palm out, and shouted, "Halt! It is Colin Harten!"

The guards at the door froze, swords at the ready, already half surrounding Shaeveran. The mixed group—composed of dwarren Riders, Alvritshai Phalanx, and Legionnaires—shot angry glances toward their respective leaders, clearly seeking orders or verifying them. Roland had stepped in front of Justinian. Ikterru, the dwarren Cochen, now stood beside Quotl, an axe in hand, two more Riders behind them.

Thaedoren waited to make certain no one would do anything drastic, then lowered his arm and bowed toward Shaeveran, more formally than he ever had before. The tension on the Alvritshai side of the room altered immediately, for his posture and the depth of the bow indicated that he considered Shaeveran not only Resue-aein—a friend of House Resue—but also the Tamaell's equal. All of the Phalanx sheathed their cattans and fell back into their previous positions. Even Saetor, who had stood to protect Moiran.

"Shaeveran. It is good to see you. Welcome to our...gathering."

Shaeveran reached up and pulled back the hood that had hidden his features. Another gasp rippled through the room, for everyone could see the darkness that stained his hands and had appeared in striations up the length of his neck. A few marks touched his face as well, looking like tattoos, except that they shifted and writhed beneath his skin.

He nodded toward the dwarren contingent and King Justinian. "I'm glad you are all here. It will make this discussion easier."

"What discussion?" GreatLord Berand asked. "Why have you interrupted this counsel uninvited? And why should we listen to you?"

"GreatLord!" Justinian snapped. "Enough."

"Shaeveran is welcome at any of my counsels," Thaedoren said coldly. "And we should listen to him because without his intervention, we would all be corpses rotting on the plains before Temeritt. He is the one responsible for the fire that swept the Wraiths and their army from the earth."

GreatLord Kobel stood. "Is this true? Were you responsible for the White Fire?"

Everyone in the room turned to Shaeveran, breath held.

He hesitated, then said, "Yes, I summoned the White Fire. It's why I've come."

The room exploded, louder and more raucous than at any time before. Thaedoren realized it wasn't going to calm down for long moments, so he moved back behind the table littered with parchment, notes, quill, and ink, and sat down. Someone produced wine and poured them all glasses. Thaedoren took a large swallow, then another, before setting the glass aside.

"We knew he was behind it," Moiran said, "but it's going to wreak havoc with the Order. They've lived too long under Lotaern's hand, have been led to distrust Shaeveran, if not despise him. They won't be swayed away from believing it was Aielan's will that easily."

"They've spent the last five days speaking to the Phalanx," Saetor interjected. "I've seen them working their way through the army. They've held multiple rituals on the plains, all well attended. They will claim Shaeveran is taking credit for an act of Aielan."

Thaedoren frowned. "Have they found a new Chosen yet?"

"There is one who appears to be leading them. His name is Couraenen."

"When this meeting ends, I will want to speak with this Couraenen."

Saetor leaned back and motioned one of his own House Phalanx forward. "Find Couraenen, a member of the Order of Aielan. Bring him here."

The guardsman nodded and departed.

On the floor, GreatLord Berand's voice began to override all of the others as he shouted, "Why should we accept your word on this? What proof do you have? Why should we believe you rather than accept the word of our patri that it was the merciful Hand of Diermani?"

The rest of the chamber quieted by the time he finished. Shaeveran had not moved the entire time, but now, with a sudden, blurred motion, he vanished and reappeared twenty steps further into the chamber, directly between the Alvritshai and dwarren tables, facing Berand. Nearly everyone pulled back in surprise.

"You may believe whatever you wish, GreatLord. It does not matter to me. But I tell you that I called the White Fire forth and I let it burn across the world. You all felt its touch, every last one of you. Some of you were affected more than others. Some were driven mad by it. But know this—for that moment, when the flames burned inside you, your souls were laid bare to me. I saw everything—your fears, your desires, all of the pettiness of your lives...and all of your strengths. I judged each and every one of you. And for those that I felt were against the three races, against the survival of Wrath Suvane, I exacted punishment. The Wraiths and all of those that followed them were trapped inside those flames. The fact that you are standing here, defying me, means that I found something decent inside of you at that moment, that there was something within you worth saving."

He'd spoken to Berand, but now he spun to include all of those gathered. "The Wraiths are not dead. I have simply captured them, imprisoned them inside the White Fire. Right now, that Fire has split and burns in three columns to the east. You must have seen the glow on the horizon during the night, especially from here at the palace. Those three pillars will burn for months, perhaps even years, but they will not burn forever. They will diminish over time, dying down until there is nothing left but a black ember for each, and then even that will cool and fade into a lump of char. But even then the Wraiths and their Horde will not be dead."

"Can't you destroy them then?" the dwarren Cochen asked. He still held his axe, cradled to his chest.

Shaeveran's shoulders sagged. "If I could, I would."

"Then what do you expect of us?" GreatLord Kobel leaned forward as he spoke. "You said that we could not return to our cities, that we could not rebuild Wrath Suvane as it was before. Why?"

At Thaedoren's side, Moiran gasped and sank back into her chair, as if she knew what Shaeveran would say.

"Because the prison is not permanent. Like the Seasonal Trees, this was never intended to be a final solution. Eventually, the remains of the White Fire will shatter and release the Wraiths and the Horde back into the world. It will not happen for hundreds of years, perhaps thousands, but you will have to be ready for when it happens. Your descendants will have to deal with them. I have simply bought you time to prepare."

And suddenly Thaedoren understood what Shaeveran intended to ask of them. "Instead of rebuilding here, you want us to find these pillars of fire and build our civilization anew around them."

For the first time since the sessions had begun, complete silence fell.

Shaeveran met his gaze. "Yes."

The enormity of what was asked smothered the room. The Alvritshai would have to abandon yet another home, as they had abandoned the lands north of the Hauttaeren over five hundred years before. Except this would be even worse. Because during that move, they had simply retreated southwards, keeping their hold on the caverns and halls already in use within the mountains themselves. This time, they would have to abandon everything, all ties to their roots, all links to their past. He had seen the remnants of the White Fire from the walls of the palace glowing on the horizon. They were hundreds upon hundreds of miles distant. Perhaps even further, since he had no idea how tall the pillars of fire were.

On the far side of the room, the Cochen and Archon were deep in whispered discussion. Arguments were beginning to break out all over, but Thaedoren could not determine the tenor of any of them. Some appeared to be arguing against Shaeveran's demand, like the Cochen. Others were arguing for it. The entire room was in turmoil again.

Thaedoren turned to his mother. "What do you think?"

"It..." she began, but halted, shaking her head. "It is a monumental demand. You know this. I...don't know what should be done."

"It is impossible," Saetor cut in. "You cannot even consider this request, Tamaell. It would mean the end of everything that is Alvritshai.

We would be abandoning all that we have ever known, for what? A land that we have never seen, for a task that, if Shaeveran is right, we must burden our children with."

"But are we not being forced to abandon our land already?" Moiran replied. "The winter that forced us from the northlands has been creeping steadily southward since we left. You know the storm that hounded us as we fled toward dwarren lands and the Provinces was not a typical winter squall. It felt like the storms in the north. It *smelled* like it. Even if we return to Caercaern and our hallowed mountain halls, even if we rebuilt them, how long before the cold drove us away? Would it not be better to abandon them now, when we have already been displaced?"

"You have no proof that the storm was not simply harsh. Who is to say it has not already broken? You would forsake our ties to the past based on a scent?" Saetor turned his attention on Thaedoren. "And you would base your decision on the word of a human tainted by the sarenavriell?"

"We owe that human our lives," Moiran hissed. "Not just our lives here at the battle before Temeritt, but for that at the Escarpment and for the decades of peace we prospered under beneath the protection of the Seasonal Tree."

"We owe him nothing." Saetor would have continued, but Thaedoren reached over and gripped his forearm, resting on the table between them. The touch choked off his next words.

"We owe him everything."

Saetor's brow creased in anger. "He is asking too much." When Thaedoren didn't falter, he relented, pulling his arm out from Thaedoren's hand. "This is not a decision that you can make alone. You will have to bring it before the Evant and let them decide."

"Agreed."

He stood. The tumult continued until the Cochen began beating the flat side of his axe onto the table, the sound cutting through the arguments that had risen close to shouts in some instances. The hall quieted, and the Cochen pointed toward Thaedoren.

The Tamaell nodded in acknowledgement, then looked at Shaeveran. "I think it's obvious that your...proposal...cannot be decided upon immediately. It's not one that the Tamaell alone can make for the Alvritshai. I will have to call a meeting of the Evant and discuss it with the other Houses. I think we should end this session for today, meet with our respective people, and return again tomorrow."

"The pillars of Fire will not remain burning for long. If you are to use them to find where the remnants will be, you must leave shortly. Do not take too long reaching your decisions."

Before anyone could respond, he vanished in a smear of movement.

After a moment of shock, everyone began to rise and file out in a flurry of excited babble, protests, and troubled expressions. Thaedoren turned to Saetor. "Convene the Evant immediately. Have Couraenen attend, if he's willing. I have a feeling reaching a decision will take longer than any of us expect."

* * *

Colin watched the meeting break up, the three races splitting into their various components as they left the chamber, runners already being dispersed in all directions. The hub of activity spread, like ripples on a pond. Soon, the entire city would be talking about the pillars, the decision, the choice.

He sighed and turned away from the corridors below, gazing out over the city from the balcony where he'd retreated. The palace courtyard and streets were bustling, mostly with people attempting to repair the city and return to their everyday lives.

But that was impossible, not after what had happened. When something this traumatic hit, lives were changed irrevocably.

He'd learned that the moment he'd drunk from the Well. Perhaps even earlier, on the streets of Portstown...or when he'd been forcibly removed from Trent by his father.

He sighed, his hand moving automatically to the pendant beneath his shirt. He pulled it out, ran his thumb over the crescent and small, empty vial. The familiar ache filled his chest. "The world is changing again, Karen. I wish you were here to see it."

He let the pendant fall, the moment of respite over. There were still people he needed to see, things he needed to accomplish.

* * *

The sun was beginning to set when he found Eraeth and Siobhaen. He was not surprised to find them together on the edges of the Rhyssal House camp below Temeritt's ruined outer walls. They were tending a small fire, Siobhaen sharpening her sword while Eraeth fried a few roots and vegetables over the flames. The meal was meager, if it was intended for both of them, and Colin knew that it was.

He released time far enough away that when he approaching he wouldn't startle them. "Can a lone traveler join you at your fire?" he asked, and halted ten paces away.

Both looked up sharply, suspiciously, and then Siobhaen's eyes widened. "Shaeveran!" She sat still, body rigid with tension, as if she didn't know what to do.

To one side, metal clanged on stone as Eraeth dropped the pan and abruptly stood. He moved forward stiffly, and for the first time Colin noticed how drawn and haggard he looked, and he suddenly realized why Eraeth's face was so stricken.

When he came close enough, Colin reached out and clasped his forearm, pulling him in for a short embrace, the most he expected from an Alvritshai. But Eraeth clung to him and he realized the Protector was trembling.

"Shaeveran." His voice cracked with emotion. "Shaeveran, Lord Aeren—"

"Is dead. I know. Walter told me. I didn't believe him—didn't want to believe him—until I couldn't find him when the White Fire passed. But I knew you both lived. I felt you in the Fire."

"They said he died protecting the Tamaell from Lord Peloroun's and Lord Orraen's forces in Caercaern, when they attacked the palace." Siobhaen had set her sword aside and stood. Her face was also drawn with grief.

Colin pulled away from Eraeth gently. "I saw Moiran and Thaedoren today at the council meeting in the palace. How is Fedaureon?"

"He's handling everything as well as can be expected. From all reports, he's been received well as Lord of House Rhysall."

"Why aren't you both with him?"

Siobhaen snorted. "I'm not even part of the Rhysall House. And Eraeth—" She cut off abruptly, turning toward him.

"I," he said, "am now obsolete. Lord Fedaureon already has a Protector and advisors. He has no need of me. In fact, they are meeting with the Tamaell and the other Lords right now."

"They are discussing my proposal." At their interested expressions, he waved them off. "You'll find out about it soon enough. You should save your dinner before it burns—" Siobhaen immediately cursed and knelt beside the fire to retrieve the pan "—and then tell me everything that you know about what happened since we departed from Artillien for dwarren lands."

* * *

The three of them talked well past sunset, darkness descending around them like a cloak. Eraeth built up the fire. Siobhaen recounted what they'd heard from those in the camp about the fall of Caercaern, from the moment Lotaern, Peloroun, and Orraen staged the assault on the palace and the Rhyssal and Baene Houses, to the storm and the abandonment of their lands under the Wraith army's continued attacks. There were long moments of somber silence. Eraeth poured mugs of human ale, both Alvritshai wrinkling their noses up at it as they drank, but it was the only alcohol readily available. After they'd described the battle at Temeritt, Colin told them what had happened after he left Yhnar. He left out nothing.

"So Walter and the Wraiths are trapped in Aielan's Light then, until these remaining coals crumble," Siobhaen said. She didn't seem disturbed upon learning that Colin had called the White Fire forth himself, that it was not an act of Aielan.

"No." At their looks, he said, "Walter was not trapped in the flames. He's still encased in the roots of the Spring Tree. I could have placed him in the fire, but I chose not to. I want him to suffer. I don't know what the White Fire is like for a Wraith, but I know that the Spring Tree is hurting him. That choice is one of the reasons that the taint of the Well has grown so much."

Siobhaen and Eraeth traded worried looks.

"I don't understand," Siobhaen said. "You said earlier that the Well wasn't changing you, that you were doing it yourself. But I thought the taint is what drove you from the Ostraell in the first place."

"I thought the Well was what was causing the changes, yes. But Walter made me realize that it only allowed the changes to occur. My choices—how I acted, how I used the power I had been given—that was what caused the taint to emerge and grow. I used it to hunt and kill the Shadows in the Ostraell, because of what they did to my family, to Karen. I hunted them out of revenge. That's when the taint appeared. Since then, I've used the Wells selfishly. The dwarren accepted the Summer Tree willingly, but I forced the Winter Tree and Autumn Tree upon the Alvritshai and the human Provinces. The Evant hadn't approved its use. I never gave the GreatLord of Temeritt a choice, simply planted the tree outside his walls. In forging the knife, I destroyed countless pieces of the Ostraell's heart. Every action I've taken that has been selfish or vengeful or cruel or destructive has slowly tainted my soul. This—" he pointed to the whorls of blackness marring the backs of his hands, made darker by the firelight "—is simply a manifestation of that. There is darkness within me. The Well simply makes it visible."

Silence hung for a long moment.

Then Eraeth snorted. "I refuse to believe that."

"I don't believe it either." Siobhaen shook her head. "I can see why *you* may believe it, and perhaps there is some truth to what you say, but I don't think it's that simple. As far as I can see, you've been selfless in the use of your power. You used it to stop the battle at the Escarpment, one that would have destroyed the Alvritshai and dwarren, perhaps beyond recover. You used it to create the Seasonal Trees in order to protect us. The Ostraell gifted you with those lengths of heartwood; it would not have done so if it felt you were abusing its gifts."

"There is darkness within all of us, Shaeveran. Perhaps the Lifeblood makes that darkness more visible, perhaps not. But you can as easily argue that drinking from the Well over and over has caused the taint to appear as well." Eraeth hesitated, then met Colin's gaze squarely. "You are the most honorable man—Alvritshai, dwarren, or human—that I have known. Aside from Lord Aeren himself, of course."

Colin was speechless. But he managed a small, respectful nod of acknowledgment.

Silence settled, broken a long time later by Siobhaen singing softly. It reminded Colin of the trek into the White Wastes with Aeren, Vaeren, Boreaus, and Petraen. When she finished, he mentioned that night in the way station hut, Petraen playing on his pipe, Boreaus cooking. Siobhaen chuckled at the memory, then launched into other memories—of her time at the Sanctuary, of other moments on their journey northward, of Lord Aeren. Eraeth picked up the thread, relating the time he and Aeren had first met Colin on the dwarren plains. They laughed and cried over lost friends and better times, until Colin finally stood.

"I need to meet with others tonight," he explained. "Lady Moiran, for one, perhaps Fedaureon. I would like to speak again with the Archon, Quotl, as well."

"I'm glad you have returned, Shaeveran."

"Oh, I intend to stay, no matter what is decided tomorrow at the council session. There will be plenty to keep me active for the foreseeable future."

Then he walked away. Eraeth said something he couldn't hear as he faded into the surrounding darkness and Siobhaen laughed. He grinned and shook his head, then focused on the camp around him, orienting himself by the glow of the fires and the lights of Temeritt on the hill. The city blocked out the view of the silver lights of the three pillars of flame to the east, but the night was clear and the stars glittered above, the moon low on the horizon.

He had halted to consider who to visit next—Moiran, he thought; he owed her that much—when a cloaked figure stepped out of the night, halting ten paces away.

Colin shifted his staff protectively before him, already reaching to seize time.

"Shaeveran?"

Colin hesitated. "Yes. Who are you? What do you want?"

The figure reached up and drew back the hood of his cloak. Colin didn't recognize him, but he was clearly Alvritshai.

The man pulled a satchel forward and removed a wrapped bundle with a familiar shape.

At the same time, Colin recognized the man. "You are a Warden of the Winter Tree."

"Yes, but the Winter Tree is dead." He held up the bundle, as long as his forearm, weighted on one end. "But Lotaern pulled this from its heart. He claimed it was the Winter Tree's seed. He gave it to me and charged me to find you and give it to you. I left before Caercaern was destroyed."

"Lotaern did this?" he asked, incredulous.

"Yes. Before the Wraith army arrived at the city."

Colin stepped forward, but didn't take the offered bundle. Instead, he drew back the folds of cloth as the Warden held it, considered the length of wood with a hand-sized knot at one end. He could sense the power within it, like what he'd felt in the Seasonal Trees before he'd planted them, but that power was also subtly different.

"Take it," the Warden said.

Colin leaned back and let the cloth drop back, concealing the seed. "No."

"But Lotaern—"

"Lotaern was right to send you here with the seed, but I will not take it. It hasn't completely finished growing yet. And even if it had, I would still ask you to keep it. It will need to be planted, yes, but not by me. Once planted, it will need to be cared for. Your duty has not ended with the death of the Winter Tree, Warden. It has only begun. You must carry this seed until we can determine how best to use it, and then you must find other Wardens, train them in the Winter Tree's care, and protect it from harm. Can you do this?"

The Warden lowered the seed. His shoulders sagged, as if burdened, then stiffened with resolve. "I can."

"Then keep the seed. Make certain you do not touch it directly until you are ready to plant it. There is enough power within you to awaken it. There will be many changes and decisions made over the course of the next few days—the next few months—but remain here, close to me, and I will find you when the time is right."

"Very well."

Colin reached out and touched his shoulder as he rewrapped the seed and returned it to his satchel. "What is your name?"

"Irroen."

"I am thankful that you found me, Irroen."

* * *

As soon as Moiran stepped into the room GreatLord Kobel had provided her in the palace at Temeritt and eased the door closed behind her, she knew someone was already inside.

"Who's there?"

From the shadows near the windows cast by the light from the fire in the hearth, and the few additional candles scattered throughout the small chamber, Shaeveran stepped forward.

She crossed the chamber, hand raised before rational thought could take shape, and slapped him, hard enough her entire hand tingled with numbness. "You killed him. You killed both of them!"

Her entire body trembled—with rage, with pent up grief, with all of the emotions she'd been forced to shove into the background since the day she'd learned Lotaern and Peloroun had seized Caercaern. She tried to contain it all, arms rigid at her side, as Shaeveran brought a hand to his cheek, where her palm print was already blooming a solid red, and turned back to face her. He didn't react in any other way, didn't reach for his staff leaning against the wall to one side, didn't attempt to restrain her.

Breathing hard, she raised her hand again.

The hand that cupped the raw mark dropped away and he raised his chin, not in defiance, but acceptance.

Moiran cracked. Her face twisted as she tried to hold everything in, but the tears tumbled out and she collapsed forward onto Shaeveran's chest. All of the pain and misery and sorrow—for her losses, for her people—poured out in heaving, wracking sobs. She felt Shaeveran hesitate, then wrap his arms around her and hold her.

He said nothing, because nothing needed to be said.

* * *

When Colin stepped into the council chamber the next day, Moiran sat composed and resolute, no sign of what had happened the night before evident. In fact, she appeared rested. He nodded in her direction as he moved from the doorway into the center of the chamber. The guards at the entrance stepped aside without protest. The groups gathered within the hall quieted. He walked normally, without the attention-grabbing tricks he'd played the day before. His gaze passed over all of those assembled— Thaedoren, Saetor, and Moiran representing the Alvritshai; Quotl and Ikterru representing the dwarren; and finally Justinian, Kobel, Berand, and Went representing the Provinces at the far end of the room. There were close to a hundred others present—lords, Riders, Phalanx, and Legion— but today he only cared about those seated at the three main tables.

He halted as he reached the center of the room, shifting his staff from one hand to the next. "Have the races of Wrath Suvane reached a decision?"

A leaden silence fell. Colin frowned as it remained unbroken. He glanced toward Thaedoren, the Tamaell seated with elbows on the table before him, fingers intertwined, chin resting upon them. He couldn't read the Tamaell's face. He shot a quick glance toward Moiran, but her gaze remained lowered.

No one from the Provinces had moved, although Berand shifted uncomfortably in his seat.

Before he could turn his heavy gaze on the dwarren, Quotl stood.

"The dwarren have considered the matter," he said, his rumbling, deep voice filling the room. "We have always protected the Land. Our charge was the preservation of the Sacred Waters, and the healing of the earth that surrounds it. But this Land has been healed for generations. With the Sacred Waters' destruction, there is nothing to hold us here. We choose to accept a new burden. We choose to protect the Land by guarding one of these cinders, to protect the Land from the Wraiths and the creatures of the Turning sealed within it. We will travel east."

Quotl sat, reaching for his pipe. Ikterru looked displeased, but he raised no objections.

Murmurs broke out around the room, but Colin turned to Thaedoren. He knew the Provinces would be the hardest to convince, because while their lands had been devastated, they still retained control of most of their major cities. The dwarren and Alvritshai had already been displaced.

"What was the decision of the Evant, Tamaell Thaedoren?"

Thaedoren stood. "The Alvritshai will also travel east."

The murmurs this time rose much higher, but died off as soon as Colin turned to face Justinian. "And the Provinces?"

Justinian squirmed in his chair, glancing toward the GreatLords at his side with a dark frown. Roland leaned forward from his standing position behind the king's right hand and whispered something into his ear and the boy sighed and nodded, facing Colin.

"The Provinces are split. It is my decision that the Provinces will remain here, on the coast of New Andover." The hall erupted, half in cheers, half in protest, as those who had not been part of the GreatLords' council the night before heard the news, but Justinian leapt to his feet and shouted, "Silence!" while glaring around at everyone in the room. "I am not yet finished."

They settled down slowly, but Justinian didn't wait for complete silence before turning back to Colin.

"As I said, the Provinces will remain behind. But we do accept the responsibility you have presented us, Colin Harten. GreatLord Kobel has agreed to abandon his city and travel to the east as our representative. Lady Laurelen Sohn wishes to join him, along with those who remain in Yhnar. Any who wish to travel with them from the other Provinces may do so. We will help with the resources necessary to make the journey for all of the parties, and any Alvritshai or dwarren who remain behind will be welcomed on our lands.

"What you are asking is a monumental task. It will take months of preparation, and more than likely months of travel and hardship for all of the races. But the Provinces will be here as support."

Colin frowned at the compromise—it was not what he had expected— then bowed his head to the king. "That is acceptable."

Then, he turned and left the hall, halting time so that no one could stop him. As Justinian had said, there was much to plan and arrange over the course of the next few months, and he wanted to make certain it began as soon as possible.

EPILOGUE

"Are the horses and gaezel ready?"

Colin glanced up from his perusal of the line of covered wagons spread out across the plains to the east of Yhnar. The squat, rounded palace cast a long shadow to the west, the sun barely above the horizon before them. Vibrantly colored pennants and banners were strung from every crenellation or dangling from windows. Men and women lined the city's outer walls and thousands more were spilling out of the gates onto the lands at their base. Colin could hear their shouts and cheers from where he stood at the front of the column of the wagon train, nearly ten times the size of the one he, Karen, his parents, and the rest of the ill-fated people of Lean-to had led out of Portstown several lifetimes ago.

Colin raised his cupped hands to his mouth and bellowed, "Horses and gaezel?"

The question passed down the line, all the way to the dwarren contingent at the far end. Men and women were scrambling to load the last minute supplies into the backs of the wagons. Children were screaming, hyped up on the excitement that had permeated Yhnar for the last two weeks, building to this moment. Preparations had been going on for over three months, slow at first, but picking up momentum as the proposed departure date crept closer.

And this was only the first wagon train that would head toward the still burning white fires on the horizon. The second was already being assembled inside Yhnar and farther west in Temeritt. Shipments from the Provinces and dwarren lands—food and supplies—were already en route for the third expedition. All of them would be staggered, each leaving a week apart, for the next three months. Reports on obstacles each train ran into would be passed back to the next train. Colin had plotted out a route east from Yhnar, until they hit the cliffs of the eastern sea. Then they'd turn northward, keeping close to the water and hopefully skirting the worst of the Flats and the Thalloran Wasteland and its deadly heat. He didn't want them passing near the Haessari that remained there either. When the sea ended, they'd cut east again.

He hadn't explored the land beyond that point. They'd be entering unknown territory.

Just as he and his family had done with their own wagon train.

To the south, he heard a sudden rumble of drums and the sharp ululations of the dwarren. With a thundering crescendo, the Riders and their gaezels leaped forward from their positions out onto the plains ahead, swift and fleet.

"Looks like the dwarren are ready to depart."

Colin turned at Fedaureon's voice. "Apparently so. Lord. Lady."

Moiran snorted. "Since when did you become so formal?"

Colin grinned. He couldn't help it. He had been so caught up in the worries and issues of the preparation that he hadn't had time to participate in the celebrations that had been held in the last week. But now the excitement of the moment was tugging at him, dredging up the same excitement that had filled him almost two hundred years before when he was twelve. "Is the Rhyssal House ready to depart?"

Fedaureon glared at the wagons to the north. "The Rhyssal House is as ready as it will ever be."

All of the Alvritshai had been skeptical about using the covered wagons as transport, but they couldn't offer anything better as a replacement. And Colin had to admit that the Alvritshai seated in the benches, reins in hand, waiting for the order to depart looked odd and uncomfortable, even though they'd been practicing. But they'd adapt.

When Fedaureon turned back, his gaze lifted over Colin's shoulder and settled on something beyond. "Here comes GreatLord Kobel and the Archon."

Colin shifted position and nodded as the two and their escorts halted a few paces away.

"Everyone appears to be ready," Kobel said. "They're simply waiting for the order."

"Or not," Quotl muttered, staring out at the Riders already a significant distance away as he puffed on his pipe. He shrugged and looked at Colin. "I spoke with the gods late last night, Shadowed One. Ilacqua and the gods of the Four Rivers have blessed us, but the journey will not be smooth."

"I didn't expect anything less."

"Then shouldn't we go? The sun does not wait for lingering souls."

"Agreed," Kobel said. "If we intend to do this, then let's do it."

"Sound the horns."

The party split, each heading back to their respective groups, calling orders as they went. Colin remained where he was, moving a few paces farther east as he waited, his staff clutched in one hand, his eyes on the horizon where he could barely see the white pulses of their destinations.

And then the horns blew.